KNOCK on ANY DOOR

John Lowe

WILLARD MOTLEY

KNOCK
on
ANY DOOR

Introduction by

ROBERT E. FLEMING

NORTHERN ILLINOIS UNIVERSITY PRESS

DeKalb, Illinois 1989

Certain quotations are reprinted in this book by the kind permission of the publishers and copyright owners on the following pages:

87: lines from *Alexander's Ragtime Band*, by Irving Berlin.
Copyright, 1911, by Irving Berlin; copyright renewed.

158, 159, 161, 162, 163, 184: lines from *Ti-Pi-Tin*, by
Maria Grever and Raymond Leveen. Copyright, 1938, by Leo
Feist, Inc. Used by permission.

203, 204, 205: from lyrics from *Oh Johnny, Oh Johnny Oh*,
by Ed Rose and Abe Olman reprinted by permission of
copyright owner and publisher, Forster Music Publisher, Inc.,
Chicago, Ill.

213, 269: lines from *Always*, by Irving Berlin. Copyright,
1925, by Irving Berlin.

299: lines from *This Love of Mine:* Copyright owner: Embassy Music Corporation.

316: lines from *Music Maestro, Please!*, reprinted by permission of copyright owner, Bourne, Inc. (copyright, 1938, by
Irving Berlin, Inc.).

331, 332, 333: lines from *The St. Louis Blues*, by W. C.
Handy, copyright, 1914, by permission of the author-proprietor.

452: quotation from Clarence Darrow, by permission of
Ruby H. Darrow.

Cover Design by Julia Fauci

Library of Congress Cataloging-in-Publication Data
Motley, Willard, 1909–1965.
Knock on any door.
I. Title.
PS3563.0888K6 1989   813'.54   88-34481
ISBN 0-87580-543-4

FOR MARY, MY MOTHER

THANK YOU

Sandy. Thanks for reading this book in manuscript and making suggestions. Thanks for your encouragement, for the phrases that are yours, the sentences that are yours.

And you, Emma. Thanks for listening while, almost nightly, I burdened you with the book's growing pains even before the words were set on paper. For the frequent "shots in the arm" you gave me when I hit bald spots.

And you, Ted, who know all the trials and tribulations, for the plastic surgery.

INTRODUCTION

Robert E. Fleming

When *Knock on Any Door* first appeared in 1947, it must have seemed to the American public an instance of Horatio Alger's myth come true—an overnight success had propelled a poor but deserving young writer, whose earlier work had appeared only in little-known travel and outdoor magazines, from obscurity to fame and wealth. Motley's novel about the poor son of Italian immigrants reverses another myth concerning newfound opportunities in the United States leading to economic and social success. Nick Romano, his young protagonist, is introduced as a model son, a good student, and an altar boy. After an accidental brush with the law, Nick begins a life of petty crime that leads to his execution for murder at the age of twenty-one. In an America that had suffered through the Depression and its second major war of the century, the book struck a sympathetic chord.

The reception of *Knock on Any Door* was a major success: 47,000 copies were sold during its first three weeks in print and 350,000 in its first two years, with orders continuing at the rate of 600 to 1000 copies per week; later *Knock on Any Door* had a long life as a paperback edition. Before it went out of print over thirty years later, the novel had sold nearly two million copies. But even these figures reveal only in part the immense impact of *Knock on Any Door* on the American public. Many people who never read the novel were nevertheless affected by it. *Omnibook Magazine* condensed *Knock on Any Door* in its October 1947 issue, which featured the book on its cover, capitalizing on the growing reputation of the unabridged novel. An even more widespread audience read a comic strip based on the novel. Running from December 15, 1947, to January 20, 1948, the comic strip produced by King Features Syndicate presented *Knock on Any Door* in excerpts, with three panels of illustration per day above short passages from the novel.[1]

Motley himself cooperated closely with another popularization of the novel, which appeared in *Look*. Accompanied by a staff photographer, Motley tramped through the Skid Row area of Chicago, calling on friends to help demonstrate the techniques of "jackrolling," or mugging, as it was practiced by Nick Romano and his friends.[2] Finally, two years after its first appearance in print, *Knock on Any Door* was filmed by Columbia Pictures with Humphrey Bogart in a major role as Romano's patron and lawyer.

Previously unknown, Motley suddenly enjoyed the attention of the literary establishment. Major literary publications such as *Saturday Review*, *Atlantic*, and *Harper's Magazine* praised both book and author; those who compared Motley with Richard Wright and James T. Farrell more often than not suggested that Motley might eclipse both. Black reviewers were unstintingly favorable in their comments: writing in *New Republic*, Horace R. Cayton, coauthor of a major sociological study of Chicago, praised *Knock on Any Door* for its accuracy in the treatment of social conflict. Cayton was especially impressed that Motley, though himself black, chose to write about poverty and crime as universal problems, affecting all races and ethnic groups. By 1949, an article on "America's Top Negro Authors" in *Color* included Motley in company with Richard Wright, W. E. B. DuBois, Ann Petry, and Langston Hughes.[3] Only two years after the publication of his first book, Willard Motley found himself famous. But Motley was anything but an overnight success. He had been writing and publishing for twenty-five years before the success of his novel and had worked on the novel itself for more than seven years.

• • •

The Genesis of *Knock on Any Door*

A precocious youngster, Motley began to write early, publishing a short story in the Chicago *Defender*, a black newspaper, in 1922 when he was just thirteen years old. The two-thousand-word story so impressed the editors that Motley was asked to take over the *Defender's* weekly children's column published under the pen name of "Bud Billiken." Motley enthusiastically wrote the column from December 19, 1922 to July 5, 1924, meanwhile dreaming of life as a professional writer.[4] Artistic pursuits ran in his family: his older brother Archibald, Jr., had made a name for himself as an artist.

On graduating from high school in 1929, however, Motley was disappointed to find that professional writing was not an easy field to enter. He had hoped to attend the University of Wisconsin, but, while his father's steady job as a Pullman porter enabled the family to live comfortably in a white middle-class neighborhood, finances prevented Motley from attending college. Instead, he took a few postgraduate courses at his old high school and then set out to educate himself by seeing America. A bicycle trip to the East Coast and two automobile trips to the West Coast gave him material to write about: he slept in jails, ate at mission houses, climbed mountains, and labored among migrant workers.

He did not immediately use his experiences in his writing. Instead, he submitted imaginative but formulaic stories to national magazines such as *Liberty* and the *Saturday Evening Post*. All were rejected. Not until 1938 did Motley finally begin to sell his work, and then it was not short stories but travel articles that he published in relatively obscure magazines such as *Ohio Motorist*, *Highway Traveler*, and *Outdoors*. More encouraging publications followed. *Commonweal* took two of his articles, including a think-piece on the dubious charity doled out to the homeless by big-city missions. *Opportunity*, a national black magazine that lived up to its name by giving a start to many young black writers, opened its pages to him for an article on Chicago's black artists.[5]

Some pieces that appeared in a small mimeographed magazine produced at Chicago's Hull House foreshadow the social consciousness of Motley's fiction: these sketches focus on the beggars, drunks, prostitutes, con-men, and minor criminals that inhabited the area of the city near Fourteenth and Union where he had moved after leaving his parents' house. He had begun to discover the sort of writing that would suit his temperament and his talent, but he had yet to integrate his social awareness into his fiction.

The subject that was to unite his social consciousness and his imagination came to him from an odd place—one of his early travel stories. "The Boy," published in the *Ohio Motorist* in 1938, told the true story of Motley's visit to a correctional institution in Denver. There he met Joe, a young Mexican-American boy who was in the reform school for stealing a bicycle. Although Joe referred to himself as if he were a real criminal, Motley saw him differently:

> There was an innocent and clean look about his face; a pathos about his clear, frank, brown eyes; a wholesomeness about his tanned slightly freckled skin; his shy, half-melancholy smile that puckered his lips. His voice had the friendliness of a puppy; a puppy that had been kicked. . . . Curse words dropped prematurely but easily from his lips in his boyish voice. And there was a streak of badness that ran through him as a minor chord. . . .[6]

Motley was greatly affected by Joe and his prospects. At thirteen, young Willard had been looking forward to life as a writer; at the same age, Joe was looking forward to applying the lessons on petty theft that he had learned from the older boys in the "correctional institution."

Worried about the boy, Motley visited him again on a second trip through Denver and wrote "The Boy Grows Up," an account of Joe's continuing descent into a life of crime. After his release from the institution, Joe had stolen another bicycle and been returned to the boys' home. Motley was sorry to see that Joe had grown tougher and more cynical since their first meeting, and he was horrified by the stories Joe told about brutal punishments in the school. Joe got into trouble again the next time he was released and fled to Chicago, where Motley housed him, found him a job, and counseled him, but to no avail. Joe became bored with the job and left for California, where Motley could only assume he would again drift into trouble with the law.

As a result of meeting Joe and other experiences during his travels through Depression-era America, Motley had become convinced that economic hardship was a primary cause of crime. This belief was at the core of the novel he began in 1940, a novel about Nick Romano, a boy who was innocent and tractable while his family prospered but who reacted to poverty by turning to crime. Motley noted in his diary that Joe was his source for the Colorado chapters of the book; but, as he wrote, he found other prototypes of the character who was evolving in his manuscript. A young Chicagoan named Mike, whom Motley met in 1940, furnished a model for the later Nick Romano. Mike had committed more serious crimes than Joe, including jackrolling and burglary. Motley tried to reform Mike while observing him. His literary task fared better than the humanitarian effort: Mike repaid Motley's help by robbing his apartment. But the author continued to have faith in Mike, and the two remained friends until Mike went to prison in 1942.

A third prototype was murderer "Knifey" Sawicki, who was tried in the fall of 1941 for the murder of four people, including a policeman. Motley was not personally involved with Sawicki, but he attended his trial and talked to the assistant public defender who handled his case. Motley took careful notes at the trial and obtained permission from the lawyer, Morton Anderson, to use part of his closing argument in the novel. Anderson, who sympathized with the lower class, approved of Motley's project and offered information on the preparation of a murder defense.[7]

Motley also engaged in more formal research while he was working on *Knock on Any Door.* In the spring of 1941 he visited the Industrial School for Boys in St. Charles, Illinois, to supplement what he knew of the correctional system Joe had experienced in Colorado. Later he would visit the Cook County Jail and view the electric chair that would have been used in Nick's execution. During a WPA assignment, he worked in Chicago's "Little Sicily," where he observed Italian boys as they drifted into lives of crime when they failed to find meaningful work. Finally, as he neared the end of his work, he submitted his manuscript to a Chicago judge whom he had known for years with the request that the judge check the sections of the book that dealt with courtroom procedure.

While it was constructed on sound if informal sociological research, the book nevertheless engaged its author's emotions deeply. Motley never forgot the real people for whom Nick Romano became a symbol, and as he worked, the protagonist and some of the other principal characters began to take on lives of their own. In 1942 he celebrated Nick's sixteenth birthday, complete with a birthday cake and candles. The day he wrote the scene in which Nick kills Officer Riley left Motley feeling emotionally drained, since he knew that Nick was passing the point of no return. Emma's death was nearly as much a crisis for Motley as for Nick, her fictional husband. But the greatest trauma for the author was the execution of his main character. He put it off as long as possible; when he had finally written the scene, he went out and got drunk to try to forget his loss.

On September 16, 1943, Motley packed his 1,951-page manuscript into a wooden box and shipped it off to Harpers. On November 3 the manuscript came back rejected. Motley was so disturbed by the rapid rejection that he did not send the book out again until January 1944. In March, Macmillan tentatively accepted the novel, and the next month grudgingly sent a small advance, ordering Motley to cut the massive manuscript to 250,000 words and to remove some of the sexual passages that might cause problems. Motley began the long job of cutting and revising his work. But in 1946, after two revisions, Macmillan decided that the manuscript still contained objectionable sexual material and rejected it. Motley then sent the last version of the novel to Appleton-Century, which accepted it without further revision. *Knock on Any Door* was published the next year and repaid Motley's faith in its worth. The long search for a publisher left its scars, however, and Motley made a legend of it.

...

Contexts

Knock on Any Door belongs to a long and distinguished tradition in American literature. As early as 1893, with the publication of Stephen Crane's *Maggie: A Girl of the Streets*, a literary case study of the life and death of a Bowery prostitute, novelists had turned from the countryside to the problems of lower-class urban Americans. Frank Norris had written of the degeneration of an unlicensed dentist who reverted to primitive savagery in *McTeague* (1899), and Theodore Dreiser had condemned the falseness of the American Dream for members of the lower class, whose ambition can lead to prison or the electric chair, in his masterpiece, *An American Tragedy* (1925).

Chicago was a popular setting for novels that examined the underside of the American Dream, beginning with Upton Sinclair's exposé of the exploitation of immigrants by the Chicago meat-packing industry, *The Jungle* (1906). Sinclair, not a native Chicagoan, was followed in the tradition by minor Chicago writers such as Albert Halper, whose *The Foundry* (1934) and *The Chute* (1937) attacked manufacturing and the mail order retail industry, and by Meyer Levin whose documentary novel *Citizens* (1940) was based on a 1937 steel strike. Famous Chicago writer, James T. Farrell thoroughly explored the dilemma of the lower middle-class

Irish immigrants of South Side Chicago in *Studs Lonigan: A Trilogy* (1935). Nelson Algren continued the tradition with his *Never Come Morning* (1942) and *The Man with the Golden Arm* (1949).

Perhaps most important to Motley, as an aspiring black writer, was Richard Wright's publication of *Native Son* (1940), a national best-seller and the first work by a black author to be selected by the Book of the Month Club. Like *An American Tragedy*, *Native Son* was especially important as a precursor to *Knock on Any Door* because both Dreiser and Wright had drawn heavily on specific criminal cases as sources for their fiction. The lessons Wright had to teach were not lost on other black writers. Ann Petry began her career with a feminine counterpart of Bigger Thomas's story in *The Street* (1946), and Chester Himes followed Wright's lead with *If He Hollers Let Him Go* (1945) and *Lonely Crusade* (1947).

But Motley did not simply follow Wright's example. Unlike Wright, Motley had not experienced segregated life as a black outsider; although he had relatives who were chauvinistic about their race, his mother had always taught him that "people are just people," that no one should be judged on the basis of skin color. Motley's experience at Englewood High School, where most of his fellow students were white, reinforced that lesson, as did his experiences on the road, where he did not identify himself racially and was often misidentified as Mexican-American rather than black. Little wonder then that Motley felt free to base his protagonist on the young Mexican-American from Denver, another Hispanic he had known in Chicago, and a Polish boy whose trial he attended and free to make his protagonists Italian because of the research he had done in Little Sicily. By writing a novel that protested against social injustice but did not tie injustice to racial prejudice, Motley helped to inaugurate a significant movement in black literary history.

Within the next few years, nearly every major black writer would experiment with a novel that was not primarily concerned with race. Ann Petry's second novel, *Country Place*, appeared in the same year as *Knock on Any Door* and treated small-town life in New England, a subject that was actually closer to Petry's own experience than that of her first novel, *The Street*. Zora Neale Hurston, who had used her life in the South and her knowledge of black folklore as the basis of two successful novels, turned to the lives of white southerners in *Seraph on the Suwanee* (1948). William Gardner Smith's second novel, *Anger at Innocence* (1950), departed from the racial theme of his first book, *Last of the Conquerors* (1948). Motley himself followed his first novel with a study of Chicago politics and organized labor and their impact on returning World War II veterans in *We Fished All Night* (1951). His commitment to the "raceless novel" is evident in that he dropped a major black character from his initial outline of the book, choosing to appeal to readers on other than racial grounds.

Even major black writers like Richard Wright, James Baldwin, and Chester Himes were caught up in the spirit of the times. Wright followed his blatantly existentialist novel *The Outsider* (1953) with *Savage Holiday* (1954), an experimental Freudian study of an upper-class white executive who is reduced to savagery after he accidentally kills a woman. Although the novel was considered a potboiler in the United States, European critics compared it to the work of Dostoevsky and saw signs that Wright was emerging from the literary ghetto that confined him to black themes. James Baldwin followed *Go Tell It on the Mountain* (1953) with *Giovanni's Room* (1956), in which the main characters were outsiders not because of their skin color but because of their sexual orientation. Finally, Himes wrote a prison novel, *Cast the First Stone* (1952), in which the principal characters were white although black prisoners appeared in minor roles.

It is not surprising that during this period discussions of the Negro novel in the pages of *Phylon* often assumed that the black novel had passed through the stage of addressing specifically black issues and would henceforth concern itself with common problems of humanity instead. Charles I. Glicksburg looked upon the earlier history of the black novel as displaying "alienation" and concluded that black writers had allowed themselves to be segregated into treating only black themes. The movement to write novels using white protagonists with universal problems thus marked the coming of age of the black novelist. Hugh Gloster took a similar point of view. Referring to black novelists of previous times as "preoccupied with racial issues and materials," he praised the authors who had helped to bring about an "emancipatory process" that allowed the black author to treat any subject.[8] *Knock on Any Door* was one of a handful of books Gloster pointed to as seminal works that had opened up the field for later writers. Saunders Redding, a poet as well as a critic, applauded the realization of the black author that "his problems were human, not racial." While Redding saw nothing wrong with continuing to employ racial material, he welcomed the new freedom that had produced the "raceless" novel.[9] The antisegregation activities of the 1950s and the black aesthetic movement of the 1960s turned the attention of black writers back toward race, but the movement to which Motley contributed so much is an important phase in the history of black literature.

...

Motley's Message and His Art

In an unpublished introduction to *Knock on Any Door* Motley stated that he had not attempted to make the novel an "artistic" book. Rather, the only obligation he acknowledged was the necessity of telling the truth. Unlike many modern writers, who cultivate a distinctive narrative voice and style, Motley had tried to submerge his own personality and just to record life as he had seen it. He believed that the writer does not belong in an ivory tower, recording the lives of "lesser" people, nor should he produce work meant merely to entertain the reader.

[xv]

> In other words, the writer approaches his subject matter—his fellow
> man—in humility and understanding, in sympathy and identifica-
> tion—but without glorification. And he tries—only the serious writer
> knows how hard—to tell the truth, frankly and unshrinkingly.[10]

Such a writer will spend much of his time exposing the injustices of the
world, and, Motley realized, he will run the risk of having his work
called propaganda, not art. But this is a chance the writer must take if he
is to be anything but a parasite to society. The other chance the realistic
writer takes is that he may alienate his readers by dwelling on the ugli-
ness of the life he describes. But Motley freely accepted the risks his view
of art entailed. The message was important enough to override personal
concerns such as literary reputation and financial success.

Because of Motley's almost sociological observations and his low-pro-
file style, many view *Knock on Any Door* as little more than a case study.
Much like a scientist, Motley tends to classify types of deviant behavior
in which his subject participated and to enumerate and analyze the forces
that influenced him. As Nick makes his transition from innocent to criminal, Motley relentlessly depicts the failures of the various institutions
that should help him but do not. Because of their old-world attitudes, the
Romano family fails to understand the forces that are changing their
youngest member, and Pa Romano's only remedy—beating Nick into
submission—fails. Both the Catholic church and the schools also fail
him. The church takes no notice of human frailty and, like Nick's father,
attempts to stamp out vice by imposing brutal punishment. The schools
Nick attends have become jungles where the strong rule the weak, fit
training grounds for children who will become young criminals. Finally,
the criminal justice system supports the indoctrination of minor criminals into the ways of serious crime by throwing first offenders into prox-
imity with hardened criminals.

Comparing *Knock on Any Door* with two sociological works that cover
the same material, however, yields differences as well as similarities.
Motley's novel shows the same patient research and comes to many of the
same conclusions as Clifford Shaw's *The Jack-Roller: A Delinquent Boy's
Own Story* and Shaw and Maurice E. Moore's *The Natural History of a Delinquent Career*,[11] but Motley heightens Nick's internal conflict by con-
trasting his early life as an altar boy with his later life as a criminal and by
depicting his continued struggle between good and evil impulses.

The novelist also employs symbolism as a shorthand to convey Nick's
more humane impulses. Nick habitually identifies with small, helpless
creatures: a mouse cornered by a cat, a puppy run over by a car, a fly
caught in a spider's web, and a small boy tormented by the reform school
system he defies. His recurring memories of these victims establish a pattern of symbolism that artistically identifies Nick as a sympathetic figure
even when his own actions are brutal.

[xvi]

Motley also depicts Nick more sympathetically than a sociological writer would by avoiding the clinical tone associated with social science writing. He does this by adapting the idiom of his third-person narrator to convey Nick's own perceptions of events even though the point of view remains technically in the third person. This technique calls for the narrator to use the same sort of slang, the short, simple sentences and fragments, and the same flat style that might be used by the character he is describing. Such writing gives the impression that the author is himself semiliterate, but Motley, like other naturalists such as James T. Farrell and James Jones, deliberately chose the style as a means of breaking down barriers between the real life that he was attempting to convey and the reading audience whose sympathy he was attempting to engage.

Finally, by deliberately exaggerating the depth of Nick Romano's fall, from the extreme innocence of his altar boy period in a middle-class area of Denver to the cynicism and brutality of his last years in the Skid Row section of Chicago, Motley made his story a tragedy. Real criminals do not often have such extremes in their life stories, but the dramatic heightening of contrasts between Nick as he is first depicted and as he is seen in the final pages of the book increases the poignancy of his story.

•••

Motley's career after *Knock on Any Door* was disappointing. Attempting to grow as a writer, he wrote about other ethnic groups, other social problems, and even another country in three later novels—*We Fished All Night* (1951), *Let No Man Write My Epitaph* (1958), and *Let Noon Be Fair* (1966). Somehow the chemistry he found in his first novel eluded him, and he never wrote a book as good as his first. However, *Knock on Any Door* establishes his reputation as a significant American novelist, author of a minor classic of naturalistic fiction.

•••

Notes

1. For an account of the reception, see Robert E. Fleming, *Willard Motley* (Boston: Twayne, 1978), pp. 59–62. The novel was condensed in *Omnibook Magazine*, 9 (October 1947), 1–46.
2. "Who Made This Boy a Murderer?" *Look*, 11 (September 30, 1947), 21–31.
3. Horace R. Cayton, "The Known City," *New Republic* (May 12, 1947), 31. Cayton also wrote of the novel in the Chicago *Tribune* and in the Pittsburgh *Courier*. "America's Top Negro Authors" appeared in *Color*, 5 (June 1949), 28–31.
4. "Sister and Brother," Chicago *Defender* (September 23, 1922), 14; (September 30), 14; (October 7), 15. For a more full account of Motley's Bud Billiken columns , see Fleming, pp. 17–19.

5. See, for example, his "Calle Olvera—America's Most Picturesque Street," *The Highway Traveler*, 10 (August-September 1938), 14–15, 41–46; "Assault on Catalina," *Outdoors*, 7 (April 1939, 30–31; "'Religion' and the Handout," *Commonweal*, 29 (March 10, 1939), 542–543; "Small Town Los Angeles," *Commonweal*, 30 (June 30, 1939), 251–252; and "Negro Art in Chicago," *Opportunity*, 18 (January 1940), 19–22, 28–31.
6. "The Boy," *Ohio Motorist* (August 1938), 14, 30–31.
7. Jerome Klinkowitz, ed. *The Diaries of Willard Motley* (Ames, Iowa: Iowa State University Press, 1979), pp. 146–182. The original diaries are in the Willard Motley Collection at Northern Illinois University, which houses most of Motley's papers.
8. Charles I. Glicksburg, "The Alienation of Negro Literature," *Phylon*, 11 (1950), 49–58; Hugh M. Gloster, "Race and the Negro Writer," *Phylon*, 11 (1950), 369–371.
9. J. Saunders Redding, "The Negro Writer—Shadow and Substance," *Phylon*, 11 (1950), 371–373. See also John S. Lash, "The Race Consciousness of the Negro Author," *Social Forces*, 28 (October 1949), 24–34 and Thomas D. Jarrett, "Toward Unfettered Creativity: A Note on the Negro Novelist's Coming of Age," *Phylon*, 11 (1950), 315.
10. The manuscript of Motley's introduction is in the Motley Collection, Northern Illinois University.
11. Clifford Shaw, *The Jack-Roller: A Delinquent Boy's Own Story* (Chicago: University of Chicago Press, 1930) and Clifford Shaw and Maurice E. Moore, *The Natural History of a Delinquent Career* (Chicago: University of Chicago Press, 1931).

* * *

Other Works by Motley

We Fished All Night. New York: Appleton-Century-Crofts, 1951.
Let No Man Write My Epitaph. New York: Random House, 1958.
Let Noon Be Fair. New York: G. P. Putnam's Sons, 1966.
The Diaries of Willard Motley. Edited by Jerome Klinkowitz. Ames, Iowa: Iowa State University Press, 1979.

* * *

Selected Works on Motley

Craig S. Abbott. "Versions of a Best-Seller: Motley's *Knock on Any Door*." *Papers of the Bibliographical Society of America*, 81 (1987), 175–185.
Robert A. Bone. *The Negro Novel in America*. Revised Edition. New Haven and London: Yale University Press, 1965.
Robert E. Fleming. "The First Nick Romano: The Origins of *Knock on*

Any Door." Mid America, II (1975), 80–87.

Robert E. Fleming. *Willard Motley*. Boston: G. K. Hall, 1978.

Blanche Houseman Gelfant. *The American City Novel*. Norman: University of Oklahoma Press, 1954.

James R. Giles. "Willard Motley's Concept of 'Style' and 'Material.'" *Studies in Black Literature*, 4, no. 1 (Spring 1973), 4–6.

James R. Giles and Jerome Klinkowitz. "The Emergence of Willard Motley in Black American Literature." *Negro American Literature Forum*, 6, no. 2 (Summer 1972), 31–34.

Jerome Klinkowitz and Karen Wood. "The Making and Unmaking of *Knock on Any Door*." *Proof*, 3 (1973), 121–137.

Ann L. Rayson. "Prototypes for Nick Romano of *Knock on Any Door*." *Negro American Literature Forum*, 8, no. 3 (Fall 1974), 248–251.

Walter P. Rideout. *The Radical Novel in the United States: 1900–1954*. Cambridge: Harvard University Press, 1956.

Alfred Weissgarber. "Willard Motley and the Sociological Novel." *Studi Americani*, 7 (1961), 299–309.

KNOCK on ANY DOOR

The sparrow sits on a telephone pole in the alley in the city.

The city is the world in microcosm.

The city lies in splendor and squalor. There are many doors to the city. Many things hide behind the many doors. More lives than one are lived in the city, more deaths than one are met within the city's gate.

The city doesn't change.

The people come and go, the visitors. They see the front yard.

But what of the city's back yard, and the alley? Who knows the lives and minds of the people who live in the alley?

Knock on any door down this street, in this alley.

1

He was at the prayer age. When St. Augustine's bell blessed the neighborhood, rolling out across the scattered red and green rooftops, sounding across the sky in a deep-throated benediction, he stood facing the sharp-pointed cross-peaked steeple, made the sign of the cross and said the Angelus, three Hail Marys, slow and reverent. He went to Holy Communion on the nine First Fridays and made novenas, praying earnestly. He formed the prayers with his child mouth, clasping his small hands over the high, carved oak rail of the last pew with all the candles and lights and crowned plaster saints shimmering around him; and the sanctuary lamp glowed steady-red from its high place over the altar where it fell straight down from the vaulted ceiling on its single gold chain and hung like a misty star for everybody to see and know that God was there. He felt small in that great church. And he felt God there, near to him.

He'd see an old woman on the street with a wrinkled face and a thin mustache, an old woman shambling along in shabby out-of-fashion clothes and he'd say five Hail Marys and five Our Fathers for her. Or a tramp would come begging at the back door and he'd go upstairs and kneel by his little bed with the quiet, sad crucifix on the stern-gray wall over the bed and pray for the hobo Ma had given sandwiches and coffee to on the back porch. (She had carefully locked the door after she had handed the sandwiches out past the chain and bolt that let the door come open only a few inches.) His lips would tremble over the prayers and his eyes raised to the outstretched Jesus, white against the ebon, would sometimes fill with tears.

Then, when he was old enough, he was an altar boy. He'd get up at twenty to six every morning and, rubbing the sleep out of his eyes with his fists, hurry up and dress and start for the church. The streets would be shrouded with the gray quiet of daybreak. Down past the streetcar tracks St. Augustine's sat in the first gray whisper

[3]

of dawn, calling its sparse early-mass worshippers, taking in the men and women. Women in dark clothing, meager against the long streets and the angular buildings and the slanting splinters of sunlight, trudged to the church. There would be a few men, but only a few. A policeman or a streetcar conductor would pass up the broad stone steps and under the high arched doors carved with the figures of saints. But mostly they were women. An old Italian woman, fat, dirty, with a black shawl pulled over her head and shoulders, always sat on the top step saying her beads until the bell died away and mass began. He thought that God, way up and way off somewhere, liked to see her there on the top step of St. Augustine's, mumbling over the black beads as they slipped one by one through her oily fingers away from the crucifix and back to it.

He had to pass the brick school building, the cinder playground inside the black iron picket fence and the convent. He always slowed up as he passed the Sisters' house. In the gray frame convent through the softly lighted windows he could see the nuns in their gentle black as they knelt at prayer, their hands like the spreading wings of doves. This always made him feel good inside and when he slipped out of the cold into the church to get into his cassock he would think of the Sisters saying their prayers all together. And some mornings he would remember his first Holy Communion, coming into the church slow and all trembly and carrying a lighted candle while the organ played and the choir sang "O Lord, I Am Not Worthy That Thou Shouldst Come to Me." And the girls all in white with white veils; the faces all turned to them as they marched up the heavily carpeted middle aisle to the front pews; faces he could feel looking at him but could not see, for he kept his head bent and his hands pointed together like the church steeple. He remembered the tinkle of the altar bell, how he stuck his tongue far out and how tenderly he held the Host in his mouth, thinking all the time of Jesus inside the wafer. He had come home that warm blue and gold Sunday morning with its little breeze ruffling the lawns and the tree leaves and the lace collars of women passing by and had sat on the front porch saying his rosary over and over, the white-bead rosary Ma had given him for making his First Communion, while he thought of Jesus putting Himself into the wafers and coming into the bodies of good people.

■■■

Ma and Pa said that they were blessed to have such a good son. Pa, standing straight-backed and square-shouldered, his face never losing that severe look, said in his stern voice, "Our Nick is a fine boy. Our Nick is going to be a priest. We are going to give our Nick to the church." And though Ma nagged him about brushing his teeth and shining his shoes he often heard her say to the neighbors, or to company, "Nick is so kind and gentle. He's like a little saint."

Her voice would tremble with pride, and she would go on: "One day by Rankin's grocery store a cat had a little bit of a mouse cornered and was playing with it—just pawing it and slapping it this way and that. A crowd of people were standing around watching. Do you know what Nick did? You couldn't guess! That child walked up, picked that mouse up and stuck it in his pocket and walked away as fast as he could! If Nick was to die he'd go straight to heaven." It was Ma's favorite story. Nick would hang his head self-consciously when he heard it. But he still thought about that mouse and felt sorry for it.

■■◀

Ang and Julian were swell. His sister Ang, who was a couple of years older than he was, liked to take him out with her, out walking or to the park. And she'd buy him ice cream sodas at Torricelli's drugstore. Julian, his brother, who was sixteen and in high school, was always helping him with his homework or making model airplanes for him or playing catch with him at St. Augustine's playground. Other fellows' big brothers didn't play catch with them. He had a keen family.

And there was Aunt Rosa, a fat, lumpy, middle-aged woman with stringy gray-streaked hair that was always hanging loose from its knot in the back, and a friendly smile and a big mole on her cheek near the corner of her mouth with one long blond-gray hair growing out of it. She came over to their house a lot. He liked his Aunt Rosa. She had a way of talking that was nice and when she talked to him it was almost like one of the fellows. She didn't go around dressed up all the time and she didn't act classy. She said she didn't go bustin' her head against the altar rail every Sunday but that she was a Christian and didn't give a damn for the hypocrites who filled the churches on Sunday mornings and in a race for heaven she bet she'd beat a lot of them by a country mile. Ma would send him out of the room when Aunt Rosa got wound up but he'd sometimes stand in the hall listening and he liked the way Aunt Rosa talked and looked and smelled. But he wished she would go to church every Sunday like it said in the prayer book that you should and he didn't like to hear her say those curse words. They hurt him inside. But she was always jolly and good-natured and slapped her leg hard and she laughed and brought him something good to eat when she came over.

Sometimes she would pinch his cheek and cluck her big tongue and say to Ma, "It's a shame to go making a priest out of Nick when he's so damn good-looking and has those big dreamy brown eyes." Ma would start freezing up but Aunt Rosa always went right on as if she enjoyed shocking people. "He could break a lot of hearts when he gets older. Damn it, people are going to be attracted by this boy. You shouldn't hide him away in a pulpit." She'd pull his ear or muss his hair while Pa's face got stormy and Ma closed her eyes and opened her mouth in a horrified gasp and Nick got redder and redder.

■ ■ ■

The best day of his life had been his twelfth birthday. Spring tumbled down over the hills and through the city making everything warm and green. The sun lay on the streets in long yellow-gold patches and the flowers and trees and lawns spread their colors everywhere. Then spring folded into summer. Summer lay over Denver, indolent and caressing. Ang and Ma sat side by side in wicker chairs on the front porch and crocheted and Julian made the high school baseball team. Aunt Rosa went away to visit friends. Pa's business was doing swell and he bought a new Buick. Ang won a cake-baking contest at the Catholic Women's Sodality's drive for funds to build a new convent. Then it was Nick's birthday and he was going to serve at High Mass.

He walked along the tree-shaded streets where the leaves threw shadow patterns on him, running down his back onto the sidewalk behind him. His fingernails had been scrubbed clean. Ma had given his neatly combed hair a final pat and pecked him on the cheek with her cool lips, straightening his tie at the same time. He walked through the sunlight now in the new suit Pa had bought for him, thinking about the sacristy where he would put on his cassock and where Father O'Neil would be waiting for him with his gentle eyes and his soft smile. He thought about being twelve and going, on that day, to serve God. It was wonderful. Today was his birthday and it was St. Augustine's day, too. There would be a ceremony for St. Augustine late in the afternoon, and vespers and Benediction. He would carry a lighted candle.

"Ad Deum, qui laetificat juventutem meam," he said, half aloud. These were his opening words when he stood at the foot of the high altar at the beginning of Mass. The sun had a warm arm around his shoulders. The small breeze wrinkled his dark hair over his forehead, tossing the end of his tie against one of his cheeks.

Nick came to the side gate of the church square. He walked along the little sidewalk close against the wall of the church and pushed open the heavy door at the back. Father O'Neil stood in the sacristy by the cabinet where the sacred vessels were kept. He stood in his flowing white alb near the tall stained-glass window through which the light streaked, showing in beams across his back. In his hands was the gold chalice that no one but the priest could touch. He turned slowly and looked down at Nick with his eyes shining and

[6]

taking light from the window. "Happy birthday, son. May God bless you."

"Thank you, Father."

Nick pulled off his coat and hung it on a hook. He took the red cassock he would wear today from the chest against the wall. He buttoned himself into it. It fell to the tops of his shoes, cardinal in color, tight around his shoulders and close to his neck. He slipped the lacy white linen surplice with the deep sleeves over his head and smoothed his hair back with his hands. Father and he worked without words getting ready for Mass. He liked Father O'Neil; better than Pa even. Father O'Neil was so kind and gentle and moved about in his long garments like a saint. His voice was so soft. Never gruff or stern like Pa's. Ma never spoke that kind. And his eyes were the nicest eyes he had ever seen. All saints must have eyes like that. It was nice just being with Father O'Neil, moving about the sacristy, not talking, helping with the candles and the sacred vessels. They didn't need words.

Nick lit the tall candles on the altar, touching them with the long taper and seeing them come alive; he genuflected before the tabernacle where Christ was, returned to the sacristy. The other altar boys had come in and were putting on their cassocks. The cruets and censers were waiting on a side table. Father O'Neil had on his silky white chasuble with the large embroidered gold cross all entwined with leaves and tiny little flowers on the back of it. Then they were ready to go into the sanctuary. The altar boys lined up. Father O'Neil put the biretta on his head. They moved slowly toward the door leading to the altar. Their garments rustled. And the carpet whispered under them.

The altar was shining white marble with the rays of the noon sun falling through the semicircle of high-arched stained-glass windows behind it, crossing and recrossing and lying golden all over it. The candles stood straight in their gold holders with their flames like crowns. Flowers were on the altar.

They moved toward the holy place. Father O'Neil was taking off his biretta, he was kissing the altar stone.

"*In nomine Patris, et Filii, et Spiritus Sancti. Amen.*"

■■■

"*Et introibo ad altare Dei: ad Deum qui laetificat juventutem meam,*" Nick said. "And I go unto the altar of God: to God who giveth joy to my youth. . . ."

The organ swelled its notes to all the walls. The people knelt with heads bowed. Father O'Neil turned to them and made the sign of the cross over them.

"*Dominus vobiscum.*"

"God be with you." That was beautiful.

[7]

"Et cum spiritu tùo," Nick answered, feeling all the people kneel-ing behind him and the soft rays of sunlight falling on Father O'Neil's shimmering chasuble and traveling to him where they were warm on his hair and forehead.

***

They had a little pile of presents for him heaped up on the cushions on the front room sofa. They were all singing "Happy Birthday to You," even Pa who didn't look like he enjoyed it. Nick opened the packages with excited fingers while Ma, Pa, Julian and Ang stood in a smiling group near the door watching. He liked Julian's present best—a football. And as soon as he had wiggled out of his new suit and hung it up on a wire hanger like Ma made him, he and Julian tried the football out in the back yard even if foot-ball season was way off yet.

At dinner Pa frowned at him proudly over the big silver serving plate of veal *scallopini;* Ma piled his plate and at dessert time gave him a second helping of spumone from Torricelli's drugstore when she wasn't telling him not to eat so fast and to take his elbows off the table. Ang, sitting next to him, sneaked her hand under the table and put it on top of his when Ma was scolding. And some-times Julian, across the table from him, winked at him. And he blew out *all* the candles on the cake.

***

The procession that evening started from the chapel, went to the church where the choir sang; forty voices lifted and the big bell in the tower rang out. The procession wound down the broad streets and the little crooked, cobbled streets of Denver near the parish. People lined the sidewalks or followed behind. The choir went in front in dark blue with two altar boys in the lead swinging censers. Then came the statue of St. Augustine borne on a crossbarred plat-form covered with flowers. Behind it Nick walked with a lighted candle in his hand. His cassock touched the cobblestones and his eyes shone. With the other altar boys he walked, their red and white garments a touch of color against the drab street. Lastly came Father O'Neil in the richly colored, heavily fringed cope fastened across his shoulders by a velvet clasp and with a cape at the back. In his hands, held high, was a relic of St. Augustine.

At dusk Nick knelt in the gold and white chapel singing the Gregorian chant. Somewhere a sparrow chirruped and the tongue of the chapel bell was solemn across the twilight.

Nick went home with every minute of that day still fresh in his boy-mind. He was named after St. Nicholas of Tolentino, he knew, and he had read the life of his patron saint. It was wonderful to him that St. Nicholas had belonged to the order of Hermits of St. Au-gustine and that here he was an altar boy at St. Augustine's. His

[8]

hair now fell all over his head, shaken loose by the wind. His eyes were dreamy. He would be like St. Nicholas. And some day he would be a priest. He thought about it all the way home and about how when he was a priest he would convert the little Jewish boys and the little colored boys. Then some day he might be a saint too, with a crowned statue in a pretty church and thousands of candles at his feet. All the way home, hardly noticing people or streets, he thought about it.

2

Then they were poor. The door opened and shut but no footsteps came into the house and Pa was standing just inside the door in the hall, leaning back against it heavily and looking as if he couldn't see anything clearly; as if everything were strange. And nothing seemed to focus for him.

He was still like that in the hall when Ma came through the house with biscuit dough on her hands, asking, "Is that you, Pa?"

Pa's face was drawn up and more stern-looking than Nick had ever seen it. But when Pa spoke his voice shook; he just reached out his hand to Ma, blindly, and said, "Lena—Lena—"

His eyes seemed to be trying to tell her something his mouth couldn't find words for. And Ma, who knew something was wrong right away, told him not to talk in front of the kids. "Come on upstairs, Pa," she pleaded, standing at the foot of the steps and staring at him with deep, troubled eyes. But Pa stood there stunned-like, not hearing her. And Ma wiped her hands on her apron and got crumbly balls of dough on the floor without noticing. "Come on, Pa," she begged gently, and finally he moved toward her as if he were feeling his way in the dark. When Ma's hand touched his coat shoulder and went around him his body shook a little. He looked as if he were going to cry. They went upstairs to their room and closed the door, Pa holding on to the banister and half pulling himself up the steps.

In the downstairs front room Nick, Julian and Ang waited quietly, fearfully. Ang sat in a corner pulling at her handkerchief until she tore it. Then, for no reason at all, she burst into tears and ran out of the room. Julian, getting more like Pa every day, had put on his grown-up face with the sad expression in his eyes. Nick stared out the window without looking at anything, and he tried to hear what the voices were saying behind the closed door upstairs. All he could hear was the low murmur without being able even to tell which was Ma and which was Pa. His whole body seemed to be beating in the front of his chest.

At last Ma came down and fixed supper just as if nothing had happened but Nick could tell that she had been crying, for her eyes were red with a dried-up look around them. The others didn't ask about Pa but Nick did. When the food was on the table he said, "Ain't Pa going to eat?"

Ma stood with the frying pan in one hand and he thought she was going to drop it, her hand shook so. She pulled in one corner of her lip and bit it. Then her free hand quivered to her hair and stayed there, fretful. The words came out hollow, then with an irritable snap to them, "No, Pa don't feel good. Nick, you're always asking too many questions. Haven't I told you about being so inquisitive?" Her voice broke. "Now you children sit here and eat. I'm going upstairs to your father."

■■■

On the way from school next day Nick walked past the store near downtown with the gold-leaf lettering on the plate glass spelling out: L. ROMANO—IMPORTER OF ITALIAN FOODS. The store was locked. The big wheels of cheese weren't in the windows, or the little dirty-looking ones that hung from ropes and were good when you cut into them past their rusty-brown outsides. Most of the cans, and the big boxes of all different kinds and shapes of spaghetti with long, funny Italian names were off the shelves. Even the bottles of olives were gone. And when Nick got home strange men were in the house, in all the rooms, examining furniture, feeling it and saying how much they'd give for it. Pa's eyes still looked half-blinded and bewildered. The sternness was only in the centers now.

The new car, only half paid for, had to go back. They had to move. They took only the table and chairs from the kitchen, two beds and a couch, and the big old-fashioned gilt frame all carved with leaves with the picture of the Blessed Virgin in it. Ma cried and Ang helped her. Julian had to quit school and that broke him up a lot. He had only a year to go and it was his biggest ambition to get a high school diploma and maybe go to college. But after a few days of moping around he took it all right and went out hunting for a job every morning. Nick couldn't go to St. Augustine's any more. It was way over on the "good" side of town.

They moved over to West Denver near Lincoln Park and Ma couldn't tell any of her friends where they were moving because that neighborhood had a bad name all over the city and Pa wouldn't stand for her telling anyone. That was where they had gangsters and holdups and killings. Everybody said that was the worst part of Denver.

They lived on Rio Street. There were four frame houses huddled close together. Only four, and their house was the worst one. The four dark rooms were bare and sullen and dingy from having been lived in by other poor people who had been unable to buy paint or wallpaper to make them look any other way. Out beyond the gate Rio Street was only a dirt road one block long, worn lumpy and gray by automobile tires, fronted by the Denver & Rio Grande Western railroad tracks swollen to eight sets of rails here. From the front porch looking across the tracks Nick could see the rear ends of a paint factory and a foundry. The weeds grew waist high against the abandoned foundry and its windows were broken, with here and there a shattered pane standing stark, with blackness behind the broken windows.

␣␣␣

Pa and Ma never had a cent in the house any more. Pa couldn't find a job. He walked all around the city looking for work and he didn't do anything, he said, but wear his shoes down and get a big appetite. "And another mouth to feed," he always added. He went to the employment agencies downtown at first but they all wanted money for a job and they didn't guarantee that he'd work long. . . .

Then Pa started going to a free place on Larimer and 18th. He came home from there one day and said, "Well, I got a job." But he didn't look any too pleased, not the way his mouth hardened down over the last word.

"Oh, *thank God! Thank God!*" Ma said.

Pa burst right in with, "It ain't much of a job. It's just piece work. Trenching celery—you dig ditches to bury the young celery in. I found that out from one of the men they hired." There was a pause. "I had to tell them I knew how." And with that Pa walked into the uncarpeted room in the new house where he and Ma slept and closed the door behind him.

When the celery gave out Pa came home to sit again, not saying much, his eyes mean brown, just wanting to be alone and not bothered.

Julian couldn't find work either but he went out all day long looking. Aunt Rosa, who had a part-time job, helped them out with a dollar or two every once in a while or brought some groceries. She'd come in and set the groceries on the middle of the table, smacking them down hard, like today, and look around for an argument. Ma looked at her as if she wanted to say, "Rosa, we can't accept it—" Ma didn't have to say anything. Aunt Rosa came out with, "Listen, Lena, damn it—!"

"Rosa, *please!* The children—"

"That's who I'm thinking about—them kids. You can be as proud as you damn please and not eat but them kids have got to have some grub." Her big hand came down on the table, bang, making the cups dance. And she started peeling potatoes and onions. There was no stopping her. Ma wiped one eye with the corner of her apron, then the other. Then Ma helped get the food together and they all ate, Aunt Rosa shoving half her food off on Nick's plate and saying, "Got to see that *my* boy is big and strong." Another trick she had was to put on her hat and coat, slap a dollar down on the table and get out of the door before anyone could stop her, just yelling, kind of madlike, "So long!"

■■■

He didn't like the new school at all. The Sisters were mean. They slapped the kids' hands hard with rulers and made the whole class stay after school writing, "I will try to please God by being quiet in class," even if only a couple of kids were bad or talked. It got so they had to stay after school two or three days a week filling paper after paper with promises to be good. Then Ma would scold him for being late when he got home.

He was an altar boy when he first started going to the new school. It was different from St. Augustine's. Father Scott always had a scowl on his face that was wrinkled like a walnut shell, and his shaggy eyebrows stuck way out from his face like two mustaches and were always drawn close together in the middle of his forehead in a deep, lined frown. His eyes were wrinkled back into his skull but they flashed out at you angrily when he leaned his head out on its long neck and stuck his face in yours. He was always sneaking up on someone in the dusty old hallways of the school, or on the street even, and you never knew he was there until it was too late. Some of the braver kids called him Father Gumshoe. But they were all afraid of him. And at Mass Nick had to have the cruets there for him at the very second he wanted them. If he didn't Father Scott would clear his throat loud or go "Humph! Humph!" deep down. And after Mass Nick would catch it.

■■■

The kids in seventh grade were all older than he was. Most of them were fourteen or fifteen years old, but he was as big as they were. Some of them came to class in overall pants and ragged sweaters and shirts. They needed haircuts and their clothes were dirty. They were tough. They were always throwing spitballs or shooting bent pins across the room or throwing erasers. And sometimes they

[12]

had fights right in the middle of the aisle with Sister trying to separate them.

You never knew what was going to happen in their room. Class would be quiet with only the sound of chalk scraping on the blackboard and geography book pages turning. And when it was quiet like that you could feel the air getting ready to explode. It was always dangerous when the room got so quiet. Maybe one of the fellows would yell "Ouch!" just for the fun of it and rub his neck as if he had been hit with something. Sister would look up at someone—maybe Tony. And he'd say, madlike, "I didn't do it! I didn't do it! Don't look at me!" Or one of the girls would turn around and slap one of the boys for pulling her hair and yell, "Sister! Sister! Make him leave me alone!" Or Ben would get up and walk out saying, "I got to go, Sister." Jack and Chuck would get up and walk out right after him. Then Tony. And Manuel and Steve. Pretty soon half of them would be gone and the rest of the kids would be giggling.

The Sister in charge had divided the room. If you were bad you had to do penance and you couldn't talk to anyone all day. One side of the room was for talkers and the other for penitents. Even so, she could hold them down just so long and then there'd be another outbreak.

3

Tony was a good kid. He liked Tony, and if they hadn't got poor and moved to that neighborhood he would never have known him. They became friends in class one day. Sister Ignatius was sore, and started fussing first thing. What made Sister really mad was the dry ice. A bunch of the fellows brought some of it to class that they got from the young guy who sold ice cream bars on the corner near the playground. Manuel put some in the big ink bottle on one of the back desks and shoved the rubber cork in tight. Pretty soon the cork popped off and ink hissed all over the back of the room. Sister Ignatius came swishing down the aisle past the desks on her short angry legs. The other fellows ducked their dry ice but Tony had ahold of a piece and was juggling it from hand to hand to keep from burning himself. Sister stopped by his desk, watching him, her heel beating up and down on the bare, warped floor. "Give that stuff to me!" Tony gave it to her. She stood there with the dry ice in her hand and her eyes leaped out at Tony while she tried to settle on his punishment. The ice lay on her palm. It ate through the outer surface of skin. Ben watched, hiding a grin behind the back of his hand. Suddenly Sister jerked her hand away fast and let out a scream. Then she stood there crying and beating Tony across the face with the back of her hand. Tony hid his face in his arms and she slapped away at his hair and skull until her knuckles got sore.

That started her off on Tony. She rode him all day. She asked him the hardest questions and gave him zero when he stuttered the answers. She kept him in at noon without any lunch and made him clean all the blackboards. Manuel sneaked an apple in to him and she made him bring it up to her desk where it sat on top of the dictionary all afternoon and she made Manuel stand out the rest of the day on the penitent's side of the room with his face to the wall.

"It's a very fine apple, isn't it, Tony?" she asked. "I am going to give it to the pupil who does the best work this afternoon."

Tony took out his handkerchief and, imitating Sister when she went back to her desk sniveling and feeling her burned hand, he sniffed into it.

"Stand up!" Sister shouted. And the girls sat upright at their desks.

"Young man, I've had enough of you," she said. The voice came out even and measured. "One more thing!—one more thing—and I'm going to expel you." Her finger wagged at him over the heads of the class with the dark robe falling from her arm and hanging deep at her elbow. Tony bobbed his head up and down in rhythm with her finger.

"Do you understand me!"

"Yes, Sister." And under his breath, "Damned old hag."

Class grew quiet after that. And the kids waited for something to happen. But nothing did. Even the most mischievous boys knew you could bend Sister Ignatius only so far. Then she snapped back at you and it was just too bad. Getting licked in the cloakroom, bringing their parents to school, getting licked again by mothers and fathers who used anything handy and held the church, Father Scott and the nuns inviolable, was carrying the punishment too far. Heads bent over books, teeth bit points on pencils, tongues licked pencil lead; and toward three o'clock Sister Ignatius' face had its usual tight-lipped calm.

Only Tony squirmed, chafing under Sister's chastisement, restless under Sister's eyes triumphant behind the silver rims. He watched the clock. He waited. Then when it was lacking only a minute to three he slipped the rubber band off his wrist from under the ravelled sweater sleeve, twisted it around his first and second fingers and fitted a bent pin into the little slingshot it made. Manuel's behind in frayed overall pants, facing out from the corner of the wall made by the blackboard and the windows, was a good target. Tony drew his right hand back slowly, took careful aim. His eyes went to Sister and back to the target. The rubber band snapped against his fingers, stinging them. The pin went true and Manuel's "Ouch!" was loud at the same minute that the bell sounded. And he rubbed himself behind with both hands.

It was an ill-chosen moment. Father Scott had come into the room on his quiet footpads and closed the door without making any noise. His old eyes leaped to the back of the room and his lumpy nose twitched with anger. Tony pulled the rubber band from his fingers and threw it on the floor. It landed in the aisle, halfway between Tony and Nick. Nick reached out with his foot, remembering that Tony would be expelled. His toe barely reached it; the rubber band was stubborn and jelly-like beneath his toe as he tried to pull it under his desk. He stooped over and picked it up, palming it quickly. As he straightened Father Scott's bony fingers closed on his collar.

"Did you do that?" It was an accusation.

"Y-y-yes, Father."

Nick was marched into the cloak room where Father Scott picked out the biggest ruler in the cabinet. And even his beads as big as marbles around his waist and his cassock and the collar turned around wrong didn't keep him from doing a good job of beating Nick. Never before had Nick, with the memory of St. Augustine's and Father O'Neil close, thought that *priests* would ever whip anyone. That was what made him cry. And right then, with the beads rattling and the ruler coming down hard, something started feeling wrong inside of him.

Tony was waiting outside. "Thanks, kid!" he said, real warm and friendly.

They walked in silence then, matching step for step. The leaves, beginning to wither, hung stiff and brittle from the trees. A ragpicker pulled his makeshift cart stacked high with old newspapers, mashed down cardboard cartons and pieces of metal along the curbstone. "Did old Gumshoe hurt you much?" Tony asked, embarrassed.

[15]

"Naw." Nick took a pleasure in hearing Father Scott called Gum-shoe.

A soiled woman carried bags of dried milk, beans, prunes home from the relief station. On the bags were printed in big letters: NOT TO BE SOLD. Off from the curb, in the street, sat a little boy playing with a broken toy truck. On one knee blood had dried. And some leaves blew in the gutter.

"It was swell of you," Tony said.

Nick blushed.

They came to Osage Street. "I go this way," Tony said. "See you tomorrow."

●●●

Nick went home feeling warm inside. He could hardly wait until tomorrow to see Tony again. He knew all the fellows tried to hang around Tony. Whatever he did everybody else tried to do. Tony had said, "Thanks, kid!"

Each day found Tony and Nick more closely allied—Tony, the roughneck leader of the school, and Nick, the "good kid." Yet each seemed to recognize in the other what he himself didn't have. And each was a little in awe of this different thing. That was what held them together.

The other fellows, Steve, Ben and the rest, tolerated Nick but they didn't like him. To them he was a kid. Too young. Too dumb. They teased Tony and referred to Nick as "your kid brother." Around them Nick wasn't himself and didn't have anything to say. But with Tony he could talk. Tony started whistling by the house evenings and they'd go to Lincoln Park to play catch or checker pool and look at the pictures in front of the shows.

Once, when Tony whistled by and Nick went out to the porch, Ma's voice came from the lighted window telling him to bring his friend in. They went up the low steps to the door and against the window they could see the swell of Ma's body, pulled into a tight hard ball in front.

They sat in the parlor on the hard kitchen chairs that were there. They didn't say much. Julian came through the room, gave Tony one sweeping look and left. He didn't come back in. Pa sat in a corner with his pipe, his eyebrows tight together up above the smoke; and every once in a while his eyes would cut from the want ads over to them. But Pa didn't say anything.

Tony came only once again. Then Pa said, "We want to keep our boy pure for the church. This Tony uses curse words and plays rough tricks." Ma agreed that he shouldn't go around with him any more. That put Nick more on Tony's side.

●●●

One evening Tony whistled by the house, low, hoping Nick's folks wouldn't hear. Nick got up quickly and slipped out the back way. He and Tony stumbled across the railroad tracks in the dark and through the high weeds by the foundry until they came under a street lamp and onto the sidewalk leading toward the park.

For a long time they didn't say anything. Then when they were alone in the park, sitting up close to the bushes, Nick said quickly, afraid he'd start and then stop, "Tony, why is my mother getting fat?"

Tony was pleased because Nick asked him; and proud that he knew. They lay in the grass, real quiet. Lightning bugs flitted around their heads. Far off a water hose hissed. A Mexican's guitar twanged while a girl was laughing. Tony told Nick. And Nick lay there with his face pressed into the green crushed-down grass, listening. And he was ashamed, ashamed.

Tony said, "My old lady told me all about those things long ago."

He wouldn't cry. He wanted to. But he wouldn't. He held his teeth together hard. All kinds of things fell pell-mell on his young brain. Then, when the storm almost came, but didn't; when he could look into the dark at the form of Tony crouched near him, he turned over on his side still clenching his teeth, letting the storm ebb away inside of him like a pain lessening.

Tony rolled the cigarette and smoked it in the dark. It went down, way small. Then, "Take a puff," he said. Nick put his lips to it and drew in the smoke fast. It made him choke and cough; his nose ran. But somehow it steadied him.

That clinched it for Tony and Nick. They were always together after that. Nick was at Tony's house more than at home. Tony forsook most of his friends for Nick. To Nick this relationship took the place of the closeness he had felt to Father O'Neil, the comradeship he had enjoyed with his brother before they moved, the sympathy Ma had never given him and the understanding Pa had always withheld.

4

Sometimes Tony and Nick would flip on the backs of trucks or stand on the bumpers of automobiles, holding onto the spare tire and crouching low so the driver couldn't see them through the rear-view mirror. They could go all over town like this. But most of all they'd ride across the Colfax Avenue bridge and go to the section where the well-to-do Jews lived in swell new houses on little hills with rolling lawns and hedges and flower beds in front of them. Tony didn't like Jews and called them kikes. Julian went over there about once a week and made sometimes a dollar, sometimes fifty cents beating rugs and scrubbing floors or washing windows. But when Tony and Nick were over there they'd just go through on their way to Sloan's Lake looking at the big houses and Tony would swear at the "dirty kikes." Sometimes, coming home after dark, he'd upset flower boxes or write dirty words in chalk on the sidewalks hoping to get a shag.

One day they took Manuel with them. The Romanos didn't have any money that day and no food in the house, so Nick went without until he got to Tony's house where Mrs. Amato made him eat with Tony. Then they called Manuel and hitched a ride on a farm truck out to beyond the bridge. They went into a store Tony knew about that was run by a little man with a graying beard and weak eyes behind heavy shell glasses. Manuel spent a nickel for candy, and when they came out he and Tony had three packs of cigarettes and two packages of Cool-ade stuck in the tops of their socks and under their belts.

They hiked out to Sloan's Lake. Out there they found a couple of milk bottles and dissolved the Cool-ade in them. Then they broke down some reeds near the lake and had a battle with them. Before they knew it, it was dark and they were hungry. They stole rides on bumpers all the way back to the neighborhood. Then Manuel said, "There won't be any more supper left at my house," and Nick, remembering, knew there wouldn't be anything at his house either.

[18]

"Say, Manuel!" Tony said, hooking an arm around Manuel's neck and tightening until their heads were close together, "Let's get some pies from the bakery. You know!"

"It's just about time, too!" Manuel said. He had been wrestling with Tony and putting him down in a hedge.

Nick knew it meant they'd steal the pies. He didn't want to go. "Come on," Tony coaxed, his arm linked in Nick's. "You don't have to take anything."

"You can just be the lookout," Manual added.

He went with them. They took to the alleys when they got near the bakery, stumbling over cans and into ash heaps in the dark, and at last walked close up to a fence where they could smell the pies. Two delivery trucks were parked in the alley behind the bakery. They walked past fast to make sure no one was in the trucks. Then they cut back. In the yard they could see the door open, light coming through from the two barred windows, and in the room were many pies cooling on long metal racks. And occasionally a man all in white with his sleeves rolled up and a baker's cap on his head would bring more pies on a long wooden thing like a shovel and put them on the rack.

"Any particular kind?" Manuel asked grinning, his shoulders dark and big in his ragged sweater.

"Boy! I like peach!" Tony said. And he pulled his cap low over his eyes. "You wait here, Nick. If anybody comes, whistle and run for it."

Tony and Manuel moved off together toward the lighted door. Nick, trembling, waited. His eyes went up and down the alley where they thought they saw shadows moving toward him. He hung close to the fence. Twice he started to whistle. A light shuddered past on the street. It seemed as if they would never come out of the bakery. Nick held his breath, expecting any minute to see the baker come back and start at them. Then finally they came out, holding the pies against their chests with their coats, and started back on the trot. At the alley they picked him up and ran, ran down alleys all the way back to Lincoln Park.

In the bushes they ate the pies that were still hot. They were gummy and sweet and good. Then when they had each eaten a whole pie they crawled out of the bushes, sailed the empty tins out onto Marietta Street and went home.

After that, half-hungry most of the time, Nick went back with Tony several times. It was easy. They never got caught.

■■■

Winter came. It would have been a tough winter but Pa got a job in a factory and that carried them through. There was even a regular Christmas dinner and a little table tree Julian had bought cheap out of his newspaper money. It had a dollar's worth of ornaments on it, and there were presents for the kids. Nick wanted a bicycle but Pa, who wasn't even making twenty dollars a week, told him they weren't millionaires and a leather jacket and a pair of shoes were a *lot*.

Aunt Rosa had Christmas dinner with them and a week later she went away to Chicago where a cousin was getting her a regular job in a dress factory. Nick remembered her going away vividly. Aunt Rosa in the depot, squatting on the bench, holding him so hard it hurt, pinching his ear, giving him two big wet kisses and saying, "Damn it, Lena, he's getting better looking every day. And big and husky. You can put him out driving a truck in another year." She had winked at Ma, then said, "You be good, Nick. Do you hear me? Or I'll come all the way from Chicago and use a baseball bat on you."

In the spring Pa lost his job and they had tough times again. Julian was sometimes lucky getting work unloading trucks at the City Market early in the mornings, and he did odd jobs. Ma went out now twice a week doing housework, so Pa got miserable and meaner than ever. Early in the summer Tony went away with his folks to do some ranch work out of the city somewhere and Nick was pretty lonely. He'd wander all over the city feeling sorry for himself and wondering what Tony was doing.

Nick's shoulders were broadening under his thin summer shirts and his arms, getting tan, were beginning to harden. Julian was the good little boy in the family now. The folks were always pointing out how wonderful Julian was and asking Nick why he wasn't like Julian. And Ma would say, "To think you used to be an altar boy! I'm ashamed to own you for my son." Tears would spout on Ma's cheeks. "Why do you treat your mother like this?" she'd say. Ma would clutch him, holding him tight against her stiff dark dress with her cheek on his head and the tears falling blop, blop on his hair, making it wet. And he was glad when he could pull away and go outside feeling guilty, kicking at stones and saying, "Aw, damn it!"

He was glad when Tony came back.

5

School started again. But they still goofed around. They had a big fat nun for the last grade. She looked like a scrubwoman with her rough hands and her red chapped face. The guys wouldn't come to school and they'd write each other's absent notes, putting fancy twists to the letters. She never caught on and before September was out they were able to cut class almost half the time. They'd ditch and go roaming over the city.

At school one day Nick heard Tony say something about ditching, so he didn't come back to class in the afternoon. He watched on the corner. When the kids were all going toward the cinder playground he saw Tony walking the other way. "Tony!" he called. Tony looked around but acted as if he didn't see him. Ben, a big guy Nick didn't like, stepped out of a doorway and fell in step with Tony. A hot flash of jealousy leaped up in Nick and he trotted after them, shouting, "Hey! Wait, Tony!"

It was Ben who turned and said, "Come on with, Nick."

They crossed Cherry Creek and started up toward town. Tony didn't even talk to him. Ben swung his arms and his shoulders and threw his big feet out. They were far enough away from school and the neighborhood to be noisy now and brave and I-don't-care. Ben started reciting a hobo poem: "We are three bums, we are three bums. . . ."

They got down by a corner with a parking lot and a little shanty sitting in the back. "You all ready?" Ben asked, looking at them. Tony saw him take them both in with his eyes and Tony turned around with his head just about where Ben's shoulders were. "Leave Nick out of this. He ain't like us."

Ben grinned meanly, "Oh—he's too *good*, huh?"

"Leave him out of it," Tony said. "You go home, Nick."

"No," Nick said stubbornly.

Tony's fists unballed then and his shoulders drooped down.

Ben said, "See, he wants to go. He wants to be one of the guys.

Don't you, Nick?" And Ben danced around Nick, slapping out with his hands and grinning meanly. Nick ducked and didn't want to slap back. But Ben kept feinting, feinting, until he caught Nick a hard one. Then they went to it, both smiling, both hitting out.

Nick got the worst of it and was breathing hard with his teeth clenched together and trying not to let his lips tremble. One thing you never did; you never let the fellows think you were yellow. That was the worst thing to be. Ouch! He almost said it aloud. Then Tony was pushing in between them, grinning with that swell grin that went all over his face. "Let's you and me, Ben," he said. And they went to it, Ben mad and swinging hard.

Tony had his shoulders hunched with his hands out in front of him alertly and he said, sort of explaining, "He ain't really stole nothin' yet."

They hit back and forth, their hands making smacking sounds when they landed. Nick leaned against a car fender, out of breath, and watched. Their faces were both red. Ben's wiry hair stood straight up. His nose was bleeding from one nostril and he licked the blood in with his tongue, not grinning now, just hitting and ducking. Some people stood on the sidewalk watching. Too many people were watching. The parking lot attendant came over to break it up.

Tony, Ben, Nick walked down the sidewalk. Tony worked his shirttail back into his pants. They were down on 19th Street. Tony said with finality, "Nick, wait here, will you?" He never saw Tony that determined before. He thought maybe Tony would even want to fight him. Tony's face was still red where Ben had slapped him and Nick knew he'd do anything Tony asked when he saw that. "All right," he said.

It was a shop where they had three balls over the door, guitars, holsters, guns, cowboy hats and jewelry in the window. Tony and Ben went in. Nick stood outside near the corner. A man walked by the shop and looked down into the show window. Tony and Ben came out, walking fast. Nick noticed the man had gone down the street only a few doors. Then he turned around and came back.

Tony and Ben met Nick at the corner and they walked together. Some blocks away Ben pulled his hand out of his pocket and with his back turned to Nick showed Tony something. Nick saw the glisten of the watch case. Right then, when Ben slipped it back into his pocket, someone was walking with them. It was the man who had gone by the pawn shop and he had Ben by the arm with his fingers sinking in. "Where'd you get the watch, kid?" he asked.

"I ain't got no watch!"

"I ain't goin' to hurt you, kid," the man said smoothly, his voice slow, playing with the words. The hand not holding Ben straightened the tidy knot of his necktie. There was a big-stoned ring on his finger.

"Honest, I ain't, mister!"

"Come on! I saw you swipe it." His voice scoffed at Ben. His black squint eyes watched Ben. He smiled with one corner of his mouth.

Ben backed away as far as the store front would let him. "What are you going to do to me?" he asked, panicky.

"Maybe I want to buy it," the man said. "Let's me and you talk it over—alone." He nodded toward Tony and Nick.

Ben and the man walked a little way into the alley. Nick could see them standing near a garbage can close up to the wall of a building and Ben showing the watch to the man.

After a while the man walked down the street and Ben came over to where they stood. Ben swaggered up. "I wasn't scared," he said. "He wants to buy it. He said he didn't have no money with him but for me to come by his house. Come on, let's go over there."

They started to hurry over to the address the man had given Ben. In the next street a truck had pulled up to the curb near an alley. The tailgate was down. There were half bushels of apples, red and green and shiny, in the truck. The driver was just carrying a basket of them into the store. "Look!" Ben said. "Let's get some."

They hopped up on the truck, Ben, Tony, Nick. The apples were under Nick's hands. He started filling his pockets, crowding them in, and into the front of his shirt next to his belly.

"Naw! Naw! Not like that!" Ben yelled. "Take a basket!"

Nick took a basket. He had just jumped down off the truck when the driver came out and started after them.

They ran across the street, couldn't make the turn into the alley, and kept going straight down the sidewalk. Somehow a policeman got into it too and the cop could run fast. Nick, forgetting that he had the basket of apples but hanging on to it with both arms wrapped around it, saw Ben and Tony turn a corner. Breathing hard, barely able to make it, he too turned the corner.

A red-headed woman saw the kids running, with apples spilling all over the sidewalk, saw the cop chasing them with his billy carried in his hand. When Nick rounded the corner out of sight with the flatfoot almost on top of him this woman stepped out of the doorway directly into the policeman's path. She tumbled a little from the speed with which he ran into her. But she grabbed his arms and held on. The cop, panting, grabbed her, holding her up and keeping himself from falling on top of her.

"Hello, Casey!" she said, her red mouth smiling at him.

He clutched one of her arms and shook her, trying to pry her loose.

"You goddamn bitch, you! Obstructin' the law—" He was indignant and angry.

Her fingers tightened into his arms playfully. "Come see me and I'll make it up to you," she said, smiling.

The cop grinned. "All right, Lottie," he said.

Nick caught up with Tony and Ben. They still ran but not so fast now with no one chasing them. Ben said, "Hey—look!" and they saw the man Ben had talked to in the alley. He stood in a doorway. When they got almost to the door his lips moved without making much noise—but they said, "In here."

They ducked in. It was dark. It stunk in the hall. They stood close together, Ben, Tony, Nick; and Nick waited, not knowing what to expect. Then the man opened a door down the hall. "Come on, kids—get in here."

They got. He closed the door. Nick set the basket of apples on the floor and looked around. There wasn't much furniture. The man stood with his back leaning against an old dresser. He was laughing at them. "Nearly got caught, uh?" From the way he said it Nick knew he was all right and wouldn't turn them in.

"Sit down, kids. On the bed—that's all right."

The man took out a shiny, gold-looking cigarette case and passed smokes around.

Nick drew in on the cigarette and looked admiringly at the man's stickpin and the coat big at the shoulders, draping down, tight at the hips. His eyes slipped down to the pants like you saw on the dummies in store windows and the sharp-pointed patent leather shoes, shiny like two mirrors. The man dropped his only half-burned cigarette on the floor and stepped on it. To Ben he said, "Let's see that watch again." Ben and the man looked at the watch together. After he had examined it all over, even opening the back, he said, "I'll give you three dollars for it."

Ben said quickly, "Chee! All right!"

The man went over to the dresser and pulled out a woman's pocketbook. He opened it and fished around inside of it. But he didn't find what he wanted and he cursed. He threw the purse on top of the dresser. "You'll have to wait a while," he said. Then his eyes came up from the watch and stared at Ben meaningly. "Maybe me and you can do a lot of business together."

None of them heard the door open or shut. The woman stood inside the room with her red hair frizzed, with the smile coming off her face, with her eyes jumping out at the man, mad. Her mouth twisted up ugly and she said, "Why you dirty little white-livered sonofabitch!"

The man looked guilty. He said, "Aw—Lottie. Pipe down, will you?"

[24]

She didn't even hear him. She was just staring at him. "I thought you were a *man*."

He shrugged angrily, said between his teeth, "Shut up!"

"Shut up?—Shut up!" There was a catch in her voice. "You ought to be ashamed of yourself. These kids—" She looked around at them blindly. She was laughing just a little but it sounded like a sob. "You no-good bastard!"

He slid around to where she was like a cat. His hand came out hard and her head jerked. He brought his hand across her face again. Again. She held on to the bedpost with one hand and gently beat the palm of the other one on top of it. But she didn't whimper.

When he was finished she lifted her head. "You ain't going to buy that watch from these kids," she said. Each word was underlined. A long scar on her cheek was white against the redness of her skin where his hand had slapped.

"All right! All right!" he said. Then his lips lifted in a sneer. "You got any money?"

She bent down, reached under her short skirt and pulled some crumpled bills out of the top of her stocking. She held them out to him. He counted them and stuffed them into his pocket.

She was boss then. She turned on Ben, Tony and Nick. "You kids get out of here. And don't you ever come back. Get out now!" Her voice was angry but her eyes were funny-like—sad and hurt.

They got. And Nick, putting the basket of apples on his shoulders, wondered why her eyes were like that.

They walked back toward the neighborhood together. After a while Nick said, "Was that his wife?" Ben laughed out loud. Tony looked at Ben and frowned. He said to Nick, "I don't know."

They couldn't go home yet because school wasn't out. They walked slow and ate apples. They found an empty factory and lay hidden in the tall weeds behind it. They filled up on apples, crunching them, not talking, throwing the cores and hearing them plink softly in the weeds. They ate lots of apples and still there were plenty more. Then it was time to go home.

They started down the sidewalk again. Ben scratched some dried blood out of the corner of his nose and looked at it. Then he pulled the watch out of his pocket. "Here, you can have it," he said, holding it out to Tony. Tony took it.

Ben turned off by the City Market. Tony and Nick, each carrying a handle of the apple basket, walked down Colfax. When they came to Cherry Creek Tony threw the watch into the creek. It made a bright, yellowish splash and was gone. Then he picked up his end of the basket and they crossed the bridge.

The sun was coming down and as it came it colored things up

[25]

and made long shadows. Nick and Tony carried the basket. Their long shadows walked along with them. Nick looked over at Tony. He wanted to say, "We're good friends, ain't we, Tony? We'll always be good friends, won't we?" But he just walked on with the wire handle of the basket cutting into the palm of his hand and making it tingly-numb, with the streets getting darkish but the lights not coming on yet, with him and Tony walking along . . . together. And every once in a while he would look over at Tony.

He was going to hide the apples out in the barn so they wouldn't ask him questions, but Ma was out in front buying a head of cabbage. She wanted to know where he got the apples. Nick thought fast. "I helped a man unload a truck at the market and he gave me these and a dime."

Ma said, "Oh, that's pretty good. You ought to go there every day after school."

◄■■

He made up his mind, after almost getting caught, not to steal any more. He didn't go out with the guys. He stayed home chopping wood after school and pulling weeds out of the backyard that was all weeds. Ma asked him, inquisitively, "How is it you never go out any more?" He'd say, "Aw, I just don't feel like it." Ma liked having him not go out. He stood by home for a whole week.

▼■■

Then Ben came by late one night. Ben had a bicycle and he was in a hurry. "Keep this in your barn for me," he said, insisting.

"I don't want to."

Ben got mad. "I'm telling you you're going to keep it for me."

"What if I get in trouble? Why don't you take it to your house?"

"We ain't got no room in that little joint where I could hide it without my old man seeing it and kicking hell out of me. Anyway you got a barn. Come on! Let me leave it here."

"No. I don't want to."

Ben had him by the arm, twisting. "I'm in a hurry. I can't stick around here. You going to put it away for me, do you hear?"

He didn't want to fight. He wished he did. He wished he had enough guts. His arm was hurting like everything. Then Ben said, "Tony's in on it."

"All right, I'll keep it," Nick said.

■■■

When the policeman came into the room with his hat off and went up to talk to Sister, Nick got scared stiff. He stuck his head way down and slipped as far down in the seat as he could. But he kept looking up at the policeman's mouth moving and Sister's mouth moving.

Sister looked worried. She called him right up to the desk. Then he had to turn around and, facing all the kids, walk out with a policeman.

The cop had him by the arm, leading him out. Nick hung his head and walked along beside him. All the kids in the room made "ppppsssssss—!!!"

He looked for Ben. Ben was sitting looking out of the window, unconcerned.

He had to pass Tony's seat. He looked at Tony. With his eyes he tried to say, "I won't snitch." Tony was looking at him real sorry and with his mouth half open as if he were going to say something.

At the door Nick looked back. The expression hadn't changed on Tony's face, only he was turned away from his seat as if he were going to get up and follow Nick. Gee, Tony looked sad. He wouldn't forget that.

6

Daylight touched the bars of the windows along the whole length of the wall. Beyond the bars there was nothing but mountains, mountains coming alive in the light, first foggy, then turning purple, green, brown. Somewhere in the room there was heavy breathing.

All the cots were empty, both rows of them down each side of the long walls. All but Nick's. Nick lay on his stomach on the dormitory bed. The army blanket was pulled down halfway so that his back was up and out of the covers. His arms were criss-crossed over his head. His hair was weedy over one wrist. The mattress moved a little with his breathing. He hadn't heard the get-up whistle. He wasn't used to whistles—yet.

Now there was a beam of sunlight on the foot of the bed. A whistle, outside the building, blew in a command. On the pillow Nick's mouth was open a little, taking the air in and letting it out. BA-OWW! Then the housefather was hitting him across the back with a strap. "Ow! You bastard!" Nick yelled, coming awake with the sting of the strap on his flesh.

And Nick woke up on his first day in reform school.

"Who you calling that! You sonofabitch!" The housefather let Nick have it.

Nick twisted around on his back and sprang to a sitting position. He grabbed the blanket up around him and threw his arms up, warding off the blows. "Wait a minute! Wait a minute!" The housefather swung the strap, not letting up for a minute.

Nick jumped out of bed. His bare feet hit the cold floor and sent him running around the dormitory putting on his clothes. The housefather chased him and laid in a couple more. Then he stood by the door watching Nick's scared eyes as Nick stuffed his shirt into his pants and tightened his belt.

"Now you get down those steps *fast*, you little sonofabitch!" His voice shook with anger.

■■■

On the green lawn in front of the dormitories all the new kids stood shoulder to shoulder. Their arms were folded across their chests tightly. Their chins were in. Their eyes were straight forward. In front of them stood an officer with a whistle clenched between his teeth.

"Get in line there," the housefather told Nick. "No breakfast for you." Then to the officer, "They're all here now."

"Thank you, Mr. Wallace."

Nick fell in line. He was scared. He didn't know anything. He withdrew into himself and waited. He was scared.

The officer, with a voice that went *Ahhhhh-ten-SHUNNN!* marched them up and down, teaching them "Forward march! Squads right! About face!" He got mad and sarcastic when they didn't catch on. Up and down they marched, with his voice in their ears shouting: "Forward march! Squads right! About face!"

At last he lined them up, arms folded stiffly across their chests again, and looked at his watch. He wouldn't let them move an inch. "Eyes straight forward! Shoulders back! Don't move!"

The superintendent came under the trees and across the flagstone walk. He was a tall, skinny man, about forty-five years old. A snap-brim hat hid most of his face. The left sleeve of his coat was empty, pinned against his coat and tucked into the pocket. In his only hand he carried a slip of paper. There was another man with him. He was a big, beefy man who might have played tackle on a college football team ten years earlier.

They walked up to where the new kids and the officer waited. The big man grinned at them. "Hello, boys!" he said. "I'm the director. My name is Mr. McGuire. I want to introduce you to our superintendent. This is Mr. Fuller." He grinned at them again and stepped back so Fuller could have the stage.

The one-armed man looked them over. His nose was thin, sharp, coming down to a straight-across mouth. You couldn't see his eyes very well because of the way his hat was pulled down. But you felt as if he were looking through you all the time he was talking: "...Each of you is given a number of credits when you arrive here. You have to work these off. You can get 125 off a month—*providing*—you have performed your various duties here properly and your behavior has been above reproach. You will be checked on your company record, school record, credit record, and departmental record. None of you has been given a sentence. You can work your way out of here. We try to keep before you the idea of good habits—personal cleanliness, honesty, obedience, cooperation, respect for property, *and* the use of clean language. Now you boys have been assigned to your dormitories according to age...."

When he had finished his speech he squinted at the slip of paper he held and read their names and the work they had been assigned to, glancing up quickly now and then to see if any of the boys were looking at his empty sleeve.

"Nick Romano, kitchen."

■■■

Superintendent Fuller went back under the trees and across the flagstone walk to the office, one side of his body looking flat with the arm missing. Director McGuire, with a new cigarette in his mouth, got into a shiny this-year's car and drove to some other part of the grounds. The new kids were marched into the big, empty gymnasium and lined up in two long straight rows, one row behind the other. They stood with their arms folded. Some had their heads down. Some squirmed uncertainly. There were big ones and little ones. They were all scared.

The gym director waited for them. He stood with his feet on the sideline stripe of the basketball court. Instead of looking at them he watched the officer trailing back up the low hill to the office. He was a short man, husky, with blue eyes and straight blond hair that was thinning. For a long while he watched the sidewalk going up to the office. Then for the first time he looked at them all standing stiffly with their arms folded. "At ease!" he yelled. He moved his head up and down the line. "Well—here you are. The law says you stay here until you're reformed. Oh, yes. You'll be reformed when you get out of here. Oh, yes."

His eyes glowered. But every once in a while they shot past the boys to the wide gymnasium door that stood open with sunlight in it in big chunks and that gave a view all the way up the little incline of hill with a long sidewalk climbing to the office building.

He went right on talking, like a quarterback yelling signals. "We mix you all up here. The clean and the unclean, the young and the old, the innocent and the guilty." He sighed heavily . His blue eyes were gray. The thing he was looking at wasn't there in the gym but way off somewhere. He looked out the door steadily and said, "If you refuse to work or are really the bad type we handcuff you to a cell in the basement and shoot the fire hose on you until the water knocks you out or you decide to behave. That's how we reform you. Oh, yes."

He looked all along the line, looking at them seriously. "My name is Roy Quinn. Call me Roy. Or Quinn. Maybe—in front of the big shots—you'll have to call me Mr. Quinn. Just don't try to kid me. I know what goes on around here. Now, I'm nobody's father. And I'm nobody's big brother. If any of you boys get in a jam come to me. And don't worry about me talking. I'm your friend—and you won't have many around here. Well, that's all." He clapped his hands together twice. "Grab a ball and some bats."

They went out into the sun that lay bright and yellow all over the reform school grounds. Far out they could see the work fields. On the baseball diamond they chose up sides and Quinn played baseball with them.

After a while, when the sun was really burning up over the mountains, a tall boy in blue denim came out across the field and spoke to Quinn where he stood in the box pitching. Quinn called all the boys around him. "Well, I've got to go to the office," he said, not pleased. "Keep on with the game. Soon they'll send an officer after you and march you off to church. You've got to go to church. Oh, yes." He had his foot on the soft indoor ball and he rolled it back and forth with the sole of his gymshoe. "Then, after lunch, you'll get your uniforms. You've got to have prison clothes. Oh, yes."

Quinn was hardly gone when a bunch of big guys in blue denim slowly wandered out to the baseball diamond and stood around. Some of them had their hair slicked down. They all had sneering mouths. Their eyes watched the new kids. They stood around with their hands in their pockets. They were *big* guys, seventeen, eighteen, nineteen years old.

Nick chased a fly that bounced foul on the base line. He couldn't get it and it rolled fast toward the bunch of fellows watching. A tall, skinny guy with pimples all over his face stooped over and picked it up. Nick trotted halfway to him and stopped with his hands held open for the ball. The fellow with the ball said, "Here comes my new babe." All the rest of them laughed.

Nick stood looking at him with his mouth half open. He wasn't any *kid*. That sounded funny. What did he mean? The new kids were yelling, "Come on! Throw it!" Nick threw the ball in to the pitching mound and trotted back to the game.

Finally the new kids were marched off to the chapel. As they went out of the brightness of the sun and over the brown dirt path between the dormitories the older boys stood back against the walls, laughing and looking them over.

*■■

Their legs, a whole line of them in the reform school blue, were going down the stone steps beyond the iron fence to the basement. Nick bent his head to get through the low door and went into the basement under the Company B dormitory where all the guys but the older fellows, those seventeen and over, had to stay after supper until they were locked up in the dormitories. He walked in his reform school uniform: denim blue pants and shirt. They were stiff and itchy. There were no shorts. Just pants, shirt, socks, heavy workshoes. And a blue denim cap. Nick stuffed the cap into his back pocket and sat on the edge of one of the benches against the wall.

Nick looked around. There was the door they had come through with a long corridor to the outside door. Someone had closed it and a couple of lucky guys were smoking, off in a corner with a bunch of the fellows hanging around them begging for butts. At the other end of the basement was another smaller room where Nick could see the long white troughs, stained and dripping water, where you took a leak. There were some shower stalls too, with drains in the floor. Beyond the troughs there was a door. Just bars, like in jail and locked with a big lock. A guard sat on a stool on the other side of the barred door at the foot of the three steps up. He was leaning sideways with his back against the bars, smoking quietly. Darkness was up the steps.

Inside the basement room where Nick was, pipes ran all around the walls. There were a couple of small, barred windows, neckhigh. The basement was crowded with fellows. They laughed and talked and wrestled. They cursed a lot. Four of them sat, tailor-fashion, in the center of the floor, playing pinochle. Two fellows sat facing each other with a bench in between their legs and a checkerboard on the bench. But most of them just horsed around.

A husky guy kicked the door open and came into the basement. He was so husky that he was sort of hunchbacked. His bushed red hair stood tangled on his head. He had a kind of flattened-out nose and freckles, big freckles. Right behind him were two other fellows walking close to him. He squinted around the room at the guys on the benches. The fellows looked up and all started saying, "Hi, Bricktop, hello, Bricktop, whatcha say, Bricktop?" But the voices were not friendly, only as if they were all telling him anxiously: We're on your side and you're a swell guy.

One of the fellows was crossing the room to the can. Bricktop

[31]

stuck out his foot and tripped him. Then he laughed. And all the fellows laughed too, looking over at Bricktop.

On a bench a fat kid polished an apple against his shirt front. Bricktop walked over, snatched it out of his hand and put his teeth halfway around it, biting in. The kid didn't say anything. He sat there empty-handed. His face got red and in a little while he got up and walked away like he was sneaking.

All the fellows watched Bricktop sinking his teeth into the apple, not turning their heads, just looking out of the corners of their eyes. But when Bricktop looked at any of them they grinned at him.

When there was nothing much left but the core he offered it to one of the boys who had come in with him, a slim good-looking fellow with light brown hair curly under his blue denim cap that was screwed around on his head so that the bill was at the back. The youth shook his head no, went over to a bench, sat down with his legs spread out in front of him and his head down and began to roll a cigarette. "Here, Slim," Bricktop said, handing the core to the other fellow who was with him.

When the cigarette was ready, Bricktop said, "Hey, Rocky, roll me a cigarette." Rocky looked up through his hair. He tossed the cigarette underhand to Bricktop and started another one for himself. Bricktop nodded his head at Slim. "Watch the door."

When Bricktop was sucking in on the cigarette greedily he noticed Nick, the new kid. For a while he stared at him, looking him over. Finally he crossed the room to where Nick was sitting on a bench trying not to be noticed.

Nick saw the big workshoes and the blue denim pants legs standing close to him and looked up. Hunchbacked Bricktop was squinting down at him with the tangle of red hair over the narrowed eyes. "I want to see you outside."

Bricktop led the way to the barred door at the back. In the dark, near the shower stalls, Nick heard scuffling. Bricktop said hello to the guard, "Hi, Charlie!" with a lot of swagger in his voice and Charlie got right up and unlocked the door for them.

The door creaked noisily and they stepped out beyond it into the hushed and cool night. They went behind the dormitory near the engine room where a tall smokestack went straight up. They squatted up close to the smokestack in the dark, Bricktop motioning Nick down beside him. Nick sat, scared.

"You look like the right kind of guy," Bricktop said.

Nick didn't say anything. His fingers scratched across the dirt gathering pebbles in a pile.

Bricktop said, "I run things around here."

The mountains were far out, black in the night. Like cut from cardboard. There were stars. Lots of stars.

Bricktop talked out of the corner of his mouth. "We call ourselves the Spiders. I'm the boss."

There was a small pile of rocks under Nick's hand. He could feel them. He pulled at the roots of crab grass. Around the corner of the building was the guard who had let them out, smoking.

"You got any money?"

Nick pressed the little pile of rocks down under his palm. He shook his head no, slowly. "No."

"You'll get some? Your folks are going to send you some?"

"Yes."

"How much?"

"Maybe a dollar."

"Well, you've got to give seventy-five cents of it to me if you want protection. Guys who don't kick in get all their stuff taken away from them. Like candy and magazines from home. Understand?"

Nick looked at the black wall of mountains curving all around like a horseshoe. "Yes," he said, hardly audible.

Bricktop didn't talk so hard boiled then. "Course we ain't goin' to let you join the gang yet. Not till we find out if you can take it."

Nick looked down into his fear and loneliness. He remembered: "You'll be reformed when you get out of here. Oh, yes." The strap was twisted in the housefather's fist and it touched the floor.

Bricktop said, "I think we'll get along."

The moon was up and beautiful over the reform school. The open square between the buildings was flooded with it. There were stars trailing down behind the mountains. In the work fields, way over, looking like they were plastered up against the mountains, the long even rows of corn rustled gently, touching their leaves together. There were spider webs; they were silvered with dew. The sugar beets sucked in the dew. The flagstones, like silver-black disks, walked under the trees into the reform school grounds. You couldn't see the flowers in the dark. But when you listened you could hear the crickets all making low, vibrating noises together.

7

The whistle screeched in a long-drawn siren howl and the forty boys got out of bed hastily.

Light spread over the mountains.

Again the bars lit up and the boys inside stooped over their beds, making them. Nick fumbled with the blanket, trying to make it fold under the foot of the bed and smooth out. Twice he tried and couldn't. Right close to him a quiet voice said, "I'll help you." Nick looked up into the serious gray eyes of a Mexican boy about his age. The boy stood in the aisle between the beds. He was skinny. His bones showed like knots in a rope. His cheekbones were pinched up high with slight shadows under them and when Nick smiled at him he averted his eyes shyly. But he moved in next to Nick and with expert hands made the bed. Bending over, tightening the blanket down, he said, "My name is Jesse."

"Mine's Nick."

When the bed was made Jesse said, "We got to sweep the dormitory." He got Nick a broom and they worked close together.

"Where do you work?" You had to listen hard to hear Jesse.

"In the kitchen," Nick said.

"I'm in the shoeshop."

Up in front, standing by the door, a houseboy in blue denims just like them was bossing the work. Once in a while he'd curse somebody, showing he was a big shot and meant business.

Jesse and Nick went down the long flight of steps together. "We got to scrub the basement." Nick followed him.

In the basement they filled pails with hot soapy water, turned up their pants, hung their shirts over the waterpipes and, stripped to the waist, started swabbing down the basement. About twelve boys worked there, splashing out the soapy water and then mopping it up. Nick and Jesse hung close together. With their backs bent they worked the heavy mops back and forth over the dirty concrete.

When they were finished they didn't have much time to wash.

They just rubbed soap and water on their faces fast, wiped it off and started pulling on their shirts. Jesse didn't have much chest to button his shirt over; all his ribs showed through his brown skin. Nick was glad he had a big chest and big shoulders. But he put on his shirt fast when Jesse, with his head half-hung, looked over at him, at his husky chest and arms.

Nick had just started buttoning when a whistle blew. "Hurry!" Jesse said, panicky. He hurried. They combed their hair as best they could with their fingers and Jesse, walking fast, led the way.

With the other boys of Company B they marched in line out of the big upstairs door, down the broad stone steps and onto the green of the lawn. The man with the soldier's cap and the whistle was standing on a little rise of ground. He blew his whistle. Every boy came stiffly to attention. In front of the other two dormitories the rest of the fellows were in straight oblong boxes of blue denim against the green lawn. The officer blew his whistle again. Companies A, B, and C fell in line in order and marched across the grounds, then back. The long formation started with the big fellows and petered down to the little kids ten and eleven years old.

They marched up and down until breakfast was ready. Then another whistle blew somewhere else and they marched in to breakfast.

Jesse, in line with Nick, said quickly, in a whisper, "I can't sit with you—don't talk!"

There were eight fellows to a table. One of the men pointed to an empty place and Nick went there. The eight boys stood by the table with their arms folded. All over the dining room it was like that. You had to say blessings with your arms folded and your head down.

Up in front, at a long table with a white cloth that was just for the officers and housefather, Superintendent Fuller stood leading the blessing. He said it as if he were God.

"...from Thy bounty through Christ our Lord, AMEN."

Then the officer who marched them in said out of the corner of his mouth, "One!—Two!—Three!"

And everybody sat down.

It was mum then. Once you hit that dining room and said the blessings you didn't talk until you got out. One guy took a chance, a fellow sitting near Nick. He whispered to the boy next to him, "Let's fog the new kid."

Arms went out everywhere, reaching, filling plates, taking doughnuts. Plates of food went right under Nick's nose to the fellow on the other side of him without stopping long enough for him to get any. Oatmeal lumped up out of bowls of milk. Jam was red on

[35]

white slices of bread. There were saucers of prunes. And the dough-nuts were brown and crisp-looking.

All the other fellows were eating greedily. But there was nothing on Nick's plate. And every platter was carefully at the other end of the table.

Each table had as a waiter a reform-school boy in a white jacket. Their waiter watched the fogging and grinned, blowing little snick-ers of laughter through his nose as he stared at Nick's empty plate and his hurt and bewildered eyes.

You couldn't say a word at the table. Not a word. The waiters brought the salt, the water, the bread and milk and stuff like that. You held up a hand and signalled what you wanted by so many fingers. Nick saw the guys get milk and later bread. Nick tried, holding up four fingers. The waiter grinned, brought over the pitcher and filled his glass with water. One of the guys laughed, blowing oatmeal across the table. He laughed almost too loud—Superintendent Fuller looked up over a spoon of iced cantaloupe and frowned.

Nick looked at his empty plate and all the fellows shoveling the food in. Then he glanced at the waiter timidly. The waiter was looking right at him, encouraging him. Nick held up his little finger.

Salt.

They were allowed just so much time to eat. Then they heard a whistle. And they went to work.

As he came into the long kitchen Nick saw his new boss. The kitchen officer was a kind of nice-looking man, not very old. His name was Kennedy and he said he used to cook on a boat. He talked to Nick and the rest of them almost as if he were young himself. He was one of those men who was always cursing.

There were six fellows working in the kitchen, two on the dishes, two on the range and two on the kettles. Kennedy laughed and told Nick. "You start on dishes but you can be promoted. You can move up to the range and then to the kettles. But only when some sonofabitch leaves."

Just before they had to rush to get the lunch ready Kennedy called Nick over. He said, "If you do anything wrong I have to fill this out and send it over to the office." Nick saw printed on top in big capitals: MISCONDUCT SLIP. "When you take one of these over there they add some more discredits to your record. I seldom send one of them in. But I just thought I'd tell you." Then he looked away, out the window, cursed and told Nick to go back to work.

The other fellow helping peel potatoes said to Nick, "Them

things go tough on you when you have to take one in. It all goes by what the officer writes down. And if he writes it down pretty strong when you get to the office they say, 'I think you better take a few. Pull them down.'" He screwed his mouth up sideways and skidded the knife around the end of the potato. "Then you pull down your pants and they let you have it. You get discredits too. I seen guys catch two hundred and fifty discredits just for whistling. It's all how the officer feels."

Then it was noon and they went back to the dining room. Between the buildings Nick met Jesse coming out of the shoeshop. They fell into step together, shyly, without words. Along the sidewalk there came a Negro, a fellow about seventeen. He was handsome like a brown, smoothly built race horse. He had the same bulging muscles that didn't really bulge but seemed to ripple like water; with shoulders straight across, and a slim waist buckled under a wide black belt, with arms coming down to big hands. His face was brown and all shiny. His shoulders were back and he walked kind of proud, with a certain challenge to the toss of his head. All the fellows said hello to him. When Nick and Jesse came along he didn't wait for Jesse to say hello. He grinned, and with it came the words, friendly-like, "How's it goin', Bones?" And he looked at Nick friendly, too.

"They call me Bones," Jesse said softly.

"Who's that guy?" Nick asked, curious.

"He's champ of the hill."

"What do you mean, champ of the hill?"

"He can fight anybody in here. The best fighter is always champ of the hill. If you want to be champ you challenge the guy who is and fight him on the hill behind the dormitories. And if you win *you* are."

They walked along toward lunch. Nick watched all the fellows in blue piling up the steps of the dining room. "What's his name?" Nick asked.

"Allen. Nobody wants to go to war with him."

Under the trees of the square Bricktop, Rocky and Slim walked toward them. They had their shirts unbuttoned all the way down to their belts and thrown open. Their shirttails were out in front and knotted with the ends standing out like bows. On their chests they had their names smashed into their skin and under their names, pinched in bruised, darkened skin was a big S for Spiders. Nick looked below the twisted-around cap and in between the long, narrow V of open shirt: *Rocky.*

Bricktop had his thumbs looped in his belt. He didn't speak to Nick. He just gave him a superior, dismissing glance and let his

[37]

eyes go over to Jesse. "Well, if it ain't the bag of bones. You still walking around?"

Jesse went red.

Rocky looked away from Jesse at Nick and Nick saw Rocky's mouth tighten a little. Then Rocky's lips twisted in a friendly smile. He bobbed his head and said, "Hi!" Nick bobbed his head too and said "Hi." Nick turned around and looked back at Rocky. All the Spiders had their shirts pulled out sloppy in the back.

After lunch they had half an hour off in the basement where they sat around. They were hardly down there, with their butts eased down on benches and some of the guys cutting up, when a kid hopped in through the door and shouted, "Here comes Fuller!"

All the fellows stopped horsing around. They all hunched up stiff and tense. Some sat with their heads down. Some watched the door. They could hear the superintendent's feet clicking on the concrete like a soldier's as he came along the hallway.

He came in. He looked around at them like he owned them. His gray eyes were just a cold stare.

Nick looked at the empty sleeve and a little shiver ran up his back. The fellows all said that he had more strength in his one arm than most men had in two.

In the only hand he had Superintendent Fuller carried a small wooden box of matches. He swung his arm back and forth with the box showing in between his lean, bony fingers. He went through to the back and they could hear him yelling at the guard, bawling hell out of him about something. Then his clicking heels carried him back through the room where they were and out of the basement.

The fellows were quiet even after he had gone.

8

Before going back to work in the kitchen Nick had to sit through two hours of English, history and geography classes. It was worse than school outside. You couldn't stall. There were only fifteen fellows in each class and the teachers could see every move you made. One of the teachers was a woman and she was worse than the men with her nasty cracks and fingers drumming on top of the desk—"Well!—Well!—Go on! I don't expect you to have any intelligence or you wouldn't be here, but is it too much for you to read a thing out of a book and then tell me what you read? Well—! Well—!" The fingers drummed on the desk.

The fellows sat with their elbows on the desks, their hands up to their faces and the books open. You couldn't glance out the window even for a minute without the fingers drumming or a man teacher coming down the aisle and twisting your head back over the book with his hand tangled in your hair. All three teachers threatened them with discredits if they didn't study hard, be mannerly, stand up right away when they were called on. The fingers drummed, the bell rang, and Nick was glad to go back to the kitchen and listen to Kennedy curse.

All the fellows crowded through the school hall. On the second floor landing one of the women teachers, a plump blonde with heavy curves, was going into a room. A bunch of the reform school boys were crowded behind her and out from somewhere came a hand grabbing her behind. Then they all ran along the corridor and down the steps.

A line of new kids trailed across the grounds toward the gymnasium. At the tail end was a little blond boy walking with his head twisted back toward still another kid at the very end of the line. "Come on, Sam!" he called. Sam hurried along on skinny bow legs inside black, knee-length stockings. His face was black. Even his lips were black. He hurried along. And he grinned a little when the other kid said, "Come on, Sam!"

●●●

In the kitchen Nick peeled more potatoes. He sat on a bench with a newspaper between his feet to catch the peelings that curled from under the blade of the knife. There was a big five-gallon can half full of water on the floor near him for the potatoes. He liked to finish a potato so he could toss it into the pail, hear it go *spah-lash!* and watch it settle down at the bottom on top of the other potatoes. The big kitchen smelled good with meat baking and pots bubbling on top of the stove where the range boys, with long spoons, took care of them. For a moment, mingled in the smell of the food and the familiar sounds of a kitchen, the faces of his parents loomed large before his eyes. . . .

He saw Pa standing straight-backed and square-shouldered, his face never losing that severe look, saying in his stern voice, "Our Nick is a fine boy. Our Nick is going to be a priest. We are going to give our Nick to the church." And Ma nagging him about brushing his teeth and shining his shoes. And Ma's favorite story. He still thought about that mouse and felt sorry for it.

■■■

...alongside of Rankin's grocery store there was a crowd of people in a circle, their legs shutting out what was going on in the circle...then, between trouser legs he could see a cat crouching over something. He moved up to the legs hesitantly, squirming in between legs and stood inside the circle...and...on the ground ...by the green and crumbly boards of the grocery store...there was a tiny little mouse with pleading eyes looking up...there was a cat playing with it but getting ready to eat it...the cat slapped, slapped, slapped...the cat didn't have its claws all the way out ...it just patted and slapped the mouse trying to make it run... trying to have fun with the scared little, black-eyed little, trembling little mouse. Black little eyes, scared little eyes...and the cat's paw reaching out...toying, slapping, playing...slapping, playing, ripping...he walked over real fast with his head down and drawn in because he was shy and ashamed and embarrassed...quickly he picked up the mouse and stuck it in his coat pocket...in the darkness of his pocket and the palm of his hand he could feel the tiny, soft little mouse trembling...and quickly he had squirmed past the legs and walked away...in the alley he let the mouse go...

■■■

Nick lowered his head. He could feel his hands trembling. He took the last of the peeling from the potato and tossed it into the pail.

He heard the low murmur of an automobile and the click-shut of the car door. Looking up he saw Mr. McGuire, the director, get out of his shiny green limousine and wait for the visitors who were easing their long legs out beyond the leather upholstery to the gravel path at the back entrance to the kitchen. Mr. McGuire wore a summer suit and spotless white shoes. As usual, he was smiling at the visitors and pointing, "This is the kitchen. We prepare four hundred meals here every day...."

The visitors were smoking cigarettes and stood squinting into the sun in the direction Mr. McGuire was pointing. Then the three of them came crunching up the gravel walk toward the screen door.

Mr. McGuire said, "Don't give any of the boys cigarettes. They'll ask for them."

They were at the screen door. One of the visitors looked at his cigarette that was more than half gone and tossed it on the ground. He stepped out only the coal of the cigarette, carefully. Mr. McGuire said, putting one white shoe-toe over the butt, "They'd have that in a minute." And he twisted around and around on it, grinding the paper and flaking the tobacco into the dirt. He smiled with one hand holding the door open and the other on the visitor's shoulder in a comradely pat. "We try to break the boys of smoking. The visitor looked doubtful. The other visitor carried his cigarette into the kitchen with him.

The kitchen door banged and Mr. McGuire led them across the white scrubbed boards. They had to pass Nick. Already the director knew his name. He said, "Hello, Nick!" and rumpled his hair. Nick didn't like that. It was like when Ma patted him.

McGuire's back was to him now, with the two men following him. Nick stared at the cigarette, then up at the man, wanting to ask for it; begging for it with his eyes. The man looked at McGuire's back, wrinkled his eyebrows in a frown and shrugged his shoulders helplessly. Nick held his glance a moment longer in grave youthfulness. There was something nice in the man's eyes, something that had been in Father O'Neil's. Serious, yet kindly and half-smiling, with sympathetic needle-points of light in their centers. And now he was smiling at him with his forehead wrinkled into the grin and his mouth twisted up at one end. He turned, walking to catch up with McGuire and the other visitor.

Nick followed him with his eyes. The man was tall and slender with loose shoulders inside an easy coat as he moved away.

They crossed the kitchen. The man, nodding toward Nick, asked McGuire, "What did that boy do?"

"I've been here seven years and I've never asked a boy what he did. I'm afraid it would prejudice me against him," Director McGuire said. They were approaching Kennedy now. McGuire put his hand on the visitor's arm. "You said your name was Holloway, didn't you?"—chuckling—"I never forget a name."

"Yes. Grant Holloway," the man said.

McGuire introduced the visitors and they shook hands. McGuire's voice went on smoothly, "Mr. Kennedy instructs the boys in cooking. When they leave here they are capable of seeking employment in a restaurant or cafeteria. This boy here—hello, Bob!"—he felt Bob's muscle—"is learning how to run a modern range." Mr. McGuire hoisted one white shoe up on the round of a stool, took a match from the box on top of the stove, struck it against the stove and lit a cigarette. Bob, behind the director's back, looked hangdog at Holloway who still carried his cigarette, and his lips said, without making noise, "Gimme a cigarette."

Nick, going to the stock room for the carrot scraper, went over to see if the man who came in smoking had thrown away the cigarette. A kid of about eleven came in from the office with the next day's menu and handed it to Kennedy. When he was gone Holloway said, "Good Lord! What could a little kid like that *do?*"

McGuire laughed pleasantly and explained like a teacher telling

[41]

somebody something. He talked about playing hooky, shoplifting in dime stores, broken families and behavior patterns. Kennedy said, "You'd be surprised what some of these god—some of these little kids can get into. They can raise—er—all kinds of devilment."

"Well, I want to show you the whole plant!" McGuire said affably. "We'll have to move on." On the way out he mussed Nick's hair again.

One of the visitors asked McGuire, "Do you give the boys any sex instruction here?"

"*Oh, no!*" McGuire looked shocked. Then he said, "They've learned about all that on the streets before they got here."

"I mean—that is—" the young man said, "I thought perhaps you directed their sex knowledge—"

"We give them religious instruction," McGuire concluded.

The two visitors fastened glances and smiled a little. McGuire didn't see. He was looking sideways up the side of a far mountain. A sudden frown passed over his features. It was like a confession and he walked to the car soberly. Then he was smiling again when he looked at them.

"You seem quite interested in what we're doing here to rehabilitate the boys," he said to the two visitors.

"Yes," the one called Holloway answered. "We're doing some research work in penology at the university." He ran his fingers into his hair and massaged his scalp. "I want to know all about these schools. So I can write about them fairly."

For a moment McGuire looked taken aback. Then he said, "Fine! Fine! Glad to help you. We'll go over to the shoeshop now. The shoeshop is a tremendous saving to the taxpayers. All the boys' shoes are made and repaired there. New shoes would cost around four dollars a pair on the market but we make them of first-class leather for about a dollar and a half. Socks are knitted in the shop for about three cents a pair...."

The car rolled slowly under the wide spread of trees. McGuire half-twisted around in the front seat while one beefy arm thrown up on the cushion pointed out buildings and the work fields "where the boys grow their own food."

■■■

Again their legs were going down the stone steps beyond the iron fence to the basement. Inside the fellows started ganging up with pals. Right away Nick saw Rocky and Rocky winked at him. Nick bobbed his head hello and started looking around for a place to sit. On the long bench against the wall he saw a colored kid—a new kid. The kid was looking right at him, and it was a scared-to-death look like when you're far away from home and don't know nobody. He watched Nick for a long moment. Then he twisted his lips in the

[42]

faint beginning of a smile. Nick grinned at him and started to go right over. Bricktop walked to the center of the floor where Nick had to pass and stood there waiting.

"Hello, Nick," he said like he was doing him a favor, but his eyes were mean. Then he said, loud enough for everybody to hear, "They brought a nigger in today." Nick looked at the kid, quick, and saw his face crumple.

Nick half-hung his head. A little, lifted curl of hair fell over his forehead. He looked over the big edge of Bricktop's shoulder at the colored kid who sat straight up on the bench with skinny shoulders and not much chest inside the blue denim jacket that was too large for him. He didn't have much hair. What there was of it was screwed down on his head like flies on fly paper. He had white eyes in a black face. And now his lower lip trembled as Bricktop said the words loud, "They brought a nigger in today." Then Nick saw the other kid, a little kid come in from the toilet, look over at Bricktop and sit down quietly on the opposite end of the bench. He was real young—only about twelve—and real small. His blond hair spilled all over his forehead without any curl at all. A little kid with big eyes that looked everywhere and skin the color of a girl's. Even his cheeks were kind of red. Nick watched, and saw him edging down the bench.

"We don't talk to no niggers in here," Bricktop was saying to Nick. Nick's eyes, hitting over Bricktop's shoulder, saw the blond kid pushing down the bench, see-sawing down its whole length. "You ain't going to talk to no niggers, are you?" Bricktop told Nick, loudly, bossing him. Nick hung his head and said, softly, hoping the colored kid, who was all of a sudden different and a nigger, wouldn't hear, "No, I won't."

"You won't what?"

"I won't talk to any niggers," Nick said, shamed.

"Don't forget."

The little blond kid had worked his way the length of the bench; he had reached the opposite end. He was right next to the other kid. He stretched out his hand and, watching Bricktop carefully, laid it on the black kid's knee. And he smiled at the nigger kid.

Nick saw and hung his head.

It was then that Bricktop looked over and saw what was going on.

"Hey you! Come here!" Bricktop yelled at the white kid; and he snapped his head in a motion that meant "and hurry up!" All the fellows were watching now.

The kid stood up, straight, almost proudly, and walked across the basement to Bricktop.

"What do you want?" His voice was as big as Bricktop even if he wasn't. And he looked straight at Bricktop.

[43]

Nick stood fastened to the floor. His chin was way, way down.

"Did you hear what I said?" Bricktop had his shoulders hunched and he was frowning with one corner of his mouth lifted, with deep and ugly wrinkles from his nose to the ends of his mouth.

"Yeah," the kid said, not backing down.

"Well, what's the big idea?"

You could tell the kid was breathing hard. And his face colored some. Not scared though. "I'll talk to anybody I want."

Bricktop put a big hand in the kid's face and shoved. The kid went off his feet, folded up in the middle and, landing on his behind, slid across the floor. It could have been funny the way he slid across the floor.

Nick, with his head still down, went outside. He didn't even hear Charlie the guard say, "You're with Bricktop. Bricktop told me it was all right."

Someone was walking with him in the dark. He didn't look. Whoever it was walked right along with him, side by side. For a long time he didn't look. Leaves, under their feet, made sad little sounds when they crumpled. The night gave its sounds under rocks, in tree limbs, across open fields. Finally Nick looked. Rocky was walking along with him.

They didn't say anything. Just walked slow. And when there were small stones in the road Rocky gently kicked them out of the way. When they came to the big square of buildings Rocky turned off.

9

Nick sat on the hard basement bench with his head leaning against the water pipes and waited for the go-to-bed whistle. He rubbed the back of his head against the water pipe. At eight o'clock you went to bed. Until then you stayed here. If you had cards you played cards. If you had checkers you played checkers. *If* you had them. If you didn't you just didn't. Then you sat around saying what you did when you were out. "This is how

[44]

I broke into a store." "This is how I stole a car." You wised each other up. And all of them had plenty of girls on the line. Lots of times the fellows had asked him what he did. I didn't steal that bike but because Tony was my pal and because he was a swell guy I didn't squeal. It's a bum rap. So you don't tell. You leave it a blank....

The whistle blew.

They marched out of the basement, each head bending a little to get under the low door, and went in a long line to the front entrance of the dormitory. In the hallway at the foot of the long ladder of steps up to the bedroom floor stood Wallace, the housefather. Wallace counted them as they came in—"One—two—three—" At the top of the steps by the door leading to the beds, old Hendricks, their night guard, recounted them—"One—two—three—"

And at the bottom—"Sixteen—seventeen—eighteen—"

They climbed the stairs with the beds waiting—"Sixteen—seventeen—eighteen—"

Wallace looked at each boy as he passed with his head down. Wallace tolled the numbers off—"Thirty-three—thirty-four—thirty-five—"

Nick came with the others, in close-locked step. Wallace looked at Nick with something meanly critical in his eyes. The Company B boys went up the steps. And Old Hendricks—"Thirty-three—thirty-four—thirty-five—" The last of the blue denim line trailed up the steps, checked and double-checked. Old Hendricks leaned over the banister with darkening light on his thinning hair, "All right, Mr. Wallace. They're all here."

The big outside door closed heavily. The bolt shot across loudly. And the key grated. Then housefather Wallace's footsteps went into the downstairs part of the dormitory.

Old Hendricks locked the upstairs door and stood inside stuffing the key in his pocket. The fellows started undressing. They folded their clothes over the foot of the beds and pulled on their nightgowns.

Nick, in the white nightgown, flattened his bare feet against the coolness of the floor and waited. You undressed in silence and stood by the beds. You didn't go up there and just hit the hay. "One—" and you kneel down; "two—three" and you pray.

Old Hendricks' voice rumbled over the heads bent on the blankets, "Our Father, Who art in heaven, hallowed be Thy name...."

You're supposed to say them to yourself. But you don't. It's a game to start low, mumbling them; then louder and louder in different parts of the room. And pretty soon different guys keep going, "Amen! Amen! AMEN! AMEN! AMEN!" and later, "We're

[45]

finished!—WE'RE FINISHED!" Then Old Hen-Pick yells, "Shut up, you sonofabitch!"

"One—" and you get off your knees, "two—three—" and you climb into bed with the nightgowns crawling up over your belly....

Nick lay on the cot, not sleeping, twisting. Around him in the room things came to life. The partitioned-off toilet way down at the end of the last beds stood out in the dark. The cots with the humped up shoulders and rear ends of the guys all around him. Sometimes a fellow got out of the bed and went like a ghost between the two long aisles of beds to the toilet and Hen-Pick snapped his flashlight on him.

Bars on end with moonlight on them.

Nick turned on the mattress. Out through the bars were hunks of mountains standing up black. No sound now. No whistles. Sometimes a fellow turning in his sleep. That made you more lonesome. All the guys asleep and you awake and alone in the night....

Brrrrrrring!

The phone went off making Nick jump. Hen-Pick's chair legs hit the floor. He took the receiver off right away. "Hendricks," Hen-Pick said. "Everything okay." Then the receiver went back on.

Nick lay real still listening for the night sounds. He strained his ears. But he could hear nothing. With his eyelids shut down tight the night was heavy against them but he couldn't sleep. If he could of just stayed out of trouble. What were they doing at home now? They'd feel bad if they knew ... how he felt....

... *rring!* ... everything ... okay....

Nick turned heavily.

A wolf howled.

... thing ... o ... kay....

It was all black. Once a rooster, thinking it was day, awoke in the chicken barns, crowed lonesomely; he sounded ... scared ... sleep came twisting in through the straight up and down bars. Hunks of it....

You can reach way down inside you, and I sat on a fence in the back yard just when the sun was going down and made things out of the clouds. That's an eagle and there goes a three-cornered lake with soft white land all around it. And oh! look at the Indian head. Like a penny. It's a man-Indian with just one big feather sticking up. A rooster opens his mouth with his head back but the sound that comes out is the sound of a whistle. It hurts my ears. There's a horse with his front legs up in the air. A big white horse. Maybe it's Sir Galahad's horse. It is Sir Galahad's horse. And when Ma says take out this paper and burn it you set the boxes in rows in the alley and set them on fire making believe it is a city on fire.

Corn-flakes boxes are big buildings like downtown.... In the straight up and down church the little bell sounds like a whistle between clenched teeth ... and tall censers ... swing ... swing ... incense in long, wrapping spirals ... swing ... swing ... it's only the chunks of night and sleep coming through the bars ... a wolf howls ... an engine hoots.... and the thoughts of....

10

McGuire pushed open the screen door, letting in flies, and came into the kitchen. He walked over to where Nick was rubbing a greasy dish rag around the bottom of a big cooking kettle. McGuire smiled at Nick and said in a big-brother voice, "How'd you like to catch some fresh air, Nick?"

"Yes, sir."

They went toward the garage behind the officers' quarters. "How are you getting along?" McGuire asked.

"All right."

"Do you like it here?"

"It's all right."

"I thought you might like to get away from the kitchen for a while," McGuire said. He ground out a cigarette. "Mr. Fuller wants his car washed. I've got one kid on the job but he needs help."

They were at the back of the garage. A red water-hose lay twisted across the broad oblong of pavement where a big cream-colored Cadillac, shiny with chrome and extra lights, was wheeled out beyond the garage doors. A kid was stooped over near one of the white-walled tires with the nozzle of the hose in a pail. The water hissed and bubbled and filled up into the pail.

"Nick," McGuire said, "this is Tommy." Nick looked and saw the kid Bricktop had shoved across the basement.

McGuire went around the corner of the building toward the office. Nick filled another pail and dipped a sponge into the cold water. It made his hands numb.

[47]

"What happened to the nig—" Nick blushed and didn't say it. "Is that colored kid in your dormitory?"

Tommy looked up from a hubcap. Sun put light in his eyes and on his straight, mussed blond hair. "Sam? Yes. He's in my dormitory."

They washed the car, scrubbed mud off the tires, pulled dead moths and grasshoppers away from the radiator grill. The sun kept streaking the windows because they didn't dry them fast enough.

"How old are you?" Nick asked Tommy.

"I'm eleven. How old are you?"

"Fourteen."

Their elbows opened and closed down as they rubbed the polish over the back of the car. "Sam's a nice kid," Tommy said suddenly. He smiled a little, "We're good pals."

It was hard reaching over the top of the car, polishing it.

"What kind of work does your father do?"

"He's dead."

"Oh—that's too bad." Nick put more polish on his rag, busy then keeping the embarrassment out of his voice.

"He wasn't there much anyway," Tommy said.

···

McGuire came back.

"All finished, boys?" he asked cheerfully.

They nodded their heads. The car stood, glistening in the sun. It was low and shiny and powerful-looking.

McGuire told Tommy that he could sweep out the garage and he gave Nick a broom, telling him to sweep the sidewalk all the way around the building.

Nick loafed near the corner of the building, not sweeping fast or much, looking up at the mountains that were beautiful as they tumbled up and down under the sun. A man, some visitor who was walking around alone, was coming toward him. When he got close he saw Nick and smiled. Right away Nick whispered, "Have you got a cigarette, mister?" Staring up into his face he recognized one of the men who had come into the kitchen the first day Nick had been in the school.

The man ran his hand into his hair and the hair stood up between his fingers. "I can't give you one here," he said. He smiled again, in a friendly sort of way. "It's heck when you want to smoke and haven't got one, isn't it? I'll walk to the end of the building and drop some on the lawn there. Then when you get a chance you can pick them up."

"All right, thanks—thanks a lot! And leave some matches too, will you?"

[48]

The man walked along near the edge of the sidewalk. His hand came out of his pocket. Nick saw the cigarettes fall out of his fingers onto the lawn.

With his head down and his eyes, under the cap, looking around everywhere, Nick bent over the broom and swept to the end of the sidewalk fast. He stooped over, picked the cigarettes up. Five of them. They were a little damp from the grass. But he had smokes.

He was standing up again when his eyes went over to the side window of the office. Superintendent Fuller had his one arm up near the pane. A long finger moved back and forth motioning Nick into the office.

Fuller sat behind his wide shiny-topped desk. His hand was up with a big opal ring shooting colors. He pointed to the desktop and Nick put the cigarettes there.

"You will report at the recreation hall tomorrow when the whistle blows for lunch."

■■■

Outside on the sidewalk, coming toward the steps, was Rocky. Like always he walked slow, with a careless grace and a loose, easy movement. He walked real slow, with his head turning and his cap, screwed around backwards, turning too. Rocky had eyebrows that made him look like he was always asking a question. One side of his hair fell over the end of his forehead. He had a wide mouth that grinned a lot. He seemed as if he was always having a good time and everything was a joke. He grinned at Nick, his eyes shutting down a little and his mouth spreading out red, showing white teeth. "Hello, Nick."

Nick liked having Rocky know his name. He said, "Hello, Rocky," and forgot about the cigarettes, the hand pointing and the recreation hall tomorrow.

■■■

The fellows all stood near the back of the gym, a whole line of them. They didn't talk much. Every once in a while they glowered up at the stern frosted windows of the building covered over with heavy webbings of iron. A fellow came up and asked, "Who is it?"

"Allen," said a fellow.

"Allen's getting licked," said another.

"What happened—? He took off?"

"Naw. The drill officer called him a name," said a fellow.

"Allen beat hell out of the bastard," said another.

They waited.

Bricktop slouched near the fence with his big arms on top of it and his chin resting on them.

"Allen can take it," said a fellow.

Then Allen came.

His brown, shiny face was unnaturally pale. Sweat beaded over it. There was a little blood soaked through on his shirt-back. But his head was up fiercely. And he had a tight-mouthed grin that circled around his teeth.

"Who did it?" a fellow asked.

"Fuller," Allen snapped.

"How many?" another fellow asked.

"Plenty, man!" The grin was tight. "I told him I had more ass than he had leather." His eyes turned mad.

Some of the fellows fell in step with him.

•••

Bricktop watched. He listened. Then he moved away with Slim. "They shoulda killed the nigger," he said.

Jesse, walking with Nick, said, "Bricktop don't like him because he can't fight him."

A fellow Nick didn't know said, "Bricktop was champ of the hill until Allen came here." He knew a lot about the beatings. "You bend over and grab your ankles or a bench. With your pants down. Or they lay you flat on a bench and tie your ankles and wrists."

"How many do you get?"

"It all depends. The least they give you is seven."

"For nothing at all—" another fellow put in, "for just talking or cussing at a officer they give you a criss-cross."

"What's that?" Nick asked.

The fellows laughed. "They run the clippers through your hair this way, then that way." He demonstrated with his fingers.

•••

In between the shoeshop and the kitchen they had a few minutes and Nick said to Jesse, "I had some cigarettes and he saw me and told me to go over to the recreation hall." Jesse paled a little. "What do they do to you?" Nick asked. "They may chain you and put water on you or—" The whistle blew. They hung close together another minute. "You—" Jesse put his hand on Nick's arm and tightened his fingers, "you won't get any lunch." From inside his shirt front he pulled a candy bar and stuck it into Nick's hand. Then he moved away toward the shoeshop quickly.

Nick went into the recreation hall. This was where they were supposed to go two nights a week instead of to the basement. Only when the outside guard came for them he'd almost always say, "You guys ain't been quiet, so you ain't going today." Nick looked around. Near the bookcases he saw a wooden chest, open, with ten-pound iron balls in it. Facing the wall all around the room with their noses against it stood about ten fellows. Their arms were stretched to their sides stiffly with their hands behind them. In each hand they held an iron ball. "Grab a couple," the guard told Nick. Nick obeyed and went on the line with the rest of the fellows. The glass door came open and someone entered the room. "Here they are. Take over," the guard said. A voice answered, "Okay."

Nick jumped a little when he heard the voice and his nose scraped around on the wall as he twisted his head toward the voice.

Rocky.

Rocky saw him and looked away quickly. The guard went out. For a long time everything was silent and the blood began to drain out of Nick's arms. He stood with his nose pushed against the wall. His fingers and wrists got tingly. He heard Rocky walk across the room. Outside a whistle blew. They were coming out for lunch.

"You're supposed to stand an hour and rest five minutes," Rocky told the fellows apologetically. The sun came in the glass door and threw a pattern of light on the floor. You couldn't get tired and drop one. You had to take it in front of the fellows.

Rocky walked over to the pool table where the balls were racked up in their many-colored, glistening triangle on top of the smooth green felt and started rolling them toward the pockets. They made soft noise on the felt and swished into the pockets. Nick couldn't feel his arms any more. They didn't belong to him.

Rocky walked across the room slowly. He leaned against the window staring outside, not looking at them, but talking to them: "I'm not like those other jerks. Because Bricktop stands high around this place they've made me a lineboy." For a while he didn't say any more; then, "I don't squeal." And behind him all the guys started relaxing.

At last the wash-up-for-supper whistle blew. Rocky said softly, "All right, guys." The fellows put the balls back in the chest, started working their arms around and rubbing them at the elbows.

Nick was going out when Rocky said quietly, "Nick." Nick came back. "Let's sneak a smoke."

Rocky pulled the smokes out. He said, explaining, "You got to know somebody in here to get along all right. I started sucking up to the big shots and got in good."

They sat on the pool table smoking and swinging their legs. Rocky said, "Whatever you've done, when you come here you're almost like an angel. They make worse crooks out of you." After a while he said, "Each house has its own mob that runs it. Kids smuggle in cigarettes and we steal them. If a kid gets two boxes of fruit and doesn't give us a box and a half we take them both. See—when you get a mob together you feel powerful."

After a while they didn't talk; both just sat thinking. Nick, remembering, pulled out the candy bar that was melting, and, breaking it in half pushed a piece at Rocky without looking up. They ate it, melting the chocolate against the roofs of their mouths with their tongues.

***

Sundays you didn't have anything to do. If your folks didn't come to see you you loafed all day. Nick would forget all about his folks, and then they'd come. When they were gone he'd feel real lonely and like crying.

This Sunday he watched Ma and Pa as they went through the big gate and it was locked behind them. He stood, staring through the wire diamonds of the fence even after they were out of sight....

Nick swallowed hard and walked around to the back of the school building where nobody would be. Rocky sat back there in a basement window ledge. "Hello, Rocky."

"Hello, Nick." He didn't lift his head but went on scratching in the dirt with a small broken-off branch.

Nick rubbed the toe of his workshoe in the dirt. "Did your folks come to see you?"

"I ain't got no folks."

Rocky went on scrawling for a long minute. Then he snapped his head back, tossing the hair out of his eyes. His mouth widened out in a smile with his lips close against his teeth. "Let's take a walk."

They struck out away from the buildings, walking under the trees down a straggly path worn and beaten into the ground with grass on either side. Their pants were rolled up several twists over their ankles. Rocky went with a long straw in his mouth. Nick picked up pebbles and tossed them ... you meet a new fellow and you like him. You walk along and don't have anything much to say. It's nice walking along. Not alone. Even if you don't talk you know he likes you and you like him....

"This ain't the only reform school I been in," Rocky said. "I was in St. John's Industrial School." Nick hit the tree with a stone. "The first thing when you get in is they want to find out how tough you are. I was a battered-up sonofabitch. It didn't take me long to find out how far down the line I stood. I was just middle class."

The sun was right over the mountains now.

"I hit town broke and hungry. And at night. Well, I ain't in town an hour and I gets in trouble. There was a store that looked easy.... Yeah, I was walking out with the joint—I had so much stuff I couldn't get my coat buttoned. First thing I knew, 'Put up your hands, you little sonofabitch!' "

[52]

"What did you take?"

"Oh, mostly cigarettes—stuff I could peddle easy."

Rocky pulled out cigarettes for both of them. With his hand on Nick's shoulder, steadying himself, he struck the match on the bottom of his workshoe. They dragged in on the cigarettes and blew smoke.

"Well, it was the industrial school for me. I got in the office, see. I'm running the switchboard in the office. Then I'm taking the mail around and going outside the gates once in a while. When I get in good and everybody thinks I'm a right guy I take a powder."

They walked way out till they were close up to the low hills that began crawling up to the mountains. They slouched down in the high grass. It tickled their necks and their ears. Nick looked at Rocky's name bruised on his chest. "How do you smash your name like that?"

Rocky sat up. "I'll do it for you." Nick unbuttoned his shirt. Rocky took the skin on Nick's chest in between his fingers and squeezed, pinched. *N* It hurt a little. *I* The skin got all red. Rocky squeezed harder. *C* Some blood came out in one place. *K* His whole name was there, big across his chest. *Plenty* red. *Real* big.

"It'll turn brown in a couple days," Rocky said.

They lay back against the soft swell of ground. Rocky lay on his back with his feet propped against a tree and slowly puffed a cigarette. He waved one arm around and said, "If you went over this joint in a airplane you'd think it was paradise."

The sun over the mountains lit up the far-off buildings in a neatly-arranged pattern. Their tile roofs, some red, some green, were pretty. In the grass a garter snake wiggled in a swift little river of color.

"You're worse when you get out of this joint. And you're sure wised up."

Under a rock somewhere a cricket made a sawing sound. A grasshopper leaped against Nick's cheek.

The sun was coming down. But it made everything beautiful and shadows were long, long across the field from west to east. Rocky sat, now, with his arms hugging his knees and his back against the tree. Nick lay with his head on his hands but turned toward Rocky. Rocky pursed his lips. The whistling notes came out clear, vibrant, echoing. The notes poured across the empty field, filling it. Nick listened, with his eyes staring at the leaves overhead but not seeing.

The whistling notes went up and out. Nick lifted his head and, through the long grass, looked at Rocky.

[53]

Rocky put his fingers in his hair with the curls sticking through them and scratched.

With his head on one side Rocky whistled. With his lips pursed, making a red circle. With his shadow large and grotesque on the wall of the gray concrete dairy building.

11

The days went by slower and slower. They couldn't be any longer. At night you were alone in the dark dormitory, stretched out on the hard bed, letting the hurt and the madness soak out of you, with just the loneliness closing in around you from all over the room. Before it was light you got up with the siren scaring you out of your sleep. When it was hot you worked. Before it was dark you were locked up in the dormitory. All the time they made you know you were bad and were being punished. You were a criminal. They didn't let you forget it. For nothing they hit you.

More days went by. Nick endured them. They ran in his memory, branded there. When your folks left on Sunday afternoons you were lined up in the basement and the office boys searched you for cigarettes or anything that could be slipped to you and that you weren't supposed to have. You had to take off all your clothes and if they found anything they asked for a cut. If you didn't come across they squealed and you were called up to the office and got some discredits slapped on. The guards really thought they were somebody because they were working there. It went to their heads. They'd have you all over the place. And they slapped you around for nothing whenever they felt like it. The only good guard was Charlie. He'd sit on his stool on the other side of the barred door smoking. And he'd toss cigarette butts inside, between the bars, so a guy could get them. Director McGuire went around rumpling their hair.

•••

One Saturday afternoon Nick and Tommy were sent to clean the chicken houses. It stunk so that every once in a while they had

[54]

to go outside, spitting to get the taste out of their noses and throats. One of the times when they stood rubbing their shoes against the ground, scraping the mess off of them, Tommy said quickly, hotly, "I'm not going to stay here."

"What do you mean?" Nick asked.

"I'm going to"—his lips tightened—"run away."

They went back into the barn. The acrid stink burned into their nostrils. They worked the hoes, scraping at the boards, raking up the fouled straw.

"Ain't you scared?" Nick asked. Then he remembered, *I'll talk to anyone I want.*

Tommy frowned and tossed the damp blond hair off his forehead. "I'm not going to stay here. Me and Sam—we're going to run away."

"Sam—he—because he's a—"

"They're mean to him. They call him names. They're always blaming him."

"I'd be scared—"

Tommy squared his immature shoulders. "Me and Sam—"

They raked some more. Tommy looked around. "A lot of the other kids say they'll go." He looked around again. "Some of them asked me if I wanted to take off with them." There was nothing but the empty barn with, outside, hens fussing. "And I told them."

Just a little kid. Nick looked at him with deep-eyed admiration. Nick said, "You've got more guts than me."

Tommy said, "And we're all going. All the fellows in our dormitory. Next Sunday night."

It came out, bit by bit, with the straw and hunks of hard chicken mess.

•••

Then it was next Sunday night. In the basement, on the way up to the dormitories, Nick managed to get up close to Rocky. "Rocky, I want to tell you something." Then he didn't tell him. But just as they were starting up the steps to bed he said, "The little kids are taking off."

"Yeah?" Rocky looked surprised.

They started in, with Wallace counting them. "Boy! I hope they make it!" Rocky whispered. "So do I!" Nick said. He clenched his fists.

They were all quiet, well-behaved in B Dormitory that night. *"The young kids are going to take off!"* Everybody seemed to know it; and they all waited tensely.

Nick lay flat and silent on the cot. The nine o'clock telephone call came in. Nick cracked his knuckles under the blanket. He could hear his heart beating.

[55]

The monotony of night settled over the dormitory. But bed springs kept squeaking. Boys kept turning on mattresses. And Hendricks, angrily, "Go to sleep! Go to sleep!"

The cricket noises came up so loud you wanted to stuff your fists in your ears. The toilet made dripping sounds. You could hear Hendricks breathing.

Then—

Then the siren came up like the wail of an animal. Spotlights went on, shooting out in the dark like snakes striking, then seesawing out across the flat, black grounds. Cutting holes in the dark, showing trees, the parts of buildings, kids running, where before there had been only blackness.

Every boy in B Dormitory jumped out of bed and ran, in a flood, to the barred windows. Hendricks' chair legs hit the floor and he jumped to his feet with his flashlight snapping on. "Get back in bed, you bastards!" "Go to hell, you sonofabitch!" That was Bricktop. Someone knocked the flashlight out of Hendricks' hand. Hendricks stood in the dark, breathing hard. Then when he saw all of them at the windows he unlocked the door swiftly, jumped past it, slammed it, locked it. His footsteps ran down the staircase. But no one saw him or heard him. They were all at the windows.

Nick was as close to the window as he could get. He saw kids ducking all over the place. Some of them had taken off in their nightshirts. The spotlights streaked, zigzagged swiftly. The siren howled on and on. He saw a spotlight pick up a kid stumbling towards the work fields with a guard almost on top of him. Nick clenched his teeth and hoped it wasn't Tommy—or Sam.

The guard had him now. He fell on top of him and was hitting him. The kid's bare legs and feet beat back and forth in the air. Then the spotlight went toward somewhere else.

Nick saw Superintendent Fuller, only partly dressed, running with his empty sleeve flying loose. He saw the lights go on in back of the garage and two cars standing outside. One of the fellows groaned, "They're going to get the cars and run up and down the highway after them."

Jesse, at the window, breathing hard and coughing a little, said to Nick, "Rocky took care of that. He punched holes in the gas tanks of all the cars tonight."

...

Daylight opened up all over the countryside. It lighted the quiet, peaceful reform school grounds. It made the buildings beautiful in their pattern-square. The dew sparkled in the sunlight.

Thirty-four boys had been in the breakout. Twenty-two had escaped.

Superintendent Fuller ate his breakfast alone in the officers' quarters and read the news in the town papers. Director McGuire went about his duties without his affable smile and he mussed no hair.

Twelve boys were locked up in solitary—the twelve who had been retaken.

The reform school boys ate, went to classes, worked. They grinned at each other all during the day.

That evening when they were locked in the basement after supper Rocky pulled something from under his belt next to his skin. It was a poster, folded in four. Rocky smoothed it out and held it up to the light for the fellows to see. It said: ESCAPED ... *Twenty-five Dollars Reward for the Capture of* ...

In the middle was a photograph. Nick looked and saw Tommy's picture. Tommy's face was like it had been when he told Bricktop, "I'll talk to anyone I want!"

Rocky said, "I swiped it at the print shop. They're printing them of all the kids still out. And they're going to put them up all over town."

Slim said, "I hear they take five bucks off from the housefather's and guard's pay for every fellow who escapes."

"Swanson won't get no pay for a year!" someone shouted and they all laughed.

Next day five more kids were caught.

Ten still out.

A week later seven out.

As they caught them they were locked up in solitary.

It took three weeks before Tommy and Sam were caught.

12

The big doors of the assembly hall were spread wide open. Under the trees, across the flagstones, came the long line of reform school boys in blue denim. At intervals, on the green smooth-cropped lawn, guards stood, keeping them in line. The slow-paced line filed into the assembly hall. Silently the boys squatted on the theatre seats where all of them could sit. They weren't allowed to talk. But heads leaned toward each other. Whispering.

Nick and Jesse sat together, waiting. Heat made their clothes sticky on them. Flies buzzed around the hall. Nick looked up at the big stage, several feet above floor level with a small platform of steps leading to it. The curtains were thrust way back. Against the wall was the white square of screen where once every two weeks they saw a movie. The lights were on brightly. They beat down hard against the stage boards, crashing away in highlights. On the stage there was only a bench with, across it, a leather strap. The strap was long, black, thick—thicker than your finger. At one end the sides had been cut in so that there would be a handle to grip it by. Nick hunched way down in his seat. A short-blast whistle blew. They should be eating. Nick shook a fly off of his arm. His eyes wandered around the hall, fearfully.

Then the little kids came. They were marched in by two guards, one in front and one in back. They were pale, tightened up, scared. They had been locked up since they were caught and their eyes squinted against the light.

On the seats there was a stir of resentment, and mumbling, and scraping of feet. The drill officer blew his whistle warningly.

The little kids were marched up to the front of the hall where the guards motioned them down on the two long benches at the foot of the stage. They sat facing the reform school audience. Their heads were bowed. Their hands, between their legs, were fastened together.

Nick looked quickly at the seated line of kid prisoners—looking for him. He saw him. First on the bench at the foot of the steps leading to the stage. Tommy's chin was almost on his chest. His blond, straight hair hung down loosely. You couldn't see anything but the hair and the thin white arms disappearing beyond the blue V of pant-legs. Sam sat next to him, turned slightly toward him. Sam's white eyes moved back and forth in his black face.

Rocky came in late and flopped down next to Nick. Flies buzzed. There wasn't any other sound. Outside a window the branch of a tree moved back and forth, slowly, lazily. Flies buzzed some more. Even the office boys and the stools were pale. And every boy in the school was there to see.

Nick dampened his lips with his tongue. He sat up straight, forcing himself against the seat. He wanted to get up and run out. He half rose. Rocky stuck his legs out in the way and tightened his hand on Nick's knee. His eyes saw a guard watching them and stepping closer. "Look. Can you do this?" Rocky asked. Then he started moving his knees back and forth with his hands on them, with his hands slipping, criss-cross, from one knee to the other. Nick slumped back against the seat. As soon as he did that Rocky stopped jiggling his knees.

It came too soon. The sharp heels crashed into the assembly hall, smacking against the hardwood boards, resounding. All the heads turned, looking at him. The eyes of the reform school boys, watching him come, met his with the impact of a blow.

The tall, narrow, one-armed body came down the wide aisle. The empty coat sleeve clung close to his side, pinned there. Nick shivered. More strength in one arm than most men have in two.

Superintendent Fuller went to the stage with a guard following him. He unbuttoned his coat and when he had to let the guard help him get out of it his eyes frowned angrily. He was even thinner without his coat, more lopsided.

Fuller walked over to the bench. He unbuttoned the collar of the white shirt and yanked the tie loose. Then he picked up the long leather strap. Experimentally he tried it, swinging it back and forth. It was lazy at the end of his hand like the tree limb swinging outside the window.

Tommy was first on the bench. And he was first on the stage. Fuller twisted him around so that his back was to the audience. He stood faced away from them with Fuller holding the strap. No boy moved, or made a sound. They were all hushed like when they were in church.

Fuller said, "Pull them down."

Tommy's small hands worked clumsily with his belt. The pants fell down to his shoetops, a circle of blue around his ankles. The immature legs were skinny. His small, narrow buttocks were exposed for everyone to see. The hard light beat down.

Fuller said, "Grab your ankles."

Nick tightened his hands into fists at the ends of stiffened arms. Jesse put his forehead down on the seat-back in front of him and didn't look up.

"Grab your ankles."

Tommy grabbed his ankles. The skin tightened out across his behind.

Fuller stood over Tommy. The light hit the top of his head where the hair, smoothed back, was thinning out and turning ugly gray. Fuller raised the strap. Nick saw the muscles coil into a knot in that one arm. Goose-pimples gathered on the surface of Nick's skin and he sucked his lips back in between his teeth. The whip poised above Tommy's bare buttocks like a snake about to strike. It fell back over Fuller's wrist, over Fuller's back. It was black against the white cloth of his shirt. Nick saw Fuller's muscle curl in his arm and then spring out as the strap came down.

As the whip fell Nick's mind leaped back to that mouse by Rankin's grocery store. He closed his eyes. He heard the horrible sharp smack of the whip. Then a silence. He heard the smack of the whip again, cutting the flesh, bringing the blood. He heard Tommy cry out loud, in a scream, and then gasp for breath—sobbing, whimpering, blubbering.

Nick opened his eyes. He was standing in the middle of the row of seats with his fists clenched. He wanted to cry out. But he sat down weakly, trembling all over. "Stop it! You sonofabitch! Stop it!" he whispered. And he was crying, blubbering, with the tears running down his cheeks fast, salty on his lips, falling off the end of his chin onto the floor. He shook his head sideways, hard, to shake the tears from his eyes. "Goddamn you! Goddamn you!" he sobbed. It was a long time before the whippings were over.

■■■

The words Tony had taught him came easily to him now. He lay on the hard mattress cot and clenched his fists and said, over and over, "Goddamn them! Goddamn them!"

He'd never be sorry for anything he ever did again. He'd never go crawling home asking for forgiveness again. He'd never try to reform now. He was on Tommy's side. All the way. For good. Forever.

He knew how men treated boys. And he knew how they reformed them. He hated the law and everything that had anything to do with it. Men like Fuller were behind it. He was against them.

For good. Forever.

13

In the few weeks since Tommy was beaten, Nick picked up five hundred discredits. He'd never get out of this joint. He seemed to be in trouble all the time. He'd never work his way out. There was only one thing he could do. . . .

Working in the vegetable garden with Wallace way over near the other end talking to a guard, Nick looked up at the far mountains. If he could only get to them. He didn't know what was over the mountains but anything was better than this. Without thinking much or figuring things out, he was running. Running away. Just to get somewhere else. Anywhere.

He didn't get far. He wasn't halfway across the lumpy work field with the high wire fence still far away when they caught him. He got three more months, with, this time, twenty lashes to be paid to him later.

••••

After that he had a reputation as a real bad kid with the officers and guards.

Everytime he had a chance now he was with Tommy. And Sam. They never talked about the licking the young kids had taken but, without even mentioning it, it tied them together. Sure he went with Sam. He didn't care. Sam was just another kid. The hell with Bricktop. Then one Sunday in the basement before all the guys Bricktop said, "I see you been hanging around with that nigger."

Nick swallowed. Here it came. What he had been afraid of. He swallowed again. "Yeah," he said.

"What did I tell you?" The big shoulders were hunched, the red hair knotted, the puffy eyes bullying.

Nick felt the heads snapping around to attention. He could feel an itching under his arms. If only Rocky was there he could look at Rocky and know what to say. Everybody was listening. Tommy had said it. Why couldn't he?

He had to say something. Bricktop was waiting. "He's all right. He's a nice kid." That was pleading.

"I told you not to talk to him."

All right, he'd say it. "What do you care if I talk to him?"

"Gettin' tough, huh?" Bricktop's thick lips sneered.

Nick ruffled a little. "I don't see why you should boss me. I don't see where it's any of your business."

Bricktop hunched his shoulders up bigger, angrily. He turned, and walking away said over his shoulder, "I'll see you on the hill after lunch."

Nick, turned inward to all his fear and panic, sat down heavily on the bench. All his strength, even of words, drained out of him. He swallowed dryly to get his heart back in place and keep his scaredness down inside him. He'd just talked himself into a fight. All the guys had heard. He couldn't back out now. He sat, leaned forward a little with his shoulders slumped and his palms clenched tightly over the splintery edge of the bench. Jesse came over and sat by him without saying anything or looking at him.

The gong rang and chilled away in the basement. It shivered up against Nick's ears. With the rest of the fellows he went out toward the food. Jesse walked right along beside him, still not saying anything. And behind him, almost tripping on his heels, came Tommy.

[61]

There was a small bunch of fellows on both sides of him and behind him. The fellows kept watching him and when he looked around they bobbed their heads. Nick bobbed his head back at them without even knowing he did. He went with lagging feet. What did I do? I talked myself into it. But I can't back out now. The guys are with me. Or rooting for me.

They went into the dining room, the fellows all moving aside and clearing a path for Nick. Nick went in and more eyes were looking at him.

I'm going to catch it. Wait till it comes. Yeah, but he's going to kick my can through.

They had good food that day. But Nick sat, not eating, taking little sneak looks at Bricktop. There was whispering going on at the table. The guys said, "Give it to him!" If I show I'm scared they won't even yell for me. But fear was in his heart, spelled in capital letters.

So the grub was over. And at noon on Sundays you didn't wait for whistles. As soon as you finished eating you walked out.

Word had passed around so fast that the whole reform school lined the hill. Bricktop was there already and Nick walked slowly out towards him. Jesse went right along with Nick. "Yeah, Nick, you can do it," Jesse said. And there was Rocky walking out to the hill carelessly with the cap twisted around. Rocky sneaked him a wink.

Bricktop was all ready with his shirt in his hand, with his pants rolled way up showing the bulge of his calves, hairy and big.

Nick walked out to the open space behind the dormitory where an ugly, half-bald hill lumped up under the sun. He still clung to the hope that some way or another Bricktop would say let's forget it. But hell no.

Nick started taking off his shirt. As the blue denim slipped out away from him the sunlight struck the muscles that moved smoothly over his arms, and his back, broad, youthfully hard.

The fellows lined the hill silently. There was nothing in the sky but its blueness and the sun straight overhead.

Nick took off the shirt slowly. Just stalling for time. He started rolling up his pants. This was Sunday, visitors' day. Maybe an officer would find out and make them postpone it and Bricktop would forget.

The officer came—with a pair of boxing gloves.

The only thing he wanted to know was, "Who's the guys?" And the fellows: "Nick,"—they all knew his name now—"and Bricktop."

Nick looked up quickly and right into Wallace's face. Wallace's lips were not quite touching, were curled away in just the faintest smile, a mean smile.

Yeah, he was going to fight Bricktop.

They were ready now. Bricktop said, "Up there?" and nodded toward the top of the hill.

They walked to the top. Wallace said, "All those on Bricktop's side over there—" The fellows picked their sides. Nick had more on his side than Bricktop, and there were fellows in Bricktop's line who looked as if they'd like to be at the other end of the hill. Wallace held out the gloves. Bricktop pushed them away. "No. Bare fists."

Wallace was saying, "Well, boys, rounds or to the finish?"

Before Nick could speak, Bricktop said, "To the finish."

Nick wouldn't, couldn't, back down. "All right. To the finish."

The fellows on the slope of hill tightened up. Nick looked over at Bricktop. Bricktop's lips tightened in a nasty way. Wallace said, "Go to it!" A couple of fellows whistled shrilly.

Nick didn't know much about fighting but he knew enough to keep away from Bricktop. He circled around Bricktop trying to keep out of range. Bricktop threw all kinds of fists at him from all kinds of angles. So fast that he couldn't duck the first one. He caught Nick. Nick stepped back. The trampled-down grass straggling up the hill was still damp from morning dew. Nick's heavy work shoe slid on a slippery tongue of grass. He slipped and fell. He felt a sharp pain shoot up in his crotch and slowly fold away.

Wallace stood over him looking down at him. The voice had an edge of satisfaction in it with an undertone of contempt. "What's the matter?"

Sitting on his rump Nick could see the big calves of Bricktop's legs disappearing into the two columns of his blue denim pants. His eyes raked the sidelines. He saw some lips sneer. He saw some eyes turn derisive. Again he looked at the silent, tightpressed ring of inmates. Their eyes were like slaps. Maybe that's what made him get up.

He climbed to his feet, holding one hand against his crotch. "I'm okay," he said. "Let's go down in the sand." The hostility relaxed in the onlookers' eyes. Rocky grinned at Nick approvingly. Tommy kept his lip between his teeth where it had been all the time. Jesse leaned against a tree breathing excitedly.

The sand was down the hill a little, near the dormitory. That gave him more time. And he realized Bricktop knew he was just stalling. He *knew* that made Bricktop mad, made him want to kick the crap out of him all the more. They started down off the bald hilltop. The sun followed them, gilding their sweaty backs.

In the sand your feet sink in almost up to your ankles. It works its way inside your shoes. In sand like that you get tired as hell.

Nick knew Bricktop realized it too and that only made Bricktop want to finish him off all the sooner.

They were fighting again, Nick keeping away, or trying to. Circling around, dodging, dragging the sand with him, plodding backwards in it with Bricktop's fists slashing out like whips, stinging, with the sun breaking sweat all over him. His arms were up warding off the hard fists, his head held down. The fists, like rocks, kept breaking against your arms, making them ... so ... tired ... with ever so often a fist coming through and turning him numb.

Bricktop bore in, carrying his weight with his sudden impetus. The big, cube-square fist found space, came through on the side of Nick's head above the temple. The sun fell, suddenly, out of the sky and bounced like a huge rubber ball, yellow, red, black. It blurred. The sonofabitch hit him so hard he forgot his name or where he was.

The hard-knuckled fist pecked solidly at Nick's head in the same place. To Nick it seemed like a hundred times.

Finally he went down. He was sent spinning half around by one of Bricktop's hammer fists. He hung in the air for a split second. Then he stumbled over forward, fell to his knees, posed there. Slowly the upper part of his body leaned way over forward until he was lying on his face with sand in his mouth and his nose and his hair.

He wanted to stay down. Wanted to terribly. Something dragged him up. He came up. Only to go down again.

Nick was mumbling inside his head, "He can't do this to me ... all my friends yelling for me ... or hoping for me ... Tommy ... Jesse ... Sam ... and Rocky ... Rocky...." From his knees and his elbows, through all the fuzz and haze and twisting sounds he saw Rocky's face with the funniest tense look in his smoky eyes. And while the buildings rocked, he tried, with his mind, with his eyes, to grasp hold of Rocky's eyes and pull himself to his feet.

He came up.

Like before, every time he came up Bricktop worked him over some more. But now he was beyond fear. He was out somewhere where you weren't afraid of anything. Where something inside of you drove you on ... on.

Nick, in a haze that had a circle of fists spinning around his head like cartwheels, started to fight back.

Not retreating now. Going in. Shaking off blows. So mad he could cry. So mad he could kill.

And was Bricktop surprised. Bricktop now gave ground, backing slowly in the heavy trampled sand, backing towards the wall of the dormitory, looping out with a hard, sweaty, defensive fist.

Nick had it in his mind to *fight*. But Bricktop changed his mind.

[64]

Bricktop beat the hell out of him some more. That's when Nick started praying for a miracle. Right then he was praying for rain, a fire or an earthquake. Anything to stop the fight. He was even hoping Bricktop would hit him so hard he wouldn't be able to get up again.

But Nick wouldn't quit. Not him. You got to kill me first.

Bricktop moved in, ready to end it. Then Nick threw one. The way Nick felt he didn't think it did anything to Bricktop. But Bricktop staggered.

There was a shout that came from all around the ring of reform school boys. One big yell—a cheer.

"Finish him, finish him. . . ." But Nick couldn't lift his arms any more. It was as if they were dragging in the sand at his ankles. Like somebody was hanging on to them. His lungs were busting. His head was busting. . . . Finally he got enough strength to walk up to Bricktop where he was leaning against the dormitory wall. Nick got up close to him and, putting all his strength together, let him have another one.

The maturing muscle, the tanned arm, the tightened fist shot out through the sunlight. Straight it went to Bricktop's face and buried iself there. Bricktop's face turned sickly white. Blood jerked out of the big, flattened-out nostrils. Bricktop slid halfway down along the building, supported only by the wall.

After he hit Bricktop Nick sort of staggered back. But that wasn't to give Bricktop a chance to get up. Hell no. That was to get his strength to hit him again.

So he went back and hit him again. And Bricktop went all the way down. He lay crumpled up against the foot of the wall. Blood all over his face, spitting like a bull, foam on his lips.

Even after Nick saw him do that he was still hoping somebody would stop the fight. If he gets up again I ain't got the strength to go back and hit him again.

Bricktop sat heavily, his large hunched shoulders crashed against the ground. He had landed by a big rock. Nick saw him with his head lying against the rock. With them heavy workshoes you can sure do some damage. Something told him to go kick Bricktop. That's when you get in the mood to kill . . . go kick him.

Wallace saw what was coming. He walked up to Nick, intercepting him. "No, you don't."

And that's where the fight ended. Bricktop said, "I've had enough."

Nick felt like getting down on his knees and thanking God for that.

"I've had enough," Bricktop said again.

■ ■ ■

[65]

Afterwards Nick staggered up the low bank of lawn and lay there, face down, tasting blood and sweat and hate.

Bricktop walked away.

14

"He licked Bricktop!"

"He licked Bricktop!"

It went all over the school. They were all saying it and they all wanted to be friends with him. And talk about respect! Bricktop had it for him now.

When Nick could spread his thinking away from his fight with Bricktop and the little kids getting beaten, he told Rocky the one thing he had on his chest. They were up over the hump of hill and out beyond the grounds near the dairy barn where they liked to go to be alone. Looking up at Rocky he said, "You know what—I ain't going straight when I get out of here."

After that it was as if he and Rocky had a large and incomplete scheme between them. Their silences seemed to mean more. The things they talked about seemed to reach far out, away from them, into some unrecorded future.

Rocky's voice was casual, "Yeah, it's tough being hungry in some strange town. So, I'm in Denver. So I'm out to make something. So, I do all right, I put the arm on a drunk for five bucks. Naw—I ain't done nothing. I asked him for five bucks. But I had to knock him down to get it. So, I eat. . . . "

Nick walked around the reform school grounds with his jaw stuck out and his eyes mean. No one better mess with him. No one did. He was always in trouble with the office now. He was catching discredits left and right. Even cussing, good-natured Kennedy had to slap a few on him. He didn't give a goddamn after the fight.

One of the first things he did was look for Gus, the older boy who had bothered him on his first day in reform school. He found him. He didn't say a thing. He just hauled off and hit him and knocked him down. When Gus got up he knocked him down again.

...

". . . So then I'm walking along the street looking for something. You don't pick on chain stores or nothing like that. They're too well protected. You find a small place in a quiet neighborhood. You hang around nights for a week. Well, I have this place spotted —and bingo!—one night I goes through the back window. It was good for thirty bucks. I made five trips carrying away the stuff. It's easy to knock a store over. . . ."

It happened in the B Dormitory vegetable garden. Nick was there with Irish and Joe, spading. Wallace stood around bossing the job. They worked until their hands hurt and their belts got uncomfortable and hot. Nick heard Wallace drag out the ugly curse word and shout it at Irish. He saw Irish lift the shovel over his head. He saw the sharp blade cut down, narrowly miss Wallace's jerked-away head, strike him on the shoulder and send him sprawling in the vegetable garden.

Then Irish was scared. But he stood his ground, poking at Wallace with the shovel, not hard, but not letting him up. Wallace lay with onion sprouts bushing out from under his shoulders. His little rat eyes were frightened and pleading, running back and forth in his head. "Come on, help me!" he called. "Don't let him hit me!"

Nick remembered the first morning in the dormitory and shrugged his shoulders. "I can't do anything," he said. Joe put his hand against Nick's arm. Joe, trying to suck up to Wallace, wanted to mix in. "Come on, let's help him." Nick pushed his hand away. "You try to mix in and you and me are going to go to town." He meant it.

After that Nick had a real build-up with the fellows as a *tough* kid.

■■■

Again it was Sunday. Nick wandered around the grounds looking for Rocky. He couldn't find him and cut back toward the administration buildings. Parents and visitors, like on every Sunday, were walking all around the grounds. A man Nick thought he recognized was coming from the opposite direction. When they were almost abreast the man happened to glance up and, seeing Nick staring at him, smiled and said, "Hi, there!" Nick pointed at him. "Aren't you the guy who gave me the cigarettes?"

"Oh, yes!—I remember you now." He stopped on the sidewalk alongside Nick. "I've only got rollings today." He seemed to be laughing at himself. Then he said, "Don't you work in the kitchen?" His voice was friendly.

"Yeah."

"I thought I saw you there. How long have you been in?"

"Too damn long!"

"When do you get out?"

"I don't know. Maybe never. Not the way I get discredits." He

[67]

looked up at the man suspiciously. "You trying to get a job here?"

"Hell no!" the man said. "I'm just casing the joint." He looked quizzically at Nick. Then his eyes moved across the grounds with curiosity and eagerness. "I've been hanging around here just to see what it's like."

"What for?"

"I told them in the superintendent's office that I was doing some research work. I'm on a trip around the country—looking these places over." He glanced at the lawn under the trees. "Let's go over there and sit down and talk."

"I don't care."

"What's your name?"

"Nick Romano."

"Mine's Grant. How old are you, Nick?"

"Fourteen."

They sat on the lawn together. Grant nodded at the handsome buildings beyond the flower garden. "Do they feed you well?"

"Oh, I guess so. Only it don't seem like it."

Grant felt around in his pocket, took out a tobacco sack and a wrinkled cigarette paper. Carefully he emptied tobacco into the paper. Nick looked at his worn coat and trousers. Grant twirled the paper into a cigarette, licked it, lighted it. "I'm from Chicago. I'm on my way to the coast." Blue smoke hung in the sunlight. "What's Chicago like?" Nick asked, remembering Ma had said they might go there to live with Aunt Rosa.

"Oh, it's big and it's dirty and there are a lot of slums there. But it's a great town. It's a man's town. It's alive."

The trees threw patterns all around them. Sunlight slanted through the branches, cut across Nick's face and laid a pattern at his feet. The breeze ruffled his hair. His chest and shoulders stood out, broadened in his blue denim shirt. Nick hung his head. He pulled at the grass with his fingers. He kept pushing the soles of his workshoes against the lawn.

"This doesn't seem to be a bad place," Grant said. Nick didn't answer. Grant smoothed the grass under his palm. "Is it all right here?"

Nick kicked the soles of his shoes against the lawn. Anger rose suddenly in him. "I hate it! They beat us. They make you think you're bad no matter what you do. They make you think you ought to be punished for everything."

Grant looked at the sagged-down shoulders in the blue denim shirt, at the legs drawn up and the workshoes pressing against the grass, cutting black wounds in the lawn. He searched for something to say and saw the watch on Nick's wrist. "Where'd you get the watch?" he asked, making his voice sound casual. "I bought it for ten cigarettes." Some boys in blue denim uniforms crossed the grounds with shovels over their shoulders. A sparrow chinned a worm out of the grass a few yards away from Grant's feet. Nick measured the fence with his eyes. "I'm going to run away. It won't be hard to get out of here." His eyes slid over the high wire fence again. The worm was all gone now but the very end, and the end waggled helplessly in the sparrow's beak. "You couldn't run far,'" Grant said, "you'd only go home and they'd find you and bring you back."

"I'd go over to Chicago by my aunt. I took off from here once but they caught me. They won't catch me next time!" His mouth and eyes were hard.

Grant rolled another cigarette, looking down into the tobacco. "The superintendent tells me that they teach you boys a trade. What do you want to learn?"

"I don't want to learn anything."

Grant shoved his fingers into his hair and rubbed. "Oh, you must want to be something," he said.

Nick leaned forward, head down. His hair touched the path of light. "Well, I did want to be a baker." He turned bitter again. "But they wouldn't let me. They said my record was too bad. No, I don't want to learn anything!"

Grant fastened his long fingers around his knees. He looked across them at Nick. "It's none of my business," he said, "but you can't get away from the law. You're only fourteen. You don't want to be chased and hounded and locked up do you? I guess they mean well here," his hand gestured impotently. "You can't understand that though. Neither can I. I think they're wrong. But keep the right slant on things. Stay here and learn a trade—" Grant stopped talking and followed Nick's eyes to where they were staring darkly and angrily at the office building. Nick tightened his lips. Then he twisted over on his stomach and with a long forefinger started searching in the grass for four-leaf clovers. After a while Grant grinned and began telling Nick about his trip, what he had seen—

Nick listened then. "Want to see the place?" he asked.

Grant rose, brushed his trousers with his hands, combed his hair with his fingers. They walked with their backs to the administration building.

"Look—" Nick said, when they had taken a few steps, "I stole a bicycle—or they said I did, anyway."

"What you did," Grant said, "doesn't worry me. It's what you'll do later."

"Let's go this way, Mr. Grant," Nick said.

"Grant," said Grant.

Nick's half-sorrowful smile came hesitantly, stayed that way. "Grant," he said and nodded.

Nick led Grant around the grounds, through the dormitory and into the shops, into the dining room where boys were setting tables. All about the grounds boys came and went with their heads down.

Finally Nick took Grant into the shoeshop. The fellows working there crowded to the door. Grant had wrapped cheap tobacco in paper. Their eyes focused on the cigarette. Each boy whispered, "Got a cigarette, mister?" Nick said, laughing and pushing them away, "Come on, guys, cut it out, will you?" and led Grant into the shoeshop. Jesse looked up, saw Nick, grinned. Nick went over. "Who is he?" Jesse asked in a half-whisper. "Mi amigo," Nick said in his newly learned Spanish words. The officer was saying to Grant, "I'll have one of the boys show you the work we do here."

Jesse advanced politely. "May I show him, Mr. White?" Grant smiled and followed Jesse around the workshop. "This is where we cut the leather," Jesse said. "Here is how the leather looks." He picked up a piece of it for Grant to see. "And this is the machine where we sew the soles on. These are the heels. We put them on too." Grant followed, listened, watched the grave thin Mexican face.

Jesse held a finished shoe in his hand. In his eyes there was a youthful pride in the work. Grant asked, "And you boys do all this?"

"Oh, yes, sir!"

Struck by his carriage, his politeness, Grant asked, "How much longer do you have to stay here?"

"Oh, I'm leaving for home next week. I'm waiting for my clothes. I've been here twelve months." His hand, holding the shoe, shook.

Grant and Nick again went across the grounds, away from the buildings, following Nick's wandering route. Nick was more restless than he had been before. "All the little kids took off a couple of weeks ago."

They walked in silence.

"Still thinking of taking off?"

"No."

Grant looked down at Nick. This kid had personality. He was well built. A sensitive face . . . very sensitive. Not a dumb kid. Could go somewhere in the world.

They walked on . . . across the baseball diamond . . . beyond the work fields the boys had plowed and planted. . . . The mountains thrust upward under their vision. Close to them was the long, low-roofed cow barn. It was open at both ends. Nick led Grant under the rafters. It was cool and quietly dim inside, with sun throwing a whole broad shaft of light through the far door, putting color in the straw that was spread across the floor. The barn smells were pleasant. Cows stood in the stalls. Their tails swished. Their udders were swollen. From the other end of the barn, small against the stalls, Tommy came toward them. He carried a pail in one hand, leaning way over to balance its weight against his strength. The pail was only inches off the ground. Water spilled over its top; Tommy limped a little.

Nick said, excitedly, "Here comes one of the kids who got licked!" And he called out through the barn, "Hey, Tommy, come here!" Tommy came with a slow limp. "Show him!" Nick said.

Tommy obeyed. He fumbled with his belt like that day on the stage. He let the pants slip down to the divide of his legs. From his thin back to where his immature legs disappeared into his trousers his flesh was black and blue, showing the rise and fall of the lash. The whip had torn away the flesh in places. One of the sores was festered. The welts could be counted.

Tommy pulled up his pants and trudged away carrying the pail. He hadn't spoken. He didn't look up. He limped out of the barn carrying the heavy pail.

Grant and Nick moved out from under the roof of the barn at its other end. Grant passed his sack of tobacco to Nick. They both rolled cigarettes. Grant's legs carried him down to the edge of the ground where the mountains were beginning to crawl up against the sky. He stopped with his legs spread, with the long light of afternoon full on him. Nick waited there too. They stood with their heads raised a little, looking out toward the mountains.

They sat with their knees drawn up tight under their chins. Time slipped around them. They were lost in long, long corridors of thought. "It's—it's like a wilderness—" Grant said, as if speaking to himself, "like those mountains over there if no one had ever been into them."

●●●

They walked back toward the grounds. Their long shadows walked in front of them. Neither spoke. And now they were back in the quadrangle, on the spaced flagstones. A whistle blew. Immediately all the boys filed out of the buildings and went across the grounds in silent lines of blue.

Grant attempted a smile. "Well—" he said.

Nick stared up at him with dark eyes and slumped shoulders. "So long, pizon," Nick said.

Grant laughed. "So long, pizon," he said.

A whistle blew again. Nick watched Grant walk past the administration building, the deep-banked beds of flowers, the neatly trimmed shrubbery to the high wire gate. The guard unlocked the gate and let him out, locked it again. Nick watched Grant until he was out of sight. Then he turned and walked under an archway back toward the command of the whistle.

15

You don't go to reform school without seeing and learning a lot of things. And each affront to one of the inmates is an affront to you. You suffer with them. Their wrongs become your wrongs; their resentment is your resentment. No boy gets beaten without your feeling the lash of the whip in your skin. It reaches out and out until you're not alone. You're all together. You're one. Against this thing they do to you. They, here, and the police outside.

And the days go by. . . .

Nick lived the days with dulled but heavy bitterness. You never let on how you really felt. You stayed in there and acted tough and kidded each other. You didn't give a damn. That was the only answer you had. Even the little kids were like that now. The little kids had been scared stiff when they first got there but after a while they were worse than anybody. Sometimes some of them ran away because the big guys did dirty things to them. If they told about it when they were caught they'd have to point somebody out. And they'd point—lots of times to the wrong guy because they were scared to get the right one.

Ma came to see Nick every visiting day that she could scrape the money together. Sometimes the whole family came. They had been there today. When they left part of him always went with them. That part knew what they did when they got back home; what they had to eat; what Ma would be saying at the table; how Ang cleared off the dishes and washed them; how sometimes without being asked Julian would roll up his sleeves and wipe them; how Pa looked sitting on the kitchen chair smoking and reading a two-day-old paper from one end to the other; how the park looked on the late Sunday afternoon; what the guys were doing. The part of him that was left in the reform school was the loneliest, bitterest part.

■■■

[72]

It was close to the end of Jesse's time in reform school. In the basement he walked over to Nick, averted his eyes, said in a shy whisper, "I've got some cigarettes." Nick looked around. Jesse couldn't pull them out there or all the guys would mooch him. "Charlie will let us out," Nick said. He led the way to the barred door. Charlie saw Nick and opened up immediately. "Don't go too far away," he said.

Nick and Jesse went behind the engine house. They lay on their stomachs with their heads close together. When the cigarettes were just tiny butts glowing in the grass they still stayed there. Jesse said, "I get out Monday. I only got—" he counted on his fingers, "—three days more!"

Neither of them heard the footsteps. They both jumped when Fuller said, "How did you boys get out here?"

They couldn't let Charlie down. "We ducked out of line," Nick said.

Fuller saw who it was. His face scowled. "What! You!" He tapped his four fingers against his thumb in a slow rhythm. "We're having a little burlap party Monday. Both of you be there—before breakfast!" He looked at Jesse, "What's your name?"

"Jesse—Garcia."

Fuller looked at Nick. "You—" he said, "come to my office every morning for a week before breakfast and clean it. Now get back in that basement."

Monday morning a heavy rain beat against the grounds, so hard that it even blotted out the mountains. Rain rattled on the tile roofs and ran down the sides of the buildings. Reform school whistles sounded hoarse and far away in it. Streaks of lightning made everything look wet green and slime gray. Thunder crashed too close overhead and rumbled into the distance.

Jesse and Nick lifted their shirt collars up around their necks and pushing their chins down into them went across the terrace to the A Dormitory basement where no visitors were allowed and where they held the burlap parties and gave the fellows all kinds of goings over. Their workshoes squished down the steps and went into the basement.

Against the wall ten or fifteen fellows waited. A guard was getting things ready. Three lineboys stood with big water hoses in their hands. Nick looked, and was glad to see that Rocky wasn't there. A lineboy handed ragged burlap sacks to Jesse, Nick and the other fellows standing against the wall. The guard said, "Go ahead." Someone turned the hoses on. The lineboys just stood there, throwing water on the concrete floor with the big hoses. It spread all over the floor, crept in large pools to the feet of Nick, Jesse and the fellows. The lineboys and the guard retreated one step up out of the basement. Outside the rain beat down, making a brittle tattoo sound against the high, barred window. The water rose almost an inch in the basement. Nick, Jesse and the others stood in it. It soaked through the leather of their shoes. The water came up even farther. Then the hoses were turned off. From the bottom step, with his head bent in the low doorway, the guard said, "Mop!"

They had to kneel down in the water, swing the burlap bags out across the floor, wring them into pails. Their pants were soaking wet up well above their knees. Their arms were slopped. Their knees hurt. Jesse and Nick worked next to each other. Jesse stooped way over in the water. His skinny body made a funny crouching angle. His thin arms moved out slowly with the old bag clutched in his long bony fingers. Once a slow shiver ran the length of him. He looked like he was going to cry. Nick, with his head close to Jesse's, saw his hair hanging over his forehead in a limp ragged mat and said, "Take it easy, Jess!"

When all the water was wiped up the floor was flooded again. The lineboys soaked it five times straight.

Drenched, they walked through the pouring rain to their dormitory. Jesse said, "I was going home today." Nick put an arm around Jesse's shoulders and walked with his head down.

They trudged through the rain to the basement of their dormitory, went down the three steps, through the small door.

That night, going to bed, Jesse wasn't in line. He wasn't in the bed next to Nick. Next morning Nick looked for him in the dining room. He wasn't there. "Where's Jesse? Has Jesse gone home?" he asked three or four times. "Jesse's in the hospital," someone told him finally.

In the morning Nick walked past the hospital and looked up fearfully at the long flat wall of windows on his way to Fuller's office.

Nick had to sweep the office, scrub it on his hands and knees, dust everything. He had even to empty the two stinking cuspidors, swab them out with a rag, and bring the brass back to color. All the time he worked he thought of Jesse in the hospital.

He went to work in the kitchen, then to lunch. He didn't eat much. He went to classes, back to work.

That night: *"Jesse's got pneumonia."*

For two more days Nick had to clean the office. During free periods he stood outside the hospital, waiting. Then Fuller told him, looking mean although his voice was softer than Nick had ever heard it and his hand worked nervously on top of the desk, "You don't have to come here any more."

The fellows who knew Jesse stood outside the hospital at one time or another during those two days. They stood around, not talking, not tough, neither boasting nor careless, just hunched up and silent.

They looked up at Jesse's window often.

Fuller went to the hospital several times each day. He walked in silently, and came out nervously. Fuller would walk off, one arm gone, one arm close against his side with the hand stuffed in his pocket.

Then: *"Jesse's dead."*

Nick went into the basement. Most of the fellows were there. They sat on the long benches in silence. Through the small, neck-high barred window, sunlight came. It hit in the middle of the worn concrete floor. Rocky sat with his head back against the wall. His cap was still turned around backwards. His smoky eyes stared at the path of sunlight on the floor. His eyelids didn't blink; he just sat staring. Sam sat in the opposite corner with tears running down his black face. Tommy sat next to him. His face was in shadow. You couldn't see it. Just the spilled blond hair where some light was and his hands knitted together on his knees. There were cigarettes going, lots of cigarettes. And fellows passed them on and on down the line, taking drags and sending them on without talking. A cockroach scuttled in the sun path. Far off the church spire marked the hour sadly.

Everybody seemed to be listening. Then Bricktop said, "Jesse was a nice kid." Nick looked up, trying to harden his lips, but they trembled.

Head down, he walked to the shower room where he could be alone. He went into one of the shower stalls, where it was dark. He sat down, way in the back. It was cold but he didn't notice. He had his arms up in a circle with his face buried in them. He wished he could cry, but he couldn't.

▪▪▪

Weeks passed and most of them forgot about Jesse. Ma came to visit Nick. She had news. "We're trying to get you out. We are moving to Chicago. Rosa is doing fine there in Chicago. She has a nice place to live in. It'll be better for the baby. There's work there. Even for women. Pa can't find anything at all, neither can Julian. I can work. I'd work if I could find anything."

Nick looked at her curiously. They might go to Chicago. Where would they get the money? Who was she trying to kid?

"Poor Julian," Ma said. "He wants to join the C.C.C.'s—he says then we wouldn't have to feed him." She put her handkerchief up to her eyes.

Ma liked to cry. Yeah!—poor Julian!

Ma was with her face bent into the handkerchief. "I told Pa there's the—the city funds."

[75]

City funds!

Her red eyes were looking at him over the top of the handkerchief. "Julian wanted me to turn in his insurance policy so that we could go to Chicago by Rosa. We've got to do something. If we could go there we could start over again—and we could get you away from all your bad influences—"

Bad influences!

•••

Chicago! It was like a magic word. Chicago. He said it in his mind. Al Capone! That's all he thought of. Al Capone and the big buildings. Aw—it's just a dream. They're kidding themselves. Ma got up to go and he was glad. He walked her to the administration building.

"Nick."

"Yeah," without interest.

"A man came to see us—Mr. Holloway—he said he had talked to you out here."

Grant! He had been over to their house!

"He was very nice. Maybe he can help me get you out."

"Naw, he can't help me."

Ma put her hand on his shoulder. She tried to pull him toward her and hug him. Nick pulled away. "Aw!"

"Nick—" she said, "Nick—"

"Don't start bawling!" he said.

Goddamn it, why couldn't she leave him alone! He hated to have her coming out here. They didn't really give a damn for him anyway. All he wanted was to be left alone.

Ma wiped her eyes. "Maybe in Chicago," she said, "you'll go back to church."

"Go back to church! What do I want in church?" He tossed his shoulders back, looked at his mother challengingly and remembered . . . at the Catholic school in the poor neighborhood . . . the priest beating him.

Ma was shaking her head and her eyes were getting red from the tears she wiped into a handkerchief. "I got to go into the dormitory," he lied.

She tried to kiss him. He turned his face away. Her lips touched his ear.

•••

Days, nights in a full succession. Nick and Rocky walked out to the place where they went when they wanted to be alone. The grass out there was way high now. When you lay in it it almost hid you. Lying in it Nick could just see Rocky's face hunched up on the palms of his hands, serious-like, and his shoes, with his feet lifted high, stretched up above the slowly waving, yellowing grass tops.

Rocky wiggled a long straw in his mouth. Nick looked at Rocky, looked away, looked at Rocky. "Where are you going to go?"

Rocky rolled the straw to the other end of his mouth. "I don't know." His smoke-blue eyes leaped, then burned down gray again. "On the road, I guess." He hooked his ankles together and rubbed one against the other.

Nick looked at him, looked away. "What's it like on the road?"

"What's it like?" Rocky stared at a tangle of bush and said, "Some days just a cup of coffee and next day maybe you hit the Salvation Army for a meal or knock on a back door or you go to the hallelujahs for coffee and." He rolled over on his back and grinned at the sky. "But you're going some place!" Rocky folded his arms across his chest. The sun came down on the pale gold hairs on his arms; it made a shiny spot on his forehead. Rocky's voice, remembering, was reciting, "Freight trains, switch yards, dicks, hobo jungles. Skid rows in every damn big city in the country. Maybe go to Chicago." He shrugged his shoulders. "Maybe go to New York." He shrugged his shoulders. "Stick around two-three months. Then leave. Trying hard to get there. Freight trains, the blinds of passengers, hit the highway and thumb a while." His eyes remembered too, now. "So I'm out there and the cars go zipping by. You get so mad you curse at them and shake your fist when they go by. Once in a while one stopping and somebody letting you in. Because he's a salesman and wants somebody to talk to. Or because maybe he's soft or dumb and not afraid I might hit him across the head with a wrench and take his car away from him. But most of the time I give them a sob story about my mother and mooch enough for something to eat with— sometimes—a little left over for a drink or a girl. Ever stop to think how many of us got sick mothers?" He grinned.

Nick felt he was out on the road with Rocky. He saw the cars and the salesmen and the strange towns. Rocky was talking, ". . . and feeling glad to have the miles jumping under the car behind you. Long hikes with your feet giving you hell. So I stop and stick cardboard inside over the holes. And pebbles coming through."

They both looked far, far out on the road. Rocky said, "Handouts. Coffee. Chili when you got the price. Down by the railroad tracks and the flop houses and the can houses. It's all the same, up and down the road."

Rocky lay back in the grass again. He stretched luxuriously. Crickets were under the rocks. Dandelions were in yellow circles. Nick pulled grass and let it blow in the wind. He looked at Rocky and tried to think how it would be there without him.

"Chicago. Omaha. Salt Lake. Frisco. L. A. All the same. Train smoke, cinders, washing up at filling stations," Rocky said. "Getting there. Glad to be there. Glad to leave."

Silence hushed over the mountains and all across the field. Rocky and Nick lying in the grass.

Whistling notes tumbled out of Rocky's mouth, up toward the tree top. The notes stopped a minute. "I wish you was going, Nick."

The whistling strides climbed up into the tree again.

■■■

Nick waited outside the dormitory. When Rocky came out, no longer in the blue denim uniform, Nick slipped over next to him. "Hi, Nick." Rocky grinned. Nick grinned too, faintly. Nick stuck his hand in his pocket, pulled out the piece of paper with his scrawling on it. He shoved it into Rocky's hand. He was a kid again. With a knot working in his throat he said, "It's my address. If you ever go there—will you—look me up?"

There wasn't much left in reform school.

■■■

It didn't seem true but finally he was sitting in the back of a car with an officer driving him out of the reform school.

Nick turned and looked out the back window. There were the buildings, clustered in the green branches of trees, sliding away from him. He narrowed his eyes at them. The gate came open. It closed. He looked back again. There was the stretch of high wire fence glistening in the sun with behind it the terrace, with around it the quadrangle of beautiful, hateful reform school buildings. The gate . . . the wire diamonds. . . .

The car bumped over the dirt road, rolled down toward town. Nick looked back once more.

Dust curdled in the road.

16

They stood, prisoner and guard, close together in the bus depot. Nick lowered his chin into the collar of his jacket and, twisting his head sideways, squinted out the window at the new city. It was good to get out. He had thought he'd never get out. His eyes were bitter as he glanced angrily at the man with him and then

[78]

once again stared out through the window at the people pushing and shoving into the noise and traffic of the street.

The man with him was a huge man, tall and broad in a blue serge suit. Between his lips was clenched a cigarette that was souped and ragged. Nick stood small and rebellious alongside of him. His clothes were in a roll of canvas under his arm. His hands were shoved down in his pockets and his shoulders were hunched up tensely as he stared through the plate glass at the strange city; he watched with deep, smouldering eyes the endless flow of automobiles and filled-up streetcars that came across the view of the windowpanes. He stuck his head back and tried to see the top of a building that was mostly white and went straight up. There were big buildings here!

"Bet you're glad to get out," the man said, laughing in short, humorless cordiality.

Nick tightened his lips and didn't answer.

"You'll like this burg," the man said.

Nick clenched his arm on his bundle of clothes and lowered his eyes. He knotted his face and ground his teeth. Don't talk to me, you bastard! Frowning he stared at the man's big feet in shiny black shoes.

Aunt Rosa came into the depot on fast fat legs, her head swinging around above the large shoulders and swollen-out breasts, her eyes searching everywhere at once for him. Nick looked at her with quick pleasure. She looked just the same. Even the mole with the fading hair growing out of it was the same. And the beginning of a black mustache.

When she saw him he came forward slowly, half-embarrassed, his lips loosening in a widening smile. He began to tremble a little.

"Nick!" She had her arms around him, all the way around. They were big, enveloping, hard-pressing. "How's *my* boy?" Her wet lips went smack! smack! against his. She held him off from her at arm's length. When she let him go she grinned and punched him on the arm playfully—but with a sting. He liked that. It wasn't like when Ma petted him. It was the way Tony or Rocky would have done it.

The man from the reform school walked over to them.

"I'm his aunt. I'll take him home," Aunt Rosa said, dismissing him.

"Lady, I got to take him to the door. I got to deliver him."

"Huh!" She blew anger and contempt through her nose. Taking Nick by the arm she moved with him to the door, the man from the reform school following them.

They pushed out into the rush of city noise. Aunt Rosa took Nick's bundle of clothes from him and lugged it under her beefy arm to the curb where, whistling like a man, she made a taxi stop. The three of them got inside.

They started over cobblestones and streetcar tracks. There were automobiles, a streetcar clanging, trucks, a top-heavy Greyhound bus rumbling past the taxi and making it low against the street.

"Your folks are staying with me," Aunt Rosa was saying. "They ain't found a place yet. They don't know their way around yet. That's why I came to meet you."

Ahead of them there were some tracks up in the air on stilts with cars hooked together like a train going along on them. They went under these tracks.

"Your Ma," Aunt Rosa said, "dragged that gilt-framed picture of the Blessed Virgin all the way to Chicago with her, carrying it between her knees." She laughed good-naturedly. "Jesus God Almighty!" she blasphemed. "She could have got one on Maxwell Street for a quarter!"

He didn't want to hear about them. He stared out the taxi window. He shivered, thinking about the reform school. Then he began relaxing. The taxi climbed a low incline of street. There were railroad tracks down in the hollow, lots of tracks branching out like fingers. Nick's eyes began to enlarge on the city. The city began to beat its throb and pulse into his consciousness. They came to a bridge. They went over it, bumping on street stones. Nick, with his face against the taxi window, saw a flow of water and—stretching his eyes—big, on-end buildings piling up against a smoked-over sky. This was all right! This was new and exciting. It wasn't small-town. Things happened here. Maybe he'd run into Rocky on the street. They went over the bridge and down the car track until they came to a big sign on a store on a corner. The taxi turned here and went down another carline. "There's a Italian store!" Aunt Rosa said, pointing. "There are lots of them around here." They didn't go but a couple of blocks when they turned again and passed a big funeral parlor with a bright, different-colored front like a show or a night club. It wasn't far then and the taxi pulled up in front of an ugly, straight-faced building, brick, with the front peeling away in crumbling, weathered leaves of red paint.

•••

Aunt Rosa's apartment was stuck up on the second floor over a grocery store. There was just a front room, kitchen and bedroom. In the kitchen there was a nailed-up door with voices on the other side of it.

Nick walked in like, Well, here I am!

They were all there. Ma had been crying. She was always crying about something. She put her arms around him but when she tried to kiss him he pulled away. He said, "Hello," to the rest of them, bobbing his head at them and, "I'm hungry."

They seemed ashamed and glad and sore at the same time. Pa

tried to explain. "We were thinking about moving when you were home. We had to do something, we were broke." Nick looked at his old man, at his beaten face without friendliness.

Ma tried to explain. "We didn't want to leave you there, son. We—we had to do something. We—we tried to get you out." She began to sniff again. With the handkerchief up to the corner of her lips she said, "Rosa has been so good to us. She sent us the money to come."

Aunt Rosa laughed good-naturedly. "Would you believe it, Nick, I won it on the horses. It was about time I hit." She snorted again. "Your Ma got pious and holy and didn't want to take it because I won it gambling."

"We sold for nothing or gave away the few sticks of furniture we had left," Julian said, and Nick's eyes met his brother's for a moment and moved away. Ang sat in a corner, looking at Nick with grave and wondering eyes.

"Well—let's eat!" Aunt Rosa said.

It was Friday, so no meat. They had fish fried in deep bubbling oil, a heaping bowl of mashed potatoes going down by the big spoonfuls, tomatoes with oil on them, a loaf of Italian bread long as your arm, spaghetti—even a bottle of red wine for Pa and Aunt Rosa. Julian shook his head no. "This is a celebration," Aunt Rosa said. "We're all together again." Nick took as much as Aunt Rosa would give him—half a glass. Ma complained about that. But Aunt Rosa said, "That'll put hair on his chest, Lena. Who the hell ever heard of a dago who didn't drink wine?" She held the bottle out toward Julian again, nodded persuasively, made a coaxing face. Again Julian said no. Ma's eyes were approving; they caressed the clean profile of Julian's face.

"Even the priests drink wine," Aunt Rosa said. Immediately Nick held out his glass with one bead of red wine slipping down to the bottom. Ma frowned. Aunt Rosa laughed with her belly shaking. Then she winked at Nick and set the bottle at her fat elbow without giving him any more.

When it was time to go to bed Ma, Ang and Aunt Rosa fitted, somehow, in the bed. Junior was in the clothes basket by the bed. Pa slept on the sofa. Julian and Nick slept on blankets on the floor with Pa's snoring going on over them.

•••

Sunday morning Ma hustled them off to church. Nick rolled himself up in the blankets on the floor and said he didn't feel good; he had a stomach-ache. Ma couldn't make him go. She said "godless" and "ungrateful" and "not a Catholic." She went off to church with Pa and the rest of the family. As soon as they were gone Nick pulled on his pants and, barefooted, went into the kitchen to look for

[81]

something to eat. He heard noise in the bedroom and, Aunt Rosa, moving heavily on the mattress, called him. Nick went to her. She propped herself up on one beefy arm. "You didn't go to church, did you?" she said, frowning. "No, ma'am."

Aunt Rosa relaxed the pretended scowl. She smiled, double chins forming, and said, "Neither did I. I didn't feel like it either. Do you think we'll go to hell?" She grinned and moved in the bed a little. "Sit down, Nick."

He sat on the edge of the bed. She wrapped the blankets about her shoulders in a small patchwork tent and sat up. She put her arm around him and pulled him back against her. "You be good, Nick," she said. "Don't give your Ma or your old man any more trouble. You be good. Aw—who am I to go giving you a lecture?" She gave him a little shove. "Clear out of here while I dress."

While Aunt Rosa made noise in the bathroom washing her teeth, Nick stood eating a slice of bread and looking out the back window. There wasn't any porch. You couldn't see much. Just a small vacant lot crowded in between the high brick walls of buildings on each side. The vacant lot lay lumpy, scaled with ashes. Tin cans caught reflections of light. A dog sniffed below the window with long, curious sniffs. Nick opened the window and threw a piece of bread to him. The dog ate it greedily.

Nick wandered around the front room. Nick opened the door and went down to the sidewalk. He watched, carefully, the way he went so that he wouldn't get lost. He crossed several streets and came to a carline. He looked up at the black and yellow sign on the post. It said: S. HALSTED ST.

He turned down this street.

17

On Halsted Street Nick heard a loud and continuous nonking of automobile horns. He turned and saw a wedding procession. Streamers of colored tissue paper were wrapped around the cars. On the backs of the cars were big, unevenly lettered signs:

The cars stopped before a photographer's shop. The wedding party went across the sidewalk in front of Nick. The bride wasn't young; she was fat and wore a lacy white veil that trailed to widened-out hips. The bridesmaids wore pink and blue and green dresses made out of stuff that looked like curtains. The men were in tuxedos with flowers in the buttonholes and the women held their arms. Nick walked past them. He looked back at the dresses that swept against the dirty sidewalks, the hands holding them up a little and the men dressed like a dead man he had seen once.

Nick walked on, looking at everything. There were Italian stores crowded together, with spaghetti, olives, tomato purée for sale. He saw baskets with live snails in them: 10¢ A POUND. Nick, thinking of people eating them, spat on the sidewalk. At the corner of 12th Street taxi drivers stood in groups, smoking and talking. The streets were crowded with people. All kinds of people. Negroes in flashy clothes—high-waisted pants, wide-brimmed hats, loud shirts. Women dragging kids by the hand. Young Mexican fellows with black hair and blue sport shirts worn outside their pants and open at the neck. Kids, lots of kids. Two gypsy women passed Nick. They wore several different-colored skirts, red and blue, yellow, green. They had big yellow earrings, dangling, and long braids; and their dresses were so low in front that if they stooped over you could have seen their belly buttons. There were beggars with sad eyes, with mouth organs, with hands held out. A blind man's cane tapped the sidewalk. Dress shops, hat shops, men's clothing stores were crowded together along Halsted, hiding the slum streets behind them. Hiding the synagogues, the Greek church, the Negro storefront churches, the taverns, the maternity center, the public bath.

Nick turned onto Maxwell Street. Before him stretched the Maxwell Street Market extending between low, weather-grimed buildings that knelt to the sidewalk on their sagging foundations. On the sidewalk were long rows of stands set one next to the other as far as he could see. On the stands were dumped anything you wanted to buy: overalls, dresses, trinkets, old clocks, ties, gloves—anything. On what space was left near the curb were pushcarts that could be wheeled away at night. There were still other rough stands—just planks set up across loose-jointed wooden horses: hats for a quarter apiece, vegetables, curtains, pyramid-piled stacks of shoes tied together by their laces—everything. From wooden beams over store fronts, over the ragged awnings, hung overcoats, dresses, suits and aprons waving in the air like pennants. The noises were radios tuned as high as they could go, recordshop victrolas playing a few circles of a song before being switched to another, men and women shouting their wares in hoarse, rasping voices, Jewish words, Italian words, Polish and Russian words, Spanish, mixed-up English. And once in a while you heard a chicken cackling or a baby crying. The smells were hot dog, garlic, fish, steam table, cheese, pickle, garbage can, mould and urine smells.

Behind Hewitt's Restaurant Nick saw the stinking garbage cans pressed full and running over. Bums were picking through the garbage, carefully and without shame. They took out scraps of meat, bones, crusts of bread. They had wrinkled brown bags. Into the bags they dumped stale buns, blue-stencilled ham fat, chewed chops, soft tomatoes. The well-dressed people coming off the curb stared at them.

Down Maxwell the people were crowded in thick, shoulder to shoulder, tripping over each other, pushing down both sides of the street in a nosey, bargain-hunting crowd. The pavement had no rest from the shuffle of their feet. They even took up every bit of room in the middle of the street as they wove around the pushcarts. The venders gestured and lifted their wares for the people to see. They shouted back and forth to each other in Yiddish over their shoes, their aprons, their vegetables.

Three boys in old clothes walked along Maxwell. One of them had a sailor's white oval of cap on the back of his head. He was blond, bowlegged. He talked huskily. When Nick saw him later he was alone and ran out of a shop with two gesticulating and cursing Jews after him and a sweater in his hands. All the Jews along the line of stalls shouted angrily, cursed, moaned. A couple of women, powdered-up and well-dressed, said, "A shame! A shame!" But when the kid ran down a side street with the Jews still after him the people squatting on the steps of the miserable little slum houses only laughed.

Nick turned off the market street. But he didn't get away from it. Down this street, on both sides, stood men in straw hats and vests and baggy pants with cages of pigeons at their feet. Foreign-appearing men, but lighter than Italians, stood around looking at the pigeons, taking them in their hands, spreading out their wings gently and examining their feet. The birds rested in the men's palms with caged tenseness. The venders talked, bargained, argued. And one vender released a homing pigeon. The pigeon flew slowly above his head, seemed to shake out his long-pinioned wings, hung there uncertainly a minute just over the heads of all the people on the street. Then, even with the factory building across the street, over the shacks and hovels, over the high-spired cross of St. Francis' Church the gray pigeon wheeled in large, widening circles. And out of sight.

[84]

Nick wandered around, up and down side streets. A short-haired, dirty-white puppy, tail working, looked back over his shoulder at his master and hopped down off a curbstone. The automobile was coming fast. It didn't stop, didn't slow. The dog yelped once, sharply, and lay in the street. "Oh!" Nick gasped, scared and with pity.

The puppy lay in the gutter belching blood. His skinny legs pawed the air. A crowd, staring, pushed in on tiptoe. The puppy's head lay in an oil puddle. His blood, spewing out of his mouth, mixed with the oil. The dog's master, unconcerned, walked on down the street. "See, that's what will happen to you if you don't stay out of the street," a woman told her small boy as she pulled him along by the hand. The boy looked back at the dog fearfully, his nose running and his eyes filling up.

Nick wandered on, not noticing things at first, thinking about the puppy. And underneath, farther from the surface, ran disconnected memories of Tommy, Jesse, Rocky.

It got later and it got more exciting. Down one street there was a fight. They were two niggers. Young guys. One was short and husky and black. The other was bigger and he was the one who pulled the knife that went zigzag in the air where the black one's face had been before he jerked it away. The black one ran. The guy with the knife was right on his tail with the knife held over his head, slashing. There were paving rocks in the alley. It didn't take the black guy long to get to them; and he started throwing them at the fellow with the knife. Nick was on the small guy's side. Because he was little and because he didn't have a knife.

A crowd of Negroes watched from the sidewalk. As a rock sailed past the tall yellow nigger's head some fellow in the crowd yelled, "Ball!—little too wide." Everybody laughed. Another rock missed his head and the fellow shouted, "Ball two!" On the porch of one of the houses an old white couple sat on the seat cushions from an automobile. They weren't scared and didn't go into the house but just sat watching indifferently. A Negro sat on a sagging balcony with his feet propped up in front of him. He chewed an apple and watched the fight. The woolly heads of three Negro women came out of the first floor windows of a shack next door. Three black hands clutching beer mugs rested on the window sills. The bums and transients at the Shelter across the street lined the fence in front of the old school building that was their home. One transient lay sleeping in the doorway. His shoes were off. His dirty toes came up out of the holes of his socks. His head, in the crushed felt hat, was on the concrete. Over him, painted on the old boards of the door, was an unevenly lettered sign some bum had painted: HOOVER HOTEL. The words were faded from rain and some later hobo had

drawn a chalk mark through the Hoover and scrawled over it:
Roosevelt.

On the stone step of a tenement sat a Mexican boy watching a
crap game in the middle of the street. After an indecisive pause
Nick sat next to him. After a while the Mexican kid pulled out a
package of cigarettes, lit one, saw Nick there on the step and shoved
the pack at him without saying anything. In the street the crap-
shooters saw nothing but the black and white cubes tangoing across
the dirty pavement.

"Two bits he don't come."

"You're covered!"

Two big-shouldered men in dark suits walked along the sidewalk,
in the shadows, watching. Nick looked at them uneasily and said to
the Mexican boy, "They're going to be raided." The Mexican
smiled and shook his head no. "You're not from around here, are
you?"

"No," Nick said.

One of the dicks caught the eye of the teen-aged fellow who was
running the game. The dick lifted a long, beckoning finger. The
youth walked over to him with his hand in his pocket. They stood
close together. Their hands touched. They walked their opposite
ways.

"Come on seven, come on seven, baby needs shoes."

"See how we do things down here," the Mexican said to Nick a
little proudly.

Nick, losing his way a dozen times, went home. Yes, they were
smart down there.

■ ■ ■

Something pulled him back to Maxwell Street. Right after supper
he got up and started for the door. "Where you going, Nick?" Ma
wanted to know.

"Aw, for a walk," and outside the door, "for Christ sake!"

"You come back here! You might get lost," Ma called.

Nick had already hit the bottom step.

■ ■ ■

This was a *big* night. The crowd, gathering from all the slum
houses, talked about the mayor coming to make a speech. The whole
neighborhood was turning out.

They came across the cracked sidewalks and the dirty street stones.

There was music at the carnival. And laughter.

The street lamps leaned drunkenly and were an easy target for
the kids' rocks. Under the now deserted Maxwell stands the cats
fought their fights. In an alley a bottle of fifteen-cents-a-pint wine
went the rounds. On a stand, blotted out by the darkness, a boy had
his arm around a girl. They looked up, through the threading trails

[86]

of smoke, at the moon. In the alley an empty bottle crashed against a brick wall and tinkled in shattered glass to the ground.

Nick walked down the carnival street, edging his way through the crowd. One end of the street had been sectioned off. Wooden horses made an uneven circle around the part that was for dancing. A crayoned sign tacked to one of the horses read: 5¢ A DANCE. A string of sickly red bulbs crossed above the dance space. There was a juke-box playing constantly. Its long electric cord went across the sidewalk to a second story window. A group of young Italian boys, fourteen to eighteen years old, loafed near the wooden horses, straddling them, laughing, joking, poking fun. The jukebox beat its drums, moaned with its saxophones, swung the music out loudly—

> Come on and hear, come on and hear
> Alexander's rag-time band—
> Come on and hear, come on and hear,—
> It's the best band in the land. . . .

The boys each grabbed another boy and, outside the circle of wooden horses, went into their wild, imitative dance.

The music said—

> Come on along, come on along—
> Let me take you by the hand
> Up to the man, up to the man
> Who's the leader of the band. . . .

The boys protruded their rear ends. They kicked their toes against the street. Some postured like girls, smirking, touching their hair, putting their cheeks up against their partners'.

A youth escorted a girl to the dance floor entrance and, embarrassed, led her out to dance on the empty pavement. The ridiculing boys, recognizing him, hurdled the horses, clapped their hands in time to the music, patted their feet to its rhythm, began chanting the words.

The boys joined hands and circled him, shouting, laughing, ribbing him.

The shuffle of feet in broken shoes, in turned-over heels, came across the night pavement and under the electric wreath of lights over the middle of the street. Nick leaned against a stand and watched them. There were women ready to drop kids into the world. There were the tough faces of boys who had known no boyhood and the broadened bodies of girls who had known everything before they were fourteen. There were little kids, looking like they belonged to no one—with just a dress pulled over their heads, with their stockings hanging down over their shoes and their shoe laces

[87]

dragging. Lots of kids. And young fellows. And girls. Boys, half-grown, with arms encircled, walked down the carnival pavement. Girls in slacks, in tight-fitting sweaters, whispered together or giggled. There were a couple of drunks staggering up to beer stalls. Negro youths, black, brown, yellow, walked down the middle of the street in baseball shirts and caps. They walked loose-jointed with all the ancient African grace retained. And when the sob of the music caught their ears it affected their feet.

Wheels of chance spun. Bingo games were in full swing with a loud voice coming out over the microphone to announce the numbers. At one stand Italian sausages on long, swordlike spears baked over charcoal pan-fires. The smoke curled up and was lost overhead. In the houses lining each side of the street people were leaning out the windows with their elbows on the sills.

The mayor came in a shiny new car, and a policeman opened up the wooden horses that blocked off the street to let his car pass.

The mayor said he had been raised in the neighborhood and pointed toward the street where his school was. The mayor said, "I came from the bottom and I'm still with the bottom!" And everybody cheered. The mayor said, "We can thank God for living in a great country and a great city." And everybody cheered. The mayor said, "Each boy in this neighborhood has the same chance I had to make his place in the world."

The mayor left. The crowd was good-natured and happy all over the carnival street. There was a colored orchestra by the dance floor now. It played hot music from the back of a truck. The crowd ringed a drunken Irishman who danced in the street, his hat sliding over his eyes. Then a colored boy and girl did a jitterbug dance while the crowd clapped hands, keeping time with the music. They could dance! Then a Jewish girl in a high school sweater with bumps and her skinny partner in loud-colored trousers and glasses took over. They were almost as good. Then, for a nickel you could dance inside the ring of wooden horses.

Only a few people danced. Fellows and girls stood around uncertain and half-embarrassed. A lean young Negro, black as the hat he wore, came out of the crowd and asked a pretty Italian girl in her teens for a dance. She smiled and nodded. Together they went under the strings of electric bulbs. Through the wild steps of the jitterbug dance he took her. They whirled across the dirty asphalt and back. They swayed to the music. They answered its harsh notes. The crowd, three-fourths white, watched, applauded when they were finished. The black boy escorted the Italian girl back to the fringe of the crowd, thanked her for the dance and went on his way.

Nick stayed late. When the carnival was no longer interesting he walked around the side streets. By the hot-dog stand on Newberry and Maxwell, propped against an empty stand were two women. One of them looked only about seventeen. She still had a childishness about her lips and an undefinable freshness. In the half-dark of the street they were smoking cigarettes.

One of the Maxwell Street merchants, a little round Jew in a straw hat, came along the sidewalk. When he saw the two women sitting there he tipped his hat to them. He said, "Hello, girls." Then he walked over closer, let his voice drop down and said confidentially, "Better be careful. The heat is on."

"How often do we have to pay them goddamn cops!" the older women complained, half-whining.

Nick sat near where the women were, listening and smoking a cigarette he had sneaked out of Aunt Rosa's pack. The two women kicked their heels against the stand. They lit cigarettes and complained about "business." "I can't make fifty cents. If I was getting drunk I know I'd make it," said the older one. "I'd run up and grab somebody."

"You gotta eat," said the young one, laughing, but her eyes didn't match her laugh.

A man came through the shadows. The young whore whispered loud enough for his ear, "Want to go home with me, honey?"

The man walked slow. He hung on the corner, uncertain. The young whore's heels struck against the sidewalk. She dug her elbow into the other woman's side and said, matter-of-fact, "Here I go again."

The man waited on the corner. She caught up with him, said something under her breath, walked half a step in front. He followed her with one hand in his pocket.

Nick smoked the second half of his cigarette and went home. On the way he went to see if the dog was still there.

He was.

He lay in the gutter. The grime of the street had sooted his white coat. Red spots were crusted on it. Flies had already commenced to carry bits of him away.

And newspapers swirled around him like the withered petals of flowers.

In the street in the dark ahead of Nick were the reform school grounds. Again he was staring through the little diamonds of its tall wire fence.

18

On his first Monday in Chicago Ma dragged him off to school, scrubbed and mad. Up the steps of St. Genevieve's, the Catholic school in the neighborhood, they went, Nick growing more lagging and sullen. On the way home Ma said it would cost her a dollar a month to keep him in school but she was willing to sacrifice that much and skimp and save just to see that he'd have the right kind of schoolmates and he ought to try and behave himself now. This speech lasted all the way home.

It was funny in Chicago without the mountains; like being in a room with no pictures on the wall. All the streets and the tall buildings and the ugly shacks shut you in. It was ugly and dirty, Chicago. And he was kind of scared there; and he didn't know anybody.

He took to walking around the neighborhood. He used to think Mr. Grant, *Grant,* lives in Chicago. Some day I will see him. Some day he will be walking on the street and we'll meet and I'll say, "Hello, pizon."

Now Julian had two pay checks. And Pa brought money home. They could move by themselves. Aunt Rosa and Ma went house-hunting evenings. Finally they found a place not far away. Ma said, "I don't know if it will be a good place to live but we can't be choosy and it's only twelve dollars a month."

It was on South Peoria Street at 1113. There was a Greek church down the street—an ortha-something church. Across the street was an ice house. Their place was behind another building. The one in the front was the color that Chicago smoke and grime leaves houses. Their place, only a few feet from the front building, was old wood. Buildings crowded it on both sides. There was a long narrow area-way leading to it from the sidewalk.

They lived on the second floor. The stairway ran up between musty, broken plaster walls with no banister or rail. There was no light in the hall. You felt your way in the dark until your eyes, widening up, got accustomed to it. The toilet was in the hall behind a broken-hinged door at the top of the landing. It made its presence felt long before you got there.

Aunt Rosa took Ma to Maxwell Street to buy what furniture they could afford right now. Julian washed the kitchen and bedroom walls nights after work. Nick, reluctant and angry, helped. They moved in.

■■■

Down the street was the school playground where all kinds of things went on like, during the day, softball games; at night, girls and crap games under the circle of light the lamppost made. But mostly girls.

Nick hung around down there. He and another dago kid got to be buddies. Angelo was a little runt, hard as nails, with a tightly screwed-up tough face. Angelo meant "angel" in dago. But he wasn't no angel. He liked Nick and got him started in the crap games with money Nick was supposed to need for paper and pencils at school. And pretty soon, in just a couple of days, Nick got to know a bunch of the guys.

Nights Angel and Nick liked to go over by Maxwell Street. It was there that Nick met a fellow he had seen his first Sunday on Maxwell. He and Angel were walking along Newberry. The blond guy was sitting in one of the window ledges in front of the Boys' Club.

"Hello, dago!"

"Hello, polack!"

"What's up?" the blond kid asked in his husky, growing-up voice. "Where you going?"

"Lookin' for trouble," Angel said, grinning. "Come on with."

Stash was the way you said it. You didn't say Stanley because that was sissified and he was a tough polack kid. Stash was the same fellow with the white oval of sailor's cap Nick had seen running out of the Maxwell Street store with the sweater.

They circled the block. They came to the grimy brick wall of the St. Francis Church and leaned against it, watching the girls. Stash was bashful and self-conscious. He always shuffled off on his bow legs, not walking close to the girls and with his head twisted away from them a little. And if he had a chance he stuck his hand in his pocket first and moved his hand up under his belt. Angel was like a man of the world. He swaggered off, looking over his shoulder at the fellows and winking. With his black hair slicked back, with his eyes looking sideways at the broad, he made the others, watching enviously, feel dumb. He looked like he knew what it was all about. Before all this worldliness Nick felt small and embarrassed. And the girls continued to hang around. Girls! He didn't like them.

[91]

Once or twice the guys tried to "fix him up" or one of the girls wanted him to come along. Like tonight.

Along Roosevelt Road came Daisy and Kitty. Daisy and Kitty weren't very old, only about fourteen. Their hair was combed smooth but bushing out around their faces at the bottom. They had their blouses pulled tight against their chests; and their chests were stuck out without much showing. Daisy had pulled the neck of her blouse down as far as it would come; there was even a small tear. Kitty's skirt had been drawn snug around her waist. They had their arms linked; there were cheap bracelets on their wrists. They glanced sideways at the boys of the neighborhood who passed them. They whispered. They giggled. All the boys whistled at them or made loud wisecracks. Sometimes they smiled at the boys. Sometimes they yelled, "Aw, shut up!" Seeing Stash and the fellows in front of the church they slowed down, hardly walking. Now you could smell the loud perfume from the dime store on Halsted Street. Nick looked up, then away quickly, feeling his face get red. Angel, grinning, said, "Oh, boy!"

When they had almost passed Stash said in his husky voice, "Hey! —where you going?"

The girls stopped, glanced back as if they had seen the fellows for the first time. "Oh! Hello, Stanley!" said Daisy.

Nobody said anything for a minute. Daisy and Kitty looked at the boys' legs spread out and the belts strapped across.

Angel piped up with, "Ain't you girls out kinda late?"

Daisy said, "What do you care?"

Angel eyed Kitty slowly from her ankles to her face. He said, "Say! You're kinda nice, Blondie!"

Daisy said, "Her name is Kitty."

"Kitty of the slums, huh?" said Angel.

"Shut up!" Kitty said contemptuously; but there was a faint grin.

"I bet I could show you a good time!" said Angel.

Kitty said, "You're too young."

Angel made a motion with his arms. He up-swung one arm and hit his muscle with his open hand.

Kitty said, "You'd like to!"

In the shadows Stash, with his hand in his pocket, made a little half-circle upward; and he fussed with his belt, tightening it.

Daisy smiled at Stash and her eyes widened up with a big, knowing question. Daisy said, "Do you want to take a walk, Stan-ley?" Stanley's face below the blond hair went red. Her eyes told him about the walk; her moist lips, spreading out in a childish red smear, told him about the walk. Stanley went a little redder and he pulled his sweater down over his belt buckle. "Well—ah—gee—yes!"

Daisy, shy now, looked away. Where she glanced she saw Nick and her eyes startled out of their coyness. She stared at him wide-eyed; surprise went across her face. She said to Stash, "Why don't you bring your friend? I don't know his name." Then bolder, "I don't know your name."

Nick didn't answer: I'll pretend like I didn't hear her.

Kitty saw Nick for the first time. "Yeah," Kitty said, interested, "come on with."

"Why are you so quiet?" Daisy asked.

Nick dropped his eyes and didn't answer.

Angel stood up and went right over by Kitty. "All right, baby," Angel said, "I'll go along."

He poked Nick in the ribs with his elbow. "Come on with."

Kitty turned her shoulder away from Angel. "Not you—him," she said, pointing at Nick.

Angel looked at Kitty with lowered black eyes and head tilted, showing the glossy sweep of black hair. Angel said, "I bet I could show you a good time."

Kitty, liking what his eyes said, smiled into his face. "Gee! you've got nice hair!"

Daisy said to Nick, "Do you want to come?" And her hand absently pulled the neck of her blouse down till the little tear yawned.

I got to say something. Nick cracked his knuckles. I got to say something. He dropped his eyes. "I'll go next time," he said.

Kitty glanced toward Halsted Street. Her face became frightened. "Come on! Hurry!" she half-whispered. "I think I see Mom coming."

Angel and Kitty, Stash and Daisy, went toward the darkness back of the church building. Nick was left alone.

Someday they'll fix me up and I'll have to go. Then what will I do?

The darkness in the back of the church scared him.

19

Out of the blur of faces at the desks and in the playground a few contracted into fellows he recognized. Don was the first one. Don wore glasses and brought his books to school in a briefcase. He had a brace holding a couple of teeth straight. Every time Sister asked a question Don's hand was straight up in the air. And Sister, proudly, "Yes, Donald?"

All the fellows who sat near him, even some of the girls, would lean over looking at his paper during tests or make motions asking for the answer. Sometimes you could hear the *ssssing* going all over the room—"Donald!—What's the answer?"

In the schoolyard Don wasn't so popular. But he stood around in the playground telling the fellows about all the stuff he stole, trying to make them like him. And he looked like a sissy.

Nick, going over to meet Stash and the guys and play baseball, laughed about Don to himself. At the corner of 12th Street stood the old policeman. He was always there during school hours to help the young kids across the wide thoroughfare. He'd stop traffic with an upstretched hand when there was a bunch of kids waiting on the curb and see that they got across safely. And sometimes he had candy stuffed down in his pockets to give them. Or pennies. He was a big cop with a round middle under the large blue coat. Up in front of Nick kids were running to meet the policeman. "Hello, Mr. O'Callahan! Hello, Mr. O'Callahan!" they all shouted at once, half-singing the words.

Nick came to the curb and stepped down. "Will ye wait a minute, lad," O'Callahan called. "What?" Nick asked hostilely. Old O'Callahan stood with one foot on the curb; he hoisted himself up to the sidewalk. "Whew!" he said, blowing air. "Sure and the divil is in me feet!"

Nick's eyes lowered sullenly. Cops ain't no damn good.

"Ye're a new lad, ain't ye?"

None of them.

"Yes."

Old O'Callahan put his hand in his pocket, saying, " 'Tis a new lad ye are in the neighborhood—" and pulled out a baseball. "Would we be interested in a baseball, lad? Sure and I got it at Wrigley Field. I cot it meself. Now what would I be doing with a baseball? 'Tis a little fat around the middle that I'm getting." He patted his belly. " 'Twas a good catch for a man of me size." He chuckled good-naturedly, went on, " 'Twas hit by Gabby Hartnett, another good Irishman."

Nick didn't take the outstretched ball. Old O'Callahan looked surprised. "Now what be the matter with ye? Take it! Ye play the game, don't ye?"

"No," Nick said.

Nick started across the street. "Here, take it anyway," O'Callahan called, making a motion as if to toss it underhand to him. "Ye've friends can use it."

"Keep it, cop," Nick said over his shoulder.

■■■

Next day in the schoolyard Don was bragging again.

"I rob a lot of stuff."

Just silence.

"I got all kinds of stuff I robbed at home."

Nick turned his mouth up in a grin.

"All—all kinds of stuff."

One of the fellows, feeling the thin arm of his coat, said, "What are you—Raffles?"

Don, not backing down, trying to impress them, trying to make them believe him, said, "I rob trucks at the South Water Market."

They all made farting sounds with their mouths.

"And I steal stuff out of the stores downtown—all the stores."

Again they made the sounds.

"Honest, I do," faster, desperately, "honest!"

Nick knew what Angel would say. Nick pushed up close. "Oh bull—!" And he followed the word out to its second syllable.

"Honest I do!" Don said, looking at Nick.

Nick put his head back, looked up at the roof of the school building and started whistling the way Rocky used to.

Don had him by the arm trying to make him listen, "Do you want to go robbing with me?"

"Sure!" Nick said quickly.

So after school Don was there by the corner where they said. As soon as they got away from the school Don took off his glasses and snapped them into a metal case and stuck the case in his back pocket. He knew the newsboy on the corner of 12th and Blue Island and when they got over there Don tossed the briefcase to the news-

[95]

boy, who opened the bottom of the stand and stuck it in there just as if he were used to doing it.

South Water Market was several buildings, blocks long. The loading platforms were circled with trucks. In between the trucks on the dividing lanes of wet and slippery pavement old men and women picked up discarded fruit and vegetables and put them in gunnysacks they carried over their shoulders. On the platforms young kids were helping load and unload trucks. *Honest* kids. Nick, looking at them, twisted his lips: I'll get mine easier.

"Come on!" Don said.

"Ain't we going to wait until it gets dark?"

"No."

Don led the way a little distance from the market where there were other trucks; trucks loaded and getting ready to pull out. Don found a truck. There wasn't anyone on the back to watch the load. "Come on!" Don ran, hooked a leg over the tail gate and climbed in among the crates of oranges. Nick, climbing in, said to himself, He's got *guts!* You couldn't tell by looks or being smart in school.

They rode the truck to over by Taylor Street. Then, in broad daylight with people and cars coming and going on the street, they hoisted a crate of oranges onto the tail gate and pushed it off. They followed over the edge of the tail gate.

The box split on the car tracks and a few oranges rolled over the cobblestones. An automobile going past honked, "Look out!" at Don and Nick; and some people in the car stared at them with curious faces on twisted necks.

Don and Nick put the orange crate on their shoulders. They didn't bother about the spilled oranges; some young boys loafing in front of a poolroom went after them.

They put the oranges in a hiding place Don knew and waited for the night. "I know a guy who runs a stand on Maxwell," Don said. "He buys anything."

Going home, after splitting up the dollar they got, Don said, "None of the guys think I can do anything because I get good marks."

Nick said, "We'll keep it to ourselves. Just you and me. That way we'll make lots of money."

Closer to home with night in the sky and stars sticking out over the roofs, Nick told Don about Tommy.

Next morning Don came to school with his briefcase and his glasses and his teeth braces shining when he talked.

At least twice a week they made a truck after that. A couple of times they went shoplifting at The Fair or the Boston Store. Nick told himself that he was robbing because they turned him that way in reform school. He didn't worry about it much.

20

At Nick's house Ang was looking in the mirror like always and Julian was reading. As soon as Nick hit the door, asking, "What's to eat?" Ma wanted to know where he had been.

"I was helping Sister after school." He said it softly, turning his eyes up innocently.

Julian looked up over the book and, cocking his head sideways a little, asked, "Are you *sure?*"

"What the crap do you care?" Nick yelled at him.

"Now, Nick, you stop that kind of talk around here!" That was Ma sounding off.

"Aw, he makes me tired."

Nick lifted the top of the steaming pot. "Gee! Cabbage again!"

"You ought to be glad to get cabbage to eat," Ma said.

Ang was setting her hair. She looked up with her fingers twisting the ends curly. "Ma," she said, "are you going to let me get the shoes Saturday?"

"Hey, I need shoes too!" Nick yelled.

The tired mother dished cabbage into a big bowl.

"He gets everything!" Ang said.

"Stop it!" Ma shouted, dishing up potatoes. "You'll get your shoes Saturday, Ang."

Ang smiled triumphantly at Nick.

"Aw, she makes me sick!" Nick waved a disgusted hand at Ang. Ang smiled brighter and Nick, coming close, lifted his arms as if he were going to hit her.

"*Ma!*"

"Why don't you two stop it and help Ma," Julian grumbled and started setting the table. "Aw, blow it!" Nick yelled, cutting his eyes at Julian. Ang started helping with the dishes. Nick got a drink and banged the glass on the sink board. "I can't have anything."

"Nick," Ma said, "I can't buy you any shoes yet. I haven't got the money."

"All right! ALL RIGHT! You don't have to preach about it."

"Hey!—Pipe down!" Julian shouted.

"You make me!" Nick shouted back. He looked at Julian angrily, then at Ma. "I'll get my shoes, don't worry!" And he started for the door.

"Nick!" Ma called. "You come back here and eat."

"I ain't hungry," Nick yelled; then, at the door, "I'll get my shoes! Watch and see!"

He slammed out.

...

Nick went looking for Don at his place. The door was unlocked and he walked in like always. Don's old man was there, lying half off the bed, drunk, seeing things, talking to something behind the mirror. Don wasn't home. So Nick went over on DeKoven Street. He hadn't seen Angel for three or four days. He called and called outside the straight-up-and-down building on DeKoven. After a while, after a long time yelling, an ugly-face woman with weeds of black hair hanging out around her face stuck her head out a second story window. "What do you want with Angelo?"

"I—we was supposed to go peddling papers."

"He ain't home. He's in reform school." The ugly eyes looked down at him, the ugly face found temporary grim humor. "Go out there if you want to see him."

The window banged down.

Nick walked away, thinking back half a year. You knew what it was like. And you knew what he'd be like when he got out because you'd already done time. . . . What about the shoes and shoplifting for them? . . . The reform school grounds and whistles and getting up before the sun tumbled in his mind.

Maybe I'd better not.

...

The next evening when Nick got home there was a new pair of shoes on the table for him. His eyes leaped triumph at Ang. He started unlacing his old shoes and was just about to try the new ones on when the door came open, slowly.

They all looked up; all of them, as if they sensed something.

The gaunt, head-bowed figure of Pa stood behind the slowly opening door. "It's no good, Ma," Pa said. "It's no good."

Ma, with her hands trembling and her flat breast heaving with the sudden intake of air, moved toward him with middle-aged agility. "It's no good," Pa said again. Pa moved wearily into the room. "I couldn't make anything. I—"

"You don't feel good, Pa."

"I'm all right.'

He filled his pipe, his hard, calloused hands uncertain on the bowl. He settled heavily into the chair and sucked in the smoke. His cheeks hollowed.

"You're sick, Pa."

"No, I'm not. Just tired."

Nick, ashamed, laced his old shoes tight again. He left the new ones on the floor without trying them on and sneaked out.

■■■

But later they had luck, lots of luck again. Pa got a job in a furniture warehouse; he even sent back money to pay the grocery bill they owed in Denver. Julian's job was lasting. He started in at night school at Crane. Nick, looking at Julian, had his private, inside sneer. The jerk!

Pa was the same old Pa, crabby as hell, trying to tell everybody in the family what to do. He said to Nick when he was in one of his half-friendly moods, "Get all the education you can, son. Look at Julian. He wants to learn."

Yeah?—Julian! Julian! Julian!

Ma cut in with, "You might as well talk to the wall. He likes the street too well."

And Pa, "Get everything you can out of school. You won't get anywhere without education."

"Bunk!" Nick said, loud enough for Pa to hear, and got up and walked out on him.

Pa sat silent for a minute or two, just staring. Then he rocked back and forth on the chair a couple of times.

Nick walked on the street.

Why don't they let me alone?

Preach! Preach! Preach! That's all they do. Why didn't he stay fixing railroad tracks? They make me sick with their preaching. Nick looked for Don or Stash or anybody. Maybe there's a crap game. But there was nobody behind the school. "Get all the educaton you can." I don't like school!

There was the school building right in front of him. He picked up a rock and hurled it, viciously, at the windows. The rock went through the center of the window. It was a damn good shot. Nick stooped to pick up another rock. A hand folded around his shoulder. Old O'Callahan, the cop, sighed wearily and said, "Sure and the divil's in ye! And why are ye after breaking the windows in the school?"

"Cause I like to."

"Now don't show me ye're spunk or 'tis the back of me hand I'll be giving ye."

Nick didn't answer. O'Callahan, scratched his neck with his free hand, looked away from Nick's hard, angry face and said, "Come now, lad, don't be like that with me. 'Tis me duty to march ye off

[99]

to jail." Nick didn't answer. Old O'Callahan shifted from one foot to the other. "Why don't ye spake, lad?"

"You're doing all the talking!"

O'Callahan sighed and slowly, elaborately straightened his hat and got a firm grip on Nick's arm. "Well—" They went a couple of blundering steps towards the gate. "I guess the only thing left is the path to the station—" Old O'Callahan heaved air heavily. When they got to the alley O'Callahan's hand was barely touching Nick's arm. O'Callahan, with his head turned away, whispered out of the corner of his mouth, "Away with ye—duck—and run—"

Nick stiffened.

"I ain't taking no favors from any goddamn cop!"

He'd never reform. He was on Tommy's side.

For good. Forever.

O'Callahan said sadly, "Why don't ye go home, lad."

Nick hated the blue uniform and the kindly voice.

O'Callahan said, "It's the gray hairs ye're putting in ye're folks' head."

Nick thought about Tony. And Tommy. And Jesse.

He had tears in his eyes.

"Aw, cut it out!" he half shouted at O'Callahan.

■■■

Ma came to the door. Her face went scared. Old O'Callahan said, "Settle yerself, ma'am. 'Tis nothing much. 'Tis after breaking the windows in the school this lad has been."

Ma took her scaredness out on Nick. "We can't do anything with him. He just ain't no good."

Pa heard the voices and came to the door. With a rough hand he dragged Nick across the sill. "I'll fix him!" Pa looked Nick in the eye. "I'll give you a beating you won't forget, young man!"

"Now 'tisn't after bayting the lad ye'd be," Old O'Callahan said. "If I thought that would do any good I would've done it meself."

Pa cooled off a little. He even opened the door wide and said, "Come in, officer." That made Nick boil inside. They preach and—and they like cops!

When O'Callahan had gone Ma said, "Why don't you be good, Nick? Why can't you behave? You worry me to death."

Pa got up and went out of the room. Ma said, "When a policeman comes up to the door that lays me out." Pa came back into the room. He had the strap, the one he used to sharpen his razor on. Ma said, "No! No, Pa!" Pa looked at her, frowning, telling her with his eyes to get out of the room.

Ma put on her coat with trembling hands and went down to the street. Pa beat the hell out of Nick. He beat him until he was sweating and panting. Nick hated to run but it hurt so much that every once in a while he had to jump around the room and cower with his arms up around his face and head.

I won't give you the satisfaction of making me cry. No, not even if you kill me.

His eyes flashed at Pa, up into Pa's hostile eyes. And there was no relenting, no breaking on the part of either. When Pa was worn out and panting, when Nick was beaten up with red welts all over his arms and legs—even with one across his face half closing his eye—Pa stopped.

Nick and Pa faced each other, staring each other down. The sting was in Nick's flesh, creeping, in needles, all over his skin. But it was deeper too. Nothing would take it out. And as they stared at each other Nick said, "You sonofabitch!" under his breath, half hoping Pa would hear him.

21

One of the other fellows Nick noticed at school was Vito. Vito was a husky guy who wore a chauffeur's cap pushed back on his head and had a sloppy way of walking. Each day he came into class, walking slouchy and unconcerned, with the cap cocked up over his broad, shiny forehead and straight nose. And Sister would say, "Haven't you forgotten something?" Vito would look under his arm at the ragged book, and behind him, then stare at Sister and shrug uncomprehendingly. Then Sister would say wearily, "Take off your hat." Every day it was the same. They all waited for it; Vito never failed them.

Half the day he read comic books—*Superman, The Flash* and *The Batman*—hiding them between the pages of his big geography book. And he had a game he played. With the flies. He'd lay for them. A fly, buzzing around the room would come and sit on Vito's desk, gliding to a stop. The fly would rub his front legs together, cleaning them. The fly would jack up his hind-end until his beady little head and round red eyes like car headlights were almost on the desktop. Then he'd wind his back legs together, rub them over his wings, paring them too. The fly would make indecisive, zigzag excursions up the desk or take quick flights only to settle back and start the leg manicuring all over again. Vito bided his time. He watched with focussing eyes. Then his hand would flash in a quick jerk and ball into a fist. And the fly was inside.

His hand, with the fingers curled in not too hard around the little buzzing piece of life, would open slowly until he could get the fly in between the first fingers of his other hand and handle him.

Then Vito set to work, methodically, tearing the fly's wings off so that the fly had to crawl on the desk, going lopsided in the big grooves where hearts and initials were carved. Vito would prod him on with the point of his pencil or push him back on the desk when he nearly went over the end. It was slow, cruel play and Nick watched with most of his sympathy on the fly's side.

When Vito got tired of torturing flies he dropped them into the ink well where they swam around and got blacker than they were before. Then he pushed their heads under with his pencil rubber. Nick watched Vito, fascinated, not liking him.

Vito stuck his nose in Nick's business one day after school. He wanted to horn in when Nick and Don were going over to the South Water Market. Nick told him to beat it and they had an argument. Without warning Vito swung and Nick was picking himself up off the sidewalk with a bloody nose. He saw red. He sailed into Vito. Right there on the corner they tangled.

It was a good fight while it lasted. They rolled over and over on the sidewalk, kicking and punching, picking up skinned elbows and knees and rips in their clothes. And, even if Vito was bigger, Nick was getting all the best of it when Vito grabbed a stick, somehow, and jabbed it in Nick's side. That made him boil.

They rolled out almost into the street and Nick managed finally to get on top. With his knees on Vito's chest he grabbed Vito by the hair and bounced his head up and down on the pavement until Don pulled him off.

Then Nick was sorry. "You can go with," he said. He picked up the chauffeur's hat and handed it to Vito.

So they went robbing at the market and Vito showed them up by getting more than they did. And he split with them. That made them pals.

Nick asked Vito what he had been thinking about for a long time. "Where did Al Capone hang around?" Vito didn't know but he told Nick: "He had all the cops in his pay, he ran a breadline for guys out of work, he pulled all kinds of jobs and nobody could pin nothin' on him—nothin'!"

Nick took Vito around to meet the guys, Stash and them. The fellows took to him and Friday or Saturday nights they'd go up to Stash's house. On the street below there was always the listless loafing of bums and drunks; the aimless shuffle of men and women, coming, going; the sudden outbursts of quarrels and cursing; the wail of a baby. Inside a bunch of the neighborhood men, polacks and lugans and a big Russian with an accordion, got together week ends. They'd be there in their shirtsleeves or their underwear tops playing cards for money and drinking. They'd be there all night in a circle around the kitchen table with their suspenders eased off their shoulders and their keesters pushed down in the chairs until they were sitting almost on their backs. They'd gamble their whole week's pay checks away.

■■■

One night the whole bunch of them—Vito, Stash, Nick, and Sleepy —a nigger kid they palled with because Vito had said that all they needed was a nigger in their gang—were walking along Halsted Street in front of a big store. From nowhere a squad car pulled up at the curb and a cop came running around the corner of 14th Street. The cops came from three directions, on the run. They were cornered. There was no way to escape unless it was up the wall. They stood there waiting for whatever was going to happen.

Stash had his hand in his pocket. A big cop pulled out his gun and pointed it at him. "You move—I shoot!"

Stash stood frozen with his hand in his pocket, his face turning from white to red, from red to white. The flatfoot frisked him.

The fellows stood, half-cowering, against the store window with suits and shirts advertised, cheap, in the show window behind them, with the cops around them on all sides. Vito, with the chauffeur's cap cocked crooked, didn't look scared. Sleepy was trembling. And that's how Nick felt.

"What are you boys doing on the street at this time of night?" a policeman asked meanly, looking at Nick.

You act tough. Even when you're scared.

"Waiting for a streetcar."

"All right, don't get smart, you punk!" the flatfoot said nasty as hell.

Another cop, seeing Vito, the big guy of the bunch, pulled his gun out right away and put it on him. "How many stores did you rob?"

"We didn't do nothin'!" Vito said it mad.

"Where do you live?"

"In a house."

WHAM! The cop cracked Vito in the face with a hard, open hand and Vito's head snapped back. His face went all red on that side. His eyes jerked up water from the sting. But his lips tightened and, through the hurt, they grinned faintly, sardonically.

"Keep a civil tongue in your mouth," the cop said. "Answer like you're supposed to."

Nick narrowed his eyes at the scowling cop.

The sonofabitch!

"*Now*—where do you live?"

In the reform school the guys who ran it were your enemies. Outside it was the cops. That's what he had felt. That's what Rocky had told him later. That's what he knew for sure now. You can't even walk on their goddamn streets.

"How come you boys are all different nationalities?" one of the cops asked.

"That ain't nothing, is it," Nick said, "in this country?"

I bet they don't go looking for gangsters. They just beat up kids.

The cops searched them; they didn't even have any keys on them.

"All right, get home! And don't let us catch you on the street again at night."

The squad went along the curb slow, keeping up with them a couple of blocks. Then the squad pulled away. And on one of the side streets, an hour after, they saw the squad car parked in front of a tavern with no one in it.

■■■

It was night and it was dark. Street lamps made evenly spaced circles of light on the asphalt, and one star stood in the sky. People were in the houses with the shades drawn down. There was no noise on the street.

Nick walked through the darkness and quiet toward Don's house feeling a strange uneasiness in him.

I ain't been near Don for a couple of weeks. Maybe he thinks I took a powder on him since I been hanging with Vito. I'll be real friendly with him. He don't have much fun. He ain't got many friends. He's a good guy.

The street lamps fell past him but the high-hung star stayed in front of him.

I'll say, "Whatcha say, Don?" just as if I saw him yesterday. And I'll come around often.

The porch steps ran straight up with a black iron rail, blacker than the night. Someone was sitting out in front on the bottom step.

"Whatcha—" Nick stopped.

Don was sitting there staring straight ahead in the dark. He was crying. Behind the glasses the tears ran out of his eyes and onto his cheeks. He was small and hunched up there on the bottom step, his briefcase leaning against his leg.

Nick didn't know what to say. He slumped down on the step next to Don. Finally Don saw him and saw who it was.

"My old man shot himself," Don said.

Nick hunched up next to Don, feeling the shock and hurt inside himself.

"My mother is coming to put me in a private school somewhere."

Don's old man drank and played the horses. His mother lived in a different house with another man. Don's old man used to say, "Everything will be rosy tomorrow," and "Tomorrow's another day." He saw things when he was drunk. He gave them cigarettes. Don cried without making noise, cried inside. Don's old man wasn't a bad old man. Better'n mine. And at school Don wanted the fellows to like him. He wanted to be one of the guys.

In the sky the lone star showed, frozen there. Nick looked up at it.

After a while he was thinking of Tommy with his bare behind and Fuller with the strap in his only hand. He clenched his teeth and he clenched his fists. He shivered a little. Rocky said it was the same up and down the road. Rocky didn't have any folks. "He's dead." That's what they said about Jesse. Because he was sick and they made him go on line and he had only a couple more days to do. "Jesse's dead." Now Don's old man was dead. And Don was crying.

Nick clenched his teeth. His head slumped down. It's a lousy world. Oh, yes. That's what Quinn used to say. Oh, yes. It's a hell of a world. All the good guys like Don and Jesse and Rocky and Tommy get it in the neck. Tommy had screamed loud.

Nick cracked one knuckle. He cracked another knuckle. Nick put his forehead against the iron rail. It was cold against his forehead.

The little cold star shivered all alone in the sky.

22

Nick lasted in the Catholic school only three weeks after he met Vito. But even that didn't separate them. When they were expelled Pa beat Nick, adding a couple of kicks in the rear end, and enrolled him in a neighborhood grammar school. As soon as Vito found out where Nick was he transferred there.

It was a tough school. The kids didn't want to learn anything. Even the girls were bad, most of them. Lots of them were like Kitty and Daisy. Pushovers. Some of the fellows even had ways so they could ask a girl right in the classroom, right under the teacher's nose. You did it with signals with your fingers. One girl had to leave school because she was going to have a baby. The boy, a big dumb fellow sixteen years old, got the reformatory. The other fellows did a lot of whispering about it and a lot of laughing because he wasn't the only one who had done it; they all had.

But the girls were not all like that. A girl named Rosemary had the job of keeping the glass on the teacher's desk filled. And Rosemary, with her stuck-up airs, went around carrying little papers for the teachers. Miss Miller was always smiling and cooing at her because she got an average of 95, belonged to the Speak Good English Club and the Honor Society.

Nick stared at the high pile of brown-gold hair with light shimmering on it, and was awed. She was pretty. She looked pretty to him anyway. He glanced at the round blue eyes that she held up-tilted, looking at space over the fellows' heads, and was awed some more.

She's proudlike and sort of different. Something like Ang; only not snooty. He was sure of that. Just different from the other girls. Dignified, he guessed.

The day he didn't forget was after school on the sidewalk going home. At first he didn't see Rosemary. What he saw was that moron-looking guy he had noticed sitting out in front of the men's shelter on Newberry waiting for mealtime. Every day for a week now he sat down a short distance from the school on the bottom step of an empty house and watched the young girls coming from school. He wore a red bow tie and a black hard-brimmed hat. All of his other clothes were ragged and dirty. All but the tie and the hat. And every time a girl came by he straightened the long ends of the red bow tie, took off the black hat, rubbed the brim clean with the sleeve of his coat and put it back over the coarse, uncut hair.

Today he looked up at the girl coming toward him. Nick followed the beady black eyes and—he got scared!—there went Rosemary passing right by the slobber-mouthed man with sunlight lying all over her gold-brown hair and with her English book under her arm.

The moron's lips slobbered open in a smile. The thick lips said, "Hello, girlie!" Rosemary was frightened and made a wide, cautious half-circle around the steps. The moron got up and followed her. Rosemary walked fast, glancing back fearfully.

Nick ran to catch up with her; and Rosemary, awfully scared, turned around on the sidewalk and stared behind her when she heard the running footsteps. Nick halted at her side. "Hello, Rosemary," he said, breathing hard.

He walked beside her. He looked back and saw the moron ducking down an alley. And right beside him Rosemary was walking slow again.

He didn't know what to say.

Am I supposed to ask her if she wants me to carry her book?

He got red thinking about it. And Rosemary, next to him, was red and silent with the blue eyes looking as if they were going to cry. For almost a block they walked that way. Then Rosemary, her voice trembling, said, "That was nice of you"—she paused—"Nick."

They had to pass his house. He hoped Ma or Ang wouldn't see. Then, going down 12th Street with lots of people there and all of them seeming to be staring at him and smiling, Nick got a funny, scared feeling inside of him.

"I got to go back," he said fast.

"Aren't you going to walk home with me?" Rosemary asked.

"My mother's waiting for me to go to the store," Nick lied.

Without even saying goodbye he turned and walked away. His face was burning. He hoped nobody had seen him. Especially Ma. No, especially the fellows.

***

The next day Rosemary lowered her clear blue eyes from up above Nick's head and looked right at him as he came into the school building. "Hello, Nick," she said, soft and musical.

"H-h-hello, Rosemary," he stammered. He flushed. He felt like running. And worst of all Vito was with him.

Rosemary threw him a little smile and started for the classroom. Vito said, "Ho!—you work fast!"

Nick colored some more. I hope she didn't hear him.

"How's it she talked to you?" Vito wanted to know.

"I don't know."

"Oh, yes you do—come on, spill it!"

"I—I walked her home."

"How about fixing me up?"

"She's a nice girl!" Nick said, indignantly.

"They're all nice to the right guy," Vito said.

...

It was only a couple of days later that Vito said to Nick, "I'm fed up on this school. Let's make them throw us out." Nick thought of Rosemary when Vito said that and had a funny feeling inside. He was ashamed to feel that way about a girl. Like he'd miss her. "All right," he said quickly.

...

A week later Vito and Nick got their walking papers at school. They were in the toilet. Nick took a pencil and over the trough he marked:

No matter how you shake and dance
The last few drops go down your pants.

Then they started a crap game. The door swished open and old lady Miller, the teacher, ran in. Nick dashed to the trough and started faking while Vito yelled at old lady Miller from the back of the toilet, "Hey, can't you read? It says Boys!"

What did he say that for? Miss Miller turned on him like a blast of steam. She beat him up and down the length of the toilet until he let her have one back. It was a pretty good fight but Vito, getting scared, quit after he had pasted her a couple, and she pulled him all the way down to the office by his tie.

Vito said, "Nick wasn't smoking in there and he wasn't shooting craps. I was but he wasn't."

The principal listened patiently, even a little bored. Miss Miller cried till her eyes got red and her face looked even older than it was. The principal said, "I'm afraid we can't do anything for you boys. You're too tough for us." The principal smiled a frosted smile and said, "I've got a little surprise for you. You're going to go to Forman where they know how to take care of incorrigibles."

Nick wondered what incorrigibles meant.

The principal wrote the transfers.

23

Around the neighborhood Nick asked, "Hey, what's Forman like?"

All the fellows knew. "It's full of polacks and niggers and dagoes. It's a reform school only they don't call it that. It's the last jump before you go to St. John's. They get them from all over the city when they ditch and send them to Forman."

"If you're retarded, too." The fellow who told him that tapped his head. "That means a little off."

At Forman they all worked on Nick. Teachers in the receiving room, the dentist, more teachers, the doctor, the psychologist. Nick was bored and careless. He slopped through the tests, but he got a kick out of them. He made fun inside himself and put down any old answer. The tests, he knew, had something to do with his I.Q.— whatever that meant—and he didn't give a damn what his I.Q. was as long as he could monkey around. Did they think they were going to keep him cooped up in this school? He'd show them just like he did at the other schools.

In the print shop with the teacher out of the room Nick asked the crowd, "How is this joint? Do you like it?"

Sarcastic, razzing voices said: "Sure, it's swell. Sure, we like it! They only keep us till two. They ought to keep us till six. We ought to have school Saturdays and Sundays."

In his last class of the day Nick heard a teacher say to one of the kids, trying to make him behave, "Did you hear me?"

The kid screwed his face up into a small, insolent, wise-cracking grin that was half scowl. "No, I'm deaf and dumb!"

The teacher laughed indulgently. She said, "Oh, all right, you didn't hear me." She didn't pay any more attention to him.

From his desk Nick stared surprise. He had never seen a teacher back down before.

• • •

As the week passed Nick found that the fellows who went there were his kind. They didn't believe in school. They came with their hair uncombed and with ridiculing mouths. They knew how to stand up for their rights, right in class. And they knew how to ditch classes, going out the side exits where they had friends on guard, and they knew how to shoot craps in the alley across the street.

There were a couple of bad things in school. If you lived over a mile away you got streetcar tokens and at the end of the day the teachers put you on the streetcar. Another lousy thing about the school was every day you had a card that was signed by the teachers to show you had been there. These cards had to be returned every morning with your old man's signature on them. Even so, if you used your head you could find a dodge and ditch just the same.

Most of the time he and Vito hung out at a dirty-windowed lunchroom across the street. There was a music box with all kinds of low-down and half-dirty records, and for a penny it played. And there was always a fellow or two from school who kept an eye on the school through the window, or a guard with a white belt across one shoulder to come and warn you when a teacher was on the way over on a raid. Over there, too, even if they didn't have a license, they sold penny cigarettes to the fellows. All the wisest guys from Forman loafed over there. They knew how to work Reggie out of sandwiches and pop for free.

Reggie looked like he was poured into his sweater and tight-fitting pants. Most of the time Reggie stood leaning over the counter with his head close to one of the newest Forman boys. Then after a while he would change to the next latest kid in school--if he was good-looking.

It was only the second time they came into the store that Nick tried to put something on the cuff. "How about it, Reggie?" he asked, wrinkling his forehead in a pleading gesture. "Come on!" And he nodded his head up and down and made his face look sad.

"Huh," said Reggie, "this isn't a relief station."

Nick, with the trick he had learned to use on Ma, widened his clear, innocent brown eyes with his head half down and said, "*Please*, Reggie."

He got his sandwich, and with it a bottle of pop. After that it was easy to mooch over there. He worked Reggie for a chump.

■■■

This neighborhood was plenty tough. That's what Vito liked about it, and that's what fascinated Nick. Like a movie. You could see tough characters and hear all sorts of stories. Murders. Robberies. Rapes. Crooked cops and good-paying rackets. And when they heard about a killing on one of the streets near the school they'd go over and look at the blood spots on the sidewalks. Most of the killings were with knives or razors. They left big spots of blood, black and grit-crusted.

If only he could see one of the knife battles! He'd like to. He wanted to. He hung around, hoping.

The young fellows who lived around here were tougher even than where Nick lived. They all carried knives. Long, sharp-bladed knives, like daggers, four and five inches long. Some had little buttons on the handles that snapped the vicious-looking blades open for action with a quick flash. And some of the heavy-lidded Negro and Mexican fellows smoked marijuana. And you couldn't go through Homer playground even as early as eight o'clock at night without seeing young guys and girls only thirteen and fourteen standing pressed close together in the shadows.

That's what the neighborhood was like.

24

The cold weather clamped down over Chicago. The ugly gray rains from a lowered sky turned to sleet. The first snowfall came, powdering the face of the neighborhood, hiding it. A white beauty heaped tenement roofs, etched in church steeples and water towers. The feet of the people and the wheels of automobiles cut ugly trails across the snow's beauty. Corner thermometers edged their threads of liquid lower and lower.

Windows were frozen over. Whole forests of silver pines showed on Halsted Street's plate glass. Ashes were scattered across sidewalks and salt ate the ice. The Jews didn't abandon their pushcart stands on Maxwell Street. They beat their hands together over little fires in tin cans hanging from wires. Their overcoats fell almost to their ankles, their caps were turned down in ear muffs. They danced little warming jigs on the icy sidewalks, pulled customers into their stores.

On street corners alongside of newsstands fires burned in garbage cans. The flames leaped high over the circle of the cans and newsboys and bums stood near them, hunching toward their warmth, holding their numbed fingers over the ragged red and yellow tongues of flame.

People crowded into streetcars in the cold morning light and again in the freezing evening dark. Tramps stood wherever there was warmth. Women and children carried pieces of wood or paper cartons home from the gutters and alleys.

Pa Romano sat behind the stove sucking on his pipe. The family was on relief. Ma went to the relief station for the checks and food orders, cooked the surplus foods given the family by the city, re-mended old clothes every night. Ang minded the baby, scrubbed the floors, washed dishes, set her hair in all different kinds of hair combs and read love stories. Aunt Rosa's boss, who owned the laundry where she worked, wasn't making any money and had to sell the place. That threw Aunt Rosa out of work and she didn't have any money saved; it had all gone on the horses. Then it was Ma's turn to say, "You're coming to live with us. We'll get along all right. I'm glad—we're glad to do something for you—after all you've done—" So Aunt Rosa came to live with them and that was something else they had to hide from the caseworker who came popping in at dif-ferent times as if she were trying to catch them at something.

Julian got odd jobs on the sneak because if the relief found out they'd stop the family's check. He sometimes helped one of the mer-chants on Maxwell Street on a Saturday or Sunday all day long for a dollar. And on Wednesdays and Fridays when he could get on he walked through the cold winter streets, up and down front porches, distributing department store handbills for three dollars and a half. Julian carried books home from the library on Roosevelt Road and studied. And now, once a week at night, he went to Hull-House to something called a Youth League. One evening, after distributing handbills, he asked Ma for thirty cents out of the money and took Nick to the Villa Theatre.

They went down Halsted, and as they passed Hull-House Julian walked slow. "There's where I go. That's Hull-House." He put his hand on Nick's shoulder. "Why don't you come here with me some-times? You'll meet some nice people."

Nick buttoned his lumberjacket up higher and stuffed his hands into his pockets. "I don't want to meet no nice people!"

"Why don't you ever go to the Boys' Club? You can get a member-ship for nothing," Julian said.

"I'm through going to Sunday school," Nick said, hard as nails.

"It isn't like that, Nick—"

"Any crap shooting?" Nick wanted to know.

■■■

Nick was home only to eat and sleep. Other times he was with Vito. Today he got up early because he and Vito were going over to Stash's house to play cards.

Nick ate the slimy relief breakfast food cooked with dried milk,

He swallowed it down fast so he could get out of the house in a hurry. He knew the relief coal was going to be delivered and he didn't want to be around.

Ang, with her hair balled on top, was burning newspapers in the stove and they had Junior propped up close to it. She wore Julian's old sweater with the sleeves rolled up over her wrists. Pa sat as close as he could to the stove with a blanket around his shoulders and was poking the stem of his pipe at the baby, playing with him. Ma saw Nick grab his lumberjacket and try to duck out. "Where are you going, Nick?" she asked.

Nick put on his angel face. "I'll be right back."

Pa looked up at him with stern, hostile eyes. Pa's eyes were always stern and hostile now when he looked at him.

Nick said, right at Pa, "I'm going out somewhere where I can get warm."

Pa stiffened as if the words had been a slap across his face. Pa put the pipestem in his mouth and forgot about the baby reaching for it with his little clutching hands.

Ma said, "I want you to help put in that coal."

"Aw, it won't be here until this afternoon," Nick told her, and went out before they could say any more.

That evening when he got home the half-ton of relief coal was dumped on the stair landing and Ang, still in Julian's sweater, was putting it in.

At the top of the steps Pa was kneeling over the toilet chopping ice out of the broken bowl.

Right away they all raised hell with him. He didn't even want to stay to eat. But he was hungry.

When he wasn't hungry any more he said, "Aw—all you do around here is preach!" And he slammed out and went looking for Vito again.

■■■

Vito led Nick over to a big factory where men worked nights. Their cars were parked in the large vacant lot against the factory where the straight-up-and-down wall threw its large shadow over them. Vito walked along trying all the car doors. Nick asked, "What are we going to do?" Vito said, "Go joy riding." Nick, following Vito, tried the cold chrome doorhandles too. Vito said, "If none of them ain't open and if some jag hasn't forgot and left the ignition key, a Ford is easiest." They went, trying doors. They were all locked.

Vito found a brand new Ford V8. He took a big screwdriver out from under his jacket and stuck it in under the crammed-up edge of the small front section of door glass. He worked the screwdriver slowly, but with continuous pressure. In the factory overhead they could hear the clatter of machines. Far on the other side of the street a man walked with his head down against the wind. Vito worked. After a long try the glass came down a fraction of an inch. Bit by bit, now, it came open, inched open. Then at last there was room to get a hand and arm through. He grabbed the inside door-handle and, with a soft click, the door came open.

Vito hopped in behind the steering wheel. "Grab ahold," he said and he and Nick grabbed the steering wheel. "It takes two guys to break a wheel," he said.

They strained, grunted a little, put all their twisting power into four arms and shoulders forcing against the little pin down inside that locked the car wheels. Their arms forced, hard, harder—and they heard a tiny click. "That's it!" Vito said triumphantly. When he turned the steering wheel now the auto wheels turned too, crunching in the frozen snow and cinders.

Vito fished in his pocket and got a nickel. He stuck his head down under the steering wheel and told Nick to do the same. With their heads close together along the steering post, Vito said, "This is how you get them started." He showed Nick the two small nuts under the ignition. He put the nickel against the two little nuts and held it there with his fingers. Then he stepped on the starter, gave gas, nursed the accelerator with his foot. The current jumped across the nickel from nut to nut.

They drove all over. On the Outer Drive Vito let Nick sit in the driver's seat and showed him how to use his feet and how to change gears. They drove way out to the South Side. They stopped the car alongside a curb on a dark street out in the Hyde Park district and left it there. Then they found a Ford that belonged over there and brought it back to their neighborhood.

Over in the neighborhood they stripped the car, taking the tires, the battery, the radio and heater and even the headlights and the horn.

They had to lug all the parts over to Stash's house, not far away. It took a lot of trips. But late that night they had all the stuff safely locked in Stash's basement. The next day they sold it to a fence Vito knew.

•••

The next night they had a big time. The fence had given them forty dollars for the car parts. They took Stash's old man a quart of whiskey. They passed packages of cigarettes around. Stash's old man sat them down at the head of the poker table. The red and blue chips came out and the game started. They lost and lost but they didn't give a damn. They were big time. And when Stash went broke Nick handed him five singles. Stash said, "Thanks. Maybe I'll win now and be able to pay you right back." Nick said, "Aw, forget it." Stash's old man laughed, slipped his suspenders off his shoulders, squirmed his hind-end down on the edge of his chair and said, dealing cards around, "The kids they got plenty the money." They lost some more. But when between them they had dropped twenty dollars they pretended like they were broke and quit. Stash's old man and the Russian wanted to give them a couple of dollars but they wouldn't take it.

...

For a few days Nick and Vito were big time. They saw all the shows downtown. They ate at restaurants. They spent plenty of money at the shooting gallery on South State Street. They lost in crap games behind the school buildings and up alleys. They just threw the money away.

When it was gone Vito said, "Let's make another car."

"Screw you!" Nick said, laughing.

25

Then it was spring.

Mud that had been packed solid loosened up. Patches of old snow turned wet brown on vacant lots and revealed ovals of last year's grass underneath. The gutters on Halsted Street gurgled. The alley smells came alive again. There were more children on the street now, more and more each day. The girls and young women came out of the dark tenements. Baby buggies appeared on the sidewalks. Boys began to play finger-muddied marble games and, shouting and laughing, played leapfrog over the cracked sidewalks. Little girls with pigtails, with white faces, black faces, brown faces, brought their dolls, their jacks, their skip-ropes out to the sidewalks. In the evenings you could hear their kid voices rising above the street noises. Fruit and vegetables bloomed on the pushcarts on Maxwell Street again. The evening skies turned delicate pink and rose-tinted orange behind the tenement roofs, the smokestacks and water towers and somebody said, "Tomorrow's going to be a good day."

And somebody sat a carnation on a window ledge in a tomato can.

And it was spring again.

• • •

Nick lay in bed. The ragged shade was halfway up. Sun had a yellow hand on the window sill and a warm yellow hand on Nick's forehead. Nick lay with his eyes half open, dreamily. Pretty soon now he'd have to go to the toilet. But right now it was warm and—pleasant—in bed. He lay there, thinking about things. Secret things. Every morning for a week now he had awakened this way. He closed his eyes and thought some more.

Ang pushed the bedroom door open and came in quietly. He didn't know she was there until she leaned way over the pillow. It was too late then to turn over on his stomach. His eyes blinked open wide. He turned them away from his sister in shame and pushed his behind down in the mattress hard so maybe she wouldn't be able to tell if she should happen to look. And he closed his eyes down right away again and pretended to be asleep.

Ang laughed at him. "Sleepyhead!" she teased. Her laughing red lips whispered the words. Her warm bare arms were tight around him, touching his neck and shoulders, making little needles tingle and stand all over his flesh. And she kissed him hard on the lips.

Nick struggled in the blankets that held him down. He pushed against her weight and sat upright in the bed. His arm came out from under the covers and he slapped her face as hard as he could.

Ang's eyes were round, startled, hurt. Tears flooded their brownness. Her mouth twisted. Her hair was all mussed.

"Don't ever do that again!" Nick yelled.

Ang, sobbing quietly, went out of the room with her hand up to her face where Nick had slapped.

Nick lay back in the bed again.

The secret thoughts flooded back to him.

Nick got up and went to the bathroom.

• • •

All day he and Vito horsed around the streets with Stash. They even forgot they were hungry. They just goofed around. All that happened was lagging pennies on the sidewalk in front of the Boys' Club, shooting craps, playing pinochle, looking through a tavern window at some drunk who was sleeping on his arms on the bar with his hat rolled off and the bartender trying to wake him up, getting a shag from a kike on Maxwell, almost having a gang fight with some niggers on Washburne, and turning garbage cans over in an alley. Then it was dark and Stash took Nick and Vito over to his house because his old lady always cooked a lot and never cared if they came over there to eat.

After they ate all they could hold they went back to the street and met the other guys. Pretty soon a couple of girls they knew came along and started talking to them. The guys felt the spring coming warmer every day and funny ideas getting into them, and these girls were feeling that way too, so right away everybody started looking and pushing and wisecracking. You'd hit a girl on the arm, not too hard. She'd hit back. You'd pull her over against you by the neck and, twisting her arm behind her, make her body come up close to you until those sweaters that bulged were pressed up against you. Nick, watching how Vito and Stash did it, only hit the girls on the arm. But that wasn't enough. Hitting their arms and mussing their hair only put a nervous urgency in him and—he looked up and down the street to see if anyone was coming. Then he grabbed the redheaded one and pulled her over toward him. But right away he itched under the arms and felt funny; he let go immediately.

The girls were what Vito said: pushovers. The fat one even goosed Stash. Nick thought that was too much when a girl did it. But you couldn't talk these girls into taking a walk. Vito and Stash tried. But the girls were too young yet or too scared yet.

The fellows grew sulky and irritable. They stopped jagging around and tried to get rid of the broads.

"Are you fellows going to be in the show Sunday?" the redhead asked.

"Naw!" Vito said. "What for? What's in it?" Stash asked. "Don't you want to take us to the show?" the fat one asked. "Aw, blow it!" Vito said, disgusted. He walked off.

Then the girls were gone and the fellows sat around still full of funny ideas.

A guy called Jinks wrestled with Stash on top of the Maxwell stand and got him down and got on top of him, forcing his legs out. Then Jinks, with his face down next to Stash's, kidded him and pushed his body down tighter and tighter on Stash's.

From around the corner came Vito. "Come on! Old man Snyder and his wife are in the bedroom!"

They sneaked down the alley and through the dark areaway. They tiptoed up the back steps with, once in a while, a board creaking under their shoes so loud that they'd stop and let the noise tremble away. They climbed around on the third floor back porch and lined up near the window with their noses close to the sill where, inside, a frayed yellow shade was pulled to within a couple of inches of the sill. They all crowded close, pushing in around the window with curious and excited eyes. And their voices whispered: "Hey! Cut shoving.... Boy, I'll be glad when I get married!... I'll stay in

bed all the time! ... Shhhhh. ... For Christ sake, cut it out! ...
Look—!"

Nick didn't look. He stood huddled into a tight knot. He only
looked at the shadows against the shade—big, convulsive, distorted.

He looked at the shadows.

When he couldn't stay there any longer he squeezed past the
fellows and sneaked away.

•••

Nick didn't go to school any more even if he wasn't old enough
to quit. He just hung around the streets with Vito. At first he didn't
tell his folks. But they found out when the truant officer came
around raising hell. That gave Pa another excuse for beating him.
Pa said, "Goddamn you, I was young but I listened to somebody."
It was the worst beating Pa ever gave him. With kicks. Pa even hit
him with his fist once.

Saturdays and Sundays were best in the neighborhood. There
were *big* crap games down there then. The young guys and the half-
grown fellows who had jobs in factories and places like that brought
their salaries with them. And grown men, men forty and fifty years
old, shot craps with them. On Sundays when church was out and
women and girls and kids came along, the biggest and best crap
games went on. Right on street corners. The women had to walk
around the circle of gamblers. All over the neighborhood, if you
took a walk, you'd see bunches of guys shooting craps.

Anywhere around there, on Sundays you could see whole checks
won and lost. And on Sundays the squad cars roved. But you ain't
got nothin' to worry about. All the cops want is a little cash. Them
cop bastards make plenty on Sundays just circling the neighborhood
collecting from the crap games. Me and Vito been at all the games.
We know. It's only when some crab calls the cops that they have to
break the games up. But people in this neighborhood mind their
own business. Most of the time when me and Vito play, the fellow
who runs the game has Vito go down with the money.

Nick, shaking the dice in his balled fist, looked over his shoulder
at Vito taking the pay-off money down the block to the cops.

26

Nick got the baking-soda off the high shelf and, standing by the sink, brushed his teeth. He brushed hard, rubbing the bristles across them like sawing wood, staring into the mirror at the spread-out lips and the teeth, white, hard, even. Then he spat in the sink.

Ma yelled.

Nick said, "Aw, she's always in the can trying to make herself beautiful."

Ang came into the kitchen with new make-up on her face. "You think it's the library," she said.

"Aw, shut up, ugly puss!" He raised his arm back across his face as if he were going to hit her with the dipper full of water he had gotten from the kettle. Behind Ma's back Ang thumbed her nose at him and stuck out her tongue. Right in front of Ma Nick threw the water in Ang's face. And Ma yelled some more.

"*All right!* ALL RIGHT!" Nick shouted. "I'm going in a minute."

But he stayed a long time, sneaking into his room to change into his newer shoes and rub a dirty sock across them, brushing down his jacket with his hands and rubbing his shirttail around in his ears. Then he put water on his hair and stood in front of the mirror, combing it.

It won't stay down. It's too curly.

...

He went over to Taylor Street an hour before school was out. He hoped he might see some of the girls come out. He sat down on the steps.

Someone came up behind him and put fingers over his eyes. It wasn't Vito or any of the fellows. The fingers were soft—and small. A thrill went through Nick that left him like a little boy. His hands that had gone up involuntarily to pull the fingers away trembled now and he took his hands down without touching the fingers.

"Guess who!" the girl's voice said, and Nick's heart almost turned over inside of him. He thought it was—but it couldn't be!

[119]

"I don't know." That came out like when he was little.

The fingers came away and he looked up at Rosemary, into her clear blue eyes.

"Hello, Nick!" The voice sounded like she was *really* glad to see him. "How are you?"

She's got gold hair. It was fixed different now, in a high pile of brown-gold without the curls. She looked almost grown up.

"What are you doing now, Nick? Are you still in school or are you working?"

Sunlight was on her hair. Funny how the sun always was in her hair, brighter than any place else. He couldn't lie to her. "I—I don't go to school any more."

Rosemary smiled.

She's pretty.

Rosemary said, "Remember the time you walked home with me."

"Un-huh." And he hung his head; pleased, embarrassed.

"Remember how embarrassed you were that day?"

"Yes," Nick said, still embarrassed.

"How bad you were in school," Rosemary said. The little smile came back. Nick got redder. Say something, you goof. What'll I say?

"Ah—what are you doing now?" The words came out all right, even a little hard boiled.

"Oh, I'm going to high school. I go to Catholic High School. I'm a freshman."

I didn't think I'd ever see her again.

"Why don't you come over to my house and see me sometimes, Nick?" Rosemary was saying.

"I—I—"

Go on, say something! Answer her.

"—would you care?"

Rosemary laughed. It was a musical laugh. "I'd like to have you come over," she said, looking at him with friendliness. "I'd like mother to meet you." She wrote her name and address on a piece of paper and gave it to him. Then, "Goodbye, Nick. Don't forget to come over!" And Rosemary threw him a little smile and started down the street.

And the street was empty and he didn't want to see the other girls.

■■■

Nick began to gather miscellaneous knowledge from "doctor books" and street guides he found scattered on the sidewalks. He remembered everything Tony and Vito had told him. He remembered the tales the guys told in reform school and on street corners. At night in bed he'd think about it. And now he looked at the dirty books Vito and Stash had.

[120]

Maybe if he could see Kitty or Daisy alone. They mess around.

Then he did see Daisy all alone one night. She was standing in a doorway pulling up her silk stockings and knotting them over her knees. Nick stepped into the dark doorway and immediately wished he could step back out. But it was too late. Daisy raised up, and in her raising up he could see the dark crease that separated her breasts. She looked right at him. Her moist lips, smeared with lipstick, came loose a little in a smile—a funny smile.

"What do you say, Daisy?"

"Oh, you're that *bashful* fellow!"

"What do you mean—bashful?" And he froze up, bashful. He didn't know what to say next.

She stood waiting. Her hand went up to the blouse, her fingers, the nails covered with the reddest polish the dime store sold, pulled the collar down as far as it would come.

"Where you going?" His voice sounded the huskiest it had ever been. Inside he said to himself: she messes around.

Her head was back against the wall of the little entrance to the door. Her hair was slicked down more than half its length. Then it bushed out in a frizzed black collar over the red blouse. "Nowhere," she whispered. And she waited. And her eyes opened up wide with a questioning stare. "Nowhere at all." Nick kind of hung his head then, not knowing what to say next.

The dark curls were lifted all over the top of his head now, unruly, without gloss in the darkness. Daisy put her hand out and her fingers stole into the curls, lifted them, played with them. "Gee! You've got nice hair!"

He felt funny all over. *All over.* He put his hand up and his fingers reached out in the half-dark, played with the tarnished brass necklace she wore. And his fingers, running up and down the chain, pulled him closer to her until he was almost on top of her. His fingers, running along the chain, guided the back of his hand up and down along the small swell of one breast.

He was trembling all over. He couldn't keep his knees still or stop shivering or make his teeth stop chattering. "Let's go someplace," he said. His voice trembled like his knees.

They went toward the darkness behind school that he had always been afraid of.

And when he got back there he wasn't scared at all. "Come on! Come on!" He was crazy.

■ ■ ■

Nick walked home, shamefaced. He was disgusted with himself. He'd be ashamed to even look at himself in the mirror. He kicked at the sidewalk. He sneaked along. His head was down. Way down.

I didn't like it.

I'll never do it again.

In a week all memory of shame and disgust had gone.

···

All the girls went for him. They liked his curly hair and his innocent eyes. With the other fellows he took walks with the broads. He didn't score all the time—*but*—he did all right. And Daisy was a pushover. Whenever he wanted.

He kept a mental score sheet.

Ten times now. He was a man now.

Nick walked along the street cockily. He knew what he had now and he knew what it was for. He gave all the girls the eye.

27

Over at Nick's house Nick and Vito would sit on the porch boards with their feet stretched out on the little square of yellow and lumpy yard that separated the front and rear buildings. They would plan things. They had a little black book and sometimes they'd write in it, just for the fun of it. They'd have the names of stores they were going to make and their death list. In it they had written the names of their enemies and the guys they were going to bump off. Julian's was the first name in the book.

Today they sat on the porch boards kicking the soles of their shoes against the knots of stubborn grass and looking over the pages of their little black book. Aunt Rosa was in the rocker reading a *Racing Form*, studying horses, jockeys, records.

Vito pushed his chauffeur's cap back off his forehead and told Nick in an undertone, "I'm going to get a gun from a guy I know."

Nick looked disbelief. Vito cocked one heel up on the porch boards and leaned over toward the little black book Nick held. "What does the book say we're going to do today?" he asked loudly.

"We got a bank to rob and a guy to bump off," Nick said loud enough for Aunt Rosa to hear.

Vito asked, "Who's the guy?"

[122]

Nick thumbed through the book importantly till he came to the death list. "Julian Romano," he said.

The middle-aged woman looked up from the pages of the *Racing Form*. For a second her lips creased in a faintly amused smile. But she straightened them immediately and said, looking at Nick and Vito, "What are you going to do when you die?"

Vito looked at Nick and, laughing, asked, "Do you still believe in that stuff?"

"Naw!" Nick said.

Aunt Rosa's face clouded and wrinkles gathered over her eyes. But she didn't say anything. She didn't even rock. And the *Racing Form* spread out on her knees was forgotten.

■■■

After they had eaten Nick got the basin out and set it in the sink so that he could wash.

Nick poured water into the basin, rubbed soap, in bubbly lather, over his face and neck and rubbed the palms of his hands into his face hard. He cupped the cold water from the faucet in his dripping hands and drank. He threw lots of water up on his face. The clear, clean water ran down his nose and dripped off the end of his chin. It ran, in little crooked rivulets, between the two square and muscular plates of his chest. Some stood in little pools in the small hollows that reached up to his shoulder blades. His chest was straight across, square. His shoulders big.

Nick stood before the mirror spreading out his chest and inhaling deeply. He tightened his belt in. He pulled in his flat stomach and barreled out his chest, poking it out as far as it would go. He turned his shoulders sideways so he could see them too. He looked at his heavy limbs. He flexed his arm, felt the smoothness and the hardness of his flesh. He put his long, square-tipped fingers over his muscle and tightened them down on it as hard as he could. But he found no softness there. And Nick was pleased with himself.

He was stuffing his shirt down into his pants when Ma came in and said, "You get in this house by ten o'clock tonight, young man!"

"Ahhh!—I'll get in when I feel like it!"

Ma had her finger wagging at him. "You're coming to a bad end. Mark my words."

Aunt Rosa said, "Aw, Nicky, why don't you do what your Ma says?"

Nick tried to harden himself against Aunt Rosa's advice. But Aunt Rosa walked over and pinched his cheek. "Those dreamy eyes—" she said. "Bedroom eyes, that's what they are."

Nick had to laugh, even if it was with embarrassment. And they all laughed. They were all free and easy and not mad any more.

[123]

The door opened and closed. They could hear Pa clear his throat. Again the whole atmosphere changed. Nick got right up and went out with Vito.

...

It took all his courage but he did go over to Rosemary's house. He rang the bell and felt like running. Before he could turn around and get down the steps the door opened and Rosemary stood there, just like he remembered her.

Her cheeks were dimpled and her lips smiled when she saw him. "Oh, Nick!" She held out her hand to him. It was small, soft, cool in his. "I'm so glad you came over!"

He stood twisting his toe on the doorsill; and he held his hat stiffly at his side. "Come on in!" Rosemary said and he followed her into the quiet, rich-looking apartment. There was a woman standing by a grand piano turning the pages of some sheet music. She wore a smock and her hair was the color of Rosemary's.

"Mother, this is Nick. We went to school together." Rosemary's mother held out her hand and shook his. He felt funny.

"How do you do, Nick?"

She looks like Rosemary, only older.

"Make yourself at home—sit down, children," the quiet voice said. Then Rosemary's mother sat at the other end of the room looking at a book.

Rosemary led him over to the sofa. She sat down and turned toward him. He held his head down a little. She talked in a soft tone about high school and taking typing, and how he liked not going to school. He didn't say much. Finally Rosemary said, "Mother, play something, won't you?"

The young woman got up immediately, put down the big book she was looking at and went to the piano. "All right, dear," she said.

Under the long fingers the keys went down and music came out: Brahms' *Lullaby* . . . Schubert's *Knight Rupert*. . . .

She had an opal ring on her finger. Nick watched it.

And she ain't got no make-up on. Only lipstick. Her face is pale white. Like Rosemary's.

Rosemary put her hand out on the sofa in a little gesture. "Do you like music, Nick?"

I don't know. Not that kind. "Un-huh," he said. And he tried to make his face serious like Julian's always was.

Mendelssohn's *Songs Without Words* were in the room now, slipping across it, bringing a softening, half-melancholy look into all their eyes.

I wish I was like them. I wish Ma was like her.

Rosemary brought the book her mother had been looking at over to the sofa and she and Nick turned the pages. It was a book with pictures on every page, pictures by famous artists. Nick's eyes sneaked up, now and then, from the pages to Rosemary's face, her lashes almost touching her cheeks. "Some of the originals are at the Art Institute," Rosemary said. Nick looked at the pictures and the slim white fingers turning the pages.

"This one is by El Greco," Rosemary said. "Don't you like it?"

"Un-huh." I wish I knew about things like that. What for?

"Why don't you make some cocoa for Nick?" Rosemary's mother asked.

Rosemary made it. She even asked Nick to stir the cocoa and sugar together. They drank it on the sofa with little cookies, all three of them.

Nick was uneasy and bashful, and most of the time he was unhappy without knowing why. "I gotta go," he said as soon as the cocoa cups were empty.

Rosemary's mother said, "Do come over again. Rosemary has talked about you." She held out her hand to him again. "I think you're a fine boy. You are welcome to come here whenever you wish."

...

It was his secret about Rosemary. He didn't tell anybody. Not even Vito. And he sneaked away from Vito when he wanted to go over there.

He had a better time when he was over there than ever before. And her mother trusted him. She'd go out and leave them together all afternoon. Rosemary got to be like a good friend with him. They'd laugh and talk and seemed to understand each other. Sometimes they'd even wrestle around a little, after he had been over lots of times, and he'd get bad ideas. Then he'd go home right away.

I'm a wrong guy, I guess.

One afternoon Rosemary and Nick had been in the house all alone for a couple of hours with her mother downtown shopping. They were standing by the piano. Rosemary was playing with one hand. Nick drummed with his forefinger, hitting the keys hard and sending his hand hopping down to hers. Their hands touched for a second and a quick shiver of feeling went through Nick. He reached over and kissed her. He couldn't help it. Just a quick, hot kiss. Then he moved back from her, looking at her. She stood still, sadlike. She said, "I'm afraid." Then Nick kissed her again, hard, rubbing it in. She stayed real serious and sadlike.

"I'm afraid," she said again. And she looked down at his shoes with her hands and arms pressed tight to her sides.

"So am I," he said, simply.

They stood silent. Afternoon sun was stealing in through the bay window. One ray made a warm, bright band on her wrist which was pressed to her side.

"Feel my heart," Nick told her.

He could feel it going *blump-blump* inside of him. It wasn't running right. It seemed to be going from side to side.

She put her hand out, trembling, and felt.

"Let's feel yours," he said, forgetting about her breasts.

She took his hand and put it on her breast over her heart.

They stood there like that for a long time. The sun rays stood still in the room. Nick's heart beat hard. And her heart, under his hand, beat against it.

Nick's fingers began to tighten over the soft material of her dresstop. Panicky at first, timidly. Then slower, more sure, more heated.

After a while he said, "Unbutton your dress a little," and he put his hand inside.

She moaned and she bled and she cried.

···

Doing that to Rosemary. That's what he was more ashamed of than anything else. She was a nice girl. You didn't mess around with nice girls. To the dirty ones you said or did anything. But you didn't make no passes at nice girls. He could never go over there again. He could never look her or her mother in the face again.

He tried to forget about what he did with Rosemary. The only way he had of forgetting was getting other girls, lots of them. He was tired of Daisy. He was branching out now. But you need lots of money for sodas and shows and like that. He wanted to make a real play for that church girl, Alice. But he needed money—

Vito was waiting for him on the corner by the pool hall. Nick said, "Hey, the Castolano family moved out! Let's go get the lead pipes!"

They climbed in through a back window. They went to work on the water pipes, not particular about how much noise they made. And when Vito used the hacksaw the water started spurting out past the sawteeth; the company hadn't turned it off yet. But they kept sawing and yanked the pipe out anyway.

Water started pouring out all over the floor. Nick found a rag and a piece of broom handle and tried to stuff it in the pipe. Vito, sawing and pounding on the lead pipe, said, "Let it flood—you ain't paying the water tax."

They must have made a lot of noise. While they were still working a flashlight beam leaped through the open window. Nick jerked his head up.

Some bastard must have called the cops!

They stood scared, trying to see the cop-face. The flashlight beam swept them. Then the cop said, seeing Vito, "Oh, it's you guys. Why the hell don't you go to bed?" And the other cop said, "Don't make so much noise, anyway."

The flash clicked off. The two pairs of feet went over the porch and down the steps. Nick and Vito heard the squad car pull away.

"It's the ones I pay off to at the crap games," Vito said. "I recognized their voices."

They gathered up the lead pipes and hauled them home.

•••

At home things were getting damn bad. Aunt Rosa was the only one he half got along with. She was always stooping over him and kissing him on the neck or cheek with her fat lips, and sometimes saying, "You damn good-looking little devil, you!" or "How many hearts did you break this week?" or "If I was young and wasn't your aunt I'd go for you in a big way." Nick would be embarrassed, pleased and mad all at the same time. Aunt Rosa seemed to know about the girls too, without the part behind school. She gave him money. "Here, go take one of your girls out."

The rest of the family stunk. Julian was sponsoring a Boys' Club at Hull-House and lorded it over him. Ang was interested in boys now but Pa wouldn't hear about it unless she brought them right into the house for him to look over; Ma let her go out sometimes but she had to be in before dark. Nick, when he was on good terms with Ang, would say, "Why do you listen to her all the time? Why don't you go out and have a good time? You're like an old lady." But most of the time he and she were squabbling. And Pa, the sonofabitch!

It was hell, living at home. Like tonight. Ma had been after him for a solid hour about going around with Vito.

"That kid's no good! No good at all!"

Christ, how he hated that!

"He treats me better than you do!" Nick snapped.

Ma banged back at him with, "Why don't you get out? Why don't you go over to his house and live? I'll pack your clothes if you want me to."

He started to say something. But Aunt Rosa came in with her easy, fat-woman's voice, "When we are young we all make mistakes, Lena."

Then Ma was bawling him out again and he was sassing her back. "I didn't ask to get born, did I?"

Julian and Pa came in. Julian glared at Nick. Pa started on him too and Ma said, "Let me handle this." Pa said, "You're too soft on him. All he understands is a clout." Pa and Ma started arguing.

When Pa walked out of the room with his lips twisted down angrily over his pipestem Julian came over and sat down across the table from Nick. "Listen—Nick—" Julian said, "acting like that isn't getting you anywhere." His eyes came over to Nick pleadingly. "Why don't you stop worrying Ma? Why don't you get a job and help Ma?"

Nick lit a cigarette. He tossed the match on the floor. Then tilting back in the chair with the front legs off the floor he looked across the round, old-fashioned table at his brother. He laughed tauntingly at Julian and Julian got up and walked out of the room. But Ma started on him all over again.

He couldn't stand it and had to walk out, slamming the door for emphasis. Outside, he couldn't put it into words. Not even for himself. But thoughts kept running around in his mind, thoughts that if he could have pieced them together would have come out: Ma is changing. She's getting hard and bitter because we live here and because we're poor. She hangs on to her religion. But it's grim and hard. She's crazy enough to hope for something better after she's dead.

As for me, I'll get mine the easy way. Little Nicky will take care of himself!

28

Sometimes now he'd stand in front of the mirror combing his curly brown-black hair and looking deep into his own eyes, admiring them and thinking how innocent they were and how Aunt Rosa said he was going to be good-looking. And he knew girls and women on the street glanced at him curious-like. And men too, in a sort of admiration. And it was easy for him to make friends. Yes, he thought, I am good-looking.

He saw his broad, square face, his wide cheekbones with their touches of tan, his cheeks not heavy yet with any beard but smooth and soft. He looked at his gently tanned skin, his clear clean eyes, his dark hair curling across his forehead, falling over it. Nick liked what he saw in the mirror. And he wondered if being handsome would help him like Aunt Rosa said.

He'd practice his innocent stare on people. On women, men at the poolroom when he was trying to mooch a dime, girls older than he was, Ma when she got after him about something. It always worked like magic. People would just melt in front of him. It became a regular trick. He could always work people by just staring at them kind of sad-like and innocent-like.

And now he stood in front of the mirror as much as Ang did. He combed his hair. He straightened his tie. He practiced the innocent stare, practiced smoking a cigarette before the mirror. He combed his hair some more. Nick looked at himself.

The guy in the mirror is good-looking.

Ang shouldered him over and, glancing in the mirror, started twisting her hat on and arranging her hair around it. "Come on, handsome!" she said viciously. "You'll wear it out. Give somebody else a break."

Nick snapped his hips sideways, hard, striking them into her, and walked away. "Oh, go to hell, will you!" he yelled.

■ ■ ■

When he met Vito over on Taylor Street, Vito said, "Do you want to go somewhere special with me?"

"Yeah!" Nick said right away.

Vito got up off the newsstand and started walking down Taylor Street. "Where we going?" Nick asked. But Vito was secretive and only said, "Oh—just for a walk." And he grinned.

They turned off Taylor onto Halsted and walked north.

It was turning dusk now. Lights began popping on. Nick and Vito walked on into the darkness. "Where are we going?" Nick asked. "Jack-rolling," Vito said. They went a few steps more, passing a Greek coffee shop with no coffee on the tables but with men sitting at all the tables playing cards.

"I never went before," Nick said hesitantly.

"Aw, there's nothing to it," Vito said.

Along the street Vito showed him how, going behind him and illustrating the grip: you slipped your arm around a guy's neck and fastened it in with all your might while you pushed your knees against the back of his legs.

They went on, along Halsted, on through the scrap-heap neighborhood. There were hotels and restaurants. Taverns now, too. The three gold balls of a hockshop hung over the sidewalk. Nick and Vito went under the sweep of elevated tracks. There were more taverns now. Vito showed Nick the jackroller's hold again. They had to wait for the light at Jackson Boulevard because traffic came fast and endless. A man on crutches leaned against the plate glass of a dark storefront and had dog's eyes and an outstretched hand. A rubberneck bus hushed along on easing brakes. A drunk, crossing in front of the Honky Tonk, found the sidewalk uneven.

. . . And the spieler's voice came loudly from the windows of the rubberneck bus: "Thirty to seventy thousand hoboes come to Chicago a year. This is the home of the hoodlum, the land of the panhandler, the avenue of the . . ." The voice was lost under the clang of a trolley car; then came up again, " . . . razor blades for sale . . . five cent beer and whiskey . . . the floater population finds its way down here. . . ."

"Here they come!" a skinny tramp yelled into the tavern. The men on the sidewalk all turned toward the bus. The drunks on the stools, the half-drunks at the tables all turned toward the street.

The bus was crawling now. It was right in front of the Honky Tonk, at the curb.

All the men, in chorus, pruned their lips and gave the rubberneck bus the razzberry—loudly, raucously.

Vito and Nick, laughing, moved on down the street. Then, on the high street-marker on the corner over a green-painted city trash box and a newsstand—W. MADISON ST.

29

PASTIME POOLROOM the sign said in a red and yellow arch over the plate glass. Cue sticks were crossed below the letters and in each triangle that the sticks made there was a billiard ball; then, lower on the window: RECREATION PARLOR—CHILI 10¢—HOT DOGS. Over the steam table inside the window the whole plate glass was adorned with a frame of frosted electric bulbs.

Next door to the poolroom on one side was a tavern. Next door on the other side was a hotel. Its sign, sticking over the sidewalk, swung back and forth a little: H O T E L—ROOMS 25¢.

Three or four fellows stood in front of the poolroom plate glass, leaning against it as if it were their only support. They were fellows in their twenties. Hats were twisted down over their faces or sideways on their heads. Fags were plastered in the corners of their mouths. Their faces were wise-looking, their eyes know-it-all.

Vito went right up to these fellows. "Wha'da ya say, Dick? Hi, Pete." Dick took another puff on the fag. "Hi, Vito!" The other fellow just stood without saying anything, looking Vito and Nick over. "Where ya been? We ain't seen you on Skid Row in a long time," Dick said. Vito nodded his head toward the poolroom door. "Let's go in."

The first thing that hit Nick's eyes was the crayon sign tacked to the wall: NO MINORS ALLOWED. But Vito, passing by the owner poked him in the stomach playfully and with a nod of his head said, "Hi, Chuck!" Chuck said, "Hello, Vito. Where have you been keeping yourself?" He said it friendly-like; and he looked at Nick, then looked away without paying any attention to him.

Vito pushed past a man playing pool at the front table. Vito nodded his head. "Hello, Barney." Barney, chalking his stick, said, "Hello, Vito." Then his eyes, sharp and black, went over to Nick's face and fastened there. Barney nodded at Nick; Barney smiled a little. Then he stepped to the table for his shot.

Nick and Vito shouldered their way deeper into the poolroom. Up by the coffee urn Chuck filled white coffee cups.

Nick looked around: inside the poolroom there was a white marbletop lunch counter near the front pane with ten stools. Against the opposite wall were a few small tables with chairs pushed up to them. Men sat at the tables with their legs stretched out over the floor and their elbows on the table, making a rest for their chins. Other men sat on a couple of the lunch counter stools, twisted around so that they could watch the pool games. At two tables the balls, disarranged on the green felt pads, glared under the hard lacquer of green-shaded lights on long cords. The players moved about the tables with their coats off, vests unbuttoned, ties pulled loose. They squinted at the balls and kidded. They bet on the games. Along the benches, against two walls, sat idlers and tramps without the price of a game.

Vito got a cue stick from the wall and was going to shoot Nick a game but Pete, coming over, pushed up to him and said, "Hey, Vito, bet I can beat you a game of banks."

Vito said to Nick, undertone, "Let me play him," then to Pete, "How much you bettin'?"

"Oh—two bits."

"You know I can take you, huh?"—grinning.

"That's what you think—make it half a buck!"

"Okay—half a rock." Vito chalked his stick and moved in toward the table as if it would be like taking candy from a baby.

Nick knew Vito didn't have fifty cents and he looked over at him.

Vito winked; and cocky, he broke the balls and said to Pete, "Go on, sucker—see what you can do!"

Pete moved in, scowled derisively and took his shot. He missed. Vito slapped the pool rail with his cue, signalling where he intended the ball to go. "End pocket!" he challenged. The ball went in. Pete said, "Lucky!"

They played; and as they played they once in a while put their heads together and talked in low voices, nodded their heads, yeah! yeah! And once Nick heard Vito say, "Me and him's goin' to work tonight." Then Pete looked over at Nick who was slumped against the Coca-Cola stand; and Pete, catching Nick's eye, lifted his eyebrows in recognition, poked out his lips in a scowl and bobbed his head, howdy.

Nick watched the game. Watched Vito, with only the price of the game in his jeans, walk around the table cool as a cucumber, take his shots and, kidding all the time, beat Pete by three balls.

A slim boy, tall, immature, stood in a corner of the poolroom with his head down a little but with his eyes looking across tables at Barney shooting pool at one of the front tables. The boy's pants were out at the knees, showing other pants under them—and one back pocket hung half off. An oval of dirty sweat shirt showed under the opened collar of his blue denim work shirt. A jacket hung in the crook of his arm and on the bench next to him was a large newspaper-wrapped bundle. When, still looking at Barney, he pushed his hair off his forehead a strip of whiter skin showed as if the smoke and grit from the blinds of a passenger train hadn't found that spot. Another fellow, a youth of about twenty, stood talking into the boy's ear. His yellow-skinned face was masked with cunning. His lips moved over big and crooked teeth and one eye was drawn down in a permanent, cross-eyed squint. His long, narrow-bridge nose was pushed to one side. He talked slowly, explaining, into the boy's ear. Someone yelled, "Hey, Squint! Wanta shoot a game?"

Squint's face came around, in the same cold mask, "Yeah, yeah, yeah. Just a minute." His lips, moving secretly, went back to the younger boy's ear. The boy nodded his head, listened attentively, nodded his head again. Squint said, in his ear, "That tall fellow playing pool. I know he's good for a dollar. Maybe more. He's all right."

Squint moved toward the front of the poolroom. He stopped by the front pool-table rail and stood next to Barney. Barney was crouched over the table for his shot. Small eyes in a sharp face measured the angle. Squint said to him, in a coaxing voice run through with cunning, "How about buying me a coke, Barney?"

The sharp face lifted from the green felt a little. But the small eyes didn't look at Squint. They looked toward the dark corner of the poolroom. The slim boy smiled at him a little; white teeth from the darkened corner. The eyes were half afraid. "Sure," Barney said, measuring the angle again. And without looking at Squint he pulled a half dollar from his pocket and put it on the table rail. "Last game," he told the man he was playing pool with.

Someone came in for a cup of coffee and a hot dog. Nick watched Vito beat Pete another game and another. Barney racked up his cue and walked out of the pool hall. Almost immediately afterward the boy came from the dark corner with his jacket under one arm and the newspaper bundle under the other. He walked nonchalantly to the outside pavement, stood for a moment looking first one direction down the street then the other. He chose the same direction Barney had taken and faded out of the lighted-up square of sidewalk in front of the poolroom. Pete said, "Christ, you're lucky!" and paid off. Vito laughed. "Come around when you learn the game," he said.

When Pete had gone Vito told Nick, "All you need is a good bluff." He bought hot dogs and pop for both of them. They played a couple of games of slop pool.

■■■

Vito and Nick walked down West Madison, slowly, wasting time until it got later. A little rain had come. The streets were slicked over with it. Neon tavern signs reflected in it. The sidewalks had turned concrete-brown. Vito said: "Friday's a good night. They're all paid. And they're out blowing it." A few steps down the sidewalk in front of them a drunken hobo stood, taking a leak on the sidewalk.

"You look for creases in their pants and shines," Vito told him. "Creases and shines mean money in their pockets."

Vito looked into a cafeteria window. The clock pointed to five after ten. "Let's walk around and see if there's any likely customers. Soon's they get drunk and start wandering around the streets we go into action."

Nick followed Vito down West Madison. Vito said, "I'm going to get a gun from Hank."

"Who Hank?" Nick asked, greatly interested.

"You know—Hank, the guy who plays football at Beecher High—"

"Oh—" Then reflectively, "Do you think you'll get it, honest?"

"Wait and see."

Nick and Vito moved on down the street. On the corner of Desplaines the hallelujahs were selling God. They stood, grouped around their leader. He was a rounded-out man with sad eyes that swept the crowd and then blinked wide at the sky. BEER—BEER—BEER, a sign spelled behind him.

They stopped to watch the show. Nick grinned contemptuously. He knew all about this religion business.

"Christ is coming again," the preacher shouted. "He's coming soon!"

"Yeah," Vito smirked. "He'll be here any minute."

An old man shouldered into the crowd, hat crooked on his head, booze on his breath, bristles of gray beard sticking up on his chin. "I preached for twelve years and stayed drunk all the time," he shouted at the evangelist. "And I'm still drunk. Yippee!"

"Accept the truth before it is too late," the evangelist's voice bawled back loudly. "The Lord has said he would destroy his enemies."

A voice in the crowd: "This is better than a circus."

Another voice: "And free."

"Let's go," Vito said, poking Nick with his elbow. They walked on down the street, looking for prosperous drunks. They trailed a couple. But either they weren't drunk enough or they wouldn't get off the main drag where it was too light. Then down almost to the Northwestern depot they saw a guy who looked like money. He wore a light gray topcoat, a new hat, and shoes that you don't buy for a couple of dollars. With new knowledge Nick saw the blade-edge of his trousers.

They fell in step behind him. "He's kind of big," Nick said doubtfully.

"So?" Vito asked, looking hard at Nick.

They trailed him for three blocks. They nearly lost him when he went into another tavern. They waited and looked through the pane that was painted halfway up. All they could see were men lining the bar, a couple of women, and schooners and shot glasses down the length of hardwood. They waited a long time.

"Won't the bastard ever come out?" Nick said.

Vito said, "I'm going to the can," and pushed into the tavern.

He came out excited. "Boy! He's got a roll! He was buying the 26-girl a shot and I saw it!" They waited some more. Then the man came out, walking unevenly, humming to himself. They got on his trail again. They went past a darkened theatre front, past a big furniture store, the drunk weaving uncertainly, and turned the corner onto Halsted behind him.

"By the alley," Vito said, "we'll grab him and pull him in."

"All right."

Nick itched under the arms. He looked around. Nobody was coming.

I ain't scared.

Nick looked at the back of the gray coat with the hat up above it, almost a head taller than he was.

I ain't scared.

[134]

All he remembered clearly of the next minute was the bar of red neon up ahead spelling out JULIUS CAFÉ.

They didn't have to grab him. The man turned into the alley, staggered into it, and started fumbling, getting his coat and pants open. He was still humming a jukebox tune, softly, under his breath. Shadows fell out of the alley heavily, in logs of blackness, criss-crossing and getting blacker in the alley depth.

Nick came alive again.

This place was cut out for it.

He walked firmly, straight-legged, broad-shouldered, up to the man's back. He hooked his arm around the man's neck like Vito had shown him. And he tightened, felt his muscle flex.

The humming stopped. Vito stumbled in the dark and muck of the alley, getting in front. Nick's knees pressed against the back of the man's legs, and big as he was Nick could feel the guy sag. "Don't struggle! Don't try to yell, you sonofabitch!" Nick hissed in his ear. The man's weight went a little deader against him and Nick, bracing himself, pulled him farther into the black-sleep of the alley. Vito's fist lashed out and drew blood out of the gasping mouth. Nick held the neck in the vise of his arm. He could feel the man's Adam's apple twitch against his arm.

They went through his pockets. They took everything. They cleaned him from top to bottom.

They dumped the guy and ran down the alley. They came out at the other end and ducked into another alley. Panting hard, they finally stopped so that they could see what they got. There was a billfold. It had fifty-four dollars in it. And pictures, a union card, a social security card. They threw the billfold away. They threw the pictures and cards away. Vito jingled his hand, knotted in a fist. Then he stopped and looked at a cut knuckle. "I scuffed myself on the bastard," he said. Then he opened his hand. "I even got his change," he boasted. He grinned professionally.

There were seventy-seven cents in Vito's hand, a couple of keys, and a St. Christopher medal. Vito threw the keys away. He even threw the medal away. They divvied the money up. Vito had snatched the drunk's hat too. It fit. So he put it on and sailed his own hat down the sidewalk. Then they got the hell out of the neighborhood.

30

Nick, Stash and Vito walked along Halsted Street laughing and joking about how drunk they'd been at Stash's house the night before. Stash held himself up by hanging onto Nick and Vito; and he laughed so hard about how his old lady had undressed Nick that his white circle of sailor cap bobbed up and down on his head and tears ran down his cheeks. Vito laughed as loud and slapped Nick across the back.

"Boy, oh boy! Your big-shot brother ought to have seen us!" Vito guffawed.

Now, some blocks down the street they were less boisterous. They walked, feeling their manhood, squaring their shoulders, eyeing the broads, throwing out their legs in long, ungainly strides, tightening their belts and cocking their hats over their eyes. Nick walked in the middle with his hands on Stash's and Vito's shoulders. Suddenly he hit Vito, playfully but hard on the shoulder. "Oh, you motherless bastard!" Vito yelled. Nick grinned, tossing his head, and walked at a defensive distance from Vito.

They bummed around some more. Then Nick and Vito shook Stash. Right away they started for West Madison.

Vito said, "I know another racket we can work. You're good-lookin' and young-lookin'."

"What?" Nick asked, interested.

"We'll play the phoneys," Vito told him.

Vito told Nick more about it, in detail, and how they'd work it.

They went to the Pastime Poolroom, pushing, big-shouldered, through the door. The Pastime was full of smoke, guys shooting pool and loud talk. Nick and Vito shoved down between the tables. Barney was angled over a shot and they had to wait until he took his shot. Then as they pushed past he saw them. His black eyes, under heavy black brows, fastened Nick's sharply. "Hi, Kid!" he said, friendly and as if he knew Nick. "Barney's okay," Vito said. Then Vito asked a fellow he didn't know, "Wanta play a game?" and they cued up. Nick slumped against the Coca-Cola case, half-sitting. Chuck, who owned the joint, walked over to Nick. His vest was still open and out over the top of the white apron with his tie down the middle. "How old are you?" Chuck asked. "Eighteen," Nick said quickly, making his voice huskier than it was and figuring, rapid-fire, what year he'd have to be born in. Chuck looked at him quizzically, not believing. "Okay," Chuck finally said and walked away.

Vito won two games and his partner quit. Nick got down a cue stick from the back wall for a game with Vito. Up at the lunch counter a man with a loud-patterned tie toyed with his second glass of milk and shifted stealthy glances at Nick's face under the full glare of the pool table light. Once, looking up over the cue ball at the number eleven, Nick looked right at the man. The man's timid eyes went away fast, fluttering down. A little later Nick looked again with Vito's new information at the surface of his mind. The man was looking at him.

Yeah, he's a phoney.

The sneer was inside of him. It didn't show in his face and the next time he lifted his head over the table rail he widened his clear, light-glistening eyes and looked straight at the man. Nick smiled at him innocently and thought the crazy, mad, mean thoughts.

Vito caught it too. As they moved around the table Vito said, "You got a live one." Then, "Can you handle him alone?"

"Yeah. He's small."

As soon as the game was over Nick racked up his cue and went out of the poolroom alone. The phoney followed him out.

Nick walked slow, pretending to be interested in the store windows. And the phoney—right behind him. Almost next to him now.

The voice sneaked over softly, "Hello."

"Hi there," Nick said. And walked on. Slow.

Nick turned off West Madison.

When he got to the alley he went down it, to the middle, as if he were going to take a leak. The phoney followed him. And when he got him in the alley Nick turned bad. He grabbed the man by the lapels of the coat with his fists balling into the expensive material. "You sonofabitch!" Nick said in his face. And remembering what Vito had told him, "Don't you know it's one to thirty for fooling with a boy?"

The man was scared stiff. He could hardly talk. "You won't tell on me?" It came out like a squeak.

"No. Not if you give me five bucks."

The phoney forked over.

■■■

Nick went back to the poolroom where Vito waited for him. They played plenty of pool then, and after filling up on hot dogs and pop they went on the street. Nick walked way ahead. It wasn't long before a man stopped him. He used the old gag. Street directions. Then he jumped the subject. "I've seen you some place before, haven't I?" he asked.

"Maybe," Nick said. "I've been lots of places."

They walked along, talking, the man edging over to the subject. And Nick had Vito about thirty feet down the sidewalk.

The man was cautious. He kept looking back over his shoulder. "Isn't that fellow following us?"

"Naw."

"Do you know him?"

"Never saw him before in my life," Nick said innocently.

Down a dark street and near an alley they ganged up on him. They konked him over the head. They took all his money and his wrist watch.

"He saw us pretty good," Nick said. "He could turn us over to the cops."

"How the hell can they squeal?" Vito said.

■■■

The little boy came whistling down the sidewalk headed toward West Madison. Nick and Vito passed him on their way home. A bootblack stand was slung over his shoulder. Farther down an elbow stuck out of an unravelled sleeve. His hat was slanted back and to the side of his head. The black gash of hair fell over his forehead. Shadows were heavy all about him and sometimes a lighted doorway threw its sharp dagger of light. Nickels and pennies struck one against the other in his pocket. His boy features were puckered and screwed together tightly, comically. He whistled.

31

Catching a glimpse of himself in a store window as he walked along Taylor Street, Nick pulled up the zipper on the black leather jacket so that it tightened against his waist and squared at his shoulders.

You gotta fix up for the girls. For them too. Yeah, its like clean-ing up and brushing your hair and looking your best for the girls. Then the phoneys notice you. Vito—he's okay. I like him better'n anybody. Better than I liked Rocky, even. Tony's small-time stuff now. It made him warm inside, thinking about Vito.

He walked into the Pastime and squatted on a stool in front of the lunch counter. On the other side Old Jake wiped the white slab of counter with a damp cloth, taking up circles of coffee, spots of chili and stew. "Jake, how about loaning me a dime for a game of pool and a hot dog?"

Old Jake laughed without moving his lips. "Aw, come on!" Nick coaxed. "Please!"

Old Jake leaned over the counter into Nick's face. "Why you no work and get your dimes?" He wiped down to the other end of the counter angrily. Nick's eyes followed him, and when Old Jake looked up they were in a pleading stare. Old Jake wiped back up the counter to in front of Nick and slapped the nickel down hard. Nick stuck his head down innocently—to hide a grin. Old Jake leaned over the counter and said, "It's no good for you here. You no belong. We got three kinds gangster here. Leetle ones, beega ones and beega ones. You go home."

Without answering, Nick got up and walked toward the pool tables. He played pool, making Old Jake's nickel last for three games because he didn't lose and the other fellow had to pay. When he lost he sneaked out a nickel, lost again and hung up his cue stick. At the oblong of fly-specked mirror he arranged his hat, sideways a little, and smoothed back the hair over one temple where it showed.

Gotto make them notice you.

He practiced the innocent stare.

In the front of the poolroom he heard the young guy curse and heard the thud of his fist. He looked across pool tables and saw the fat, puff-faced man leaning against the wall holding the side of his face. The tall Greek boy flushed through his dark skin. "He came up to me and asked me if I wanted a room. You know what that means on Madison Street." His voice trembled.

Nick walked out of the poolroom fast, ashamed. He saw himself standing in front of the discolored mirror practicing to make the phoneys look at him and ask him questions like that. He walked around the street and back along another street. As he passed St. Patrick's Church, just off from West Madison and the bums and drunks, he jerked automatically at his hat, tipping it to the little prone Jesus in the sacred cup inside the tabernacle. Then after a while, walking, kicking his heels, seeing some guy without legs pushing himself along on a rollerskate framework with pads held

[139]

in his hands, Nick wasn't sore about everything any more. He wasn't even sore at himself.

When he had regained all Vito's I-don't-give-a-damn air about things he went back to the poolroom.

Vito was there now. Nick went over and Vito said, "Let's go."

On the sidewalk outside Vito said, "We'll go to the Paris. There's always a lot doing there."

They went up to the balcony. When they looked for seats five or six men's heads came around, looking at Nick.

Nick sat in the last row. There weren't many people in the balcony of the show and Nick had the whole row to himself—except for a man who sat in the aisle seat. Vito stood in the aisle behind the seats, leaning back against the wall. He was hidden in the dark.

The man at the end of the row of seats where Nick sat moved over next to Nick. He looked sideways at Nick. Nick tossed him a half-friendly glance and again looked down at the screen. For a while the man was quiet. But Nick could feel him edging over in the seat as close to him as he could get. Now he had some coins in his hand, jingling them. He nudged Nick again, showing him a row of quarters.

That's when Vito stepped into the picture. He hooked his arm under the guy's chin and clamped. Nick, leaning over, said to the man, "Don't make a sound, you bastard!" and loosened the quarters out of the man's clenching hand.

Nick moved to the opposite end of the balcony where he was half-hidden by the projection room. He had hardly sat down when he had company. And Vito was right there at the right moment.

They went through four guys.

Coming out of the show Vito said, "Let's go to the Nickel Plate. They walked along Madison. They went up the long flight of steps with blue and white signs on them like on the elevated steps: N I C K E L P L A T E—*Open Night and Day.*

The Nickel Plate was big, with the smell of grease and food and the musty odor of old clothes. Vito and Nick pushed down the metal rail, picking up trays and silverware. They filled their trays with food, even two slices of pie apiece and two bottles of Pepsi-Cola. They had money, easy money.

The Nickel Plate was tables with old faces under hats and coffee cups coming up to mouths with spoons stuck in them and held still by worn thumbs. The Nickel Plate was coffee at three cents a cup, squint eyes bent close to day-old newspapers, bums, tramps, drunks, panhandlers, jackrollers, road-kids, a few phoneys, and—at night—no women.

"This place is all right!" Nick said approvingly.

Late that night when they were almost home Vito turned down

an alley, put his hand in his pocket and pulled out a gun. 'See, I got it!" he told Nick. "I got a stick-up job to pull with Pete and Dick tonight." He wouldn't let Nick go with him.

Nick was envious, angry, hurt.

■■■

The next day Nick went to the poolroom. Vito didn't show up. Nick asked Squint, "Where's Vito? Have you seen Vito?"

Squint said, "They made two hundred bucks on a holdup last night. They went to New York. It was too hot around here for them."

32

Nick walked around Taylor Street slowly and listlessly. There was nothing down here for him any more. This was kid stuff around here. Up on West Madison it was different. There was excitement and something always happening. He walked around, looking the neighborhood over scornfully. I'll go to West Madison.

■■■

He stood inside the Pastime looking out through the plate glass. The sign on the window said CHILI 10¢ and above it billiard sticks were crossed. He leaned against the gum machine with his hands crossed over its dull red top and his chin on the back of his hands. He stared gloomily through the windowpane. The sun, slipping behind the western range of buildings, fingered the upper stories of the Nelson building. The lower floors lay in deepening shadows. Lights were coming on in the hash houses. The marquee of the Paris Theatre across the street started winking at the passing crowd.

Squint came into the poolroom and Nick happened to look up at him. "Hi," Squint said without any real friendliness. "Hi," Nick said.

Nick looked out the window again and thought about Vito and the good times they used to have.

I wonder what he's doing in New York. I wonder who he hangs around with. Gee, two hundred bucks!

Squint poked him in the side and said, nodding toward the back of the poolroom, "Barney wants to see you."

Nick flushed.

"Barney's all right," Squint said.

Barney had a cue stick in his hand and was pointing to a pool table with it. He jerked his head at Nick, motioning for him to come on down there.

Flushing, Nick walked slowly to the pool table.

"Want to play a game, kid?" Barney asked, his narrow lips smiling at Nick.

"I'm broke."

"Oh, that's all right."

Barney beat him. That made him mad. Barney said, "Tough luck, Nick," and banged for the houseman to rack them up again. "Want a coke?" he asked, looking at Nick sideways.

"All right."

Jim, the houseman, set the bottles on a bench. Barney broke. Nick chalked his stick.

He treats. Vito said he's all right.

Nick loosened up. Nick became an innocent smile and clear brown eyes. And Barney paid for the games, bought him a hot dog and another coke. But Barney beat him.

When they had finished playing and Barney said, "I'll see you around," Nick went out onto West Madison Street. Someone caught up with him. It was Squint.

"What do you say?"

"Nothing." They walked in silence.

The puffed-out blue uniform came from the opposite direction with light from store windows making the blue coat and the dull-shining brass buttons look like one big bulge of metal. The heavy metal star sticking out on the blue uniformed chest shouted: *I am the law!* In one paw the cop held an unsheathed billy, swinging it slowly, rhythmically, swinging it with the gait of his big-footed stride. He jerked his head around looking in all the tavern windows, all the hash house windows. The last coat button was loosened so that the bottom part of the coat that couldn't take the full roll of belly was open. There was a wide black belt with a silver buckle over the big stomach. The cop's awkward, oversized body rolled from side to side a little as he came along West Madison on his big feet in copper's shoes. Light cut down from street lamps, throwing angles across his burly shoulders and stuck-out chest. Neon colored his hard, protruding jaw. The policeman cap had a black bill. Under the black bill was a swollen, lumpy nose, red, big-pored.

Below the big nose was a big mouth twisted up at one end, half sneer, half command.

Squint stepped against the wall of a building, as far into the shadows as he could draw himself. He dropped his head and his eyes.

The cop was abreast of them now. Nick had his head half down but looked up with his eyes. The mean cop face smacked into his like a fist. The eyes were cold, hard, menacing.

Then the cop was moving, flat-footed, on down the street past them.

Squint had Nick by the wrist of his jacket. Unconsciously he was shaking Nick's arm hard. "Look out for him!" Squint said apprehensively. "That's Riley. He's the meanest sonofabitch down here. He'd just as soon brass knuckle you or drag you in as look at you." His voice was scared. "He's *plenty* tough!" Squint said.

"If they push me around they'll get pushed right back," Nick said.

Squint said, "He's killed three men."

••••

In the Nickel Plate that night Nick was sitting with Squint. A slim Mexican youth walked to the table. A copper-colored Mexican youth in a light tan topcoat. When he smiled his cheeks came up to meet his eyes and his lips widened into a half-circle, showing teeth white in the copper face. He grinned. Nick liked his looks and smiled at him. Squint looked over his shoulder. "Hello, Juan." Juan leaned over and, grinning at Nick, winked confidentially. "I got a broad waiting," he said. "See you later." He went out.

When Nick tiptoed up the steps at twelve-thirty that night and knocked on the side wall where Julian could hear him and get up to let him in, nothing happened. He knocked a long time.

He knows I'm out here but he won't let me in.

Nick knocked louder, cursing Julian under his breath.

Then the door opened and things started flying. The old man had a shoe in his hand and beat Nick across the head with it. Mad, Nick threw up his fist and caught Pa on the wrist, sending the shoe flying. Pa came at him. The old man was on top of him, crowding him in a corner, giving him a good beating.

When the old man quit, mumbling to himself, Nick ran into the front bedroom.

Goddamn Julian! He woke the old man up so I could get hit.

Julian lay in the bed sleeping, his legs drawn up toward his stomach. Nick went right up to the bed, blood in his eye, and hit Julian as hard as he could. Then he ran out of the house.

He went back to West Madison. Squint was still at the Nickel

Plate. He said, "Are you carrying the banner too, kid?" When Nick looked puzzled, he said, explaining, "Sitting up all night."

"Yeah," Nick said. Then not knowing what to say he asked, "Where's the others?"

"Some of 'em went to see what they could find on the street. Maybe they scored enough to get a bed."

A hunch-shouldered fellow in an old coat with the collar turned up around his face and expressionless eyes stood by the table. He sat down and jumped into the conversation. "Them guys ain't got guts enough to put the arm on nobody," he said.

"What do you know about it, Kid? You goddamn cheap pan-handler!" Squint said, not unfriendly.

"Yeah? Well, you don't never see me without something to eat, do you?" He laughed mirthlessly. "Look, I'm forty-two and I ain't worked a day in my life. Not one goddamn day. The sonofabitch ain't born I'd work for." Again the mirthless laugh came past the heavy lips without moving them.

Nick looked at the ugly, middle-aged face and wondered why he was called Kid.

He turned to Nick. "You new on the street, kid?"

"Yeah."

He became confidential. "Well, you stick with me, and I'll teach you the ropes. I'll show you everything I know." His thumb pulled back the top of the watch pocket of his pants and under the table he showed Nick the folded edge of a worn dollar bill. "The Kid always has money in his pockets." He laughed, the sound snorting through his nose. His eyes shifted around the room. "I'm a gambler," he said. "What I don't make one way I make another. Know where Jefferson Park is? Hot days there's a bunch of men sleep on the lawn over there. I go over there when I need money and lay down near one of them and pretend like I'm asleep. Then when I'm sure he's sleeping I pick his pockets." He laughed, hard-edged. Lifting his hands he looked at his fingers. "Kid Fingers," he said. He put his head close to Nick's. "I carry a razor blade with me. I don't bother puttin' my hands inside and take a chance waking them up. I rip their pockets open with the razor blade. Easy, kid! You just stick with The Kid and you'll get along!" He patted Nick on the shoulder and chuckled through his nose. "I'll smarten you up!"

A young fellow came over to their table with black eyes under the snap-brim of a hat. "Hello," the fellows all said and Butch sat down. When he saw Nick, a young newcomer, he said, "You want coffee?" and put the money down in front of The Kid. "For him," Butch said, motioning his head at Nick. The Kid got right up and went for it. He hurled back a sneaky, flashing look at Butch.

They drifted into the Nickel Plate and out, carrying the banner.

Nick sat all night, listening to all of them; absorbing part of the thinking of all of them.

...

Every day I been playing pool with him. On him. Every day I been eating. For free. For a week he's been treating me.

Nick leaned over the pool table, half-stretched across it to reach, with his cue stick, the difficult-angled shot. A twisting fold of his curly hair hung over his forehead. His forehead was wrinkled a little. And his eyes took careful, clear-eyed aim.

I haven't paid for a game of pool since I've been playing with him. Win or lose. It's good I met him. I'm always broke now Vito isn't here and we don't make money. I guess I ain't got guts enough to go jack-rolling by myself. And I need money. To play pool and go to shows and stuff like that. Barney's all right. I'm glad I lucked up on him.

Nick, ready for his shot, looked up at Barney. "Bet I make it!" he said cockily.

Barney's eyes were already on him. Barney said, "Bet you a coke!"

"You're on!"

Nick took careful aim. He made it. Barney shouted to the houseman, "Hey, Jim! Bring a coke. Open it."

Nick was posed for his next shot. He looked up at Barney, smiled conceitedly, said, "You don't want to bet on this one, do you?" The cord-dangling pool table light was glistening in Nick's hair. The smile came slowly off Barney's face. The sharp eyes in the sharp face concentrated on Nick as he moved the cue stick back and forth, slowly, on a line with the cue ball. Barney stepped closer to Nick. "Why don't you drop up to my place tonight?" he said.

For a week he's been trying to get me to go up there.

Nick looked up, then down. "Aw, I don't want to go up there tonight. Some other time."

Every day he asks me.

Nick shot and the ball rolled into the end pocket.

Jim sat the opened bottle on the bench and there was a silence until he had walked to the front of the poolroom again.

"What are you afraid of?" Barney asked. "Are you afraid somebody's going to hurt you?"

Nick was poised for his next shot. "No." Some of his hair had fallen, curly, into his eye. He shook it back off his forehead.

"Come on! Nobody's going to hurt you," Barney said, joking with him, but with an urgent tenseness under it. Nick wrinkled his eyes and mouth no but didn't answer. Barney moved a little closer to him. His voice dropped. "I got some money up there for you—in

case you're broke and want to go to the show or play pool when I
ain't around. I got two dollars you can have."

Nick looked up. He widened his eyes in an innocent stare. It was
a naïve, brown-eyed smile. "All right," he said.

Maybe I can get him to give me the money for free. Maybe I can
stall him off. I could sure use the dough.

■■■

Going up the steps, following behind Barney, all his life seemed
to roll before him like a movie running backwards. He closed his
eyes, guiding himself by running his hand along the banister.

The pictures of the past were glued inside his eyelids.

I don't want to go! I don't want to go! No! No! Don't go!

Nick stopped on the steps. "I ain't going."

Barney turned toward him. "What do you mean you ain't going?"
Barney smiled. "Ain't I been good to you?" He put his fingers on
Nick's arm and fastened them. "Ain't I been treating you to pool
and things?" He smiled again. He was big. He was husky. Nick
followed him up the steps, scared.

His mind had him running away from Barney, running wildly
down the street. But his feet dragged him, slowly, unwillingly, up
the steps.

In the hall, while Barney fumbled with the key, Nick was for a
brief but frozen fraction of a second an altar boy kneeling at Father
O'Neil's feet in his red cassock and lacy white surplice ... *ad Deum
qui laetificat juventutem meam ... to God who giveth joy to my
youth....*

The Latin words rang in his ears. And Barney's shoes were heavy
across the floor.

...Dominus vobiscum ... et cum....

Nick stepped into the room. Barney took off his coat, tossing it
across a chair, almost gaily. He wore a polo shirt. The sleeves were
short. He had hairy arms.

Barney patted Nick on the shoulder, chummy. Barney walked
around the room, turning on the radio, getting an unopened bottle
of wine.

Nick flopped down in a chair by the table. He felt weak and
scared. Barney smiled at him, showing gold-edged teeth. Nick
looked at Barney. Nick's eyes were pleading. All the cunning, all
the scheming was gone.

He ran his hand along the edge of the table and dampening his
lips, averting his eyes, said, "I don't feel good."

Barney laughed. "Who you trying to kid?" he said.

Nick was silent a moment. Then he said, "I'm going."

Barney opened the bottle of wine. "All right, kid," he said. "Here,
have a glass of wine." Nick looked at him gratefully and drank the

[146]

wine. Barney immediately filled their glasses again. "I only came because I'm broke," Nick said. "I hope you ain't sore at me." Barney laughed. He emptied his glass and said, "Drink up!" Nick drank slowly; and with the heat of the wine a cunning came to his eyes. "Maybe," he said, "you'll just let me have the money and I'll give it back to you when I get it."

"We'll see," Barney said.

And then the bottle was empty and Barney was getting a second bottle from the shelf. "Why don't you stay," he said, "and I'll give you the money."

And now Barney had the wine bottle in his hands, wrestling with the stopper. The polo shirt was short. Nick saw the arm. A man's arm. Heavy-veined. Hairy. Muscular. The hairs black, stiff, curling. They ran all the way down. They were long and black almost to the tips of his fingers.

All the revulsion in Nick rose. He felt sick. He put his arm on the table and laid his head on it.

Barney, going across the room with the glasses that gently tinkled together, laid his hand on Nick's shoulder, And, in his mind, behind his tightly clenched eyelids Nick could see Barney's arm. The black-haired arm. The heavy, blood-filled veins. A man's arm.

"What's the matter, kid?" Barney asked.

"Nothing."

Nick felt like he was going to cry. To keep from bawling, to stop his bottom lip from trembling, he put his teeth over it and fastened down.

33

Nick was ashamed to go back to the Pastime at first. He went into the Pioneer and ate. When he came out the first faint cracking of dawn was sidling, smoke-gray, over West Madison. He went to the Pastime. Already it was open. Inside Old Jake was getting ready for the day's business; filling up the stained brown sack for the coffee urn, wiping off the white lunch counter, setting sugar bowls on top of it. At one of the small tables near the door reading the morning paper sat Chris, one of the fellows who hung around the poolroom all day. He needed a shave, his dirty shirt cuffs hung beyond the sleeves of the worn lumberjacket. He looked up, saw Nick. "Hey, come here a minute, kid." Nick went over. "Sit down." Chris pushed out a chair with his foot.

Nick sat down. Then, looking at Chris—

I wonder if he's a phoney?

Christ—not everybody.

Chris said, "Look, kid, why don't you get off Skid Row? This street isn't any good." He pointed with the open newspaper to the window. On the awakening Madison Street sidewalks, in the murky, cigarette-smoke colored fog, old tramps already floated back and forth, yawning, rubbing their eyes, scratching. "Look—" Chris said. "You'll get just like me. Twenty-nine and I'm a bum. I went a year to college, too. This street gets in your blood and you just can't get away from it. You leave and you come back. It pulls you back." Chris stared out into the fog at the indistinguishable, all-alike tramp figures that floated back and forth.

Old Jake had come from behind the lunch counter. He stood with the backs of his hands on his hips where the top of the apron hit him. "He's right. He's right. Why you no go home?"

"I don't like it at home."

Chris sat staring out the window with the newspaper trailing from one hand onto the floor. Out beyond the pane the hobo figures floated . . . back and forth . . . back and forth.

Nick pushed the chair away from the table and stood up. Chris looked up at him. "That was good advice I gave you, kid."

Old Jake, back behind the counter, was slamming the heavy white cups on the shelf near the coffee urn. From near the back of the poolroom came low-keyed, even snoring.

Good advice! Who the hell wants advice! Do as you please! Don't listen to nobody!

Nick walked over to Old Jake with almost three dollars hidden in his sweater band. "How about a cup of coffee?" he asked, leaning over the lunch counter with his elbows on it.

"Maybe—when it's ready," Old Jake said angrily.

Nick smirked. "I don't want any," he said. "I just wanted to see if you were Scotch." He smiled at Old Jake. "You can give me a bottle of coke if you want."

"I got nothing for you!" Old Jake shouted. "You crazy in the head. You got good home." He tapped his own forehead with a slow, illustrating finger. "Crazy in the head." But he pushed the coke across the counter at Nick. Nick grinned with his eyes shut down, making it look innocent. Old Jake said, "Drink that. Then you go back and sleep. I wake you when it get busy. You crazy fellow." He tapped his head again, angrily.

Going past the benches to the one along the back wall Nick saw The Kid stretched out in his rags, sleeping with his mouth open and one leg up on the bench in an upright angle.

Nick went to the back bench, pushed his behind down against it, leaned over sideways against the stacked pop bottles and fell asleep.

When he woke up, sitting near him Nick saw a colored fellow maybe a couple of years older than he was. Nick had seen him in the poolroom before and knew that everybody called him Sunshine.

Sunshine was leaning against the stacked cases of empty pop bottles looking unhappy. His brown, almost black face was shiny, greasy-looking on his forehead, on his cheekbones and across his flat nose. His kinky hair stood up all over his head and was in a tall cockscomb just at the front. His lips were pushed out in a sad pout.

Nick leaned over and said, "Hey, Sunshine, come on over."

Only the eyes were alive in the sad brown-black face. They came around sideways, showing white. All the rest of him was in a dead, lazy droop. Sunshine got up slowly, slowly shuffled over to Nick. His eyes watched Nick eat.

"You hungry, Sunshine?" Nick asked.

"Man—" Sunshine drawled, "I ain't et since yesterday morning."

Immediately Nick's hand went in the sweater band and pulled out the first coin it touched. "Get something to eat, Sunshine."

Later Juan came in and he and Nick played pool. Between games Juan pointed to a man at the front table. "See that flashy dresser?" he asked. Nick looked, saw the neatly fitted drape coat with the tapered waist and the nailhead pattern, the silk shirt and perfectly knotted cravat. And when the man stretched the length of the table with one leg thrown up on it, Nick saw the iridescent lining where the coat fell open, the diamond ring on the hand that bridged for the shot.

"Yeah," Nick said.

"He's a pimp. Boy! he's got the life!" Juan's cheeks and slits of smiling eyes met. "A woman to dress him up and money in his pockets all the time and a broad whenever he wants one."

The pimp gained stature before Nick's eyes.

Yeah, that's right.

Nick hung around a while. When he was leaving the poolroom, thinking about maybe showing up home for a while, he bumped into a man. "Why don't you watch where you're going?" the man asked angrily.

"Why don't you?"

"Trouble with you young snots is you hit Skid Row and you think you're men," the fellow growled.

"Who you calling a snot?" Nick challenged.

They stood facing each other, lipping off at each other some more. The man said, "Go ahead, move on before I slap you a few."

Sunshine had been standing, leaned against the plate glass with PASTIME in an arch over his shoulders and street lights making his face shiny. Sunshine walked over and with one punch knocked the man down.

He was out cold. Sunshine and Nick stood looking down at him. With the toe of his shoe Nick pushed against the lifeless sleeve curiously. "I hit him kinda hard, huh?" Sunshine drawled. Nick grinned. "Yeah," he said.

Nick gave Sunshine a dime. "Ah'm going to the show," Sunshine said.

"Yeah, see you around," Nick said.

∎∎∎

The next night Nick, Juan and Butch went to a show on South State Street. When they were coming out they spotted a guy who looked like he'd have money. Juan went first and nailed him—

That's what I like about him. He's got guts.

—and he and Butch were right there to help.

They split the take three ways. "Now let's go to the Long Bar," Butch said.

They went back to West Madison. Even before they went under the red neon and into the tavern, jukebox music burst out at them—

He said he was glad he met herrrr
*And some day he would come back and get herrrr....**

In the doorway Butch pushed his social security card into Nick's hand. "Here. Just in case they want to say you ain't old enough."

Nick wasn't challenged. They sat with their lips pressed down over cigarettes, with steins of beer on the table, with their eyes scowled wisely, importantly.

At the bar were men from Madison Street with enough for a drink. And a few men from neighborhoods far south or far north, out for some fun. There were a couple of women on the make. Near the end of the bar stood three men leaning together with their arms loosely thrown around each other, their bodies close. Walking toward them now was another man, slightly switching his hips and behind. A hostess, coming from the toilet, was very angry. "There's too much competition here for a woman," she said to the 26-girl.

It got late. People got drunk. There were a couple of fights but

* From *Ti-Pi-Tin*, by Maria Grever and Raymond Leveen. Copyright, 1938, by Leo Feist, Inc. Used by permission.

no one paid any attention except the bartenders who pried them loose. Nick, Butch and Juan got plenty drunk. The redheaded hostess noticed them and came over to sit at their table and work them for drinks. They sat, all leaned over toward her. Butch had a handful of bills spread on the table and was pounding his fist down on them. "We got plenty money! Plenty!" Juan held his glass to her lips coaxing her to drink from it, saying with a slow, slit-eyed smile, "Let's all of us go somewhere."

Butch saying, "Plenty of money!"

Nick, with his hand on her knee under the table, said, "And there's plenty more where that came from."

■■■

The next week end Nick went to the Long Bar alone because Juan wasn't around and because Butch hated the phoneys and beat them up every time he got a chance. The Long Bar was a good place to meet them.

Nick played them.

He was good-looking and he got all the trade.

He played them and threw the money away on girls.

If they were respectable business men they tried to take him to the downtown hotels and register him as "son" or "brother."

He played them.

I shouldn't do this. I need money. I oughta stop. It ain't right. I gotta have money. I'm used to having money in my pockets all the time.

When he thought like this he was ashamed of himself and mad at himself. But he did it for money anyway, the shame becoming more and more intense.

Nick played them.

He had money jingling in his pockets again.

34

Nick, Butch and Juan walked along West Madison each a separate and individual, unalike yet alike, set of hard-boiled mannerisms; each a small fleck of undeveloped malehood swaggering, big-footed, square-shouldered, down the street. Their chests were stuck out. Their hats were on the sides of their heads. Cigarettes were stuck in the sides of their mouths. They came down the street feeling their masculineness and their toughness and their worldliness. If they found out about a good broad they passed the word around and they never turned anything down. The kid stuff didn't go any more. You didn't go around hitting each other on the arm and goosing each other. You were men now.

Swollen out in their own importance they walked along West Madison looking for trouble, or for broads, or for someone to jack-roll.

They turned into the Pastime. Sunshine looked up and said, "Do you want me to do anything for you, Nick?"

Nick reached over and patted him on the shoulder. "No, Sunshine," he said, pleased and embarrassed.

I liked him best of them all. I think he'd give his right arm for me.

Nick reached out again and rubbed Sunshine's woolly head.

"Don't do that, man!" Sunshine protested, trying to make his hair lie down. It crinkled from under his hand and stood straight up.

Nick walked over to where Barney was shooting a game of banks. "I'm broke," he told Barney, looking up at him guilelessly. "Could you loan me a dime to shoot some pool?"

Barney gave it to him. Then Barney said, just to him, "When are you going to come over and see me?"

"Oh—some time," Nick said, indefinitely.

Nick, Butch and Juan sat twisted on the lunch-counter stools, watching a game.

In a few hours it will be late enough and we can go jack-rolling.

Juan kept glancing up at the clock. Pretty soon he said, grinning, "I gotta go see my broad."

Nick looked, side-eye at him.

He's okay when he keeps his mind on business.

"Hurry it up!" Butch said. "We're going out tonight."

When he starts meeting broads in the taverns he stalls and stays with them.

"Yeahyeahyeah. I'll be back soon," Juan said. He hurried out.

Well, I won't say nothin' because there's Butch to go jack-rolling with and, when he ain't around, plenty other guys.

"Hey, Butch, gimme a cigarette."

"I ain't sleeping with you," Butch wisecracked; but he gave Nick one and they played pool.

Nick could hold his own with Butch now. He shot a good stick. Right now Nick made a hard combination shot and Butch whistled slowly, said, "Boy! I'd rather see you shoot pool than eat breakfast!" Nick grinned and poked Butch in the stomach with the butt of his cue stick. "Out of my way!" he commanded and moved around the table for his next shot. The ball went in. Nick acted like it was nothing and walked around the table to his next shot.

Sitting on a bench, watching Nick admiringly, was a pink-faced boy who had been coming into the poolroom for three days. He was blond, slim, good-looking with regular features. He was a very tall, very young boy, clean in a blue and gray lumberjacket and his cheeks were without fuzz. He had a pink and white complexion.

Butch said to Nick, "You're too hot for me tonight," and quit. Nick looked for someone to play with. He saw the pink-faced boy. "Wanta play?"

"Yeah!" before Nick had it out of his mouth.

They played. The pink-faced boy was no competition for Nick and lost his dime in a hurry. But he hung around Nick asking questions. "How's things in this town? Is there any work? What's this jack-rolling like? Does it pay good? How's panhandling in this town?"

"Jack-rolling's best," Nick told him. And he told him how to go about it.

"Hey—" the pink-faced boy said, blushing, "will you show me the hold?"

Nick went around behind him and, expertly, showed him the hold. Then he went out into the street.

●●●

Things tore at him. He couldn't understand them. He felt hurt and alone. For a minute a picture of Father O'Neil stood up in front of him. And he could hear, with his memory, Rocky whistling.

He went under the sign that blinked blue-orange, blue-orange: HAYMARKET—ALL SEATS 15¢. A young fellow all dressed up like in

[153]

his first pair of long pants stepped up to him and asked, "Hey, Bud, where can I find a woman around here?" Nick stood sizing him up. "I'm not sure," he said. "Wait here. I'll be right back."

He came back with Butch. They led the fellow to the door of a flop house where the hallway was dark. "Up this way," Butch told him. They stepped into the semi-black hall and Nick put his foot against the bottom of the door so no one could enter. In front of them was just the stairway going up with the brass step-treads shining dully. Nick had his arm fastened around in the method he knew so well now. Butch was in front going through the fellow's pockets. The gink was scared stiff. He trembled all over.

He had only a couple of bucks.

"Give me carfare," he whimpered. "I live way over on the South Side."

Butch got mad; he wanted to hit him because he asked for carfare.

"Don't hit that kid!" Nick told Butch and Butch got sore, but he didn't hit him.

Going out of the hall Nick stuck his hand behind him and, without looking at the fellow, slipped him a dime.

Butch said, "Let's go scoff."

They went to a restaurant and scoffed good. Juan joined them. Nick hadn't noticed but Butch motioned with his fork to the table against the wall. "There's the heat," Butch said. "Riley and Big Tim."

Nick looked, remembering Red telling about Big Tim.

He's the shakedown man. Crooked cop.

Riley was talking through his nose to Big Tim, "With that he rushes me and my gat comes down on his head, sort of sideways. The magazine hit him, not the butt. When I got the bastard to the emergency hospital he had twenty-seven stitches taken in his scalp and my revolver was bent out of line."

Riley sat with his back to Nick, with his dead, pistol-barrel eyes turned away, with his wide-spread hips going out past the seat of the chair. His neck was red and big with a roll of fat coming around and sticking over the wide blue collar of his uniform in back. His holster, with the pistol butt sticking out, was hooked around his shapeless waist and hung sloppily over the hip. Nick's eyes fell on the belt; saw the three notches, one new-cut and still clean in the darkened leather of the belt.

■■■

He's killed three men.

Nick fastened his teeth; and he fastened his mind in a knot of hate. And the hate passed into him, beyond the moment, beyond the surface of his mind. It smouldered at the very center of him.

35

Then he was sixteen.

He stood in front of the mirror, combing his hair. He stood, in love with himself, looking in the mirror at himself. His hands halted; the comb rested half-drawn through the curling dark hair. Sixteen! He looked like he was eighteen or nineteen. He was grown up. He was a wise guy now. He had all the answers. He knew all the goddamn answers. Yeah, he knew about whores and pimps and phoneys and crooked cops and gambling joints and playing the horses. He turned his face, slowly, first to one side then the other, looking at it out of the corners of his eyes, studying his profile. Let anybody try to kid him or make a sucker out of him. He'd show the bastards! He looked up into his eyes. He widened them, made them boyish and innocent. He grinned and winked at himself. Whistling, he got his hat, put it on, tilted it over his forehead a little and posed in front of the mirror. He pushed it to the back of his head and posed again. He squared back his shoulders. What a sap Julian is! Jesus-on-a-stick. Twenty, and making ten dollars a week working nine hours a day and glad to get it. Look at his old man. Too damn honest. Worse off than he had ever been before. Well, little Nicky Romano would get his and get it the easy way! He took one parting look at himself in the mirror and swaggered out of the room.

Crime didn't pay, eh? Maybe not after you were caught. But it sure did up until then.

"So long, Ma!" he shouted, waving, big-shot, with his arm and walking out.

•••

Late that night Nick sat in the Nickel Plate. The big-armed Polish busboy was clearing tables. When he got to where Nick sat he leaned over and said, "I know where you can get a job. Dishwashing and your meals."

Nick twisted his lips back. "Only suckers work!" he said.

Now there came to the Nickel Plate a man who sat alone in a

corner almost every night. He was about forty, a man once beefy, now beginning to go soft all over. He had loose blond hair and gray-blue eyes that had a sad look in them, deep down and way back. He was always fairly well dressed and sat there every night reading all the evening papers and sometimes the next day's *Trib*.

Nick looked over at him.

He looks sad.

Maybe he don't get along with his wife and doesn't want to go home.

He looks plenty unhappy.

■ ■ ■

Nick was well known on West Madison now. Everybody knew him by name. Everybody knew that he was tough and clever and a jack-roller. Some of them knew other things about him: how he got his extra money. Sometimes he would bring a dollar home, or five dollars and tell Ma he won it on a horse or gambling. Julian would look up and ask, quizzically, "Are you *sure?*"

"Sure," Nick lied easily. "I'm lucky."

Because Ma needed the money she took it.

■ ■ ■

One night when he got to the Nickel Plate a bunch of the fellows were there. He threw up a hand in a hello gesture and walked down the railed aisle toward the food. When he came to the table he carried a tray of coffee and pie for all of them. "Look at Nick popping for all of us!" Red said. "You must have scored heavy," Squint said enviously.

Nick showed them some folded bills. He grinned again and tilted his chair back until it touched the wall. He put his foot up on the seat of Squint's chair. "They *all* go for Nick!" he said.

After a while, when he could catch Sunshine's eyes he made a let's go motion with his head and they got up and left. They went to the Long Bar and in a corner behind the edge of the bandstand they ordered beer after beer. The Kid came over and, on the mootch like always, bought one round of beer, then drank on Nick the rest of the time. And Nick, feeling his drinks, began telling, "She was sitting on my lap and I was feeding her beer. I had to go to the can. When I came back she crawled back on my lap and I fed her more beer." He leaned his head back and drank from the bottle. "Then we went into the bedroom and I went to town."

The Kid laughed his nasty laugh. "Did you score?"

"Did I score?" Nick wrinkled his mouth in a grin.

"How was the score?"

"I ain't complaining."

Nick pounded the table for more drinks. "It was a party Juan took me to. I got the money to go out of a guy."

When the beer came Nick lifted and tilted the brown liquid in past the yellow foam. "Live fast, die young and have a good-looking corpse!" he said with a toss of his head. That was something he had picked up somewhere and he'd say it all the time now. Always with a cocky toss of his head.

It was after closing time. A bartender shut the lights low and went on selling drinks. After a while Nick and Sunshine got up to go. The Kid put on a sad face. With a soliciting hand on Nick's shoulder he said, "I ain't got a flop. Can you let me have the price?"

"Sure!" Nick flipped a quarter out on the table with a noisy ring.

Nick and Sunshine went on rubber legs toward the door. Two cops leaned against the bar near the door, drinking. Nick pulled himself up straight-legged. When he passed he brushed against their blue uniforms on purpose. "Cops in taverns are no good!" he snarled loud enough for them to hear him.

Nick and Sunshine, holding each other up, climbed up the steps of the Nickel Plate to grab a couple of hours' sleep. They got, confusedly, past the chairs and tables to the round table behind the post. Almost automatically Nick looked over toward the table by the window. The unhappy man was there with his paper spread out on the table.

Nick saw him through a drunken blur that filmed his eyes. He looked at the drooped mouth and sad eyes. Nick felt sorry for him without knowing why.

He's got something on his mind. He's sad about something. He's got the blues.

Poor guy.

Nick wanted to tell Sunshine about it. He twisted slowly in his chair toward Sunshine. Sunshine had his eyes closed and his mouth open. Greasy smears of light were on his face.

Nick rose, almost knocking the chair over. Untangling himself from it he walked, unsteadily, toward the window table. He flopped down there. He said to the unhappy man, "The world ain't that sad." He said, "Take it easy. Loosen up." He said, "Live fast...."

Nick put his head down on the table and fell asleep.

36

"YOU'RE IN CHICAGO NOW! IS EVERYBODY HAPPY?" the drunken guy shouted hilariously over the blare of the jukebox. He sat on a chair against the wall grinning at the opposite wall. He was twisted half off the chair, balancing himself uncertainly. His hat was crooked on his head and his hair bushed over his forehead and eyes. He tapped his foot against the floor to the tune of the music, loudly, banging it, almost dancing on it. He was very happy. *"You're in Chicago Now!"*

The bar was filled up its whole length with glasses, big and little, slopped pools of liquor, beer rings, elbows, smoke-trailing cigarettes, heads and shoulders; and farther down, rounded-out rear ends parked on narrow stools. The tables were all taken; cigarette smoke and the noise of loud talk rose from their square surfaces. The floor was crowded. People bumped, pushed, staggered into each other; squeezed past. The smell of beer and sweat and tobacco smoke rose to the ceiling, spread sideways, settled to the floor. The music was noise with rhythm hidden in it somewhere under the noise—

> *But she said "No, no,*
> *I cannot go*
> *Until I know you betterrrr...."* *

Outside a small crowd of men without the price of beer gawked in through the dirty window. Leaning against the glass near the door was a panhandler or two; and a couple of jackrollers.

An old, toothless woman sat at a front table leering at men coming into the tavern. The 26-girl leaned over the front edge of the bar. Her breast, heavy and full in the low-cut dress, almost touched the green felt where the dice rolled. Light was on her, on the tight blondined curls that stood all over her head. Powder went down her neck, over the uncovered part of her breasts and down inside the dress. The man holding the leather dice-cup looked covertly where the double swell of the breast ended and the dress began.

A hostess hung over the bar with a man. The dress took the curve with her hips and fell not quite to her knees. The man said, "When are you going to sing again?"

"Buy me a drink, honey," the woman said.

"I think you have a swell voice, baby," the man said. "You belong at the Chez Paree, not in a dump like this. A girl with your voice—"

She turned eyes, heavily made up, painted purple on the lids, at the man. She put the palm of her hand against his cheek and ran it along his close shave in a slow caress. "Do you want me to sing something sentimental?" she asked, cooing. He tried to put his arm around her. Slowly she pulled her hip away; so slowly that he hardly realized it had been where he reached. She nodded toward her glass. "I'm down to the bottom, Harry," she said. "That's what you said your name is, didn't you?"

"What do you want?" the man asked.

"The same thing." She pushed her glass across the bar and gave the bartender a sly glance. She watched the billfold come open. The man shook the inch height of beer that remained in his glass and emptied it. "Why don't you try beer? Nothing like it!" he said.

"I don't like beer," she whined. "It makes me sick." She ordered a thirty-five cent drink.

Ti-pi ti-pi-tin, ti-pi-tin
*Ti-pi-ton, ti-pi-ton.***

A young man sat at the far end of the bar with his peach-colored sport shirt thrown open and worn outside his loud sports coat in two hand-stiched, pointed V's. His hand was up to his cheek with the fingers spread. He leaned on his arms. He smoked a long, cork-tipped cigarette and exhaled long, lazy clouds of smoke.

There were two women on the floor. One was skinny, with her hair like a mop hung over a banister to dry, with a caved-in chest, with a dirty black dress hitched up over her knees in an uneven hem and gathered around her waist. She staggered among the tables looking vacant-eyed at the men for a man. The other woman was dumpy, without shape. Her shoulders rolled down and folded into her hips. She was about forty-five. She stood in the middle of the floor reserved for dancing. Her arms were hurled wide and wild. She shook her head from side to side, tossing the mat of dirt-brown hair about her face and head. She grinned. She shook her shoulders. She threw her legs out sideways and went down into a half-squat. She rose slowly, twisting, posturing vulgarly; and she howled—a howl that was part giggle, part gasp for breath. A man was shouting, "Shake it but don't break it!"

■■■

* From *Ti-Pi-Tin*, by Maria Grever and Raymond Leveen. Copyright, 1938, by Leo Feist, Inc. Used by permission.

[159]

The bartender looked over tables at Nick and his friends and grinned. He saw the empty glasses. He went over and stood with his towel over his arm, waiting for them to order up again. Juan came down the length of the bar and over to their table.

Juan sat down and, pushing change on the table, bought drinks for all of them. When they were drinking, he said, "Did you hear? Big Tim got transferred way over to the North Side."

"Yeah," Butch said, tightening his lips, "I know all about it. He gave us a farewell party at the Nickel Plate. The sonofabitch came in and used his club on everybody who wasn't eating. Old men and all. You should have seen those guys getting down the steps." He laughed shortly, bitterly.

Nick said, "If any of them push me around they'll get pushed right back!"

Butch took off his hat and for the first time showed them the lump on his head. "That's what I got."

You could cut the smoke with a knife. "Ti-Pi-Tin" was a sure thing for the Hit Parade. Tonight would be a swell night to work. Lots of drunks.

Across the tavern floor he heard someone shout, "Nick! Nick!" with a surprised and pleased ring in it. "Nick Romano!"

Nick turned around, looking for the voice. He stood half-swaying, his feet widely spread. As his head went around, searching, he felt a tightening at his throat. He knew that voice!

His eyes found the voice. He could feel his face burn; he tried to pull himself up straight-shouldered and was only half successful.

Some day I will see him and I'll say, *Hi, Pizon.*

Grant Holloway sat at a small table crowded up against the wall next to the bandstand. Half-risen, now, from the chair, he had his arm in the air to catch Nick's attention.

Embarrassed, trying to make his legs behave, Nick walked toward Grant's table.... He banged into a woman. "Excuse me."... *Like those mountains if no one had ever been into them....* Unnaturally stiff he walked towards Grant's table.... And all the time he looked over tables, over heads, and into Grant's face. He saw the bare head and the large friendly eyes. Again he looked at the serious eyes and the wide square mouth that smiled at him. Then he was standing at the table. They were shaking hands. Nick's eyes slid away from the needles of brown light. "What do ya say?" he said. His drinking had given a surly touch to his eyes and a nasty edge to his mouth.

Grant pulled out the other chair. "Sit down, Nick." Nick sat down.

He gave me cigarettes.

Grant was saying, "I often wondered what had happened to you."

Grant was saying, "What are you doing here?" With just a little twist of a smile he said it.

Nick reddened. He said, "Want some beer? Let me buy for us."

Grant, quietly smiling, said, "I think you've had enough, Nick."

Nick was shamed; but he said, "Aw, don't go preaching at me. I get enough of that at home."

"How are your parents?"

"The old man ain't working. We're on relief," accusingly.

Grant slipped a flat gold cigarette case from his pocket. "Have a cigarette?"

"Thanks."

"You've grown up."

"Yeah."

Nick put his hand against the edge of the table and looked at it. Then he said, "I don't like anything at home," as if that explained everything.

The bartender was standing at the table. "Bring me a glass of beer," Grant said. "—Bring two."

> *He said he was glad he met her*
> *And some day he would come back and get her....**

The beer came. Nick tilted the glass to his lips. He wiped his mouth against the back of his hand. He grinned. "I'm goddamn glad to see you again." The curse word was casual, easy.

Grant held out the cigarette case with the long, spread-out G.H. on it. Nick chuckled. "You don't smoke roll-your-owns any more, huh?"

Grant smiled. "No."

"Boy, that's a keen case you got there."

"Oh," Grant said, "it's a present from a girl I know."

Nick secretly started looking Grant over.

He's got good clothes now. That's sure a swell coat. You don't get that kind on Halsted Street. He wears his clothes sloppy though, like he don't give a damn.

Grant rubbed his fingers against his scalp. The hair stuck up between his fingers. Nick grinned. It still needs cutting.

Grant sat remembering the Nick who had said, "They beat us. I hate it here. I'll never reform now!" He remembered a Mexican boy with a shoe in his hand and his hand shaking when he said, "I'm going home." He remembered a little boy pulling his pants down and showing him his behind. Only two years ago.

Grant looked around the smoky, noise-filled tavern of drunks,

* From *Ti-Pi-Tin*, by Maria Grever and Raymond Leveen. Copyright, 1938, by Leo Feist, Inc. Used by permission.

jackrollers, bums, painted women. A woman's voice cut across the tavern laughing and cursing.

Grant's eyes came back to the youthful face, flushed with liquor. "They've done a lot to you, Nick, haven't they?" he asked as if he were talking to himself.

"Huh? Who?"

Grant didn't answer. He shook his head, nothing, instead.

They smoked from the gold cigarette case. Nick said, "It's my turn." He drained his glass and paid for another round.

> But she said "No, no
> I cannot go
> Until I know you better...." *

"What do you get out of hanging in a place like this?" Grant asked.

Nick hung his head. "Gimme a cigarette, huh?" He didn't look at Grant when he took it. For something to say he asked, "What have you been doing since I saw you?"

"What have I been doing?" Grant tossed his head in a small gesture of self-condemnation. "Oh, writing a lot—" He took the beer a third of the way down in the long length of glass. The square mouth flattened out. The brown eyes grew sullen, then wistful. He swallowed a big swallow of beer. "I'm not doing what I want to do. I write lots of stuff I don't believe in."

Grant drank again. "Successful young writer. Oh, yes—!" He blew a heavy cloud of smoke toward the ceiling. He waved a gesturing hand at the tavern. "I haven't forgotten all of this—and the things I'd like to write." He smiled. "Maybe that's why I come down here sometimes."

"You're in Chicago Now!"

At the other table Butch was yelling across, "Hey, Nick! Are you going to stay all night?"

Nick looked at Grant. "I gotta go." ..

"Where do you live?" Grant asked.

"Twelfth and Peoria."

"Come on, Nick!"

"I'll see you later!" Nick told Grant....

"Who's the guy?" Butch wanted to know.

"A friend of mine."

"Why don't you call him over?"

"All right."

"He might pop for the drinks," Whitey put in.

Nick threw Whitey a disgusted look.

Nick yelled across, "Wanta come over?"

Grant nodded, smiled his twisted smile and came over.

[162]

The bartender stood at the table. Grant counted heads. "Five beers, please."

"I don't want any more," Nick said.

Grant zippered open his billfold and pulled out a bill. The broken-nosed man stared intently. "Lay off!" Nick snarled in an undertone.

The beer came. Grant sat, slowly sipping. . . . Nick measuring the fence with his eyes. "I ain't going to reform!"

They drank more beer; all of them but Nick and Grant. They smoked Grant's cigarettes. Then Butch said, "Come on, let's get to work." Nick gave Butch a meaningful look. "We got a job cleaning up a tavern down the street for three dollars," Nick told Grant. Grant leaned over toward Nick. "You're going jackrolling, eh?" he asked in an undertone.

"No, I'm not!" Nick said, his guiltless eyes looking at Grant squarely.

They got up. Nick said, "I'll see you around!" He went out with Whitey, Butch and the broken-faced man.

Grant sat alone, staring around the tavern. The music said—

> Ti-pi ti-pi-tin, ti-pi-tin,
> Ti-pi-ton, ti-pi-ton.*

Grant sat a long time.

The drunken voice shouted: *"You're in Chicago! Yippee!"*

Grant got up and walked out.

37

The unhappy man sat at his table by the window. He sat with his hand up to his face, with his eyes in the shadow of his hand and the newspaper folded to the crossword puzzle. When Nick walked into the Nickel Plate the unhappy man looked up.

* From *Ti-Pi-Tin*, by Maria Grever and Raymond Leveen. Copyright, 1938, by Leo Feist, Inc. Used by permission.

The Nickel Plate was crowded. Nick looked around for a place to sit. He saw that the other chair at the unhappy man's table was empty and, squeezing past tables, he went to it, twisted it out away from the table and sat down with his back to the window. He threw the ankle of one foot over the knee of his other leg. Holding his ankle he took the sole of his shoe between his fingers and examined it. The unhappy man was looking over the edge of the table at the broken and worn sole of Nick's shoe too. He looked at it intently with his sad eyes. Then he looked up into Nick's face. Nick grinned at him. "They do look bad," said the unhappy man.

"Yeah!" Nick said, laughing and lifting his brows in amusement.

Carefully the unhappy man folded his paper and put it in his pocket. Carefully he took out his wallet. From it he drew five single dollars, folded them, laid them on the table near Nick. "Get yourself a pair of shoes." As soon as he had put the money on the table he got up and walked out.

       ...

The next evening Nick walked into the Nickel Plate in new shoes. He went to the window table with his eyes staring innocently and just the touch of a smile curving his lips. He flopped down and stuck a foot out where the unhappy man could see it. "How do you like them?" he asked, twisting the new shoe around on the floor. The unhappy man looked at it, nodded his approval, and a minute later got up and walked out.

After that Nick always smiled at the unhappy man when he saw him. And once in a while he went over and talked to him.

He's a good guy.

The unhappy man never had much to say. He never seemed quite glad to see Nick.

       ...

Nick drifted into the Pastime, walking with straight-bodied swagger. He stared in surprise when he saw Grant there, then sat on a bench alongside of him. "Hello, pizon," Nick said.

"Hello, Nick!"

Nick looked at Grant with narrowed and suspicious eyes. What does he want down here? "What brings you down here?"

Grant grinned. "Oh, just looking around. Anything wrong with that?" He grinned again.

"I don't suppose so," Nick said without friendliness, then added, "So long's you ain't keepin' an eye on me and don't start telling me what to do."

Grant laughed. "Okay, pizon." He lit a cigarette and passed his case to Nick. Nick lit up.

Nick was silent a moment; then he said, "I haven't eaten in three days."

Grant smiled.

"Honest I haven't. And I haven't slept in four days."

"You're an awful liar, Nick."

Nick sat, his innocent eyes divided between Grant and a pool game where Butch was beating Whitey and there was half a dollar on the game.

"Come on, I'll take you to dinner. You lead the way." Grant said.

Nick took him to the Nickel Plate.

They were silent during the meal. Occasionally Nick looked up over a chop bone and grinned. When he had finished the second slab of pie he wiped his mouth with the back of his hand and said, "Boy, I was hungry!"

"What did you do last night?" Grant asked.

"Aw, I borrowed some money from a guy. First I had to put the arm on him. Me and Sunshine. You don't know Sunshine, huh? He's all right. Sunshine lives with a lady and a gentleman that ain't married." Nick grinned.

Grant laughed; then seriously, "Why do you do it?"

"I don't know. I bet you think I'm no good."

Looking at the clean-cut face, Grant said, "You have to take people as you find them. Not as you'd like to have them on a blueprint."

After that Nick was more honest with Grant. He even demonstrated the sleeper to him and told how they left their victims in the alley and made a getaway.

Several times Grant said, "I'm coming by your house someday."

"No. Don't go over there," Nick always told him. And Nick was worried and afraid, ashamed of his parents and his home, worried that if Grant went there he might meddle in his business. He was all right to talk to on West Madison, an audience to dramatize himself before and to try to shock with inside information about jackrolling and the gambling dens, but he didn't want him at his house where he might spill the beans and where he would see the way his family lived.

Grant talked to Nick in his serious moods, in his bitter moments, when he was off guard. Nick always told him, "I'm worse now than I was when I went to reform school."

•••

Tonight, for a change, Nick stayed home. He lay full length on the sag-spring front room sofa with his legs over the armrest and a comic book propped up before his face. On the floor beside him was an ash tray, several twisted butts in it, ashes all around it where he had aimed and missed. A knock came on the door. Nick, putting a shoe up on the armrest, twisted himself around on the couch and yelled back toward the kitchen where Pa, Ma, Julian and

[165]

Aunt Rosa were, "For Christ's sake, what's the matter with your ears? Somebody's at the door."

Julian came through the room. "It wouldn't hurt you to get up and go."

Julian opened the door. There was a mumble of voices. "It's someone to see you, Nick."

Nick squirmed to sitting position. Grant was standing grinning down at him. "Hello, Nick. I didn't have anything to do so I thought I'd drop by." Embarrassed, Nick said, "Come in and sit down." He motioned toward Julian. "This is my brother Julian. This is Grant—Grant Holloway." They shook hands. Julian said, "I'll take your coat for you."

Alone with Grant, Nick looked around the bare room, ashamed. He gestured with his hand—"Well, sit down." With his foot he secretly pushed the ash tray under the sofa.

They all came in, serious-eyed, to look at Mr. Grant. Pa shook hands, "I'm glad to know you, Mr. Holloway,' and sat down stiffly. Grant said, "Just call me Grant." Aunt Rosa, pumping his hand, said, "Hi, Grant!"

Ma came in last. She had Junior in her arms. Ma switched his weight over to one arm and held out a bony hand. "I'm very glad to see you again. I hope you have been well."

Nick got small on the edge of the couch.

Pa went out and came back with a small bottle of dago red and glasses. He poured for Grant, Aunt Rosa and himself. Grant, rubbing his lips over the taste of the dago red, nodded his head. "It's good stuff!"

Aunt Rosa said, "Say! Do you play pinochle, Grant!"

"I sure do!" Grant said with a wide grin.

He's all right. On the edge of the couch, nervous, Nick thought that when he saw the grin.

"Well," Aunt Rosa said, "let's me and you beat the socks off anybody who wants to take us on!"

They scraped chairs up to the table. Grant asked, "Would anybody like some beer?"

"We all drink it!" Aunt Rosa retorted. Grant's tan face wrinkled in a smile and he stuffed his hand into his pocket. Aunt Rosa said, "You go for it, Jule."

After the door closed Nick told Grant loudly, meanly, "He's ashamed to go in taverns. He don't drink, he don't smoke, he ain't got no faults!" Already Aunt Rosa's fat hands were rumpling the cards.

Julian came back, lugging the half-gallon bottle. They cut for partners and the cards said Grant and Aunt Rosa. Grant yanked his tie loose and unbuttoned his collar. His long fingers made the cards dance under them as he shuffled. Ma brought pieces of brown bread and cheese on blue glass plates. "How do you like them dishes, Grant?" Aunt Rosa asked. "I won them at the show."

Grant dealt around. Aunt Rosa took the bid. Pa, Julian and Grant got their meld down. Aunt Rosa said, "You better get everything down you got—I'm going to puke!" and laid down a run and half of pinochle.

Julian said, "J'ever see such luck!"

Aunt Rosa went, "Huh!" To Grant she said, "We'll lick the pants off them or there ain't a cow in Texas and that's a cattle state!"

Nick, sitting in shadow at the corner of the sofa, sipped his beer.

■ ■ ■ı

After that Grant started dropping by the house once in a while. One night he came in bringing big cuts of sirloin steak and all the trimmings. He gave the packages to Ma without looking at her and said, "Mrs. Romano, you'll know what to do with these—I've been dying for some." There was enough for a week. Julian was kidding around with Pa. He had an arm clenched around Pa's neck and was rubbing Pa's stubble of beard. Pa, breaking away, said jokingly, "I'll smack you in the nose!"

Nick, uncomfortable under the scrutiny of Grant in the house with the friendly feeling growing up there, slipped into his coat. At the door he said, "I got to see a friend of mine."

Grant winked at him. "Take it easy!" he said.

Nick looked at Grant sheepishly. For a moment he started to pull off his hat and stay. But his hand opened the door and he slipped past it and into the hallway.

Nick walked toward West Madison Street.

. . . Good guy. He don't preach. When he looks at me I feel ashamed. I ought to try to be like I was when I first saw him. I'm going to quit robbing.

I don't think I can.

Sure I can. I will.

■ ■ ■

In less than an hour Nick was in the Long Bar, smiling his innocent wide-eyed smile and twirling a watch at the end of a gold chain, around and around on one finger. He slipped his other hand into his pocket and pulled out a bill. "Give me a beer," he said. "No, make it a whiskey."

38

Nick walked along DeKoven on his way over to say hello to Stash. There was warmth in the winter night, and some snow was coming, gently, from the leaden sky. Big flakes once in a while touched his face, clung there, damp and large. There wasn't enough on the ground to kick your feet in. But it felt good, walking along on big steps, feeling the swing of your legs, the tickle of snow, sometimes, down your neck. And the Palmolive Beacon cut across the sky ever so often in a wide path. You tried to time it by counting until it came around again. There it was—

He stood in front of Stash's house, looking up, counting. A girl was coming toward him. He watched her coming, looking at the legs smooth as marble in their silk under the dim light of street lamps. He was still looking at her legs and hips when she was almost up on top of him. He looked up into her face.

Rosemary!

"Rosemary!"

She stood locked to the sidewalk, her face as red as it possibly could get. And he stood there too, his face also pumping up red.

"H-h-hello, Nick." Her voice trembled a lot.

Nick hung his head. "Hello, Rosemary."

She didn't go. He said, "How—have you been?"

"All right."

"Where—where you been keeping yourself?"

"School—and—and I go to Hull-House all the time," Rosemary said. "Mother teaches the piano over there."

Then they were silent and awkward, standing facing each other on the sidewalk.

He looked around panicky. She was there. She might go. There was Stash's old man's car. "Let's sit in the car," he said. She nodded, not answering. He took her arm. They climbed into the back seat and, quietly, he closed the door.

Rosemary sat away from him, almost pressed against the opposite end of the seat. She stared at him. She kept staring.

[168]

"What's the matter?" he asked, sitting far away from her.

"Nothing."

He felt uncomfortable; her nearness excited him.

"Well, don't stare then," he kidded and moved a little closer to her. "Are you mad at me?"

She shook her head no. He moved a little closer to her. She shut her eyes. He put his arm around her and kissed her. To kiss her he had to half stand up, for her head was drawn away and pressed against the seat cushion.

Slowly, carefully, he unbuttoned her coat, the jacket of her suit. He could see her lips tremble a little. He looked at her face, clean, regular-featured; her eyelids pressed tight, some of her golden hair loose and mussed across her forehead from under the black band of her hat.

Nick took his hands away. Shamefaced he looked at her opened clothes. He put his hands up to his face for a moment. "No," he said into them.

He fastened her clothes back on her; and all the while she lay crushed up against the seat, not saying anything, trembling all over.

He straightened her clothes with hands trembling like her limbs. Then he leaned back against the cushions and laughed loudly, laughed and laughed. Rosemary, next to him, was still crushed against the seat.

He took her arm, roughly, and got her out of the car. He walked her to Halsted Street, all the time holding her elbow, squeezing his fingers into it tightly, twisting it, feeling her arm quivering under his grasp. "I'm not your kind," he told her roughly. "You'd better keep away from me. Get it!"

■■■

He hung in the Pastime till late that night shooting pool. A couple times Squint, hanging around watching the game, said, "Bet you don't make it!"

"How much?" Nick yelled.

"A dime."

"Ho! Make it worth my while!"

"All right! All right! Bill Hoppe—a quarter."

"That talks a little louder—put up!" Nick said. He aimed carefully and, as you have to do in banks, called his shot. It was a perfect bank; a thrill went through him. But he acted like it was nothing and dusted the palms of his hands again. Squint said, coldly, "Lucky!"

"You ought to see me when I really get hot," Nick said. Squint said, "You think you're All-American hell, don't you?" Nick said, "*Think?*" and made a sour, wisecracking face. Squint, mad, trying to get some of his money back, said, "Bet you a buck you can't make the eleven ball on a double bank in the end pocket," pointing out one of the hardest shots on the table. Nick tossed his head. He counted change and gave Butch his money to hold. "Put up or shut up!" he told Squint. Squint's good eye glared. He tossed a dollar bill on the green felt of the pool table. Nick let a tight smile stretch out over his face as he aimed.

Here's where I drop a buck.

Damn if I'll let him call me on it though.

He aimed carefully. It went in.

Every time Squint put it on the line Nick was lucky; he took Squint for all he had. The yellow, tight-drawn mask that Squint had for a face turned yellower. Nick told him, "You ought to know better'n to bet against me!" Squint moved away with his face down in a scowl.

Late that night Nick went along Halsted between Madison and Washington wondering where the hell everybody was so early. He heard someone say, out of a half-dark doorway, "There goes All-American hell." Nick threw a glance back over his shoulder. He saw Squint standing there with two pals; and when he kept walking he heard Squint laugh nastily. That was too much. He walked back, measuring the situation with narrowed eyes. One of the fellows he knew, Lefty. Lefty nodded a little and said quietly, "Hello, Nick." Nick nodded. Lefty wasn't for him, he guessed; but he wasn't against him either.

"What's the trouble?" Nick asked walking right up to Squint.

"You think you're *good,* don't you?" Squint's one eye was down; but his lips lifted up off his teeth.

"Yeah!" Nick had his face in Squint's.

Without warning, like a flash, Squint's hand went in and came out of his pocket with an opened knife. Nick moved back quickly. The streak went down where his face had been. Nick stood not far away from Squint, fists clenched, toes clenched. He let his eyes go sideways for only a moment, then back to Squint's ugly, scowling face. In the moment he said to Lefty, "Have you got a schieve?" Squint said, "Come on!" Lefty said, "No." Nick dropped his knees a little, pushing himself down into a half-squat, and made a grab for Squint's wrist with his left hand. He grabbed blade instead and the knife tore through the flesh of his hand. At the same time he sent Squint's lip through his teeth with his other fist.

Squint went down. Nick kicked him in the face. A drunk, a straggler and a couple of other people walking by watched casually. Lefty and Squint's other pal turned around and walked away.

Nick could feel blood curl around his hand and run over the back of it. He stopped kicking and looked down at his hand. Someone asked, "Did you get cut bad?"

Nick stared across streaks of blood at the unhappy man. "Naw!" Nick said angrily. "Just a scratch!" And his mad eyes looked down at Squint lying moaning at his feet with his arms folded up around his face protectively.

More people had stopped to gawk. The unhappy man said, "Hurry!" He and Nick walked away fast.

They walked. They didn't talk.

Nick wound his handkerchief around his hand.

For a long time they didn't talk. Then: "Does it hurt?"

"Naw—it's numb from the cold. That's all.—Thanks for the shoes."

"Oh, that's all right."

Again they walked along silently.

"That bastard pulled a knife on me."

"I know."

"Hey," Nick asked, "where are we going?"

"To my house. I'll see that your hand is fixed up."

Nick glanced at him quickly, wondering.

Close to Henry Street they went up slabs of worn and rusted limestone steps with iron banisters running up and a box-shaped bay window hanging over the porch that didn't have any roof.

Nick went in thinking, yeah, I guess so. Well, he'd wait and see what the score was.

The unhappy man led him into a high-ceilinged room with tall, shuttered windows painted gray. He nodded toward a large, overstuffed plush couch with a big-flowered cretonne slip drawn tightly over it and a couple of pillows thrown on it. "Sit down." The unhappy man went into another room.

Nick looked around. At each end of the sofa were small end tables. There was, by one of the windows, a big chair with a leather hassock covered with oilcloth, and by the arm of that chair was a thin-legged table with a small white radio on it.

Nice layout!

With his feet close together on the worn, flowered-pattern rug and his hand on his knee Nick unwound the handkerchief from around his wound, pulling it loose where the blood had crusted.

It ain't so bad. Not deep at all.

He had his hand up to his face, examining it, when the unhappy man came back carrying a basin of hot water, a towel and a red rubber-corked bottle. He pulled an end table around in front of Nick and put the basin on it. He took Nick's hand and put it down into the hot water. Nick winced. With the end of the bath towel the unhappy man gently laved the open flesh. Then he dried it on the other end of the towel. Looking at the cut with Nick's hand pulled over on his knee, the unhappy man asked, "Does it hurt, Nicky?"

[171]

Nick grinned tight-lipped and shook his head, no; then, as he heard, "Oh, you know my name."

"Yes."

The man tore the arm off a good white shirt and bound the wound up.... "Ow! That's too tight!" Then the man said, "Just like new," and went out of the room with the basin.

Nick looked around. He saw, by the other window, a small gold-fish bowl on a stand, fishfood near it. By the big chair was a floor lamp. In the other corner was a liquor cabinet.

The unhappy man came back with a bowl of soup and set it on the end table in front of Nick. "Gee! It's good!" Nick said, tasting it and burning his lips. When it was gone the unhappy man poured a small glass, a thimbleful, of wine and gave it to Nick. "Here, drink this."

Nick drank it. "I better go—thanks for everything." He started to stand up but the unhappy man motioned for him to stay where he was. "You don't need to hurry."

"I might wake someone up."

"I live here alone."

Nick looked around approvingly. "Gee!" he said. "It's swell to have a dump of your own like this!"

"Do you think so?" The man handed him a magazine to read and then sat in the big chair at the opposite end of the room.

There on the sofa arm Nick grabbed up a couple of hours' sleep. When he awoke there was a blanket over him. The unhappy man was in the far chair, doing a crossword puzzle. He looked up, smiling slowly.

"I'm going to go," Nick said, standing up; and with his hat on. "Thanks a lot!"

"That's all right. You know where I live now. Come over again if you want to." He didn't try to make Nick stay. Nick was surprised and relieved.

"Okay! So long!"

Nick stuck his head back in the door and frowned. "Hey! What's your name?"

"Owen," said the unhappy man.

39

Nick stood in the poolroom, out from the wall a little, posing. He was all dressed up. Neatly pressed suit, white shirt, tie smoothly knotted and pulled up away from the shirt blouse a little, cuffs pulled down showing an inch, trouser cuffs just touching the highly polished shoes. He had his head and chin pulled in, his freshly cleaned hat on the side of his head a trifle, showing the gloss of just-combed hair. In the loop of one arm a topcoat was carefully folded and draped down, part of the lining showing. In his other hand, between two fingers, he held a newly lighted cigarette. His eyes, under lowered lids, watched the pool games with a bored and superior look.

Juan came in all dressed up too. Nick offered him a cigarette and asked, "What are you doing tonight?"

"I got a broad on the line."

"Have you seen Sunshine or Butch?"

"Ain't you heard?" Juan said. "They're in the can. They caught time for jackrolling."

"No fooling! What did they catch?"

"Butch got thirty days and Sunshine got sixty days."

Juan left. Nick stood around with no one he knew in the poolroom. He went up to the Nickel Plate and loafed at the table. A big guy tapped him on the shoulder. "I want to see you." Nick looked over his shoulder at the big guy and then away, not moving.

"Did you hear me!"

"Well, I don't want to see you," Nick retorted.

The big guy pulled back his coat, showing a badge. "Read it and weep, bozo—I'm the law!"

Nick hardened up some more and didn't move. "I'm a customer here."

"Come on!" The law had him by the shoulder lifting him up off the chair and another flatfoot came over from near the door.

They took him to the station. Riley, who had killed three men, leaned over the cage sill, talking in to the sergeant. Riley had his coat off. His holster hung sloppily over his pushed-out hip. Three cuts were in his belt, in close to the stomach of his shirt. He wheeled around and, standing over Nick, asked, "What's your name?"

Nick stood up straight, like when you're making yourself strong. "Nick Romano." Then he waited for the clout across the face. It came. He clumped back against the grillwork of the cage, clenching his teeth, hating cops, goddamn it! Hating them.

Riley took him downstairs to the damp and stinking basement. There was a turnkey's desk at the foot of the stairs. Behind the turnkey's desk was the lockup. There were three rows of cells: one for the drunks and bums, one for the prisoners ready to go to court upstairs some time in the morning near noon, and one for prisoners who weren't booked on any charge but were held "open." Bums and drunks sat and lay on the floors of the cells.

In front of each cell door, sitting on the concrete floor, was a gallon tomato can full of water for drinking. In each cell was a tin cup. You stuck your hand and the cup through the bars and dipped into the rusty tomato can when you wanted water. In each cell was a bunk of iron grillwork. There was no mattress on the bunk and no blanket. The whole basement reeked of Lysol, urine and the smell of the breaths of drunks. The toilet was a small ditch cut in the floor and running through the cells from one end of each tier to the other. It was there you took a leak, standing like a horse, or there you squatted like out in the country, holding your pants in your hands as best you could. A slow trickle of water ran in the inch-deep trough from one end of the row of cells to the other. Nick slumped down on the iron bunk and started spitting at the trough, trying to hit center. One of the prisoners a few cells ahead plugged the trough with paper so the water wouldn't pass through and in a little while the three back cells were flooded over. Nick and the other prisoners at that end climbed up on their bunks and started cursing.

As the night went on they brought in more and more fellows. Pretty soon the jail was just about filled up with the drunks off West Madison and they started singing and raising hell. And once the turnkey came back with a pail of water and threw it in between the bars on one of the drunks who wouldn't keep quiet. Occasionally, when the noise died down, a sewer rat came out of the cracks and holes in the wall and crept around the floor. On the walls were cockroaches and bedbugs.

Nick sat staring through the bars. You couldn't tell whether it was day or night. There were no windows through the bars. All you could see was a concrete wall. If you had twenty-five cents against your name upstairs where they searched you, you could buy a pack of cigarettes.

In the morning they gave you a cup of black, unsugared coffee and a hunk of bread. Noon and night they gave you a hunk of baloney between bread.

Nick gnawed at the hard bread and the tough gristly baloney, waiting to make the eight P.M. showup over at headquarters.

The paddy patrol backed into the runway in the alley behind headquarters. With others they herded Nick out of the wagon and into the building.

■■■

They took the prisoners into an elevator and shot them up to the upper floor. They were locked in cells. When the clock had jerked noisily to four minutes past eight, they took the prisoners from their cells and marched them toward the stage.

■■■

Nick was herded out under the lights with seven other caged prisoners and made to face the gathered mob, spotlights overhead hitting them in the face. And there were footlights that reflected their glare on them too.

In the harshness and whiteness of the lights Nick's face was pasty, his features washed out. With the others he was pushed back against the measuring rule painted across the wall at their backs which catalogued them by numbers painted at intervals.

Nick stared straight ahead.

That's crap about not being able to see anybody.

Nick stared. The angry, miscellaneous and unsure crowd stared back, muttering. Nick and the other seven stood in unreal cockiness, shoulders back, faces chalky. Some ties and collars were pulled loose.

On the chairs, facing the stage as if in boxes at a theatre, sat the mob. They were mostly women, well dressed, powdered. Down each aisle police officers in uniform were lined.

The prisoners stood under the lights. The officer read out the name and charge against each man. . . . "John Andrews, suspect. . . . Charles Boyle, picked up seven times in suspicion of strong-arming. . . . Suspicion . . . suspicion. . . ." There was a microphone on wheels that was trundled down in front of each prisoner. They made him talk into it for the benefit of the crowd.

"What's your name?"

"John Fenski."

"What's your alias?"

"I haven't got one."

"*Speak up louder!*—Where do you work?"

"I—I'm not working. I can't find a job. I was just walking along the street late at night and—"

"How many times have you been arrested?"

"This is the first time."

"What alias do you use?"

"I told you I haven't got an alias."

"Nick Romano. . . ."

Nick scowled, squinted his eyes, twisted his mouth and made his voice different to help keep from getting a finger.

He didn't get a finger. He was free. . . .

Coming out feeling crummy, mad and hungry, Nick headed back toward his haunt. When the street got ugly and dirty, when bums and drunks were wandering along the sidewalk he felt at ease again and squared back his shoulders. A wino came up and tried to put the bum on him. "Go on!—Beat it!" Nick told the drunk. But it felt good to be back on the street.

Nick walked to Washington. He remembered the building. He went up the scaled limestone steps. He had to knock hard. Then Owen, with a book in his hand, opened the door. Owen looked surprised. "Hello, Nicky! Come on in!"

"You told me to come over."

"Yes."

"I just got out of the jug. Can I take a bath here?"

It was a *swell* bathroom. There was a big, low tub, slick white, lots of soft towels. He looked around at the broad top of the chiffonier filled with men's shaving lotion, silver-backed military brushes, an electric razor, jars of shaving cream. He picked up the electric shaver and, laughing, puffed out one cheek. Then, suddenly he sat down on the fancy toilet mat and, whistling, began to pull his clothes off.

In the bathroom Nick splashed in the water and whistled loudly.

Owen got up. He went to the window and, pulling the flowered cretonne curtains back, stared down onto the street. On the street automobiles chased one another.

Owen was still gazing down through the dirty pane of window when Nick came out of the bathroom. "Oh, you're finished."

"Un-huh," grinning. "It was swell!"

Owen sat down. Nick pulled a straight-backed chair to the middle of the worn flowered rug. He put his arms, one folded over the other, on the back of the chair and, straddling it, dropped his chin down on his arms. His brown-black hair, unruly, healthy from soap and water, curled over his brows and over his ears. Nick, gazing from the rest his arms made, said, "Gee, you've got a swell place!"

Owen dragged his eyes away. He stood up. "I've got to dress to go out," he said.

[176]

Nick combed his hair while Owen watched. It kept curling back away from the comb. Nick put on his coat and hat. Owen said, "Come back soon. Whenever you want."

40

The city had just pushed its way up out of the night and onto the gray shoulders of the winter dawn. Pa Romano got down off the streetcar and with the WPA-402 order went toward the project site, proud of the chance to work again. He walked onto the large vacant lot. It was black dirt, frozen. All around the lot were men in overalls, sweaters, blue jeans, and shabby overcoats. There were Italians, Poles, Negroes, Swedes, Mexicans.

Pa walked through the muck in line with the others. The tool man gave him a pick. With the pick over his shoulder, he straggled off with the others, away from the vacant lot to a street, the concrete of which was already chopped up.

He looked around. Most of them were just like him—worn out, used up. Some swung their tools slowly, hacking dead-faced at the hunks of concrete. Others leaned disconsolately on their shovels.

The sun came, taking the frost away. Across the street, beyond the dead green lawn, newspaper-wrapped sandwiches and lunches in brown paper bags were stuck between the boards of a picket fence. In the lumped-up concrete of the street several kids of school age were pounding with sledgehammers and wheeling the broken concrete away. They ran with the wheelbarrows and goosed each other, playing while they worked.

Pa Romano, with the other men, stood hunched over in the street, picking at the stubborn concrete. The skin began to rub and pinch on his palms. The soreness started in his fingers and climbed up his arms until it sat on his shoulders and hung there, heavy. He stooped closer and closer over the rock pile . . . remembering.

. . . *It will be over there. It will come out of there—out of the mist and the sea. . . . The tired soil had given them no more. The land was brutal as it was sunny. Rocky hillside. Barren mountain. Trees,*

[177]

*stark, twisted. "A rivederci, Dio ti guarda."... Tears from the sig-
nore. Tight smiles from the men. Hands waving....Into the mist
and the sea. ... They flattened back against one another, nine hundred of them. Greeks, Swedes, Russians, Poles, Italians, Jews, mute
Lithuanian peasants. ... Long rows of bunks side by side. ... Sitting down on a lower berth and bumping his head on the top one
with no room for his knees in the aisle. ... And under him the tremendous blows against the side of the ship. Over him the rattling
bars and chains. Around him the sighs of the sick. ... Into the night
and the sea and the new. ...*

*...New York. Trying to get to the West. Denver. The padrone,
the foreman of the labor gang on the railroad. ... Tracks. A boxcar
for a home. ... "Luigi, we are going into business." ... The pushcart. Alleys. And then better and better with the bananas and apples
and oranges. Soon green salads with olive oil and the good, hard-
crusted bread like—back there. Provolone. And one day, after many
days, letters on the window of a little store: L. ROMANO—IMPORTER
OF ITALIAN FOODS. ... Good times, years of good times ... then the
depression. ... Strange men came to the house, in all the rooms,
examining the furniture ... and worse and worse ... and Nick
more stubborn every day. ... His boy he was saving for the church
in reform school ... and always on the street now. ...*

It will come out of there—out of the mist and the sea.

Pa lifted the pick again. "I don't ask him to work. I don't want
him to work yet. I want him to go to school." Pa looked around,
embarrassed, to see if anyone had heard him.

■■■)

Noon, and the men all trudged away from the street toward the
picket fence where their lunches were. A little man had fallen in
step with Pa. "A hell of a long morning, huh, my friend?" Pa, blowing his nose, looked sideways and shook his head yes. The men
walked across the dead lawn and unfolded their dried sandwiches
from the newspaper wrappings. Pa stood chilled, his warm skin,
filmed with perspiration, feeling the wind. Pa and the men crowded
into the hallway of a two-story flat building to get out of the cold.
They chewed their sandwiches, their onions, their raw carrots. The
little man said to Pa, "Listen, my friend, I'm a musician. I play the
guitar. Gene Mack, the playing cowboy—and here I am pounding a
hammer. I won a prize on the Morris B. Sachs amateur hour a year
ago. Five dollars for five minutes." He pulled a harmonica out of
his pocket "Play a mouth organ, too. And I really tear it up. My
music touches the heart strings."

The whistle sounded. The men trudged back into the street. Gene
Mack told Pa, "I play for the working man. The hell with the millionaires. Chop their heads off."

Again Pa Romano went on line with the rest of the men. That afternoon they worked in the alley, digging it eight inches deep and carting the dirt away in wheelbarrows to trucks where it was loaded. . . .

Rain came, cold, stinging. The men left their tools and ran to protection under the front porches and down concrete stairways leading to basements. Men stood, looking out at the gray rush of rain, grumbling, hoping it kept raining, hoping the foreman would send them home.

It was a real downpour. In fifteen minutes the foreman poked his dripping cap and face under the porch. "All right, men, check in and go home."

Pa started away from the WPA tool lot on slow feet, unmindful of the rain that was soaking him. Someone slapped him on the shoulder. Pa looked across at Gene Mack. "It's a hell of a day," Gene Mack said. "Let's go have a drink. Too early to go home yet."

"All right," Pa said.

In the neighborhood tavern Gene Mack said, "Stan, you bring us a bottle of wine and two glasses, huh?"

Stan brought it. It was dull red in the long-necked bottle. The stove brought its heat over, warming, to the table. Gene Mack poured the glasses full. *"Prosit!"* he said, hoisting his glass.

Pa drained his glass.

The rain had stopped. When it stopped it left the sky black with night. In the bottle on the table the redness had gone halfway down.

Pa and Gene Mack sat drinking together.

The second quart was more than half gone now. Pa, leaning over the table suddenly, said to Gene Mack, "I got trouble with my boy. He won't go to school. All the time he stays on the street." Pa's eyes stared at Gene Mack with hurt and shame, asking him an answer.

"You got to bend your kids the way you want them to grow. You got to be hard on kids," Gene Mack said, throwing off his wine at a toss. "My old man he was from the old country and he beat hell out of me. I was so scared of him I wouldn't say a word wrong when he was around. Once he tied me to the bed and beat me with a horsewhip."

Pa loosened the muscles in his throat and took all his wine down. Pa filled the glasses again.

Gene Mack said, "I told myself I wouldn't treat any kid of mine like that. Now I got a son in the penitentiary. I was too easy on him. Gave him everything. That's how I got paid off." He drank. "My old man was right. He knew how to raise kids."

The little circle in the bottom of the second bottle was a small

[179]

red pool now. The bottle was turned over on its side on the table. The tavernkeeper started turning off the lights.

■■■

Pa, feeling along the sides of the wall with his hands, climbed up the rickety steps toward the hallway. The door came open, sending a triangle of light into the black hall. Ma stood in the triangle of light. "Pa!—I've been worried sick! What happened? Where—?"

Pa walked in past her, not looking at her. "Ohhh!—Pa, you've been drinking!"

Pa walked toward the front of the house. Ma, following him, whined, "Pa, it ain't like you to drink. What's the matter with you, Pa?" He pushed her away from him and walked into Nick's and Julian's bedroom.

"He's here," Pa said, as if he were satisfied.

"What are you going to do?" Ma whined. Not paying any attention to her, Pa let his overcoat fall off on the floor and unbuttoned his under-coat. "Oh, leave him alone! Leave him alone!" Ma begged hysterically.

Pa unloosened his belt, yanked it out of the loops around his trousers and held it in his fist, the buckle picking up light and dangling loosely. He walked over to the bed and yanked the covers back.

Nick lay on his stomach. He was sleeping in his shorts. Below them were the two white lines of his legs. Above them were his back and shoulders, broad, husky; his arms were doubled under him. He lay relaxed, peaceful. Next to him, also asleep, lay Julian.

The belt buckle came down hard, cutting into the flesh of Nick's back, leaving broken skin, bringing a smear of blood. Again the metal and leather came down as Nick, waking and twisting away from the pain, turned over on his side with his arms and legs drawn in.

"OW!" Nick pulled himself into a sitting position. The buckle hit him in the arm, setting his elbow off into paralyzing jabs of pain. It slipped off his funny bone and grazed his chin, leaving a red mark.

"You dirty bastard!" Nick yelled, warding off the belt, aware now of where he was and what was happening.

The belt came again and again. And all the time Pa was beating Nick, Julian lay on his stomach close to the wall with his face buried in the crook of his arm. From under the cover his fist showed, clenching, relaxing, clenching, relaxing with the rise and fall of the belt. Ma cried, with her hands up to her eyes.

Aunt Rosa, her hair in a braid down her back, burst into the room, pulling on a robe and almost tripping over her long flannel nightgown. "What the hell's all the commotion!" she demanded.

Then, seeing what was happening, she rushed toward the bed on her bare feet. Catching a blow of the belt across her back, she grabbed it and twisted it, angrily, out of Pa's hand. Her braided hair, streaked gray, jumped over her shoulder and hung between her heaving breasts. She threw the belt across the room, and panting, faced Pa. "You ought to be ashamed of yourself! A grown man like you beating on that kid! Your own flesh and blood too! I'll be damned if I'll stay in your house!" She stamped out.

Nick was dressing, twisting into his clothes as fast as he could. All the time he stared hate at his father, the hate of enemy for enemy, daring him with his eyes to start again.

Now Nick stood up, dressed. He grabbed his coat. "I'm getting out, see! I've had enough of you and your goddamn beatings!"

He strode past his father, past the old man who with stooped shoulders still stood in front of the bed. He walked past his mother, leaning against the wall crying with her aged palms up to her face, past her without looking at her. He passed Ang who stared at him with scared, sad, half-awake eyes.

In the hallway Aunt Rosa waited. She was still barefooted. Her bathrobe was open and her braid of hair lay there where it was open. She had some bills crushed in her hand. She held the money out to Nick. "Here, Nick, take this. You'll need it." Her voice was hard-boiled and shaky with tears at the same time.

"That's all right," Nick said, not taking the money. He hardened his lips. But his eyes filled with tears.

■■■

When Nick was gone his father sat on the side of the bed and cried.

41

Nick knocked hard. Owen opened the door. He wore a dressing gown over his pajamas and was pushing his long straight hair off his forehead. "Oh!—" He stared in half-sleeping surprise. "Hello, Nicky!" He stood to the side of the door and Nick went in. "Can I stay here all night, Owen?"

"Why, of course, Nicky!" The surprise was fading now and his face flushed up concern. "What's the matter? What happened?"

"I left home."

Owen tied the fringed sash of his robe and motioned to a chair. "Sit down."

"I'm going to the bathroom," Nick said.

He walked into the bathroom and turned on the light. He walked over and looked at himself in the mirror. His eyes narrowed on the long thin streak of red the belt buckle had left across his chin. He clamped his teeth together, clenching them to keep from bawling; the muscles jumped at each end of his jaw.

The sonofabitch! The sonofabitch!

When he went back into the parlor, his bed was made down on the sofa, fresh sheets, a woolly blanket tucked all the way around, a fold of the blanket thrown back to a soft pillow with a clean slip, its creases still showing. One of the end tables was drawn up in front of the sofa. On it was a cup of coffee, slow steam rising from its khaki-colored surface. Nick glanced around the room. Owen wasn't there; his bedroom door was closed.

In the morning Owen had oatmeal, orange juice, toast and two eggs ready for him, with slices of bacon next to the eggs. "You can stay here," Owen said. Owen didn't look at him when he said it.

"No," Nick said, "I don't want to mooch on nobody."

•••

He hung on West Madison Street, at the Pastime and at the Nickel Plate. He went jackrolling, or mooched, or played the queers for his money. He was never going back home again.

One night he stood out in front of the Pastime with Juan. The sweater band was empty. "Have you got a dime, Juan?"

Juan grinned. "If I had a dime I'd be drinking or shooting pool. More and I'd be with a broad."

He started to ask Juan if he wanted to work tonight—he glanced down the street—

Down the long canyon of street came Owen. Nick stepped out farther on the sidewalk, blocking it. "Hello, Owen."

"Oh! Hello, Nicky!" His eyes looked into Nick's. They were gloomy. "Where have you been for the last few days?"

"Oh, I've been around," Nick said.

"I—" Owen said, "haven't seen you."

Nick slanted his eyes up into Owen's. He gave his mouth a pleading droop. "Hey, Owen, buy me something to eat, will you?" Owen glanced at him, and away. "I'll meet you in the Nickel Plate in fifteen minutes." He moved on down the street.

Juan squinted his eyes. "Hey," he asked, "is he a phoney?"

"No!" Nick said angrily. "Do you think something's wrong with everybody? He's a good friend of mine!"

Nick went up to the Nickel Plate to wait for Owen. When Owen came, Nick said, "Boy! I could eat a cow!" Owen handed him a dollar. "Spend all of it if you want." Owen's dusk-gray eyes watched Nick as he walked toward the food.

Back at the table Nick dug in with his elbows on the table and his head bent over the dish. Owen looked at the top of his head, black hair going every direction in curls. When Nick was almost finished, when he was leaning his neck back with the small bottle of milk tilted to his lips and a white trickle coming down his chin, he became conscious of Owen's gaze. With the bottle still at his lips, he grinned.

"Is it good?" Owen asked. Owen looked at the heavy, tapering lashes. The tip of the nose. His hands, in his lap, hidden by the tabletop, fastened together tensely. Owen said, "Nicky—come over tonight. . . . Won't you, Nicky?"

Nick's hand didn't touch the spoon. It stayed poised as he looked up, hearing a quality he had never before heard in Owen's voice. He looked at Owen. His hand came down to rest on the table slowly. One hand took the spoon, the other the fork. His arms spread out slowly, on the tabletop. Nick stared at Owen, a slow flush coming to his face. Owen's eyes dropped. Owen rearranged his face. He looked over the edge of the table at the floor. Nick took the end of his lip between his teeth and bit down on it hard. When he knew his voice would be all right he said, "Let's get out of here."

They went down the steps. On the sidewalk, his voice trembling, not looking at Nick, Owen asked. "When will I see you?"

"Well, ain't we going over to your house?" Nick asked roughly.

They walked to the corner. Owen didn't walk very close to Nick. And Nick, feeling different about Owen, went along. "I thought maybe you might like to listen to the radio," Owen said. His voice still shook. Nick didn't answer for almost a block. Then Nick said, quietly and evenly, "I think I know what you mean."

When they turned onto Washington, still not having anything more to say to each other, Nick thought, Gee, I'm dumb!

The sucker! I'll take him for all I can!

Then Nick talked, talked a lot. Kidded and laughed just as if nothing was different.

They went up the steps and into Owen's apartment. Even the apartment looked different. The fish bowl and tiny wafers. Big flowers on the sofa cover. And in the bathroom fuzzy, different-colored bath towels he couldn't see but remembered.

Nick dropped down on the sofa and, with his head twisted a little, smiled up at Owen with clear, artless eyes. Owen was em-

barrassed. He turned on the radio. They were still playing it. It
filled the room—

> *He said he was glad he met her*
> *And some day he would come back and get her....* *

Nick sat, drinking, turning the slick pages of the *Esquire* magazine, laughing at the cartoons. Ha ha. "Hey, this is a good one!"
Owen came over to see and moved quickly away. With the glass at
his elbow Nick turned pages, stopping only at the cartoons. Every
time he looked up, Owen was looking at him.

Owen drank some more. So did Nick. Owen drank some more.
Now he had so much in him that he staggered a little. And, no
longer embarrassed, he came over and sat near Nick. Nick sat there,
not caring. His lips were drawn back in a tight-skinned sneer, showing hard white teeth. But his eyes were wide and innocent.

42

Nick lay staring at the ceiling. The ceiling was sun-
patterned, even with the shade drawn to the sill. Daylight stood in
the room, sour-sad. Nick stared at the ceiling. A long crack in the
plaster directly overhead, jagged, thinning out, like a river.

Nick threw the sheet down to his stomach and sat on the side of
the couch with the sheet over his lap and legs. There was movement
in the room.

"Nicky...."

"I'm going."

Nick reached for his shorts. Slipped into them. He buckled his
trousers.

"Stay for breakfast," Owen said.

"I ain't hungry."

Sitting on a chair, Nick put on his socks, tied his shoes.

"Please stay."

"Oh, all right."

* From *Ti-Pi-Tin*, by Maria Grever and Raymond Leveen. Copyright, 1938,
by Leo Feist, Inc. Used by permission.

Nick stood at the dresser, combing his hair. "Nicky. . . ." Owen looked into the mirror. With his back to Owen, Nick met Owen's eyes in the mirror.

Nick walked into the front room. Owen followed him.

"Nicky, I—I—"

Nick glanced down at the toe of his shoe. He forgot to be hard-boiled and don't give a damn. Owen's money had bought the shoes. "Look—" he said, "I'm no good. You don't want to mess around with me. You're all right. I don't care what you are. You're all right." Nick got up. "I'm going." He put on his jacket, stood whistling unconcerned as he stared at himself in the mirror and fixed his hat on the way he liked it.

"When will I see you?" Owen asked.

Nick turned from the mirror, a sly expression sneaking over his face. "Hey, I'm broke!" Immediately Owen opened his wallet and gave Nick the three dollars that was in it.

"I warned you," Nick said.

"That's all right," Owen said.

"I'm money crazy," Nick said.

"That's all right," Owen said.

When he got to the door, Nick looked back, straight at Owen, and said, "I'll see you Saturday."

•••

The first person he ran into on West Madison was Grant.

"Hello, Nick!" He almost shouted it.

Nick flushed with shame. "Hello, pizon."

Grant said, "Come on, we'll have something to eat."

Nick lowered his shoulder so that Grant's fingers slipped off. "No. You don't want to have anything to do with me."

Grant looked surprised. "Okay, Nick," he said quietly.

Nick twisted away and walked off, almost running.

But that night Grant found Nick again at the Pastime. He motioned his head toward the door. Nick got up and followed him out. "Eat?"

"All right."

They sat in the restaurant with twisted cigarette butts in the used plates. "Why the sad face?" Grant asked.

"Nothing."

Grant leaned over the table. "Look, fellow," he said, "why don't you take it easy? You're not doing yourself any good down here. Stealing—sleeping in shows. Why don't you go home, Nick?" Nick didn't answer. Grant paused for a moment, then went on, "Listen, you've got to look out for yourself. You've got to say, 'I'm Nick Romano. I want to stay out of jail. I want to live.' "

Nick smiled, tight-faced. "You can't give me any advice. Don't you

[185]

know that?" he asked. "I know what I'm doing. I've got my eyes wide open. I'm fed up on everything, see. I don't care what happens to me, see." His grin grew brittle-bright. "Live fast, die young and have a good-looking corpse." The smirk was still across his face, mostly in his eyes when he finished.

Grant snapped his cigarette case open.

"Cigarette?"

"Thanks."

...

Think I'll go see how the old lady's getting along.

He had only been home once since the beating. He started out for home just before dark, knowing he wouldn't hang around the dump long.

Closer to home, with darkness coming over the sky, he separated a dollar from his other money so he could give it to the old lady. And he knew he'd be mad and embarrassed giving it to her. Embarrassed when he said, "Here, Ma." Mad when she started whining and wanting to know where it came from.

The old man was sick. There was the smell of medicine and his door closed with the murmur of Aunt Rosa's and Ma's voices whispering out. Nick handed the dollar to Ang. "Here, give this to Ma. I'm taking a sneak."

Ang's eyes were red. "Why don't you go in and see Pa? He's been asking where you were." Nick shook her hand off his shoulder.

"Don't be so sentimental!"

It was then Ma came out of the bedroom. Her eyes were circled. The bunched little networks of wrinkles scratched in red and brown gave a dragged look to her face. Her lips, cracked, were like leather. Her hair looked as if it hadn't been combed the last couple of days.

Ma walked over to him. She was calmer, more tensed-out than it was like her to be. She said thinly, "Go in and see Pa, won't you?"

Nick squinted his eyes and scowled his mouth. "Aw, he never has a kind word for me. He hates me. I'm going to take in a show." He turned and started for the door. At the door he looked over his shoulder. "I'll be back in a couple of hours, Ma."

He came back in a week. By then his father was dead and buried.

43

The family pulled itself together as best it could. Ma put on mourning and wore herself out crying. The second day after the funeral Ang came home, put her handbag on the dresser and sat down on the edge of the bed. "Feel better, Ma?" Ma nodded her head without answering, silent tears streaming down her cheeks. Ang put her young hands over her mother's old hands. For a long time Ang sat there and, something like Nick, rubbed the sole of one shoe against the floor. "Ma—" The elderly woman's eyes opened. Aunt Rosa came into the bedroom bringing coffee into which she had sneaked a little whiskey. Ma's eyes moved to Aunt Rosa's face without her head moving. "Ma," Ang said again. Ma looked at her.

"I got a job today."

Aunt Rosa said, "That's swell, Ang! Just swell! Now you won't have to go back on that damn relief, Lena. You can tell the relief to go to hell." Ma, grateful and heartbroken and worn, moved one of her hands up over Ang's and pressed. Aunt Rosa said, "Me and Ang and Julian working. Hell! We'll get along just fine!" Julian, gaunt-faced and tight-mouthed, was working seven days a week now and was donating two nights to volunteer work at Hull-House.

And Nick. . . .

...

Nick sat in the Nickel Plate with his feet cocked up on a chair, a bottle of coke stuck up to his face and his hat pushed back on his head.

What do I want to hang around there for? He didn't have no use for me. What good would it do me to be there? I ain't—no, I ain't sorry.

With Butch he went into the Pastime where The Kid had a bottle of yankeedock and gave them both a swig. Nick shot a couple of games of pool. Then he counted what change he had left and sneaked it in his sweater. At the mirror he carefully adjusted his hat.

...

Owen opened the door. Nick, making his face real sad, walked in.

"Nicky!" Owen stared at him. "What's the matter?"

"I'm in trouble. I'm on the spot."

"What did you do? What happened?" Owen's voice quivered in fear.

"How much money you got, Owen?"

"Seven dollars."

"That's how much I need."

"Oh, Nicky!" Owen's mouth drooped. "I can't give you that much. It's all I've got to live on."

"I've got to have it. I've got to buy my way out."

Owen grew more calm now. His eyes watched Nick's face, saw the slight, uncertain shift of his eyes. "I don't believe you, Nicky."

"You don't have to." He squared his shoulders angrily. "So I'm in trouble and you can't help me out. All right! All right!" He talked fast. Loud. He turned and, picking up his hat, started for the door.

Owen got to the door first, blocking its panels with his back. His voice took on a high-pitched tone. He was humble before Nick. "No, I can't let you go now," he said. He put both hands on Nick's shoulders and hung his head.

A faint smile quivered at the corners of Nick's mouth. "Move! I'm going!" he said roughly.

"No—no. I'll give it to you."

Nick came away from the door then and sat down. Owen went into the bedroom and came out with the seven dollars in his hand.

When Nick had his hat on and Owen was looking at him sadly, Nick said, "I'm no friggin' good. You'd be better off if we called it quits right now. I'll just take you for everything I can. I'll be after you all the time for money."

"Why don't you stay, Nicky?"

"No."

He walked out.

Owen stood leaning against the door with his head and his long hair against the panel.

...

Nick went to the tavern next door to the Pastime. Juan had a room in the hotel upstairs with his rent paid up two weeks in advance. But Juan had been spending the week with some married broad on the South Side, so Nick to keep a good room from going to waste slept in Juan's room when he felt like it. There was a woman called Mazie next door—

He ordered up and started drinking off Owen's money. He drank and kept thinking about Mazie upstairs. His mind kept dragging him up the stairs to the sagging bed there.

[188]

Unable to stand it any longer he climbed the steps, opened the door quietly and, without putting on the light, undressed. He slipped under the covers, naked, and lay waiting. His mind ran away with him. He lay there tight, unrelaxed. At last he saw a crack of light around the door leading to the adjoining room and heard Mazie inside, drunk, mumbling to herself, undressing. He moved himself up and down on the springs making them squeak loudly—and hoped.

At last she heard him. The door across the bed opened. He saw her outlined in light, a big, broad-hipped woman in her thirties, wearing only a slip. "Are you there—?" her voice asked. "I was sleeping," he said from the covers; and he put his bare arm out where she could see it. "Come on in and close the door." She did....

Nick went over to Owen's house quite a bit; almost every time he needed money, and sometimes when he didn't. Sometimes Owen wanted him to stay, but not always. He seemed to like to have Nick near him. For Nick a certain liking and friendship had grown up. Owen was somebody who understood. Maybe because Owen, in his way, lived outside the law, too.

Nick told Owen, "I tell you things I wouldn't tell anybody." And he told Owen all about his family, about his old man and the beatings. About the reform school and Tommy. He told everybody, sooner or later, about Tommy, and his eyes would get hard and he'd tighten his lips when he told. But nobody seemed to be much interested or even to half listen. Only a few people did. Grant. Owen. Julian.

Funny Julian should listen.

When Nick didn't go near Owen for a week or two Owen would come around asking, "Has Nick been here?" Sometimes Owen would find him sitting alone in some tavern, drunk. Owen would say, "Come on, Nicky, come out of here," or "Come and go over to my house, Nicky." Nick would tell him, "Aw, go on, you phoney!" And Owen would get mad.

This evening Owen found Nick at the Pastime and Nick went over to his place with him. After they had eaten they sat on the big cretonne flowers, with glasses of wine. Owen was sad-faced. "What's going to happen when you get married?" Owen asked. Nick said, "I'm not going to get married for a long time—maybe never." Owen stared at him sadly. "Oh, yes, you will." Nick leaned back against the cretonne flowers. "Well," Nick said, "we'll be good friends like we are now."

"Do you mean it?"

"Yeah." Nick doubled his fist and playfully rubbed it against Owen's jaw. "You're all right with me."

44

Grant found Nick at the Pastime one night. "Want to go for a ride?"

"Sure! Here, Sunshine—finish the game!"

They went out to the brand-new Buick. Grinning, Nick examined all the dials, dim-glowing under the lights. "Boy! A radio and everything!" Grant eased himself under the steering wheel.

Along West Madison they drove and onto the slick pavement of Michigan Boulevard, polka-dotted with the reflection of street lamps. The Outer Drive stretched its long finger out to them along the indistinct margin of lake. "Oh, I forgot to tell you—we're going up to Wisconsin for a few days," Grant said casually. He nodded toward the rear seat of the car piled with camping equipment, rifles, fishing rods.

"Oh," Nick said, "so you're kidnapping me! I got you on a charge of kidnapping."

Grant laughed. With one hand guiding the steering wheel he snapped open his cigarette case, passed it to Nick, took one himself. As Nick held the match for him and he squinted against the smoke, Grant said, "Truth of the matter is I want to get out of town for a while. I have to think something over."

"I thought you knew all the answers."

"Not always."

They drove in silence for a while. Grant rolled the window down and tossed his cigarette butt out. "'I nearly got married," he said.

"How come you didn't?"

"I talked fast," Grant said, grinning.

"Gave her the air, huh?"

"No, it isn't settled. She's a swell person. I'll take you over there some time. You'd like her. I've told her about you."

"What did you tell her?" Nick asked suspiciously.

"Oh—what you're like. How I met you."

"My pal!" Nick said.

"She wants to meet you," Grant said.

Night spun past them, endless, in two black sheets. Nick slept on the front seat. Through the night Grant drove and most of the next day. Toward late afternoon Nick asked shyly, "Can I—drive a while?"

"Sure." And Grant let him.

Night came again. In a clearing off the highway they saw a sign: LONE PINE TOURIST CABINS. They spent the night there in a cabin that lay low alongside the highway.

Morning found them on the road again, under the harsh glitter of sunlight. Wisconsin climbed green under the sky, stumbling, catching its balance, edging up to the big pines and the jagged, heavily piled clouds, white against blue that stretched like an endless, timeless door. Open but secret. Grant watched Wisconsin curve around him, spin, reach up, stand in wild sun-splashed green; and Grant caught his breath. He looked at Nick: something in nature should take him. Because he is young. Do something to him.

Nick showed no interest in the scenery.

Toward evening they wound among pine trees. Grant had said no more about it. "So you're in love," Nick said.

"I don't know. I'm very fond of her."

"Is she rich?" Nick asked.

"She has some money," Grant said.

He thought of Wanda's friends. Most of them were rich. Were they any better than the denizens of West Madison? Cleaner, more subtle in their methods, perhaps. But that was all.

"It would be a pretty soft life for you, wouldn't it?" Nick asked.

"Yes, it would be that."

"I think you'd be a damn fool not to marry her."

"I don't know."

∎∎∎

The pine cabin was far from any road, deep in the fold of a hill, hidden by arrow-straight evergreens. The water came from a well, cold like the wind. Night shrouded them; campfire licked the night. Their rifles sounded across the day. Lakes silvered under the moon with stars studding them and trees peering in. Air smelled of sunlight and dew and growing things. There was nothing except their own footsteps and the occasional call of a bird.

And Nick. . . .

Nick enjoyed carrying a gun and shooting at things. For an hour each day he set a can in the fork of a tree and fired away at it. He didn't like the long hikes. "Hey, Grant, how much farther do we have to walk?" He never woke in time to see a sunrise. He complained about the mosquitoes. He left all the dishes for Grant to do. Grant broke into his shell only once. With rucksacks on their backs and leaning against the on-end hills, they had come through the

[191]

pines on a trail to the deer country where at night they bedded down in sleeping bags beside the rim of a lake. Dawn came, bitter cold, splitting the sky like a long rip in a blue-gray evening gown. The dim stars were there, then gone. Clouds fed, like lambs, on the edge of the horizon. And the sun, emerging from the lake, dripped color across the water, shook color across the sky. The silence of night broke into a hundred pieces. Grant shook Nick, shook him hard. At last he awakened; he sat up, searching the lake and the sky with wide brown eyes. Grant watched him. All the color of nature reflected in his eyes. They were more childish than Grant had ever seen them before. For a long time Nick said nothing. His curly hair fell over his forehead, glistening with the sun. His lips trembled, unsmiling.

"Gosh!" he said.

■■■

That night they huddled before the campfire, their backs against tree trunks. They hadn't spoken for a long time. At last Nick broke the silence. "You going to get married?" he asked.

"I'll let it ride a while," Grant said.

"I think you're crazy."

"Well, I don't know. I don't want to sell out. If I married her—"

Grant lit a cigarette, tossed the match away angrily. "Once you're padded around the middle it's damn easy to forget a lot of things," he said, looking into the fire. "You know what I was interested in when I met you—juvenile delinquency and so on. I wrote some articles about the reform school you were in. I went out to see your folks after I met you so I could understand you better and what had put you in a place like that. I became interested in your case. Then in you as a human being. You got bigger than the problem—" Grant tossed his cigarette away with an angry snap. "When I was writing those things you could have called me a reformer or one of those well-meaning liberals. But you can't stay in one place. One thing moves on into the next or you're standing still. The problem gets bigger than the individual—" He shrugged and pushed his hand into his hair. "That's why I don't know whether a *nice* woman like this is my dish or not."

Nick glanced at Grant with an expression that was curious and interested but not convinced. Grant leaned forward. He grinned. "Lecture's over," he said. "Let's hit the hay," he said.

"She still sounds good to me," Nick said.

■■■

They stayed in the north woods almost a week. One afternoon Grant put on old clothes and picked up a fishing rod. "Want to do some fishing?" he asked. Nick looked up moodily. "No."

Several hours later Grant came back up the trail. He whistled sharply, single notes, signalling his good luck. As he neared the door that stood open he shouted, "Put on the frying pan, Nick—we eat!" No answer. He went in. Nick wasn't there. On the table, hanging half over the edge, was the wallet Grant had left behind. It had been zippered open. He looked inside, saw that half the money was missing. He walked to the window: the car's still there. He sat down and smoked a cigarette: he just went haywire for a minute, that's all. Grant smoked still another cigarette.

Grant fried and ate the fish. He sat a long time on the ground outside the cabin with his knees drawn up to his chin, smoking. He went to bed and lay staring out through the square of window at the black, starless sky.

It hurt as if he had lost something.

Next day Grant drove back to Chicago, alone.

He knew where to find Nick. He went back to West Madison. But for several weeks Nick avoided him. Then one evening Grant ran into him in a tavern. Grant crossed the room. "Hello, pizon," Grant said.

"Oh, hello there, Grant!" His eyes were innocent. "Got a cigarette?" Grant gave him one; he sat down.

"I'm sorry about leaving you but I had some business in the city," Nick said. No mention of the money. No shame in his wide brown eyes.

A day or two later though, when Nick walked into the Nickel Plate and found Grant there, he sat down next to him. He looked sheepish. "Hello, pizon."

"Hello, Nick," Grant said.

Nick couldn't meet his eyes. He drew thirty dollars out of his pocket, already folded, and lay it on the table next to Grant. "There's your money."

Grant looked at him, slipped the money off the edge of the table and stuffed it in his pocket. "Want some coffee or something to eat?" he asked.

"No," Nick said. He choked.

■■■

That night Nick hooked up with Lucky and Bill in the Long Bar. They were pretty drunk and got drunker. About three in the morning they walked down West Madison. As they passed the Shamrock a man came out carrying a violin case.

"Shall we nail him?" Lucky asked. Without any of them having to say yes they knew that they were going to, and they all tensed up, trailing him.

Down by the *Daily News* building, just before the fellow hit the bridge, they put the arm on him. Nick did it, choking off the scream that tried to escape from the little violinist's throat.

They dumped him and ran through the plaza of the *Daily News* building with the violin. Then they took an alley and got out onto

West Madison at Halsted. They were passing a chili joint when Nick saw Whitey inside. Nick said, "Let's go in here a minute."

He went up to Whitey. "Hey," he said, "you know the waiter. Have him put this in the basement for us." Nick held out the violin. Whitey's crafty eyes looked at the case. "Sure thing, Nick! What's my cut if I peddle it for you?" Nick patted him on the shoulder. "If you get enough we'll see that you're treated right."

● ● ●

In the Pastime the next day Nick sat on a bench against the wall, waiting for Whitey, who was peddling the violin, to show up. He didn't know where Lucky and Bill had disappeared but they didn't need to worry none, they'd get their cut.

Whitey walked in. But right behind him was Riley, towering over him and staring into the poolroom, his eyes like two pointed barrels of automatic colts. Whitey looked scared stiff. "The guy I ask for a cigarette," he whispered to Riley with his head down and his eyes unable to look at anyone in the poolroom.

Nick didn't see him until he was standing beside him. "Got a cigarette, Nick?" His voice was a mumble in his throat.

Nick gave him one. Right then Riley walked up with a foot-and-a-half blackjack in his hand. He told the proprietor, shouting it, "Call the wagon!" Nick sat, looking up at Whitey, grinning at him. His grin said: you yellow rat, you! Whitey stood, stoop-shouldered, looking at the floor. The cigarette he had taken from Nick was between his lips, unlit. Nick said, "What's the big idea, cop?" Riley, backing Nick against the wall, shouted, "Strong-arming a guy and taking his violin away from him, that's what!" Nick said, "I don't know anything about it—don't push me!"

At the police station they all faced each other—Nick, Lucky, Bill and Whitey. Whitey still hadn't lit the cigarette. It was souped, wet and ragged halfway to its end. Nick's face wore a hard smile. His eyes riveted Lucky and Bill, saying: keep your mouths shut! Lucky sat on a chair with his chin on his shirt front. The other kid was full of welts and blood. "Well—did you do it?" Riley shouted, prodding them with his blackjack. "Yeah, we did it, we did it," the two kids admitted; they didn't have guts enough to look at Nick. "No!" Nick said.

Lucky, Bill and Whitey were taken down to the lockup. In the room Nick was alone with Riley.

"Well?—How about it?—Are you going to confess?"

"Look—I don't know what you're talking about."

Riley's mean cop face came close to Nick's. "No?" *Wham!* His open paw slapped Nick's face, making his teeth rattle. Nick straightened his shoulders and showed him a hard, tight-lipped face.

Riley's jaw was hard-lined and protruding like the butt of a horseshoe. "Are you going to talk?" Riley's face was in Nick's.

When he talked a little spit hissed out past his lips and dotted Nick's cheek. Then, standing close to Nick he slammed his fist suddenly into the hollow above Nick's hip bone where no marks would be left. "*Ohhhh!* YOU SONOFABITCH!" Nick staggered back. Bent over he looked up at Riley's six feet two inches through eyes that smouldered in pain and hate. In the back of his mind he thought: He killed three men.

The killer walked in and hit Nick behind the ear, rabbit-punching him. Nick staggered back again. Then he rushed at Riley and flailed out with both fists. Riley stepped aside and stuck out his foot, tripping Nick. At the same time he brought his fist down on the back of Nick's neck as he fell. And he laughed. Leaning over him on lumbering feet, Riley said, "Now will you talk?"

"No, you bastard!"

Every time Nick got up Riley punched him in the neck and sent him down again. He beat him cleverly, leaving no marks.

"Are you ready to confess?"

It took a long time to get the words out now. They were: "No, you bastard!"

Riley left him on the floor a while. Then he came back and beat him some more.

You got to kill me first!

Nick didn't talk.

45

Old Jake stopped wiping the counter and waggled all the fingers of one hand, excitedly, in a come-here gesture. When Grant was leaning over the counter, Old Jake said, "Your friend, they got him by police station."

"What happened?" Grant asked.

"Something he steal. They come in here get him."

■ ■ ■

Nick sat on the side of the bunk with his head dully paining from Riley's rabbit punches and ripped open the package of cigarettes that had got down to him from Grant.

Grant's all right. That guy's all right. After the way I treated him, too.

He lit a cigarette.

Gee, I don't want to go to the adolescent home. I hear it's worse than jail. Lucky was smart when he told them he was eighteen. I'm going to tell them I'm eighteen. I don't want to make that joint.

"*Romano!*"

It was the turnkey yelling his name. Ma was outside the bars. Before he had a chance to say anything, she said, "I can't do anything for you. You got into trouble and you'll have to get yourself out."

"Hey, I told them I was eighteen. Don't go telling them I ain't," Nick said.

Ma said, "I left some sandwiches for you and a couple of apples and one of those nickel lemon cream pies you like. The man upstairs says he'd see you got them."

Ma stopped at the desk on the way out. "My boy is only sixteen," she said. "He won't be seventeen for more than a month yet."

•••

Riley unlocked the cell door and said, "Come on, kid." He said it real friendly. And he said, "Your mother's upstairs waiting for you."

Nick followed him. His eyes narrowed on Riley's bull neck, hating him, but his eyes were misty too, thinking of Ma upstairs doing all she could for him.

I'm going to get out of it.

Riley walked slow. He put a big paw on Nick's shoulder. "You ain't going to tell anybody I hit you, are you? And I'm going to let you go."

Nick jerked his shoulder away hard, making the cop's hand fall off.

Riley, standing at the foot of the stairs, not taking him up yet, said again, "I'm going to let you go, kid."

Nick believed him. But he didn't shake the paw Riley held out.

•••

They climbed up out of the basement.

Ma was there. He went over and sat down by her. "Why did you tell them how old I was?" Cops went back and forth. There was one who had an eye on him all the time.

In about five minutes a policeman from the home came in. "Where's the juvenile?" he asked, looking around for Nick. Another policeman pointed Nick out. "That's him." The cop from the adolescent home laughed. "What are you trying to do—kid me? Why, that guy's nineteen or twenty."

"No," the other policeman said. "That's the kid you want."

The adolescent home officer came over. "Come on, kid," he said. He took Nick by the sleeve and marched him to the police car. Ma followed right behind him.

On the way out Nick turned and gave Riley a dirty look. You bastard!—You lying sonofabitch!

...

They brought him inside, into the red brick building with a high stone wall around it, in past a door that opened with a buzzer. Ma had to leave him there.

In the receiving room they left him alone with a guard and a woman all in white. A nurse. She came over and looked in his hair, parting it. They were under a light. She searched with her nose close and her sharp fingers hard against his scalp. She took a comb with some stuff smeared on it and combed his hair good with it, adding more of the stuff a couple of times.

Nick, humiliated, submitted meekly.

She washed her hands. Nick looked at the low-heeled white shoes, the legs, the still young and slightly pretty face with the straight mouth and business-like eyes. She walked over to him and gave him a pill. Without water. He couldn't even swallow it; it kept catching in his throat. The nurse went out.

The guard telling Nick to get out of his clothes, said, "Take them off!" Just then another nurse came through. A prettier one. Nick stood blushing. Again the guard said, "Take them off!" The nurse looked at Nick and smiled a little; then she walked away so that he could undress.

He stripped off his clothes. The guard put them in a locker. He took all Nick's valuables, too, and locked them up—his comb, his keys, his knife, his billfold. You can't have any money. No smokes and no gum.

The door opened and a man came in. He was an elderly man gray-haired and smelling of medicine. The doc didn't look at him right away. He went to a cabinet, got out some things and a chart. Then he walked over and started making Nick turn around, bend down, turn back around, say ahhh! Nick, flushed and mad, did what he was told.

The doc got a chair and sat down in front of Nick. The doc cleared his throat. "Are you sure you never had any girls?"

They keep asking me that.

Nick got panicky.

He said, "No! No!"

He could have told. But he figured they'd just put him more in jail.

...

Nick came out of the showers. He was all alone down there with no one to tell him anything. There was a bunch of overalls.

I guess I take a pair.

None of them fitted. Most of them came halfway up his legs, making his shins and feet, sticking out, look funny. The others he wrapped around like this—too big—

There was a bunch of doors; it was all doors and he didn't know where to go next. A guard looked in and said, "You're a new guy, ain't you? You go straight through that door and if you don't behave we're going to knock the hell out of you." He was an ugly-looking bastard.

Nick walked through the door and a little farther, and found a place where they were boxing. He stood watching. It was pretty mean fighting. They stood whaling the hell out of each other. If a kid said, "No, I don't want to," the guard socked him. And you couldn't quit. In the ring when they knocked a guy down you didn't keep hitting him; and if you were taking too bad a beating they stopped it. Not here. The guard would tell you when to quit. A kid would say, "I've had enough. I've had enough." Then the guard would let the other guy beat him up some more.

"Let that new guy fight," one of the inmates said, pointing. "That guy there."

"Yeah," said another fellow.

"All right, you—" the guard said at Nick; then he looked around. "You—" he said at another boy.

Nick stepped right up.

I gotta show 'em right away.

He showed them right away.

In the adolescent home you can fight any time. Them friggin' guards like to see fights all the time.

If trouble came Nick would just get right up and start tangling.

∎∎∎

Nick came out two months later, mad at the world. Still thinking about Riley's rabbit punches, he went over to Maxwell Street and into a store. It was a pawnshop. A safe held up one end of the ceiling. Nick waited until the store was empty. Then he went up to the fence he and Vito had done business with. He talked alone with the fence for a long time. When he came out he had a package. He took it home. With the bedroom door closed and a chair under the knob he unwrapped the package. In it was a rusty, old-fashioned rod. He took it apart and oiled it good. He filled it. In a sporting goods store he bought a jockstrap. When he went out on a job after that he wore the jockstrap and stuck the gun down inside of it, in front.

The next cop who tries to take me in is going to have to shoot it out with me.

He swore it.

46

For two years Nick hung on West Madison Street. And in those two years he never aged a day. He knew a good-looking kid could get along on West Madison. He could pick out the phoneys at a glance, and the girls who looked easy. He was gambling heavily now. Every day the horses got a part of the money he had stolen or cheated someone out of, and stuss or poker took the rest of it from him. He was often drunk—more often than he was sober. Every woman on the street knew him. They still turned to look over their shoulder at him when he passed. Many of them gave him money. He always kept his clothes at home. They were immaculate and he never went on the street without first glancing into a mirror and adjusting his hat. And his eyes still held that innocent stare. The street hid in some secret tissue of his body. The street was in his blood. He lived fast....

▪▪▪

Before going in Nick looked up at the house at 1113 South Peoria and grinned. The family sure is highfalutin now, moving out of the second floor shack in back and moving on the second floor in front. Even having a telephone and a brand new radio with push buttons for the stations. That's one good thing about Julian. He thinks of the house. He likes to see everything new in the house. Still giving Ma his whole check. Hah!

Nick went up the wooden steps, across the warped porch boards and into the hall. Ang was in the dark hallway kissing some fellow. They pulled apart when the door came open. Ang's round eyes looked at him out of the dark. "Nick—this is—Abe." Nick nodded his head, hard-boiled, and said, "Hi!" Abe went out of the hall right away and Ang ran up the steps to catch Nick. Halfway up she put her hand on his arm. "Don't tell Ma," Ang said.

"It's none of my business what you do!" Nick said. He shook her hand off his arm.

"It isn't that, Nick. It's—he—isn't a Catholic."

Nick went up the steps laughing at her.

Junior was whining for Ma to give him some money for candy.

[199]

and Julian sat in the front room on the new sofa with a notebook on his knees. "Hey!" Nick asked Ma, "did my suit come back from the cleaner's yet?"

"Why don't you look," Ma said, nodding at the pole fastened across the door separating the dining room and the front room and from which Nick's suit hung in a brown paper bag.

Nick went right away to the bathroom and started cleaning up. The phone rang and Julian shouted, *"Nick!"* Nick came through the house and, flopping down on the sofa near Julian, picked up the phone. "Hello."

"Hello—Nicky?"

"Yeah."

"How are you you haven't been over I wondered what had happened to you you aren't mad about anything are you when will I see you everything's all right isn't it won't you drop over for a while tonight?" the voice whined.

"Yeah, yeah, yeah," Nick said. "Yeah, I'll see you," and hung up.

Ma called them all to the supper table. When Nick had hurriedly eaten and was pushing away from the table, Ma said, "Tomorrow's Thanksgiving. See if you can't come home to dinner tomorrow, Nick." She looked up at the large colored photograph of Pa on the wall over the table that, for the enlargement, had cost fifteen dollars. Pa looked back, stern-faced and out of focus.

"All right, Ma," Nick said.

Nick went into the bedroom and back into the closet. From under a pile of junk he hauled a pair of knee-height lace boots. He stuck his hand down in one of them and pulled out the gun he had bought from the fence on Maxwell Street. He held it in the palm of his hand, looking down at it and grinning. He patted it. "I may need you tonight, baby!" He put it in the pocket of his topcoat and tossed the coat across his arm carelessly, then went through the house and down onto the street.

■■■

In the Pastime late the next afternoon Nick and Juan stood with pool sticks in their hands and grinned at each other over the night's experience with two broads they had picked up. Sleepy-eyed, rubbing the sleep away, Juan said, "The redhead was sure swell packing, Jack!" and let a moon grin slip across his teeth. Yawning and remembering, they walked around the table, poking lazily at the pool balls.

Claude, up in the front of the poolroom, yelled, "Oh Nick!" and grinned. A girl was standing just outside the poolroom door in a wrinkled tan coat. She wasn't bad-looking, but was pale and her mousy hair was showing from under the brim of a red hat. Two fingers were out through her gloves. She stood half-shrinking against the gum-ball machine. Nick grinned at Juan and strutted over toward the front pane. "What do you want?" he asked roughly.

"You know," she said.

"Yeah, I know."

Lifting gray eyes to his, the girl said tensely, "Come on home with me."

"Aw, go on, Nellie, go on up there. You got the key. I'll be up later."

"Come on now," she whined.

"Look—I'll take care of you later."

"Come on, Nick, I waited for you last night." Her voice took on an edge of despair. "And you didn't show up. Come on." Her eyes got watery.

"No." he whispered it, forming his lips around it hardboiled, with finality. She pulled her bare fingers in beyond the holes in the glove. "You'll come later?" She was begging now. "What time will you come?"

"How the hell do I know what time!" He walked away from her and back to Juan. "Who's the broad?" Juan asked, grinning.

"Oh, just a little plaything of mine."

"Say! She's all right!"

"You telling me? I get money off her. She buys me eats and everything. This shirt—" He pulled at the shirt.

"Where's she from?"

"She slings hash on North Clark Street," Nick said.

"Are you packing her steady?"

"Whenever I want."

After three more games Juan racked his stick and said, "I'm going home. I ain't seen the old lady in a month. She likes to have us all together on the holidays." Combing his hair before the wall mirror, he asked over his shoulder, "You going home?"

"Not me!" Nick said.

Juan left. Nick looked up at the clock. Four. He thought of Ma. She can wait.

Nick went next door to the tavern and got sloppy drunk. Outside, under the neon sign that said ROOMS—25¢ A NIGHT, Nellie was waiting for him. "Let's go, Nick," she whined.

"Go on!—Beat it!" he told her.

"See how you are," she whined. She moved over close to him. "See how you are." He shook her fingers off his arm.

"Say, are you looking for a fat lip? I told you to beat it!" Her fingers were on his lapels.

"Aw, Nick!"

"Take a powder," he said.

"Please don't be like that, Nick." She stopped a tear with a finger that came up beyond the worn hole in her glove. The tear ran along it and soaked the frayed black cloth.

Nick looked at her disgustedly. He moved back from her. "Look —I'm going to punch you in the mouth if you don't beat it." He turned and walked down the street. She followed him.

"You dirty bastard!" she called after him.

47

The wind was red in his face and stiff in his hands. The heat had breathed against the window front and beyond the sad, drooping Christmas decorations of the Ideal Cafeteria the pane wore a fine bead of sweat. Behind him a drunk said, "Wake me up at seven o'clock, willya, waiter?" and laid his face in his arms. Nick walked over to the counter, got coffee and a pastry for a nickel.

You're no good, Nick. You're just like the rest of them down here. Christ!

He stood at the window looking out.... Forget it! ... Listening to the wind howl past; seeing it push stragglers along with it.... Go out and get drunk.

He turned up his coat collar and went out in the night and the cold.... Drinking kills everything.... Get drunk....Pick up a broad. ... Get drunk. ... Yeah. ...

He stumbled along in the cold. ... Live fast, die young and have a good-looking corpse!

Far off in the night a slow-stroked chime counted the hour.

St. Augustine's! ... A kid with a dad who said, "We're going to give our boy to the church." ... In the bed, warm, snuggled close to Ma.

...

He hunted up Juan and Butch. He found them at Ace's place. "How much you got?" he asked.

"You want to gamble?—We'll stake you," they said.

"No. Loan me some dough." Butch gave him two bucks. Juan handed him a fivespot.

At the Pastime he found Sunshine. "How much dough you got?" Sunshine took him back to the can where nobody could see and showed him twelve dollars. "Loan me half of it, Sunshine."

Sunshine put the whole wad in Nick's hand. "Take it all. Ah got my room paid. You do me favors."

He went to the Penguin Club.

It was a better class of joint. Bars of neon in small sections against the wall and ceiling cast indirect dimness, threw discreet lighting sparsely about the room. A black velvet drape hung from the ceiling all the way across the back wall. In front of the curtain a man in a dress suit and top hat was singing over a microphone.

Next to him a girl danced with nothing on, without a strip, without a rag, oh boy! Nick looked. *Oh boy!* He slid up against the bar, watching. The girl twisted, wiggled, quivered from head to foot. She snaked her hands, fingers groping, convulsing, over her legs, her hips, her quivering breasts. The waiter was saying, "Yes, sir?"

"A shot," Nick told him without taking his eyes from the dancer. He threw the shot down, and the small chaser of beer. It was then that a girl in a long dress open at the bosom, dropped over to the bar next to Nick.

"Will you give me a cigarette?" He gave her one.

"Buy me a drink." Without answering, he moved to one of the white-cloth covered tables.

A waitress in a maroon and white outfit brought him his drink. Sixty cents. He had just put it to his lips when a girl with her breasts bobbing out sat down next to him. "Give me a cigarette, will you?" He held the pack for her. She took one and said, "Buy me a drink, will you?" She smiled at him with half-sleepy eyes.

"Hey—what's this—a parade? You're the second one," Nick said. The girl stood up, mad. She broke the cigarette in half and threw it in his face.

Nick grabbed her bare arm and laughed. "Hey, come here! You're all right! I like a girl with guts. Have a drink!"

She sat down again. "Well—if you insist," she said, rubbing her arm where he had grabbed her. She looked across at him. "Say, you're good-looking!"

Nick leaned over the table. "I been told that, baby." He took hold of her arm. "I ain't as good as I look either."

Smiling she shook him off and blew smoke in his face. "Not so fast!"

Nick popped for drinks at eighty cents a crack. The jukebox filled the place. Bonnie Baker was singing—

> *Oh Johnny! Oh Johnny!*
> *How you can love....* *

The girl at Nick's table smiled out of her red mouth and purple eyelids. "Is your name Johnny?" she asked.

* Reprinted by permission of copyright owner of the song.

[203]

"No—but I can love."

"Sez you."

"Sez I—let's dance. . . . My name is Nick. What's yours?"

"Lucille, honey."

They danced in the darkest corner, standing in one place, not lifting their feet off the floor, moving their legs in against one another.

She looked at him, eye to eye. She opened her mouth with her lower lip pulled in over her teeth and, leaning in his arms, pushed her legs in close under him. "Oh, Nicky! Oh, Nicky!"

> *I just*
> *Oh Johnny! Oh Johnny! OH!* *

Nick danced backwards slowly. Her stomach pivoted against his. His hand patted her back.

They sat again at the table and again drank. After a while Nick got up and went to the toilet.

Drinking doesn't kill what's inside of you, you go on thinking about it. Live fast—

He swaggered out of the toilet smirking. Someone grabbed him by the arm. "Hey, Nick, there's some broad outside told me to come in here and get you. Said her name was Nellie," Butch said.

"Tell her I ain't here."

"She saw you. She said you'd say that." Butch grinned.

"Wait a minute," Nick said. He went back to the table where Lucille was. "I got to go somewhere, baby. I got to do a friend a favor." He put Sunshine's five-dollar bill on the table. "Wait for me here. Buy yourself some drinks."

Lucille looked up through sleepy, purple-lidded eyes.

"I'll be waiting—see. I won't let any bastard horn in," she said.

Outside Nellie waited. "Ho, here you are! Come on over to my place."

"Christ! You give me a pain," Nick said.

"I got my pay tonight. You didn't forget that, did you?" Nellie asked nastily.

"Come on!" Nick told her roughly; he grabbed her arm. Over his shoulder he motioned with his head for Butch to come along. "Where's he going?" Nellie asked. "With," Nick said.

On the darkened side street Nick took her purse, took what he wanted and handed it back to her. They went up the steps to her two rooms. In the hallway she paused, trying to stand so that Butch couldn't go in. Nick pushed Butch in ahead of him.

As soon as they got inside Nellie started toward the bedroom. "What about my pal here?" Nick asked, jerking his thumb toward Butch.

* Reprinted by permission of copyright owner of the song.

She had her arm curved around his neck and her body pulled in against him. She was crying as Nick pulled away and went back down the stairs.

...

"I see you're still around, baby."

"I said I'd wait."

Nick sat down, pulled out some of Nellie's money and paid for drinks.

You're a dirty bastard, Nick!

So what!

He grinned, hard-eyed, at Lucille. "Let's dance."

They danced.

> *But when I—*
> *Look—*
> *At—*
> *You—*
> *I just—*
> *Oh Johnny! Oh Johnny! OH!* *

"Oh, Nicky! Oh, Nicky! OH!" She stood wiggling against him, rumpling his hair with both hands.

"Kiss me!" Lucille said, and that wasn't hard to do.

"Oh, you fool!" she said. "I'm crazy about you!"

At the table he pulled his chair up close to hers. His shoulders swayed a little and his elbows supported him on the table. He said, "You're hot stuff, baby!" He liked that; he said it again, "You're hot stuff, baby! I go for you." She kissed him, pulling him over to her, pulling his head over on her breast. "Want to go to my room?" she asked.

...

At home Ma said, "Mr. Grant was here this afternoon. He wanted to see you, Nick. He's worried about you."

"What did he have to say?"

"He's coming over tomorrow night to play pinochle," Aunt Rosa said. "He said if you and Julian wasn't here he'd play me some two-hand."

Nick had a wad he had won in a crap game. He offered Ma five dollars. She wouldn't take it. He put it on the table. "Well, there it is. You may use it."

"I wouldn't touch it! I wouldn't touch it!" Ma said.

He left it there anyway.

All during dinner Ang sat watching Nick. When he got up and left she grabbed her coat and ran down the steps after him. "Wait a minute, Nick."

He walked a little slower so that she could catch her breath.

* Reprinted by permission of copyright owner of the song.

My sister, he thought. He put down the sentimental feeling. Sis. He blushed thinking it and tightened the muscles in his jaws. She's a good-looking broad. Some guy's going to be lucky. Good figure, too.

They were at the corner but she kept coming right along with him.

"Nick," she said, putting her head down, "I'm in love." Her head touched the shoulder of his coat.

"That's swell, Ang."

"Nick—he—he's Jewish. But I love him—I love him." Her fingers tightened a trifle on his arm.

"Does he love you?"

She nodded without answering.

"Well?"

"Ma—she doesn't know. She—he—it would just about kill her. You know how she feels about being a Catholic."

Nick turned so that he could look at Ang. "The hell with Ma," he said. "Don't let her live your life for you. You love him, he loves you. Marry the guy."

"Oh Nick, I can't—Ma's had so much trouble and worry."

Nick shrugged. "I think you're a damn fool," he said.

■■■

Nick stood in front of the washbowl combing his hair and getting into his shirt. "Hey, Owen," he called, "bring my coat." Owen brought it. Standing with it on his arm, Owen felt its heaviness and stuck his hand in the pocket. When he pulled his hand out the gun came with it.

"What's this, Nicky?" His eyes were large and frightened.

Nick wheeled around and immediately took the gun from Owen, immediately stuck it out of sight. With his behind propped against the washbowl he looked up at Owen. "It's a rod. What do you think it is?"

Owen was staring at him. "What are you going to do with it?"

Nick made his eyes innocent and looked at Owen guiltlessly. Then he smiled and said, "Maybe I'm going to use it on you." He walked into the front room. "I got to go."

Owen followed him. "Please, Nicky—don't take that gun out of here."

He kept begging Nick not to, so at last Nick said, "Oh, all right!" and put it under the mattress on Owen's bed.

■■■■

All day it was Pastime, the Haymarket, the bookie's, Ace's place, then the taverns. He was drunk that night. He and Red. They came staggering along the street. In front of a flophouse Riley the cop grabbed him by the shoulder. "I want to see you, Romano. What are you doing on the street this time of night?"

Nick stood motionless. The drunkenness slipped away from him.
It's Riley.

The rabbit punches.

It's Riley and he's going to rabbit-punch me again. It's Riley and
I put it under the mattress at Owen's.

Riley was trying to frisk him. He had Nick shoved against the
wall.

"No, you don't!"

Riley had Nick's head against the bricks of the flophouse with
his forearm hard against Nick's neck.

Three notches in his belt and he's going to give it to me. No, he
ain't!

"You dirty killer!"

Riley let go, stood big-shouldered a little distance from Nick.
"Go ahead, Romano, run, so I can plug you. All I want is an excuse to shoot you."

Nick twisted his lips in a grin; he tossed his head and laughed.
Riley grabbed him and tried again to frisk him. Nick swung at
him. Riley swung.

Nick was too drunk to do anything.

■■■

Nick woke up in jail. He searched his pockets for a cigarette
butt. I'm in it. That bastard is going to bum-rap hell out of me.
He's going to frame me. Good thing Owen made me leave the gun.

He stayed caged all day. In the evening the turnkey came down.
"Somebody's going to bail you." He was taken upstairs where
Grant stood paying fifty dollars and signing a paper. Nick had to
sign too and did so, looking at Grant sheepishly. "Be in court at
nine tomorrow morning," the sergeant said.

■■■

The red Packard was out in front of the joint and Nick sighed
a little easier. He walked into the inner office. Ace was sitting with
a silver decanter in front of him. "Hi, Ace," Nick said and sat
down.

Ace looked out of baggy eyes and smiled with his tight lips.
"Howdy. Have a drink."

Nick shook his head no. "I'm on the spot, Ace."

Ace looked across the table at him.

"Riley picked me up last night and I know he's going to railroad
me. I go to court in the morning."

Ace laughed. The dry, amused laugh rolled out of his mouth in
an ugly whisper. Nick glanced up quickly. "Can you fix it?"

Ace leaned back in the chair and, looking straight at Nick,
stopped laughing. The thin lips came down hard over the big
teeth. "I can fix just about anything in this town." He filled a glass

and pushed it across the table at Nick. This time Nick drank. Ace again laughed through slightly parted lips. "Take it easy," he said. "You ain't got a thing to worry about. Not a thing ... not a thing. In the morning just tell Wagner I sent you around to see him. He's the chief bailiff over there. You may have to salt his hand a little."

Nick, easy again, lit a cigarette and stood up. "I'm going to blow. Thanks a lot."

Ace waved his thanks away. "I stand pat in this town. Any time you want any favors done just drop around."

...

Nick's case was called. He and Grant stood in front of His Honor. His Honor, by some method or mark or instruction on the sheet of paper handed up to him by his chief bailiff, knew how to dispose of the case. Without bothering to look up at the defendant before the bar, he said, "Case dismissed."

In the courtroom the bums and drunks stood before the bench in their long line while the other cases were all disposed of. Then His Honor narrowed his eyes upon them, counted them, heard their cases, dismissed two-thirds of them to West Madison Street, twenty-five-cent bottles of rotgut, taverns, mission meals and doorway beds again. Among the dismissals were sentences—few-worded, without sympathy, without interest, without looking up: "Rockpile—rockpile—ten days on the rockpile—five days—rockpile."

....

Grant and Nick ate in a nearby restaurant. When they had finished Nick asked Grant, "What are you thinking—that I'm no good?"

Grant stuck his hand in his hair and rubbed. "I was thinking about a lot of things." He was quiet for a long time.

"I'm no good, huh?" Nick asked again.

"No, I wouldn't say that."

"Go on, say it if you think it."

Grant looked at him. "I'm afraid you're piling up a lot of trouble for yourself."

"Maybe so. What the hell do I care."

"I'll be around to do what I can," Grant said.

"You'd be a sucker to help me then."

"Maybe so." Grant shrugged. He got up. "So long, pizon." He didn't smile.

48

Spring had come to West Madison Street again. Nick sniffed it in—gasoline fumes, beer bars, flophouses—but the scent of spring was there too. Oozy mud on the cobblestones at street crossings, the fresh scent of promised rain coming down from around the shoulders of the grimy buildings, even the sun bringing a warm, pleasant smell of—something.

The sidewalk was crowded with hoboes wandering aimlessly down the street, leaning against storefronts, sitting on the curbstone. Every freight that snorted across the wide prairies brought its shipment of bums and distributed them along the pavements. The hoboes sitting along the curbs on newspapers looked like weeds that had mushroomed up through the sidewalks overnight. They were like sparrows. As alike and as colorless. And some of them stood on the curb searching the gutters for snipes.

In front of the Pastime a young hobo sat with the others. He might have jumped off a freight the night before or just been released from jail. There was a sultry defiance in his eyes, grim hatred in the straight-line tightness of his mouth. He sat on the curbstone transferring snipe tobacco into a cigarette paper.

Nick glanced over his shoulder at him.

His hair falling loosely over his forehead reminded Nick of Rocky.

Restless, Nick wandered down the street.

•••

Ang walked along Michigan Boulevard, window-shopping in front of all the exclusive women's apparel shops, looking with large eyes beyond the clear glass panes. Ahead of her she saw a girl in a tan swagger jacket. There was something familiar about the girl. Ang walked fast—to get closer—to make sure.

Yes, it was Emma Schultz.

"Emma! Emma!"

The girl turned half around, her hand still holding the wind-blown hair; then all the way around, her mouth breaking into a delighted smile. "Ang! Oh Ang! How are you?"

They stood holding each other's hands, looking shiny-eyed at each other, talking both at the same time.

"Gosh, Emma! It's so good to see you! I haven't seen you in such a long time! I can't remember how long ago it was."

"Not since just after we worked at the packer's together!"

"I was afraid we'd never see each other again. How are you? What are you doing now?"

"I'm at Spiegel's—typing. What are you doing, Ang?"

"I'm still at the stockyards packing bacon." Ang made a dour face; then laughing, squeezing Emma's hands, she asked, "Will you come over to my house tomorrow?"

Emma looked at her gratefully. "I'd be glad to, Ang." She looked away. "There was a reason why I never asked you to come over to see me. My mother—" She took her lip between her teeth. She hung her head. "It's—it's—I can't have anybody over. None of my friends."

Under the elevated structure on Wabash Avenue they waited for the southbound streetcar. "I want you to meet my brother Julian. You'll like him. He's swell!" Ang said.

Ang went home and cleaned the house from top to bottom. At supper she said, "Julian, there's someone I want you to meet tomorrow. You'll be home, won't you?" She looked hopefully into her brother's eyes.

...

There were plenty of streetcars but he walked downtown to Ace's place. He went past the bar and to the roulette wheel in the back where well-dressed men and women, some in evening clothes, stood playing. For two months now he had been working there, watching people, acting boyish and innocent, but not letting any of the men get away with big winnings. Tipping off the jackrollers Ace had in the downstairs tavern; or sometimes doing the job himself.

Nick stayed only five minutes. He walked along Michigan Boulevard. Grant Park spread its green aprons out to the lake front. From the avenues the people came. Women in colored dresses and big hats, men with shirts open at the throat, children licking ice cream cones. On the benches, encircling the bandstand like embracing arms, the music lovers listened.

Nick sat far from the bandstand, but not too far away to hear. The music welled up in him, big, bursting, flowing away, trembling inside of him, breaking, leaving him empty and quivering, waiting for its return. It hurt as it throbbed through him again. . . . He cracked his knuckles and looked at the white arch of his hands in the night. He smoked one cigarette after another.

I wonder what happened to Rocky. . . . I ain't seen Rosemary since that day . . . I shouldn't have tried nothing with her.

He rolled over on his stomach and lay on the grass, digging holes with the toes of his shoes. He lay with his mouth on one wrist, open, his teeth pressed gently against his wrist.

The music trembled in the night, broke over him like waves. Gee....

Something in him reached up and out; and something in him pressed him against the grass like a stone.

When he awoke he was chilled. He sat up, shivering. He was all alone in the park. The moon had grown pale in the sky. The sky was taking on light tones, showing the form of the buildings on Michigan Avenue. Nick rubbed his face with his hands. At the water fountain he got a drink and walked out of the park, squint- ing against the headlights of automobiles that straggled along the black flatness of boulevard.

He went up the stairs at home and into the dining room. Glancing toward the parlor he saw Ang's legs in sheer silk stockings drawn up gracefully against the sofa base, calves touching, heels against the rug. He grinned and wound up underhand with the ball.

Watch her jump! He grinned again.

He let go swiftly and ran into the parlor after the ball as if it were a football, a fumble, and he was going to fall on it and recover for his side.

He stopped dead in his tracks, his mouth dropping open in surprise, black hair over his forehead, eyes stretched wide. A keen- looking girl stood by the sofa, her mouth open too, looking down at her feet, startled. Her hair fell from around her temples in long loose curls. She looked up at Nick. The startled open circle of mouth spread in a slow smile. Little amused wrinkles gathered on her forehead. And her hazel eyes, looking at him, glistened liquidly with amusement and teasing. "You scared me!" she said. The *scared* was drawn out, musical, husky. Her voice laughed at him and at herself. She put her chin up and shook her head, tossing her hair into place. The hair went back away from her cheeks like water flowing. She smiled again.

She's got dimples.

The itchiness and embarrassment cooled down in Nick a little. He looked at her with amazement.

Light in the room touched the back of her head, flamed her hair, came across one shoulder, touched the tip of her nose, left the hol- lows under her high cheekbones in deepness. "Are you Julian?" she asked, clasping her hands behind her back, looking up at him frankly and still laughing. Her teeth were even and white.

She's got a nice voice. Like—a little girl's. Happy sounding.

Nick stood near her. "I—I—" He made a vague, circular motion with his hand. "—I gotta go in there."

Feeling like a fool, not looking at her any more, he walked into the kitchen. All the womenfolk were in there fussing around with food. Aunt Rosa saw him first. "Hello, handsome!" she half shouted. "You must have known Ang was having company. Or did you smell the pots?" Ang walked into the pantry. Nick hurried in after her. "Hey! Who's she?"

"She's my friend," Ang said coldly.

"Yeah—but who is she?"

"Just a friend of mine."

"Come on, give me a knockdown to her!" He had his arm half around her, coaxing.

"After a while," Ang said.

Nick went into the bathroom and combed carefully. He looked at himself critically in the mirror. Then without Ang or any of them noticing he walked into the parlor.

As soon as he got there he was tied in knots again. He sat down in a far corner and picked up the funnies. He held them on his knees and his head bent down over them. His neck began to burn.

He looked up, slowly. She was looking at him, smiling, only one dimple creased a little. He dropped his eyes quickly.

She's got a turned-up nose.

She was looking at him frankly, friendly, her lips parted in a faint smile as if she were going to say something.

"Do you want to listen to the radio?" he asked suddenly.

It was the first thing he could think of. It wasn't his voice. It sounded funny in the room. And loud!

I hope I ain't blushing.

He almost jumped up. With his shoulders and face turned from her he pushed one of the buttons on Julian's new and shiny radio. A popular orchestra sent music into the room:

> I'll be loving you, always,
> With a love that's true, always....
> Not for just an hour, not for just a day,
> Not for just a year,
> But always.

Embarrassed by the music, Nick turned back toward her. "I'm Nick," he said. His voice was husky.

"I'm Emma," she said. "Ang and I are old friends."

...

Then it was time to eat. They sat at the table: Julian and Emma side by side where Ang had placed them, Ang and Nick across from them, Ma at the head of the table and Aunt Rosa at the foot. Ma made the sign of the cross and said the blessing.

Nick looked at Julian in his shiny but pressed serge suit.

[212]

He's got a tie on.

Aunt Rosa was telling a joke and they were all laughing. Nick looked at Emma quickly. She was laughing with one cheek down on her shoulder and her eyes crinkled.

They were all talking and eating in a friendly Sunday group about the table. All but Nick. He ate silently, not finding anything to say, looking across at Emma, then averting his eyes.

She's real pretty.

She ate slowly, handling her fork gracefully. She and Julian sometimes turned toward each other, talking.

I wish I could act like him.

Suddenly she was looking straight at him, smiling with her eyes. "Why are you so quiet, Nicky?"

Nicky!—The way she said it. He felt the muscles in his throat tighten and burn. He swallowed. "I don't know. I guess I just ain't got nothing to say." He felt the flush rise all over his face. He tightened his teeth together, mad at himself. Under the table he pushed the sole of one shoe against the toe of the other, hard, angrily.

Don't be like that, damn it! Don't act like a kid.

Over dessert Emma looked around at all of them, at Ma Romano in particular. "I've enjoyed myself more here today than I can remember in a long time," she said. And when the chairs were scraped out away from the table, Emma started gathering up dirty dishes.

"I wish you'd just sit and talk to me while I do them," Ang said, but Emma said, "Aw, come on, now!" and was already filling the dishpan with water.

Nick walked into the kitchen. He saw her wrists in the dish water. That's what he noticed first. Next to her stood Ang, drying. Julian sat on a stool by the window with his feet on the round of the stool and his long legs up near his chin. Emma had her head turned toward him and they were talking, excitedly, about some book.

Nick stood in the doorway. "I'm going to go," he said, loudly, even a little gruffly; he meant it only for her. Her head turned away from Julian to him. "I'm—" he swallowed, "I'm glad I met you."

She took her hands out of the dish water and dried them. She held out her hand. "I'm glad I met you, Nicky." Her hand was small in his. "I hope I see you again soon."

"Yeah," he said. He turned and walked out of the room. He could feel his neck burn.

49

Nick slept at home every night for a week. During the day he took long, restless walks, then strolled into the Pastime or a bookie's, then out. I never thought Ang knew any swell broads like that. Evenings he loafed over at Stash's house until about nine o'clock when Stash, always tired now, went to bed. Then he loitered around the empty Maxwell Street stands, smoking, or sat in the dark on a bench at the Homer Playground. She wouldn't look at me twice. He'd sometimes stay on the bench until midnight, lying on it full length, staring at the sky.

He dragged himself around. When Sunday again came he stood by home playing solitaire to kill time. Then she walked in. "Hello, Nicky!"

Her voice had a glad ring in it. He looked at her with large and serious eyes. "Hello, Emma." And right away he thought of somewhere he had to go. When she and Ang were talking, he sneaked out.

On West Madison when Nellie or Marcella or the others were hanging around him he'd tell them, "Go on, beat it, bitch!"

Owen couldn't find him.

Then the night came when he walked in and she was still there. He couldn't go back out, so he sat down in the dining room where he could glance in at her without being noticed. He got the paper and sat there smoking. Julian was at Hull-House yet. Emma got ready to go. Ang said, "I'll walk to the car with you." But Aunt Rosa shouted, "Walk her to the carline, Nick."

"Would you mind, Nicky?" Emma asked.

Nick went down the steps with her. He walked along the sidewalk next to her, on the wrong side. He glanced shyly at her. He didn't know what to say to a decent girl.

They walked silently. He listened to the clicking of her heels.

"Isn't it a nice night?" she said.

"Un-huh."

There was a moon. There were boys and girls walking together along the sidewalk. She carried her hat in her hand and looked nice that way with her hair blowing just a little. Her legs swung in stride with his. It was night and it was good to be walking beside her in the night. There was a breeze against his cheeks. It made him feel good and like crying at the same time.

"Are you always so quiet, Nicky?" she asked.

"I guess I haven't got anything to say."

They walked on. Without words. *I'm no good and it's night and we're walking along together ... I'm no good and I like you I'm not like the rest of my family I rob and drink and do bad things ... she's pretty with her hair blowing ... lots of stars ... I'm no good and I like you.*

They were just at the corner of Halsted. "Oh! there comes my car!" She looked at it, then at him. "I'll see you Sunday, Nicky!" She ran to the corner. He stood watching as she grabbed the platform bar and hopped on the car.

She likes me a little.

Next Sunday evening she said, "Nicky will walk me to the car, won't you?"

"Sure. Come on," he said gruffly.

They were even quieter than the other time. She said, "I like your family."

"Yeah, they're all right, I guess," he said.

That was all they said. When they were almost to the corner of 12th and Peoria, Nick slowed up. "Look—did Ang ever tell you about me?"

Emma shook her head. They walked the two blocks to Halsted in silence. When they got there, when the car came and she stepped down off the curb to catch it, he said, "Ask her some time."

■ ■ ■

He found them kissing in the darkened hallway and said to her, "Break the clinch. I want to talk to you."

Their arms fell away from each other embarrassedly. They stood white-faced in the dark. Abe said, "I'm going to go, Ang."

Nick said, "No. Stay. I just want to talk to her for a second." He shoved a pack of cigarettes at Abe.

Nick went out the door slowly and Ang followed him, leaving Abe in the hallway. Nick walked far over to the side of the porch and leaned against the crumbly, paint-blistered facing of the house. Ang stood near him, her shoulders slumped against the house, too. Her mouth was open a little and her eyes looked at him. He lit a cigarette so that Ang could take a puff. She took a puff, her eyes on his face all the time. Together they smoked it halfway down. Nick put one foot up against the house in back of him, and with his shoulders and head stooped looked down at the red dot on the end of the cigarette. "Ang," he said. He didn't say anything more for a while. Then, "Tell her about me, will you?"

Ang didn't say anything. They finished the cigarette together. He tossed the butt. Over the banister it was a red arch. Then nothing.

He put his foot down from against the house. "That's all I wanted," he said. He moved away, on down the steps.

••••

Tonight when she got ready to go he almost jumped to get his coat and walk with her.

Tonight she talked to him more. And she was more friendly. One of the things she said was, "What are you interested in, Nicky?"

"Nothing, I guess."

When they were almost at the car stop, he suddenly asked, "Did Ang say anything to you about me?"

"Maybe," Emma said.

The car came. He hopped on. "I'm going with," he said.

They found a seat at the back of the car.

"Have you ever been to the Art Institute?"

"No," Nick said, "but I knew a girl once who had a book with paintings in it."

. . . and she had gold hair and my hand hopped down the piano keys until it touched her's and I did it and it was wrong and she cried . . . and she was pretty but not as pretty as Emma and I spoiled everything and I won't again. . . .

"Would you like to go to the Institute sometime?"

"Huh? Oh, I don't know."

The Halsted Street car bumped south through the night. He couldn't sit there and say nothing. He asked her, "What's your job like?" She told him all about the work she did at Spiegel's.

Nick didn't listen. He watched her. How she used her mouth and her hands, how she leaned against the seat with her slim body inside the loose dress. He asked her questions. She did all the talking.

What color are her eyes? They're pretty eyes whatever color they are. The wind blows pieces of hair at them.

"Tell me about you, Nicky? What were you like when you were little? What do you like to do?"

He shrugged his shoulders and spread his arm expressively. "Me— I—I always been like I am. I don't do nothing but hang around pool halls." He wanted to stop but he went on. "I just bum around. I don't even work."

Her hand was on his shoulder, sympathetically. "Oh, you're not that bad, Nicky! I think you're nice."

They got off. She led the way to her house. He followed her. "Now tell me about you," he said.

"Oh, I"——she laughed throatily—"I was always a tomboy. I used to run around in boy's pants with Leo. That's my cousin—you'd like Leo! We used to go swimming in the woods and climbing trees —oh, everything!" She stopped still on the sidewalk. Her eyes shone in the light from a street lamp. Her lips spread, smiling. "Why, Nicky! You know what?—I even had a tree house in my back yard!"

There are many doors to the city. There are hopes and dreams and a path from the door of home. And beyond the door is the neighborhood, the city, the world.

In each room there are whispers and hopes and dreams. There are many paths.

50

She had been all legs and arms; all hair and eyes. Her mother was German and old-fashioned. Her father died when she was eight. They were always poor. When that bad day came when her father went away never to come back she stood with her small face, all hair and eyes, sticking over the tabletop, asking, "But Mommy, where is Papa going? Why can't he ever come back? I don't want Papa to go away." Mommy didn't answer. Mommy put her face down on the table and cried and cried.

Then the next thing that happened was people in the house; flowers, but not like they were in the woods; a man with a camera taking a picture of Papa. Right after the man took the picture and something went—bang!—burning her eyes and making them go shut, Mommy lifted her up and walked her over to where Papa was. Mommy had to lift her up high. And Kate and Maggie were there, standing on the floor, tugging at Mommy's shirt, waiting their turn, asking, "Is Papa up there?" Mommy, tears running down her cheeks and her voice high and quivery, said, "Tell Papa goodbye." Mommy leaned her down, way down, "Kiss Papa *auf Wiedersehen*." Papa had his hands folded over his chest and his eyes weren't open, blue and smiling like Papa's eyes were. "Kiss Papa *auf Wiedersehen*." Her dark hair fell around Papa's face. Her lips went down, next to Papa's. Papa's lips were cold—*cold!* She screamed and wiggled, fought her way out of Mommy's arms, ran to the outdoors.

She always went to the woods. When anything was too big for her she went to the woods. When she was sad or didn't understand. When Mommy scolded. It was best, alone, hiding herself. Even when she was happy, when gladness was so good, so big inside of her that she couldn't control it, she had to be there with lots and lots of sunshine and trees; not in the dark little house they lived in, not in the cramped little back yard where it was all bald and lumpy dirt. But today she didn't quite get to the woods. She stumbled. She fell

[219]

in high grass and weeds. She lay crumpled there. She sobbed. Something was wrong in their house. She didn't know what.

When she had cried herself out, when dry sobs and catches of her breath shook her and went away, she lay with her face buried in grass. Mommy was a funny Mommy. Mommy cried a lot. She was always so big; she was really skinny but she always stuck out—here. She couldn't bend over. Papa would say, "What! *Again, Katrina?*" Then they would tell her about the little brother she was going to have. But the new baby never came. Mommy was sweet and good but she cried all the time. Her hair was dark brown. It hung down her back and was thick and wavy and she brushed it a lot. Sometimes when she combed it in the dark you could see sparks fly. Mommy was always tired and lying down when she didn't have to work. Papa had a leather chair, all cracked. He would sit in it smoking with a big happy laugh coming out and now Papa had gone away and would never come back. In the crushed-down grass she shook with sobs again.

The drying weeds made noise. Mommy was calling her but she didn't answer. The weeds made louder, closer noise. Mommy had found her. Mommy sat down. *"Was ist los, Kind?"* It wasn't Mommy's voice.

They were there, wordless, mute, clutching at each other like animals; hanging on to each other in their anguish.

At last Mommy said, "Come, Emma—we go back to the house." It wasn't Mommy's voice. It was a frightened, tender, quivery voice from far off somewhere.

■■■

Things were different in the house now. Mommy had to work a lot more. Always Mommy was working now. Every morning she piled dirty clothes on the floor, clothes that didn't belong to them. In the evenings Emma had to help her mother. When she wasn't taking care of Maggie and Kate she was doing dishes; when she wasn't doing dishes she had to help sprinkle the clothes, dampening them and wrapping them into balls, putting them in a clean peach basket with newspaper in the bottom of it.

Mommy was a stern and tired Mommy. Mommy was a mean Mommy. She almost never kissed Emma or petted her. Sometimes she did with the little kids, but clumsily. And just about never were there any stories Mommy would tell her. Sometimes Emma would beg, "Please, Mommy, tell me a story!" Tonight when Emma asked, Mommy shook her head yes and went on finishing up the last three pieces of ironing. Emma waited, serious-eyed. When Mommy was finished, she set the irons up on their ends on the window sill and said, "Come on, Emma."

She put two cups on the table and poured the black coffee into them. Emma watching, felt her eyes sting with sudden water. It was good to have a nice Mommy take care of you. If only Papa would come back.

Mommy sawed two thick slices of bread from the loaf. On one she smeared some butter and put it in front of Emma. She sat down on a chair at the table. Then she said, "The story." Emma went right over. She dragged the chair with its back sawed off over to Mommy's chair—as close as she could get it. She put her hand in Mommy's hand. Mommy slowly took her hand away and picked up the cup of coffee. Emma put her head down on Mommy's lap. Mommy raised her up. "Now! Now, Emma!" She patted Emma's shoulder twice. Her fingers were stiff and unfamiliar. "The story," she said, and began to tell it, *"Der schlimmen Fritz—"*

"Uncle Fritz, Mommy?"

"No, not Uncle Fritz—*lief vom Hause fort, und der Wolf frass ihn."*

That was all; the story was over. Emma didn't notice the shortness; her eyes were big, round, sad with the story. "Mommy—" she said. "Don't you know any happy stories?"

Mommy started again: *"Es war einmal ein braver Fritz...."*

Emma listened in German and English: "There was once a good little Fritz...."

"His name was Fritzie, too, Mommy?"

"Yes, this was good Fritz."

"Was he Uncle Fritz?"

"No...*und er sagte: Ich gehe nicht in der Wald, und er ging auch richtig nicht in der Wald. Da kam plötzlich kein Wolf und frass den braven Fritz nicht."* Mommy turned Emma around and started braiding her hair. "Mommy, I'm glad little Fritz didn't get eaten by the wolf." And later: "It wasn't Uncle Fritz when he was little, Mommy?"

She liked her Uncle Fritz. He came over a lot. Uncle Fritz had hair the color of dried weeds and a long and heavy mustache, ragged along his lip, curled way up over his cheeks at each end.

Uncle Fritz had a fiddle. He always brought it along when he came over to their house. On it he played the most wonderful songs Emma had ever heard; songs that made her go shivery all the way up her back. Before he played he'd go out and get beer in a can like a lunch pail. The beer, on top, was like the soap suds in Mommy's washtub, and, like it, ran over the top and down the side of the sweating and beaded pail. He and Mommy and sometimes the grocer, without his white apron on, would sit around in the kitchen drinking beer. Uncle Fritz or Mommy would stick the poker in the fire and get it so red that it was beginning to turn white and sparked a little when they drew it out of the fire. Then they'd stick the poker in the beer—fffzzzzz!—they called it mulling the beer. Always they did this before drinking it. "Like in the old country, Katrina," Uncle Fritz said. Then Uncle Fritz, getting the ragged end of his mustache wet in the mug and having suds white and funny-looking on it, would put the fiddle under his chin and start playing. But, before he started playing, before the beer, he always took Emma by the hand and said, "Come on, Emmie, we'll go get some candy." It wasn't the candy she went for; it was the stories. Today they went over the sidewalk and through sunlight and a chilly wind, Uncle Fritz acting the story out. "... and Jack climbed the beanstalk—like this, Emmie—" Standing just off the sidewalk he showed her, his hands moving up and down, his eyes looking up to the top of the beanstalk. "... And then he was on top...." Uncle Fritz wiped his forehead with the back of his hand and went "Whew!" showing how tired Jack was.

Coming back with the licorice stick in her mouth, the cinnamon balls and chocolate soldiers in the little paper sack and Jack's adventures with the awful giant and the goose that laid the golden eggs, Emma said, "Tell me again, Uncle Fritz"—her eyes shining—"about Hansel and Gretel!"

The time to look out, Mommy said, was when Uncle Fritz came over with the fiddle under one arm and a big jug of wine hooked in a finger at the end of the other arm. This happened on Friday nights.

"*Guten Abend, Katrina.*"

"*Wie geht's, Fritz?*"

"*Gut! Jawohl, gut!*"

He'd set the jug of wine on the floor in the kitchen near his foot and put the fiddle under his chin and his handlebar mustache would scrape the strings as he played. The fiddle bow went back and forth, dancing. The wine went down in the bottle, inch by inch. Mommy nodded with her elbow on the table and her hand up to the side of her face. Uncle Fritz sang songs. German songs. His feet patted the bare wooden boards of the kitchen floor. His mustache scraped the strings. Mommy chased Emma off to bed. Upstairs—in bed with Maggie and Kate—Emma could hear the songs and the fiddle bow pulling the tunes out of the fiddle for ... a ... long time....

In the morning when she came down and Mommy was poking in the stove, trying to make it burn, Uncle Fritz would still be there in the chair by the window. But he would be asleep with the fiddle bow still clutched in his hand and his arm stretched out across the floor with the empty jug kicked over near his feet.

Mommy said, with her lips drawn tight, "He acts disgraceful! Disgraceful! I don't know what's going to happen to poor Leo."

Poor Leo was the boy who came along with Uncle Fritz. "*Dein Vetter,* Leo. Kiss *dein Vetter,* Leo," Mommy said. Leo pulled her hair and made faces at her. She stuck out her tongue and kicked his shins.

So, at their house it was Mommy and Kate and Maggie and her, with sometimes Uncle Fritz and Leo. But home meant work to her. Her little sisters were lots of trouble. Kate was a year younger'n her. Maggie was only six and bawled a lot. She had to mind them. She had to undress them and put them to bed. Kate was skinny like she didn't get enough milk; that's what Mommy said anyway. Maggie always had a snotty nose. To keep her sisters quiet Emma made paper dolls for them and told them the stories Uncle Fritz had told her.

■■■

She could hop good on one leg. Jump-rope was too sissified. That was for little-bitty girls. She was *ten* now. She could walk a fence balancing herself with her hands out to either side and her hair blowing out away from her head. She wished she had a pair of roller skates but Mommy was too poor. Uncle Fritz heard her wish for the skates and one day—"Here, Emmie—you want skates? Your Uncle Fritz got skates for you." He kissed her, tickling her with his mustache. "You love your Uncle Fritz?" he asked. Her small arms fastened about him tightly, her face lifted to the tickling mustache was answer.

In no time she could skate good. Across the sidewalk and in the midde of the street she went

> gruuuu-eeeer!
> gruuuu-eeeer!
> chuuu! chuuu!

And if she fell, if she skinned a knee, bringing blood, she just said, "Oh, heck!" climbed to her feet, pulled the torn skin off and skated on. She could even skate backwards

> gruuueer-chuuu!
> gruuueer-chuuu!

She played with boys. She shot marbles with them, even winning lots of times. She went home with sand ground into her knees. Mommy took the scrub brush to her knees and threatened her about the marbles but nothing Mommy could say or do could stop her from playing.

The outdoors was for climbing trees. For playing and having fun. There wasn't any other purpose for the outdoors. That's where God was too. When she wanted something real bad, like for Mommy not to have to work so hard and be unhappy all the time, she would pray like mad.

Mommy needed praying for. Mommy was always complaining

[223]

about being poor; her face looked as if she cried a lot when she was alone. Mommy worried about things. Not Emma. There were so many wonderful things in the world. The world was opening out to her like a flower bud unloosening its petals one after another to the wind that came down over the country when spring was there. There was the woods; nothing was as good as the woods. Running near them was a ditch along the railroad tracks where the mud squoozed through your toes when you played there barefooted. On the little siding, sunflowers and weeds grew, grasshoppers jumping away from them when you came near. You caught the grasshoppers and made them spit tobacco. You caught them, bunches of them, till you had a whole Mason jar full. Dragon flies were pretty. In the woods there were trees over your head and flowers running wild all around your feet. The wide, flat water spot full of reeds but with enough room for swimming. Leo taught her how. She and Leo always went there. Leo liked the woods too. That was what was nice about Leo. They pulled off all their clothes. With their bodies naked, with their belly buttons like the belly buttons on gingerbread men they went into the water. With the sun on your body, with the warm wind tickling your back and your small, narrow hips it was nice. But you didn't tell Mommy about it.

■■■

Mom was always trying to get ahold of her and curl her hair like the *nice little girls* who went to school with their hair in sausages all around their heads. Mom said she'd make a lady out of her or kill her. Mom would set her on a chair, twist her hair around the rung off a chair that she saved for the purpose, and brush it in one sausage after another, pulling the chair rung out carefully and going on to the next piece of hair until her hair looked just like Marion's and Dorothy's and Frieda's and all the other girls at school. Darn! She didn't want it curled. She liked it loose, flying over her shoulders and down her back. Soon as she got out of sight of the house she tore the red ribbon out and pulled all the curls loose. When she got home she told Mom, "I lost the ribbon."

What she liked next to the woods was reading. Her favorite books were boys' books. She and Leo read all the Ralph Henry Barbour books about boys' schools and academies where they won football and baseball games on the last page. She finished them as fast as she could get them from the library: *The Crimson Sweater, Rivals for the Team, The Spirit of the School* and all the rest of the sport story books until there weren't any more on the shelf in the children's side of the library that she hadn't read. Always, when she read them, Leo was the hero or she was the hero.

Their house, out near the end of Chicago where the city and the

[224]

country got lost in each other, looked like a barn except that it had a porch on each end and more windows. The green paint had turned almost black. Boards hung loose from the side of the house. There was no bottom under it, only boards all around with a little door on rusted hinges at the back. It was fun sometimes going under the house with your head bent, smelling the funny damp smell, feeling your way past the round crumbly-splintery posts in the dark, getting spider webs in your eyes and on your lips, sometimes stopping dead in your tracks and shivering all over when you heard a rat running to its hiding place, making believe you were in Africa. That's what she and Leo did under there. Houses had skeletons like people; you could see the rafters that held the house together when Leo lit a match.

Inside the house there were only three rooms and the little attic bedroom with the blue calcimine peeling off where she and Maggie and Kate slept on a pipestem bed painted gold. There were steps leading up there but you had to push your head against the trap door cut in the ceiling to go in. The one little window up there looked out over the tree house and the black twisted limbs of the cottonwood tree to the big factory building and the street lamps cutting crazy across town. She and Leo built the tree house. It was way up, as high as they could get it, in a big fork of the tree. The tree house was just for her and Leo. Nobody else could go up there. Nobody else had better get caught up there!

Besides washing clothes, Mom worked in a restaurant some of the time, washing dishes and cooking for people over on 63rd and Blackstone. Mom would bring home some leftovers and warm them, shoving sticks of wood in the stove and, when she had it, throwing some kerosene on the wood. Whoooof! the stove would go. Then the flames would go racing up the chimney, making noise; the wood, under the lids, would begin crackling. She and Maggie and Kate sat, waiting, stretching their noses to smell what was in the pot, watching every move Mom made, feeling their insides hurting for the food.

And now it was getting cold. Inside their house the coldness smacked through worse than outdoors. Outdoors you were running and playing. In the house to keep warm you had to go to bed or sit with your chair almost on top of the stove.

Cold mornings Mom would send her out with the bucket to pick up lumps of coal off the railroad siding where they had fallen, shaken off the rattling coal cars that had gone by. In the real cold weather sometimes Mom would come too. When Mom leaned over picking up a lump, when Mom walked back toward the house, a shawl drawn over her head, her body stiff, her legs taking clumsy steps from the weight of the coal in the bucket, Emma would feel a sting of water in her eyes and her heart getting big, swollen with tears inside of her.

...

Emma sat on the bottom step of the front porch feeling the spring come. She raised her turned-up pinch of nose and her small nostrils to it and sniffed. She could smell the rain and the warmness and the still concealed odor of the buds on the lilac bushes, that were small, green, pinched like her nose. A small wind played in the hair at her temples, lifting it, letting it fall back over her ears. She looked at the blueness of the sky. She felt sad and happy all at once. Soon the woods would be ready for her. She saw the tree branches with wind shaking the new leaves, beyond them the sky, blue, with clouds white and frothy, moving quickly across the sky. Emma's eyes filled with tears. Her light brown eyes reflected, in their glistening wetness, the blueness of the sky, the white clouds racing across, the tree limbs browner than the color of her eyes.

Emma half hung her head, still with the feeling of happiness and sadness mixed in her. Where she looked she saw a puddle of rainwater on the sidewalk at her feet. In it she saw her own reflection. She had to laugh. The small, pinched nose, turned up a little at the end. The wild, free-curling hair. Her brownish tapering face. Shadowed hollows under her broad cheekbones. Her eyes, not blue, not gray, not brown. No color. The smile slowly faded away. Her forehead puckered. She leaned over closer to the pool, staring at herself in the rainwater. Gosh! she was plain-looking. She'd never be beautiful she guessed. Sometimes now she thought about what she was going to look like when she grew up because she was so darn plain-looking—and it worried her.

That same day Leo came over. She was on the step fooling around with some of those play glasses that were just rims. Leo said, "For gosh sakes', take them off! They make you look uglier than you are." He flipped his leg over the banister and started cutting his initials in it. Emma sat stiffly, in the same position she had been in when he said it. She stared down at her shoelaces, afraid to look in the puddle of water again. She was hurt. Sad.

"Let's go for a walk," Leo said.

"No—I—I—have to do some work in the house."

She got up and went into the house. She pushed her head against the trap door and went into the attic bedroom. She lay across the pipestem bed. Ugly Emma! Ugly Emma! It was almost a tune. Outside she could hear Leo whistling. Maybe he wouldn't marry her. A few tears splashed her cheeks, just a few. She got up, sneaked out of the house and went to the woods.

The woods were ugly yet. They were ugly like her. She tramped around, putting her feet down heavily and making twigs crack under them. She picked up a rock and threw it. It hit a tree. She picked up more rocks and, using a tree for a target, began firing away. Pretty soon it was fun. She didn't care if she was ugly. Well—she didn't much. But there was nothing you could do about it.

•••

She began, that spring, romanticizing about herself. She made up her own stories about what was going to happen to her. She was always going to be a tragic figure. She was the Lily Maid of Astolat. She imagined the whole thing out. She even went into the woods once and covered herself over with leaves and lilacs she had brought, and lay still, dead under them, smelling their sweetness.

51

One day Mom said, "We're going to move. I found a house closer to work. It costs only eight dollars a month."

Emma's heart beat hard. She didn't want to move. She thought of the little attic bedroom and the tree house. She didn't want to leave them. She thought of the woods not very far away. She felt like crying.

The new house was on a second floor above streetcar tracks. Mom worked three days every week in the restaurant on 63rd Street and, after she became better known in the neighborhood, started taking in washing. Saying, *"Mein Gott!* but three girls can eat!" Mom started doing tags for a big company in the neighborhood.

Nights they'd all sit in the little second floor kitchen with a wash-tub in the middle of the floor. Mom and Emma and Kate did tags every night after supper, putting the strings or wires through the holes, trying the strings, twisting the wires—tag after tag. Every thousand tags was seven cents earned. "Another loaf of bread . . . another pound of sugar," Mom would say when she counted out a thousand and put them back into a box.

Emma liked doing tags and seeing Mom with her head soft in the dimly lit room. Emptying boxes went fast. Even Maggie tried to help but she only twisted the wires all up. Soon as a tag was finished they'd throw it in the washtub. On some nights they'd fill the tub. It was nice there in the kitchen with the kerosene lamp burning and streetcars clanging past, and the feeling of being together. A family. Feeling sad and happy at the same time—feeling *close*.

At nine o'clock sharp Mom would say, "Bedtime!" Emma and her sisters had better get right up and go to bed then.

Emma always looked back from the bedroom door and said, "Good night, Mom." She wanted, terribly, to rush back, throw her arms around her mother and kiss her. But Mom would say, through unemotional lips, *"Gute Nacht,"* and Emma, hanging her head went farther into the darkness of the bedroom. If only once she could have Mom put her arms around her and hold her tight and kiss her. If only she had someone who loved her, *really* loved her. If only she had someone who really belonged to her. Again she'd look at her mother. Mom would have her head bent toward the kerosene lamp, her eyes straining, her fingers carefully putting the wire through the hole.

On her bed in the dark room with her eyes closed Emma could see Mom like that, old, ugly, unhappy. Almost every night Emma cried herself to sleep.

Friday nights Mom would just barely drag in from work and flop down in a chair. Fridays she never did tags. That was the night Uncle Fritz came over, lugging his violin. Uncle Fritz would say from the door, sticking his handlebar mustache beyond the panel, "How about some beer, Katrina? *Jawohl?*"

"Ja," Mom would say, all worn out and without spirit. Every Friday night it was the same. Mom would fill the glasses, saying the same thing, "I'm German and I show it—I like my beer."

One evening Mom didn't come home from work alone. A man was with her. He was a handsome, smiling man and he had candy bars for them. Mom sat looking at him, her face stern and proud. He said to them, "Will you be real good kids while I take your mother to the show?" They promised. Mom went to get ready. Emma never saw her mother fix up so carefully before. From a window she watched Mom and the handsome, smiling man. They looked so nice walking on the sidewalk together, only, "He's almost ten years younger than I am and I feel funny about that," Mom said when she got home. But he took her to the show once every week after that. They called him Uncle Jim.

•••

Emma graduated from grammar school. The night of graduation when her mother said "Bedtime!" Emma undressed but didn't get into bed. When she got up enough courage she sneaked out into the kitchen. "Mom—" She moved a little more into the room. "Mom—" Mrs. Schultz looked up, squinting at her with her head on the end of a long neck. "Yes, Emma?"

Emma came quickly then and sat at the table. She hung her head, trying to put words together into a sentence. "I—I don't want to go to high school. I want to get a job. I want to help you." She spilled it out, quickly.

Mrs. Schultz's hands shook so much she had to lay the tag down. "You're only fourteen, Emma."

"I can do something. I can tell them I'm older. You've been working for us a long time. I want to help you—" She stopped, near tears.

"I had hoped—" Mom said. Mom brushed her lap with her hand. She said, "Maybe Kate can go to high school—maybe Maggie. One of my girls—"

Emma didn't get a job right away. She stayed home doing housework, the tags and washing clothes Mom took in. Then, when she was fifteen, she got a job in a hand laundry ironing shirts all day. Every night she was all tired out and felt like going to bed right after supper; but on Saturdays, handing Mom her pay check, she felt proud. Maggie and Kate were growing like weeds. Kate said she wasn't going to go to high school either; she was going to get a job like Emma. Maggie didn't want to be called Maggie any more. "My name is Margaret," she'd say. "Don't call me Maggie! Call me by my name!"

●●●

Mom called all of them into the room. Mom's face was serious but Mom was happy and excited about something and looked from one of them to the other. "Girls, how would you like to have a father?" she asked. Her voice shook.

"Who? Who? Uncle Jim?" Margaret yelled, jumping up and down. Mom nodded her head yes real fast and they all laughed and cried; even Mom. And Emma and Margaret and Kate all hugged her at once.

Papa Jim was swell. They all liked him. He took their side when Mom bawled them out. He went walking with them and to the park. Even to the show on Sundays. Mom said, "You love children, don't you, Jim? I think you married me for the girls." The first thing he said to them when he came to live at their house was, "I never want to be mean to you or fuss at you." And he kept his word. He was like a pal to them. Evenings when they wanted to go for a walk or sit on the steps and Mom didn't want them to, he'd say, "Aw, let the kids have some fun, Katherine." Then he'd open the door and say, "If I let you out will you be good kids and come right in when I whistle?" They'd promise and, throwing him grateful glances, sneak out. They had electric lights now and Mom didn't have to work.

...

Emma, almost sixteen now, felt most disappointed about the way life was. It was not like the story books she read. When she walked along the street and young fellows turned around looking at her and whistling at her, she always pretended that she didn't know what they meant.

Every Saturday she took a long, wandering walk. It was something she did to think. It would be so much better if she had someone to talk to. But there was no one. Maid of Astolat, she'd think, Lily Maid of Astolat. She'd smile. But she'd feel like crying.

Mostly she'd lie under the trees and think things she couldn't figure out. All the jumbled thoughts and ideas tangled together in her mind. And sometimes she had bad thoughts. *Stript off the case and read the naked shield: now guessed a hidden meaning....* She'd feel ashamed and guilty. She knew it was wrong. Even the bad dreams she had. Dreams sometimes with Leo in them, sometimes boys she had seen at work; even boys she had never seen, the foreman, even her stepfather once. She blushed. She hid her face in her hands and lay on her stomach. *That someone put this diamond in her hand, and that it was too slippery to be held....*

She rubbed the rough laces of her shoe against her leg, scratching it. Lily Maid. Lily Maid. She tossed her heavy hair off her cheek and with her palms one on top of the other on the ground put her chin on them. She stared at the tree trunks that let sunlight through. There... must be... something more to life.... *Now made a pretty history to herself....* She had read books, nice love stories about pretty girls and handsome heroes and she knew that somewhere was the wonderful boy she would marry. She thought about the children they were going to have and what they'd name them. She blushed, deeply, to the roots of her long hair. Again she hid her face against the ground. Lily Maid. Lily Maid. Everything between a boy and girl should be pure. It should be as it was in books and in the movies.

Sitting under a tree she wrapped her brown arms around her knees and put her forehead on knees. She longed for something, someone who was all hers.

The wind lifted her hair, spilled it over her arms and her knees.

52

Emma came out into the kitchen for breakfast before going to work. "Good morning, Mom," Emma said. There was no answer. Her mother sat at the table with one hand stretched out in front of her and she stared straight ahead, not seeing anything. "Mom! What's the matter?" There was no answer. Emma put her hand on her mother's shoulder and shook her a little. "Mom!"

"Don't touch me!" The eyes stared straight ahead, unblinking.

"Oh, Mom!"

"Go away!" harsh, bitter.

Then Emma saw her mother's hand stretched across the table with a crumpled sheet of paper in it. Emma unloosened her fingers, took the paper—

DEAR KATHERINE—
Blanche and I are going away together. I'm sorry that I'm doing this to you. You are a fine and a good woman. I guess it isn't goodness that I want. There's no use to try to make excuses or alibis for this thing I'm doing to you. I'm sorry. Please don't hate me too much. Please try to understand.
Kiss the girls for me. Ask them not to hate me.

JIM.

"Oh, Mom!" Emma tried to put her arms around her mother. "Don't touch me! Don't touch me!"

All that morning and afternoon Mom sat at the table in the same position, stiff and unmoving. Emma sat across the room from her, sharing her hurt and her sorrow. Then at last Mrs. Schultz broke. Her face crumpled, her body sagged over onto the table and let her arms take her face and head into their circle. She sobbed brokenly. As an old woman sobs.

Emma ran to her mother's side, threw her arms around her. Emma cried with her; their voices blended, whimpering. Mrs. Schultz opened her arms and took Emma into them, blindly clutch-

[231]

ing at her daughter. For the first time since her father had died Mom was hugging her. For this, too, Emma cried. For all the empty, loveless years between, for her mother's sorrow, for the loss even in memory of the good, kind stepfather she had had. Emma slipped onto her knees beside her mother with her arms thrown about her and her head in her lap. She cried until there were no more tears in her, until little dry catches of breath were in her throat. Above her, her mother was sobbing and saying, over and over, "Next week would have been our anniversary"— And later—"There's nothing left for me. I have nothing—nothing—nothing—"

The tears and sobs came out of Emma again. She tightened her arms around her mother. "You have me, Mom. I'll never leave you, Mom."

■■■

For a whole week Mom sat by the window nights crying and rocking and eating very little. Then, two Saturdays after Papa Jim left, Uncle Fritz came with the fiddle and the gallon of wine. That night Mom drank glass for glass with Uncle Fritz.

In her room Emma lay on the bed, dressed, hearing the glasses fill time after time. At last she fell asleep. When she awoke, chilled, and put her feet down on the floor she could see light beyond the partly opened bedroom door but heard no sound from the kitchen. She stood up and went on tiptoe to the kitchen.

Uncle Fritz was gone. The back door stood open. Mom lay sprawled across the table, sleeping, one side of her face on the bare table, her arms in their drab black crepe sleeves spread out. Emma leaned her mother up against the chair back and, with trembling hands on her shoulders, tried to awaken her. Mom's arms dangled, her head lay on her shoulder. Emma, frightened, washed Mom's face with a wet cloth. At last she awakened her. Mom was sick. Emma got the basin. She washed her mother's face again. Mom was weak and flabby in Emma's arms. Mom came back to half-consciousness. She pulled Emma's hair, cursed her. Emma had never heard her mother curse before. Emma bent her head, trying to crowd out the short and ugly words. When she lifted her head Mom had passed out again. Emma called Kate. Together they got Mom to her bedroom, undressed her and put her to bed.

■■■

Mom recoiled with bitterness. She said no man will ever fool any daughter of mine. She preached at all of them, in German and in English, telling them that she didn't want them to go with boys. Every Friday and Saturday night she sat with Uncle Fritz drinking beer or wine in the kitchen and telling him that no man would ever get the better of her daughters. She told Emma and her sisters that they were growing up, that the fellows they'd meet would want only

[232]

one thing and that if any fellows came around her house to spoil any of her girls she'd kill them.

When Mom talked like that Emma had to get out of the room. She'd go to the bedroom and clamp her hands over her ears as hard as she could get them. She'd end by crying.

Mom began to drink more and more. Then it got so she just didn't care and drank all the time. She even drank whiskey. It was awful coming home from work and finding her half-drunk every night. Later in the night when it wasn't long until daylight Mom's hair would come loose from its ball on top and hang down around her face wildly. Her motions, reaching for the glass, holding herself up off the table with her arms, her gestures when she talked were awkward, jerky in their loss of control. Behind the loose-hanging hair were her eyes. Her eyelids were always slits when she was like that: behind the slits her eyes were glassy. She laughed easily and she cried easily. When Uncle Fritz or the girls weren't there to talk to, she talked to herself.

One Saturday afternoon one of the fellows Emma worked with asked her to go to the show with him. When she got home Mom, half-drunk, stood facing her with her hands on her hips and demanding to know where she had been. "I went to the show with a boy from work."

Mrs. Schultz marched to the bedroom door. "You Emma! Come here!" Emma went. Mrs. Schultz pulled all Emma's clothes off, half tearing them. "I'm going to see what you've been up to," she said, squint-eyed, her hard-knuckled fingers tight on Emma's clothes, rough against Emma's flesh. Emma submitted, humbly but tearfully.

When her mother left her standing nude in the bare light in the middle of the bedroom, Emma pulled the light cord and slipped between the covers. Lay in a ball as tightly curled as she could get herself with the covers over her head. Shamed.

There was soft noise at the door. There was motion in the room. "Emma." It was an old-woman voice. Broken. "Emmike." Mom sat on the side of the bed.

Emma sat up. She felt in the dark for her mother. Her hand touched the sagged and withered cheek, felt the stream of wetness there. Mrs. Schultz leaned against Emma. She cried on Emma's shoulder. The hot tears ran down Emma's bare shoulder, cooling themselves. Mrs. Schultz's rough hair pressed heavily against Emma's breast and neck with her forehead behind the hair. "Your old Ma means well, Emma. You're all I've got. The others don't love me like you do. Don't leave me, Emma, don't leave me."

•••

Kate had finished school now and was working at the laundry with Emma. It wasn't long until Margaret was in the eighth grade.

Margaret, cute, blond, was already interested in boys. Emma was laid off at the laundry and was out of work for a while. Then she got a job in a book bindery, piece work.

On Sundays when Mom was home in bed, sick from too much drink, when Kate and Margaret were at the show, Emma sat in the park. It was comfortable there with the sun on her back and neck. It was nice to relax on a bench or on the lawn. And, also, unexplainable thoughts, *bad* thoughts kept cropping up in her mind. There would be boys, playing ball or walking through the park. She'd sit, watching them, secretly observing their legs in their tight-fitting pants, their loins. She'd look when they stooped to stop a grounder or leaped to catch a fly. Then she'd pull her eyes away, blushing and shamed. And if a good-looking boy passed close to her she'd look up at him, hoping he'd be looking at her; but whether he was or not she would immediately drop her eyes guiltily. When he had passed, was safely down a way, she watched him out of the corners of her eyes, tracing his back, his hips, his legs with her eyes. She was his girl and she was with him. They were alone somewhere. They were sitting on the grass and he was forcing her back, making her kiss him. She didn't want to, but his lips were strong against hers. His lips were sweet on hers. She could feel his leg over hers while he forced her to kiss him. Again she blushed and thought how wicked she was. At home she had, hidden under the mattress, a wrinkled *Physical Culture* magazine with pictures of muscular men posing with nothing on but a pair of white tights that were just a string in back over their buttocks. In the pages of the magazine, too, was a photograph of a nude male statue without the fig leaf that she had torn from a book on art in the public library. At work she sometimes listened to what the girls said to one another about boys and to the dirty jokes they told one another in the toilet. But that only disgusted her.

They had no life in the house. They were always squabbling, or trying to quiet Mom, or hiding Mom's bottle. It was wake up at six o'clock, go to work, come home, a couple of hours just sitting trying to get up enough energy to start fixing her clothes for work the next day and then bed. Every day was the same as the day before. Only some days were worse. On those days Mom was drunk bad and had to be put to bed.

All the money she and Kate together made went into paying the rent, light and gas and keeping enough food in the house. Emma didn't even have enough left over to buy herself a dress or a pair of shoes. And Mom always wormed enough out of her or Kate for a bottle no matter how hard they swore they weren't going to give her money for drinks. The mirror showed Emma a round face without make-up. Tired-looking eyes when she pushed her head close

[234]

and looked at herself in the mirror evenings after work. A kind of funny nose; not big, straight, with just a little turn-up on the end. A mouth, red without lipstick. Olive skin. Margaret, in the freshman year at high school, told her she'd never catch a beau unless she fixed herself up.

There came a day when Emma looked at herself in the mirror, really looked. She looked at her no-color eyes; hazel, she guessed, was the word they had for them. She looked at her hair, curly by itself. I'm not ugly, she thought, maybe even a little bit nice-looking. I want something out of life. I'll get old without ever having anything.

She began to think about what she wanted. I don't like working in factories and places like that. I want to amount to something and have nice clothes and fix up the house for Mom and maybe get Mom straightened out. I'd like to take shorthand and typing.

She saved up five dollars out of her spending money, going without new stockings and a pair of shoes, and enrolled in night school at Englewood High School. She even took a class in English Literature.

In her literature class there was a boy who was Miss Mitchell's smartest student. His name was Vernon. He gave Miss Mitchell some of his poems and she read them to the class, saying they were advanced for his age. He seemed to like Emma and struck up an acquaintanceship with her, often walking her to the streetcar after class, talking all the time about writing. Then once he gave her a poem he had written to her. Emma took it home. She read it over and over. Every few days she read it.

That was how she and Vernon started going out together.

She had her excuse for Saturdays and Sundays. She told Mom she was going to the show, going to the woods, going over to a girl friend's house.

She loved to sit next to Vernon in the park, looking at him, admiring him, when he wasn't looking. He stirred some undefined longing in her. When he wrote other poems for her she would hear a small tune in her head say: Lily Maid! Lily Maid!

They sat on a bench in Jackson Park. Vernon was sad, shaken in his confidence, defeated today. He told her about some poems he had sent to *Harper's* and *Poetry Magazine* and about the rejection slips. "I don't suppose I'll ever amount to anything," he said. He had his head in his hands like a hurt little boy. Emma couldn't resist the desire to help him out of the dumps; she put her arm around him, leaned over and kissed him on the cheek. As soon as she had done it she pulled away, blushing. Vernon raised up, took both her hands in his and said in a shaking voice, "Does that mean you love me?"

She didn't know what love was but she shook her head yes.

After a while, when it was getting dark, Vernon said, "Let's go sit where it's soft," and led her toward some bushes where they sat with their shoulders touching. "I've got to go in a little while," she said. "My mother will be after me."

"Not yet," Vernon said, putting his hand on top of hers. "Tell her anything."

Emma looked up at the moon. Her eyes filled with tears, happily. She knew Vernon loved her. She could imagine him at home in bed thinking about her as she thought about him every night before she went to sleep, thinking of him as a famous writer with everybody talking about how wonderful he wrote and he and her sitting in the park together while he wrote. Only when he lay in bed he made up poems to her. She was his inspiration. And they could both look out the window and see the same moon.

He had his arm around her waist. His hand, his long fingers, were above her waist line, close under her arm. She was overcome with feeling. His hand was up a little higher. She wanted to push it down. But she couldn't! Not wanting . . . to be touched. Craving a physical touch of some kind. But not this. Admiration. Fondness. His hand was higher, sneaking across the swell of her chest. She wanted to push it down. But she couldn't. He had his hand on her *breast!* She tried to straighten herself up to a full sitting position but couldn't. She was overcome with warmth and discomfort and fear. He was pressing her back. The small branches of the bush caught in her hair and scratched her cheek. "Ow!" she said. He was working his lips against hers, hard. Her lips were all slobbery wet. She twisted her head away. Hot, soundless tears ran down her cheeks. "No! No! No! Don't—oh, please!—please!" His voice and his breath were hot on her twisted-away cheek. He was biting her neck; and all the time his fingers tore at her clothes—pulling them up. She twisted her face back towards his. She bit him. She could feel her strong teeth sinking in, tasted the blood, salty, that ran from his cheek into her mouth. She heard his startled cry. She got her arms from under him in that moment. He fell back from her, cursing. Emma leaped to her feet. She ran wildly through the park toward the driveway.

She didn't want to have anything to do with boys any more. She was through with them.

...

Emma stood at the sewing machine Mrs. Schwartz had assigned her, not knowing how to turn on the power. The head girl came over with a pile of cloth and heaped it on the small wooden horse on Emma's right side. "Here, you do the front making," she said. Emma sat, her head hidden by the pile of blue, yellow, red cloth.

[236]

trying to find the power switch. The girl at the machine next to her's noticed her confusion and embarrassment. She left her sewing and came over, whispering, "Here, I'll show you." Emma looked up gratefully.

That night, going out of the factory, Emma walked fast to catch up with the girl who had been nice to her. She caught her and shyly touched her on the arm. The girl turned around. "Oh—hello!" she said with friendliness.

"I—thanks for—showing me how to turn on the power," Emma said.

"Oh, that's all right," said the girl. "Going my way? I'm going as far as 12th Street."

Emma nodded. "I can catch my car there," she told the girl.

"How much did you make?" the girl asked.

"Ninety-three cents," Emma said, sticking her head down.

"Aw," the girl said, touching Emma's arm, "don't let it bother you. You'll do better tomorrow." She laughed, showing even white teeth and dimples. "I made less than that when I started."

Each night afterwards they walked to 12th Street together; and at noon they ate lunch together. They exchanged names:

"My name is Emma Schultz."

"My name is Ang Romano."

The dress factory was the best place she had worked yet. The girls were all nice. They were mostly Italian and Jewish girls, some Mexicans, a couple of colored girls. Sometimes on Saturdays after work Ang and Emma would have a soda together or buy something on Maxwell Street just to be together. Neither of them seemed in a hurry to go home. Once Ang said, "Some day you'll have to come over to my house—" and stopped, remembering the dingy little rear apartment rooms all running on a slant toward one end of the house. And Emma said, "Oh, yes, Ang! And you'll have to come over, too!" It was out; she blushed, remembering her mother drunk most of the time, staggering around the house, yelling and making her go down for a bottle. So both of them thought how nice it would be to invite the other over to her house without doing it.

Jerry was the boy who lived down the street. Margaret had introduced him to Emma and told her that he was a nice kid. Every time Jerry saw her on the street he asked her to go to the show, to the park, for a walk with him. She always said no. He kept pestering her; kept saying, "Aw, please!" and "I'm going to kidnap you! You'll see!" One evening, coming home from work he looked so sad and was so insistent that she promised to go to the show with him.

They went to the show. They came back home. They hadn't

talked more than a few words. Now he said, "Can I take you again next week?" His forehead was pinched in a little pleading frown. She nodded her head yes and ran up the steps.

He took her again the next Saturday and the next and the next. She tried to break it off. She told him, "Your name starts with J just like his did."

"What are you talking about?" he asked, puzzling his eyebrows. She shook her head, nothing. But she remembered Papa Jim.

"Say! What's this all about?"

"Nothing." He mussed her hair and twisted her arm behind her back and made her say uncle.

▪▪▪

Jerry was quiet and earnest. He had a serious voice. He told her that he had finished the two-year course at Wilson Junior College and was working in a dental laboratory downtown. That was just marking time. He was going to be an aviator. He was waiting for an appointment to the flying school at San Antonio. When they walked now, through the park or far from home, they held hands. One day when she had been going with him for five months, he said as they stood in the downstairs hallway at her house, "Emma, I'm going to ask you a favor. Will you—kiss me good night?" She didn't answer. She put her forehead down on the shoulder of his coat. He lifted her face with his finger under her chin. He kissed her gently on the lips. There was no little furrow of frowns on his forehead.

▪▪▪

Emma got out of the bathtub and rubbed her firm body dry with a towel; her skin came up rosy, glowing. She slipped into her bathrobe and went to the bedroom. The bedroom was dark. A column of moonlight, chromium in the blackness of the room, came through the window, slantwise to the floor. Emma went to the window, and stood there in the dark. She reached to the top of the window with her arms and stretched, slowly, thoroughly, rising on her toes. Her bathrobe fell open. The moonlight seemed to pass into her body. She looked out at the dark lacy images of the trees, saw the moon round and good and white in the low sky. Lily Maid. Lily Maid.

Emma pulled down the shade and switched on the light. She stood in front of the mirror and let the bathrobe fall to a broken circle of cloth about her bare feet. She stood examining her body, turning, looking at her firm and shapely legs; her lithe back; her flat stomach; her breasts, solid, brown-nippled; her smooth and rounded shoulders with her coil of brown hair over one of them. She stood looking, admiring. Then she blushed; saw her blush in the mirror and pulled on her bathrobe.

[238]

She sat down before the mirror. She looked into her hazel eyes, at her hair, tossing it back by shaking her head so that she could see her face better. She saw its roundness, the slight lift of cheekbones, the firmness but smoothness of the flesh. She took Kate's powder puff and lightly brushed it over her face, dusting only a little powder onto her skin. She took the flesh-colored lipstick and put only a light cream of red over her already red lips. She touched rouge to her cheekbones. Then she looked into the mirror.

Her eyes rounded with astonishment.

"I'm beautiful! I'm actually beautiful!"

The knowledge astonished her and frightened her.

53

Three blocks before the streetcar got to her corner Emma squeezed and pushed along the aisle between the seats to the front of the car. Slowly she worked her way through the people who were crowded shoulder to shoulder, hip to hip. She edged past the men crowded behind the motorman and got off at her corner.

Not wanting to go home she walked along the sidewalk thinking about the dingy little rooms and Mom probably drunk; and if not, nagging about everything. She brushed damp hair off her cheeks and, straightening her clothes that the crowd on the streetcar had mussed, walked as slowly as possible, already thinking of what would be said at home, how, once she stepped inside the door she would be a different person, how everything happy and free in her would be sapped out. Why did things have to be the way they were ... Mom ... Kate, drab and unattractive. Flat-chested in her dark, straight-cut dresses. Hardworking, plain-looking, too skinny. Kate with the seams in her stockings never straight. Kate looking like a younger, but not much younger Mom.... Margaret who had changed her name again; who wanted to be called Margie now and had a large scrolled pin in imitation gold that came from the dime store and that she wore over her breast. Margie who was boy-crazy and clothes-crazy. Margie who had quit school but wouldn't find a job; sleeping every day until noon and going to the movies two and three times a week. Emma saying, "Well, it's a poor family that can't afford one lady," and sometimes even slipping her fifty cents or a dollar to get a new blouse or some stockings. Margie *was* cute, though. It was too bad she couldn't meet a nice fellow and some day marry him. It would be better if Margie didn't stay at home. Emma was ashamed of the thought. She put it away. She thought of herself. What was she getting out of life? What did she have? Jerry and Ang—

She didn't know what she would do without Ang. She was a real friend. It was wonderful to have someone to talk to, confide in. The good times they had together too, just walking, or eating lunch, or at the show with a box of candy on their knees. And Jerry—

He was everything to her. She could never love anyone as much. He wasn't like the other fellows. He wasn't after her for just one thing. He really loved her. What was even more he *liked* her. She lived for Saturday nights with him.

They'd stop at the Owl Inn way out on the highway at the south end of the city. A neon owl blinked in the dark. Inside was a rustic restaurant and tavern. In the booth Jerry would put a long leg up on the booth and, grinning across at her, ask, "What are you going to have, fellow?" Maybe that was the way Papa Jim had been with Mom. Maybe that was why Mom was like she was now. It hurt about Mom. Emma's no-color eyes filled up. Poor Mom. She knew how Mom felt. That was why she would never leave her....
Jerry bought her anything she wanted—frogs' legs, chicken or charcoal-broiled steaks. Jerry would have beer. Sometimes he'd take a bottle to the car with him and drink it slowly, setting it on the running board and lifting it through the window when he wanted a swallow. A couple of times she had tasted it, because his lips had been on the bottle, but it was bitter and she didn't like it. Jerry was shy without the beer. With the beer down in the bottle, though, he talked about what he wanted in life.

They would sit in the car late, until three or four o'clock in the morning. She'd stay, not caring what Mom said, holding on to every minute. They'd look at each other, eyes a little watery. And they'd laugh, both covering up their real feelings. In his arms everything was whole, nothing mattered. They had drifted to the point where gently, tenderly his fingers circled her breasts, where their lips met, clung, pressed, clung. Nothing more. He loved her, she loved him; they could wait.

■■■

When she got home next evening, Emma dragged into the kitchen and tossed her purse on the ice box. Kate was straightening up. Margie was at the round table with jars, nail polish and mascara spread out before her. She had a towel twisted around her neck.

Staring into a mirror, she was tweezing her eyebrows into narrow arched lines. Although the sun was still in the room, she had the electric light turned on.

"Where's Mom?" Emma asked.

"At Uncle Fritz's," Kate said tonelessly.

"You know what that means," Margie said, looking sideways. Kate, passing the table with dirty clothes piled in her arms, pulled off the light. Emma went into the bathroom and washed her face. When she came back the light was on again and Margie was curling her eyelashes with a little rubber and metal contraption.

Margie carefully put orange polish on her sharp-filed nails. Emma twisted off her shoes and sat with a cup of coffee untouched in front of her. Margie said, "What's to eat, Kate?" Kate stared angrily at the back of her sister's too-blond and sausage-curled head. But she got up without saying anything and broke eggs into a frying pan. "I'll do it, Kate," Emma said, taking the frying pan from her sister; and to Margie, "Where are you going, Marge?"

"I'm going out with Chaaahr-lee." Her voice caressed his name.

"Who's Charlie?"

"He's a prize fighter." Margie cocked her head up at an angle.

"Huh!" Kate said through her nose.

"I met him at White City."

Emma scrambled the eggs, put them on a plate in front of Margie.

Kate began sweeping the kitchen. She swept around Margie, raising as much dust as she could. Margie finally got up, said angrily, 'Oh! you—!" and sailed out of the room with her head high.

When she came back into the room she was all dressed up and stood in the middle of the floor curling her hair off her neck with both hands, standing so that her sisters couldn't fail to see her.

You could see her. She wore a red dress. There was a green pillbox hat perched on the top of her head with curls showing all around it. You could hear her. A link-chain bracelet clicked on her wrist. A necklace dangled around her neck. You could smell her. Cheap perfume floated away from her.

"Me and Chaaahr-lee's going to the Trianon," she said loudly. Her high heels, cheap patent leather, clicked noisily against the bare boards of the kitchen floor. "Goodbye!"

"Huh!" Kate said through her nose.

"Have a good time," Emma said.

You could hear a giggle going out the door with the perfume; you could hear high heels running down the back steps.

Emma sat at the table alone. She saw Mom's dark hat and two empty beer bottles set on the oven. She saw Kate's wrinkled cloth coat thrown over the chairback. On the table were Margie's nail polish, tweezers, kurl-lash and disk of rouge where she had left them. Emma put her arms on the table and put her forehead down on them. She lifted her head up again immediately. She set up the ironing board, put an iron on the stove and took Kate's coat from the back of the chair.

••••

Margie came home one day, bringing a fellow into the house with her. Mrs. Schultz stood up, greeting them with her hands on her hips and her eyes screwed up in a scowl.

"Ma this is Chaaahr-lee—Chaaahr-lee this is Ma—"

Mrs. Schultz breathed hard through her nose. Her raw liquor breath came angrily from her nostrils. Margie looked scared. But she went on, looking first at Kate and Emma, then back at her mother. "Me and Chaaahr-lee was married today."

Mrs. Schultz nodded her head toward the bedroom. "Come here, young lady!" Mrs. Schultz marched into the bedroom. Margie's face was red and scared; her legs moved forward, carrying her like a little girl to the room where her mother waited.

In the kitchen they waited. They could hear the sharp cracks of the slaps—smack!—smack!—smack!

Margie stumbled out of the bedroom. Mrs. Schultz walked into the hall behind her. Tears ran down Margie's powder-caked face. "You old drunken slob!" she yelled, her voice weepy. "Come on, Charlie, let's get out of here!"

••••

Only two months later Kate told Emma, whispering to her in the bedroom while their mother mumbled in the kitchen and moved the bottle about on top of the table, "I'm going to get married, Emma. It's Mr. Olsen at the laundry."

"Oh no!—No, Kate! He's almost twice your age."

"He's only thirty-five, Emma. I don't love him but he thinks he wants me and he'll be good to me." Her voice quivered, grew steady, quivered. "I don't ask for love. But I want something. Even if it's just security and—and—not this. Come and see us, Emma. I'll help on the bills, Emma—"

She wept noiselessly on Emma's shoulder.

••••

The vision of growing old there with her mother grew black in Emma's mind. The thought that she and Jerry would probably never be able to marry grew gray, dull and heavy in her mind. The knowledge that she couldn't run out on Mom reflected itself in her automatic and uninterested packing of bacon and chipped beef at the yards where she and Ang were working now, her listless attendance at night school, her tiredness in the evenings and desire to crawl in bed and at least sleep, the almost frantic way she clung in Jerry's arms on Saturday nights. Finally she was laid off.

[242]

She didn't tell her mother that she wasn't working. Every morning she got up early, bought the paper, had a cup of coffee on 69th Street and sat looking at the ads. At last she got a job as a clerk and order filler. It wasn't any better than the stockyards; harder even. But it paid more and a job was a job. She'd stay. If she stayed long enough she'd get a couple of raises and maybe even work up to a typist. She and Jerry could maybe get married.

Emma stayed on the job even though she began to hate it. She at first saw Ang every week. They would meet at the show or at a soda fountain. Then later they saw each other only about once a month, and still later not at all any more. On Sundays Kate came over, and, making Mr. Olson wait downstairs in the car, stayed with Mom for about half an hour and left a couple of dollars, sometimes five. Margie never came. She'd just send an envelope with a dollar, maybe two, between white sheets of writing paper about once a month. But she invited Emma and Kate over to her little kitchenette apartment way over on the east side, two rooms. When they arrived she always put on the dog, serving them burned or half-cooked chicken, lettuce salad, cake from Hillman's. She had about three dresses; but she had a cheap fur chubby and that made everything all right.

She asked a lot of questions about Mom but none of their pleading would make her come to see her mother. The last time they had been over to Margie's she told them, giggling and drawing her dress tight about her stomach, "Me and Chaaahr-lee are going to have a baby. Isn't that wonderful!"

...

The days dragged for Emma. Coming home wearily from night school at almost ten-thirty she set her sociology book on the table, opened it and sat there with coffee and one of the rolls that was for her breakfast. Her eyes burned; her whole body felt numb. She put water on the stove and when it was hot washed out a blouse, her undies and the one pair of good stockings she owned that had to be washed every night and hung over the back of a kitchen chair until they wore out and she bought another pair. She put the roll of pink undies on a bath towel in the bottom of a chair and hauled the ironing board out of the pantry. When it was hot she ironed her clothes dry. She made sandwiches for tomorrow's lunch, filled the coffee pot and put it on the stove ready for a match in the morning. She turned off the kitchen light. In the bedroom she wound the alarm clock, looked at the dial with the small hand already on twelve and the large, ticking hand moving quickly toward it. Emma looked to see that the alarm hand was at six and pulled up the alarm button. Then she undressed and crawled between the sheets. Yesterday, today, tomorrow. All the same.

[243]

She awoke with a face swollen with sleep, tossed water against her eyes, got into her clothes, washed, combed, and powdered. She swallowed the hard crust of a roll and the scalding coffee with one eye on the clock, grabbed her hat, coat, purse, ran down the steps toward the carline.

Emma's days tolled themselves out, all alike.

···

Again it was Saturday and they rode down the highway, within the distance the neon owl blinking at them, winking at them.

She and Jerry stayed at the roadhouse only long enough to eat. Then he said, "Let's go for a ride." He grinned at her and she felt warm inside about him.

A policeman was leaning up against the front wall of the Owl Inn as Emma and Jerry stepped outside. He was drunk. His cap had slipped askew over his eyes and the wall was his only support as his knees sagged. He looked about ready to fall asleep. Emma and Jerry went past him and toward the car.

Down the road two men and a woman stood between the parked cars arguing in the half-light. All three were shouting and cursing at the same time. The woman's long hair hung in her eyes and she raised her voice higher and higher in drunken hysteria. One of the men held a wine bottle in his hand. His other arm was around the woman. The other man was trying to pull the woman away from him. "Police!" the woman screamed. "Police!"

The cop came staggering down the cinder lane toward them. "Go on, shut up! Break it up, goddamn it," he yelled as he came. He was fumbling for his pistol.

Jerry moved Emma past them toward the car. Just then the man lifted the wine bottle to hit the woman. Jerry started to grab his wrist. The policeman, seesawing his gun back and forth, staggered toward the group. The woman screamed.

Then abruptly, without warning, the pistol exploded. Exploded again. Jerry fell on his knees against the side of a car. There were screams in the roadhouse. The heads of a couple of men poked out. The cop turned menacingly toward them.

Emma didn't remember much until the ambulance came. She got in beside the stretcher on which lay the strangely still and skinny Jerry. Emma held his hand. It didn't move.

The ambulance rolled down the highway, down its black length into the night. The siren rose—higher—*higher*—*HIGHER*. Night went past on both sides. RAILROAD X RAILROAD X. Bumping over tracks. In the distance behind them the neon owl grew smaller, blinking on-off, on-off at the red taillight of the ambulance.

Jerry died on the way to the hospital.

[244]

Who is bigger than the city, or the city's streets, or the city's will? Who is stronger than this twisted sky of trolley wires and this roof of smoke? Who is taller than these chimneys belching soot or these watertowers? And who can breathe against the sky with these smokestacks?

Who is broader than the city's walls? Who is muscled like these buildings? Who is tougher than these rusted fire-escapes? Who can stay awake in the leer of the neon night? Who can sleep and dream beneath these roofs?

Who is willed beyond the people of his breath and bread?

Who can best the neighborhood?

54

The next time Emma came over to the Romanos' Nick took her home on the streetcar again. They said almost nothing to each other and got off at her stop, walking close together on the sidewalk, their hands sometimes accidentally brushing.

They were alongside of her house. She looked up and saw the light behind the kitchen shade. "Mom is still up," she said.

"I'll go up with you and meet your mother," he said.

In the dark her eyes looked scared. "All right," she said.

Mrs. Schultz was fussing around the kitchen, straightening things up. Her face was old, reddish, shiny from cold water. Her hair was in a ball on top of her head with one large piece of hair that had come loose and hung raggedly down her back. "Oh," she said when she saw the young man with Emma. Her eyes took on fear.

"Mom—this is—Nick."

"How do you do," Emma's mother said with curt politeness and snapped her head in a short nod.

Nick bowed his head slowly without speaking and his eyes stayed on her face seriously.

Mrs. Schultz came to the round kitchen table, sat down, motioned for him to sit down. Mrs. Schultz looked across the circle of oilcloth at Nick. "It's warm. It's so warm," she said. She put her skinny arms up on the table and laced her fingers together, held at arm's length on the tabletop. Her eyes went, fearfully, from Nick's face to Emma's and back to Nick's. She clenched and unclenched her fingers stiffly. "It's awful warm tonight," she said again. Her eyes watched their faces. They seemed to say: they took my other daughters away from me. Have you come to take all I've got left? She clenched her fingers. "All day I've been dying for a little beer," she said; and she laughed a small, toneless laugh. Her thin and aging lips folded away the faint and helpless smile that had for a moment flickered on them. "I'm German, you know," she said. And all the time she watched them, trying to read what had happened so far, what was going to happen, how far it had gone, if Emma was going to leave her. Her fingers loosened. *"Himmel,* so hot in here! What I wouldn't give for a glass of beer." Her fingers clenched, loosened, clenched.

Nick pushed his chair back from the table slowly. "I'll get you some beer—Mom," he said gravely.

When he came back, climbing the steps two at a time with the cold and sweaty half gallon bottle of beer, knocking, then going right in, Emma sat where he had left her, white-faced. She looked up at him gravely. She was all hair and eyes.

"Sit down! Sit down!" Mrs. Schultz told Nick, half-friendly.

Nick drank only one glass. Then he said, "I don't want any more, I bought it for you." Mrs. Schultz said, "Well, I wanted only a glass—only a glass." She filled her glass a second time. Her hand fastened tightly on the glass, then loosened. Her eyes never left his face or Emma's face. She talked to Nick. She told him about her good first husband, about how hard she, a poor widowed woman, and an old woman too, had to work to raise three little girls. She told him about how ungrateful her other two daughters had been, how they had run out on her and got married. She filled a third glass. Looking at it she pressed the palms of her hands hard against the sticky oilcloth. "Emma's all I've got left," she said. "Emma says she'll never leave her old mother."

Then laughing, trying to be friendly, she told him stories about what a bad little girl Emma had been, how she had climbed trees and ripped her stockings. The third glass was empty. She half reached for the bottle. She looked at Emma embarrassedly. Pushing the bottle away from her she told Nick, "I'll save the rest for to-morrow."

Nick said he had to go. Mrs. Schultz said, "I'm glad you came," but she watched him with suspicious eyes as he moved toward the door. Emma went to the door with him. As they left the room Mrs. Schultz pulled the beer bottle over and filled her glass.

Emma and Nick stood on the porch together. "Thank you for bringing me home, Nicky." He took her hand. She smiled a trifle with serious-sad eyes. He felt her hand slip out from his. "I think you're very nice," she told him.

Nick stood on the sidewalk below the house. He looked up. He brought a clenched fist up to his mouth and bit hard into the flesh on the back of his hand. Emma, I love you! I love you!

He walked away from the house with his fists clenched at his side.

"You got to leave her alone. Don't screw up her life for her," he whispered to himself.

•••

She's a good kid. I ain't going to mess things up.

Nick walked out of the sun and heat and stink of West Madison Street and into the Pastime. He looked for someone to shoot pool with and saw Sunshine. He nodded his head toward the table in a let's-play gesture.

Boy, she's nice!

Nick scowled with his face close to the table's green pad.... Christ! why should I let any dame get under my skin ... and his eyes even with the table rail ... forget about her. Don't think about it. ...He missed the shot.... "Goddamn it!" he muttered angrily.

While Sunshine was razzing him for missing the shot and was moving in for his turn, Nick ... *Live fast* ... chalked his cue stick ...*die young*... and glanced over its tip at Sunshine shooting ... *and have a good-looking corpse....*

He stayed away from her. He didn't see her for two weeks.

●●●

Emma walked into the poolroom looking for Nick. She stood just inside the door where Nellie and others had waited. She was fresh-looking, well-dressed, a pride in her eyes; and she was frightened and flushed with embarrassment. She touched the arm of a middle-aged tramp who loafed near the door. "Would you please ask that young man to come here a minute?" she asked, pointing at Nick.

"Sure thing, sister!" All the eyes near the front of the poolroom slid from her face down to her legs, clung there.

Emma stepped outside and waited.

The hobo went over and told Nick, nodding his head toward the door. Nick looked up, saw Emma on the other side of the dirty, fly-specked plate glass with her back turned to it. Red-faced, he leaned the pool stick against the table and went out immediately.

He stood looking at her with shock and surprise. "You shouldn't have come down here," he told her.

"Walk to the streetcar with me, will you, Nicky?" she said, turning her face away from him. He walked back toward Halsted with her. He swallowed and choked and swallowed. He couldn't find anything to say. She didn't help matters any; she didn't want to say anything.

"What are you trying to do, reform me?" he said at last, kidding gruffly, trying to break the ice.

"Maybe," she said, laughing slightly. Her laugh sounded more disappointed than mad; but she was silent again.

"How did you know where I was?" Nick asked.

"Julian told me."

"Julian!"

"Yes."

"What did he say about me?" Nick asked, suspiciously and angrily.

"Nothing," she said.

They walked a few more steps.

"He didn't want to tell me where I could find you," she said.

They went past the Penguin Club and the Nickel Plate. They waited for the traffic light to change. "I'm sorry I didn't show up last Saturday."

"That's all right," she said. "You didn't say for sure."

On the other side of the street Emma got her carfare from her purse. "Ang and Abe are going to meet downtown Saturday and see a show. I'm going too. Do you—" she fingered the dime, "want to come?"

"Yes," he said; the car was approaching, "I'll see you before then. I'll see you when you come over."

He walked back into the Pastime and toward the table where he and Sunshine had been playing. Juan stopped him and, grinning, said, "Say! That was some broad! You packing her?" Nick caved in the smirk with a hard fist in the mouth that sprawled Juan half across the green top of the table before he knew what he was doing. He pushed the hair off his forehead and looked around angrily, challengingly, at the other men and young fellows pausing with cue sticks in their hands or looking up from the long bench against the wall. "Anybody else got any question?"

"Take it easy!" Butch said.

"Ah'm no trouble, Nick," Sunshine said woefully.

Nick racked up his stick and left the poolroom, made some money at Ace's. Coming along West Madison on his way back, he saw Juan up in front of him. He walked fast, caught up with him. Juan looked at him with unfriendly, half-menacing eyes. "I'm sorry," Nick said.

Juan said, "That's all right." His voice trembled emotionally.

That night Nick felt the urge lie on his flesh like bars of red-hot iron. He looked around for a broad, any old bag at all. He saw one in the Cobra Tap that wasn't bad. Three or four guys were mauling her and trying to proposition her. Nick caught her eye and made his face interested. He drew a five-dollar bill from his pocket and held it up in his hand.

She saw it. Laughing, she left the other fellows and came over to his table. They had a couple of drinks together. Nick said, "Let's go to your place." She stood up right away.

They turned off West Madison onto a darker street. She was holding his arm, squeezing it and pretending she couldn't wait.

Nick half opened his mouth to wisecrack. Then he thought of Emma.

She came to the poolroom for me. She must like me.

"I bet you've had a lot of experience, a good-looking guy like you," the broad said, tightening and loosening her fingers on his muscle.

Emma had said, I think you're nice. Nice! He stopped on the sidewalk. "I'm not going with you," he said.

"What d'you mean, you ain't going?" Her lips curled back in anger.

"I'm not going."

"Why, you dirty bastard, you!" The broad shouted, "You dragged me away from all them customers for nothing—why, you—"

"Here," he said, shoving the five-dollar bill in her face. "Now, go on. Beat it!" He pushed her away from him.

He went halfway into the first tavern he came to, turned around and walked out.

He gritted his teeth.

After a while he was wandering around aimlessly, like a dog without destination, sniffing at heels.

He felt like crying, so he cursed.

...

It was too late. He couldn't stay away from her. At least twice a week they were together. And the long summer was drawing to its close.

55

Emma stood in front of the mirror with her head raised and tilted back. She touched rouge to her cheekbones. She lowered her head and looked at her reflection. You like him, don't you? She glanced down at the dressertop, her hand lying in front of her still holding the rouge. She glanced back at her reflection. A lot? She stared herself straight in the eye. A lot. Her hands came up to each side of her neck; her fingers arranged her hair. Again she was looking into her own eyes. She shook her head a little. You could never marry anyone. The slight shaking of her head steadied itself. Mom needs you. What would she do? What would become of her? Her eyes were hazel-misty. They widened, the lashes curling out, the

[251]

irises staring at each other frankly. I'm a woman. I want something.
I couldn't do that. She flushed.

•••

They walked along the highway silently, listening to the soft pat-
ter of their feet. Emma led the way to a low curl of hill. From the
top they saw a few trees, then more. "Come on!" she said excitedly.

She crossed a field, came to the railroad tracks. Balancing herself
she walked along the rail. Nick did the same thing, slipped off, got
back on, went a few steps, slipped again. Ahead of him Emma
walked steadily, surely.

I hope she don't look back.

The railroad tracks began skirting the woods in a slim, curving
line. Emma abandoned the tracks and, looking towards the woods,
waited for Nick to catch up. Then they cut across a long field to
the first trees. Overhead the branches of trees became thick, with
small patches of blue here and there and bands of sunlight falling
through.

Clear-eyed, Nick followed Emma deep into the woods.

The woods were like home to Emma. She took him all around,
showing him things. "Oh, look at the snake hole!" Hurrying along
a straggly path through the bushes, past trees, to a spot where the
bushes lowered showing an uneven and ragged surface of brownish-
green water. "This is where Leo and I used to go swimming! This
is the very log we used to dive from!"

She sat on the tree stump and pulled off her tennis shoes, rolled
her stockings down. Nick followed, with his eyes, the rolled-up blue
slacks, the light brown stockings coming down between excited fingers, white legs coming down out of the blue slacks. Emma stuffed
her stockings in her shoes, stuck the shoes under the end of the log.
She looked at Nick, pushing hair off her forehead. He saw her profile sharp against the background of water and sky. Sunlight was
behind it, making her hair gossamer brown, her skin sun-tan, putting gloss in her eyes. His heart was like a piece of paper inside of
him that someone was crumbling up into a ball.

Her lips smiled at him liquidly. "Come on, take yours off!" she
said.

The grass was soft, twigs were hard. The sun was hot on their feet
and ankles. They edged out along the log and sat side by side, swinging their feet in the water. They looked down at their ankles with
the green-brown water closing around them, saw water circles widen
out away from their ankles like bracelets.

Walking in the grass dried their feet. Emma couldn't find any
frogs but she caught a snake. Shouting with pleasure she showed it
to Nick. The slim green length of snake circled around Emma's

[252]

wrist. Holding it behind its head with her thumb and forefinger, she offered the snake length to Nick. "Naw! I don't want it! I'd kill it!"

He was scared.

Emma let it go. The snake, part of the woods again, went swiftly between the parting grass.

There weren't any frogs around anywhere, only their sounds, always far away. But near the water Emma went up to her elbow in a crawfish hole and showed Nick a crawfish.

■■■

Nick and Emma lay near the green-brown water hemmed in by bushes and the trunks of trees. Sun spotted them. A tree shaded them. "Tell me all about you," he said.

"Me?" She told him all she could remember about being a little girl, the oldest girl, in a family that had no father.

They were silent for a long while, feeling good together, good to be in the woods, against the swell of green earth. Nick shut his eyes down. Emma looked up at the pattern of leaves overhead, watched their slow sway back and forth in the breeze. Still watching the leaves, she told Nick about Papa Jim.

Nick rolled over till he could look at her. He watched her lips. The story seemed ended now. They were silent. Then Emma said, "After that Mom started drinking." She put the crook of her arm over her eyes and lay still. Nick looked at her arm, her lips parted, breathing; the slow curl of her hair in the breeze. Emma said, "My mother drinks a lot now. A lot, Nicky." She bit her lip.

"That ain't nothing," Nick said softly. Then more matter-of-fact: "She's got to do something. She loved the guy."

They were silent. The sunlight withdrew from the woods a little.

"I like her," Nick said.

At length they sat up. There was a strong breeze coming across the grass, cooling. When Emma looked at Nick he grinned and patted his stomach. "If we had some bread we could have some ham sandwiches if we had some ham."

"I'm hungry too," she said.

Nick said, "I'll go get something. Come on with."

"No. I'd rather sit here, Nicky."

"Ain't you scared?"

"Afraid? Of what? No."

He started out. She watched him go until the trees hid him from her. She lay on her stomach and put her head down in the crook of her arms with the grass pressed against her face. Don't! Don't, stupid! she told herself. Although her lips trembled she didn't give way. She sat up with her back to a tree. Then she saw him coming back, straight-legged and grinning, a brown bag in one arm, a quart milk bottle of water swinging from the other.

The bag was full of hot dogs, potato chips, two oranges and a half pint of ice cream with wooden spoons for each of them. They ate there on the ground in the clearing near the sluggish and rusty water. Nick lay on his stomach using his elbows for props and stuffed in three hot dogs. Emma sat near him, getting mustard on her chin and laughing. Nick rolled over on his side and they helped themselves to potato chips out of the same crinkly bag. Sometimes their hands met and wouldn't fit in the bag. This made them laugh. They turned back the flaps on the ice cream cartons and dug into the strawberry coldness. Nick licked the carton, turning his eyes up at Emma and grinning, and they were finished.

"Orange?" he asked. She shook her head no. Then suddenly she jumped to her feet, took the orange and, standing wide-legged a little distance from him, said, "Hey! let's play catch!" They did, laughing. Then they sat again, sharing the same tree trunk. They were suddenly shy and withdrawn from each other. The sun was falling, now, in the west. Twilight crept closer to their tree, to the two oranges under it, to Nick's crumpled sweater, to their shoes and stockings where they had brought them and left them tumbled on the ground near their bare feet.

They sat with their legs drawn under them, turned toward each other. Looking at each other.

The best day of my life. And she's going.

Nick made a slow gesture toward her with his hands. "Let's stay all night."

She looked at him with deep eyes, frankly, not smiling. "All right, Nicky."

"It will be all right," he told her.

Touching his hand, "I know, Nicky. I—I believe in you."

They eased themselves against the swell of earth again. They were suddenly awkward and embarrassed. They didn't talk. They didn't move. The night was over them.

The woods deepened in silence and darkness. Light retreated from the farthest leaves on the highest branches. The evening stars were blurring the sky. The moon came up big, round and full and wandered through the black tree-trunks, then climbed up the tree limbs and on up and up like a balloon escaping from the earth.

Nick took the low branch of a bush between his fingers and pulled it down until the leaves were gently brushing Emma's face where she lay on the slight swell of earth, staring into the night. She closed her eyes against them and, smiling, turned on her side to face him. Her throat made low laughter. "You know what, Nicky?" she said, softly but very seriously. "When I was a little girl I used to come into the woods and cover myself with lilacs and pretend I was the Lily Maid." Again she chuckled softly. "If there weren't any lilacs I used leaves. I was the Lily Maid and I was dead. It—" laughing gently, "was very romantic...."

Words trailed away. The night came closer, heavier, lay next to their thoughts. Somewhere a bird's wings made muted beatings in the leaves of a tree limb.

"Who was the Lily Maid?" Nick asked.

Lying close to him Emma told him the story of the Lily Maid. And some of the poem she remembered. Blushing self-consciously she recited what she remembered.... " *'Elaine the fair, Elaine the loveable, Elaine the Lily Maid of Astolat, high in her chamber up ...up in a tower to the east....'*" Her words drew a long and solemn note from the woods; he listened, everything in him slipping down to a low hush. " *'...Now guessed a ...now guessed a hidden meaning in his arms...now made a pretty history to herself of... every dint a sword had beated in it and ...every scratch a ...lance had made upon it....'* That's all I remember, Nicky...Oh," her lips smiled, "the part I liked, it goes—*'In her right hand the lily, in her other the letter, all her bright hair streaming down, and she ... she did not seem dead but fast asleep.'*" Leaning on her elbows, Emma smiled gravely at Nick. Nick's eyes came back from Camelot.

"I think she was dumb," he said.

Again words, movement, reality trailed away. The moon was there and gone and there. Nick and Emma sat hugging their knees, leaning their backs against a tree trunk. Their shoulders touched but they did not look at each other.

He tried to think of something to tell her. All he could remember was going around with Tony, and reform school and Rocky and Tommy. He told her about them, what swell fellows they were, leaving out all the bad things like gambling and stealing. In the night, there beside her, telling her, nothing they had done seemed bad at all. He longed just once more to be with them, to bum around with them with nothing to do but be kids and have a good time.

He even told her about Butch and Sunshine and Juan. He painted the black parts white. And most of all he wanted to tell her about Tommy, about the guts that kid had and the licking he had taken. But he couldn't.

Emma ran her fingers along the grass. "Ang told me you were an altar boy."

"Yeah—a long time ago."

They sat again, not talking. They sat a long while. Silence closed with the darkness about them. It was then she noticed the stars. She looked at one, reciting in a child voice:

[255]

> *"Star light, star bright,*
> *First star I've seen tonight,*
> *I wish I may, I wish I might,*
> *Have the wish I wish tonight."*

He watched her. "What did you wish?"

"Oh," she said, turning her face away, "if I told you it wouldn't come true."

They rose and walked a way looking for wood. "Did you make a wish?" she asked.

"Yeah," he said, "only none of my wishes ever come true."

The night was warm. There was no breeze at all, but a warm movement back and forth over the grass. The sky was like a blanket over them. Nick sat with his knees drawn up to his chin and his face concealed in the circle of his arms. Over his arms his hair tumbled black and curly.

...His arms...the big flowers on the sofa...fishbowl don't leave me I'm still around ain't I...sad eyes drawing him back I know what I'm doing PARIS THEATER *Daisykittyalicemarthahelen: ...darkness behind St. Francis' schoolyard Nickel Plate are you hungry kid? play them all live fast....*

"What are you thinking of, Nicky?" Her voice, soft, almost a whisper, was like a shock. He jumped a little. His forehead came up off his knees with the hair lifting.

"Huh?—Oh, nothing." He put the palms of his hands against his face and rubbed hard, with eyes closed, trying to push his thoughts back out of his memory.

A slight wind murmured above their heads. She told him about Jerry. How they used to sit in the car together at night. She told him how nice and how fine Jerry was. She told him about Jerry's dreams. His ambitions.

She cried quietly in that brief, brokenhearted moment.

And Nick sat next to her with his head turned away, feeling awful, wanting to touch her, tell her not to. Unable to do so. Clenching his teeth. Crying inside. Crying about Jerry and Emma and himself.

She said, "I'm sorry," and stopped.

When he was able to look at her she had her eyes closed. He felt small and hurt and like a little boy inside.

It must have been half an hour later. "Asleep?" He formed the word with his lips and whispered it. "No." He pushed himself down against the ground and lay next to her. He stared at the sky, unblinking.

The night was as warm as the day.

No sound, now, in the night. No movement.

[256]

"Sleep?"

She shook her head. Her hair brushed his cheek, tickling.

The stars marched all around the sky. The moon threw its silver. Nick rolled away from the touch of her shoulder. "Sleep?" he whispered. She didn't answer, by words or movement. Nick stood up. Getting his sweater he folded it, gently, over her, around her shoulders. Then he again sat next to her, but leaning over her slightly. He looked at her. It was a little-girl face. Her lips were parted. Her breast rising slightly, falling slightly.

So slowly that there was no movement in the depth of the forest he brought the fingers of his hand in contact with the long ends of her hair where they lay on the shoulder of his sweater and curled loosely over it onto the grass. He touched them gently, pressing them softly against the grass. He looked at her hair and smoothed the ends of it with his fingers. His lips said, without making sound, "Don't go away, Emma. Don't ever leave me, Emma." He became afraid that she might awaken. He pushed himself back onto the ground. Slowly, painstakingly, he moved closer and closer to her, closer, until once more their shoulders touched. Again he stared, unblinking, at the sky.

...

Sun warmed the woods. Touched color to the leaves. Fell, in slimness, through the leaves onto the two sleeping bodies huddled close together. It came warmer. It fell on Nick's cheek, across his closed eyes. Slowly he opened his eyes. He saw her face near his, the round and tanned face, the brown hair with fingers of sunlight in it, the green grass for a pillow. He saw his sweater pulled up close about her neck and, seeing it there, around her, his heart was again a piece of paper being crumpled into a ball. And right then she opened her eyes. The lids, long-lashed, blinked a few times. Then her eyes met his. "Hello, Nicky!" she said.

"Hello, Emma." It wasn't his voice. It was a strange and husky and curiously soft voice.

Emma sat up, rubbing her eyes, lazily handing his sweater across to him. They stood up, she holding her hand to him to be helped to her feet. Awake now, hearing the awakening woods sounds.

He hadn't taken his eyes from her. They stood looking at each other. She was smiling up at him happily. He was deep-eyed and solemn. She tilted her head a little and, looking at him, smiling at him, almost laughing at him, said, "Why don't you say it, Nicky?"

His eyes turned to the ground. "Say what?"

She laughed and, leaping away from him, ran through the woods. Her laughter came over her shoulder, streaming behind her as her hair streamed. He wanted to stay where he was but his feet followed her, his legs kept running after her.

[257]

She was ahead, ducking past trees, running toward a blue sky. Then she was closer. Then he had caught her and she was panting. He held her by the shoulders and she kept her head down. His hands tightened on her shoulders. He drew her near to him. Then he was crying with his face in his hands. Crying for the first time since he was a young boy standing in an assembly hall in reform school seeing a younger boy getting beaten. "I'm no good, Emma. I'm no good."

And Emma was kneeling on the ground with his head against her breast, kissing his hair, and his neck, and his face. Holding him as his mother had held him before everything that had happened to him had happened. Emma was kissing his hair, and his neck, and his face.

56

The smell of beer was heavy in the kitchen. Emma, coming home from staying all night in the woods, stood staring in. Her mother sat at the round kitchen table holding her face up with hands propped to each side of it and her elbows hard against the table. Her black hair, streaked with gray, streamed down her face and straggled out at the back of her neck. Her half-asleep mouth was open. It was loose and ugly in its drunkenness and there was slobber on her lower lip. Her long black skirt showed two inches of petticoat going past it and touching the floor at the leg of the chair. Bottles were on the table, some standing up, some knocked over. Glass rings were gummy-wet on the oilcloth.

Mrs. Schultz lifted her head and pushed the hair from in front of her face. Her eyes blinked. Then she looked at the figure standing in the door. "There's my little Emmike!" she bawled in recognition. "Come kiss your old Ma." She held her arms out away from the table toward Emma drunkenly. Her eyes were bright with alcohol. Again she said, "Come give your Ma a big kiss, *Kind*."

Emma stood looking at her mother. She wavered a little and tightened her hand around the doorknob to steady herself. Her lips that had been humming and smiling when she opened the door began to tremble.

Mrs. Schultz banged the beer glass down on the table. A new expression came into her eyes. "You, Emma! Where have you been all night?" Mrs. Schultz spat at her. She spat at her again. "*Du Dirne,* you dirty little whore, you! Whore! Whore!" She was pounding both hands on the table, angrily and drunkenly. "Where did you stay all night!"

Emma looked slowly into her mother's face. She felt a shiver curl up her spine and through the roots of her hair. She stepped backwards across the sill and onto the porch and pulled the door shut.

Emma stumbled toward the steps, ran down them, the rail flashing through her fingers. She ran around the side of the house and out to the front sidewalk. Kept running, as fast as she could. But she couldn't get away from the sound of her mother's words. She couldn't run away from the tears. She was crying, bitterly and heartbrokenly. And she was out of breath and couldn't run any more. She had to stop and walk. People were looking at her. Her hair was tangled, her face red and blotched from crying. She took out her handkerchief, twisted the knot open and tore out a dime. She boarded a streetcar and sat in the back seat with her face away from people but hurt so badly that she didn't care if they saw or what they thought. Past her blurry eyes the houses all ran together.

■■■

Julian opened the door. His mouth loosened in surprise when he saw Emma's red eyes and her tear-swollen face.

"Is Nicky here?" She stepped past Julian without any real recognition. Julian seemed not to hear her. "Where's Nicky?" Emma asked, standing inside the door and looking around the room.

Ang heard Emma. She came to her quickly and took her hands. "Emma, what's the matter?"

Emma withdrew her hands. "Where's Nicky?" She walked into the house blindly. Julian and Ang followed her.

The bathroom door was open. Nick stood at the washbasin in his undershirt, roughly lathering his face with his hands. Emma walked in and closed the door. With her hands behind her back she locked the door. Nick heard the bolt go across and looked up sideways from his cupped hands that dripped soap suds. "Emma!"

She stood leaning against the door, looking at him. "Nicky, will you marry me? Will you marry me right away? Oh, Nicky, I don't ever want to go home again! I don't ever want to go back there!"

He was holding her hands. "Emma! Poor kid!" His hands were cold, soapy, wet over hers.

"I can't go back there!"

[259]

His arms were around her. "Don't cry—please—" He had his arms around her tightly.

"I can't, Nicky! I can't! I can't ever go back there!" He was kissing her, getting soapsuds all over her face and hair and neither of them noticing. Her forehead was on his shoulder, on the underwear strap and the bare skin with tears running down his chest. "I can't! I can't!"

His knee was up on the toilet seat, his bare arms were around her. In her hair his voice said, "Emma, I love you. I'll marry you anytime you want me."

They stood like this a long time. The tears and the choked, whimpering sobbing became less. "Oh Nicky...."

He joggled her a little in his arms and rocked back and forth with her. "Please stop crying." He took her by the wrist. "Your eyes are red." He drew her over toward the washbowl and, looking at her, grinning at her, fished with a searching hand behind him for the washcloth. It came out of the bowl wet and cold. "We'll fix them!" he said; and he tried to wash her face in cold water.

She struggled. He laughed. He got the back of her head in the crook of one arm and the cold, dripping cloth up near her face. She bumped into the bowl. "Shh! Nicky! Don't!" They were giggling softly and struggling until finally she had to give in and stood, pushed against the wall with her eyes clamped tight, letting him dab at her face and eyes with the wet cloth. It took a long while, for every time he got her washed a few more tears would run down her cheeks.

When he was finally finished, she said in a small, shamed voice,"I don't know what to say to your family." Nick handed her his comb. "I'm scared!" she said in a smaller voice.

"Hey! Are you going to fix your hair?" he asked. "Or do I have to do that too?"

"Please, Nicky!" She moved to the mirror and combed her hair. Watching her, he felt himself choke.

She was ready to go out. She looked up at him timidly.

They moved o the door. She put her fingers against his wrist for a moment. "I'm scared!" she said.

"I'll fix it," he said.

●●●

He saved the news for supper. He waited until they were all finished eating. Then he said loudly, "Emma and me are going to get married." He looked straight at Julian when he said it. He seemed to be saying it to Julian alone, to be showing him. And he smiled at his brother a little, tight-lipped.

Nobody said anything for almost a full minute. Ma set down her fork in her surprise. In the sudden silence it made a loud, clicking sound.

Aunt Rosa spoke first. "That's swell! That's just swell!"

Emma was every color. Julian stood up, now that the family had absorbed its surprise, and held out his hand to Nick. Nick took his brother's hand and smiled without showing his teeth. "That's the best thing that could happen to you, Nick. Congratulations. Emma's a swell girl."

Nick's smile took on an edge of ridicule.

Just what I thought—he'd make a speech.

Nick let go his hand. "Yeah."

Julian held out his hand to Emma. He looked at her very seriously. He said, almost as Pa would have said, "I hope you will be very happy, Emma. We're all glad that you'll be one of the family."

"Thank you, Julian."

Ma sat just as she had been when Nick hurled the news at them. Her eyes looked from one to the other and filled up. Then she got out of her chair, went up to each of them, kissed each of them on the forehead.

Nick felt cheap as a penny. Aunt Rosa leaned back in her chair with her arms folded and looking at them. She bobbed her head up and down a couple of times as if something had been completely put over on her. She pushed her chair from the table. "You know what? —I'm going to buy a bottle of wine so we can all drink on it. Damn it! but it's great to be young and in love! Nothin' like it! I wish I was young again. I'd sure get married this trip! Maybe I ain't too old to catch a man yet!" Aunt Rosa chuckled again, then yelled, "Well, here's the money for the wine. Damned if I'm going after it, wedding or no wedding!"

···

The next evening they sat together on the front steps. Emma was staying there, sharing Ang's room. For half an hour they didn't say a word. There were stars over the row of two and three story shacks across the street and over the icehouse. Finally Nick said, as if he had been thinking and thinking about it, "Do you really want to, Emma?"

She was quiet so long that he wondered if she had heard him or really didn't want to after all.

When he was straining his ears for her answer, she finally said, drawing her fingers across the boards of the porch and holding her head down, "You don't have to if you don't want to, Nicky. I—I shouldn't have asked you. I'm ashamed of coming here—and—asking you—"

He put his hand on her shoulder and took it off. "It ain't that— It's—" He stared at the black wall of the icehouse. "You don't know

[261]

what I'm like. I've even been in reform school. I ain't even got a job."

"Oh, Nicky! Don't worry about that. I believe in you. You'll get a job."

She believes in me!

The wall didn't look so black.

"I wouldn't of had the nerve to ask you," he said.

■■■

Ma Romano insisted that they be married by the priest. It was a lot of trouble. The priest talked to them very seriously about if they were sure, the sacredness of marriage, an indissoluble state. He used a lot of big and solemn words. There was a great long talk about the jurisdiction of the church over marriage, about the church demands that all the children born of mixed marriages be brought up Catholics. Catholics are not really married if they go to anybody else but the priest and are living in a state of public sin. They had to sign papers saying any children they had would be raised Catholics.

Nick listened bored and angry.

Yeah, and I'll have to kick in with some money. And it can't be in the church because Emma ain't Catholic.

■■■

Nick walked in without knocking. Owen was lying crumpled down on the sofa gazing moodily at the fishbowl in which the one goldfish turned ever around and around in a lonely circle.

Nick walked over quietly. "Hello, Owen."

Owen's body responded with a small involuntary jerk. "Oh—hello, Nicky." His eyes looked up, unrelieved and sad. "I was thinking about you."

"It don't look like they were good thoughts," Nick said. His attempted kidding came out thinly. He looked down at Owen, at the forehead with the long hair going back from it in straight and limp wisps, the downcast eyes and the loose, unhappy mouth. "I'm going to get married, Owen."

Owen's eyes blinked wide. His lips loosened as if he had run a long distance.

"*Married!*"

Nick looked away when he saw Owen's eyes. The daylight stood still in the room. There was no sound.

Nick walked over to the window and looked down on Washington Boulevard. Automobiles were going along the asphalt. Behind him Owen asked, "Is she a nice girl, Nicky?"

The row of buildings across the street stood cardboard stiff in the sunlight. A beggar had nothing and had asked for just a little with his hand stretched out like a cup. The other man was moving away down the sidewalk and the beggar stood with his outstretched hand empty.

Nick heard the echo of the words: "Is she a nice girl, Nicky?" He knew Owen was looking at him. Without answering he nodded his head, yes.

You hurt somebody bad. You wouldn't do it but you have to.

A fly buzzed and struck against the window.

Owen's voice came, softly, from the other end of the room. "What's her name, Nicky?"

"Emma."

"She loves you a lot?"

Nick nodded.

"She couldn't help it, Nicky. She couldn't help loving you." His voice shook; he laughed to steady it.

"When does it happen?"

"Sunday."

"That—that's day after tomorrow."

Silence folded around them in the room bright with sunlight. Nick lit a cigarette and smoked it standing by the window with his back to Owen. Smoked it low.

Owen moved on the sofa. He heard Owen coming across the room. Owen stood next to him, looking down on the street too. Owen turned and looked at Nick a long time, at his face in profile, remembering it, imprinting it in his loneliness.

Owen put his hand on Nick's shoulder. "Come over tomorrow."

Nick nodded yes.

■■■

It was their last day together. Nick came over early in the morning. Owen hadn't completely dressed yet or combed his hair; but his eyes, looking at Nick, rounded like a child's and lit up with pleasure and surprise.

"Hi!" Nick said. "What are you trying to do, sleep all day?"

"You came!" Owen said, as if he hadn't really expected Nick to show up.

"What are we going to eat?" Nick asked, tossing his hat on the sofa and walking toward the kitchen. While Owen was brushing his teeth, washing and combing, Nick peeled potatoes, put on the coffee and unpeeled the greasy paper on half a pound of bacon. Owen came into the kitchen with a strained face and deep eyes but a mouth that smiled when Nick looked at him. Nick grinned at Owen. "You didn't know I could cook, huh?"

They ate.

Later they went downtown to the show. When they came out Nick said, "Hey! there's a picture at the Oriental I want to see!" and they went there too. After they were seated Owen went out to the lobby and came back with an apple. He handed it, in the dark, to Nick. "I know you like them."

After the show Nick said, "Let's walk," and they walked back down Madison Street. Twilight lowered the sky. Night began to scatter into the dusk.

On the bridge between the Civic Opera House and the *Daily News* building Nick and Owen hung over the rail for a while, silently looking down the river. Then they moved on along West Madison again.

Nick and Owen came almost to Halsted. In front of the steps that ran up to the Nickel Plate Owen fastened his fingers around Nick's arm urgently. "Let's go in for a cup of coffee," he said.

"All right."

"That's where I first saw you and where you talked to me first."

Then afterwards they were on Washington and nothing more had been said. After several long silent steps, Owen said, "Remember how drunk you were the first night you talked to me?"

"Yeah!" Nick grinned. Then he said, "You bought me shoes." His voice was serious. His eyes, in the night, stared straight ahead. Owen's voice came in, "You recited your favorite line— 'Live fast, die young and have a good-looking corpse,' only when you got as far as 'live fast' you fell asleep."

They walked a block looking straight ahead into the night. Then Owen said, "The very first thing you said to me was 'The world isn't that sad. . . .' "

They didn't say any more. They came to the limestone front of the building and went in.

Owen fried steak and they ate. They drank one glass of wine, silently. Nick looked down into his, tasting it. Owen sipped, then held the glass up, draining it. They sat on the cretonne flowers and remembered.

"Remember the fight?"

"Yes—you got an awful cut."

Silence for a while.

"You took me home with you and fixed it. You tore up a shirt to fix it. . . . And the night my old man beat me up . . . I came over by you."

Another long silence.

Nick grinned. "I used to mooch you for plenty."

Owen smiled faintly, nodded.

"I knew you were lying that time when you said you were in trouble and needed seven dollars."

They read back, relived all the incidents that had made up their friendship. Owen talked them and found strength in them. Like a

[264]

fist clutched around something ... this is mine. Nothing can take it away from me.

"What are you thinking?" Nick asked.

"Nothing."

They sat thinking nothing, thinking everything, for a long time. At last Nick sat up straight.

"I've got to go," Nick said.

"Yes," said Owen.

Nick pounded his open hand against Owen's knee hard. "You've always been okay with me," he said seriously.

They stood up. Owen said with his eyes drawn away from Nick, "There's something for you and Emma over there."

He walked to the table and Nick followed. There were two packages on the table, neatly wrapped and tied. Owen put his hand on one of the packages. "This one is the—the wedding present. The other one is for—for your first anniversary. Don't open it until then."

Nick stood with his head down, feeling cheap, tracing the worn floral design of the rug with his eyes.

Owen said, "Nicky, I'm your friend. Come to me if you ever need anything. Anything."

Owen was holding his hand out. Nick put his out too. Owen shook with him as a wrestler would have. Nick put the two packages under his arm. Then he went down the steps and onto the street.

57

It's Sunday and it's today.

Nick sneaked a hand under one arm and scratched where it itched. Ang and Emma were in the bedroom looking again at the clothes Emma had bought at Sachs out on the South Side to get married in and the lingerie Ang had bought Emma for a wedding present. Nick looked at Ma and Julian and Aunt Rosa. He fingered nervously in his pocket to make sure the ring was there. "Tell her—I'll meet her over there."

He wandered around the streets in a daze. He didn't even know where he was. At last he thought of somewhere to go. He walked in and yelled, "Hi, Maw!" at Stash's old lady. Stash's old lady yelled his name a couple of times and patted his back and Stash came out of the bedroom where he had been lying across the bed. He had a shirt on but it wasn't buttoned and the tail wasn't in his pants. He limped tiredly as if the steel mills had sucked all the strength out of him. Stash and his old lady stood around, excitedly admiring Nick's new clothes and the old lady asked, "Why you so dressed dandy? Where's funeral?"

Nick stood in the middle of the floor in the new shoes, new suit, the shirt Ang had bought him for a wedding present and the perfectly knotted tie. He felt the redness go to the roots of his hair. "I'm not going to a funeral," he said in dead earnest.

"Come eat, Nick," Stash's old lady said. "We eat. But you eat."

"I couldn't eat nothing," Nick stammered. "I ain't hungry."

Stash went into the pantry. He came back with a bottle of whiskey. Nick said he didn't want any but they kept insisting and the old lady got three shot glasses so he took one drink. Stash's old lady said, "We play rummy, yes?"

She dealt the cards out. They played. Nick held the cards tightly. He kept making dumb plays. After the game had been going for an hour he began asking what time it was. He asked about every five minutes. Then suddenly he stood up. "I gotta go." Stash's old lady shook her head. "You act funny today," she said.

Outside Nick cupped his hand up to his mouth blowing to see if he could smell whiskey. At the corner he bought a stick of gum and chewed it hard.

■■■

Nick waited in front of the buildings where the church and St. Michael High School lined themselves in a solemn wall with the grammar school he had gone to back of them.

They didn't even see him. They came along the sidewalk, Emma, Ang, Ma, Julian, Aunt Rosa—even Junior. They were going right past him. "Hey, wait a minute," he gulped. They saw him and stopped. He looked at Emma and felt his heart turn upside down. She wore a powder-blue suit. He could see a white blouse underneath. Her hair was in a soft coil about her neck. It touched her shoulders. She wore a blue hat to match her suit and there was a wisp of veil the same color that didn't come below the tip of her nose. Beyond the veil her eyes were staring at him. There wasn't even a piece of a smile in her eyes. "Hello, Nicky," she said. He swallowed. His eyes dropped down to her white gloves and white purse, they dropped down to her white kid sandals. Nick pulled something from behind his back and thrust it at her. It was a little spray of flowers in a twist of florist paper. "Here," he said. Emma tore the paper away and pressed her face down into them.

"Come on, you two!" Aunt Rosa yelled. Emma took Nick's arm. Her fingers were trembling. "I wish Leo was here," she said and they were on the first step.

One—two—three—Nick counted them to himself. At the top there was a door—ten—eleven—twelve— He felt in his pocket—it was there ... there were sixteen steps and he was going into the building to get married.

They were in the hall. They were going into the priest's parlor and the family was pressing in behind them. Emma had her cheek down on her shoulder. She looked up at Nick, shy and frightened. "You look—so—so holy, Nicky." Her hand trembled on his arm.

And they were in the room waiting for the priest. They were alone on the rug in front of the table. All alone. And Emma, with none of her family there, with none of them even knowing, was going to marry him. He stole a glance at her. She looked so scared and like a little girl that he filled up inside. Him and her ... all alone ... behind him from a long distance he could barely hear Junior asking, "What are they going to do now?" and Ma saying, "Keep quiet, Junior!"

"Good afternoon, my children!" It was the priest. He came in smiling, a very old priest with his head tilted on one side to see them the better. "How is everybody?" The murmur of the family, and the old priest with his gray hair, making jokes, "Sorry I'm a little late ... but when you get old ... the hinges get rusty".... Bending down, rubbing his knees with his hands, moving onto the little island of carpet. "A very handsome couple!" The priest getting things ready with nervous but unhurried hands, saying, "Now don't look so frightened, children, this isn't going to hurt!" Everything was ready now. The old priest had the witnesses step in close; and Aunt Rosa was right behind Nick because she was going to stand up when "her boy" got married; and Ang stood at Emma's side. Nick felt in his pocket.

It's there.

The priest saying....

"Nicholas, wilt thou take Emma, here present, for thy lawful wife?"

Nick gulped and wet his lips with his tongue. Behind the heavy drapes a streetcar clanged by on 12th Street and Nick was so scared that he wished he was on it.

"Ye—I will."

"Emma, wilt thou take Nicholas here present. . . ."

Nick listened, watching the small reddish veins on the priest's nose. Aunt Rosa, behind him, had her fingers pressed into his arm tightly and kept sniffing but smiling broadly at the same time. The table. The glass top. The cloth underneath.

The ring. His hand catching in his pocket a moment. The priest with his head tilted, waiting. The ring. Emma with the white glove off. Their hands trembling together, fumbling.

He wet his lips again. "With this ring I thee wed, and I plight unto thee my troth. . . ."

"By the authority committed to me I pronounce you. . . ."

Another streetcar going by.

". . . united in the bonds of matrimony."

• • •

At home there was a big feast Ma had spent all day preparing; and a huge cake Aunt Rosa had bought on Taylor and Halsted that had a bride and groom on the very tip-top of it. On the sideboard in the front room were wrapped packages—the wedding presents. Nick and Emma, self-conscious and shy, were pushed toward them and told to open them. From Ma there was a set of good substantial dishes for when they went housekeeping. Emma moved down to the next package that had scrawled on top, "To my kids from Aunt Rosa." They all crowded up close to see the ornate spread and the pillow slips, one with NICK and the other with EMMA embroidered on it. Nick was fingering a large brown-paper-wrapped oblong that stood on the floor leaning against the sideboard. His fingers felt through the paper to a frame of some sort. "I bet this is from Julian," he said and tore the paper off. Out of the paper, revealing itself, came a Japanese print. "Oh, Julian!" Emma said, going to him and kissing him.

Nick picked up the square package Owen had given them, and with his head twisted, shook it near his ear. He opened it. It was an electric clock. "It's beautiful!" Emma said. "Who gave it to us?"

"A friend of mine," Nick said. Emma touched the other box.

"Who is this from?" she asked.

"He gave us that too."

Emma slipped her finger under the string to break it. "Oh, don't!" Nick said. "He told me we wasn't supposed to open it until a year after we was married."

"Oh, let's open it, Nicky! Let's open it!" Emma coaxed.

"All right," Nick consented.

The paper came off and Emma peered in past the cover. Immediately she dropped the lid and turned red to the roots of her hair. Everybody was asking, "What is it?" Nick pushed over to the box. "Let's see." He pulled the top off. In the box was a layette. A small white yarn coat, baby socks, tiny knitted boots gay with blue ribbon trimmings. Nick turned and walked away from the sideboard.

[268]

After dinner Rosa and Ma went out. Julian had gone to Hull-House.

They sat in the parlor without anything to say to each other, even too self-conscious to look at each other. "Let's go for a walk, huh?"

Emma almost jumped up. "Yes!"

On the street they walked self-consciously, sure that everyone was looking at them and knew.

They walked down 12th Street past Racine, past Loomis. "We'll go to Moon's," Nick said. They sat in a booth near the window, looking out, sodas they didn't want in front of them. Nick put a nickel in the jukebox—

> I'll be loving you, always
> With a love that's true, always. . . .

"Remember?" Nick asked, and Emma nodded.

They walked around; all the way to the bridge on 12th Street they walked. They looked over the edge of the bridge.

They walked toward home. They walked as slow as they could in the dark. But even then they couldn't make the walk long enough and they were home. They went slowly up the steps, not letting their bodies touch. They went inside and listened to the radio until they were sleepy, and tense, and unsleepy again.

She knew that they had to go to bed, sooner or later, but it seemed like something that should be postponed indefinitely.

Sleepy . . . then tense. . . .

At last they had to give in. Nick said, "Let's hit the hay." Emma didn't move for a full minute. Then she got up and walked toward the bedroom. Her hand trembled on the switch, turning on the light. Nick looked at her funny as if that was the wrong thing to do. He closed and locked the door. Emma trembled. They were in the bedroom together, more tense than they had been that whole day.

Nick sat on the side of the bed. Emma sat far at the other end of the bed. She looked over at him with her head down. "Nicky—" Her voice made him look at her questioningly. "I've got to tell you something."

"What?"

She started blushing. She turned her face away from him.

"Hey!" Nick moved close to her, putting his hands on her shoulders and gently wrestling her around until she was looking at him. "What are you holding out?"

She shook her head no.

"Come on, tell me!"

"I—I can't."

"Aw, come on!" He had pulled her over and was rubbing his chin against her neck.

"I want to but I can't... Nicky... turn out the light and don't look at me and I'll tell you."

He turned out the light and sat next to her on the bed again.

"Don't look at me," she said. And she told him; she told him that she was a virgin.

His thoughts stood still—then crashed forward.

I knew it all the time only—only—

He thought about Rosemary and how—how—

Forget about it. Don't think about it.

He put his arm around Emma. His hands were hot and excited. Nicky became less Nicky and more Nick. He started kissing her, loosening her blouse. "Let's go to bed, huh?"

"Please don't, Nicky!" Her voice trembled.

"Let's go to bed, huh?" he said again, more urgently; and she knew she had to undress and that was dreadful. "Please go over there and don't—don't look until—until I get in—bed."

Nick stood up, moody and embarrassed and walked across the room. She got behind a chair and undressed with just her head sticking over it in the half-dark.

Then they were alone in the room, facing each other. Naked. But not as it had been when she and Leo were nude in the woods. Not like that.

Nick, male and urgent, strode toward her. Nick had his arms around her hard. All his embarrassment and shyness was in a heap on the floor with his clothes. He was holding her hard against him. He was kissing her hard. He was dragging her toward the bed.

He almost threw her into the bed. Oh, Nicky, you're awful. You—you—why do we have to do this?

He was in bed beside her. It was awful. The bed was narrow and she was against the wall with her eyes clamped tight and her teeth clenched together. The wall was cold and hard and he was pressed close against her. His clumsy hands were on her body. His voice was husky and passionate. His breath was hot on her flesh and made her cringe farther against the cold and hard wall. No! No! No! She wanted to talk. Just talk and talk. Anything to postpone it.

Nick didn't try to excite her. He was just driven on, forcefully, in his maleness, toward taking her. *Stript off the case and read the naked shield....*

She was scared. She held back. Her modesty cried inside of her like a string being tightened on a violin. There wasn't one nice thing about it. His sweaty body. Her sweaty body. He—approaching her. She—trying to hold him off.

Then—she heard the family close the front door and walk into the house! They walked softly and talked low and didn't turn on the lights but she heard them and her body flamed with embarrassment.

The wall bruised her back. "No, Nicky!—Your folks are home—they'll hear!"

"The hell with them!" Nick said.

Nick calmed a little. He became more affectionate. He petted her and moved her closer and closer against the wall until there was no room between their bodies. She felt helpless.

She began to have awakening feelings. A warmness put itself across her flesh like sunlight. She had feelings—but they went away with the shock and hurt—a sharp pain—then numbness.

She lay like a piece of paper that had been crumpled, thrown on the floor.

All she could think was, I'll never be the same person.

Nick was finished. He went to sleep soon.

She lay broken, unhappy.

■■■

Daylight spread slowly across the bed. Emma, awake, lay on her side looking at Nick curiously. He turned toward her in his sleep. The first ray of sunlight fell across his hair, his cheek. He awakened, just his eyes. They looked at her. Brown. His lips smiled a little and his eyes closed. Again he stirred in the bed. In his sleep he reached out and put his arm around her. Emma ran her hand over his cheek, gently, so as not to awaken him. She kissed his forehead, barely touching her lips to it. Her fingers smoothed his hair back. "My Nicky!" she whispered.

58

Two days married. The alarm clock went off. Nick rolled over on his side and knotted his face into a hard frown; wrinkles folded tightly around his clenched eyes and his arms pulled the cover over his head. Emma got up and turned off the alarm. She dressed quietly. She looked toward the bed and saw the swell of

Nick's back and his shoulders under the covers. She tiptoed to the bed. Gently she leaned over and touched her lips against his curl-mussed hair. Then she tiptoed out of the room.

Julian had already gone to work. His washed coffee cup and plate were turned down on the sink to dry. The warmed coffee had just begun again to jump slowly up the elevation of glass and Ang was setting cups on the table. She and Emma exchanged sleepy good mornings. Aunt Rosa came out of her bedroom arranging her hair and yawning. "Where's Nick?" Ang asked. "Is he going to get up?"

Emma looked down at the table edge. "He said he'd be out soon. He's dressing."

Nick stepped into the kitchen. He looked at them shame-faced. "Maybe I can find a job," he said.

Emma didn't get home until late. She waited until Nick came into the bedroom. Not looking at him, she said, "Nicky, I looked at a place today." He didn't say anything. "You don't care if we move by ourselves, do you?" She lifted her eyes to him. He looked away and shook his head no. "It's on the South Side. Do you care if we live out there?"

"Whatever you want," he said.

"It's near night school and near Mom," Emma told him, "and it won't be hard for us to get over here." Nick looked at the edge of Emma's shoulder. "I'm looking for a good job. I'll get something soon," he said.

...

It was furnished rooms, two and a half of them in the Princeton Hotel, a long, flat frame building with a porch all the way across the front. Emma was cooking her first meal over the twin-burner gas plate when someone ran up the steps two at a time and pounded on the door. "Oh, Nicky!" Emma said, panicky, "we're having our first visitor!" Nick went toward the door. "Wait," Emma said, unty-ing her apron and smoothing back her hair. The pounding came again and they opened the door.

Grant stood on the other side of the sill grinning at them with eyes that crinkled; and he put his hand out and shook with both of them. "I just heard!" he said. "It's great news! I wish I could have been here. I was in Mexico." He took a big box of candy from under his arm and handed it to Emma. "It's swell news!" he said again.

After they had all eaten, Grant and Nick made Emma stay out of the kitchen while they did the dishes, then Grant said, "I've got my car downstairs. Come on, kids, I'll take you for a ride!"

He made them sit in the back and, turning the radio low, chauf-feured them through Washington, through Jackson Park, along the lake, along the Outer Drive. They sat with their heads against the

seat. Emma's hand turned over under Nick's, her fingers found his
...Elaine the Lily Maid....

•••

Several days later after work Emma said, "We've got to go see my
mother. I—I haven't seen her for two weeks."

They walked in sheepishly.

Mrs. Schultz was sitting at the table with her hands stretched out
tensely in front of her and her fingers clutched together. When she
heard the door open and looked up and saw them standing there
she stared at them for a long time. Then she stood up by the table,
steadying herself against it. Her voice, her eyes came from a long
distance. "You've come to tell me you're married," she said. She
walked toward Emma. They met in the middle of the room. "You
did right," Mrs. Schultz said. She patted Emma's hand and her
cheek. She shook hands with Nick.

Nick left them alone and went down to the street. Out in front
of the house he lit and smoked several cigarettes. Then he walked
to the corner and bought a half gallon of beer. When he went back
in Emma and her mother looked as if they had both been crying.
"Look what I brought us, Mom," Nick said. His voice was strained
with forced cheerfulness.

Mrs. Schultz barely touched the beer.

•••

A week married. The alarm clock went off. Nick groaned and
rolled around on the bed. Emma got up and turned it off. He
watched her dress, but when she turned toward the bed, he shut his
eyes, pretending that he was asleep. She leaned over him and kissed
him on the cheek. She took her hat and coat and walked quietly out
of the room. Nick rolled over and went to sleep.

When he awoke it was eleven o'clock. His place was set at the
table. Propped up against a milk bottle was a note for him:

*Dear Nicky, you will find your breakfast on the stove. I love you!
Emma.*

At the side of the plate was money for carfare and lunch.

He rode out to where the factories were. He went in and out of
factories and warehouses. He went in wishing they'd hire him and
wishing they wouldn't. At first he looked hard.

It's hot. It's no fun walking around.

He tried a lot of places. He knew before he asked they'd say no.
They said no.

Gritting his teeth, grinding them together, he walked out.

He found himself walking toward West Madison Street.

I'll look tomorrow.

•••

Sunshine was in the Pastime. Sunshine stood leaning against the wall with his coat collar bunched up at his neck and his arms held protectively around his chest. "Hello, Sunshine." Sunshine looked at him with a sad face and loosened the coat. "Look," he said. Nick peered in. He saw a small yellow head, little black eyes and a shivering puppy body. "Well, for Christ's sake! Where'd you get that?"

"Ah broke into a house and there was them puppies. First they scared me. Then they started whining and licking mah shoes." Sunshine grinned. "Ah got a bottle of milk and some po'k chops out of the icebox and fed them. This one was the hungriest so ah took him." Sunshine's voice became serious. "That's all ah took."

Nick put his hand inside Sunshine's coat and rubbed the puppy. It shivered with ecstasy, yapped and licked Nick's hand. Nick and Sunshine sat on a bench, put the puppy on their knees and played with him. They had a lot of fun tightening their hands over his jaw, shaking, teasing him, making him yap and snap and get mad, rolling him on his back, tickling his ears and seeing his tail wag like mad. "What are you going to do with him, Sunshine?"

"Ah don't know."

"Give him to me, will you?"

"All right."

"Hey, I'm going to take you home!" Nick said excitedly, standing up and putting the puppy in his shirt front. Sunshine called after Nick, "His name's Po'kchop. Ah call him that 'cause he was so hungry."

When he got home, Nick showed Emma what was down the front of his shirt. "Meet Porkchop," he said, grinning. She lifted him out and, holding him in her hands, rubbed her face against him. She looked at Nick over the happily shivering yellow ball and said, "We've got a whole family now!"

Nick looked at her and caught his breath.

What color are her eyes?

●●●

Because he was so tired from walking the day before, he didn't get up until one o'clock. The eggs were shrivelled in hardened grease; the buns were dried. He stepped in what Porkchop had left all over the kitchen floor. There was an I-love-you note on the table and carfare. He felt ashamed of himself. Porkchop was whining and waggling at the toes and the heels of his shoes, running in a little circle around Nick's feet. Nick took toilet paper and cleaned up. He fed Porkchop. The fool didn't know how to lap milk right. You had to push his face into the saucer until his head came up with his nose and whiskers white and dripping. Nick sat on the sofa and played with Porkchop. Then it was three o'clock. He sneaked down the

steps, out onto the veranda porch and out onto the sidewalk feeling
that everybody in the whole damn neighborhood saw him.

He went over to Stash's house. He waited around until Stash got
home. "Hey," he said, "can I get a job out at the steel mills?"

Stash scratched his blond hair, grinned, looked at Nick. "What's
the matter with you?" he asked.

"Nothing," Nick said embarrassedly, "I just want a job."

"Well, be here at five-thirty tomorrow morning and I'll take you
out there. I don't know. You might be able to get on."

"Five-thirty!" Nick said. Stash grinned. "Bet you won't be here!"
he said.

Nick was there. He got a job out at the steel mills as a laborer.

•••

Two weeks married. As soon as she got something out of marriage, right away she thought, well, gee! it would be swell to have a
baby! Almost as if when you reach one complete experience you
want to go on to the next. In the moon-darkness of the room she lay
on her side looking at Nick with large and tender eyes.

She lay next to him, happy. She had him. He had her. She could
feel the rise and fall of his breathing. The window pane darkened,
lightened, with a cloud passing across the moon. She snuggled close
to him, feeling her breath against his. She closed her eyes. With a
good job for him she could have children. Mom? . . . That wasn't
Nicky's responsibility. That was hers. Maybe she couldn't have children for a long time. She tightened her arm around him and lay as
close to him as she could get.

•••

Three weeks married. Sunlight put its yellowness across the bed.
Emma awoke, sat up in bed, yawning, stretching her arms, shaking
her hair back over her shoulders. No alarm clocks. No hot coffee to
swallow at the last minute. No crowded streetcar. Sunday was wonderful! Her yawn was pleasant and comforting. She looked at Nick
asleep next to her. He looks like a little boy. His face all puckered.
She smiled. He lay flat on his back. His arms lay naked on the
covers with sunlight catching fire in their slight hairs. She moved
next to him in the bed again and ran her fingers along his arm.
Nick awakened. His eyes looked at her and his lips grinned at her.
"Hello," he said.

"This is our anniversary!" she said. "We've been married three
weeks today!" He was lying lazily, had one hand reached out with
his fingers twisting the ends of her hair and was looking at it curiously. He gazed into her eyes. "What color are your eyes?" he asked.
She leaned over and kissed him. "Nicky! *My* Nicky! You're the only
thing that has ever belonged to me." She was staring at him seriously, almost sadly. Her eyes trembled away to the edge of his shoul-

der. "Oh, Nicky! you've got freckles on you!" She touched them with the tips of her fingers. The brown spots on his shoulder, his chest, his upper arm, his stomach. She rubbed her nose, her cheek against his chest. She put her arm around him, her lips against his upper ribs, and lay there.

59

Nick stood in safety shoes, overall pants and heavy gloves as for several days he had stood at the steel mills. He leaned his shovel against his leg and yanked off one of the stiff gloves. He wiped the palm of his hand across his face angrily. It came away dripping with sweat. He looked at it and shook it disgustedly.

What the hell am I? A slave?

The sweat splashed down against the hot, soot-dry ground, sending tiny sprays of dust rising at the steel toes of his safety shoes. Nick's face, where he had wiped, stood out hot, moist, clean-streaked. The rest of his face and neck were black with dirt, dust, scales of grit. His arms ached; his back was breaking. Nick kicked his shovel away from him and walked over to the foreman, stamping his feet heavily.

"I quit!"

■■■

He didn't tell Emma.

I'll find a better job. Then I'll tell her.

That night he lay in bed staring at the ceiling in the dark. Emma had her arm over his chest and her face against the muscle of his arm. Her lips said, "I love you, Nicky." He didn't answer. He told himself that he was tired. "I'm so happy," her voice whispered against his muscle. He pretended that he was asleep.

With his eyes closed his thoughts came down even closer to him.

He was tired. He didn't feel like it. It was funny being married— any time you wanted to.

He grew helpless and sad and uncomfortable in the bed.

She was funny. Different. Not like the others. That was more

[276]

exciting. You slapped a broad across the can as you went up the steps and into the room with her. You were in the dark unbuttoning each other's clothes, almost tearing them off. The broad was almost as anxious as you. Not shy and holding back all the time like—like Emma.

He thought of Rosemary. The last time he saw her and not being able to.

"Nicky, are you asleep?"

He didn't answer.

It wasn't like he thought it would be, him and Emma. He loved her, yeah—only—

He thought of all the messing around he had done on West Madison. He was awake long after Emma had gone to sleep.

■■■

Nick, on Monday, got a job as a laborer. The first time the boss jumped him he threw down his shovel and quit. Tuesday he went to work in a foundry. He stayed until Thursday, drew his pay and quit. He told Emma he got laid off. She said, "Oh, Nicky, that's too bad! But you'll find another job." And she kissed him. He was more ashamed when she kissed him than he had ever been in his life.

Because he remembered how her eyes had clouded in sympathy, then cleared and looked at him bravely, and the way she had put her hands on his shoulders and leaned toward him when she kissed him, he got up early Monday morning. He had her breakfast ready for her and went out job-hunting again. It took almost a week to find anything. This one was in a factory. "Goddamn you, you're going to stay here!" he told himself.

It was hot and dirty and hard. It was awful not to be boss of yourself but to have to punch a time clock and be somewhere you didn't want to be all day long, five and a half days a week. But he gritted his teeth and cursed and stayed on the job. He brought his first week's check home and handed it to her. She told him it was his money. He told her she knew how to pay the bills better than he did, so she took part of it for the bills and gave him the rest.

At the end of the second week he lined up with the other men before the cage for their checks. He got his pay and was going across the basement to the showers. By the back entrance the men were having a crap game with their week's earnings. Nick went over and stood watching the game. A fellow he knew yelled, "Come on and play, Romano!"

"Aw, I've got to go," Nick said. "Anyway, I ain't cashed my check yet."

"Oh, that's all right!" another man said. "Just sign it and some-body'll cash it for you when the winnings get high enough."

[277]

I can't be a bum sport. Anyway—I worked hard enough for it to have a little fun.

Somebody shoved an indelible pencil at him and he knelt on the concrete floor and signed the check.

Anyway maybe I'll win.

"Your dice, Romano!"

He took them, blew on them and rattled them together hard.

I can't be a piker. "Two bucks!" he said and tossed his check down on the concrete. It floated slowly and settled against the dirty and oily floor. Some old man about sixty covered him. Nick threw and won. The old man said, "Jesus! wouldn't that beat you!" and walked away.

Nick covered the foreman. Five bucks.

They played, fifteen or twenty men with wives and families; played with the money it had taken them a week of eight-hour days to earn.

Nick rolled the dice. A one turned up on each of the cubes and stayed that way. "Snake eyes!" a couple of the men yelled.

"Snake eyes!" Nick said, grinning. "I lose." He stood up, smiled and tossed his head a little. With his toe he pushed his check over to the houseman. "It's yours."

"You broke? —Did you lose it all?" the men wanted to know.

"That's right," Nick said, laughing. He turned and walked out, laughing so that they could hear him.

A young kid said, "That guy sure can take it!"

As soon as he was beyond the door the smile dried up off Nick's face.

You goddamn fool, you! You'll never learn! No, you'll never learn. A whole week's pay! What am I going to tell her?

Hurry up, think of something!

He went over west of Ogden on Madison Street. What if I get caught! What if I get caught! He was scared stiff.

He jack-rolled the man. When he was far enough away he counted the money. Fifty-six dollars!

When he got home he told Emma, "I had to work overtime," and gave her money for the rent and the food for next week.

He didn't go back to the factory. All week he slept until twelve and one o'clock. In the afternoon he went to the movies. Saturday he gave Emma money that was supposed to be out of his pay check. This worked a couple of weeks. Then the money was all gone. He looked in the want ads and among them saw advertised a job as a baker's apprentice. He remembered how when he was a kid he had wanted to be a baker, how at reform school they wouldn't let him. He went over to see about the job. It was a small neighborhood shop. The baker's wife must have liked his looks. "He's a nice

[278]

young man—he's nice-looking—he'll be honest," she told her husband and the baker said to come to work the next morning.

It was hot. It wasn't any good. It was scraping pans and separating eggs and carrying in hundred-pound sacks of flour and scrubbing the floor to keep the roaches down.

If I don't stay here I won't stay anywhere.

In bed that night Emma kept running her fingers through his hair and kissing him. "Gee, I'm tired," he told her. He tried to get worked up. "I'm tired," he said again and didn't try any more.

In the morning she came to kiss him goodbye and to set the clock for seven-thirty for him. "Your lunch is on the table, Nicky," she told him and kissed him again. He went to sleep. It seemed as if he had just closed his eyes when the alarm went off, drilling loudly into his ears. He reached out a fumbling hand and pushed the alarm button down.

I gotta get up. I gotta get up. If I don't get....

His eyes closed and blinked open again; then closed. He wanted to get up—but—

He rolled over and went to sleep.

■■■

Two days later Nick walked along Halsted Street.

I can't live off of her.

He turned down West Madison. The red Packard was parked outside with a blond in it. Nick found Ace in his office sitting at his desk with his hand stretched out toward the silver decanter. A cork-tipped cigarette was smoking on the silver ash tray. Ace looked up at him with his baggy eyes and smiled. He pushed a chair out with his foot and Nick sat down. "Nice-looking broad," Nick said, remembering the blond.

"Oh, not bad ... not bad," Ace said casually. He poured Nick a drink.

"She looks like she's tired of waiting," Nick said.

Ace laughed loudly; he said, "She's only been waiting an hour. I needed a drink ... needed a little pickup."

Nick swallowed his drink. "How about giving me my old job back?"

Ace poured himself another drink. "That's gone now. I got somebody else on that. But I can work you in over here on something." Ace showed his big teeth, like kernels on an ear of corn. "Glad you're back ... sure glad you're back."

Nick went to work for Ace. It took only a couple of hours a week to make good money. He told Emma he hadn't found anything yet and the money he gave her he said was won playing the horses. When he really played the horses or gambled, he lost and had to do an extra job or so for Ace.

[279]

It felt swell to get back on the street, see all the fellows, play pool with them and stand around shooting the bull. But he couldn't screw around down there too much because he didn't want Emma to find out what the score really was and he had to be home when she got there.

It went all over West Madison that he was married. The fellows shook their heads and said, "Poor girl. A guy like you getting married. Christ! Your wife don't know what she's letting herself in for!" Every time any of the fellows saw him they'd ask, "Where you going, home to the wife and kids?" And those who remembered her coming down to the poolroom for Nick that time said, "She sure is a good-looker. If you get tired of her—"

...

When Nick got home from West Madison one evening, Emma had surprising news for him.

"Ang was over," she said.

"Yeah? What did she have to say?"

"Julian is getting married next Sunday."

"*What!*" Nick whistled in a long-drawn exhalation of surprise and sat down on a chair and began to fan himself with his hat. "Say that again!"

"Isn't it swell?" Emma said.

Nick leaned back in the chair and fanned himself some more.

I didn't think he had brains enough to get a woman. I didn't think he knew what it was for. Christ! Who'd marry him? She must really be something! I gotta get a look at that broad!

Emma told him about Julian and his wife going to live at home because Julian wanted to help his mother.

Nick curled his nose and laughed inside. Yeah, just like him.

Emma said, "What will we get them for a wedding present?"

Nick said, "I don't know. I ain't going."

Emma pleaded with him but he said no he wasn't going. She bought the present, showed it to him and wrote from Nick and Emma on it. Getting dressed Sunday she kept looking at him. At last, picking up the present, she said, making her voice steady, "I'm going, Nicky. I'll see you later."

On his way over to Ace's place the day after Julian's wedding Nick got off the car at 12th Street.

She must be a prize! I gotta get a squint at that broad.

He looked up at the house. He thought he saw someone in the window. Going up the stairs he pushed the door open slowly. "Hey!" he yelled. "Who's home?"

Nobody answered.

He pushed the door all the way open, stepped in and started closing it.

A girl stood behind the door staring at him. Her mouth was open a little as if she were going to say something. Her arms were pressed to her sides. When she saw Nick she dropped her eyes.

Rosemary!

"Rosemary!"

"Hello, Nick," Rosemary said. It was so low he barely heard her.

"What are you doing here, Rosemary!"

She looked up, slowly, with embarrassed eyes. "I'm Julian's wife."

"Well, for Christ's sake!" That was all Nick could say. He stood staring at her in astonishment.

Rosemary could talk now. Her words rushed out. "I met Julian at Hull-House. I was doing social work over there. He's—he's wonderful, Nick—so earnest and—and—"

Nick started laughing.

I thought he'd get some old hag. Rosemary. Of everybody in the world. It was funny. It was very funny.

Rosemary put her hand out on his shoulder.

"Please—please don't—" She sounded as if she were going to cry.

Nick stopped. "I was just laughing because—because—look, I've stopped." He gazed at her seriously. "I think you and Julian will make a fine couple."

Rosemary's voice was still unsteady and her blue eyes panicky. "Please, Nick, don't tell him about—about—over at my house—"

Nick became dead serious. "We'll tell them I introduced myself to you over here." He patted her shoulder.

■■■

He walked down Halsted to Madison and into the Pastime still in a daze.

Jesus! Who would of thought that could happen!

Butch said, "What about a game?"

Nick shook his head no. "Later," he said.

He stood thinking, watching the balls roll across the green pad without really seeing them. Some one came up behind him and hit him on the arm with his fist, hard. "What do you think you're doing, you sonofa—" Nick whirled around.

It was Vito.

"—Well for Christ sake!"

They stood, pumping each other's hands up and down, grinning, looking at each other, slapping each other on the shoulder, both saying, "Christ! It's good to see you!"

Nick said for the fifth time, "Boy! am I glad to see you!" And Vito said, "It's sure swell to be back. I'd of been back long ago only they had me in the pen for two years."

"Good old Vito!" Nick said, pounding his shoulder and grinning at him.

"Remember the car we made?" Vito said.

"Boy! And how!"

"How's things around here? Can I make some easy money?" Vito asked, and he grinned.

"Good old Vito!" Nick said.

60

Emma came home from work and dropped down on the sofa by the window. She hung her head. He doesn't love me. If he did—

Her head went down lower until her chin touched the little hollow at the end of her neck and her face burned with the consciousness of what she was thinking about. Consciousness of shame didn't inhibit her thoughts.

He's not the same. Not like he was that first night . . . and for a little while after that . . . maybe there was something the matter with her. Was he ashamed to tell her?

Nick found her alone on the sofa with her head down. He sat next to her. "What's the matter?" She shook her head, nothing. He put his hand on top of her hands where they lay on her lap. "Are you sorry?"

"Oh, Nicky, how can you say that?"

"Is it about me not working steady?"

She leaned over and put her head against his shoulder. "Nothing's the matter, Nicky."

They sat silent for a while, then Nick said, "Are you going to night school tonight?" She shook her head no against his shoulder. "I want to go out for a while if you don't care," Nick said. "A friend of mine just got in Chicago and I want to see him."

"You go if you want," Emma said. "I'll go see Mom for a while."

...

Nick went to meet Vito. They went to the Long Bar and drank at one of the tables with their feet propped up on empty chairs and their chairs tilted back against the wall. They talked over old times.

And Vito told Nick everything he had done in New York before he got caught.

He and Vito put on a party, just the two of them. Nick popped for all the drinks, shoving Vito's hand with bills in it away and yelling for the bartender to set them up again. The jukebox was loud in Nick's ears, making him feel at home. Good old Vito was next to him at the table, making him feel like old times. He put his arm up on Vito's shoulder and again they relived the schools they had been kicked out of, the broads behind St. Francis', the jack-rolling.

When Nick came home he was pretty drunk. He undressed and got quickly into bed, without night clothes. He woke Emma up. He pawed her a little. She waited tensely, with her arms tightened around him, ashamed of his drunken breath, near tears.

Nick pawed her, but after a while he didn't feel like it any more. He said, "I'm tired," and rolled over on his back away from her and immediately went to sleep.

Emma lay awake, staring, blinking at the dark. Her body and her nerves were stretched taut. Emotion and frustration rasped against her, ground her. Her breath came in defeated gasps. She couldn't relax. The bed was hot and uncomfortable. She rolled on it, cease-lessly changing the position of her legs, her arms. Next to her Nick breathed heavily in his sleep. His breath smelled of liquor. She curled her nose away and rolled far to the other end of the bed. I hate him! I hate him! She tightened herself into a knot and tried to sleep. She couldn't. She rolled back again, rolled next to him. I hate you! She was as close as she could get to him; and he was like wood, like a stone, like dead. "I hate you!" she sobbed dryly, too miserable for tears.

■■■

Nick started hanging around the poolroom with Vito and Butch on nights Emma went to school. Sometimes in the Pastime there would also be Juan and Sunshine and a stringbean of a guy called Stretch. Butch had a big old-model car now that they'd sit in at night. They'd get a couple half gallon bottles of beer, pass them around, drinking out of the bottle, and smoke cigarettes. They'd roll the windows down, and all piled in the car sprawled out against each other, they'd stick their feet out the windows or prop them up on the steering wheel, or up on the dashboard near the windshield. They'd yell and shout and curse and tell dirty jokes out there in Butch's car drawn up to the curb in front of the Pastime.

Sometimes when they were out there Riley passed by, walking his beat. His ugly face on its bull neck would turn toward the car, his pistol-barrel eyes would shoot over at the legs hanging out the win-dows and the faces inside. Nick, in the car, always tightened his jaw

[283]

and stared back at Riley, even if Riley hadn't noticed him. With his teeth clenched Nick would mutter, "The sonofabitch!"

Nick started hanging over there a lot. A few times he didn't go home in time for dinner and a couple of times not until Emma was washing her stockings and getting ready to go to bed. She never said anything, but she looked like she had been crying or was going to cry. Nick would feel bad, but when he was with the fellows he forgot all about home; he was happy. It was good to be back. The street pulled you back. It got in your blood.

Nick made the rounds of all the taverns with the fellows. It got so the bartenders and hostesses recognized them when they shouldered in, dressed up like bigtime hoods—neatly knotted cravats, starched shirts, topcoats, hats pulled over their eyes a little or tilted on the sides of their heads. It got so the 26-girls kidded them when they stood around rolling for drinks; it got so the 26-girls were open for propositioning. Most of them tried to get next to Nick.

Every day or so it seemed that he and Riley were passing each other on the street. He stared at Riley and Riley stared at him. Cold. With hate. They recognized each other without showing it.

Riley didn't bother him. But his pistol eyes seemed to be always waiting. Under his coat, the pistol on the belt with the three notches cut into it seemed to be waiting.

■■■

Vito had a room of his own. When he had been in town a few weeks he took Nick up there and showed him a gat. Then he told Nick what he was planning. The idea gripped Nick's imagination as Vito told him how easy it was and what a lot of money was in it. "I'm kind of broke now and could use some dough and it's sure easy money," Vito said. "Want to come along?"

"Yeah!" Nick said without thinking. "You can count me in! When do we start?"

"Right away—as soon as you can pick up your rod. Butch is coming by in his car. He's going to work with us—he's a good wheelman."

Butch drove them over to where Nick lived.

I hope she ain't home. I hope she ain't home.

She had already gone to night school. His plate was on the table, the supper in dishes near it. His eyes filled up. There was a note on his plate for him. He didn't look at it but instead got the old gun from its hiding place and went down to the car.

They were driving down Princeton Avenue. All of a sudden Vito said, "Hey! Park here!" Butch parked. Vito said, "Shut off the lights." Butch did. They sat smoking cigarettes in the dark. Up in front of them were the El tracks with, once in a while, a train of cars going past overhead, brakes screeching on the curve of tracks, wheels throwing sparks in the night. Nick's mind jumped back to the day he came to Chicago, the first time he had seen the El. Tracks in the air on stilts.

At last a single car came along, going fast. All of its shades were down. But it was fully lighted and the light showed along the edges of all the windows. "What time is it?" Vito asked. Butch held his watch up close to the windshield and looked. Nick drew in on his cigarette, making it glow so that there would be more light. "Eight-thirty," Butch said. Vito nodded. "That was the pay car. It picks up the station money along the line. I wanted to find out what time it got here. Let's go."

He told Butch where to drive. They went there and Butch parked the car a couple of doors from the El entrance with the motor running.

ENTRANCE. Blue enameled letters on white enamel. Vito and Nick went in through the swinging door.

Inside it was just like all the other El stations. On the right-hand side there was a cage completely surrounded by iron grillwork, painted black with a little oval for people to push their fares to the ticket taker, and a door at the far side for going in and out of the cage. Inside the cage on a swivel chair sat the operator at a high desk. There was an aisle along which you went to pay your fare. On the walls were posters advertising the Civic Opera House, a play at the Blackstone. On the inside of the iron grill opposite the ticket taker's cage was a potbellied stove, a couple of benches. At the far end of the wall were doors, TO CITY and FROM CITY, that led to the upper platform where you boarded the trains. There were several electric bulbs on a board next to the doors that flashed on and off, making a buzzing sound and signalling that a train was leaving the platform of the next station.

Nick walked not to the ticket taker but to the side of the entrance door and over to the peanut machine as if he were going to buy some peanuts, so that he could cover anybody who came in. In his pocket his hand was on his gun.

Vito walked up to the ticket taker and, shielding his gun from the street entrance with his back and shoulders, pointed it into the oval in the iron grill. "This is a stick-up! Keep your mouth shut and fork over!"

Nick thrilled to Vito's words.

He watched the door and couldn't look. He'd give anything if he could see the ticket taker's face!

"The bills in the drawer, too!" Vito's voice snarled.

The lights blinked, on-off, repeatedly, the buzzer jangled warningly. A long line of cars was leaving the station, one down the line.

"Hurry up, you bitch!" Vito's voice said, "or I'll plug you!"

Then Vito was cramming the bills in his pocket, raking the loose change into his other hand, and Nick had turned around to face and cover the ticket taker. Then they were going out the door fast. Then they were hopping in the car past the door Butch had thrown open.

An El train passed overhead, slowing, throwing sparks, drawing up to the platform. Butch, Vito and Nick were speeding away from the scene before the train stopped.

They hopped three stations down the line. They pulled a job there. Then they drove two miles away, fast, to another station on the Jackson Park line. When they parked Nick said, "Let me pull this one!" and Vito let him.

Recklessly they pulled five jobs. After the fifth hoist they decided they better let that be enough before the goddamn cops caught up with them. They had over three hundred dollars in bills and change.

■■■

Only two nights after they had pulled the robberies, Vito said, "Let's go make them again. They don't expect to get hit so soon again." That sounded like good sense to Nick. "Okay, let's break them this time," he said.

Before they set out their confidence was lowered a little and they decided they'd make only a couple of places. Tonight they went to the North Side and pulled three jobs. They split the money up and got sixty dollars apiece.

Over on West Madison after the job Nick swaggered around with Butch and Vito, feeling good, tough, like a big shot, sticking his hand down in his pocket every once in a while to double it around the bulging billfold.

They swaggered down the street and, going under the neon sign, turned into the Long Bar. They drank shots for a quick kick. Sunshine came in and they got him drunk, coaxing him to take one after another, whiskeys and beer, kidding him, telling him he couldn't take it. Juan came in and they started feeding him drinks too. Juan had five or six. Then his eyes got dreamy; he stood up, grinned, hoisted his pants. They knew what was wrong with him before he said it. "I got a broad on the line," he said, grinned again, and walked unevenly toward the door.

A couple of girls came over and, unasked, sat down, muscled in, smiling and kidding them. So they bought drinks for the broads too. They lapped it up. Verne had her arms around Butch and Vito, Nick sat twisted toward Dot, motioning at her with his glass. "Come on! Drink! What did you come over here for?" She smiled at him. She drank. Like a man. Swilling the shot down in one swallow. Making no face. She put her hand out and ran her fingers through Nick's hair. He jerked his head away.

They drank until it seemed to float around inside of them. Vito told Verne, "Let's get a room somewhere," and Dot looked at Nick meaningly.

"I got a wife I gotta go home to," Nick said.

Vito said, "Aw, what she don't know won't hurt her," and the whole bunch kept coaxing him, so finally he said, "All right." And inside, she won't find out.

When they got to the place, Dot went up the steps ahead of Nick. Nick started patting her. Yeah, this is more like it!

•••

It wasn't fun. No kick at all.

Out on West Madison Street alone, staggering down the street in a half-daze, he told himself that he had been too drunk. He walked on, unconscious of his direction.

I can't go home like this.

He pulled up on drunken legs in front of the Nickel Plate. He bought a cup of black coffee, hot. It burned his lips. He got another. He could hardly keep awake, drinking it. Staggering down to the counter, he got still another cup of coffee and brought it back to the table.

I gotta sober up ... gotta ... sober up. . . .

•••

When he finally got home he turned on the bedroom light. Emma was crying. The chain dangled noisily against the bulb. "For Christ sake!" Nick said. "What the hell's the matter with you? What are you bawling about? Just because I went out and had a good time?" He undressed, leaving his clothes scattered all over the floor. He fell asleep as soon as he hit the bed.

The next morning when he woke up his clothes were folded across a chair. Emma had gone to work. Porkchop was scratching against the door to get out. Nick dressed and went to see Vito. Butch was there already. They had bought all the papers, morning and afternoon editions. The story was there.

> ...the bandits were youths about twenty and twenty-two years of age. The younger was described by Miss Mary Morgan, ticket taker at the Pine Street station at the time of the robbery, as being handsome, with brown eyes and curly black hair. The other bandit was about five-foot-nine and wore a gray hat and topcoat. . . .

Nick didn't stay long. They said they better take it easy, Butch was lucky he was the wheelman and didn't have anybody looking at him, oh hell, they won't catch us, how many guys in Chicago answer

[287]

that description, thousands of them, they ain't got a chance to pin it on us. In the doorway Nick looked down the street both ways before stepping out on the sidewalk. He looked both ways before he waited on the corner for his car.

At home with Emma he was sorry for the way he had acted last night and tried to make it up by peeling potatoes, drying the dishes, kidding with her a little and talking to her all evening about whatever he could think of. She seemed to have forgotten about last night. On the sofa she sat close to him with her head on his shoulder.

He was as nice to her as he could be all evening. But that night in bed he failed her again.

• • •

Memory of the newspaper articles with the half-descriptions of the bandits and the fear of getting caught preyed on Nick's mind. He got so that for a couple of weeks he was almost scared to go out on the street. But he wouldn't admit it to himself. He brazened it out. Sure, he went down on West Madison Street. But whenever he walked out of a door, he hesitated and looked up and down the street. If he saw a cop he stiffened, ready to duck out of sight. All but Riley. If Riley messed around with him—

For two weeks they were scared off. Then the money ran low with stuss and poker and the horses. Then one night it was all gone and Nick and Vito walked along West Madison broke. Vito poked Nick with his elbow. "Let's go on another job."

"I ain't got my gun."

"I've got mine," Vito said, patting his pocket.

They found Butch in his room. Butch was drunk and stretched across the bed. Vito went through his pockets and took the key for the car. He and Nick drove down to the Douglas Park branch. They went into the station as if they were customers, even paying their fares. Then Vito went quickly to the door leading into the cage, threw it open and levelled his gun at the ticket taker. "Please— please—I'll lose my job—" the middle-aged man whined.

"Get down from there, you sonofabitch, and hand over that money!" Vito commanded.

The guy was so scared he couldn't move. "Kneel down, you bastard!" Vito said. Nick stepped up to the ticket counter. The money was in a little box on top, stacked in piles of nickels, dimes, quarters. The ticket taker knelt down at Nick's feet and Vito had the gun against his skull. Just then the lights blinked and the buzzer sounded, telling them that a train was leaving the Hurst Avenue station. "Take your coat off!" Vito told Nick. "Act like you're the ticket taker." Nick struggled out of his coat and let it fall on the floor. Vito quickly straightened the remaining stacks of nickels and dimes. They heard the train rumble up to the platform. Vito ducked down out of sight whispering, "Keep quiet, you bastard, or I'll plug you!" The train rumbled again, rolling on toward the next stop.

Some people came down from the platform. At the same time two women came in for tickets. They were tishing and saying, "Oh dear, we just missed that train." Nick kept his eyes lowered, afraid that they might look at him and know. They left their dimes and went through the To City door. Nick rang the customer register and put the dimes in his pocket. Vito, out of sight, crawled over to the safe and took the stacked bills out of the cash drawer. Another customer came in. Nick, grinning, took the man's dime. It was a lot of fun! But then Vito said, "Let's go!" and to the ticket taker, "Don't move from there till we get out of here—get it!"

In the car, leaping away from the curb, they laughed.

They had just switched on the car lights, making a hole of brightness in the alley when the squad car came down the alley. Nick pushed the starter; and his whole chest jumped up into his throat. Under his foot the starter whirred and didn't turn the motor over. The squad car was drawn up next to them with three cops jumping out with drawn guns levelled at their heads. Vito was trying to get his gun out of his pocket. But it was too late. The cops had the drop on them.

•••

Emma walked into the barred cell where at last they let her see him. "It isn't your fault! It isn't your fault, Nicky!" She moved quickly toward him, almost running. "It's what reform school did to you, the way you grew up." She threw herself hard against him, her fingernails scratching down the material of his coat at his shoulders, digging into his back. "I love you, Nicky, I love you!" With his face buried against her hair and her neck, Nick choked and didn't answer. With his arms around her he patted her back, gently.

•••

Vito and Nick stood before the judge. Vito, with his bad record, his times in jail, on the desk before the judge, said, "Naw, Nick didn't have anything to do with it. I handled the money and I handled the gun. He was just the lookout."

The judge read Vito's sentence. "One year to life."

Nick opened his mouth and swallowed; he tightened his fingers on Vito's arm.

The judge removed his glasses, squinted, massaged the bridge of his nose with his thumb and forefinger. He twisted his swivel chair around and leaned over the bench. "You're a young man," he said, looking down at Nick. "You're not even twenty-one yet.

Your whole life is ahead of you. I have a lot of sympathy for you. . . ."

After that he said, "One year in the county jail."

•••

A year! A year!

Nick slumped down on the bunk in his cell at the county jail. He put his hand on the back of his neck and hung his head. The bars stood up, black, heavy, in front of him. His shadow loomed up large and black on the wall.

A year!

Nick lay on his back on the bunk. His shadow lay down with him. He pulled the blanket over his face and knotted his arms in it.

61

364 more days. Nick sat in the bull pen starting his stretch. The hard daylight fell through the prison bars, fell on Nick's bowed head and his knuckles. He stared at his knuckles. He kept cracking them.

Well, I guess the smart guy got too smart.

Alone in his cell.

I'll be waiting for you.

He whispered her name, over and over. He felt like bawling; and with the tears inside of him he was angry at himself, hated himself. He lay, twisting on the cot, unable to sleep. Then in the night, late in the night, on the other side of the wall he heard the young inmate who had arrived just that day twist on his cot and sob hysterically. Nick got off the bunk and tried to talk to the prisoner on the other side by knocking on the wall with his shoe.

Morning. The bull pen. The fellows laughing and kidding, playing cards and cursing.

He couldn't bear to think of the awful and dragging months ahead—and yet he did think about them. That was all he thought about. And he kept score—

Only one day in here.
Only twelve days.
A month. Eleven to go.
Christ!

■■■)

The days were as cruel to Emma. She went to work. She came home. She went to night school, doggedly, three times a week. She dreaded going home, cooking, getting into the large and lonely bed. Often she ate at a restaurant and walked home to tire herself out.

She didn't cry. Her loneliness was beyond tears, her wretched-ness beyond expession. Often she lay face down on the sofa under the window in the small front room until it was time to wash her stockings and underwear and go to bed. Porkchop would lie on the floor near the sofa, sleeping. Or he would paw the sofa cushions, whine, nuzzle her neck and shoulder. That was more heartbreaking than anything—the dog's loyalty, his faithfulness to her. It pointed up her waiting for Nick.

Ang came over. Ang and Rosemary came over. They tried to cheer her up. They made her get dressed and go walking with them. They dragged her to shows. She went because they were nice to her. Her lips even laughed with them. In her mind there was no smile, no laughter. Bread without butter. Sleep without rest. Death without dying. In the crowds to walk alone. A year! A year!

■■■

In the jail the horrible monotony weaves blackly around you. Closer and closer it walls you in. It is the only reality you know. You can put your hands out and press against it, trying to push it back. Your eyes get dead. They look back. They see nothing but meanness and hate in life.

Forget it! Don't think about it!

You can't forget it. You think of getting your revenge.

■■■

Emma went to see her mother once a week, taking her a house dress, bringing her some food or paying a bill for her. When Mom asked about Nick, why he never came to see her, Emma lied, say-ing he was working nights.

Sundays she spent at Ma Romano's, glad for their good friend-ship. Ma hugging her and telling her everything would be all right. Aunt Rosa kidding her out of the blues. Julian with a box of candy for her. Glad for the feeling of belonging, glad to get away by herself again. The Lily Maid in a tower, without love. She in Chicago, in two and a half furnished rooms, without him.

■■■

Nick sat looking at the words Emma had put on paper. *"Rose-mary and Julian are going to have a baby."* He tried to make them click in his mind.

I didn't think he had it in him!

He read the letter several times.

Emma should have a baby. She'd give anything to have a baby.

In his cell, lying on the hard cot, he thought about it. He was thinking about it when he fell asleep ... he walked into the yellow room. The walls were yellow, the floor and ceiling yellow. Foggy wisps of the floor and ceiling rose, filtering through the air. Yellowness was everywhere like oil, sickly, thick, congealing. It was really a solid yellow cube with him in the middle of it. In his hand he held a huge key. The end was broken off. Lost. He held the butt of the key in his hand. The jagged, broken end was dull metal and blunted. On a higher level of yellow cube was Emma. She stood on a precipitous, smooth-sided vertical with a flat and narrow top. There were no steps up to her. At the foot of the cube, far below her was a yellow sea of crashing waves, licking, thundering over jagged yellow rocks. There was no boat to make the crossing in. There were no steps, not even broken ones, up to her height. She had slowly shrunken to doll size. She sat, swollen like Buddha; then dried, shrunken like a mummy. Her eyes looked, sadly, down from the cube top, across the yellow sea at him. He looked at her casually, then away, paying no more attention to her. The broken key in his hand. He could feel the coldness of its metal. It crept up into his arm, crept through him, making his arm metal, changing him into metal with a death-cold Midas touch. Hard, cold, yellow-colored metal. He couldn't move. The boyishness was frozen in his eyes, on his cheeks and lips. He was fixed to the spot. Then he was moving. Something under him, like a disk, was turning him around until he faced away from Emma. He was faced into yellow space. At his foot he could see a dismembered arm. Swollen. The tissues ragged at one end. The nerves throbbing in it. An arm with thick, curling black hairs on it. A man's arm. He stared into yellow nothingness. . . .

Days in—three hundred.

●●●

Nick couldn't believe he was getting out Wednesday.

He paced the floor. He thought again of what his suit looked like. He thought of it downstairs in the bundle cage where Emma had left it for him. He didn't fall asleep those last nights until two or three o'clock. When he slept he had all kinds of cockeyed dreams. Wish dreams. Hope dreams. Fear dreams.

●●●

Today's the day! Each second was like drowning. Then—he was in his own clothes. He was walking out toward freedom. He stood waiting for the door to open. It rumbled open. He moved forward. The bars fell over his back in shadow, slipped off, lay on the concrete behind him.

In the sunlight on the sidewalk Emma waited. She wore a tan coat and a hat with a veil. She didn't speak. She came toward him quickly, put her hand up to the veil and threw it back over the top of her hat, put her arms around him, lifted her lips to him to be kissed.

62

Nick wanted to move. He wanted to forget. They found a second-floor apartment in a small two-story building near 57th and Halsted. Nick got a job in a factory.

A few days later Nick went down to West Madison to see the boys and to let them know he was back in circulation again. He big-shouldered his way into the Pastime and posed in the doorway for a minute. Old Jake was wiping the counter just like always. Everything was the same down there. A year didn't make any difference. He walked over to the counter. When he let go of Old Jake's hand he picked up a coketop and hurled it at the middle pool table. Sunshine wheeled around and Butch, poised for a shot, looked up. Their eyes met.

"Hello, you bastards!" Nick shouted.

"Nick!"

"Nick!"

They came on the hustle, grinning. They yanked his hand up and down. They pounded his back and beat in his hat. Chris came over. The Kid came over; his lips twisted nastily, "You're out, huh?" He laughed meanly and walked away. Nick grinned; he looked around at all of them. "Yeah, little Nicky's back in circulation!" he said, hard-boiled.

Just then Juan walked into the poolroom. When he saw who

it was, he rushed over to Nick, shook him by the shoulders, pumped his hand, hugged him and then kept his arm around Nick, shaking him affectionately.

"Let's get some beer! We gotta celebrate," Nick said. He popped for it and Butch, grumbling but not minding, went next door for the half gallon. Old Jake put glasses on the counter and, in his apron and rolled-up shirtsleeves, drank with them. Butch popped for the next half gallon. They stood around, drinking and talking, Nick telling them how he did the year rap standing on his head, telling it and laughing, big-shot, about it.

They had a couple more drinks. Then Nick whispered to Juan when the others weren't paying any attention, "I want to get a broad. Know any fast numbers around here?"

"I know them all!" Juan boasted. "I can fix you up with a broad and you won't have to pay."

"No," Nick said, "I want a live wire."

"There's a new one hit Skid Row since you was here. She's from Frisco. French Lulu." Juan's hand made descriptive gestures.

"Yeah, that's what I want," Nick said.

• ■ ■

He went with Lulu. She was a tall broad, sag-breasted, stringy haired, with gaunt gray eyes in a hollow-cheeked, painted face. Going to her room he started singing her the song he knew when he was a kid on Taylor Street, "I took my Lulu to the circus to see what we could see. . . ." He put in all the dirty words. In the hall, going up the steps he put his hand where her dress wobbled behind. She said, her voice dropping to a professionally passionate and throaty tone, "What have you got for me, big boy?"

He went home from Lulu shamefaced. Emma was sitting by the window gazing out. When he saw her something reminded him of himself staring through the bars in jail. When she turned her face to him it looked as if she had been crying. "Hi," he said gruffly.

"How are you, Nicky?"

"I'm okay," he said, monotone.

"Nicky—"

She had gotten up and was coming toward him. She smelled him. "Oh, Nicky—you've been drinking."

"Yes, I've been drinking." He imitated her and watched her wince; enjoyed it.

"Nicky—" she said; her voice was cool. "Rosemary had her baby today—" Her voice trembled. "A baby boy."

She turned and went, quickly, to the bedroom.

Nick stood for a minute where he had been when she told him. Then he followed her, slowly. She was sitting in a chair in the

[294]

dark. He stood in the doorway looking in at her. After a long time he said hollowly. "You want a baby, don't you?"

She glanced over her shoulder at him, then back out the window. She nodded her head yes.

Nick looked down at his hands. He lifted them. He looked at them helplessly. He moved his fingers, watching them move in the dark.

In the dark he undressed, got into bed, turned on his side with his face to the wall and lay that way.

···

It was then that he saw Owen again. Owen had been so damned decent to him. He was the only real friend he had. A guy he could depend on any time for anything. Only once he and Owen hadn't been on the level when they were together.

Nick, at home, had pulled a new shirt from the dresser and started unbuttoning it.

"Where are you going?" Emma asked.

"Oh, just for a couple of games of pool."

Instead he stopped for a few drinks, and a few more, and went up to Owen's place, on sudden impulse.

It was late and he had to knock hard. At last the light went on and Owen stood in the open door blinking out into the hall and tying the sash of his bathrobe.

Nick grinned without showing his teeth, hard dimples forming at the ends of his mouth. He walked in. "Surprised to see me this late?" he asked.

Owen closed and locked the door. He stood near it staring at Nick. "What are you doing here at this time of night?"

Nick shrugged. "Just thought I'd come to see you." He grinned again.

"You've been drinking," Owen said.

"Yeah, I been drinking," Nick said, imitating Owen.

"Go home, Nicky," Owen said.

Nick grinned. He turned and walked through the rooms to the pantry and came back with a bottle of wine and two glasses. Owen stood near the door where Nick had left him.

Nick sat down. He put the glasses on the floor and uncorked the bottle, leaning over until his shoulders were almost touching his knees. He filled the glasses. "Come on over and have a drink," Nick said.

Owen came slowly. His eyes didn't leave Nick's face. He sat at the other end of the couch and took the glass of wine Nick shoved at him. "Why don't you go home?"

"I want to hang around."

Nick drained his glass and motioned to Owen. "Drink up." Owen stared at the wine, then at Nick. Leaning over Nick filled his own glass again.

"Go home, Nicky," Owen said.

"*No.*" Nick pronounced it slowly, echoing it in the emphatic open circle of his lips.

Owen drank his wine.

■■■

Emma sat in the kitchen near the double windows, looking out. Nick came in and pulled out the light. The room snapped to darkness. Emma looked over her shoulder at Nick, then back out the window. The chain jangled against the bulb for a moment, then hushed into silence. Nick drew a chair up near Emma's. The chair scraped against the floor like a fingernail across a blackboard.

They sat looking out the window.

A pale bath of cold light fell in the back yard. On each side of the yard was a fence, over one of which drooped the branches, still leafless, of a lilac bush. They were black, brittle, in the night, twisted snares in the dark. The back stretch of fence sagged in the middle where a couple of boards were missing. The gate hung half open on one hinge. Beyond the fence was an alley, beyond the alley an empty lot, beyond the empty lot the railroad tracks on a high, level parapet of limestone blocks. The season's first flakes of snow were streaking intermittently across the sky. They were small, cold, hard. They were a white, powdered crystal across the night. They coated the hard, brittle branches of the lilac bush, edged the top rail of the back fence, brushed the yard in weedy, uneven ovals. Wind swirled them across the vacant lot. Wind beat them against the limestones of the railroad tracks. Wind touched them against the black panes of window in front of Nick and Emma with a pecking sound.

Nick opened his mouth a couple of times without speaking. Nick opened his mouth and closed it. His armpits itched. His insides rose and fell, rose and fell. He fastened the soles of his shoes against the floor. His eyes stared out the window without seeing.

"Do you know why I can't be a real husband to you?" His voice was almost a whisper, hoarse. His heart beat so hard he could hear it. He went on, talking fast so that he'd get it all out without stopping, blurting it out, gruffly, almost hard-boiled. "I was no good from the time I was sixteen. There were men and women. A lot of them." He could hear his own voice rush on loudly, scaring him. "They gave me money. I always needed money. There was every whore and slut on West Madison." He stopped. He waited.

No sound. No sound. In the room no sound but the wild beating of his own heart.

The wind trod on the roof. The snow crystals pecked at the window.

Inside the room it was so quiet he could hear his conscience condemning him, reading back his sins to him; he could feel the rope his conscience had put around his neck. He swallowed. He stared straight ahead at the black, snow-streaked window without seeing. His knuckles made loud popping sounds as he twisted his fingers madly together.

That minute went on . . . on . . . on. . . .

The only sound. His knuckles cracking, his heart pounding, his temples thumping against the skin of his forehead.

Window. Me. Emma. Told her.

Emma's chair squeaked a little.

Nick started and began to tremble. His forehead was hot. A shiver ran up his back and shook him.

The cords in Emma's neck swelled. She could feel the tears lump up in her throat. Her mind repeated his words, echoed them through her consciousness, sent them, slowly, one by one, through her mind.

From—the—time—

I—was—sixteen—

for better, for worse . . .

sluts—

for richer for poorer . . .

men—

in sickness and in health . . .

whores—

forbetterforworse

lots—of—

forricherforpoorer

them

in sickness and in health.

They sat staring out the window. That minute went on an hour, a day, a year.

63

Nick waited on the corner for Emma. She came along the sidewalk toward him. The wind blew her skirt and she held the brim of her hat with her hand. He looked down at her and she said hello, removing her hat and shaking her hair back over her shoulders. She took his arm and they walked on. He took secret side glances at her. She leaned toward him slightly as they walked.

They went into the restaurant and ordered dinner. "It's nice, Nicky, to eat downtown and not to have to fix supper," she said, and the waitress brought the soup. Nick glanced at her and lowered his eyes. She looked across the table at him. His eyes, with the spoon tilted to his lips, were looking at her, seriously, childishly grave. A pang of emotion squeezed at her. All during the meal her eyes looked at him protectively.

They went to a show and then home. Nick turned on the light and stood looking at her with his hand still on the switch. Emma raised her eyes. . . .

Lifted her eyes and read in his lineaments the guilt he bore. . . .

She walked quickly into the kitchen. She ran the cold water and got a drink. Moving to the window to pull down the shades she stood there a moment looking out with her hand on the sill.

". . . If you want to call it off, Emma—I don't see why you hang around. I ain't no good."

"I love you, Nicky. That's all I know. That's all that matters. Nothing else matters. . . ."

Her eyes filled with tears. She blinked hard. She stared, unseeing, down into the moon-flooded and vacant back yard. Over the fence leaned the branches of the lilac bush. They were heavy with the twisted green knots of buds. Her eyes focussed on the green buds without seeing them. The slim branches, the buds full to bursting, swam in the tears of her eyes. She walked from the window, forgetting to draw the shades, and into the front room.

Nick stood by the radio. He turned and looked over his shoulder at her. Standing in the doorway she smiled quickly when he glanced at her. "Want to hear the radio?" he asked. She nodded her head without answering . . . .

Marr'd as he was, he seemed the goodliest man . . . .

The radio button clicked on. Music filled the room. Emma moved across the room swiftly to him. Her hair swayed on her shoulders as she walked. She stood next to him. She didn't speak but put her arms up around him. They kissed. He put his face down against her hair and her neck and clung to her. He could smell the sweet and clean odor of her skin. He could smell the soap she used. He clung to her. "Emma! Emma!"

*This love of mine goes on and on . . .**

Nick turned the radio down and grinned. "Kind of loud, huh?"

*I ask the sun and the moon—the stars that shine—
What's to become of it?
This love of mine.**

They lay in bed. Oh, I love you. I love you. Oh, please, please. Why does life have to be like this? God, if there is a God, help me. Please help me. What have I done? Help me. No, don't help me. Help him. Please, please, God. I love him so. Please, God. You don't know what it's like. Loving somebody so much—please, God, please. I don't mean to be a baby but, please, please.

She lay clenching her teeth, holding the tears inside of her, letting them drain down through her, begging. Slowly she felt with her hand for him, touched his arm, her fingers falling on the rise and swell of his muscle. A thrill ran through her, making her shiver. She clenched her teeth. Oh, please! She moved her hand down over his muscle, curious, affectionately. Her fingers moved over his forearm, across the slight roughness of the curled hairs there. Her fingers smoothed the hairs, mussed them, smoothed them. Nicky! Nicky! She lifted his arm and put it around her. It came over limp, lay in a limp half circle around her.

He lay, his hair mussed on the pillow, his eyes staring at the ceiling. Her face was pressed against his shoulder. Her eyes were clamped tight. He could feel her breath against his arm. Her hair, touched his cheek, tickling it. On the roof was rain. Her voice whispered, pleaded, in the dark. "Couldn't we try? Couldn't you . . .?" He moved his hand down along her body to her waist. He could feel her shiver under his touch. He drew her, unheatedly, toward him. She strained against him. She was whimpering. Her lips were fastened to his. He accepted the kiss. Nicky! Nicky!

* Copyright Owner: EMBASSY MUSIC CORPORATION.

What in hell's wrong with me! My God, what's wrong with me! He lay limp in her tight embrace. Damn you! Damn you! His arms, not tight, grew tired. His body felt cramped, unexcited. You dirty louse. He lay another minute in the straining circle of her arms. Then slowly, unnoticeably, he drew away from her . . . then farther away . . . no use. They lay apart in the bed.

On the dresser glowed numbers in a bright yellow-green aura, with the hands spread far apart. On the roof was the rain. Outside was the night. The hands of the clock. The small hand and the large hand stretched away from each other. The large hand fanning slowly, moving farther away. The dark. The rain. The night.

Live fast, die young and have a good-looking corpse. Hahaha. That's funny. Goddamn funny. Forget it! Yeah . . . forget it. Yeah! The tattoo of the rain on the roof. Drumming. Trying to get through. The clock. It made no noise in the dark. It moved, green-yellow, in the dark.

When he thought she was asleep Nick slipped out of the bed and dressed quietly. He let himself out the back door and into the slow drizzle of rain. A fragrance, rain-born, scented the night. The rain misted his hair. In the night his hair began to lift and curl. He walked around, slump-shouldered in the rain and the night.

What the Christ!

I guess I did it.

I guess I screwed her up.

64

Nick came down the alley and through the back gate on his way home from work. Across the walk in front of him the branches of the lilac bush, now blossom-heavy, hung over the fence from the yard next door. They moved their purple color in front of him, gently, and lifted their scent up to him. Nick broke off several of the flower-heavy branches and carried them up the steps and into the house. "Look, Emma, the lilacs are blooming."

Emma's eyes, smiling at him, dropped to the flowers, then lifted back to his, wide, grave. "Yes . . . the lilacs are blooming."

She took them from his hands. Their fingers touched for a moment.

She dished up the food and set it on the table. They sat down to eat.

Emma only picked at the food on her plate. As soon as they had finished she said, "I'm going to see Mom," and, pulling on her hat, stroking her hair back over her shoulders with both hands, she went out.

···

Emma opened the door softly. In the low light from a shaded lamp she could see her mother sitting in a corner, old, alone. Her head was bowed. Dim light showed on the graying hair. The eyes under wrinkled lids were looking down at the veined and folded hands. Her whole body in its old black dress slumped on the chair, leaned toward the long dead past. She now reached to the table for the glass that stood near the quart bottle of beer. She drew it over to her lap and sat staring at it. The brown liquid took dull highlight from the lamp. The old eyes looked into the beer, down past the foam.

Emma closed the door softly and stood leaning back against its panels. "Mom."

The old face looked up across the table at her.

"Emma . . . Emma."

"Mom."

Emma moved quickly to the low chair where her mother sat.

"Mom."

She stood gazing down at her mother with wide, frightened little-girl eyes.

Her mother put the glass back onto the table and pushed it away from her. "I was just drinking a bit so that I could sleep," she said.

Emma leaned over and put her arms around her mother. She slipped down on her mother's lap. The old woman's arms went tightly around her. She could feel the bony fingers through her dress, clutching her. "Mom . . . Mom. . . ." She lay in her mother's arms, crying softly. The old woman held her, rocking gently on the chair with her. Their heads lay close together. Their arms encircled each other. The old woman was crying too. They were hot tears. Tears down a wrinkled face. They struck, almost scalding, against Emma's face, against her dress. "My girls do come to see me now and then," the old woman said against Emma's hair and her neck. *"Meine kleine Mädchen . . .* my little Emmike," she said, rocking back and forth with Emma held on her lap.

At last her mother drew one arm from around Emma. She fumbled in her pocket and pulled out a handkerchief. With it she wiped the tears off her cheeks. Then she patted it gently against Emma's face, drying her tears.

Emma lay in her mother's arms with her head against her mother's shoulder, no longer crying. Her breath caught, occasionally, in her throat and made her gasp. Her mother rocked back and forth and stroked Emma's hair with her skinny fingers. "There, there! Emmike. . . ." Her mother drew Emma's hands down into her lap and held them. Emma could feel the thinness, the coldness, the boniness of her mother's hands. She turned them over and looked down at their palms. "Mom, you worked so hard for us. You did so many tags. You took in washing." She looked up into the old and tired eyes. She put her arms around her mother and hugged her tightly, clung there. Then, quickly, she got up. From her pocket she unfolded some bills. "Here, Mom." She thrust them into her mother's hands. The tired old eyes looked down at them.

"Oh, Emma, this is too much!" She pushed the two ten-dollar bills and the five-dollar bill back at Emma.

"You keep it, Mom." Again Emma kissed her mother and went quickly toward the door.

She saw the panels of the door in front of her. She turned and moved quickly back to her mother, almost running. She put her arms around her mother and kissed her again without speaking, pressing her lips hard against her mother's thin and cracked lips. Then she went right out.

■■■

At home, late that night, Emma lay in bed, propped up on one elbow. The room was black. The cloak of blackness settled heavily on everything, covering everything like warm wool. The oblong cut of window was silver with black behind it. The four panes let in some of the chromium moonlight. There was a square of it on the floor near the bed. Porkchop lay curled in it, sleeping. In the room objects stood up black with highlights of moonlight on them. The foot of the bed. A chair. The dresser. On top of the dresser the lilacs in their vase. They were black. As if sculptured from ebony. The clock dial showed its yellow-green radium: 11 ... 12 .... The clock. The bed. The black lilacs.

Emma sat propped up in bed looking at Nick lying on his back, sleeping. The vagrant patches of moonlight that had sifted into the room fell across his high cheekbones, got lost in the mussed black curls on his forehead. One of his hands was out from under the covers and lay across his stomach. His shoulders were square, swelling at their ends into the muscles of his arms. The straps of his underwear top went across them. His chest rose and fell with his even and rhythmical breathing. Emma looked at him deeply, drawing him into herself. Her eyes moved across his face, slowly, back and forth. Her eyes looked at every mussed black curl on his head. Her eyes looked at his ears, pointed slightly, and the innocent little-boy face asleep on the pillow. Her lips smiled faintly, sadly. She looked at the forehead splashed with one broad spot of moonlight. She looked at the high, square cheekbones, the deep hollows of shadow under them. In the night, far off, a train whistle blew, sending a stab into her. She reached and stroked his forearm, smoothing the insignificant hairs there.

Night. Darkness. Yellow-green glare of the clock dial: 1 . . . 2. . . . Lilacs outlined in black. Emma's fingers twisted in the curls of Nick's hair, slowly, over and over. She looked, with wonder, at his face. Her heart contracted, expanded, in rhythm with his breathing. Her forefinger traced the outline of one of his slightly arched and slowly tapering eyebrows. Her fingers slipped through his hair again, felt its curly ends slide through them. Her fingers smoothed his hair back from his forehead, smoothed it back, felt the warmness of his forehead under them. She leaned over quietly and kissed him. Lowering herself in the bed she put her head against his chest, against his heart. She listened, curiously, to its beating, lying there with one arm around him. In the moon-square at the foot of the bed Porkchop dreamed, whined frightenedly, tried to shake off the fearful dream. His muscles jerked convulsively.

The darkness. The clock dial: 2 . . . 3. . . . The black lilacs.

Emma looked at Nick, drawing his features down into her. She looked at his lips, peacefully and slightly parted. She bent her head. Her hair, dark against the moonlight, fell around her face. She lowered her face to his. Her hair fell around his face. Her lips touched his. Against the windowpane the lilacs stood up full-blossomed and black.

...

In the morning Emma came out into the kitchen wearing her blue housecoat. Her face was lightly brushed with powder. Her hair, loose, flowed curly about her neck and shoulders. Nick looked at her with large eyes. "Gee, you look pretty!"

She fixed breakfast and made his lunch. She sat across the table looking at him with her no-color eyes.

Nick pushed back the chair and got up to go to work. Her eyes rose with him and stood in his. He picked up his lunch and came around the table to where she sat. He leaned over and kissed her lips. He moved toward the kitchen door and, sitting as he had left her, she watched him, looked at the broad shoulders and the black head. His hand touched the doorknob, opened the door.

"*Nicky!*"

Nick turned around at the sound of her voice calling him back from the door.

[303]

"What's the matter, hon?" he asked gently, smiling a little.

Emma got up quickly and met him at the door. "Kiss me, Nicky! Kiss me hard."

He put his arms around her. He kissed her lips hard. He could feel her lips moving tightly on his, saying, "I love you, Nicky." One of his hands went up under her breast and tightened. Her hand came on top of his, pushing it down slowly, forcefully. His fingers slid down away from her breast, over her ribs and off her figure. "No, Nicky, no," she said. "This has got to be real." She was holding his hands in hers, holding him away from her and looking at him. Her eyes moved back and forth and then up and down across his face. She looked at his hair, his nose, his lips. She looked for the shadows under his high cheekbones. Then her eyes were looking into him, were fastened into his as if tied there. And just a faint smile whispered around her lips. Her fingers released his, slowly, with a pressing, a caressing touch. "Smile at me, Nicky."

They stood apart, looking at each other. "Now go to work, Nicky," she said quietly.

She closed the door and stood with her back pressed against it, her head back against the panels. Her eyes were clenched tight. Tears forced their way out and down past her lashes. She called Porkchop who came to her quickly, wagging his tail and jumping against her legs. She bent down and patted the dog. Her fingers on his yellow head were cold, impersonal, withdrawn. She opened the door and let him out. She closed the door and again stood with her back to it. She stood staring into the room. She moved away from the door and toward the stove. The back of her hand touched the coffee pot as if to feel if it were still warm.

•••

Nick came down the alley on his way from work that evening whistling *Always*. Under his arm he carried a box of candy for Emma. When he came into the back yard, Porkchop jumped against his legs and scratched frantically. Then Porkchop ran halfway toward the steps and back to Nick, again jumping against his legs and scratching. "Get down! Get down!" Nick yelled. Porkchop ran up the steps and disappeared on the second floor landing. When Nick got to the top of the steps Porkchop was whining and scratching at the boards in front of the door. "Hey! get out of there!" Nick yelled. The dog paid no attention to him but kept scratching, kept putting his nose against the crack under the door.

Nick pushed him away with his foot and put his key into the lock. To open the door he had to lean against it so that the key would turn. Holding the box of candy under one arm he turned the key in the lock. As he did so and as the door cracked open he noticed that the kitchen shades were drawn down to the sill. Then he stiffened.

[304]

The door came wider open under his hand. The smell of gas crept to him across the sill like a shadow. He flung the door open. He stood paralyzed, the smell of gas twisting up into his nostrils. He dropped the box of candy. He rushed into the kitchen, beyond the kitchen, ran into the bedroom. "Emma! Emma!"

She was there. She lay on the bed in her blue housecoat. Her lips were parted slightly, as if she smiled. Her face, her neck and throat, her bare arms were ghastly white, ashy. Her lips stood up pink from her ashy-white face. They were the pink of rose petals. Her eyes were closed, the lids drawn down over them like thin curves of wax. Her lashes drooped down from them, over her white cheeks. Her hair was mussed on the neatly spread bed coverlet. It was in a cloud about her head. She was all hair and eyes. She lay on her back. Her arms were at her sides, spread away from her body a little, with her fingers curled up toward her palms. The shade was drawn down to the sill. An unnatural half-dusk stood in the room. In their vase on the dresser the lilacs drooped on their stems.

"Emma! Emma!"

Nick stood in the middle of the room. The gas fumes twisted around him. They twirled up into his nose. From the kitchen came the steady hiss of gas. Nick ran into the kitchen. All the burners were turned on. The oven door and the broiler door were stretched open. Nick staggered toward the stove. The half-sweet smell of the gas gagged in his nose and throat. His eyes smarted. He twisted the burners off. He fought for his breath and ran back into the bed-room. He pulled the shade up. It went up noisily and twirled around and around at the top. He tried to get the window open. It wouldn't come up. With his fist and his forearm he broke out the panes. Fresh air poured in through the jagged and broken glass. His arm came away bloody. He ran into the kitchen again and opened the windows there and in the front room.

He rushed back to the bedroom. For a second he stood by the bed looking down; then he knelt with his arms around Emma, pulling at her, trying to lift her.

"Emma! Emma!"

She fell out of his arms, slipped back against the bed, stiff, cold. He tried to wrap her arms around him, he tried to make them bend at the elbow, he tried to uncurl her fingers from their tight, half-cupped position. He touched her face, trying to move her head. Her neck was stiff. Her skin was cold. When he touched her cheek his fingers sank in and left a discolored spot. Her hair curled on the bedspread. Nick knelt beside the bed. Beyond his shoulders and his back her hands lay stiff, the palms turned up, empty, the fingers curled inward a little. At his feet Porkchop had Nick's pant cuff fastened between his teeth and was shaking his head hard, back and forth. The dog whined and shook, shook and whined. Porkchop stood with his feet braced against the floor, pulling at Nick's pant cuff.

Nick knelt beside the bed with his arms tightened around Emma's stiff body and his face pressed against her neck and her still breast.

I did it, Emma. I killed you, I killed you. . . .

65

Emma didn't have anything to do with him now. He couldn't see her like that. He just stood outside against a wall, miserable, holding his hat in his hand. Outside, half a block away from the funeral parlor, hidden by the building, his back and shoulders pressed against the wall so that none of them would see him. Outside with his hat in his hand. With his head down and his eyes, deep with agony, watching. Inside she would be with her empty hands turned up and her fingers curled in. With her ashen white face and her pink lips in the ashen face smiling a little. With her curly hair mussed about her head and her no-color eyes closed down tight. Candles trembling their flames on long wax tapers the color of her cheeks. Flowers stuck in vases and standing on the floor.

No lilacs. No, no. Please, no lilacs.

I did it, Emma, I killed you.

His body waited. His insides waited. Quiet as night. Trembling like the flames on their candles. Twilight like the solemn dimness inside the chapel.

Please forgive me, Emma—please—

He waited. Nothing to give. No prayer. Empty like her hands, turned, palms up. Empty as her no-color eyes under the waxen lids.

He closed his eyes. A shiver passed through him, shaking him violently. He clenched his teeth and tightened his lips.

Emma—Emma—!

At last he opened his eyes. He stood pressed against the wall, slumped against it. Sag of a scarecrow. Eyes of a dog, beaten.

A car at the curb. Another. Low. Black. The smoke of the exhaust breathing close to the asphalt, purple in the dull day. The driver's hand coming out the window to open the back door, his hand white against the dark body of the limousine. The driver in his dark clothes helping someone out of the car. Her mother. Her two sisters. Three black-clothed figures in front of the funeral parlor. Three, yet one. Clinging together. Mrs. Schultz almost unable to stand, the black veil hiding all of her face, trembling about her neck in the low breeze, her black dress falling almost to her shoetops. Margie and Kate supporting her, leading her slowly toward where Emma and the candles and the flowers were. Kate with her arm around her mother. Margie holding her too, saying, over and over, "Ma, Ma, please, Ma...." Tears rolling down both sides of her face as she said it, her tight yellow curls trembling from under the front of her black hat and on her forehead as she walked with her mother toward the door.

Each figure sent a stab through him ... *I did it ... I did it. ...*

Behind the three women Charlie and Mr. Olson, carrying their hats in their hands, their heads bowed. From the other car, coming now behind Mrs. Schultz and her daughters, Ma Romano and her family. Ma had her head turned down, her chin shoved into the collar of her black coat, her hand holding a handkerchief up to her nose and mouth. Ma walking swiftly in past the oak doors. Behind her came Ang. A man stopped on the sidewalk, took off his hat and waited, politely, for them to go into the chapel. Ang stopped stock-still on the sidewalk. She stood looking up at the building, its pressed and twisted architecture, with her arms held tightly at her sides. She stared, wild-eyed, for a moment. She put both hands up to her eyes, shielding them, and sobbed, swaying a little. Julian put his arm around her and walked with her toward the door. Nick, seeing her, again clamped his eyes tight, clenched his teeth. She staggered toward the door, leaning on Julian. Behind Julian came Rosemary. Last of all came Aunt Rosa. Her jolly face was a twisted and wrinkled, red and fat old-lady face. She stood outside, indecisively, looking up and down the sidewalk as if she were searching for him, and then went in.

Nick waited.

It's so long—Nicky—a year—
I'll be right where you left me—waiting for you—
Kiss me, Nicky—
Now go to work, Nicky—
Numbness folded in around him.

■■■

The sad-colored hearse pulling slowly to the curb, long and gloomy in front of the funeral parlor. The other cars lining up behind it, the flower car and two others. Now the undertaker in his business black, in his white shirt and black tie, opening the doors. Now they came, the family. Mom Schultz held up by her crying daughters. Her hands in fists up at either side of the black veil where her mouth was. Charlie and Mr. Olson still with their heads down, still with their hats in their hands, walking automatically. Ma Romano, Ang and Rosemary, with their heads twisted away and their faces hidden. Julian walking stiff and straight. Aunt Rosa again looking up and down the sidewalk with squinted and puffed eyes, then getting into the car. A few splashes of rain falling on Nick's forehead like autumn leaves unloosening from a tree. Two women passing him on the sidewalk with heavy brown shopping bags of groceries, saying, "The poor things!" saying, "It's such a small funeral," saying, "It must be a sister or a brother," saying, "When my Joe died we gave him a big funeral. We spent every cent of the insurance on the funeral. We had twenty cars. And the flowers! Why, you never saw so many flowers!" saying, "I think you should. It's little enough you can do."

In the two cars they waited. Behind the hearse the heaped flower car. Pink, purple, white. Now through the chapel doors—

In the cars women's heads in black leaned together crying. Mrs. Schultz, Kate, Margie. Ma Romano and Ang. Julian staring straight ahead at the back of the driver's head. Rosemary with her body leaned far to the side of the seat, her face toward the window, her eyes staring out at automobiles passing along the street. Aunt Rosa hunched in the car, still looking for Nick.

The gray-over sky. Through the chapel doors—

The gray casket being carried out.

Nick leaned against the wall and closed his eyes, unashamed of the tears that ran down his cheeks.

The gray casket being carried across the sidewalk. A little girl skating along the rain-dotted sidewalk—*gruuuu—gruuuu*—her hair streaming, her head turned back, her eyes looking back curiously.

The little girl skated past Nick. The cars, black, slow, silent in the slow slant of rain-mist that was wetting down the pavements, pulled away from the funeral parlor, past him, carrying Emma away from him forever. He watched the slow cars go, saw them turn the corner.

"Goodbye, Emma, goodbye—"

Each year the city's dead torso gives birth.
Each year the stillborn of the city roam in the night.
Winter or fall, spring and summer
Each year a number is given, a time,
A place, and a whispered word.
Each year the crop ripens.

66

He couldn't go back to the flat. He went to Owen's. Owen slept on the couch and left him the bedroom all to himself. While Owen was at work he sat in the front room, staring at the walls or out the window onto the boulevard. When Owen was home Nick sat staring at the flower pattern in the rug and didn't talk. Or he locked himself up in the bathroom. It was a dream. It hadn't happened. He would wake up. Just a bad dream. He passed his hand over his eyes again. Just a nightmare. He rubbed his hand over his forehead, trying to get the numbness out of it, trying to smooth the dull headache away. Keep your face still. Keep your body still. No matter what. Don't crack. Not in front of Owen, don't crack. Just a dream. It never happened. He stared at the wall.

For three days he was like this, numb, dull, feeling the unreality of everything, the silent, dreamlike quality. For three days he was silent; then he sat grinding his teeth, cracking his knuckles, hearing the loud popping sound they made. He was conscious of Owen's sad eyes staring across the room at him.

Nick stood up quickly. His face was twisted with pain. He went to the sofa and sat down. "Get me something to drink, Owen." His hands were trembling on his knees.

He heard Owen go out the door. He leaned over and fastened his teeth into the fist of one hand, fastened them down. Hard, hard! He was still sitting like that when Owen came in with the bottle.

His hands shook, taking the bottle to his lips.

He finished it in ten minutes. "Get me something to drink, Owen, get me something to drink!" It was half whining, half crying.

•••

After ten days of it he passed out cold on the bed. Owen undressed him and spread the covers up over him.

At the end of two weeks he pulled himself together a little. Pale, shaken, he dressed himself with trembling hands, washed his face in cold water. Not bothering to comb his hair he walked past Owen and out the door.

He climbed the stairs at 1113 South Peoria and went in. All of their eyes picked him up, sympathetic, pitying eyes. He stood in the door a minute. Then he walked through the house to the bathroom. He turned on the cold water, fast as it would go. He slapped water against his face automatically. He rubbed soap into the palms of his hands and brought the lather up to his face. The soap smelled of Emma. He sat on the toilet stool and bawled.

He was in there a long time. When he came out his face was pale and masklike. He looked at Julian, no one else. "Hey, do me a favor, will you?"

On the street he said, "Drive me over there to get my clothes." They got into Julian's second-hand Ford. They bumped over the Halsted Street carline to 57th Street. Neither of them spoke all the way. Julian drove the car up in front of the apartment. Nick shoved the key at Julian. "Get them for me—huh?"

Julian was gone a long time. When he came out he had all of Nick's clothes. "Did you get my hightop boots? They're under a pile of old newspapers in the closet. Get them!"

Julian went back for them. Nick saw the light flash on, two oblongs of it where the windows were. Then he saw the wall go black again and Julian was on the curbstone alongside the car. Julian got in next to him. "Did you look in them?" Nick asked roughly.

"What would I want to look in them for?"

"You're so damn nosey."

···

Back at his mother's house he went to the bedroom, set the boots on the floor, dug down into one of them and got the gun. He stood staring at it a long time. Then he put it in his pocket. He rolled his clothes in newspaper and put them under his arm. He walked out of the bedroom and out of the house. Their eyes, contorted with pity, followed him.

He went back to Owen's place. Putting his clothes that were still wrapped in newspaper on Owen's bed, he went through the apartment and to the door. Owen sat on the couch with his hands in his lap, watching Nick. Nick twisted his head around at Owen. "Goddamn it, don't ask me where I'm going!" He walked out.

····

He was drunk all the time. For a month he dragged around West Madison. South State. North Clark. West Madison again. He made every joint on the damn street. He told Butch and Sunshine and Juan to leave him alone. They didn't get sore. They shrugged their shoulders and let him alone. He went lone wolf, drunk all the time. He picked up broads and gave them what they wanted. Nellie was still around and still chasing after him. If he went broke he bummed money off of her. She whined about it but she shelled out to him whenever she had it. She begged him to come and live with her. He'd laugh at her and tell her, sure, when he was real hard up; then he'd ask her for money. With her money he bought drinks down on the street.

One night when he was sloppy drunk at a bar someone sat down across from him. "I've been looking for you, Nick. I've been damn worried about what had happened to you—after I heard." Nick looked up bleary-eyed. Grant. Nick's eyes snapped to anger. "Look— I'm getting along all right, see. Can the lecture!"

"Cigarette?" Grant asked. Nick acted as if he didn't hear him. Grant lit a cigarette; then he lit another and laid it where Nick could get it. He put his hand out and tapped Nick's shoulder hard. "Tough luck, pizon." he said.

"Get out of here, you sonofabitch, will you! Leave me alone!"

■■■

For six weeks he dragged around. Peg was all right. Peg was about forty. She bought him drinks and got a kick out of a young and good-looking guy making a play for her. Tonight, almost broke, he sat screwed around toward her on a chair in the tavern where she played the piano. His leg touched hers. She was wearing more paint than usual; a few gray hairs were combed under her mop of stringy hair. He stayed there with her until it was almost closing time, making his mind numb with liquor. She said, "How long are you going to keep me guessing, baby?"

He grinned. "What do you mean?"

"When are we going to get together?" she asked, looking straight at him.

"What's wrong with tonight?" he asked.

She was a coarse, big-boned woman; broad-hipped, big-breasted. All of her flesh was sensual.

●●●

He woke up in the bed with her at noon the next day. She wanted more loving. He pushed her away. She didn't want to be pushed away. Nick said, "What do you want to do, kill me?" and got up.

When he was dressed and ready to go, he said, "Give me some money." She faced him contemptuously, and with twisted lips. "What do you mean—give you some money! Don't make me laugh! Why, you can't even satisfy a woman. You're too good-looking. I think you're a—I think something's wrong with you."

Nick was shaky from so much drinking; he faced her angrily. He was so mad that tears came into his eyes. "If you was a man I'd kick the hell out of you," he said and walked out, slamming the door.

[313]

67

Then he was sober and sore; sore at the whole goddamn world.

Take what you want! Don't let nothing stand in your way!

What do I want? he asked himself bitterly.

Plenty of money. Easy money. A good time. Yeah, that's right. Lots of money and lots of good times.

Take what you want!

He walked along mad. Damn mad. Mad at the whole world. Hell of a world . . . hell of a world.

He saw a cop who looked something like Riley get into a squad car.

He ground his teeth.

He wandered into the Pastime, looking for some of the guys. Butch was there. Nick skipped the preliminaries; he didn't even say hello. "You want to work?" he asked. Butch put his stick down off the table. "What? Now?"

"Yes—now!"

Butch grinned. "Say, fellow, it's broad daylight! What are you trying to do—commit suicide?"

Nick grabbed the lapels of Butch's coat and twisted until his fingers became fists. "Don't say that!" he yelled.

Butch wasn't smiling any more. "Hey, take it easy!" he warned, pulling Nick's fingers out of his coat lapels. "What's eating you anyway?"

"Nothing! Goddamn it! Nothing!" Nick shouted.

He went out onto West Madison, squinting against the afternoon sun, looking for a customer.

It didn't take him long before he spotted a guy with creases in his pants and his shoes shined. Nick tailed him down Skid Row, sizing him up. Then in broad daylight with several people on the street Nick grabbed him, strangle-hold from behind, and dragged him toward the alley. "Come on, fork over! And make it snappy!"

[314]

The man didn't make a sound. He obeyed quickly and meekly, his hands shaking as he passed the billfold to Nick. Nick took the billfold with his free hand. He ruffled it open. His eyes glanced angrily at the two one-dollar bills. Because the fellow didn't have more than that Nick hit him and let him go.

Later that afternoon on West Madison The Kid edged up to Nick and started telling him about what bum luck he was having, how a horse had cleaned him right after he won at craps, how he was dead broke—he slipped his thumb in under his belt—"Christ, I didn't eat today yet." Nick didn't catch it so The Kid came out with it, plain. "Hey, Nick—" his voice got servile, his eyes looked sideways from under the brim of the hat, "could you pop for some coffee and? I'll pay you back. You know I'll pay you back."

Nick said sure and they went to the Nickel Plate where Nick bought him a full meal. They had hardly started to eat when The Kid followed up, catching Nick when he felt generous. "How about letting me have the price of a flop? You'll get it back—I'll hit at poker tomorrow—you'll get it back."

Nick put a half-dollar on the table and said, "Forget it."

Squint came in. Nick looked at him coolly. "Whatcha say, Nick?" Squint asked nervously. The lid of his disfigured eye quivered. "Oh, okay," Nick said. It was the first time he had talked to Squint since Squint had tried to knife him and Owen had bandaged his hand. Squint immediately began talking about a drunk he had been on. Telling about it he happened to glance up from the table. "I gotta scram," he said. Nick looked where Squint's good eye was staring. He saw Riley going down the floor toward the food. Nick's mind flooded with one thought: *he killed three men.* He stared at him as if he were trying to look a hole in him.

He better not mess with me! He better not say nothing to me! I got my protection along. Boy! How I'd like to!

Nick looked at the big paws, one in front of the plate in a half-closed fist and one wrapped around the fork. Immediately he remembered the hard, sledge-hammer rabbit punches Riley had landed time after time against his neck. Nick dropped his eyes to the police belt strapped across Riley's elephant hips. He looked at the three notches, and at the row of bullets fastened to the back of the belt. It made him feel like pulling a job. It made him sore all over. He got up and stamped out of the cafeteria.

The next evening Nick sat with Butch, Sunshine and Juan getting them and himself drunk.

Butch said, "What's been eating you lately, anyway?"

Nick said, "Not a goddamn thing!"

Sunshine, putting his hand on the sleeve of Nick's coat, said, "You ain't foolin' us, Nick. Honest, man, something's wrong. Take it easy, man. You's killin' yo'self."

Nick pulled his arm away angrily. He turned his face up mean and stared at them. "What the Christ's wrong! What are you guys beefing about? I'm buying, ain't I? Sit there and drink!" He looked at them with hard, almost hostile eyes. "And keep quiet!"

Juan shrugged slowly. Butch and Sunshine looked at each other. Nick lifted his glass and grinned at his pals.

The drinks came again. Nick lifted his glass, "Live fast, die young and have a good-looking corpse!" he said.

The drinks came again. A new song had hit the juke boxes. In the tavern it pounded out loudly—

> *Tonight—I mustn't think of her.*
> *Music, Maestro, please!* *

"Let's drink—let's drink!" Nick said.

> *Tonight I must forget how much I need her,*
> *So Mister Leader, play your lilting melodies....* *

"Let's get out of here," Nick said.

They went to another tavern. The song chased him out of there too. They went to another clip joint and another hot spot. The song followed them.

Nick moved them around. They started complaining. And behind Nick in this tavern the jukebox said—

> *Swing out—tonight I must forget.*
> *Music, Maestro, please!* *

Nick put a ten-spot on the table. "Here. You guys keep the party going. I'm sleepy." He walked out of the tavern.

Outside he went along with his head and shoulders down, in the night, under the beer signs and the rusty fire escapes attached to the faces of the flophouse buildings. He crossed the street and climbed up the curb on the other side on half-drunk legs. He squared back his shoulders, lifted his head, hard-boiled. He grinned at the night and the neon signs and the dirty-faced buildings. A girl was waiting for him in the darkened doorway of the transient hotel next door to the Pastime. She stepped out of the dark and put her hand on his arm.

"Nick."

"Yeah, Baby." He put his arm around her loosely, and started patting her back. He looked down into her face.

"ANG!"

* Reprinted by permission of copyright owner, BOURNE, INC. (copyright, 1938, by Irving Berlin, Inc.) .

[316]

"Nick—I had to see you."

Seeing his sister there on West Madison late at night sobered him. "What are you doing here, Ang? What's up?" He had her by the shoulder and his voice was run through with alarm.

"I've got to talk to you, Nick."

Nick stood on the sidewalk, helpless, not knowing where to take her so that they could talk. She had a handkerchief in her hands and was twisting it around and around her fingers, pulling it loose, twisting it around again.

"Come on," Nick said. He took her by the arm and started down West Madison.

•••

Owen was sitting on the sofa reading a magazine when Nick opened the door. Nick pushed his sister into the room ahead of him. Owen looked up. His face got very red. He rose and put the magazine down on the sofa behind him.

"Hey—take a walk, will you?" Nick said.

Owen's face couldn't get any redder. Looking at Nick and Ang, looking at them with beaten eyes, he went to where his coat and hat lay across a chair. He didn't look back. As Owen opened the door to go, Nick said, "She's my sister."

Ang sat on the sofa with her head down. Her fingers pulled at the handkerchief. Her feet were drawn together with the shoes touching. Nick sat next to her, close to her, and asked her gently, "What's the matter?"

"Nick—I—I—"

Her fingers twisted the handkerchief. She was silent for a long time with her head down, shadowing her face. Nick looked at her with deep eyes. He rubbed the toe of his shoe against the rug, looking at it. "Come on—" he said, very quietly, "you can tell me."

"Nick—I—I—" She stopped. Her hand wrapped the handkerchief around two fingers hard, like a bandage, and pulled it as tight as she could. "I know I can tell you, Nick. You're the only one I can tell. I couldn't even tell Aunt Rosa—" She stopped again, with her lip caught between her teeth. But only for a moment. "I'm going to have a baby."

Silence hit the room.

Ang's fingers twisted. "It's Abe's."

Again the room was silent. At length Ang said, "I've got to get rid of it." She went on swiftly then, "I—I don't know who to go to—what doctor—or what you do or anything." Her voice was trembling again. "You were the only one I could ask." She spoke so low he could hardly hear her. "Please tell me where I can go, Nick."

"Why do you want to throw the kid down the drain? Why don't you have him?" Nick said, his voice hardening.

[317]

"I—I can't, Nick. Oh, I can't. You know Ma—that would kill her. Me not married and—and—Abe being Jewish. She wouldn't let me marry him. You know that."

"You have to live your own life," Nick said, hard-boiled. "She lived her life, didn't she? The hell with her!"

"No, Nick, I've got to think about her." Ang was turned toward him with her hand on top of his. "She's had so much trouble. You know all the trouble she's had. Pa dying—and—and—she's had a lot of trouble."

"Me—go ahead and say it!" Nick told her.

Ang shook her head no. She twisted her handkerchief around and around, looking at her slim helpless fingers.

Nick looked at his sister. Something squeezed inside of him and wouldn't let go. He put his hand on her shoulder. "I'll find out tomorrow about a doctor who'll do it."

She cried. He kept his arm around her. Leaning against him she cried herself out.

"It—it isn't murder, is it, Nick?" she asked wretchedly.

He shook his head no.

"Will God forgive me, Nick?" she asked like a little girl.

"*Sure,* he will!" Nick said.

"I love Abe. I don't care.

"Is it bad not to be ashamed?" she asked.

"No, Ang. No, it isn't bad."

My sister, his mind said, my sister.

And he held her in his arms.

At last she had finished crying and sat up. Embarrassed, she couldn't look at him. Her voice, less disturbed now, said, "I better go."

Nick shoved his hand into his pocket and pulled out all the money he had, crushed bills adding up to about forty dollars. He handed them to her without counting or looking at them. "You'll have to pay the doctor," he told her. He was unable to look at her. Ang's eyes filled again and she didn't want to take the money. "Don't be crazy," he said, gruffly. "Where will you get the money to pay him?"

Ang looked at Nick with gratitude and then opened her handbag and put the money inside. "Hey!" Nick said, "Powder your face. You look like hell."

She powdered. For the first time she glanced around the room. "Do you live here?" she asked.

"My friend lives here. The guy you saw go out," Nick said. "Sometimes I stay by him."

...

[318]

He walked her to the carline and put her on a streetcar. Leaving the corner he heard someone call him. Grant. "Hello, Grant," he said. His tone was neither friendly nor unfriendly.

They walked for a while in silence. Then Grant said, "You're still on Skid Row, huh?"

"Yeah," tonelessly, trying to discourage Grant.

"When are you going to clear out?" Grant asked.

"I ain't."

"Look here, Nick," Grant said, slowing him down, "you're just piling up trouble for yourself."

"So what?"

"Do you want to stay down here all your life? You'll get just like every other bum."

"It's my own goddamn business!"

"Emma would surely be proud of you," Grant said, glancing at Nick.

"Leave her out of it!" Nick snapped.

That was lousy of me, Grant thought. "You need somebody to beat hell out of you!" he said.

"Do I?" Nick said hard, grinning.

"More than anybody I ever knew! You might get wise to yourself if somebody pushed you around a little!" He had his hand tightly clamped on Nick's shoulder. He could see himself taking off his coat, folding it carefully, giving Nick a lesson. Stop dramatizing yourself, Grant, he thought. What good would it do? It would only make him sore and you'd probably get beaten up. Grant's smile widened. He tightened his lips so that Nick wouldn't see it.

Nick was saying, "Go ahead—hit me if you want to. I wouldn't hit you back. Go ahead—go ahead!" He said it as if he wanted Grant to hit him.

Grant had him by the shoulder. Grant was shaking him. Nick was surprised by the grip of the hard, slim fingers biting into his shoulder.

"You're afraid of life. You couldn't make an honest living," Grant said. The fingers tightened more. "You're a coward."

"That's right," Nick said, licked.

"You're a goddamn fool."

"You're right."

"You're not a little boy any more. You're a man. Act like a man!" Nick was grinning, brittle-bright.

Grant stopped. "Oh, hell!—What's the use? I'm going."

"Yeah—" Nick said, "I'll see you."

He watched Grant walk away, saw him turn the corner. Nick stood staring at the empty street. His conscience pricked him.

[319]

Nick walked around for an hour. Emma... Grant... Ang. Ang ...Grant... Emma....

Aw, forget it! Don't think about it!

He walked around for another hour. He didn't think about it so much. He went up to Nellie's. She was so glad to see him that she cried. He flopped with her all night.

. . .

The next evening he dressed himself up. He went downtown. Where it said: D^DA^IN^NC^EE with the words jerking into each other in red and blue neon he went in. Ace sat at a large mahogany table with his silver liquor bottle in front of him and a cigarette held to his lips. His baggy eyes looked at Nick and the smoke curled up in front of them toward his slightly graying hair. "Hello, Nick. Thought you were dead." He poured two glasses and motioned to the seat across from him.

Nick sat down and came to the point. "I'm ready to go back to work for you. I got a favor to ask of you. I got a girl in trouble. She's got to get rid of a bundle." Ace showed his tight lips and his big teeth. "I've got to have a good doctor, I don't want nothing to happen to her."

Ace took out an Eversharp and scrawled the name without saying anything. He pushed the slip of paper across the table at Nick with the end of the pencil.

Nick looked at it and put it in his pocket. "Thanks, Ace. Thanks!" He stood up.

Ace held up his hand, like it's nothing. As if he were talking to himself he mumbled, "You're tough and you're hard and you don't look like a crook ... don't look like a crook." He laughed a hollow laugh. Then he said, "I'm going to put you on something new. Dangerous stuff." His baggy eyes looked at Nick. "In a tight pinch you'll have to go to bat for yourself ... dangerous stuff."

"Anything you say, Ace," Nick said.

"See you tomorrow." Ace's hollow laugh, tight as a drum, followed Nick out.

. . .

Nick did Ace's dirty work. Delivering drugs. Bribes. Rackets. He made enough money at it to drink and gamble as much as he wanted. But he wasn't satisfied. Some restlessness in him sent him around the street jackrolling and fighting and getting into drunken brawls. He jackrolled not because he needed the money but recklessly, as if he wanted to get caught. And he threw the money away as fast as he got it.

68

The sky darkened early and unnaturally, taking a slate brown color, almost red. There was a lull in the air. The stillness stirred. Nick sat in the Nickel Plate listening to the big drops begin to hit the windows. He saw the windows flash occasionally as lightning dodged across the sky. The lightning was the color of flashes from the street trolleys. He sat staring at the floor.

The rain stopped as quickly as it had started. Only the sidewalks showed where it had fallen. In the night the neon darkened. The thunder still rumbled.

Nick got up and went down toward the Pastime. He moved down the street, the neons throwing redness on his hair and shoulders. Ahead of him in the dark he saw some men standing in front of a flophouse. A young fellow in tramp clothes with a black cowboy hat tilted way over the side of his forehead sat on the fender of a car looking at the doorway. Nick went over and asked him, "What happened?"

"Some old guy croaked in there." Nick stood waiting with the curious crowd. Always their eyes went back to the door. Through the glass was a dirty lobby with a clerk's cage and stairs disappearing up to the layers of twenty-five-cent rooms, rooms just large enough for a bed and chair, partitioned halfway up, with chicken wire going the rest of the way to the ceiling.

Nick's eyes saw the blue legs of a policeman coming down. Then hands holding the ends of a stretcher and the stretcher coming down at a steep angle. A stretcher wrapped in black canvas and tied at both ends with a rope.

The men watched the thing being carried out, slight under the canvas. Nick looked too, but he felt nothing. From under the canvas the dead man's feet stuck out. They were bloodless, stiff. They turned in toward each other with the rope knotted tightly around the ankles.

The policemen carried the dead man to the curb where the patrol wagon was backed. They shoved the stretcher in and it banged against the floor.

The men stood watching the taillight of the paddy wagon move down the street. Then they began to trickle away aimlessly down the sidewalk, under the neon signs, under the fire escapes. A couple of the men turned into the first tavern.

The rain began again. It became a slow, steady drizzle. Nick lifted his collar against it and walked with his hands in his pockets. In the sky in front of him there was lightning, harsher now and quicker. The rain came harder, harder.

Nick ran for it and ducked into the Pastime. Just inside the door was Squint's ugly face. Nick turned his back and stared out the window.

Butch and Sunshine came over. Butch put his elbow on Nick's shoulder and leaned on him. Nick lowered his shoulder. "You got a grouch on?" Butch asked. Nick shook his head no, without answering.

"You look worse than the weather, and that's sure something!" Sunshine looked at him mournfully and puzzled and then moved over to the pool tables again.

Nick stood at the window listening to the steady and monotonous drizzle of the rain. Then, fed up, he walked out into it. He went to the doorway of the Nickel Plate. Out of the rain at the foot of the steps stood The Kid, dripping wet in his baggy second-hand coat several sizes too large for him. "Jesus Christ!" he said, "I'm glad to see you. I gotta put the bee on you for the night. Christ!—I can't sleep out in this!"

Nick said, "Sure thing, Kid!" and pulled what money he had out of his pocket. In his palm there were a quarter and two nickels.

"Is that all you got?" The Kid asked, as if wondering about how Nick would get along.

"Don't worry about me!" Nick said, and gave The Kid the quarter.

"You're the only right guy on this whole goddamn street! That's no crap, Nick!" The Kid's eyes crawled and his voice licked Nick's hand.

Nick laughed, "Go get your bed," he said and went up the steps to the Nickel Plate.

With one of the two nickels he had left he bought a cup of coffee and two doughnuts and took them to a table against the window. He put his elbows up on the table and stared out the window. The rain beat hard against the dirty pane, and beyond its wrinkled surface Nick could see the fronts of the buildings across the street. The rain beat on the sidewalk with hissing sounds. And over the street, some of the raindrops got caught in the trolley wires. They beaded there, dripped down.

Nick sat with the heavy white cup in front of him. The coffee was untouched. There was only one bite out of the top doughnut. With out-of-focus eyes Nick sat, thinking, trying not to think.

All the tables began to fill up. The smell of wet and foul clothes hung in the damp air. Old shoes squeaked across the floor leaving marks. Water soaked in through worn soles. It sucked into ragged socks, making feet wet and cold and uncomfortable. Men coughed.

Up the steps of the Nickel Plate an old man haltingly climbed. His hair was gray and dripped water. His cheeks were so hollow and sunken that they seemed to touch inside his mouth.

At Nick's table the other chair was empty. The old man sat down without looking up. He put his glass of water and his two penny-apiece biscuits on the table. With a wet and sticky hand he lifted one of the dry biscuits and put it between his uncertain teeth. Nick stood up and pulled out his last nickel. He shoved it on the table in front of the old man. Embarrassed, he walked quickly toward the door. One of his pockets hung heavier than the other.

Halfway down the steps a bolt of lightning and a crack of thunder jarred in the sky. Nick stood stock-still, waiting for it to stop. With his eyes half-closed he waited. Then, when the rumble of the thunder had passed, he continued down to the bottom landing and stood out of the rain for a moment, watching it strike against the sidewalk.

Nick looked down to the corner where the neon sign blinked on and off, lighting up, going dark, the LIQUORS and CIGARS, EAT, DRINK changing into each other. Rain fell in a sheet before it. Nick turned up his collar and moved in the direction of the Three-Eighty. He walked fast. The rain drenched him. He stood under an awning next door for a minute. The rain beat and foamed at his feet. Then, with his coat turned up and his hair hanging down wetly over his forehead, he moved quickly to the door of the Three-Eighty and walked in.

He went to the front end of the bar and stood there next to the cigarette counter. His eyes raked the place from one end to the other.

Lucky. Nobody there.

He waited with his hand in his pocket. The bartender came down along the inside of the bar to the cash register. He was a biggish man, about forty. He wore a bar apron, a white shirt with the sleeves rolled halfway up. There was a tattoo on his forearm. He stood waiting for Nick to say what he wanted. "Gimme a pack of Luckies." The man turned his back to get them.

Nick's hand came out of his pocket. When the man turned

around with the cigarettes, the gun was already levelled at his heart. His eyes blinked a little. His lips hardened. He put his hands, as if relaxing them, on top of the glass case. He looked at the black barrel of the gun and then up into Nick's eyes. His hand tapped the pack of cigarettes against the glass top of the counter.

Nick looked at him hard-eyed. And Nick's mind listened, intently, for the sound of the door opening; it listened for steps coming up from the gambling den in the basement. His mind said: if anybody comes up I'll pour a slug down on him.

"This is a stick-up. Shell out!" he said. Behind him the lightning cracked in the sky like a cat-o'-nine-tails and the rain beat against the chrome and glass door in hard staccato.

The man's eyes looked across the counter at Nick. His fingers still tapped the cigarettes gently against the counter. "Come and get it," he said. His voice was cool and even.

Nick took one step—two steps—back. He lifted the pistol. "It's your funeral, buddy," he said.

"Okay—you win," the man said.

Nick stepped up to the counter, hiding the gun from the view of the window with his back. The pistol barrel levelled out with the third button on the man's shirt, left side. The man punched the cash register. No SALE stood up in the glass, red and white. That was funny. Even in Nick's tenseness that was funny. Damn funny. The whirring sound of the drawer coming open echoed loudly. "Just the bills," Nick said, hard-lipped. His eyes didn't leave the man. The gun barrel was a stiffly-held, unwavering threat pointed straight at the bartender's heart.

The bills were thick, bound together with heavy rubber bands. Nick stuffed them quickly into his pocket. "The cigarettes too," he said in grim humor. They went into his pocket with the money. Quietly he backed to the door, the gun still pointing. He stepped out through the door and onto the sidewalk.

The rain was stopping. Swiftly Nick dropped his hand to his side and pushed the gun out of sight. He broke into a trot, north on Halsted toward the alley behind West Madison.

He heard a shout. *"Halt!"*

Running, he jerked his head around. Riley! *Riley* coming out of the doorway across the street and running across the car tracks after him. Riley running out into the street after him while the traffic light was wet and red and automobiles splashed across his path. Riley wrestling with his gun, getting it out of the holster, shooting at Nick even before he had the gun levelled. The report. The bartender running out of the Three-Eighty with a gun in his hand.

A slight whizzing past Nick's head, twice past ... *blip* ... *blip*.

He didn't realize that they were real bullets being fired at him. His mind was off from him, detached, observing, while his heart choked up in his throat and his temples pounded against his skull. *They don't sound like they do in the movies,* his mind said and his legs carried him, stumbling, over the slippery sidewalk toward the alley. But when a bullet went through the window of a car parked under a street lamp at the curb and he heard the glass crash behind him and fall into the street he knew they were real bullets—his mind whirled back. He went tense, scared, scared to death. *It's Riley! It's Riley and he's going to kill me! He wants to kill me! The alley! The alley!*

Behind him he heard Riley's big feet striking the pavement hard. Again the report of Riley's gun. A bullet hit up near Nick's shoulder and glanced off the brick wall. *He's killed three men! I'm number four! I'm four! I'm four!* Wildly Nick lifted his gun over his shoulder, and without looking, wildly fired it, once, twice, three times. End of the building. Ragged black board-fence in front of him. Alley. Alley in between. Narrow. L-shaped. Cutting behind the Pastime and opening out onto the avenue. *In there!*

He ducked into the alley. Blackness took him. He stumbled over the heaped garbage. He staggered ahead. So black he couldn't see where he was going. So narrow he could almost touch the walls on either side. Walls going straight up, blackly. He plowed over the garbage. Cans rattled. He slopped through the mud and water. The water went in over the tops of his shoes. Mud oozed around his shoes, sucked at his feet. He pulled hard, panting, fighting to free his feet. He fell. His knees hit in the mud. The mud and water soaked in through his pants to his skin. His hands went down, catching him. The palm of one hand slipped, slid away from him in the mud, breaking his support. In the other hand the gun struck the mud and garbage. The barrel struck hard and almost tore loose from his grip. Over his head the thunder.

Sound of Riley running. . . .

Nick pulling himself erect. He staggered forward—into the darkness. . . .

Thunder rolled like logs in a river.

Riley at the entrance of the alley. Riley not rushing in. Creeping along the fence in the dark. Foot hitting a tin can, sending it rolling.

Silence.

Rush of rain.

Riley's heavy breathing. The sound of his heavy panting; the tearing of air through his big nostrils . . . and beyond the bend in the alley Nick's breathing, coming more naturally now.

Lightning.

[325]

Nick tensing, drawing closer against the wall, bruising his back against the rough bricks, making himself breathe quietly, clenching his teeth so hard that the muscles jumped at the ends of his jaw ... GODDAMN ... SONOFABITCH ... BASTARD ... Riley lying out there—sneaking. Playing for the kill. Coming along the fence in the dark.

Lightning twisted across the sky.

Nick moved slowly, quietly, toward the avenue end of the alley. Crouching, he moved, shadow with shadow, back scraping along the wall, breath held, eyes hard, mean, hateful, staring in the dark where the burly blue-clothed figure would appear.

Thunder knotted in the sky and struck like fists.

Riley——————————————————————Nick.

Clap of thunder.

Flash of lightning.

Tangle of fire escapes over Nick's head. Zigzag of fire escapes going up and out of sight. Water dripping from them loudly, hitting in the alley loudly. The rush of water from broken rain gutters hanging from flophouses. Rain running from his long hair.

Nick stood erect against the wall in the dark. He moved slowly along the wall. Garbage can in the way, heaped, running over. Crouching. Going past the garbage can. Back against the wall again.

Lightning.

Nick inched along the wall. Recess of a door. Back door of the Pastime. He backed into it. Darkness covered him. He stood as straight and tight-pressed against the wall as he could. He stared straight ahead from his corner of darkness. He felt a bigness in himself, a bigness bigger than himself. He felt unnaturally calm and satisfied.

This is what I was born to do.

He smiled. His lips were drawn back tightly over the smile. His teeth showed even and white. He stared straight ahead from his corner of darkness. Not moving a muscle. Not blinking an eyelid. Smiling. Dimples showed in his cheeks. Exultation hit him. He stood erect against the wall in the darkness. Smiling.

A lull in the storm. No lightning. No thunder. The rain slackening. Behind him Nick heard, clearly, sharply, the hard click of pool balls striking together.

In the alley—pistol shots. Nick fired. Riley fired back. Silence wrapped around the two shots.

Nick, looking out of the dark with squinting eyes, saw him—the beak of his copper's cap suddenly reflecting light. Nick fired. He fired again. Riley fired back. Nick squeezed the trigger. There was a dry click. Quickly he broke the gun. His hand scrambled for the loose bullets in the pocket of his coat. Found them. Pushing back against the wall as hard as he could, his fingers frantically stuffed the bullets into the cylinder. Riley's silence panicked him. Carefully Nick slid along the wall, waiting, watching. . . .

A shot. The bullet struck Nick in the fleshy butt of his hand. Nick's hand went numb. He felt nothing in it. No pain. No weight of the gun. Nick transferred the gun into his left hand, holding his right hand on top of his left. The gun went lopsided. Nick straightened it, gripped it with two hands. Holding the gun in both hands he pointed it out of the dark. Only the tip of the muzzle showed light, picking up reflection from the street lamp on Atlantic Avenue at the end of the alley. Leaning back against the wall he fired again. Then he put his right hand down at his side and rubbed it, hit it, beat it against the wall trying to take the numbness out of it.

Riley fired twice. Nick hung against the wall with his back biting into the panel of the poolroom door. The bullets hit the bricks, chipping them, sending sprays of rock against his face and chest.

Riley and Nick . . . in their dark barricades.

Nick rubbed his hand against the rough bricks, bringing feeling back into it, feeling the pain, feeling blood running down it and curling around his little finger. Hanging against the panel of the poolroom door he changed the gun back to his right hand. He clenched the gun. Slowly he lifted it. Again its black barrel caught reflection. He aimed it at the black spot from which Riley's shot had come.

Before he could fire, Riley shot at him—once—twice—and came running, lumbering toward Nick with the gun held for the kill.

Lightning cracked in the sky like a whip.

Nick fired.

Riley stopped the slug. He kept coming. Nick fired again. Point-blank. Riley fell forward, plunging on his shoulder, sliding in the mud and twisting grotesquely over on his back.

Nick didn't run. He walked over deliberately. He walked through the puddle of water. He walked over garbage and horse manure. He stood over Riley. He stood in the alley with the Maxwell Street hockshop gun steady now, in his hand. Light glinted down from the street lamp at the end of the alley. It smeared Nick's hard chin, the barrel end of the smoking gun, the pointed-up star on Riley's chest. Nick pointed the gun down and emptied it into Riley. The lead ripped into the blue uniform. It buried itself in the big head. He kept pulling the trigger. And Nick laughed. It was a hard laugh. Bitter. Tough. Glad. He had the gun pointed down and kept pulling the trigger. The trigger made an empty, clicking sound. Blood spewed out of Riley's mouth and his nostrils. A dark red stain of blood ran from the left side of his lips, down over his cheek and under his head. It trickled down into the mud and water of the alley. Riley's eyes were hard with hate. But the pistol-barrel eyes had shot their fire. The hate was freezing out of them. They were blank, staring, glazed. Nick looked down. He heard the empty clicking of the gun. He took the gun and threw it in Riley's face.

At the corner of the alley seven or eight people stood looking into the alley, curious, fearful, horrified.

Nick stood looking down at Riley. Water ran from his long black hair. He remembered the rabbit punches. He lifted his foot and kicked Riley. He remembered how Riley had kicked him when he was down on his hands and knees in the basement of the police station. He kicked Riley, hard, in the stomach. Thunder split the alley. The wind came in a rush. Cans rattled over the alley.

Suddenly Nick lifted his head. He looked out of the alley with wild eyes. He turned away from Riley. He walked out of the alley slowly. There was a crowd there. Dazed, he looked into their faces. His lips were twisted meanly. His eyes were defiant. He looked ... Sunshine ... Butch ... Squint. He saw them. Others. He thought he saw The Kid. He blinked his eyes. He remembered that he was Nick and he wanted to live.

His heart pounded hard. It was up in his throat, beating against his Adam's apple, choking him. He started to run. He ran toward West Madison. *Hide in the show.* He stumbled forward. *No! No! Crazy! Might be cornered there!* He turned back toward Washington, running insanely over the sidewalk, down the middle of the avenue, then up the sidewalk. He ran under rough board signs: Rooms; We Buy and Sell Clothing. He fled into an alley again. Rag of sky over him, pelting rain. Slimy, rain-running cobblestones under his feet....

●●●

Butch nudged Sunshine. "Let's take a powder."

They took a powder. Squint had already disappeared.

69

North, Washington Boulevard. South, Monroe Street, brightly lit up. West, Halsted, traffic. East—*east!* He ran east. A gangway between a flophouse and a high fence. He started down the gangway. *Dead end! Dead end!* his mind told him. He staggered forward two steps more and stopped. He stood cornered. His mind whirled. His stomach tightened. *They're going to catch me! They're going to catch me!* Wildly, obeying mad impulse, he ran out of the gangway and back into the alley. The sheet of rain and roaring thunder followed him. He fled east down the alley. His mind told him No! No! Downtown that way! Run into the arms of the cops! His feet carried him ahead anyway. He staggered on. He came to the end of the alley, light meeting him and picking him up. He turned toward West Madison. The raw, cutting air in his lungs choked him. He ran across West Madison. A streetcar clanged and slammed its brakes to keep from hitting him. Lightning beat its hard whiteness against the black sky. The steeple of St. Patrick's Church stood out black in the night. The lightning made him run faster. He was stumbling under a huge beer sign. Board sidewalk sign: SLEEP—10¢. Narrow alley. He ducked into it. Fire escape overhead. Rusted and twisted iron with newspapers, battered by rain, hanging from it. A turn in the alley. He ran down the twist of alley behind West Madison. His mind stood up, showing him the Three-Eighty, his own figure backing out of the door onto the sidewalk and Riley yelling "Halt!" *Running in a circle! Back where I started from! Where I pulled the job!* At the same time the light hit him and he was halfway across the car tracks. He jerked his head looking toward Madison. Beyond it—the Three-Eighty with the door open, people looking in the door and through the window.

Factory buildings heaped in the night. Running . . . BRICK LAYERS' HALL . . . lungs bursting. Legs dead. Heart beating harder, harder, harder. *They want to catch me!* Wire fence. Garbage trucks inside.

Is he dead? I wonder if he's dead. *Catch me!* Two more blocks...
running...three blocks...running ... thunder beating against his
eardrums...running...breaking them ...
...the alley...if I can ... make ... the alley....

He made the alley He staggered into it on weak and shaking
legs. He tottered into its blackness. The alley gobbled him up.
Wooden barns and fences patched with sheets of rusty tin. Wall....
He leaned weakly against the wall. He put his forehead against it
and gasped for breath, strangling, sobbing. He knotted his fists
and held them tightly at his sides. He shook all over. He pulled
his shoulders and his arms and his legs in stiffly, trying to stop their
shaking. The rain beat on his head. He lifted his hands. He beat
them against the brick wall until his knuckles were bloody. His
mouth was sagged open. He sobbed for air. He sobbed in fear and
anger and impotence.

At last he gained control of his shaking limbs. At last his mind
stopped whirling away from him in long, ever-extending spirals
and concentrated in a tight and weary knot. He lifted himself away
from the wall. He tossed his head and the hair whipped back off his
forehead. Wearily he walked down the alley, stumbling, tripping
over his feet...so tired...not caring...so tired....

He walked slowly deeper into the alley.

70

In a telephone booth a voice shouted, "Police 13-13."
In another telephone booth a finger began dialing P—O—

POLICE HEADQUARTERS: The police call shot up to the fifth floor.
The operator saw the round bead of light and heard the buzzing
of the switchboard. She plugged the call in. "Police department,
Operator 6-o."

"A policeman has just been shot in the alley behind West
Madison Street!"

"Huh? Where?"

"Near Atlantic Avenue."

The radio squad operator swung his mouth around to the microphone—

The radio operator's voice said into every squad car in the city, "...a policeman shot in the alley at West Madison and Atlantic...."

THE BUREAU SQUAD prowled up and down streets over the city, slowly. "...a policeman shot in the alley at West Madison and Atlantic...." The bureau squad swung sharply, in a wide U-turn. The siren wailed out across the street. It rose higher and higher. The spotlight cut back and forth, weaving through the night and the rain, clearing the street of traffic.

The hunt was on.

The reporters waited three or four minutes in the pressroom at headquarters. The phone rang. "There it is," one of them said quietly, matter-of-fact. The squad operator said into the phone, "One of the boys has been shot. That was the real McCoy that came in just now."

"It's a good one!" Sanders shouted. The reporters all grabbed for the phones and called their papers. The phones with direct wires got to the newspaper offices quickest. "City desk!" ... "City desk!" ... "City desk!"

■■■

Nick walked deeper into the alley. Shadows fell across his back, darker and darker. With his fingers doubled he brought his hands up to his face. He put them up against his eyes and stood, tottering in the alley. Behind him a rat scuttled for cover against a wall. Nick jumped and started running again. He ran over the broken lot toward the rear of a building. The rain came in a last rush; it beat him and he staggered against it toward the rear of the building where a door was opened an inch or two. He leaned against the building with his forehead pressed to the bricks. Music, piano music, came through the door with the light; music came out on the smell of beer—

> St. Lou-ie woman—
> With her Dia-mon'—rings!
> St. Lou-ie woman
> With her DIA-mon'—rings—!

The piano music broke out past the door, blue and low-down. The keys caught their rhythm up off the strings and hurled it through the back door—

> St. Lou-ie wo-MAN—

Nick leaned with his head and shoulders slumped down against the wall and the music twisted around him. The slow ache of his

hand where the bullet had creased it began to burn and pull. It
rose, hot, then numbing, up his arm. Up to his elbow, beyond it.

The music twisted around him. There was, in all the world, just
the wild beating of his heart, the scared tightness of his throat and
the sound of the music. The rain and the night. The numbness in
him and the thumping of the music across his numbness—

> Got the St.—Lou-ie—Blues—
> Got the blues, got the blues, St. Louis blues—

Nick moved slowly and silently toward the crack of the door.

■■■

Sirens came up noisily. Spotlights cut through the dark and the
slowing rain, seesawing across the street. Spotlights and sirens and
the sound of brakes bringing squad cars to a jolting stop. Bureau
squad. Newspaper reporters. News photographers. Flash of bulbs
as the newshounds recorded the scene, the body, the pulpy face.
Flash of bulbs as the homicide photographer carefully and unhur-
riedly took photos from different angles for position of the body,
distance from the wall, path the killer had taken. Men from the
homicide squad stooping in the slow drizzle with measuring tapes
between their fingers. Playing the tape out, holding it taut, making
notations on slips of paper. Rain touching gently against the yellow, black-striped tape, dampening it. Rain dampening the slips of
paper and making them hard to write on. Detectives moving
through the small crowd, asking, "Did you see it?" Picking up a
couple of tramps to hold for investigation. Riley's swollen face,
pushed down into the mud, blood drying across his head and face,
the rain streaking it, melting its coagulation a little. His blue uniform cap rolled away from him and lying upside down in a puddle
of rain.

"Hey!—There's a gun here!"

A large hand, holding a handkerchief, wrapping carefully around
the gun and lifting it out of the mud and water near Riley's ripped-
open skull.

■■■

Nick stepped into the room and quietly closed the door. Swiftly
he moved toward the other door and its small square of glass so
that he could look through into the tavern, see who was out there
and decide what to do, where to hide, maybe to lock the door leading to the tavern. Halfway to the door he saw it swing open and
a woman step into the back room. She was an older woman, still
handsome in a hard, glittering, rundown way. A smile had just
come off her face, leaving it tired-looking. Her hair was dyed red
and was frizzed; it showed gray at the roots. Where the gray roots

[332]

and the dyed hair began to blend it was orange. Her clothes were old, faded. Her body had begun to relax in fatness. Only her face tried to keep up appearance. It was a face getting flabby and wrinkled; a face caked with powder. Over the powder on her cheeks was rouge, reaching up to her cheekbones and smoothing out almost to her ears. Mascara stood thick and black in her lashes. Her eyebrows looked as if they were painted on her forehead. Across her face, going the length of one cheek, was the thin scar a knife or razor had left. It had been powdered but the powder and rouge had slipped past it without taking, leaving it white. Her face, held down in shadow, was worn and sad. Only her eyes looked young; but even there the youth had a tired film over it. She stood there in front of the door, an old woman, weary of the game of make-believe. She sighed. And now she looked up into the room.

She saw Nick, and stood staring at him in surprise.

Nick, with his head twisted down, stared back at her. His heart beat hard against his chest. He stood there with nothing with which to protect himself but his bare hands. He took a step back. His mouth was open a little and he took another step backwards, still watching her. Scared.

The surprised look left the woman's face. "You're in trouble, kid." Her voice was throaty. It had a kindly huskiness in it. "You're in trouble, kid," she said again. His shoulders touched the wall. He stood facing her and she kept coming. He shrunk back against the wall. When she was quite close to him she stopped and smiled at him. It was a slow, sympathetic smile, twisting the corners of her lips. She looked up at his wet hair, down at his hands hanging stiffly at his side, one dripping blood, down at his wet and muddy shoes. He hung his head, unable to look at her.

"Come on in and have a seat," she said quietly. Her fat hand with the blood-red nail polish motioned to an old sofa against the wall near a small oil heater. He moved carefully and slowly toward the sofa, watching her out of the corners of his eyes. She said, her voice dropping to a confidential whisper, "I'm going to lock the place up." Immediately she threw the bolt on the back door and, paying no attention to him, turned her back and walked to the door leading to the tavern.

...got the blues, got the blues, St. Louis blues....

Nick leaped up and rushed across the room to the door. He fastened his face against the glass and looked into the tavern. *If she tries to turn me in I'll kill her! Kill her! Kill her! Kill the bitch!*

The woman was saying, "All right, boys, that's all. I'm locking up. I'm tired tonight." She walked down the uneven and warped floor

[333]

toward the front of the tavern. "Let's go, boys," the woman said again, wearily.

The Negro stopped playing. The Irishman said, "Aw, Lottie! Just when we were beginning to have a good time!"

Lottie smiled with her practiced lips. "All right," she said, "we'll all have a drink, then you've got to clear out." Her voice sounded weary without showing that she was trying to get rid of them and her eyes moved down the tavern toward the back room. Going behind the bar she poured whiskey for the three of them. "Here's mud in your eye!" she said, tilting her head and tossing the whiskey off in one swallow. The Negro and the Irishman did the same thing.

In the front of the tavern against the plate glass stood a boy with a bootblack stand. He was a boy of about twelve. His brown-black hair was curled over his head and forehead and around his ears. His face was lightly tanned. His dark eyes were clear and innocent. His sleeves were ravelled. The strap of the bootblack stand was across his shoulder. Nick stared at him curiously.

Lottie was easing the two men out. There was just the boy now, standing against the plate glass. "All right, sonny boy!" Lottie said. "The rain's stopped. You can come back tomorrow and I'll let you shine all the shoes I got." She pressed a coin into his hand.

Lottie locked the door. She put the lights out and came toward the back room. Nick moved swiftly to the sofa and when she entered was sitting as if he had never left it.

"Hi!" Lottie said, smiling. She came over and sat next to Nick. He watched her out of the corners of his eyes, looking at her profile, the long white scar on her cheek. "Cigarette?" she asked. holding the pack out to him. He took one with his uninjured hand.

Nick's voice trembled and he said, "I got to tell you something—"

She said, "Button your lip!" She was laughing a little.

"I'm in trouble," Nick said.

"Shhh!" Smiling, she put her fingers over his lips. They were cool against the trembling of his. Wearily, all his strength and his knotted hard-boiledness came down. His head seemed to whirl. His eyes were heavy and burning. He was leaning against her shoulder. After a little she put her arm up around his shoulder. He sobbed dryly. "I'm glad I did it," he said, "I'm glad I did it—" He opened his eyes and closed them. "It ain't fair to you—"

"All I know is you're in trouble. Anything's fair that helps somebody in trouble," she told him.

"You don't know—" he said, "you don't know—" He leaned with his eyes closed, with his pupils throbbing against his lids. His lips trembled. Under his eyelids he saw Riley's gray, blood-soaked face

[334]

and he saw himself throwing the gun down at the ugly, hateful face. His limbs trembled. "I'm glad I did it—" he said, "I'm glad—"

He leaned against her shoulder with his eyes closed. He was quiet now. Every muscle still. He felt as he had when a little kid; and he stayed against her shoulder.

Outside the rain cleared; wind wiped it all out of the sky. But the thunder rumbled and occasionally there was lightning.

For a long time they sat on the sofa. Finally Lottie looked at him, believing he was asleep. She saw his hand held between his knees, blood dripping on the warped and dirty floor between his feet in a small, gathering pool.

She got up and went into the side room. He sat upright, tensed into fear. Then he slowly relaxed again.

When she came back he was staring vacantly at a cockroach on the floor. She had a basin, hot water, gauze, iodine, tape. Without looking at him she said, "You've got a bad—a bad—cut there."

She put the basin of almost boiling water on a beer case. He looked down at the wound. Black. Red from blood. The bullet had torn the flesh deeply and passed through. It had cut only the flesh, striking in the fatty butt of his hand, away from the bones. "Get a knife," he said.

It was sharp, pearl-handled, a woman's knife. He opened it with his teeth. He put his hand down on the beer case. Lottie turned her head away, shutting her eyes. Nick clenched his teeth. With his left hand he cut the wound deep so that it would flow freely with clean blood.

"Light me a cigarette, will you?"

She lit and handed him a cigarette.

Lottie put his hand into the almost boiling water. She washed it clean with cloth, watching the water turn pinkish-red. She washed it again with new water and new cotton. She applied iodine. She bound it tightly.

All the time she worked on him he looked at the red hair bent over his hand and the long knife or razor scar going thinly the length of one cheek.

Afterwards Nick sat hunched up on the end of the sofa staring at the floor. Lottie said, "It's time to hit the hay." She hauled blankets out of her bedroom and brought them to the sofa.

"You need some sleep," Lottie said.

Lottie locked up. She pulled the shades down beyond the sills. She carefully put the chain and the iron bar across the back door. "Good night, kid," she said and turned the lights off. Then, stumbling through the dark, she felt again for the iron bar across the back door to make sure that it was securely fastened.

Then she went through the dark to her bedroom.

The rain was over. The buildings on West Madison Street came away from it with a fresh and clean look. A star showed over the neon signs and over the roofs. People appeared once again on the streets. A big-shouldered boy followed a well-dressed man out of a tavern and down the street. A girl in a thin dress and silk stockings stopped a man on the street and whispered to him. A man stood under the darkened marquee of the Paris Theatre with secret eyes watching the men who passed along, looking up at them quickly, then dropping his eyes.

West Madison Street hides many things. Night and West Madison hide them all. Jackroller. Crooked cop. Whore. Dope fiend. Thief. West Madison puts them away in secret cubbyholes. West Madison puts them all to bed and blankets them over with darkness and secrecy.

71

Nick awoke with terror. Someone had him by the shoulder. He blinked his eyes open with fear and struggled to a sitting position, ready to fight, run, die. Then he saw the red hair and the long razor scar.

The covers had slid down to the floor and he sat on the edge of the sofa fully dressed, staring at her with round, fearful eyes, his mouth held open. Lottie was smiling at him. "I'm goin' to get us some grub, kid."

In a little while she put the plates on the small kitchen table. "Let's eat!" she said cheerfully.

There were no chairs. They sat on upturned beer cases. Lottie ate. Nick only poked at the food with his fork. He drank three, four cups of coffee and smoked innumerable cigarettes.

•••

Lottie went into the tavern to open up.

Sun lay brightly on the dirty floor. Sun poured through the opening door as the newsboy came in. "Lady, here's your paper." He was a young kid, very ragged. "Okay, Sport!" Lottie said.

POLICEMAN KILLED
ON WEST MADISON

Lottie read the headline. For a while she stared out of the dirty plate glass of the tavern and onto the street where bums had already begun to drift up and down. A policeman, patrolling the street, went past, looking in. He lifted his hand to her and she could see his lips saying, "Hello, Lottie." She waved back. He moved on down the street.

When Lottie went into the back room, Nick was washing the dishes with one hand. His head jerked around toward her, his eyes fearful. Lottie smiled at him. "You don't have to do that, kid," she said.

"Did you see the paper?" he asked.

"I never read the papers. I ain't got time," Lottie said. She helped him with the dishes and when they were finished said, "Why don't you sit in my bedroom? It's more comfortable in there." She moved back toward the tavern.

POLICE–KILLER AT LARGE

He went into the semi-dark bedroom and sat tensely on the edge of the unmade bed. There was the smell of powder, cheap perfume and incense. On the end of the dresser was a Buddha, potbellied, watchful.

Nick sat on the bed with his shoulders drawn down and his head up, staring at the Buddha. He kept bringing the cigarette up to his lips and drawing in hard. Lottie at the door made him jump. "How you doing, kid?"

"All right."

She had a shot of whiskey for him. He gulped it down. "Thanks."

Lottie said, "Take it easy!" She left him there.

She knows! She knows!

Again his eyes swept the dressertop. His mind kept telling him, over and over, the names of the things on the dresser. Over and over. He lay back on the bed with the crook of his arm over his eyes. His lower lip caught between his teeth.

Lottie came in a couple of times, once with a sandwich, once with a pack of cigarettes and a deck of cards. For a while he played solitaire, holding the cards clumsily in the bandaged hand to shuffle them, laying them out with his left hand. The Buddha watched him.

He played until he couldn't stand it any more. Again he lay with his eyes behind the crook of his arm. He sat up, remembering, for the first time, the money he had robbed. He put it on his knees and, moving the rubber bands back with his fingers, counted it. There was almost five hundred dollars.

The biggest haul I ever made. And I had to kill a guy to get it.
He stared vacantly.

• • •

He stayed in the bedroom all that day and all that evening. About seven o'clock Lottie brought him a bowl of chili and some fried fish. "We'll have supper after I close up," she told him.

He stayed there, first lying across the bed, then trying to play cards, always ending up sitting on the side of the bed staring. He smoked one cigarette after the other. The Buddha watched him with cold, impersonal eyes.

It must be nine o'clock. He smoked again.

It must be ten o'clock.

He stood up suddenly. He stood beside the bed a moment thinking of wanting to run away from reform school. Of wanting to get away from there, over the mountains, anywhere. He walked to the mirror and for a full minute looked in the space where Lottie's fingers had wiped. His fright-filled eyes stared back at him. Where to now?

Nick took the fat roll of bills out of his pocket. Holding it against his side with his right wrist he pulled out ten ten-dollar bills and put them on the dresser. Opening the drawer he took out the first paper he saw, an envelope. With an eyebrow pencil, writing awkwardly with his injured hand, he scrawled *Thanks* across the front of the envelope. He propped it up against a cold cream jar with the money in front of it. Looking at the dresser he saw her black gloves. He picked one up and stuffed it into his pocket. He didn't know why.

Nick moved quickly to the back door, the warped boards cracking under his feet and making his heart pound hard. He quietly took the chain off the door and quietly pushed the bolt back. Then he stepped outside and softly closed the door. The chill air hit him.

I shouldn't of thrown my gun away. Dumb.

In a daze, stiff-legged, he walked down the alley, out onto the street. His shoulders were humped tensely. Neon was hung over the buildings. There were people on the street.

Just like nothin' happened.

A little shiver went through him. Tense and dazed he walked along the street. He found his legs carrying him into a tavern. Dazed, he followed them. He went through to the toilet and stood at the trough. He stood there after he was finished. He stared at the wall: SANITUBE—*The Original Navy Prophylactic.*

He dragged his eyes away from the sign without remembering what he had read. He walked out to the bar and asked for a shot. He could see his reflection in the mirror back of the bar.

[338]

Still handsome. Innocent-looking. Hahaha.

With out-of-focus eyes he stared over the bar straight ahead. CALVERT . . . I'm glad I did it . . . HIRAM WALKER . . . glad . . . MATTINGLY & MOORE . . . can't stay here. . . .

He walked out and down the street in a daze.

In the night he walked now, knowing where his legs were taking him.

He went down the street one block over. He went under the black cut of driveway at the icehouse. He stood in the dark looking up at the windows of his house. Behind the shades was light. It was warm and—and—it was home. Behind the shades would be Ma, darning.

He stood there a long time. Then he moved away.

■■■

He walked a long, long way. He went up the steps to the second floor. In the hall he waited a while. Then, softly, he stepped inside and closed the door. She was drunk. She sat at the table with her hair streaming down, over her shoulders and face. She pushed her hair out of her face to reach for the bottle and she saw him. "Nick."

"Hello, Mom," he said solemnly.

Again she said, dully, "Nick." Then she put her head down in her arms and started crying, loudly and miserably. "My poor little Emmike! —My poor little Emmike! My baby! —My baby!"

Nick walked to the table and stood over her. She kept crying and calling Emma's name. He sat down on a chair facing her. He started shaking her by the shoulder, gently, then harder and harder. She went on crying. He had a lot of bills in his hands. He kept only a few for himself. "Here," he said. He put the money on the table. He lifted her up with both hands. "Don't tell nobody I was here." Her eyes were closed tight and the tears ran down her withered cheeks. "Do you understand?" he asked.

"Yes! Yes!" she said hysterically; and she nodded her head up and down, hard, like a child. He got up and walked quickly out of the room. She put her head back on her arms and started crying loudly, miserably. "My little Emmike! —My little Emmike!" Going down the steps he still heard her.

■■■

Again he walked down the streets, blindly, trying to think. His mind went cold. His body went numb. He found himself walking back toward West Madison.

Yeah, he will help me. I done a lot for him. He'll help me.

COMB CITY FOR KILLER

He's a right guy. He'll know what to do.

Nick knocked softly on the iron door in the West Madison Street alley, then harder. At last a slot of opening showed light and he could hear Ace's voice ask, cold and thin, "Who's there?"

"It's me, Ace—Nick."

The door came open. Ace stood there with a gun in his hand. The light was behind his back and Nick couldn't see his face. "Yeah?" Ace said coldly.

"I'm in a hole, Ace." Nick's voice began to tremble. "Can you get me out of town or something. Just get me out of town—that's all!"

Ace didn't answer. Nick saw his head slowly moving back and forth, no. Fear welled up into Nick's eyes. "Can't you let me have a gun, Ace? So—so they won't get me."

"Sorry," Ace said, cold and impersonal, "I don't want to get mixed up in it... don't want to have anything to do with it."

All Nick could see were Ace's big teeth, white in the dark, and the gun held casually at his side. Nick squared back his shoulders and tossed his head. "Oh—okay," he said. His voice was cold like Ace's. He grinned. The dimples showed in his cheeks. He kept grinning.

...

But when the door closed he stood in terror, alone in the dark alley. Afraid of the dark, afraid of the light out on the street. He slid into blacker blackness. He crouched there, blinking his eyes, making them accustomed to the dark. Owen. I shoulda gone to Owen. He'd do anything for me. But Nick was afraid to venture out. He cowered against the brick wall, hearing rats in the garbage near his feet. Five minutes... ten....

He looked around. A fire escape. He went up the fire escape in the dark, and across a second story roof. On the wall ahead of him there were sheets of galvanized tin over the back windows of a vacant flat. From one of them the tin had been partially ripped off. Nick bent it back and, when the gap was large enough, put his knee over the window sill and worked his body inside.

When his heart was no longer trip-hammering he moved into the black cube, feeling his way with his hands out in front of him. The old and musty smell of the vacant flat curled up into his nostrils. He went through it to a second room, stretching his eyes in the dark. He struck a match and a large shadow rose against the wall. Nick's fingers shielded the match flame. In its yellow glow his face was lit up. His eyes were hollows with black pupils of fear looking out of them. He moved, slowly, silently across the room. The shadow of him against the wall grew larger and larger. Plaster crunched under his feet. Rat claws kindled muted noises in the wall.

Nick went to the front room. Boards were across the windows. Moonlight was in the chinks. Three stories below him traffic moved along West Madison. Nick stood a long time in the middle of the

[340]

room, listening . . . listening . . . straining his ears . . . and his eyes.

In the wall the rat noises. On the street below the rush of an occasional automobile or trolley. Then silence, dead and thick.

I'm alone. There ain't nobody here.

He went slowly and sat with his head down and his shoulders small against the wide and bare wall. He felt in his pocket and drew out the one cigarette he had left. He lit and smoked it halfway down. Then he put out its coal carefully and stuffed the remaining half back into his pocket. He sat silent and scared, with his knees drawn up close to his chin and his shoulders pressed against the plaster-crumbling wall. He trembled from the cold and the alone-ness. He put his arms on his knees and his head on his arms.

I ain't got any friends.

Only Owen and Grant.

DRAGNET THROWN AROUND CITY

Nick came awake. He lay with his eyes closed, shivering with fear. He lay perfectly still trying to remember where he was. He opened his eyes slowly.

Riley!

He remembered and he blinked his eyes wide open. Then he squinted against the hard sunlight that fell across his face in warm yellow bands. He squirmed his head around on old and musty newspapers, balled into a pillow. His eyes went slowly around the ceiling and the walls. Bare laths grinned in jagged sections of the wall. There were spider webs in the corners and a spider muscled its way toward the ceiling on a long chain of web. Clear sunlight fell through the chinks of the boarded-up windows in long angular brightness and smeared in the dirt and plaster dust of the floor. Far off and way down, traffic moved endlessly along West Madison.

Nick shivered from the cold. He tried to keep warm by moving his arms around in circles and quietly pacing back and forth.

Somebody downstairs! Maybe somebody downstairs! Can't go out of here!

Nick turned his collar up around his neck and stuffed his hands under his armpits, trying to warm them. His fingers were so cold he could feel the shape of their bones. The tip of his nose was cold, and his ankles.

The morning came in through the boards, cold and hazy.

Christ!

In one corner of the vacant flat Nick found an old bucket and took it to the small, windowless closet. He stripped off wallpaper and crumpled it into the pail. On the floor he found some laths. He broke one across his knee. It cracked so loudly that he could hear his heart thump. He put a match to the crumpled wallpaper. Fire licked up over the top of the pail. Nick stretched his fingers down to it. The flames leaped up and the smoke rose. The smoke scared him.

Somebody will smell it!

And he put the fire out.

He sat on the floor and smoked the remaining half of his cigarette.

And the morning wore itself away.

Cold. Hungry.

Cold.

That woman was good to me.

And the afternoon showed bald and grayish over West Madison Street.

TRACE KILLER'S GUN TO
MAXWELL STREET HOCKSHOP

The evening put gray into the blue-gray afternoon. Night wrapped around the buildings and around the faces of men and women. Night darkened the chinks of the boarded-up windows. Night closed around him. Every strange noise made him shake with fear. He knotted himself into a tighter ball. See what you did to yourself, his mind said accusingly.

He put his folded thumb between his teeth and pressed hard.

Little Nicky Romano the wise guy! Always one ahead of the game!

Nick's eyes swam with tears of fear and impotence.

He couldn't stand it any longer.

He went through the vacant flat and crawled beyond the bend of galvanized tin. He went across the roof, and down the fire escape toward the alley.

You're in trouble so you're going to run to Grant.

He'd be a sucker to help you.

He stepped off the bottom rung of the fire escape and went across the lot to the alley. He saw a policeman patrolling the street. He flattened back into the dark, and wheeling around sneaked hurriedly down the alley to the other end. A squad car was going along the street slowly. Its headlights lit him up. He jumped back and, turning, ran down the alley. The headlights were all over his head and his shoulders and his running legs.

Nick ran to the fire escape. He leaped up it, taking two steps at a time. The squad car bumped over the empty lot and came to a jolting stop. The car doors banged open.

"Halt! HALT!"

It made him go faster. He reached the top. The feet of the police,

[342]

running, sounded behind him. He saw the jagged, bent-back tin at the window and his mind saw the bare rooms: no way out but through the window.

Caught like a rat in a hole! He ran past the window, along the wall. At its end his eyes saw a ladder of iron rungs set into the bricks. His hands grabbed them.

"HALT!"

Sound of a shot.

Nick went up the handles and footholds of the iron ladder set into the wall. He gained the top. He struggled from his elbows and stomach to a standing position on the roof. He ran over noisy and sliding pebbles.

In front of him the low cornice of the building . . . behind him the police gaining the top of the ladder.

Nick ran to the edge of the roof. He looked down giddily onto West Madison Street. His head grew dizzy; he grew sick as he swayed there. Below him the cobblestones; the dirty, bum-strewn sidewalks, the neon signs, the taut network of streetcar cables.

He turned his back to the street and faced the ladder up which the police would come. Behind him the empty sky reflected street light, threw it in dull smears across his back. His fists were clenched tight. He stood, a taut silhouette against the sky, waiting.

They came running at him across the roof. He could hear the pebbles sliding away from their big feet. They came with their guns drawn. A flashlight leaped at him like a snake striking. Hit him in the face, like tons of cold water pouring over him. He stood blinded. He stood staring into its whiteness with his teeth clenched and his hands in fists at his sides.

They stuck their guns in his ribs. They dragged him from the edge of the roof and beat him with their clubs, across the shoulders and neck. He swayed but stood. They clamped handcuffs on his wrists above his balled fists. They dragged him across the roof. They forced him, between them, to climb down the iron ladder and go down the iron steps of the fire escape. They frisked him. Then they bundled him into the squad car, roughly shoving him in with their clubs.

72

They stopped the squad car behind the station.

"Yeah, he answers the description, all right."

"Yeah—young—good-looking—"

"Black hair—"

"This is the bastard, all right."

"Yeah," said the two policemen together. The flashlight clicked and went off. In the dark Nick could see the form of their faces close to his and feel their bodies pressing in on him from either side in the cramped back seat. Their breath was hot in his face.

"You killed Riley—*didn't you?*"

"I don't know what you're talking about. I didn't kill nobody, SEE!" He hissed it at them.

"What were you doing in that alley?"

"Why did you run when you saw the squad car?"

He didn't answer.

"Talk, you bastard!"

He didn't answer.

"We'll make you talk, you sonofabitch!"

They slapped his face with their hard, open hands. His teeth rattled. He gritted them.

Again they slapped his face. The slapping sounds smacked loudly in the dark and silent alley.

"Are you going to talk?"

Nick didn't answer. There was a moment of silence. Then their fists swung. Nick felt a jab of pain in the pit of his stomach. "OH!— YOU SONOFA—" Again the pain knotted him double.

"We're going to take in a confession!" one of the cops said. Their fists came again, cracking his ribs and his stomach and his neck. Nick, locked in the handcuffs, took their blows doubled in half.

They dragged him into the station. The sergeant booked him open. "Take him down to cold storage," the sergeant said.

Seventy-two hours they could hold him open. Seventy-two hours

[344]

they could grill him. For three days they could give him the third degree.

...

In the morning the sergeant and a policeman came down. They looked in through the bars at him. "You ready to talk?" the sergeant asked. Nick stared back at them and sneered.

They left him there all day. They gave him nothing to eat and nothing to drink.

That evening the sergeant and a policeman came down again. "Are you ready to talk?" Nick didn't answer. The sergeant said, "Take him upstairs to see the goldfish."

They took him to a small room with nothing but a desk and two chairs. There were spotlights fastened to the ceiling, drilling down on the desk. The cop said, "Face the wall!" Nick looked at him hard-eyed, then turned, facing the wall. Immediately he remembered going on line in reform school with the heavy weights in his hands and his nose and forehead pressed against the wall.... Rocky sent to watch them ... he and Rocky sitting on the pool table after it was over, smoking and swinging their legs.... They had divided a chocolate bar....

He had had no food for two days and his stomach retched at the thought of the chocolate.

The policeman sat on a chair and put his feet up on the desk. "If you know anything you better spill it before the dicks get here," he said. "They'll make you talk all right, all right ... they'll beat the living crap out of you." Then he was silent, with his feet on the desk, smoking.

They kept him standing there for two hours. Another policeman came to relieve the one on guard. When the door closed, the new policeman said, "Come on over and sit down, buddy." Nick moved from the wall and sat on the other chair. "Cigarette?"

Nick took one. "Thanks," he said. He smoked the cigarette with both hands held close by handcuffs.

"Take a tip from an old-timer, kid," the policeman said. "If you know anything you better tell it. It'll go a lot easier on you." Nick looked across the handcuffs. "I don't know nothing. I ain't got nothing to tell!"

The detectives came into the room, four or five of them. They were big with soft-brim hats snapped down over their eyes. Their burly figures took up almost all the space in the small room. The policeman slid out of the room, his eyes looking them over admiringly. They came over to the desk where Nick sat, stoop-shouldered. All of them looked at Nick, silently and searchingly, with hostility. And Nick, tightening his lips, stared back at them.

For a moment, as their scrutiny continued, there was no sound in

[345]

the room. Then the one in the chair opposite Nick said, "What can you tell us, kid, about this?"

"About what?"

"You can account for yourself, can't you? All we want to know is where you were. Well—what have you got to say?"

"About what!"

"You know Riley's been killed."

"No."

"You knew Riley, didn't you?"

"No."

"You were in a jam with him one time."

"No, I wasn't."

"Oh, yes, you were." The dick's voice was very slow and pleasant, but with a snap.

They stared at each other.

"Riley was killed Saturday night," the detective said. Nick looked at him squarely, eye to eye, and didn't blink a lid.

The detective's tone got a little friendlier. "Now you were running over rooftops when the police brought you in, but that doesn't mean a thing. We're just as anxious to throw you out of here as we are to bring the real killer in. Get away from the idea that cops are out to get everybody they pick up—they're not. But remember this, kid—*the whole world is out to get every cop-killer.*" He bit the last words off.

The whole world is out to get every cop-killer! The words rang in Nick's ears; they stood up before his eyes in foot-high letters. Nick's eyelids twitched but he continued looking across the table into the detective's face. "I don't know nothing about it."

"*Where were you!* . . . Were you on West Madison that night? . . . What did you do that night? . . . Who were you with? . . . You took in a show, didn't you?" They shot the questions at him, back and forth, from all sides.

Nick lifted and tossed his head. He said, laughing at them, "You ain't got nothing on me. I don't know nothing—see!"

One of the dicks lifted Nick's manacled hands. "Where'd you get the cut on your hand?" he asked, saying it slowly and softly. "And what are your knuckles doing scuffed up?" He looked steadily at Nick. The detective on the other side of the desk asked, "Ever have a gun that came out of a hockshop on Maxwell Street?"

That hit Nick like a rock. His head swung around at the dick who had asked it. But he let his eyes fall immediately.

"Well—did you?"

"No!"

"Did you?" asked the bull on the other side of the desk, poking him. Nick's eyes and head swung around to meet the bull's glance.

[346]

"No!"

"Did you?"

"No! —I said no!"

The bull across the desk leaned in Nick's face again. *"Well—where were you?"*

Nick lifted his chained hands to his face and, moving them up over his eyes, pushed the hair off his forehead. "Well—I—" His thoughts tumbled through his brain in a jumble. All he could see was himself standing over Riley pumping the bullets down into him. "—I—was at the poolroom and—at the Nickel Plate. . . ."

"Who did you talk to?" the detective followed up quickly.

"Juan and—" As he said Juan his mind threw words at him in a flood: *Keep your friends out of it!* "—and—and—Squint. . . ."

"And Squint sang!" the detective across the table said. He leaned back in the chair, watching Nick closely.

Nick went crazy. "That goddamn polack don't know nothing! You ain't got nothing on me!" Sweat stood on his forehead. A lick of black hair hung down over his forehead.

The detectives sat silent, stone-faced. Their eyes stared at him. "Nothin'—*you ain't got nothin' on me!*" He heard his voice shouting; and he sat down, weakly. He wet his lips with his tongue. *Owen. Squint. You think you're All-American hell, don't you? Zigzag of the knife tearing the flesh of his hand. Kicking Squint in the face. Owen bandaging the hand.* The detective was staring at him from across the desk. "What did he say?" Nick asked; and immediately tried to swallow the words back.

The detective was smiling. "Nick—that's your first break."

Nick's ears rang and his heart pounded. "I want a lawyer!" he shouted. His lips hung open, ugly.

The detective was cool and soft-voiced now. "Kid, you've been around enough to know that we can hold you incommunicado for a long, long time." His voice went ugly again. *"Forget about lawyers!"* He leaned his face into Nick's. "And tell us the truth."

"You can't hold me more than seventy-two hours!"

The dick smiled. "Listen, punk, you been around that mob of yours long enough to know that you can sit on your can in every police station in the city and no deputy with a springing writ is going to be able to find you."

"I ain't talking," Nick said.

Without words the bull got up out of the chair and the dicks all got off the desk. They left the room.

In the hall leaning casually against the wall stood a man. As the detectives moved past him, one of them shook his head no. The man was elderly and distinguished-looking. As the dicks went along the hall one of them called a policeman. "Pick up Juan—some Mexican, I guess."

The detectives came back with lengths of hose, blackjacks and night sticks in their hands. As they went past the elderly man he inhaled deeply and dropped the still long, cork-tipped cigarette on the floor. He stepped on it. Standing outside the door he leaned his head back and exhaled lazily.

The detectives went back into the room and locked the door. They piled the lengths of hose, blackjacks and night sticks on the table in front of Nick. Their faces were angry and they scowled. They took off their coats, folded them neatly. They rolled up their sleeves. Nick watched them white-faced.

One detective picked up a length of hose. No word was spoken, or needed. The other detectives selected tools of punishment. They stepped toward Nick. Just then a knock sounded. They unlocked the door.

The elderly man stepped into the room. He looked around, frowning, first at the table, then at the detectives. "What's the meaning of this?" he asked sternly. His tone and looks demanded an answer.

"Chuck was just trying to loosen his tongue a little, sir," one of the detectives said.

"Since when have you used gangsters' methods?" the elderly man asked severely. His eyes frowned at them. He looked at Nick. His face grew slowly sympathetic. He glanced at one of the detectives. "Take those handcuffs off that boy!" The detective obeyed humbly. "Now all of you leave this room. If ever I hear of anything as atrocious as this again I'll see that all of you are broken." There was righteous anger in his voice. His face was fatherly.

The elderly man moved around behind Nick, putting his hand on his shoulder for a second. Nick drew his shoulder away from the touch. The elderly man sat opposite Nick, glancing at him silently and sympathetically for a while, then down at the desk and what was on it, as if he were embarrassed. He said, "My boy, don't you think you had better tell me what you know about this case?" His eyes came up, met Nick's sincerely. "You don't have to be afraid of me. I'm not a policeman and I'm not a detective. I'm here to help you and I'm not going to let them handle you roughly. All I want you to do is tell me, as nearly as you can, where you were and what you did last Saturday night."

Nick sensed the phoney ring in his voice. *Copper*, his mind said, *copper, like the rest of them.* "I'm not talking to anybody till I see a lawyer."

At last the man, still looking at Nick sadly, sighed and said, "Well—I think you're acting foolishly. I could make things easy for you—but—" He lifted his hands helplessly. "You know what you want to do." He walked out slowly, so that Nick could call him back if he wanted to. When he was in the hall he nodded his head angrily and the detectives who were waiting there went back in. They locked the door behind them.

One of them rolled up his sleeves and critically selected a rubber hose. The one called Chuck, picking up a blackjack, said, "This is your last chance." Nick didn't answer.

The bulls moved in closer, surrounding the chair. The spotlights had been turned on and beat down in Nick's face. Detective Chuck lifted the blackjack. Nick ducked to avoid the blow. Another bull jerked him back by the hair and a third twisted his arm behind him. The blackjack struck. "Ow! —You bastards!"

They shoved him down into the chair. For five minutes they pounded him, methodically, without excitement, in well-practiced technique. Then the detectives paused, panting, looking down at him.

Nick hung, leaned-over in the chair with his arms folded up around his face and the back of his neck.

"You ready to talk?"

When he didn't answer a big hand came around hard, slapping the side of his head, spinning it. "You ready to talk!"

You gotta kill me first! his mind shouted at them.

They gave Nick the third degree some more.

He took it, all they gave, with his teeth grinding together and the angry tears running down his cheeks.

Again the bull-necked detectives rested. And one of them got a bottle of whiskey out of the desk drawer. "This will make the bastard talk!"

They held him. They pulled his head back by his hair. They forced his jaws open with the butts of their hands. They stuck the bottle neck between his teeth and held it there. The hot and raw whiskey hit Nick's throat. It spilled over his lips and down his shirt. They let go of him. He staggered to his feet, the chair falling over backwards behind him. The whiskey hit his stomach where no food had been for two days. It came up, strangling him. He spewed it out. Part of it went on two of the detectives. This maddened them. They forced him against the wall. He stood there with them all around him, one arm hanging limp and numb at his side from the twisting. They rushed in on him, stepping up the tempo of the beating. They punched him and used the lengths of hose on him.

"Don't mark up this pretty sonofabitch!" one of the dicks said through his teeth. "What the hell!" said one of the others. "We can say he fell down the steps." Nevertheless they kept their beating down low where it wouldn't show.

They beat him.

[349]

You gotta kill me first!

They didn't get a confession.

They left him lying unconscious on the floor.

●●●

They gave him a little something to eat the next day. And that evening they got him ready for the showup. They took him over in the patrol wagon. On the way they pounded him a little. Just to show him that they had him where they wanted him.

They marched him out under the lights in line with the others. The cops tipped the newspaper men off: "We think we got the Riley killer." A number of reporters crowded into the large room where the showup is held. Among others on the seats facing the stage like a theatre sat the bartender from the Three-Eighty Club.

Nick and the rest of the line were made to stand facing out, turn left, turn right, facing out. The light beat in his face. The officer in charge called out to the audience: "Anybody here recognize the man who held up the Three-Eighty Club ... anybody here recognize the man who ran out of the alley at Madison and Atlantic last Saturday when Officer Dennis Riley was murdered—?" A man stood up. It was the bartender. His voice struck the silence. It rocked against Nick's ears. "That's the fellow there! Number three!" Nick's heart turned over sideways.

A hard silence hit the room. It stayed only a second. There was a low rumble of voices, excitement, Nick being moved from the line. People were standing to get a look at him. Only the top of his head was over the backs and shoulders of the blue-uniformed police. His face was drained of all its color.

The glamour boys from the daily papers rushed into the press-room. "Did they finger him? ... Anybody finger him? ... They sure did! —He'll burn sure! ... City desk! ... City desk!"

●●●

The news photographers rushed down to his cell with their cameras poised. The bartender was there, looking in, again identifying him. "Yeah—that's him all right." The news photographers closed in around the bars. One of them said to the bartender, "Point your finger at him." Another said, "Hold it!" They squatted around the cell on their heels, their tightening-out rumps bulging out under their classy tweed sport coats.

Nick stared out beyond the bars at them. All he could think was that the guys on West Madison would see his picture. He lifted one end of his mouth in a hard-boiled smile, showing he could take it.

The flash bulbs began exploding.

●●●

The police unlocked the cell and the newshounds went in. "We'd like to get a story from you, Romano. String along with us and we'll

[350]

give you the breaks. We'll see that you get written up the right way. How about something exclusive?" One of the photographers was fooling with his camera, making adjustments, focussing.

Nick sat on the edge of the bunk with one foot up on it, his forearm on his knee and his forehead down on his arm. "Get the hell out of here." A flash bulb went off. Dazed Nick sat staring into the cameras. His mouth was open a little. His eyes were dark and innocent-looking. The bulbs kept going off.

"Ho! A pretty boy!" one of the reporters said.

"Yeah—Pretty Boy Romano," said another reporter.

"Pretty Boy Romano." They all said it, reflecting how it would look in headlines.

■■■

They took him to the grilling room to sweat him some more. "Do you want to tell us what you know?"

"I ain't talking!" He whipped the words at them.

They couldn't make him talk. When he wouldn't talk one of them said, panting a little. "Get the handcuffs."

They taped his wrists first so that the handcuffs would leave no marks. Then they handcuffed him with his hands behind his back. They put a mask over his face. "You'll be wearing one of these in the chair damn soon!" one of the cops said. Then they fastened the cuffs to a roped pulley on the back of the door and stood him there facing them. They lifted the pulley ropes a few notches until only his toes were on the floor. Their technique was excellent. They lined up and went past him, each hitting him below the ribs and in the small of the back. "Come clean! . . . Come clean!" . . . *Whack! Whack!* . . . "Come clean!"

He didn't talk.

The pulley was hoisted a few notches. "Come clean!" The pulley was hoisted another notch.

They didn't get anything out of him.

The reporters were hanging out in the hall. "Did he talk? . . . Haven't you got that confession *yet?*"

Word passed around about the cop-killer, and patrolmen going to and from duty stopped in on Nick. Even cops who didn't know Riley came to administer punishment.

They stopped in by ones, by twos. They stayed in the locked room a while. On their faces a sneer as if to say—we have the divine right. They seemed to get some sensual enjoyment out of it. Some terrific kick. Some exhilaration. And when they came out their faces were relaxed, like sighing after a crisis is over.

73

POLICE–SLAYER TRAPPED

Pretty Boy Romano Leers
As Bartender Identifies Him

The newspapers were playing the case up big.

ROMANO BOUND OVER
TO GRAND JURY

Grant read the story and after a long, long time pulled himself to
his feet. He went to the phone.

"Hello—Mort? Look, Mort, I want you to do me a favor. I want
you to take a case for me."

There was a short silence. Then the voice on the other end of the
line chuckled. "What have you been doing? Well—I'll try to get
you off."

"No, it's a friend of mine who is in trouble. A young fellow by
the name of Romano."

"Romano! You know him?"

"Yes, ever since he was fourteen."

"He's in a bad hole."

"Will you take the case?"

"You know I will. I think we'd better meet for dinner. I'd like to
know all about the boy before I see him. I've been reading the
papers. They are surely riding hell out of him. You know, I was
thinking of dropping in on the kid to see if he had any friends—if
he was broke and couldn't get a lawyer." The voice on the other
end of the line chuckled again and said, "By the way—who is he? A
bastard son of yours?"

"Fight the case," Grant said, "as if he were."

•••

Andrew Morton went in through the huge door of the county jail
and to the reception window. He looked beyond the glass and the

bars and said into the little cut at the bottom, "Hello, Jim." He was immediately recognized.

"Oh! Hello, Mr. Morton!" the police attendant said.

"I've been retained to look after Nick Romano," Mr. Morton said.

"Are you his attorney then? He sure will be glad to see you. Without you it don't look like he's got a chance."

Mr. Morton was admitted to the consultation room. The police brought Nick in and locked the door. Nick sat in a chair with his head and shoulders down and his hands in his lap. Morton studied the drawn, colorless face with the eyelids pulled down over the eyes and the eyes staring down at the hands.

Nick glanced up at Morton and looked away, back, letting his eyes slowly drop.

He don't seem like no cop of any kind.

Morton glanced across at the policeman and handed him a five-dollar bill. "Here, Roy, get yourself some cigars." The policeman pocketed the bill and went to the far end of the room where he couldn't hear what would be said.

Morton pulled up a chair and sat facing Nick. "I came to see what I could do for you," he said quietly.

"Nothing," Nick said, not looking up.

"Oh, I don't know," Morton said, and his voice took on a more cheerful note. "Your friend Grant sent me to see you and told me to do everything I could."

Your friend Grant.

Nick looked straight into Morton's deep-set and sympathetic gray eyes. Morton saw Nick's eyes film with tears. "Grant sent you?"

"Yes."

"He ain't through with me?" Nick asked in surprised disbelief.

Morton shook his head no; then, watching Nick closely all the time he said, "You were an altar boy, weren't you?"

"Yeah—that's right," Nick said, as if he hardly remembered.

For five minutes Morton talked about his own boyhood, chuckling and telling little jokes about the scrapes he had got into. All the time he was talking he studied Nick's face. Then suddenly he sat up in the chair and asked, very quietly, "Nick, did you have anything to do with the shooting of Riley?"

Nick's lips twisted in a tight smile. "A mouthpiece works better when he thinks his client is innocent, don't he?"

Morton sighed heavily and relaxed against the chair back. "Look, son—" he said, "a case isn't a matter of facts but of evidence." Morton sat up and then leaned toward Nick with his elbows on the arms of the chair and his gray eyes showing anger. "The prosecution is interested in only one thing—a verdict—and it doesn't care how it gets it. Their lawyers don't care if a man is innocent or guilty.

They're out to make a record for themselves. They want to publish to the world—through the newspapers—the number of convictions they make. Everything the police and the lawyers can do to get a verdict they will do. Whether you're innocent or guilty they'll go after you for a conviction just as hard." Morton stopped. He took a cigarette from his case and passed Nick one. They smoked in silence. Finally Morton said, "You've been having a tough time, haven't you?"

Nick's eyes hardened. "Yeah!"

"What did they do to you?"

"They beat the hell out of me! That's what the bastards did!"

"You didn't talk? You didn't sign any papers?"

"No, I didn't talk! They coulda killed me and I wouldn't of talked!"

Morton sighed as if he were relieved. "Part of the code not to talk, eh?" And his eyes twinkled.

Nick glanced at him hard. "Part of what code? What do you know about a code?" Morton laughed. Nick said quickly, answering his own question, "You don't talk! You don't squeal on nobody!"

Morton lowered his lids, looking at Nick. "Squint squealed."

"Squint don't know nothing!"

"The police—tell me exactly what they did to you."

Nick told him and as he did so something happened to Morton's eyes behind the shadow of his hand. When Nick had finished Morton asked, "Would you know them?"

"Yeah, I'd know them all right!"

Morton slipped to another subject. "Where were you the night Riley was killed?"

Nick thought a minute. All he could see was himself in the alley emptying the gun into Riley, throwing it at Riley, kicking him. "I—I was down on West Madison."

"Who did you see?"

"There was a dead man."

"Where was that?" Morton's eyes studied Nick.

"They were carrying him out of a flophouse and it was raining."

"Where did you go that night?"

It was all hazy. Everything was hazy but Riley lying in the alley with his brains blown out.

"I was at the Nickel Plate."

"Where else?"

Nick's mind seemed able to dwell on only one subject at a time: "I gave a man a nickel in the Nickel Plate."

"Who did you talk to?" Morton's eyes studied him.

"I was at the Pastime too . . . I remember that. I talked to Butch and—and Sunshine."

"Who are Butch and Sunshine?"

"Two of my best friends."

Then Morton let the question go: "What grudge did you have against Riley?"

Nick and Morton were looking into each other's eyes. Nick was staring at him innocently. Morton said quietly, "My business is to defend you. I don't care whether you did it or not. The police say you did. Squint says you did. Kid Fingers says you did."

"The Kid—why that dirty—!"

"The Mexican boy talked too," Morton said.

"What Mexican?" All feeling drained out of Nick as he waited for the answer.

"Juan."

Nick's mouth crumpled. He tried to clench his teeth but they wouldn't clench. His lips trembled.

"What did Riley ever do to you?" Morton asked.

Nick went dead and thought.

At last he said, "Suppose I did have a grudge against him—would that mean I killed him?"

"The police are satisfied and the Attorney's Office is satisfied that you did and that your death warrant is signed. That's why I asked you if Riley had ever done anything to you that would make you want to kill him. Whoever shot Riley didn't stop there, for after he was dead his face was kicked in. They say this shows an absolute hatred and desire for vengeance on the part of the killer. If you want to tell me anything that will help me to help you, do it now."

Nick said, "Give me a cigarette, will you?"

When he had finished smoking it in dead silence, he said, "I'll tell you."

He told Morton all about it—about the three notches in Riley's belt and the rabbit punches in the basement of the jail. When he had finished he asked for another cigarette.

"Did Kid Fingers see it?"

"I don't know."

"Did Squint see it?"

"I—I think so." Nick's lips trembled on the cigarette.

Morton said, "I'm going to send a physician in to examine you and see if he can verify that third degree they gave you. And I'll send a photographer too." He pushed the hair off his forehead. He stood up. "We can build a case on insanity or temporary insanity."

Nick flushed. He looked at Morton; all the broad flatness of his wide cheekbones showed the flush. His brown-black hair fell over his forehead and curled near his ears. "No. I ain't going to cop no plea on insanity! Leave that angle out, see!"

[355]

Morton looked down at him. Morton stroked his chin; he seemed
to be talking to himself. "You're good-looking, all right. No jury—
the majority women—would execute...." He picked up his hat.
"Take it easy and don't talk to anyone about the case."

MORTON ENGAGED FOR PRETTY BOY!
Chicago's Most Eminent Lawyer Takes Case

Ma came to see him on visiting day. Julian was with her. Ma
looked through the little section of glass at him. Her haggard old
eyes drew his face deeply into her. "You didn't do it, son, did you?"
she asked.

"Naw, I didn't do it," Nick said.

Julian looked in at him with unhappy eyes.

Ma started crying. "Oh, my boy! my boy!" she sobbed. She pressed
her wrinkled face as close to the section of glass and steel as she
could get it. "Cut it out, Ma!" Nick said hard-boiled; but he felt
the numb and heavy beat of his heart.

···

Andrew Morton began work on the case.

The first thing he did was drop into the Three-Eighty Club. He
went in quietly and stood just inside the door for a while, looking
at the two bartenders. When he was certain. from the newspaper
photographs which one was Swanson, the bartender Nick had held
up, he stepped to the bar and ordered a glass of port. The bartender
brought it. Morton immediately struck up a conversation. "Oh, you
had a holdup recently, didn't you?"

"Yeah, that's right," the bartender said. "Everybody asks about it
when they come in here. They got the guy, you know. I identified
him."

"A policeman was killed, wasn't he?"

"Yeah. Right down the alley here."

"Are you sure it was the same fellow who held up this place?"

"Christ, yes! It happened right down the alley and only a couple
minutes later—the cop was chasing him down the alley."

Morton finished his wine and pushed the glass across the bar at
Swanson. "Give me another." The bartender filled the glass again.
Morton started to pick it up. His hand struck the glass and the
wine spilled down Swanson's shirt and bar apron.

"Oh! I'm awfully sorry!" Morton said, as Swanson stood behind
the bar mopping his shirt with a towel, "that was entirely my fault!
Let me buy you another shirt."

"Aw, that's all right," Swanson said. "The cleaners will take it
out. Christ, that happens all the time with all the drunks we have
coming in here."

"Well—buy a drink for yourself—" Morton put a dollar on the bar, "and keep the change." He left the tavern immediately.

•••

Grant came to see Nick. He smiled a little and said, "Hi, pizon." Nick couldn't quite meet his eyes. "I bet you think I'm no good," Nick said.

Grant shook his head slowly, very seriously. "No, I don't," he said; and after a pause, "I don't know if you did it or not and I don't care. I want to see you get fair treatment, that's all."

Nick held his head down.

Grant's voice became dead-earnest and almost stern. "If you did, I can understand why you did it. Morton will do everything he can to help you. He's a real guy. Anyway, I'm on your side."

Nick nodded without looking up.

•••

Pastime Poolroom. Old Jake stood wiping down the counter and shaking his head sadly. The fellows sat on benches talking about the case. Chris said, "I talked to him. I tried to get him off this street. He wouldn't listen. I know what this street does to a fellow. If I had stayed in college—" He looked out through the front pane with its crossed cue sticks. "I hope he beats the rap. He wasn't a bad kid."

Old Jake said, "You right. The beega crooks make him bad. I see him when he first come down here. He nice, soft boy. That Vito—he do it. Butch, he to blame too. And that Keed. He tell him all the time how do a lot of things."

"I hope he beats the rap," Goosey said.

"He's got a good mouthpiece," Claude said.

"The best in the business," said Jim, the houseman.

"If Morton can't do it, nobody can," Texas Slim said. "I'd like to get my hands on that goddamn Kid Fingers—just once! Christ! He used to have his hand out to Nick for money regular. Nick never refused him. Nick was all right."

"Imagine Juan turnin' State's evidence! After he and Nick used to pal all over the street together!" Claude said.

"That bastard!" Red said.

"Butch took a powder, huh?" someone said.

"Yeah."

"He and Nick used to be buddies," someone else said.

Four or five pairs of shoulders came up, shrugging.

Way in the back of the poolroom Sunshine sat on a bench. His hair stood straight up in front in a kinky cockscomb. His eyes were mournful in his dark face and he looked as if he had been crying.

The door opened and Grant walked in. Red nudged Jim with his elbow. "It's that friend of Nick's."

[357]

Grant walked up to them. Old Jake said, "Hello. Our friend, he get in trouble." Grant nodded.

Sunshine got up immediately and came from the back of the poolroom. "Mr. Grant, he didn't do it, he didn't do it, Mr. Grant. Ah was with him all that night."

The fellows stared at Sunshine. Grant was staring at him too; and now a large smile spread out across his face. He put his arm around Sunshine's shoulders and hugged him. "Come on, Sunshine!" he said. "We're going over to see Morton!"

They went out the door. All the fellows, the ones who knew Nick had killed Riley and that Sunshine had seen him do it, and the ones who didn't know stood with their mouths open.

All the way over to Morton's home Sunshine said, "He was with me. He didn't do it."

They went into Morton's study where there was a fire in the fireplace and law books and papers were piled on the desk, on the seats of chairs, and on footstools. "This is Sunshine, Mort."

Andrew Morton put out his hand and, smiling, said, "Glad to know you, Sunshine. Sit down."

Grant said, "Nick didn't do it! Sunshine was with him that night."

Morton looked at Sunshine closely. Sunshine looked at the edge of the red leather chair with scared white eyes in a chocolate-brown face. "You were with him?" Morton asked sharply.

"Yes, sah, ah was with him."

"You're lying, Sunshine!" Morton's eyes kept staring at him.

"No, ah ain't, mister! No, ah ain't! Ah was with him! Honest, ah was! He didn't kill nobody, honest, he didn't kill nobody."

Morton looked at Grant. "You might as well know, Grant," Morton said, "Nick killed Riley all right."

"I don't care if he did, Mort," Grant said. "I know what goes on inside that kid. I know what he's been up against all his life."

Morton turned to Sunshine. "You're a good friend of Nick's, aren't you, Sunshine?"

"He was good to me. We was buddies."

"Nick needs an alibi bad," Morton said.

"Ah'll say whatever you wants me to," Sunshine said.

"Nothing could make you change your story?"

"Nothin' mister! Ah swears it!"

Morton studied him a long time. "I'll tell you what to say. You come over here tomorrow. Don't talk to anyone about Nick—and stay away from West Madison."

Grant stood up. "You come home with me, Sunshine. You can stay there. There's lots of room."

"Ah'll keep your car clean, Mr. Grant."

"You don't need to do that!"

They went out.

•••

Two days before they were to go into court again Morton sat with Nick in the consultation room. Morton rubbed the palms of his hands against his eyes. "I don't know if the court will allow us another continuance or not—we've had three."

"Let's get it over with, Mr. Morton," Nick said.

"Nick—" Morton drew his chair close to Nick's until their knees almost touched. His voice sounded disturbed. He laid his hand on Nick's knee. "We've got a tough one. They always yell for vengeance when a policeman is killed. Innocent men—" He leaned back in the chair, studying the cut of Nick's head the curl-rumpled hair, the even and handsome features, and, most of all, the innocent-brown stare of his eyes. "Grant bought you three suits. I want you to wear them into court."

Morton sat with his elbows on the arms of the chair. He touched the tips of his fingers together, one after the other, reflectively. He now looked across the peak his finger tips made. "You have a way of looking at people—that jury isn't going to think you did it! I'm going to get as many women on it as I can—" He paused a moment, then said, "Now you've got to do just as I tell you. . . . I'm going to have your chair at the counsel table turned so that you are facing the jury. You've got to play up to them, Nick! I want you to look at them. Don't take your eyes off of them! You've got a way of looking at people—they aren't going to believe you did it!"

•••

On the eve of the trial they brought the reporters in. They circled around him, shooting their questions at him. "Well, how's everything, Nick? . . . How are you going to take it? . . . Well, tomorrow's the big day. How do you feel about things, Pretty Boy? . . . I'm betting you don't crack in court, fellow. . . . How about it? Give us a statement—'Sure I can take it! Me and Morton will beat the rap!'—something like that, you know."

Nick laughed through his nose at them and didn't answer.

•••

EDITORIAL . . .

Almost six months ago a killer stood in an alley behind West Madison Street with a flaming gun and murdered a police officer. The killer stood over the dead body of the policeman and kicked him until the face was almost unrecognizable, in one of the most brutal and callous murders in the annals of criminal history in the City of Chicago.

The victim was Dennis Riley who for twenty-five years was a policeman here in Chicago. In those twenty-five years he made a record for himself as one of the best men on the force. In fact on three different occasions while enforcing the law he was fired on by burglars and potential killers. Officer Riley refused promotion, preferring to remain in the humble position of a policeman.

Today a young man of twenty-one by the name of Nick Romano goes on trial for the murder of Officer Riley....

74

Across the front of the building the words say COVRT HOVSE. A sidewalk leads to the building. There is grass on either side of it. It is very green. There are yellow circles of dandelions in the grass.

The courthouse is of limestone, and it is set far back on the grass, a massive, heaped block of stone. The front of the building rises behind giant columns. High at the top, standing on the pillars, are sculptured figures—Law, Justice, Liberty, Peace. Law is Moses holding the Ten Commandments. At the top corners of the building on even higher peaks than the stone figures, are Latin words: LEX—IVSTITIA—LIBERTAS—PAX. The promises are very encouraging.

Beyond the doors of the courthouse the lobby is wide, rich in tone, color, design. The marble floor is soft-toned, with a tint of pink in it. The high ceiling is raftered in deep-set squares. Bronze floor torches stand against the marble walls and reflect discreet light to the ceiling. At the far end of the hall is the Criminal Court call board with the names of judges and the day's cases thumbtacked to it—

JUDGE DRAKE

A-809   James Scott .... Atty.: Public Defender . *Larceny*
A-812   Ray Evans .... Atty.: .... *Rape*
L-404   Nicholas Romano .. Atty.: Andrew Morton . *Murder*

Alongside the call board is a sign reading: *Bondsmen are strictly prohibited from soliciting in or around this building.* Stand

[360]

ing around the board with their faces turned up to it were shyster lawyers with briefcases, bond-bail con-men, people with friends or relatives in trouble, idlers, and a few cranks. The last were dubbed "carrion crows" by the reporters. They were there to enjoy and be entertained by the troubles of others.

The group around the call board moved toward the elevators.

∎∎∎

Above in the courtroom the clerk said loudly, "Hear ye! Hear ye! This honorable branch of the County Court is now in session."

Everybody was standing. The clock showed fifteen minutes past ten. Judge Drake, in his dark robes, had just mounted the steps to his high place.

On the benches sat Ma Romano with her family, Ang, Julian, Aunt Rosa. On the last bench, sitting stiffly, was Owen.

The court clerk read loudly, "The People versus Nicholas Romano!"

∎∎∎

In the anteroom Nick sat up straight in the chair as if a lash had been struck across his back. He looked at Morton, his eyes fixed on Morton like an animal's—scared, pleading. "Well, I guess this is it, son," Morton said. Nick stood up as if in a trance. Morton put his arm around Nick's shoulders. "Take it easy, boy," he said.

Under the feel of his arm Nick's shoulders went back straight and he lifted his head. He grinned. "You remind me of my Aunt Rosa!" he said. Morton chuckled.

The deputy appeared at the door. "Hello, ugly!" Nick said cockily. Morton sighed with relief.

The deputy grinned and said in a whisper as if profoundly surprised, "W-e-l-l—if it ain't Pretty Boy Romano!"

"That's right!" Nick said. "And if they get me, I'll will you my looks!"

In the hallway he stopped to comb his hair and straighten his tie.

They moved toward the courtroom. Nick walked with the loose grace of an animal, straight-legged, broad-backed, swaggering a little. When he hit the courtroom there was a wide grin plastered on his face.

He looked around, picking out as many faces as he could. The first one he saw was Ma's. For a moment the smile flickered. He had to clench his teeth to keep it there.

...Aunt Rosa...Ang...Julian. Julian! —that surprised him.

They marched him in front of the judge's high place and stood him there. Kerman, the prosecutor, immediately stepped up next to him, as if to claim him.

"The People versus Nicholas Romano...."

[361]

Nick stared straight ahead.

Now the whole goddamn world is against me!

Kerman rubbed his hands together and looking up at Judge Drake, said sharply, "Ready!" His round red face and glasses were the picture of satisfaction. His mustache bristled.

Morton said quietly, "If it please the Court—and not to unduly tax the patience of the Court, I am again compelled to ask a continuance."

Judge Drake sighed heavily and asked why.

"For these reasons—" Morton said. "The newspapers have already tried the case and found my client guilty." Kerman exasperatedly opened his lips to talk. Judge Drake silenced him with his hand. Morton went on, "... It would be impossible to get a jury that hasn't read all about this case in the papers and formed an opinion. They just won't let us alone." He exhibited the morning editions with photographs large in the picture sections and the story on the front pages. He slapped the paper down on the bar and tapped the palm of his hand against it several times. "How is it possible—"

"Your Honor—!" Kerman cut in angrily.

"—to get anything that could resemble a fair and unbiased jury? This editorial alone—" Morton continued.

"Your Honor! If it please the Court—!" Kerman yelled.

Judge Drake swung his swivel chair around squarely and lifted his hands. For a moment he looked down at Morton and Kerman. Then he tried to joke. "It's my opinion that very few people read the editorial pages," he said. "You can ascertain in your examination of the jurors whether or not they're biased, Mr. Morton. The clerk will call the jurors—"

"We except," Morton said.

A man and a woman bailiff went down to the jurors' assembly room for the panel.

Morton walked to the large and flat shiny-topped counsel table. He seated Nick carefully so that he would be squarely on a line with the middle of the jury box. His chair was turned at an angle so that he was facing the jury box rather than the judge's rostrum. Nick saw Grant seated in the chair behind him, his tan face unnaturally pale.

"Hi, Grant!" Nick said cheerfully and sat down. He leaned over toward Grant. "Thanks." He dropped his eyes.

Morton leaned over the back of Nick's chair with his hand on it and talked to Grant for a while. Then Morton sat in the chair in front of Nick and pulled his briefcase across the table to the space directly in front of him. On the other side of the table Kerman and Brooks, his assistant, had their chairs facing the judge's rostrum. Their legs were crossed and their arms were folded. They sat up straight in their chairs with their big shoulders pressed against the backs and their eyes looking up at Judge Drake.

Across the counsel table Nick was slumped down in his chair with his head against its back. Nick's hair was black, neatly combed, shiny with brilliantine. Half a dozen newspaper photographers, began taking pictures of Nick from all angles, of Nick and Morton, of Nick with Morton leaning over whispering in his ear. One of the newspaper cartoonists began sketching Nick. On the benches the eyes seesawed back and forth to get a better view of him.

The photographers were allowed to play around snapping pictures of Nick for ten minutes. A bailiff even raised the Venetian blinds for them so there would be more light. Nick, remembering the hard-boiled role the neighborhood and the newspapers had cut out for him to play, grinned at the cameras or leaned his head way back and stared up at the ceiling as if he were bored.

■ ■ ■

The two bailiffs led the jury panel to Judge Drake's courtroom.

The court clerk instructed the prospective jurors to rise and hold up their right hands. "You and each of you do solemnly swear . . ." the clerk mumbled, "that you true answers will make to all questions that may be put to you by Court or counsel touching your qualifications to serve as jurors in this case now on trial, swelpyougod."

Then a bailiff instructed the first twelve men and women to take seats in the jury box.

Nick stared at them. His lips were parted a little. He sat, leaning forward in his chair. His eyes were dull brown. He could hear the beating of his heart and feel the itching that crept up into the pits of his arms. A photographer's flash bulb went off.

Kerman twisted his chair around on the floor noisily until it faced the jury box. He smiled cheerfully at the jurors. "Good morning, ladies and gentlemen!" he said. His voice almost cooed. Brooks handed Kerman data that had been gathered concerning each prospective juror. Morton turned his chair toward the jury box and, putting his elbow on the counsel table, rested his head against his hand. His head was large, squarely cut; his features strong, dramatic; his large nose straight and forceful. Under his eyes were finely etched wrinkles. His position in the chair, his tenseness, his large gray eyes watching every movement of the jurors gave the impression that he and his client were one, that Nick's feelings, Nick's tension, was his.

Kerman said, "You ladies and gentlemen understand that a man is on trial for murder here. You feel that you can be fair and impartial, don't you—*to the State*—as well as to the defendant—" His eyes went over Morton's head to Nick. "You won't be swayed by sympathy toward the defendant for any reason whatsoever, will you? And you will listen to the evidence and decide the case on the evidence." His voice had a snap to it. Then, almost caressingly, he added, "The first gentleman there, what is your name, sir?"

The gentleman there said, "Morris Glenn."

"And where do you live?"

"1345 North Wells."

"Anda—what kind of work do you do?"

"I'm a truck driver."

Kerman looked down at his notes. He found the name Morris Glenn. Next to it was penciled, *Sonofabitch—voted acquittal last time.* Kerman frowned at the paper. He looked up and said half angrily, "Anda you would be fair to the State—you would be fair to both sides?"

"Yes."

"Anda you would decide the case on the evidence?" Kerman said carelessly, knowing that he could dismiss Glenn on one of his twenty peremptory challenges if he couldn't get rid of him any other way. The juror was nodding yes when Kerman had already begun questioning the next juror. "What is your name, sir?"

"Louis Rabinovitz," the young voice said quickly.

"Where do you live?"

"2601 North Leavitt."

Kerman continued his questioning. Morton studied the young and earnest face. He looks all right, hope he sticks. Kerman said, "Is there any reason, as you sit there, why you feel you cannot serve on this jury?"

"Yes!" the young voice said with a crisp ring.

Judge Drake looked down attentively. Morton looked up. Nick looked up. "Why?" Kerman bellowed.

"I don't believe in capital punishment!" The young man said it flatly, his eyes looking directly at Kerman.

"Step down!" Judge Drake said.

Kerman turned his eyes to the next prospective juror. "And what is your name, madam?"

"Helen Clark."

"Anda where are you employed?"

"I'm a housewife."

Kerman looked down at his notes—*okay, voted first degree last time.* He arranged his face in a smile and looked up at Mrs. Clark "Are you opposed to capital punishment, Mrs. Clark?" Kerman asked pleasantly.

"No, I'm not," Mrs. Clark said decisively.

Kerman smiled at her very pleasantly and slipped to the next juror. "And your name, madam?"

"Miss Phyllis King."

Kerman had no notation of previous jury duty against her name. He frowned a little and toyed with his red pencil; but he looked up smilingly. He questioned her for ten minutes. She was not opposed to capital punishment either. Kerman turned toward Morton and said, smiling tightfaced over his shoulder, "You may have them."

Andrew Morton sat up in his chair and drew his eyes away from the first panel of three remaining jurors. He had been minutely reading them all the time, watching what they did with their hands, how they answered Kerman's questions, what their eyes said when their lips were speaking, whether Glenn touched his tie or not, and whether the women straightened their dresses, touched their hair, dampened their lips with their tongues before speaking. He looked down at his notes. He looked quickly at Nick who sat in profile, staring at the jurors. Then he turned his eyes toward the first panel. Across the counsel table in front of him Kerman and Brooks had their heads together, whispering and looking up into the jury box at Glenn, who had voted acquittal last time.

"The lady in the rear, may I have your name, please?" Andrew Morton said politely.

"Mrs. Helen Clark."

Morton leaned forward with his elbows on the counsel table and one hand clasping the other. He opened his lips and paused a moment. He looked up at Judge Drake in a slight and friendly challenge. Then he looked back at the juror. "Did you read the morning paper on your way to court, Mrs. Clark?" he asked respectfully.

"Yes, I did."

"Did you read the article in the paper about the defendant here?"

"Yes, sir, I read it all the way through."

"But you would have to have all the testimony before you could possibly decide this case if you were chosen a juror here?"

"It would have to be strong testimony."

"Step down!" Judge Drake said in a large and echoing voice.

Andrew Morton had his head down and his hands spread on the table, holding his notes in place. He put on his silver-rimmed reading glasses. He saw the name Glenn with *okay* written after it. He ruffled the sheets back, looking at Phyllis King. He lifted his glasses off his nose and looked at her. "Your name is Phyllis King?"

"Yes, sir."

"You have read the morning papers, Miss King?" She nodded her head yes. "You saw the story and the picture of the accused—" He motioned his hand with the palm up toward Nick, next to him at the table.

"Y-y-yes." She nodded her head slowly.

[365]

"Have you a fixed opinion of the defendant's guilt after reading the papers?"

"I t-h-i-n-k I have," she said.

"Step down!" Judge Drake said with his hand against his face.

"Thank you," Morton said to Miss King, "for your honest answer."

Kerman pulled his coat around his waist angrily. Morton's eyes went slowly to the remaining talesman. "Mr. Glenn, you have heard me ask these other jurors if they had read the papers. Have you read anything about this case in the papers?"

"No, I haven't—that is, only a little."

Kerman tightened his lips.

"What do you mean when you say, 'Only a little,' Mr. Glenn?" Morton asked.

"Well, I saw the picture on the back page." He grinned. "You don't get much time to read when you drive a truck."

Morton smiled with him sympathetically. "Yes—I know." He leaned to the side of his chair and said, "You aren't going to start out with any bias in favor of the state or prejudice against the defendant after seeing that picture in the paper, are you?"

"No." Morton liked the way he shook his head no.

"You don't believe a man is guilty until he is proven so beyond any reasonable doubt, do you?"

Again Glenn shook his head emphatically and said, "No."

Morton dug deeper. "You will give the same credence to the testimony given by a man engaged in another occupation as you would to that of a—policeman?" He pronounced the last word slowly and after a pause. Kerman gritted his teeth; behind the glasses his eyes frowned.

"Yes, sir—I would," Glenn said.

"Have you formed an opinion from the picture of the defendant and the caption under it that you saw in the paper this morning concerning his innocence or guilt—?" Morton made a slight gesture of humbleness with his hand. "I take it that you don't object to our asking you these questions?" Then he waited for the answer with the frame of his glasses against his lips.

"Well—a—sort of an idea."

"Now then—Mr. Glenn—" Morton said slowly, "have you a fixed opinion that couldn't be changed by evidence, or is it just an impression and will your verdict be reached by a consideration of the evidence?"

Kerman was on his feet. "The juror has said that he has a fixed opinion!" he told the judge loudly.

Judge Drake swung his chair around and looked over the bench. "No, he hasn't—"

"I request that the court excuse the juror for cause," Kerman demanded.

Judge Drake said, "Mr. Morton is merely ascertaining whether or not the juror is unbiased."

"If it please the Court—" Kerman said.

"Overruled!" Judge Drake cut him short; and to Morton, "You may continue, Mr. Morton."

To the juror Morton said, continuing unruffled, "You then believe, Mr. Glenn, that your verdict would be made only on the—"

"The State will excuse Mr. Glenn!" Kerman cut in loudly, using one of his precious direct challenges.

The first panel of four had been wiped away.

The State and Andrew Morton started all over again trying to pick a jury.

PRETTY BOY ROMANO
SNEERS AS TRIAL OPENS

Walking into court in a new brown suit and with his curly black hair neatly combed, Nick (Pretty Boy) Romano smiled broadly and looked around the courtroom for friends and admirers before taking his place at the counsel table next to nationally famous Andrew Morton, criminal defense lawyer, in Judge James K. Drake's . . . .

Kerman kept three people on the next panel of four. They said no, they hadn't read the papers. They dampened their lips or shook their heads as they said it, but their eyes twitched slightly when Morton asked them.

"And what did you say your occupation was, Mr. Caldwell?" Morton asked.

"I'm a butcher." Against Caldwell's name on his data sheet Kerman had marked: *Possible foreman, okay.* On Morton's list was scribbled: *Don't touch.*

Morton dismissed the entire panel. He dismissed them as a group in order to trick Kerman into carelessness. He hoped the prosecution would use up its challenges. Keep the other fellow on the run, stay ahead of him. A lawsuit isn't testimony alone, isn't black or white; it's a damned hard battle. . . .

Kerman and Morton duelled throughout the afternoon. They shuffled the jurors. They fought with their wits and brains. Kerman viciously; Morton quietly, taking care to give no one in the courtroom, least of all the jurors, the idea that he was strenuously fighting Kerman on every issue, all the way.

[367]

Nick, hunched tensely in his seat, sensed the tooth-and-nail fight for his life. And he grew frightened when he saw Morton's dead earnestness and Kerman's cold viciousness.

I'm Nick Romano and I want to live!

He tightened in his chair and stared, scared-eyed, at the men and women who came and left the jury box. But when he remembered that he was the tough guy, that the courtroom was packed and the reporters there because of him, he leaned back against the chair playing the part, looking bored, glancing up at the clock every once in a while as if he wished they'd get it over with.

"The state will excuse Mr. Gentilio and Mrs. Fransetti."

"The defense will excuse Mrs. Hall."

Others came and went. Kerman questioned them from the prosecution's point of view. Morton questioned them psychologically. He encouraged them with little pleasantries. He framed his questions so the answers would, in the long run, reveal any tinge of prejudice even in those who felt they had none. He marked their employments, their ages, their social positions. And he tried for people close to Nick's economic level.

FIRST PANEL OF JURY
PICKED IN ROMANO CASE

Three Women, Man Chosen

Thus far three women and a man have been tentatively accepted as jurors as the Pretty Boy Romano trial opened in Judge Drake's courtroom. All of the jurors tentatively selected are under the age of 30 with the exception of Mrs. Laura Green, 348 West Marquette Road, who is 61 years old.

They started all over again the next day trying to fill the rest of the jury. By noon Judge Drake had said "Step down!" many times wearily.

In the early afternoon Morton got his truck driver. "Do you believe, Mr. Erickson, what you read in the papers?"

"Hell, no!—" It was out; he caught himself, flushed, and as the audience roared with laughter, said, "—Heck, no."

Morton was smiling at him. They were smiling at each other, and Morton was figuring . . . age, thirty-three, truck driver, been around, knows what it's all about, maybe did some strong-arming himself once or twice, whored around some, probably still does, perhaps stole when he was a kid. Keep him.

There was a woman on the panel, a woman of forty-eight. Kerman seemed to want her. Morton looked at his notes—son and daughter. Morton rubbed his chin. Son about Nick's age. He passed her.

Seven jurors.

Long afternoon, fishing for jurors. Eight jurors now.

Recess. Ten jurors.

All afternoon questioning jurors. Close to four-thirty. Kerman angry and sweating. Kerman, with Morton having tricked him into rushing to the jury box and shouting, "The prosecution will excuse Mrs. Ronchetto!"

Morton looked up out of the shadow of his hand at Kerman.... Goodbye, Kerman—that was your last challenge.

And Morton with three challenges left.

Morton had the picking of the last two jurors to himself. He sighed. This would save Nick's life. These two and Nick's life. He leaned over and put his arm around Nick's chair. "Keep your chin up!" For the first time since the case had opened Morton really smiled.

Kerman was questioning a girl of twenty-four who was slim, wore little make-up and was dressed in plain clothes. "And what did you say your occupation was?"

"I'm a social worker."

Morton sat up attentively. He kept the hooked end of his glasses between his lips, studying her ... sociology, field work, brushing elbows with the people in the slums, census sheets, charts showing crime, death rate, nutrition, social diseases, prostitution, slums, poverty, case histories. He held his breath, expecting a vicious Kerman attack aimed to discredit the juror and have her excused by Judge Drake.

Kerman's first question was, "Do you believe in capital punishment, Miss Hoffman?"

"Oh, yes. I believe that the unfit, those who are absolutely useless to society and to themselves, should be eliminated."

Morton sat up in his chair. He leaned over the counsel table toward the youthful girl who was a social worker. "Miss Hoffman," he said slowly, "when Judge Drake tells you that the defendant who sits here is presumed innocent until he is proven guilty beyond all reasonable doubt—and he will so instruct you—you will take that instruction into the jury room with you and weigh the evidence in that light, will you not? And if you could not do so you would tell us, wouldn't you?"

"Yes, I would."

"You are a college graduate, I take it?"

"Yes."

"You have studied sociology?"

"Yes." Her eyes didn't leave his face.

"You have a knowledge of environment and its influences?" She nodded her head yes, slowly. "You believe that policemen are capable of falsification as well as—we common human beings?" A smile and yes. "—and you believe that they eat and sleep and drink and curse like anyone else?" A broader smile and yes.

"And you believe that they put their trousers on one leg at a time like ordinary human beings?"

Margaret Hoffman, holding his eye and laughing now, nodded yes,

Morton was laughing. "That's all, Miss Hoffman, keep your seat and keep an eye on the police!"

Judge Drake could not suppress a smile, but admonished Morton: "Now, the attorney for the defendant knows that is highly improper!"

For his last juror Morton chose Anthony Fontana, an Italian.

Andrew Morton looked around at the twelve jurors. He had three challenges remaining. He looked from face to face. He took five minutes to study the group. For a moment he started to pull out Bennett, the shoemaker, but his age was thirty-two. He thought of pulling out Mrs. Green and replacing her with a younger woman. But she had two children, one a boy about Nick's age. He looked from face to face. He looked at each a long time. Mix them well, he told himself—racially, politically, economically, religiously. He stared gray-eyed at them. A social worker. Good. A Jewish girl. She would know of persecution and of slums. An elderly woman of sixty-one with gray hair. Churchgoer. Believer in the gentle Christ. A blonde who was a beautician. She would be conscious of a person's looks. Handsome Nick. Good. An Italian juror, blood and water. Good. A truck driver who had been around. Good. Housewife and mother. Good. Mix well and shake before using. His eyes, looking at them, smiled a little. They are young. Good. The young for the young, the young won't kill the young. Do they believe in capital punishment? No. Young Nick and his young jury. He looked at them with Nick's eyes and Nick's feelings. A life is at stake here. He rubbed his hand over his eyes wearily. His life is in your hands, now, Mort. You alone can save him. He again rubbed his hand over his eyes wearily. He seemed to have aged in the last two days. He looked up at Judge Drake and then back at the jurors. "Thank you, ladies and gentlemen."

The jury was picked.

Judge Drake said, "Ladies and gentlemen of the jury, during this recess of court do not talk about this case among yourselves nor

[370]

permit anyone else to talk to you about it. Return here at nine-thirty tomorrow morning."

The papers said—

SEVEN WOMEN ON PRETTY
BOY ROMANO JURY

Young Jury Picked;
Average Age is 35

75

The cop-killer walked into the courtroom. He wore the new gray suit today. His tie was precisely knotted. There was a handkerchief in his breast pocket. His curly black hair was neatly combed, with just a little of it beginning to rise on his forehead. He was smiling. His teeth were white. His dimples were hard. Camera bulbs began flashing with eye-blinking regularity. Smiling with one corner of his mouth twisted up, he loosened his coat, adjusted it and rebuttoned it. The crowd on the benches strained forward to get a look at him. Their necks strained. They stared at him. And some of them stood up so that they could see him. He looked around the courtroom at them casually. His eyes slipped quickly away from his mother's and, keeping his face carefully arranged in its don't-give-a-damn smile, he stared deeply into the courtroom. He saw a round face with pitifully sad eyes, long blond hair; the fleshy body leaned out into the aisle on the last bench in the courtroom. Nick's mouth opened in surprise and the smile faded as he looked at Owen.

I shoulda known he'd stick.

Nick clamped the smile back on. He lifted his head in a nod of recognition and continued to his chair at the counsel table, swaggering, playing the part cut out for him by the neighborhood and the newspapers.

His guard of two deputies sat in the chairs behind him. Grant was already at the table. Nick twisted his chair around until it was facing the jury box. Turning his face to Grant, he said casually, "Hello, pizon."

"Hello, Nick," Grant answered, but he nervously combed his hair with his fingers.

Nick looked at the crowd curiously. They stared back curiously. Nick's lips twisted in a smile. Under cover of the table his fingers tightened together.

The newspapers had done a good job. Every seat was taken. People were still coming to the courtroom and lining themselves down the corridors against the walls. They were old and middle-aged people, men and women. The people wore tense faces and staring eyes, mouths open as if to drink in every word or as if the excitement and thrill of a man, a healthy young man, on trial for his life left them panting a trifle. Better than a movie. Better than a book. The real thing. There were many women in the crowd. Some had brought their lunch and held it on their knees in hard-clutching hands. And there were girls sixteen and seventeen years old. Their hair was frizzed in artificial curls and their lips loud with paint. They were cheaply perfumed. Their skirts were short. They came in pairs or in threes. Some of them chewed gum. Others rattled bags of candy. They whispered. They squirmed on the benches trying to get a good look at the handsome killer. And when they found a spot over a head or between shoulders they stared at Nick curiously, excitedly, even passionately. Their eyes stayed with him, tracing his looks. Their lips were slightly parted as if to receive a kiss. And a girl, only about fourteen years old, said, "I want to see his face!" And an elderly woman said, "I want to see his face!"

There were many potential Nicks on the benches. They wore sweaters and sloppy or almost worn-out clothes. Already their eyes, their slouches, the twist of their lips, their long dishevelled hair that needed cutting had taken on the unmistakable stamp of the neighborhoods that dump their young men down onto West Madison Street, South State Street, North Clark Street.

Inside the rail in front of the courtroom a long table had been set for the reporters. They were there in a row, looking like detectives or bigtime hoodlums, but dressed like the movies. Under the windows inside the rail sat the photographers with their cameras on the deep marble window sills.

The marble clock on the wall with its ornamental hands showed five minutes after ten. Judge Drake sat high up on the bench between two bronze lamps, with his arms on the rostrum in front of him.

The jury, led by a man and a woman bailiff, filed into the court-room and into the jury box. "Holy Christ!" said a young fellow

[372]

watching them come into the courtroom. "All women! He'll never get the chair!"

Even before the jurors sat down they were looking out over the rail at Nick. Nick looked back at them, deep-eyed. They sat down in their swivel chairs to sit in judgment on him. His dark eyes looked at them with fear, panic, desperation.

"Hear ye! Hear ye!"

Everybody in the courtroom was standing.

Kerman stepped quickly to the bar in front of the jury. He stood there in his freshly pressed suit, a handkerchief sticking jauntily out of his breast pocket. "Good morning, ladies and gentlemen of the jury! It is a privilege for me to stand before a jury of my intelligent and honest peers in the name of the people of this state. . . . It is my privilege and duty and burden to present the case of the prosecution to you. The prosecution will *prove*—beyond *any* reasonable doubt— that Nick Romano—the man sitting there—" He half turned toward the counsel table. His eyes struck Nick and his red pencil pointed at him. "—murdered Police Officer Dennis Riley in cold blood—" His glasses flashed angrily at the jurors. "We will prove that his was the hand that held the gun! The State will prove that he pumped—one—two—three—*five!*—five bullets into the body of Officer Riley!" The shocked eyes of the jurors looked away from Kerman and up over the rail at Nick, staring at him. Nick's brown eyes stared back at them innocently. Kerman's lips twisted and went on speaking. "We will prove that he stood over the dead body of Police Officer—"

"Object!" Morton said. He lifted his face toward Judge Drake. "This case has to do with the killing of Officer Riley—with nothing else. Object on the grounds that the prosecuting attorney's statement was made to induce passion and prejudice and was meant only to inflame the jury against my client."

"Sustained!"

Kerman, angry, cut back and recapitulated his case, almost shouting it to the jury, "There was a robbery at the Three-Eighty Club. Nick Romano—ran out of the tavern. Eventually in an alley at West Madison and Atlantic the defendant—" Kerman's pencil jabbed at Nick again, "shot five bullets into the body of the gallant officer who fell dead." To get his point home again he poured the words out swiftly. "Not satisfied with murder, we will show you beyond a reasonable doubt that this fiend then *brutally kicked the defender of civic security in the face and body!*"

"Object!"

"Objection sustained! The jury will disregard the last remark of Mr. Kerman."

Kerman went on heatedly, "Captured by associates of the slain officer he was taken to a police station, where, with the characteristics of the hoodlum killer he is, he refused to—"

Morton said loudly, "Object—your Honor!" He was standing up and facing the judge with his hands clasped behind him. "I must object this time, your Honor, to the use of the words 'hoodlum killer.' "

"Yes," Judge Drake said, clearing his throat. He leaned over to the side of his swivel chair and said, "The jury will disregard the words 'hoodlum killer.' " Kerman moved his shoulders in irritation. But he smiled at the jury as if he and they understood and were in agreement. "The defendant refused to make any statement as to his whereabouts on the night of the tragedy. When properly questioned by the police he refused to tell where he was." His voice dropped a tone. "Your police department, the protectors of your lives and homes, and the Attorney's Office have gathered the evidence and it is this evidence that we today present to you. The evidence will be so conclusive as to be beyond dispute or contradiction. It will be so clear—so concise and overwhelming—that there will be nothing left for you ladies and gentlemen to do, when you retire to your jury room with only your conscience and your God to guide you, but to return a verdict of guilty of—*murder!*—as charged in the indictment. The penalty for this type of murder is—*death!* And whatever your sympathy may be, remember that the four millions of people in this county who depend for their security and safety of person and property upon such men as Dennis Riley expect such a verdict! Thank you!"

Kerman turned from the jury box and walked to his chair at the counsel table. His eyes disregarded Judge Drake, Morton, Brooks, and looked straight into Nick's like knives stuck into a wall. Nick stared back at him squarely, eye to eye.

Judge Drake leaned forward and asked, "Do you care to make your opening statement now, Mr. Morton?"

"No, your Honor—we will reserve until ready to introduce our evidence, thank you."

STATE ASKS DEATH
IN ROMANO CASE

"Call your first witness, Mr. Kerman," Judge Drake said.

Kerman stood up and a large woman in black stood up too. Kerman assisted her to the witness box. She half clung to him, holding a handkerchief to her lips.

"...And, Mrs. Riley, would you please tell us how long you and the deceased were married?" Kerman said in low and sympathetic tones.

[374]

"Twenty-nine years." She touched the corners of her eyes with her handkerchief. The jurors leaned in their chairs and had to strain to hear her. Their eyes looked at her sympathetically.

"Then you lived together for twenty-nine years—except for the time he was in the last war?"

"Yes."

"Was the deceased a kind and loving husband?"

"He was very good to me." Her voice trembled, went on, "There was nothing I wanted for. He— he—" She began to cry.

In a moment, however, she had gained composure and looked up at Kerman with red eyes. "May we proceed, Mrs. Riley?" Kerman asked gently; and then after a pause, "When did you last see the deceased?"

"When he—" her lips trembled, "left me that night when he— when he was killed."

"What did he say to you, Mrs. Riley?"

"He kissed me goodbye and—" The tears came again and the voice trembled in the ears of the jurors and the audience. "—He kissed me and told me what he wanted to eat when he got home."

"When next did you see him?" Kerman asked. His voice had lost its gentleness; it was emphatic. "In the morgue!" Mrs. Riley said, half-screaming the answer.

Kerman moved quickly to a suitcase set on the counsel table. "The prosecution would like to introduce Exhibit A, the uniform worn by the deceased Riley at the time of the murder."

Mrs. Riley began to sob. Morton was on his feet. "Object! Your Honor! The uniform won't prove or tend to prove any issue in this case! In his opening statement the prosecuting attorney—*my very learned friend*—told the jury that Officer Riley was patrolling his beat at the time of the alleged holdup, therefore it is incompetent, irrelevant and immaterial what the prosecution may offer to prove by the production of the uniform because it must be assumed that the officer was wearing the same uniform when he began the pursuit of *an un-i-den-ti-fied holdup man.*"

Judge Drake, with his customary admonition to the jury to talk to no one about the case, excused the jury while the attorneys argued their point at the foot of the rostrum. "If it please the Court," Kerman said, "while it may appear irrelevant at the time, yet the prosecution promises the Court that we will, by proper evidence, show that the *bloodstained, bullet-torn, mud-spattered* garments were those worn by Officer Riley at the time he left his wife and children and until his lifeless corpse was lifted by loving hands into a mortuary."

"Oh, now!" Judge Drake said. He rubbed the end of his chin. Then, despite Morton's argument against introduction of the garment, Judge Drake said, "With these statements from the prosecuting attorney the Court will permit the introduction of the garment."

"Except!" Morton said loudly.

"Mr. Deputy, bring in the jury," said Judge Drake.

Morton moved to counsel table. Nick looked up at him admiringly.

Boy, he's got some big words!

The jury filed into its box. Mrs. Riley, still being supported, was assisted back to the witness stand. Kerman moved to the suitcase on the counsel table. The blue uniform came out of the suitcase, crushed, smeared with caked mud, perforated with bullet holes, spotted with large stains of blood.

There was an audible gasp throughout the courtroom.

Kerman walked past the jury box, one slow step at a time, holding the jacket so that none of the jurors could help seeing it. They looked at it in horror. Nick looked at it casually and without feeling anything. His eyes went beyond it and to the jurors. They were all staring at him in horror. His dark eyes looked back innocently.

Kerman walked to the witness stand and held the jacket out as if to offer it to Mrs. Riley. "Is this the jacket your husband was wearing when he left you?"

Mrs. Riley screamed and collapsed in the witness chair.

She was carried from the courtroom.

PRETTY BOY ROMANO DEAF TO
SOBS OF OFFICER RILEY'S WIDOW

"...And what did your examination reveal, doctor?"

"I examined the body visually and found evidence of the entrance of foreign matter, and immediately notified the coroner's office."

Nick sat with his head against the back of the chair. His eyes traced the ceiling.

"And all this happened on November 7th...?"

"Yes, sir."

Kerman turned his head toward Morton slightly and said over his shoulder, "Mr. Morton?"

"No cross-examination," Morton said.

"That will be all, doctor. Thank you, doctor," Kerman said pleasantly.

Nick combed his hair.

...

McGregor, ballistic expert, was next on the stand. There was a silence; a silence planned by Kerman. He walked to the counsel table and slowly took five bullets out of the grip, one at a time, lin-

[376]

ing them on the table noisily until they were in a row of five. The jurors' eyes reached toward the bullets. The spectators strained in their seats to see what was going on. Nick tilted his chair back a little, stretching and yawning.

For a moment Kerman looked down through his glasses at the bullets. Then he swept them up off the table and walked to the witness stand. "I now show you Exhibit B. Are these the bullets that were extracted from the deceased Riley's body?"

The expert looked at them for a moment. "They are," he said curtly. Kerman walked back to the table and again lined them up where the jurors could see them. He reached into the grip and pulled out the gun. All eyes looked at it. Nick glanced at it casually and impersonally, then at the jurors. Most of their eyes were coming from the gun to him; then all of their eyes were on him. He looked at them innocently.

Kerman was again standing alongside the witness. "I now show you Exhibit C." Kerman broke the gun and looked inside; he said, "This is a thirty-two Colt revolver numbered 769722 on the barrel and under the handle." He handed the gun across the rail of the witness box. "Is this the gun from which the bullets I showed you a moment ago were fired?"

"It is," McGregor said curtly.

"Fine! Thank you, Mr. McGregor!" Kerman glanced in Morton's direction. "Cross-examination."

"No cross!"

Kerman brought his next witness to the stand. "Mr. Gleason, you are a Chicago officer are you not?"

"Yes, sir."

Nick narrowed his eyes, remembering. The sonofabitch!

"Is there any particular thing fastened in your memory as to the events of the morning of November 7th . . . ?"

"Yes, sir."

"Tell the jury."

Gleason put his big hand on the rail of the witness stand and ignored Nick's hating eyes. "We were ordered to go to the alley at Madison and Atlantic to investigate the killing of a police officer. We photographed the scene of the crime and the body. We made measurements and looked for clues."

"Were there any clues?"

"Oh, yes!" Gleason sat up importantly. "I found the gun."

"This gun here—Exhibit C?"

Gleason leaned back in the swivel chair importantly. "That's it."

Brooks leaned over and whispered to Kerman. Kerman nodded yes. "Where did you find it?" Kerman asked.

"I found it near Riley's head. It was down in the mud and

water—" Kerman nodded his head up and down to Gleason as if encouraging him to tell some unrevealed thing. "I picked it up with a handkerchief so that—"

Kerman frowned and cut in. "You say it was down alongside of Riley's head. What did that indicate to you?"

"That it had been thrown down into his face. There was a scar on the bridge of—"

"Object, your Honor. Move to strike out as a conclusion of the witness."

"Maybe the officer has a right to his opinion and I will let it stand for what it is worth for the time being. Overruled, Mr. Morton."

"Did you ever see the defendant before today in this courtroom?" Kerman asked Gleason.

"Yes, sir. Twice."

Kerman sat up straight in his chair. "When was that?" Kerman's eyes frowned a little as if this had not been rehearsed in his office. Nevertheless he went on, feeling his way in the dark.

"The second time was at the showup and when he was questioned at headquarters."

"Tell us about the *first* time you saw him, Mr. Gleason."

"I saw him at Madison Street and Maine, running off of Madison onto Maine when we were on our way to the scene of the crime."

"Cross-examination!" Kerman shouted quickly.

Morton was whispering to Nick; Nick nodded and whispered back. Then Morton, with his elbow on the counsel table, rubbed his nose with his finger, and looking over the finger he said in low, unhurried tones, "What time, please, was it when you got to the scene of the crime?"

"Twelve-thirty," Gleason said quickly.

"Twelve-thirty? And Riley was dead at the time?"

"Yes, sir."

"You helped take those photographs and measurements you told us about? How long did that take?"

"Ah—I'd say half an hour. Maybe longer."

"And you arrived on the scene at twelve-thirty. Then it was one o'clock when you finished your investigation?"

"I'd say about that time."

"Riley had been dead almost an hour then?"

"I don't know how long he had been dead," Gleason said a trifle angrily.

"Sorry—but he was dead when you arrived?"

"Yes."

"And what time did you say that was?"

"Twelve-thirty."

"You went directly to the scene?"

"Yes."

"You stopped nowhere?"

"No."

"Then it took you twenty minutes to get there?"

"I guess so."

"Well now, Riley was killed at approximately twelve-ten and you say you arrived at twelve-thirty. How long is that?"

"Twenty minutes," Gleason said sullenly.

Morton had arisen and, in his low conversational tones, said, "I notice that you wear glasses. I take it that your eyesight isn't as good as it could be."

Judge Drake was leaning over the bench looking at Morton and following the questioning with interest. "Are they bifocals, Mr. Gleason?"

"Yes."

Morton had turned his back to the witness. He was staring out at the crowd, his deep eyes passing over them slowly. "Mr. Gleason," he said, talking to the crowd, "tell me this, won't you?" Morton had now turned and was facing the jurors. He put his question to them. "Were there any fingerprints on the gun?" Morton was looking at the jury and waiting for the answer. The answer was no. Morton turned slowly around. "Ohhhh—there were no fingerprints on the gun?"

"It was found in the mud and water—that's why," Gleason said.

Morton had his hands stuffed down in his trouser pockets and stood looking down at the floor in front of his feet. "It was a pretty bad night the night Riley was killed, wasn't it?" His eyes came up slowly to the witness.

"Yes," Gleason said shortly.

"It rained, didn't it?"

"Yes."

Morton chuckled. His back was again turned to Gleason and he was again facing the crowd. You could feel the crowd warm to him. He spoke to the audience rather than to Gleason. His chuckling words said, "Do you have the same trouble I do with my glasses when it rains? Do they steam up?"

Gleason didn't answer. Morton went on casually, standing now with his elbow on the bar in front of the jury box and his eyes looking at Gleason gently. "Your windshield was dripping rain, wasn't it?" Gleason didn't answer. "Wasn't it?" Morton insisted quietly.

"I don't remember," sullenly.

"The rain was falling very hard, wasn't it?"

"I don't remember," stubbornly.

Morton said slowly, "You should have remembered this one—"

[379]

He paused. "How many blocks is it from Atlantic and Madison to Maine and Madison?"

The words were like a firecracker. Gleason sat a long time in dead silence. His face began slowly to drain of its color. The crowd in the courtroom was hushed and surprised. The jurors who knew began figuring to themselves. Gleason sat without speaking. Morton said coaxingly, "Come, come, Mr. Gleason! You remember that, don't you?" His voice took on a small note of derision.

"Three blocks," Gleason said at last.

"Pardon me, but you did arrive at twelve-thirty?" Morton asked quietly.

"Yes," Gleason said very low.

Morton put his elbows on the bar in front of the jury box and, turning his head sideways until he was looking at Gleason, he said, "Then, Mr. Gleason, you want us to believe that the defendant, having murdered Riley, ran out of the alley at twelve-ten but that he—*still running*—by your own testimony—had run only three blocks eighteen or nineteen minutes later. Thank you, Mr. Gleason. That's all. But please stay around the courtroom. We shall want to know a little about your second—and less imaginary—meeting with the defendant."

Judge Drake stood up. "We will have a fifteen-minute recess."

●●●

Court convened again. The prosecution called Harry Mann. Nick sat erect in his chair and watched the Maxwell Street fence go slowly to the stand. Nick's lips smiled. Under the counsel table his fingers clutched each other tightly.

... When he was sixteen. When he had just left the adolescent home he had gone to Harry the Hog's hockshop, still with the feel of Riley's rabbit punches on his neck. Him and Vito had done a lot of business with this fence. He stayed in Harry's place a long time talking to him. Harry the Hog hadn't wanted to. He said: *Be careful, kid, don't get me in no spot, I don't think they can trace it anyhow.* When he went out of the pawnshop he carried a package....

The hockshop gun was on the counsel table. The Maxwell Street pawnbroker and fence was on the witness stand.

"I show you a gun, Exhibit C. It is numbered 769722. Have you ever seen this gun before?"

Harry Mann nodded his head slowly and looked up at Judge Drake.

"Please speak your answers, Mr. Mann," Kerman said; and again, "Have you seen this gun before?"

Nick dampened his lips with his tongue.

"Yes," Mann said, looking furtively at the jury.

[380]

"Where?"

"In my shop."

"Did you sell this gun to the defendant here or to anyone else?"

"No."

Nick's fingers unloosened themselves from each other.

"How far is the home of the defendant—1113 South Peoria—from your shop?"

"Two and a half blocks."

"How did the gun manage to leave your shop?"

"It was stolen."

"Oh—it was stolen?"

"Yes, sir." The fingers inched the hat around in a circle.

"That's all, thank you!" Kerman said.

"Just a minute," Morton said, immediately leaving his chair; and Mann, frightened, sat down hard. Morton stood at the far end of the jury box. "How long ago, Mr. Mann, was the gun stolen?"

Mann had to raise his voice so that Morton at the far end of the jury box could hear. "A—about six years ago."

Morton's voice sounded surprised. "After all these years! That's the same gun? You positively identify it?"

Mann nodded, then remembering, said, "Yes."

"Is that memory or records?" Morton asked.

"Records."

"You, of course, reported the robbery to the police?"

"No, sir."

"And how's that?"

"Well—I didn't know it was stolen for a long time."

"How long is a long time?"

"Maybe a year—maybe more—I don't know. I—I have a lot of stuff."

"Could it have been two years before then?"

"It could of."

"Why do you say it could have been two years before then?" Morton asked encouragingly.

"Because it could of. I had newer guns on display. I kept the old stuff stacked away because my place is so small."

"Could it have been stolen three years before then?"

"Yes, sir—but not earlier than that. I'm positive of that."

"Did you know that at that time the defendant was only twelve years old and was an altar boy in Denver?"

"No, sir."

"In other words you hadn't *positively* seen this gun for nine years until the police traced it to you. Is that right?"

"Yes, sir."

"In other words, although Mr. Kerman had you state that the

defendant lived but two and a half blocks from your shop, implying that he stole it, any one of the four million people so glibly mentioned by Mr. Kerman this morning could have stolen it?"

Harry the Hog smiled a little. "Yes, sir," he said.

In the courtroom you could feel the division in the crowd. You could feel the applause of the hangers-on who were rooting for the prisoner. You could feel the silent applause for Morton. It even showed in the eyes of the jurors.

76

Nick walked into the courtroom what his friends and the newspapers had made him. He came with a swagger, one shoulder carried higher than the other. Every eye in the packed courtroom hit him. Along the benches there went a stir of movement and of whispers. Nick sneered a little. The eyes bored into him and the heads seesawed back and forth, getting a good look at him. Nick could feel his heart pull harder with embarrassment and fear. But, smiling, he walked to his chair at the counsel table. With his hands stuffed into the pockets of the new black suit Grant's money had bought, he slumped down in the chair, facing the jury.

The jurors filed into the courtroom and into the jury box. Some of them looked into the audience. A couple of them smiled at friends who had come not only to hear the case but to see them taking part in a murder trial. Some of them had their heads turned toward the counsel table as if they were seeing Nick for the first time. Nick stared back, innocent-eyed. Rachel Goldberg lifted her hand casually to a friend. Mrs. Green sat down and picked Nick up with her eyes. Erickson, the truck driver, looked at Nick intently. The well-shaped blonde beautician was going into the box now. Nick's eyes dropped down to her legs.

The prosecution called its first witness for the day, Swanson, the bartender from the Three-Eighty Club. A flood of scaredness burned up inside Nick as he looked at him. This was the only guy who knew he had held him up and that Riley had chased him.

Swanson told the story of the holdup in full detail.

"Now then, Mr. Swanson," Kerman said, "be very careful in your answer—did you get a good look at the holdup man?" Swanson nodded his head slowly. "Yes."

"Do you see him in this courtroom?"

"Yes, sir."

"Point him out to the jury!" Kerman's voice snapped.

Swanson stood up in the box. He put his finger on Nick again. "That's him."

Kerman said viciously, "You mean the young man—the pretty boy—sitting next to Mr. Morton?" Morton laughed and shrugged his shoulders. Kerman's lips twisted and the hard bristles of mustache stood up. "Mr. Morton objects, your Honor, and if he desires I will withdraw the appellation—pretty boy—his cherubic countenance and assumed innocence made me forget the black heart that beats in the bosom of that wanton murderer! Cross-examination!" Kerman sat down hard.

Morton, smiling slowly, got up. He looked over the counsel table at the audience. He glanced at the jury. He stood at the table slowly putting his glasses in his pocket and buttoning his coat. For a moment more he peered out at the jurors with his hand on the back of Nick's chair, directing their attention to him. Then Morton walked quietly around the table, slowly, while everyone watched him. He stood at the near end of the jury box only a few feet from Swanson. He put his hands up on the bar in front of the jury box and, leaning on it, looked at Swanson. "Mr. Swanson," he said, "my name is Andrew Morton. I am the counsel for the defendant here." He paused a moment. Then he asked his first question and held his breath. "Have you ever seen me before?"

"No, sir," the bartender said. Morton breathed easier.

"The man who held you up—what color was his hair?"

"The same as his."

Morton looked around at Nick. "The same color as the defendant's is now?"

"Yes."

"Not darker?"

"No."

"You're sure of that?"

"Positive."

"Positive?"

"Yes—and that's him right there!" Swanson pointed at Nick.

"It was raining that night, very hard, was it not?"

"Yes."

"Did the unidentified holdup man wear a hat or cap?"

"No. He was bareheaded."

"Was his hair hanging over his face?" Morton asked pleasantly.

"I don't know," Swanson's eyes narrowed. "But that's him right there!"

"You understand that my client's life is at stake, don't you, Mr. Swanson, and we want to be certain about these things, don't we?"

"I am certain!" Swanson said positively.

Morton turned, facing the jurors, then back to Swanson. "Now let's get back to the hair. The holdup man's hair was wet, was it not?"

"Yes, sir."

"You have said it was the exact shade of that the defendant's now is. And you have said it was wet. Was it curly or straight?"

"Curly."

"You will grant me, won't you, that curly hair rises and curls when it is wet, whereas straight hair lies flat and becomes plastered to the head."

"Yes—I think so."

"Then the holdup man's hair was mussed on his head and not neatly combed as the defendant's now is?"

Swanson looked at Nick. "No," he said.

"The defendant would look differently if his hair were wet and mussed, would he not?"

"I guess so—but that's him there. I have a good memory."

"You never forget a face?"

"That's right, I never forget a face."

Morton and the bartender were looking steadily at each other. Morton was smiling a little. Still smiling, he asked, "What color eyes did the holdup man have?"

Swanson looked quickly toward Nick. Morton moved in front of him, hiding Nick. "What color, please?"

"Dark—I think."

Morton lifted his eyebrows. "You think?" His voice was very gentle.

"They were dark," Swanson said.

"Dark brown or dark black?"

Swanson had his lips parted and held them open for a while before answering. "Black," he said.

At the table Nick's shoulders relaxed. They're brown. Nick grinned. He looked at Morton admiringly. Boy, he's got a lot on the ball!

Judge Drake rubbed his hands together a little, put his arms on the rostrum and, leaning forward, put his chin down on them. He followed the questioning attentively.

Morton was saying, "You never forget a face, Mr. Swanson?"

"That's right," Swanson said in a surly tone.

"You have said that the holdup man's hair was the same color as the defendant's now is. You have said that he had black eyes. Do you stick by that?"

"Yes," Swanson said defiantly.

"Did you know that hair looks much darker when it is wet?" No answer. "Did you know that the defendant has brown eyes?" No answer.

"You have said you never forget a face?"

"Yeah."

Morton leaned against the jury box with his back to the jurors. "With whom have you talked about this case, Mr. Bartender?"

"Nobody."

"Oh, come now, Mr. Swanson, you talked to the police."

"Yeah." Swanson was sullen and disgusted.

"To newspaper men?"

"Yeah."

"Customers?"

"Yeah."

"The prosecuting attorneys?"

"Yeah."

"Kerman?"

"Yeah."

Morton put his hands behind his head and looked at Swanson. "Now then! All these people to whom you talked add up to nobody —do they?"

In the jury box all eyes watched Morton. Outside the rail the crowd was silent under Morton's cross-examination. "You testified at the coroner's inquest, did you not, Mr. Swanson?" Morton picked up the photostatic copy of the coroner's jury's report. He shook it in his hand and flipped back pages. "Now let me read to you from the transcript of the evidence taken there. This is what you said: *Question: 'Can you identify the holdup man?' Answer: 'I don't think so.'* That was true at the time, wasn't it, Mr. Swanson, and you didn't change your mind or convince yourself that you could identify the holdup man until after interviews with newspaper men, police officers—plainclothes and uniformed—and the prosecuting attorneys and your employer?"

"My boss didn't say nothing to me!" the witness said.

Morton stood there smiling. For a moment he stood silent in the hushed courtroom. Then he moved very close to the witness box and stood directly in front of it. "You have said you never forget a face, Mr. Swanson."

"That's right," the bartender said sulkily. "I never forget a face."

Morton moved halfway down the bar, away from Swanson but facing him. "Do you remember a glass of port wine that was spilled

[385]

on your shirt?" Morton moved to the far end of the bar just in front of the rail inside the spectators' benches. Swanson's lips parted slowly in surprise and embarrassment. His light face was dyed red. His eyes stared at Morton. From the far end of the bar Morton asked loudly, "Do you remember me now?" His words echoed in the quiet courtroom. And Morton continued in a loud voice, "You don't remember me—but—to refresh your memory do you recall my mentioning this killing to you?" He waited. Swanson only stared red-faced. "Do you remember I spilled a glass of port wine on your shirt and in the bigness of your heart you wouldn't let me pay for it? Do you remember that now, Mr. Swanson?" He shouted the last sentence. And he walked down along the jurors' bar with his hands on it. He walked to a spot directly in front of the witness stand. "And we talked for fifteen or twenty minutes, didn't we?" Morton said. "Didn't we?" Morton whispered.

He stood in front of Swanson, waiting. Swanson grew redder in the new silence. At last he found his voice and said, while Morton and the courtroom waited, "Well, maybe fifteen minutes." His voice was almost inaudible.

Morton's voice was now calm, deliberate, low. "Altogether we talked fifteen minutes, didn't we?" Morton turned, facing the jury; he turned completely around and looked at the audience. He spun around to Swanson. "Mr. Swanson—will you be good enough—to tell the jury—why you could not identify me—after we had talked together for fifteen minutes—but you could identify the alleged holdup man—" Morton's voice dropped to a whisper, but a whisper that could be heard back to the marble-framed rear doors of the courtroom—"who was with you only a couple of minutes." Then he shouted, "TELL THAT TO THE JURY!"

Morton swung around to the jurors. He put his hands, wide spread, on the bar in front of them. Talking to Swanson but looking at the jury, he said, "Do you identify him because the police told you they had the man who stuck you up?" He paused, looking into the faces of the jury. His eyes picked up the truck driver, then the blonde, the old lady, the Jewish girl, the social worker. "That's all, Mr. Swanson," he said quietly.

●●●

The prosecution called Patrolman Liam Murphy. In civilian clothes he moved toward the witness box.

"Do you solemnly swear before the ever-living God that the testimony you are about to give in this cause shall be the truth, the whole truth and nothing but the truth?" the bailiff said in a routine mumble.

"I do," the policeman said and sat down.

Policeman Murphy testified to having arrested Nick. "That's all,

Officer, thank you." Kerman gave Morton his profile. "Your witness," he said.

Morton continued to stare at the witness as if he hadn't heard
Kerman. Then he turned and looked at Nick. Nick nodded yes.
Morton got up, lifted his chair and carried it over in front of the
witness stand. Everyone watched him. He sat down directly in front
of Kerman.

"Mr. Murphy," he said affably, "did you ever strike a prisoner?"

"OBJECT!" Kerman shouted. He was up and standing at the foot
of Judge Drake's rostrum. Judge Drake looked down at Morton
and said in a conversational tone, "Now, counsel, you know full
well that that is grossly improper. It will be disregarded by the
jury."

When the courtroom was again quiet Morton asked the witness
with his face turned away from Judge Drake, "Did you ever kick
any prisoner?"

Judge Drake looked down. "Mr. Morton," he said, "I will not
permit your going farther along this line of inquiry. In the proper
direction I will allow you the greatest latitude but in this manner—"
He shook his head no.

Morton didn't seem to hear the judge. "Have you a direct interest
in this case, Mr. Murphy?" Murphy's face twisted angrily. Morton
held his hand up, palm toward Murphy, silencing him, and went on
quickly, "Do you—doesn't the police department—want a conviction
—a conviction based on revenge for the killing of a policeman?"

"He won't answer that!" Judge Drake said.

Kerman was up again and, pounding his fist against his palm,
shouted, "The police are not on trial—it's that killer there!" He
pointed at Nick with his finger held arm's length across the counsel
table. Kerman shouted, "There is no confession! He can't claim
that the confession was obtained by duress!" Judge Drake leaned
over the bench about to speak. *"No confession!"* Kerman screeched.
Judge Drake motioned to Morton. Kerman yelled, "May I address
the court now?"

"No, you may not!" Judge Drake said firmly. Morton walked to
the bench. Kerman moved close to him suspiciously. Judge Drake
leaned way over the bench. "Mr. Morton," he said in low tones,
"won't you please try to confine your cross-examination to this
case and its facts?"

Morton turned to the witness. "Now then, Mr. Murphy," he
asked good-naturedly, "when was the first time you hit this boy
who sits at the counsel table?"

"Never touched him!" the cop mumbled.

Lifting his head from the back of the chair, Nick looked at the
cop with smiling lips and hard eyes.

[387]

"Wasn't the first time in the squad car?" Morton asked, not raising his voice.

"Never hit him!"

"Now then, as a matter of fact, didn't you tell him in the squad car, 'You killed Riley, you bastard!' and didn't you tell him you were going to *take in a confession?*"

"No!" Murphy's voice slurred out nastily across the courtroom.

Morton's voice lowered itself. "Did he kick you—or struggle with you or in any way endeavor to escape from car?"

"Yes," the cap snapped. "He called us dirty names and tried to get out of the car."

"What did you do, Officer?"

"I just grabbed for him."

"Now what were the names he called you?"

"They were filthy names."

"Was it because they were truthful words that you became angered and smashed this boy in the jaw?"

"I didn't smash him! I just held onto his legs." Murphy flared.

"Officer, you had a gun, a blackjack and handcuffs?"

"Yes."

Morton stood up. "Officer, are you going to tell this jury that the words of the defendant were so horrible that they crazed you and yet all you did in response was to hold him gently by the legs?"

A giggle went over the courtroom. Judge Drake rapped sharply for order.

...

That afternoon the captain of the station at which Nick had been held was sworn in.

"State your name, please," Kerman said.

"Joseph McGillicuddy."

"How long have you been in the police department, Captain?"

"Twenty years."

"You remember Dennis Riley?"

"Yes. He was one of the patrolmen attached to my station."

"Good officer, was he?"

"Oh, yes, on a very tough post."

"And you found Riley an efficient man?"

"He had to be, for many times people attempted to murder him."

"When did you see the defendant—if you did—after the killing of Dennis Riley?"

"The morning after he was arrested."

"Was he charged with the murder then?"

"No, we were holding him for investigation."

"Did you have a conversation with him?"

"He wouldn't talk."

"You say, Captain McGillicuddy, that the deceased officer had been shot at three times. Is that correct?" Morton asked amiably.

"No, more than three times."

The jury leaned forward, the crowd was silent. The courtroom waited.

"But he killed three people who shot at him? When did he kill the second man?—If you don't know we will excuse you until you can go to the station and get the record."

"About eight years ago," McGillicuddy mumbled.

"Louder!" Morton shouted.

"Eight years ago."

"And the third man?"

"About six or seven years ago."

"And now the first man he killed?"

"About nine years ago."

"Then this Riley—" Morton put his arms on the jury rail and looked from face to face, "this Three-Notch Riley was always a killer?"

"Object!—irrelevant—no bearing—immaterial!" Kerman shouted.

"You needn't answer," Judge Drake said to McGillicuddy; and to the court reporter, "Strike it out, Miss Simpson."

Morton turned his head slowly to Kerman. Looking directly at him he said, "Immaterial?" He echoed the word through the courtroom. "Although it is immaterial, Captain, that Three-Notch Riley killed three men, he was very proud of his feat, was he not?"

At the counsel table Nick had his teeth clenched together.

I'm glad I did it! I'm glad I did it!

"I don't know—and I mean I don't know!" McGillicuddy said helplessly. Several of the jurors giggled. Morton looked at them sympathetically and smiled too. Then he moved a little closer to McGillicuddy.

"You do know about this picture, though, don't you, Captain?" Morton slowly took a folded newspaper clipping from his pocket and elaborately unfolded it. He held it up in his fingertips and so that the jury as well as McGillicuddy could see it. The jurors craned their necks. Their swivel chairs made noise under them. Morton talked over the top of the clipping. "I show you a photograph taken from a Chicago newspaper seven years ago. It is a photograph which purports to show the—efficient—Riley pointing to the third notch and smiling for the camera. There is a picture of you here too, Captain, also smiling. Now I ask you, Captain, was he or was he not—*proud of those three notches?*"

The clock inside its polished marble frame jerked its large hand a point before McGillicuddy said, "I guess he was."

When quiet tenseness had settled over the courtroom, Morton

again turned to McGillicuddy and stood at the far end of the jury box with one foot crossed over the other and his arm resting easily on the edge of the box. He said, almost apologetically, "Your men picked my client up as a suspect, did they not, and he was held at your station?"

"Yes." McGillicuddy's lips tightened.

"Now, Captain, how was my client booked?"

"Open."

"And that, Captain, means—?"

"There is no charge lodged against the prisoner."

"He isn't booked for any crime, you mean, and no one knows he's in jail. Is that right?"

"Yes."

"How long may you hold a man 'open?' "

"Seventy-two hours."

"That's three days, Captain?"

"That's right."

"In other words, Captain, you policemen can loosely kidnap or falsely arrest any citizen you want and unlawfully imprison him and hold him incommunicado for at least three days?"

"Objection!"

"Sustained."

Morton went on, unruffled, "As a matter of fact, Captain, although the Court did not permit you to testify as to your knowledge of law yet it is a fact, is it not, that such is the practice?"

"Object!" Kerman shouted. "Reason as before!"

"No, Mr. Kerman," Judge Drake said loftily, "the witness is testifying as to his knowledge of practice and makes no pretense of construing the law. Objection overruled."

"We are waiting, Captain," Morton said affably. McGillicuddy sat stonily in the witness chair. "Reread the question, Miss Reporter," Morton said. Miss Simpson reread the question. "Now, Captain, what is your answer?" Morton asked politely.

"Yes," Captain McGillicuddy said, hardly audible.

"And the police may employ the use of unfair pressure to get evidence and confessions?"

No answer.

"You want to see justice done, don't you?"

"Yes," Captain McGillicuddy said moodily.

"Is beating a prisoner your idea of justice?"

"No—it isn't."

"Then why did you beat him?"

"We didn't beat him!"

"You just talked to him?"

"That's right." Angrily.

"You were satisfied, weren't you? You weren't worried. You knew that eventually you'd get him to talk, didn't you?" he asked with caution and skill.

"We knew that sooner or later he'd tell us what we wanted to know."

"What was that, Captain?"

"That he killed Riley."

"I see," Morton said quietly.

McGillicuddy's answer and Morton's reply had a profound effect on the jury. The jurors stared at McGillicuddy with deep, surprised, revealing eyes. The social worker and the truck driver looked at McGillicuddy angrily. And their eyes went across the counsel table to Nick, sympathetically.

Morton took out his glasses and wiped them.

"But you have said that he never talked, did you not?"

"Yeah."

"Did one of your men twist this boy's testicles until he fainted?"

A gasp of shock and horror went over the courtroom.

"NO!"

Morton put his glasses back into his pocket. He stood up and sighed. "Captain McGillicuddy," he said, "when I bring testimony and proof that this boy at the counsel table was severely beaten while in the custody of the police you will have a lot of explaining to do from this witness box, won't you?" Morton cleared his throat noisily in the hushed courtroom and, turning from McGillicuddy, said politely, "You are excused, Captain McGillicuddy."

For the first time since the trial had begun, Morton seemed to be completely angry. *"Recall Officer Liam Murphy!"* he shouted.

He stood with his arms folded, waiting for him. The policeman took the stand. "You are the gentlemanly patrolman who so tenderly embraced the defendant's legs, are you not?"

"I'm the arrestin' officer!" Murphy said, hard-voiced.

"Did you tell the defendant that you were going to get a statement?"

The cop smiled with his fat face. "I don't remember."

Morton leaned back in his chair and folded his arms. "Well—we will wait until you do remember."

After his words the courtroom became silent. The ornamental hand of the clock moved a notch. Kerman stood up to say something. Judge Drake's hand went up immediately, silencing him. The long brass finger of the clock moved to its second notch. Morton sat quietly with his eyes closed. Judge Drake had his eyes slanted down at Murphy. Nick sat tense but smiling. The clock moved another notch. Kerman gritted his teeth. Nick was almost laughing aloud.

Judge Drake had his eyes closed now too and his head propped against his hand. Morton cleared his throat again.

"Yes," Murphy said into the awful silence.

Morton kept his eyes closed and yawned exaggeratedly. "You just held him in the car?"

"Yes."

"What conversation did you have with the defendant?"

Murphy looked at Kerman and chanced it. "I don't remember."

Morton's eyes came open and he sat up in the chair. Liam Murphy involuntarily shrank back against his chair in the witness stand.

"Mr. Policeman," he said, and he pointed his finger at Murphy, "didn't the police hold the defendant, force a bottle of whiskey between his teeth and pour it down his throat to try to get him to talk?"

Murphy grew bolder. "No!"

"Don't you mean you don't know?" Morton asked gently.

"I don't know anything about the whiskey!" Murphy said.

"Isn't it true," Morton asked, leaning forward, "that every time you talked to the defendant you tried to get him to make a written statement?"

"Well, how many times did I talk to him?"

"Well, how many times did you beat him?"

"I didn't beat him!"

Morton stood up and put his hand on the back of his chair. "You never beat any prisoner at any time, did you, Officer?"

"No," Murphy said.

Morton was still smiling. When he spoke it was very gently. "Were you with the police at the Republic Steel Works on Memorial Day, 1937?"

Murphy stared at Morton, large-eyed. "Y-y-yes," he admitted.

"And ten persons were killed by the police, were they not?"

"OBJECT!" Kerman's voice shouted, cutting in. "The police department is not on trial, as I have said over and over during this case, and I don't know what Mr. Morton is trying to prove but it's purely irrelevant and has no bearing on this case!"

Judge Drake looked down. "What have you to say, Mr. Morton?"

"Only this, your Honor, that the witness testified that he never abused anyone, but that he was with the police force at the Republic Steel Works on the date mentioned, on which ten persons were killed, and my question goes to the extent of testing his recollection and veracity."

Judge Drake chuckled in spite of himself. "Very clever, Mr. Morton," he said. "You have brought it all out and made it pertinent by your last few words, 'It goes to the extent of testing his recollection and veracity.'—Overruled, Mr. Kerman."

And Kerman went crazy.

Morton turned to Liam Murphy. "Answer the question, please. Were ten persons killed in this affair mentioned in which you took part?"

"Y-y-yes," Murphy said.

"You are excused," Morton said genially. He looked up at the clock, then at Judge Drake. "I move for recess," he said.

"Granted."

77

Nick walked into the courtroom. His head was up, his shoulders back, his chin in, his long lashes drawn halfway down over his eyes. The crowd gawked. He enjoyed their staring eyes, their mouths held open a little, their silence and attention. He swaggered toward his chair at the counsel table. The news photographers started taking pictures of him. He grinned broadly.

I didn't know I was such a big shot!

The bailiff was mumbling loudly, "Hear ye! Hear ye! This honorable court..." and the day's session of court began.

Kerman, pressed and polished, called one West Madison Street character after the other to the witness stand. He called bums and hoboes, hostesses and prostitutes, tavern owners and panhandlers. Do you know the defendant? Did he spend a great deal of time on the street down there?... Did you see him on West Madison on the night of November 7th of last year?... Yeah, he was on the street that night...Yeah, I saw him... Yeah, we saw him....

They gave their testimony slowly, dampening their lips and looking around the courtroom with lowered and fearful eyes. They gave their testimony without looking at Nick and hesitantly, as if betraying one of their own.

When Morton cross-examined he spoke quietly to the wretched, life-hardened faces of the witnesses. He asked only, "What time was it when you saw the defendant?... Are you positive that you are correct about the time?... That's all, thank you." And his hand would go back against the side of his face. He asked each witness the same question; nothing more. Time, time, time; he was careful about the time.

No one had seen Nick any later than fifteen minutes to twelve on the night of Riley's death.

"Call Bruno Ringolsky!" Kerman's voice said loudly.

Nick looked around. Who the hell is that?

He saw Kid Fingers walking toward the witness stand. He and The Kid looked at each other. They both grinned a little because Nick had never known him by any name but The Kid; and The Kid because, aside from election day when he got four bits for his vote, he never remembered his name himself.

Nick grinned at The Kid; then, remembering, pulled his eyes away and twisted his mouth into a hard and nasty line. And I gave him my last quarter. The dirty bastard! The lousy stool!

Kerman's mustache bristled with the faintest smile as he started his questioning. Then, more keenly certain, he said, "Now, Mr. Ringolsky, calling your attention to the night of November 7th—"

Morton looked up from his chair at the foot of Judge Drake's rostrum. "Just a minute—if it please the court—I have only one question and it is direct."

Judge Drake glanced down at him. "Proceed."

Morton's deep eyes fastened The Kid. "What is your occupation, mister?" Morton motioned with his hand to Kerman. "Mr. Kerman neglected, unfortunately, to ask you."

"Why—I—I—" The Kid's face reddened in the blue-scraped cheeks. "I dunno—I do odd jobs—"

Morton looked up at Judge Drake again. "With your Honor's forbearance there is only one more thing and it is connected with the last question."

"Proceed."

Morton looked at The Kid again. "Isn't that address you give a hotel, better known by the residents of West Madison as a flop-house?"

"Yes," The Kid said, not looking at him.

Morton followed up, speaking quickly and with heat in his voice, "As a matter of fact, Mr. Ringolsky—by the way—you're better known by the alias of 'Kid Fingers,' are you not, and have no permanent residence?"

And The Kid had to say yes to both questions.

"Thank you, your Honor," Morton said; and Kerman continued his questioning.

"How long have you known the defendant?"

"About seven years."

"Anda . . . knowing him that long would you be able to recognize him—" Kerman paused; he glanced at the jury, *at any time?*"

The Kid's face grew whiter and he hung his head. "Yes."

"Tell us what you saw happen on the night Officer Dennis Riley was slain, if you know." Again Kerman's faint smile bristled his mustache.

For a second The Kid's eyes sneaked across the counsel table, looking at Nick with a pleading stare. Then The Kid told his story with his head down. Several times Kerman said loudly, "Speak up so that the jury can hear you!" And Kerman drew him out, making him go into details about every incident. Then Kerman asked the questions all over again in a different way. Cleverly Kerman wound the story of the killing into a fifty-minute recital; over and over he pecked away at the exact time, the unmistakable identification on The Kid's part. Three times he had The Kid set the moment he had seen Nick come out of the alley at somewhere between 12:05 and 12:10.

On the benches those who knew Nick and The Kid, the boys from the city's slums, muttered angrily, "The bastard!—The dirty stool! —The rat!"

From the jury box the jurors stared over the long rail at Nick. Clear-eyed, innocent, Nick looked straight into their eyes.

I didn't do it.

His eyes held them.

"Cross-examination!" Kerman said cheerfully, triumphantly.

Morton cleared his throat. "How old did you say you are?" he asked.

Nick, keeping his eyes away from where Ma sat, looked around the courtroom curiously. He saw Owen on the last bench where he had been every day since the trial began. Nick felt a warmth. He saw Stash and Stash's old lady. He felt a deeper warmth.

I ain't alone.

His throat filled with emotion.

"Forty-nine," The Kid said in answer to Morton's question.

"You're not a kid then?" He waited.

"No," The Kid said.

"You were forty-two, weren't you, when you first met Nick Romano? And Nick Romano was only fifteen years old at the time?" The Kid floundered helplessly.

"You have testified," Morton said, "that you saw the defendant continually at that time. What were you teaching him?"

"I didn't teach him nothin'!"

"What was your object in seeing him continually, then?"

The Kid shrugged. "He just hung around down there, that's all."

Morton got up slowly from his chair. He walked slowly with his head down and his eyes pinched halfway closed as if he were alone in his study, thinking retrospectively. Unconscious of the eyes of the courtroom he walked around the counsel table. The eyes followed him. He put his hand on the back of Nick's chair and his head down near Nick's lips for Nick's words. The jury looked over the rail at Nick, watching his face. Morton walked back to the jury rail. "You never told him to hang around with you and you'd show him the ropes when he first came down to West Madison, did you?"

"No." The Kid's voice barely reached him.

"You had no influence on the young defendant? You're just a poor unfortunate down there who never got a break in life, aren't you?"

The Kid took the bait. "Yeah—yeah, that's right."

Walking to the counsel table Morton said sharply, "How many times have you been convicted of crime?"

The Kid looked up fearfully. "Twice."

"Wait a minute—!" Morton said, folding back the photostatic copies and starting to count, "...one...two...oh!" He looked up at The Kid sharply. "Now then, remember you're under oath—are you sure of that?" He waved three photostatic copies at The Kid.

"Oh—ah—three or four times—I don't know," The Kid said, hardly audible.

Morton, standing at the counsel table, looked down at the copies. "And the first time was for what? Tell the jury."

The Kid flared with temporary anger. "You seem to know!"

"Yes, I do know, but the jury doesn't—tell the jury."

Kerman leaped to his feet, shouting, "Objection!"

"He may answer," Judge Drake said.

"Now tell the jury," Morton said, still waving his papers, "when the first time was and what the offense was."

"I don't remember."

"Wasn't it pandering—procuring boys and women for unlawful purposes? And how long did you serve for that offense?" Morton slipped on his glasses and looked down at the papers carefully. The women jurors looked at the witness with shocked eyes.

"One year," The Kid said; he remembered that all right.

"Mmmmmm!...Oh, yes! —and now the next time?"

The Kid hesitated, made an answer, corrected it. "That was about seven years ago."

"And of what were you convicted then?"

The Kid hesitated. "Panhandling," he said at last.

"Tell the jury what is meant by panhandling."

The Kid's sneaky eyes glanced sideways at the jurors and came immediately away. "Asking people to help you."

Morton lifted his eyebrows. "You mean begging?"

"Yeah."

[396]

Morton stood at the counsel table looking across at the jury. "And what was the offense the next time you were arrested?"

"Well...ah...it was panhandling again."

Morton was flipping the pages of his copy. "As a matter of fact, Mr. Ringolsky, you were caught taking money from the pockets of a man who was asleep in Union Park and whose pocket you had slit with a razor blade—isn't that true? And you served one year—isn't that true?" The Kid nodded. Morton looked at the jury again. "Now Mr. Glingolsky, these are the three crimes of which you were convicted in Chicago—" And Morton grabbed another batch of papers from the counsel table. "Now, tell us where you were for the thirteen months before you came back to Chicago in October, 1936."

The Kid lowered his chin against the knot of his necktie. "Federal penitentiary at Leavenworth."

"Of what were you convicted!"

"Takin' a relief check from a mailbox," The Kid said from his necktie.

"Then... from the time that Nick Romano was fifteen until he was arrested on this charge a good bit of your life had been spent in penal institutions, hadn't it?"

"Yes," The Kid grunted.

Morton walked to his chair, pulled it over in front of the jury box and sat down. "As a matter of fact..." he said slowly, "you sleep where you can—hallways, under trucks, in the Nickel Plate, Union Park in the summer—and the only time you have a residence is the night thirty days before election when you claim a numbered house on a numbered street as your permanent abode lest you be deprived of the honorarium of fifty cents that an intelligent, patriotic, loyal precinct captain hands you with a marked ballot. Isn't that right? I mean—you don't live anywhere! You have no home! —Right?"

Kerman was up shouting objections. Judge Drake pointed a finger at Kerman. Looking at Kerman, he said over the side of the bench to Morton, "He may answer!"

"*Isn't that right?*" Morton shot at The Kid. The Kid nodded yes.

"Where were you at eleven-thirty on the night of November 7th of last year?" Morton asked sternly.

"Walkin' along West Madison."

"Panhandling?"

"Don't answer that!" Kerman shouted.

"Sustained."

Morton turned back to the witness. "Mr. Jingolsky, didn't the defendant give you twenty-five cents for a bed on the night Officer Riley was killed?"

The Kid looked quickly at Nick. Nick stared back at him with

[397]

hard eyes. The Kid hung his head and said yes. "Didn't he often give you money for a bed or for something to eat?"

"Yeah."

Morton tired The Kid out with questions; he drove him to the point of becoming sullen and answering hesitatingly or not at all. Then he asked, "Mr. Rumgolsky, don't you realize that you are giving the effect of lying by your stammering and half-answered answers?" The Kid didn't answer. Morton leaned against the back of his chair. "Mr. Kringelsky—"

"That ain't my name," The Kid said.

"I beg your pardon—but, anyway—are these garments you are wearing the same you wear when you are panhandling?"

"No."

"Ahhhh! —Who gave them to you? —Or did you panhandle them?"

"Mr. Kerman," The Kid said.

Morton lifted his eyebrows and looked up at Judge Drake, then at the jury, then around behind him at the audience. His voice had a loud and greatly surprised ring in it. "You mean——" he held his mouth open in surprise, *the prosecuting attorney*—gave you the clothing you are wearing?" He waited, looking at the jury with his mouth still held open a little.

"Yeah—he said he wanted me to look—"

"Object!" Kerman screamed. "Won't prove or tend to prove anything in this case where he got the clothes whether it's true or isn't!"

Morton swung around in his chair and stabbed his finger at Kerman as if it were a dagger. "The social worker doesn't want his good deeds told in court, huh?" he said in derision. "It goes to the very root of the prosecution, your Honor! If this despicable character is being supplied with presentable clothes by the prosecuting attorney's office, it needs no stretch of the imagination to convince any intelligent person that his testimony is biased!"

Kerman had flung angrily from his chair and stood at the foot of the rostrum too. "Counsel for the defendant is intimating that the prosecuting attorney's office would stoop so low as to procure unfair testimony!"

"Your Honor! I am insinuating nothing! I am *charging!*"

Judge Drake leaned back. "Objection overruled at this time, Mr. Kerman," he said. Kerman sat down so hard he almost bounced. He and Brooks glared at each other. Morton sat quietly in his chair before the witness.

"Now . . . Mr. er . . . ah . . . Wingolski," he said, twisting the name on purpose again, "you went as far in your testimony as to say 'he wanted me to be,' and then you were temporarily silenced. Proceed!"

"He wanted me to be looking respectable," The Kid mumbled.

"Mmmmm—weeelll—clothes do help ... and did he pay for your shave, shine and haircut this morning?"

Kerman was looking at The Kid trying to silence him. The Kid was so scared that he saw nothing but his tie. "No, he gave me the money last night."

"Ohhhhh!" Morton swung at a tangent. "Now then ... you testified that you heard the shots. How far apart were they?"

"Five or six seconds."

"Were there other shots fired?"

"Yes."

"And how long between these later shots?"

"A minute."

"Well then ..." Morton said, scratching his head, "that would make a minute and thirty seconds—ninety seconds, wouldn't it, Mr. Rogos—

"The name of the witness is Ringolsky!" Kerman said with a snap.

"Thank you, Mr. Kerman," Morton said. "I'll make a note of that and—you'll pardon me, the error was unintentional. Now tnen, Mr. Roogos—er-ah—Ringolsky—your hearing is very good?"

"Yeah."

"And you can count?"

"Yeah," sullenly.

"Well now ... will you close your eyes ... now keep them closed ... and count aloud ... twenty-two seconds—from one to twenty-two—a second in between ... now ... I am handing a stop watch to the court reporter ... thank you, Miss Simpson ... who will tell you when to start counting as she starts her watch and will stop the watch when you reach twenty-two." Morton nodded to Miss Simpson. The Kid sat with his eyes closed, the heavy lids quivering fearfully, and his mouth open. Miss Simpson said, "Start!"

The Kid dragged the numbers from one to twenty-two.

When he said twenty-two, Miss Simpson stopped the watch and handed it to Judge Drake. Judge Drake called both attorneys to the bench to see the watch and said, "This watch indicates that one minute and three seconds elapsed between the time the witness started to count and reached the conclusion of his count."

"I don't know what this circus trick is about!" Kerman said irritably.

"It isn't a trick, your Honor," Morton said, looking up at Judge Drake. "What I wanted to prove and what the witness has proved for me is that he has no conception of time—that he didn't see any shooting—he doesn't know who did the shooting and he doesn't know how long it took to kill this unfortunate officer."

"The jury may consider it," Judge Drake said.

Morton said, looking at his card, "Mr.....er...er-ah...Ring-olsky, is the rest of your testimony any more accurate than your idea of time?"

"I don't know," The Kid said helplessly.

"Thank you—that's what I thought. Oh! by the way...and this is the last question—" Morton's voice came up loudly and with ring-ing sarcasm, "do you keep the clothes?"

78

"Call Walter Zinski!" Kerman commanded.

Nick saw Squint moving swiftly toward the witness chair.

The polack sonofabitch!

"Take the stand, please—" the bailiff said. "Kindly raise your right hand...."

"State your name, address and age, please," Kerman said.

The good eye looked at Kerman and the bad one squinted at him. "Walter Zinski, 726 Atlantic Avenue, twenty-five years old."

Kerman rubbed his palms together. "Do you know Nick Romano?"

"Yeah, I know him."

"Is he in this courtroom now?"

"Yeah!"

"Point him out to the jury!"

Squint twisted his face around until his good eye was looking at Nick. Their hate met. They stared at each other. Squint lifted his hand over the rail and pointed. "That's him there!"

Kerman looked over his arms, folded on his chest, at the jury. "Calling your attention to the night of November 7th of last year ...was there anything extraordinary that happened that night that fastened on your memory?"

"Yeah—there sure was!"

Kerman leaned back against the jury rail, arrogance in his muddy eyes. "Tell the jury, please, what it was."

"Well, I was in the poolroom playing a game when I hears shooting. So I puts my cue stick right down and runs outside. It sounded like it was right behind the poolroom. When I got down there I see the cop—I see Officer Riley—"

Kerman cut in, holding up a long red pencil to attract Squint's attention, "As you went to the alley entrance did you observe anyone leaving it?"

Squint looked out of his good eye. "No—not then. But I saw the fellow who shot Riley leaning over him with the gun pointed right in his face blasting away."

Kerman's mustache bristled with a smile that everyone saw. *"Who did you see?"*

"Nick Romano!" Squint said it loudly. His good eye glared at Nick.

Kerman waited, letting it sink in. "Who was with you, if anyone?"

Squint leaned back in the witness chair. "Butch and The Kid."

Nick's eyes went from Squint's face; Nick's eyes filled with brown innocence and looked at the jurors.

I didn't do it.

They were all looking at him. Their eyes, looking back, seemed not to believe the testimony.

"What time was it, Mr. Zinski?" Kerman asked.

The questions and answers came in vicious summary.

"Your witness!" Kerman flung at Morton triumphantly.

Judge Drake looked up at the clock. "We will recess for lunch," he said and gave the jurors his usual admonition.

Morton walked through the courtroom past Ma Romano and the family. All their eyes looked at him pleadingly. His eyes could offer them nothing. In his impotence he nodded hello and turned away.

In the hallway a man stepped up to him. "My name is Owen Hall. I am a friend of Nick's. I—I want to tell you something."

Morton looked around at the eight or ten people smoking and loafing in the hallway. "Shall we walk?" Morton asked.

···

Outside Judge Drake's courtroom two men stood talking. "Well, I don't know ... I don't believe in capital punishment. I wouldn't make a good juror. I don't think anybody should be killed." The other man said, "Oh, Christ!" and waved a disgusted hand at him. "I could do it—easy! You should hear Judge Buchanan on the fourth floor! He says it so sweet it's a pleasure to listen to him!" The man smiled and held one hand as if he were writing on it with the finger of the other. " 'I sentence you to death in the electric chair on October twenty-fifth—take him away!' "

···

Squint was back on the stand. Morton said, "You realize, don't you, that you cannot invent answers quicker than I can invent ques-

[401]

tions?" He didn't wait for an answer. "You say you have no occupation, is that right?"

"Yeah."

"You are opposed to shooting and stabbing, aren't you, Mr. Zinski?"

Squint looked up out of his good eye suspiciously. "Yeah."

Morton looked over the benches of spectators to where Owen sat; then he turned back to Squint. "But you weren't opposed to cutting when you endeavored to stab Nick Romano with a knife a few years ago, were you?"

"Well, I was mad!"

"This isn't your revenge now, is it?"

"Naw!" Squint said.

"You were convicted of crime how many times?"

"Four or five—I don't know—but it wasn't nothin' but panhandlin' and vagrancy—nothin' like this killin'!"

And Kerman grinned.

"... Now, Mr. Zinski—alias Squint—do you mean to tell this jury that after hearing the shots fired, you and Kid Fingers traversed that distance and found Nick Romano still in the alley—not having made an escape?"

"*Yes!*" Squint said positively.

Morton took Squint back over the story. He told it in the same words. "Didn't Mr. Kerman coach you up on your testimony in his office this morning?"

"No!"

Morton skipped around to different parts of the story, introducing other questions between each part of Squint's version of the killing. Squint floundered, stammered, but told it again. Morton had him tell it backwards. Squint told it haltingly.

"Don't you know the jury thinks you're lying, Squint?" Morton asked dryly.

"Well, I ain't!" Squint shouted.

"Oh, now!" Morton chuckled: he twisted his head away. "Dismissed."

As soon as Squint stood up, Morton said, "Were you ever charged with the commission of this murder, Mr. Zinski?"

"*No, sir!*" Squint said. "I saw it though, and I thought it over for a couple of days and then I thought about that poor woman and her kids and how this fellow had killed a man after robbin' the tavern and I just couldn't stand it, so I went to the police and told them what I seen."

"You didn't get any third degree, did you?" Morton asked. "Nobody threatened to beat you up, did they? You are just a loyal, patriotic, justice-loving citizen who volunteered the information you had—isn't that right?"

"Yes, sir."

Kerman grinned.

"Just—a—minute—" It was Morton's voice coming in dryly. "It was loyalty, patriotism and love of justice that made you go to the police and tell them this story, was it?"

"Yes, sir."

"Now . . . you say you thought over the matter for two or three days?"

"Yes, sir."

"And you read the newspapers and read that a reward was issued for the arrest of the man who had committed the offense?"

"Yes," Squint admitted.

"But that didn't have anything to do with your telling the police this story—did it?"

"No, sir."

"Have you been promised a cut in the reward?" Morton looked at Kerman, smiling.

Kerman was already standing. "Incompetent! Irrelevant! Immaterial! Not proving or tending to prove anything in this case! An unfounded aspersion on the prosecuting attorney's office!"

Judge Drake's voice came down from the bench calmly. "Ohhh— I think it's relevant. I've heard of cases where men's testimony was influenced by the payment or promise of reward. . . . Overruled."

Morton had his glasses on and was looking at his notes. "You testified that one of the reasons you volunteered your statement to the police was that a tavern had been robbed and that, coupled with the killing, satisfied you of your duty to society. Now . . . isn't it a fact, Squint, that Nick Romano's name wasn't mentioned in the newspapers until three days after the shooting and until a bartender pointed him out as the alleged robber?"

"Object!"

"*Overruled!* . . . You let down the bars, Mr. Kerman, and you cannot object if Mr. Morton drives his cattle through."

Morton looked at Squint. "SO! Instead of thinking over the matter two days—you actually thought of it—four days—that is, until after Nick had been arrested and identified by the bartender as the alleged robber . . . isn't that right?"

"Well—I don't remember exactly!"

"Why didn't you give this information to the police when they arrived on the scene?"

"I wasn't there then. Ah—I went to my—I left town."

"Were you afraid that because of previous convictions you might be charged with the offense?"

[403]

"Well—you don't know what cops will do—they may grab every-body."

"I think that would meet with Mr. Kerman's approbation," Morton said dryly.

"Now . . . now . . . Mr. Morton," Judge Drake said, "the jury will disregard that aside."

Morton looked at Judge Drake. "I apologize, your Honor—but I still believe it."

The courtroom smiled.

Morton swung back to Squint. "Oh—by the way—where have you been living since this affair?"

"Same place."

"You mean that flophouse hotel on Atlantic Avenue?"

"Yeah," angrily.

"As you're not working, who pays your expenses?"

"Object—" Kerman said. "Won't prove any issue in this case."

"It may go to test the truth of the witness' testimony . . . over-ruled."

Squint squirmed on the swivel chair. "Well—I win at pool . . . I'm pretty good at pool."

Morton was standing at the counsel table looking at the jury and putting the question to them: "Now—as a matter of fact—every week since you volunteered this testimony, there has been an envelope handed you containing a ten-dollar bill—isn't that right!"

"Well, I don't know where it comes from," Squint said quickly.

Morton sat down, his deep-set eyes looking at the jury. "And you have no idea where it comes from, of course?"

"No."

Morton smiled. "Dismissed," he said quietly.

Squint stood up in the box. "Yeah! He did it! I saw him! I tell ya —Don't you think I know him!"

Judge Drake pounded his gavel. He pointed it at Squint. "The jury will disregard the remark of the former witness as repetition of his direct testimony. And you—witness!—if ever you are again called as a witness don't let your prejudices and passions manifest them-selves after you leave the witness chair!"

"Call Juan Rodriguez!" Kerman commanded.

79

Juan Rodriguez!"

Nick looked up. I thought he was my friend . . . we loaned each other money . . . drank together . . . loved the same girl . . . Juan of all the guys . . . after all the good times we had together. . . .

Nick lowered his head.

On the witness stand Juan's face was pale and his lips trembled. Juan's head was down. His long and straight black hair hung in black scythes at each side of his forehead. He pressed his lips together to try to stop their trembling.

Kerman put his thumbs under the lapels of his coat and moved along the jury rail. "Do you know the defendant, Nicholas Romano?"

Juan's lips trembled. "Yes," he said.

"Tell us if you saw him the night Officer Riley was killed."

Juan glanced up at Judge Drake. "I don't remember," he said.

Kerman's eyes blinked open wide. "You don't remember what?"

"If I saw him."

"Well, were you on the street that night?" Kerman's voice was sharp.

"I don't remember."

Morton had looked up at Juan from the shadow of his hand. Kerman half rushed to the witness rail. *"What?"*

Juan looked straight at him. "I don't remember."

Kerman ground his teeth. "Were you at the poolroom that night at twelve o'clock?"

"I don't remember."

"Were you standing at the end of the alley on Atlantic Avenue and West Madison at a little after twelve o'clock the night Officer Riley was killed?" Kerman commanded.

"I don't remember."

"You were standing at the entrance of that alley—weren't you?" Kerman yelled.

[405]

"I don't remember."

Kerman was staggered by the answer. He seemed about to have an epileptic fit in front of the witness box. His face became red, his arms gesticulated at Juan, his mouth twisted and his nostrils enlarged. "How is it you don't seem to remember anything?" he shouted.

"The cops don't remember when they're on the stand," Juan said loudly and with an angry ring in his voice.

Nick looked up at Juan and grinned widely. Even Judge Drake smiled a little; but he straightened his lips and pounded his gavel. Kerman looked up at Judge Drake. "I ask your Honor to instruct the witness not to volunteer anything!"

Judge Drake's eyes twinkled a little. "Just answer the counsel's questions," he said kindly.

Kerman paced down the length of the jury rail with his brows knotted angrily. He stuck his face in Juan's. "What *do* you remember about this case?"

"I remember that the police picked me up and took me over to the station and beat me up and threatened to kill me if I didn't say I saw Nick coming out of the alley—!" Juan's voice grew loud, insolent, angry in the hushed courtroom. It had the sound of fiery truth in it.

Kerman rushed to the foot of Judge Drake's rostrum. "The witness is lying! —The witness has perjured himself! —He should be arrested! —I withdraw him as a State's witness!"

"Just a minute!" Morton said, putting his shoulder in front of Kerman. "He won't be withdrawn until I have questioned him on cross-examination." Morton looked up at Judge Drake. "The prosecution called this witness—he is theirs—*not ours!* They cannot withdraw him until I have had my questions."

"He's a hostile witness! He must be recalled by his Honor as a friend of the Court!" Kerman screamed.

"Not so fast! Not so fast!" Morton told Kerman angrily; and over his shoulder he said loudly, to the whole courtroom, "I hope the newspapers are here to hear this!"

Kerman shouted above him, "I move that anything Mr. Morton has to say—I move that we argue this point out of hearing of the jury." Judge Drake nodded. He ordered the jury to be taken to their room and that Juan be taken to the witness room. Kerman and Morton turned their faces up to Judge Drake and both began talking at once.

"One at a time!" Judge Drake shouted at them.

Kerman put in an instruction. "The prosecution has been amazed by the perjury of the witness who made a signed statement to the police that he *saw the defendant* at the scene of the crime immedi·

ately after its commission, and I want to introduce the officers who took and witnessed the statement."

And Morton, "We admit that he made a statement such as you describe. But he also told *why he made it and the circumstances under which he made it!* Your police will say that brutality is never practiced but your own witness has testified that it was—on him!"

Morton and Kerman were again both talking at once. Judge Drake looked from one to the other and said, grumbling, "You give me too much to think about at one time." Kerman told Judge Drake what to do again. Judge Drake stared down at him angrily. "I wish you wouldn't conduct my trial for me," he said, ruffled out of his precise English.

Morton stood with his back to Kerman but with his arm and hand behind him, pointing at Kerman. "This man who took an oath—" Morton's voice took on a sarcastic edge. " '*I shall defend the innocent. . . .*' " Kerman raised his voice in objection and shouted, "The witness lied from the stand! Romano is guilty!"

Morton wheeled around and stood shoulder to shoulder with Kerman. "This witness is invited into the confines of the prosecuting attorney's office before the *apostle of justice!* . . . And the apostle of justice says to him—'This is your testimony. This is what you're going to say from the stand *or else* . . .' And the *apostle of justice* again threatens his witness with his Gestapo! *Now* he wants to withdraw his witness because his witness wants to tell the truth!" Morton was shoulder to shoulder, eye to eye, with Kerman. Slowly Kerman moved back, and slowly Morton moved with him. "I too am an officer in this court."

And Kerman shouted, giving ground to Morton, "I want to see that the poor deceased doesn't go to his grave unrevenged!"

Morton, his voice over Kerman's, his words ringing out strongly, went on, "The prosecuting attorney took an oath in a courtroom on a stack of Bibles. . . ." His voice dropped to mocking tones. " '. . . *I will protect the innocent as well as prosecute the guilty!*' This man who represents the dignity of the State . . . seems to believe justice lives only in his household. . . . Not only is he a congenital liar but he wants to build a reputation—. . . this con-man!"

"Object!" Kerman shouted, looking over Morton and up at Judge Drake.

"I don't like it," Judge Drake said.

"I'm talking about Mr. Kerman—not Mr. Prosecuting Attorney, your Honor!" Morton said, his voice quivering with anger.

Behind him you could almost hear the applause of the packed courtroom.

Kerman's voice now strode through the room, loud, proud, angry, defensive. "I want it to go down in the annals of our city that Kerman prosecutes the killers in the name of the poor fellows who die at the ends of their guns ... *and-when-I* ... take them up to try them—" Realizing how that sounded, he quickly amended, "—As attorney for all the people—*I-try-them!*"

Judge Drake pointed his finger at Kerman from out of the deep sleeve of his judge's garment. "You are attorney for Nick Romano as well as for the State."

Kerman retreated a little. "If it please the Court I move that the Court swear in Juan Rodriguez as its witness."

Judge Drake frowned. "I don't think that would be fair to the defendant," he said.

Morton started to say something. Kerman quickly shouted, *"He can't cross-examine!* He has no right to question a witness I have withdrawn! Let the testimony be struck out and he can have Rodriguez as his witness or the Court can have him. *We don't want him!"*

Morton said, "The testimony—whether it be struck from the record or not—has been given to the jury and I stand on my right of cross-examination on every point you brought out."

"Yes," Judge Drake said, nodding. He stood up. "We will take a fifteen-minute recess and, gentlemen, let's be a little more ... ah, orderly ... when we return."

•••

The jury filed back into the courtroom. Juan took the witness stand again.

"Now, to whom have you been talking about this case?" Kerman demanded.

"You and the police."

Kerman pointed the red pencil at Juan. "And you told the police and me that you saw Romano—did you not?"

"Yeah—but I lied."

"You're lying now, too, aren't you?"

Morton stood up. "Just a minute—we object."

"You needn't state your objections, Mr. Morton," Judge Drake said. "He is trying to impeach his own witness. ... Objection sustained."

Kerman narrowed his eyes. "Did you sign a statement that Romano did the killing?"

"Yes."

"Was that the truth?"

"No."

"I have here a photostatic copy of a statement taken by the police. ... I read to you what you said at that time. ... '*Yes, I saw Nick Romano kill Officer Dennis Riley.*' ... Did you ever tell that to the police?"

[408]

"Yes—but I was lying."

"Did you testify before the Grand Jury that you saw the killing?"

"Yes, I lied to the Grand Jury, too."

Kerman stood up. "You've lied all the time then, *haven't you?* And you're lying now, aren't you? *Aren't you?*"

"Object!"

"Sustained!"

Kerman, standing in front of Juan, was jabbing the red pencil in his face. "You're going to be arrested before you leave this building! I'm going to send you up for this!"

Judge Drake shot up to a standing position. He pounded his gavel so loudly that you could hear it clearly through the courtroom. He pointed it at Kerman. "I hold you in contempt! You're not going to threaten any witness in my presence! The witness is under the protection of this Court!" he said.

Morton asked quietly and dryly, "Are you finished, Mr. Kerman?" Kerman didn't answer. With his chair turned toward the witness box and his face in the shadow of his hand, Morton asked the witness, "Did you or did you not see Nick Romano come out of the alley on the night Riley was slain, Juan?"

Juan looked straight into Morton's eyes. "I did not."

"When and where did the police pick you up?"

"A couple of days after Riley got killed."

"What did they do?" Morton had his chin on his hands and was leaning forward in the chair looking at Juan.

"They took me to the station and told me that they knew Nick had killed Riley and that I had better tell them he did. I told them I didn't know anything about it."

"That's when they beat you?"

"The first time, yes."

"How many times were you beaten up, Juan?"

"Three times, by four or five policemen."

"Then they got their statement?"

"Yes, sir."

Morton stood up and looked around the courtroom. "Are any of the police officers who beat you in this courtroom now?"

"Yes, sir," Juan said.

Morton's eyes swept the chairs that lined the wall under the windows in the business half of the courtroom. "Will you point them out to the jury, Juan?"

Juan stood up in the witness box. "That one there—" He pointed to Murphy.

"Do you mean Officer Murphy?" Morton asked.

"Yes, sir."

"Are any of the others here?"

[409]

"—And the little fat copper slapped me and kicked me in the stomach," Juan said.

"You mean Captain McGillicuddy?" Morton asked in pretended surprise.

"Yes."

"Please stand up, Captain McGillicuddy," Morton said apologetically. "I don't want the witness to make *any* mistakes."

McGillicuddy, holding his coat on his lap, stood up, flushing and angry-faced.

"That's him," Juan said.

From the benches you could hear the thrill of the crowd. Judge Drake tapped his gavel.

Morton sat down. "Well now," he said calmly, "you say they beat you up ... tell the jury just what they did."

Juan looked at the jury. "The first two times they beat me with rubber hoses and kicked me." His eyes moved to Morton. "And the last time they threatened to ... to. ..." And Juan, being the ladies' man he was, flushed and grew angry. "That's when I told them I'd say what they wanted me to."

"After they got their statement what did they do?" Morton asked.

"They let me go—but I had to report three times a week at the station."

"Is there anything else that you remember?"

"Yes—they wanted to give me money after I signed the statement. I told them I didn't want their damn money!"

"You lied to the police, then, Juan, to keep them from beating you a fourth time—is that right?"

"Yes, sir."

"You know—they have a slang expression for their third degree. They say, 'Take the prisoner down and show him the goldfish—' " Morton said that to the spectators. "These beatings they gave you were the famed third degree that Mr. McGillicuddy, Mr. Murphy and Mr. Gleason swore from that witness stand never occurs—" Morton said that to the jury. "Isn't that right, Juan?"

"Yes, sir," Juan said.

"And you told the truth here from the witness stand because you didn't want an innocent person to suffer—is that right?"

"Yes, sir."

"And regardless of anything else, you wanted to see justice done?"

"Yes, sir."

"You didn't think of yourself? You volunteered this information? You realized that telling the truth might put you in bad with the police?"

Juan looked over the witness rail. His head was up. It was held up and tilted back with Mexican pride and loyalty. The dark eyes

[410]

looked straight out. "I don't care what happens to me. I just ain't a rat and I ain't going to lie so that they can burn Nick!"

"Thank you, Juan," Morton said quietly. "I know you told the truth."

Juan was excused from the witness stand amid a breathless silence throughout the courtroom. He stood up. He smoothed his long black hair back over his head with the palm of his hand. He stepped from the box and went proudly across the courtroom. The jurors watched him go. Every eye was on him.

OLD PAL TRIES TO SAVE
PRETTY BOY FROM CHAIR

80

He was headlines. He walked into the courtroom with a smile plastered on his face. He walked in, conscious of the headlines, conscious of the fact that everybody was reading about him, talking about his being able to take it. His grin grew broader. He tilted his head cockily as the first camera bulb flashed. *He* was headlines. Lines of type had been pressed out by the thousands. His name had appeared in headlines throughout the country. With a hard-boiled grin he looked around the packed courtroom. The show was on again. *He* was headlines. He swaggered to the counsel table, showing his dimples, and sat down.

The day's session started. Kerman had one more witness. He was written into the record as Samuel Bailey, proprietor of a men's hotel on West Madison. He was a quietly dressed middle-aged man. He claimed that he had just gotten off the bus and started for the hotel in the rain; that he had seen the killing. He said he had known Nick for five years; that he got a good look at the killer and was almost positive it had been Nick.

On cross-examination Morton brought out the fact that Bailey had seen Nick only two or three times in five years when Nick had come up there with a man named Barney. Morton turned to the witness. "You say it was midnight. There was no moon, no stars. It was raining. The killer held a gun—" Morton, facing the witness, illustrated.

"Pardon—" Kerman said sarcastically, "do you want the gun?" He had picked it up off the table and held it out to Morton. Morton walked quickly to the counsel table. "I'll take that gun now!" he said angrily and jerked it out of Kerman's hand. He walked back to the witness box, illustrating again. "The killer was crouched over with the gun in his hand. He had his foot lifted—!" Morton was crouching over the imaginary Riley with his foot lifted, the gun pointed down. He raised up to his full height, suddenly, and folded his arms with the gun still held in one hand. "Which hand did the killer have the gun in?" he shouted.

"I—I don't know."

"With which foot did he kick?"

"I'm not sure."

"On which side of the body was he standing?"

"I—I think the left."

"The medical evidence shows he was standing on the right side of the body!" Morton shouted. He walked to the counsel table and banged the gun down. He turned from the table. All the eyes were on him. The applause was audible. *"Now*—tell the jury, Mr. Bailey —whether or not you saw the defendant—*anywhere*—on the night in question!"

"I am almost sure it was him."

"You have nothing but a hazy idea as to whether or not you saw him, haven't you?"

"Why—I—I—"

And Morton bellowed, "Yes or no, Mr. Bailey! —You were there!"

"Yes." Bailey seemed firm about it even after Morton's questioning.

"That's all—thank you."

Judge Drake allowed a twenty-minute recess.

●●●

When court convened Morton stood in front of the bar giving his opening address: "If it please the Court—and you, ladies and gentlemen of the jury"—his eyes met theirs—"I promise that the testimony for the defense will not consume your time as did the testimony for the prosecution. It was not until after I learned many *facts* that I decided to appear in defense of this unhappy boy. Because I have for so long known the workings of the police department—the inflammatory articles in newspapers, where editors take it upon themselves to *try* the criminal cases themselves—and the vindictiveness of prosecutors—I concluded that I would be recreant to my obligation as an attorney and would become a collaborator with

[412]

the forces of oppression if I failed to raise my voice in protest against the *legalized murder* of this youth. Our testimony will be a complete denial of the killing, or any connection with it. We will show how the prosecuting attorney and the police officers have terrorized men and *women* alike in an attempt to fasten this dastardly deed upon my client. And I may say right at this time, asking you to bear it in mind—*we don't have to prove our innocence.* The prosecution *must* prove our *guilt* beyond a reasonable doubt.... So, when we have concluded, I expect nothing from your hands but a verdict of—*not guilty!* Thank you."

Morton immediately hit Kerman hard. His first witness was Nellie Watkins. She was called to the stand and sworn in. Morton asked, "Are you employed, Miss Watkins?" Her voice trembled as she said no. "Do you remember the night of November 7th, last year?"

"Yes, sir," she said timidly.

"Did you see Nick Romano that night?"

"No, sir."

"Do you know Mr. Kerman"—Morton motioned to him with his hand— "the distinguished gentleman on the other side of the table?"

"Yes, sir." Her blond strings of hair stuck out from under her hat.

"Did you ever talk to him about this case?"

"Yes, sir." Her eyes looked at Kerman fearfully, then at Morton. "I was picked up by the police when I was quitting work at two o'clock in the morning just after the policeman was killed. I was kept in jail until the next morning when they took me to Mr. Kerman's office. He asked me if I hadn't been Nick's sweetheart and I said yes. And then he said well you know he killed Riley don't you and I said no I don't and I don't believe it, and he said you saw Romano on the street at about eleven-thirty, and I said no and he said you did." Her weak blue eyes were wide and tear-filled. "I said no I didn't and he told me well you're—you're going to testify that you did or I'll find a way to send you away for a long time as an accessory to the murder."

Morton said, "Miss Simpson, please read that back to the jury," getting it in twice. "Is that all, Miss Watkins?" he asked Nellie.

"Yes, sir—only he said I'd have to come to court and testify. Then he said I could go home."

"How is it, Miss Watkins, that you weren't subpoenaed to appear in court?"

"I got scared and quit my job and went away and hid because I didn't know what he would do to me if I didn't testify the way he wanted me to." She tried to hide her holey gloves in her lap. "Then when Nick had to come to court I came to see you and I told you that we had been sweethearts and I didn't believe he'd do anything like that." It all came out in a rush and she was crying.

[413]

"How much of your story is true?" Kerman shouted on cross-examination.

"All of it," Nellie sobbed.

"Didn't you know that the defendant was going to hold up that bartender?"

"All I know is that you had me picked up and I had to quit my job." The tears ran down her cheeks.

"Wasn't he at your room? Didn't he plan this with you?"

"No—no—no—" It was almost a wail, trailing into a half-sob.

"Didn't he live with you—*Miss*—Watkins? Didn't you support him half the time—?" Nick narrowed his eyes and gritted his teeth. The sonofabitch! "Didn't you give him money?" Nellie's scared eyes stared at Kerman from under the crushed felt hat. "No . . . no. . . ."

When Nellie half stumbled from the witness box and walked across the courtroom toward a seat in the audience, still stopping the tears with the fingers of her gloves, her large eyes looked at Nick. Nick smiled at her, trying to tell her with his eyes, you're all right, trying to tell her, Christ! I'm sorry. . . .

Judge Drake looked up at the clock and recessed court for the noon hour.

●●●

Grant and Morton went down to the sidewalk together. "How does it look, Mort?"

"Only so-so. Everything depends on the testimony of Sunshine and Butch. If the prosecution hadn't called any witnesses after Juan threw the monkey-wrench in their case—if they had rested when he was excused from the stand—we would have rested without introducing any witnesses. I think we would have won this case right there. The Kid and Squint alone couldn't have hurt us. It's the hotel man—the jury will be inclined to believe him. The jury will feel that he is—as he is—the only respectable witness who has appeared and that his testimony as an unbiased witness, a reluctant witness who had to be found by Kerman, is the truth."

"Am I respectable?" Grant asked. Morton chuckled. Grant said, "I was with Nick from eleven-thirty on the night of the killing until the next morning. I've already told my wife, and she agrees."

Morton shook his head. "No," he said, "I—I want to win this case worse than any case I ever had. Believe that—but I can't let you do that. I can't let you get mixed up in this to the extent of wrecking your reputation and having you brought to trial yourself." Morton frowned. "I'm not going to let them burn him—damn them!" He lit a cigarette and said, "If our testimony doesn't hold up too well I'll put Nick on the stand. I don't want to! I don't want to! If ever a defendant cracks it's when he's on the stand testifying for himself. I've seen absolutely innocent defendants crack up under

[414]

brutal cross-examination." Morton smiled slowly. He kept smiling. Then he said, "Nick is tough—I don't think he'd crack." Morton thought about it a while. Then he said, almost as if talking to himself, "He's good-looking...he looks innocent...the jury is young ...and many women, as I hoped...many juries think a defendant is guilty if he doesn't testify...Nick is innocent looking...on the stand he could free himself...maybe I will...."

They lapsed into silence. Grant said, rubbing his scalp, "I was still with him all that night if you want it that way."

Morton shook his head. "No, you just see him to the tavern door and inside as we planned." Smiling, he tapped Grant on the shoulder. "Let's go have a cup of coffee before we ᴏo back to court."

81

Grant was sworn in. The clock hands, in their round of green marble, showed ten minutes past ten.

"What is your profession, Mr. Holloway?" Morton asked.

"I am a writer."

Morton asked, "What do you write about?"

"Economics and the social sciences."

"Are you an authority in this field?" Morton put the question half humorously.

"I have been called one."

"Do you know the defendant, Nick Romano?"

Grant's brown eyes looked from Morton to Nick. "I know him well."

"How long have you known him, Mr. Holloway?"

"About seven years—since he was fourteen."

"Would you please tell the jury, Mr. Holloway, where and how you met him?"

"When he was a kid in a reform school which I was visiting to investigate conditions." Grant smiled, "We talked about Chicago."

Kerman had jumped up angrily. "I object! Incompetent, irrelevant, immaterial! While this may be very entrancing it won't prove or tend to prove anything in connection with this dastardly killing with which this heretofore angel-faced boy—even though in a reform school at an early age—is charged!"

"Ohh," Judge Drake said, musing, "I think all of this is preliminary to something—though I confess I'm not sure what it is. But I'm equally sure that counsel for the defense knows where he's going. Overruled." Then he said, "The witness may proceed."

And Grant, "He told me, 'They turn you bad in this place. They beat you. They don't reform you here.'"

Nick wasn't acting now. He wasn't the tough guy showing how he could take it. He wasn't the smiling killer neighborhoods and newspapers make. He sat with his head down. His lips quivered.

And the jury saw.

"...What, if anything, did the defendant say about his home life?"

"That his family was poor and that his father beat him."

"And when was the next time you saw him?"

"Here in Chicago in a tavern on West Madison Street."

"When was this, Mr. Holloway?"

"When he was sixteen."

"Had he been drinking?"

"Yes."

"You mean that a tavern owner was serving liquor to a sixteen-year-old boy!"

Brooks whispered to Kerman, "Do something! Stop him!" Kerman said, "Drake's a hostile judge—let them talk—just gassing. It doesn't mean a thing." He gritted his teeth. "We'll tear a hole in them!"

"Where else did you see him?"

"In gambling dens and bookie joints."

Morton said, "These gambling joints and bookie joints allowed the defendant, then a boy of sixteen, to place bets and to gamble?"

On the bench Ma Romano wept.

"How many times, to your knowledge, was Nick picked up by the police and taken to the showup?"

"Ten at least."

Nick sat staring at his belt buckle.

"Mr. Holloway, do you remember the night of November 7th of last year?"

"Yes...I do," Grant said slowly.

"Did you see the defendant that night?"

"Yes, I did." The tempo of the questions and answers had slowed down.

"At what time, please?" Morton said.

"At about eleven-thirty."

Good old Grant! Good old Grant....

[416]

Nick felt warm and sad; he cried inside.

"How do you fix the time, Mr. Holloway?" Morton's quiet voice asked.

"Because I had just come from the Civic Opera House. I didn't want to go home yet—my wife was away—I didn't feel like working that night. It was raining—I like to drive around in the rain and started to head for the boulevard. I hadn't seen Nick in some time and wondered what he was doing. Well—I drove down to Halsted Street thinking that perhaps I would find him in the Nickel Plate. When I drove up he was standing out of the rain in the doorway. I swung my car door open and yelled at him. He ran over and jumped in. I said, 'Let's take a ride.' He said no, he had to meet Butch and Sunshine at the Cobra Tap on West Madison. I offered to drive him down there. When we got there Nick said, 'Come on in and have a drink.'"

At the counsel table Nick held his head down . . . .

Look, fellow, you've got to say, "I'm Nick Romano—I want to live."

"I went in," Grant was saying. "Butch was standing at the bar. We had two rounds of beer and I left."

"What kind of beer were you drinking, if you remember?"

"Pabst Blue Ribbon."

"What time was this, Mr. Holloway, when you left the Cobra Tap?"

"Exactly twelve midnight."

"How do you fix the time?"

"I had left the radio playing in my car. As I climbed in behind the wheel I heard the radio time signal and heard the announcer say that it was exactly midnight. I looked at my dashboard clock. It was on the minute. I looked at my wristwatch, which was a little fast, and set it."

"Thank you, Mr. Holloway," Morton said. "Cross-examination."

Kerman's face had an angry and tightly drawn look.

"How old are you, Mr. Holloway?"

"Thirty-nine."

"Are you married?"

"Yes."

"How long have you lived in Chicago?"

"All my life."

"And you're a writer? Are you a radical writer?"

"I am interested in facts, not political philosophies."

Kerman ground his teeth. "Your name is in *Who's Who* among the notables of America, isn't it?"

"I believe so."

"Well *my* name isn't in it—is it?" Kerman said.

"I've never looked to see, Mr. Kerman. In fact the only time I have ever seen your name in print was once when the newspapers reported you as saying— 'When I persecute—I persecute!' "

The truck driver grinned. So did the baker.

"The word is prosecute!" Kerman shouted. Grant shrugged.

Kerman lowered his eyes angrily. "Now then—" he said. "You are privileged to walk among the elite because of your successes—but you spend more time on West Madison, apparently, than you do at your writing—why?"

Grant said quietly, "I find the people on West Madison interesting."

"Well—" Kerman's eyes narrowed. "Don't you find your North Shore friends more congenial companions than slum-dwellers, gangsters, murderers and thieves?"

Grant pulled his tie loose a little—almost with the same gesture with which a man takes off his coat to fight. Grant said, "I don't know any gangsters or murderers—and many of the people I have met on West Madison are more honest and more congenial than many other acquaintances including some with whom I have come in contact in this courtroom."

Everybody laughed.

"Move to strike as not responsive!" Kerman shouted.

Judge Drake said, smiling, "Sustained—but is definitely responsive!"

"You've known the defendant for the last seven years?"

"Yes."

"You have taken a great interest in him, haven't you?"

"Yes."

"And during this long period that you have known him, was he at any school other than the reform school?"

"Oh, yes."

"Well—have you known him to attend any school since you renewed your acquaintance with him on West Madison Street?"

"No."

"Did he ever do an honest day's work in his life?"

"Yes—I know when he did honest work."

"Now then," Kerman said, getting angrier, "you said that you were at the Civic Opera House on the night of November 7th? How long did it take you to drive from the Civic Opera House where you say you were—"

"Where I was."

"All right! To the Nickel Plate?"

"A very few minutes."

"And you drove to the rat-trap dance hall—tavern—whatever it is? Who's this Butch you say you met there?"

"I don't know his name."

"Are you used to drinking with people whose names you don't know, bums on West Madison Street?"

"I drink with anyone I please," Grant snapped.

"But—ah—" Kerman said, "the radio announcer said it was twelve o'clock when you left there?"

"That's right."

Brooks leaned over in his chair and whispered to Kerman, "You're making a mistake. You're fastening that Romano was there. Try to tear him down on something else." Kerman pulled his head away and moved his shoulder irritably.

"Mr. Holloway, you're very much interested in the outcome of this case, aren't you? What is there about this defendant"—Kerman's voice took on a high tone— "that fastened your interest upon him and has fastened it upon him all these years!"

"I like him," Grant said.

"Mr. Holloway," Kerman yelled harshly, "*why* are you—tell the jury honestly—*honestly!*—why you are interested in this defendant?"

Grant pulled his tie loose a little more and said, "I am interested because I have seen a boy who lived in squalor and misery sent to reform school for a crime he didn't commit. . . . I have seen him during the formative years of his life driven from home by a father who did not understand him, onto the slum streets of the city, where he found companionship and sympathy and understanding. . . . I have seen him charged with murder . . . and my belief in the brotherhood of man forces me to do everything in my power to save the life of a boy who is—I believe—the victim of his environment."

For a moment a silence fell in the courtroom. Then Kerman was on his feet shouting, "Move to strike—*all of it.*"

"You asked for it, Mr. Kerman . . . overruled!" Judge Drake said.

Kerman walked to his chair and banged down into it. "Mr. Holloway," he yelled, "you spoke of the brotherhood of man—are you a—Communist?"

"No—" Grant said, "I try to be a Christian."

Kerman glared. "You said you'd do anything to have this fellow escape the consequence of his crime—"

"I did not say that. I said I wanted to do all I could to help him escape the bonds which his persecutors are endeavoring to fasten around him."

Brooks leaned over and whispered in Kerman's ear again: "You better let him go!" Kerman pulled away angrily.

"Do you know Andrew Morton, the eminent gentleman on the other side of the table?"

"I do," Grant said.

"How long have you known him?"

"Eight years."

"And you want him to win this case, don't you?"

"I do—because the life of a friend is at stake."

Kerman ground his teeth. "You say you object to persecution?"

"I do."

"Have you ever persecuted anyone?"

"Oh—some of the people I have written about may have felt that I persecuted them," Grant said.

"Oh! You didn't do them justice, eh?"

"I—ah—I tried to do them justice but maybe I didn't show them mercy."

"That's all!" Kerman shouted.

Grant walked to the counsel table. A couple of spectators stood up to get a good look at him. Grant stuck his long legs under the table and sat down. Nick, in the chair next to him, looked up at him with his head held down.

"Hello, pizon," Grant said under his breath to Nick.

82

Butch told his story of the night of the killing. He was supposed to meet Nick and Sunshine at the Cobra Tap. Nick came in early with Mr. Grant. They had a couple of drinks and Mr. Grant left. Sunshine didn't get there until way after twelve—it musta been twelve-thirty. Sunshine was excited and told them Riley had been killed. "Well—we were scared we'd get picked up—they pick up anybody they want down there. Me and Sunshine said we was clearing out. But Nick said—that we hadn't done nothin' so why should we hide out from the cops . . . he ordered up drinks for us. We had a couple more after that. Then I said I'm going, and Nick laughed at me—he talked Sunshine into going on down to the poolroom to work—but me, I took a powder."

"What time, approximately, was it when you left the Cobra Tap?"

"About one o'clock—Sunshine and me left together. I knew the time 'cause Sunshine had to go clean the poolroom up when it closed at one o'clock."

Nick looked at Butch.

I got good friends ... good friends.

"Why didn't you tell the police that Nick was with you?" Morton asked.

"I was afraid they'd frame me too—" Butch said. "You don't know them!"

Morton smiled. "That's all, thank you."

Kerman got up from his chair and stood at the bar near the jury box. "Walter Zinski—Squint—testified that you went out of the poolroom with him and around to the alley when he heard the shots fired that killed Officer Riley," he said.

"He's a liar!" Butch said. "I was with Nick at the Cobra Tap."

"Is that what Mr. Morton told you to say?"

"He told me just to tell the truth."

"Your name's Gus Pappas?"

"Yeah."

"What kind of beer were you drinking that night?"

"Budweiser."

"You're sure it was Budweiser?"

"Yeah."

"The defendant here"— Kerman jabbed his thumb over his shoulder at Nick—"is Italian. You're Greek. That—the other one was Mexican. What is that—a gang you had down there on West Madison? Why do you fellows of different nationalities hang around together down there?"

"Ain't that what America is?" Butch said.

"I'm not here to answer questions but to ask them! You had a gang, didn't you?"

"No, we didn't have no gang."

"Ever been in reform school?"

"Hey! —I ain't on trial here!" Butch flared.

Judge Drake leaned over the side of his bench. "Answer the question," he said.

"Yes," Butch said.

"How long?"

"Four and a half years," Butch said in a low voice.

"Do you work?"

"In my father's dairy."

"Oh—you work! Very unusual." Kerman swung around and pointed his red pencil at Nick. "Romano is your pal, isn't he? You want to alibi him, don't you?"

"No! I just don't want him to go to the chair for something he didn't do!"

[421]

Kerman pounded away at Butch like a boxer when he has his opponent on the ropes. "What stool at the tavern did you sit on? Oh, you don't know—then it could have been in some other tavern? What did Grant Holloway talk about? What time was it when he left? Couldn't it have been eleven-thirty?"

Kerman pounded his questions like a carpenter hammering spikes. "Was there a floor show? Just a strip tease? You don't remember whether the little lady was blond or brunette?"

"I wasn't lookin' at her hair. Look—Nick didn't do it! He was with me and Sunshine."

Good old Butch!

"Who is Sunshine?"

"A friend of Nick's and mine."

"What nationality is he?"

"Colored."

"Oh! Colored. A Negro! He was in your gang too, eh?"

"We didn't have no gang!"

"Exactly what did Sunshine say when he came into the tavern?"

"That Riley had been killed."

"Were you sorry?"

"I didn't care one way or the other."

Kerman smiled at the jury. "That's all!" he said.

MORTON CALLS SOCIAL AND SLUM WORLD TO STAND IN ATTEMPT TO SAVE PRETTY BOY FROM CHAIR

Sunshine raised his dark brown hand and was sworn in. "Jim Jackson—they call me 'Sunshine.' Ah'm twenty-four," he said in a slow frightened drawl. Morton questioned him in a voice that wrapped a friendly arm around Sunshine's shoulders.

From the stand Sunshine said, keeping his eyes carefully glued on Morton and his shoulders tense under his coat, that he had been in the Long Bar when someone came in and said that Riley had been killed. "What time was this, Sunshine, if you know?"

Sunshine remembered the story well. "Ah looked up at the clock—it's over the 26-girl's booth.... It was twenty minutes aftah twelve then. Ah started to go out and look. Then ah remembered that ah was colored and they might blame me and ah remembered ah was supposed to meet Butch and Nick ... at the Cobra Tap...."

Nick, with his head down a little, looked up at Sunshine.

Good friends.

Sunshine told the story.

Morton moved his fingers across his chin. "How did you happen to become a witness for the defense, Sunshine?"

"Ah was in the poolroom where ah was workin' and in comes Mr. Grant. Ah went right up to him and told him Nick didn't do it, Nick was with me...."

Good old Sunshine!

"Mr. Grant, he says for me to come over with him to see you. You told me that ah had to stay away from West Madison because that man"—his head nodded at Kerman—"would have the police pick me up if he knew ah was for Nick and maybe have me arrested." Sunshine's voice went on, almost in a low wail, and the jurors leaned over and listened attentively. "So Mr. Grant, he says for me to come stay at his place so the police won't get me."

"Thank you, Sunshine," Morton said.

Kerman drew his chair right up to the witness stand. "Hello, Sunshine," he said condescendingly. "Are you a Christian, Sunshine?"

"Huh?" Sunshine asked, still staring at Morton for support.

"Are you a Christian?"

Sunshine shrank back against the witness chair. "Yes, sah."

"So you brought the news of the killing to Nick?"

"Yes, sah."

Kerman stood so that Sunshine couldn't see Morton. "How old are you?"

"Twenty-four."

"Minutes or days?" Kerman asked sarcastically.

"Years," Sunshine said solemnly.

"How many times have you been picked up by the police?" Sunshine hung his head. "Suspicion of strong-arming—wasn't it?"

"No—ah guess they didn't like mah color—Nick said so anyway." That got to the jury. Their eyes all came over and rested on Sunshine's face sympathetically.

"Just answer the question!" Kerman shouted. His voice dropped to softer tones. "You like Romano, don't you?"

"Yes, sah!"

"You want him to get out of this, don't you?"

"Yes, sah! He didn't do it—he was with me!"

"Where were you born and raised?"

"Jo'jah."

"Ever been in a chain gang?"

"No, sah!"

"You should have been!"

Morton stood up. "Move to strike—meant only to prejudice the jury."

"Yes—strike it, Miss Simpson," Judge Drake said.

"Did you see Officer Riley being murdered!" Kerman asked loudly.

"No," quaveringly.

"Were you sorry he was killed?"

Sunshine's sad, pouted face looked all around, up at Judge Drake, at Nick, at the jury. He looked up at Judge Drake again. "Do ah have to answer?" he asked.

"Yes!" Kerman shouted, "and you better tell the truth!"

Judge Drake pounded his gavel. "Yes, answer the question." His eyes were still narrowed on Kerman.

"No," Sunshine said.

"You were glad, weren't you?"

"Ah didn't care."

Kerman turned his face halfway to the jury. "Can you write?"

"Yes, sah."

"Read?"

"Yes, sah."

"Ever read the Bible?"

Sunshine nodded.

"Do you remember the commandment, 'Thou shalt not bear false witness'?"

Sunshine tried to look around Kerman at Morton; Kerman moved with Sunshine's head, blocking the way. "Yes, sah," Sunshine said in a low voice.

"Do you remember the commandment, 'Thou shalt not kill'? Well, do you remember it?"

"Yes," Sunshine said, hardly audible.

"Know what perjury is?"

"Yes, sah—it's when you swear to a lie in court."

"Know what happens when you lie?"

"You go to jail."

"Oh, no. The law says that. But you, you go to hell! You took an oath in the name of God." Kerman's eyes held Sunshine's. Kerman's thick lips lifted up off his big teeth. "Do you want your soul to writhe around in hell fire forever?' Sunshine was helpless in the stare of Kerman's muddy eyes. All the teachings and superstitions of the plantation cabin in Georgia flooded back to him, beat back at him. He opened his lips twice to speak. Perspiration stood in tiny balls on his shiny forehead. He moved his hand nervously over his wiry hair, pushing the cockscomb down. "Do you?" Kerman shouted. "Do you?"

"No, sah—no—no—"

Sunshine began to tremble. "Sunshine—unless you tell the truth you will never see God—your soul will be tortured in fire forever!" The words came in a burst of flame, then spread themselves out softly as Kerman said in a low, whispered tone, "You don't want that to happen, do you?"

[424]

"No, sah—no!"

Kerman's voice rose again, shouting in Sunshine's face, "Then why don't you tell the truth! You were standing just outside the alley, weren't you? You saw Romano come out of it, didn't you—didn't you?"

"Ah—ah—" For a terrible moment, while the courtroom waited, Sunshine sat with his quivering lips parted. Then loyalty came back, like a wave. "He was with me all that night—that's all ah know!" Sunshine tore his eyes away from Kerman's. He wiped his forehead with the sleeve of his coat.

"You saw him!" Kerman shouted. "You saw him but you don't want to testify! Isn't that true? Isn't it? —Answer me!"

Morton flung from his chair and stood at the foot of the rostrum. "We object, your Honor, to the argumentative disputation, the threatening language and the attitude of the prosecuting attorney because it is incompetent and intended only to create passion and prejudice against the defendant."

"Sustained."

On the witness chair Sunshine was saying in a long wail, "Nick was with me ah tell you—he was with me."

Kerman pointed his finger in Sunshine's face. "You lied when you answered Mr. Morton's questions, didn't you!"

"No—ah stuck to mah story."

"Oh—your story? Then it is a story?" Kerman whirled back into Sunshine's face. "What kind of beer did you drink?"

"Pabst—Nick likes it," Sunshine said.

Kerman smiled and crossed his arms. "Your friend Butch says that you drank Budweiser. He was mistaken, was he?"

"Ah thought it was Pabst—ah don't know—all ah know is Nick and Butch and me was together."

"Didn't you tell this story over and over to Mr. Morton?" Kerman said.

"Yes—but ah told him the truth all the time."

Kerman stood with his arms folded in front of the witness and thought a moment, squinting his eyes. He knew it was true of some of the taverns on Skid Row that tried to go high class. A shot in the dark, but it was worth trying. He smiled at Sunshine. "You've told the truth all the time, haven't you, Sunshine? And you were in the Cobra Tap as you say?"

"Yes, sah."

Kerman folded his arms. "Perhaps you don't know, Mr. Sunshine," he said loudly but slowly, "that Negroes are not served in the Cobra Tap! *That's all! Excused.*" Kerman crossed his legs as he sat down and leaned his head against the back of the chair. Morton's eyes blinked in the shadow of his hand ... a mistake; a mistake ...

he should have investigated and made sure of his tavern . . . on Skid Row, of all places.

Kerman said, with his eyes closed, "Do you try to represent yourself or pass for a white man, Sunshine?" His lips smiled, his mustache bristled.

Morton was standing. "Objection! . . . This comes from my heart, your Honor. I am compelled to use the most opprobrious term that can be applied to a member of the bar—that in view of the appearance of the witness the question is designed only to insult, demean and degrade the witness and prejudice the defendant in the eyes of the jury, the question is not that of an ethical lawyer but"—his voice went into a crescendo—"of a shyster!"

...

Morton saw Nick in the lockup.

Nick said, "Gee, Mr. Morton, I'm sorry—Sunshine did the best he could. You tell him for me it's all right. Will you, huh?"

Morton stood looking through the barred window with his back to Nick. He sighed heavily. "That—with the thing about the beer that Butch got mixed up on—has given the case a bad turn."

"You tell Butch it's all right. Tell him I said that, will you?"

Morton sighed again and turned around. "These are the facts," he said, looking at Nick seriously. "The prosecution hasn't a good case. The police lied and the jury knows it. Their testimony didn't amount to much, especially after Juan threw a monkey-wrench into their case—until Kerman dug up the hotel man, Bailey. But now they have a case—not a good one—but a case."

Nick's heart beat fast.

I'm Nick Romano! I want to live!

Morton put his hand on Nick's shoulder. "Now then," he said, "you and I know what the facts are and you must decide—and you alone—what to do—"

"I'll do whatever you tell me to, Mr. Morton."

"No," Morton said, "you must decide—whether we go to the jury with what we have or whether I put you on the stand. You'll have to take all the venom, vindictiveness and cruelty that Kerman can think up. Now . . . don't answer me right away—think it over for half an hour, because your whole future rests on your answer. And I will do whatever you decide."

I want to live! I don't want to die! I want to live!

Nick tossed his head a little, throwing hair off his forehead. "I'll take the stand," he said.

From the window Morton shook his head no. He turned around slowly. "Not so fast, son. This is a big step you are taking. I have seen defendants on trial for their lives convict themselves when they were testifying in their own behalf. You will be fighting for your life every minute that you're on the witness stand and Kerman will try everything in his power to convict you...." Again Morton sighed and put his hand on Nick's shoulder. "You think it over for half an hour, son."

Alone in the lockup Nick tightened his fists and leaned his forehead against the steel bars of the cell window.

I'm Nick Romano!

I want to live! I want to live!

He tightened his teeth, hard, hard as he could and fought against the scared and helpless tears that filled his eyes. The steel bars were cool against his forehead.

He was still standing there half an hour later when Morton returned. Nick turned away from the bars and grinned boyishly. "Okay, Mr. Morton!" he said.

Morton looked him straight in the eye. "You understand that the verdict will probably depend on what you say and do on the stand?"

Nick nodded.

Morton sat on the side of the bunk and looking up at Nick patted the spot next to him. Nick sat down.

Morton talked. Nick listened. They sat there with their heads bent forward, Nick's down, Morton's turned toward Nick. They looked, on the side of the bunk, almost like two high school boys plotting the strategy for a football game. But Morton's voice was very, very serious.

"You've taken all the grilling and beating the police could give you, Nick, and you didn't break, you didn't confess. And because you didn't, I have every reason to believe that Kerman can't break you on the stand.... Whatever you do, Nick, don't touch that gun! Kerman is going to shove it at you and ask you if that isn't the gun you killed Riley with. Don't touch it! Don't touch it! They always take the gun. It drives them crazy. They relive it when they have the gun in their hands. Don't touch that gun! ... I'm going to stand at the far end of the jury box...."

I want to live!

"...You address your answers to the jury—not to me...."

I'm Nick Romano and I want to live!

"...Look at them, Nick! You know you look innocent. Look into their eyes, son. That jury isn't going to convict you!"

Morton pounded Nick's knee hard with his hand and stood up. "Take it easy—and don't forget what I told you," he said.

Nick nodded his head.

I want to live!

"I'll see you tomorrow," Morton said.

83

MORTON TO PUT ROMANO ON STAND!

It was a blazing headline in every Chicago paper.

•••

Ma Romano got up off her knees at early Mass, crossed herself and trudged toward the courtroom.

Ang, Julian and Aunt Rosa got on the streetcar.

Owen stood looking up at the beautiful court building for a moment before moving toward it.

Stash came from the bedroom and caught his old lady wiping her eyes on the corner of her apron. "You going to work today?" she asked gruffly. "You know damn well I ain't, Ma," Stash said. "Let's go."

Lottie locked the door of her tavern.

Kerman walked into the courthouse briskly with his briefcase under his arm.

Morton walked under the tall pillars topped with statues.

Abe waited against the wall in the lobby to see Ang come in.

Grant sat out in front in his car a long time before going up the broad steps.

Juan, Sunshine and Butch sat on the last bench in the courtroom with their shoulders slumped and touching, their eyes staring straight ahead.

The courtroom was packed, jammed. They were already standing in the aisles.

Judge Drake, in his black court robes, mounted to his bench. The jurors filed in. Grant slumped down in his chair at the counsel table. Owen tensed on a back bench.

"Hear ye! Hear ye!"

A sigh, almost a sob of relief and pleasure eased through the courtroom.

Nick walked into the courtroom smiling. The jurors stared at him

[428]

large-eyed. The eyes on the benches bored into him. The jurors' eyes followed him to his seat at the counsel table.

Nick sat down. "Hello, pizon," he whispered to Grant.

For a moment Nick hung his head. Morton came into the courtroom and, leaning in his chair, whispered to Nick. Looking at the jury innocently, deep-brown-eyed, and with his lips slightly parted, Nick nodded his head up and down, yes, yes sir, yes, yes. . . .

Nick stood up and slipped past the counsel table. He moved gracefully to the witness stand with his head up and his shoulders back. The eyes of the jurors followed him. A flash bulb went off.

He was standing now, facing his accusers, facing Society in open court.

Nick's right hand was raised. His gaze was deep, brown, innocent. His lips were already parted to answer the bailiff. A flash bulb went off.

"Do you solemnly swear before the ever-living God that the testimony you are about to give in this cause shall be the truth, the whole truth and nothing but the truth?" the bailiff said in his monotone.

Nick nodded. "Yes—I do," he said. A flash bulb went off.

His voice was frank, honest, even-toned; it could be heard everywhere in the courtroom. Innocent-looking Nick sat down in the witness chair. He looked over the rail frankly at his judges, his twelve peers who were to decide whether or not he was fit to go on living. All twelve pairs of eyes sought his.

I'm Nick and I didn't do it.

His eyes widened in innocence.

I didn't do it. . . . The jurors' eyes began to fall away from his in shame and embarrassment, began to come back to him in curiosity, sympathy and doubt. A flash bulb went off. Morton was moving toward the bar in front of the jury box. Fontana stared at Nick. The blonde stared at him. *I'm innocent.* The old lady stared. And the Jewish girl. *I'm innocent.* The truck driver. The social worker. The baker. *I'm innocent.* The housewives. *I didn't do it.* They all stared at him. *I didn't do it.* A flash bulb went off.

Nick looked out toward Morton and toward the courtroom crowd. His face paled with fear. Morton stood at the far end of the jury box, in a position that forced Nick to sit with his face turned toward the jurors. Morton's face was very serious now. "State your name, son," he said.

Nick parted his lips and held them that way for a moment.

I'm Nick and I want to live!

"Nick Romano," he said.

I want to live!

"Where do you live?" Morton asked quietly.

"1113 South Peoria."

"How old are you?"

"Twenty-one."

He looked at the jury. I'm innocent. I didn't do it.

"Do you remember the night of November 7th, last year?" Morton asked, very quietly, very dryly. The jurors' ears pricked up; the benches strained forward.

"Yes, sir . . . it rained very hard."

"What other reason have you for remembering that night?"

Nick looked at the jurors and spoke. "I remember it because two nights later I was picked up by the police and accused of killing Mr. Riley." The hushed, ear-cupped silence in the courtroom was so intense that every word he said could be heard to the farthest corner.

"And where were you that evening just before it got dark?"

"I was walking along Halsted Street."

"Where were you from then until eleven o'clock, if you remember?"

"I walked round . . . there was a dead man being carried out of a flophouse . . . it started to rain hard and I went to the Nickel Plate. . . ."

I want to live!

". . . I stayed there for a long time and then I went to the poolroom for a while and I went back to the Nickel Plate. I stayed there the rest of the time. It was raining real hard."

"Then at eleven o'clock you were up in the Nickel Plate?"

"Yes, sir."

"What time was it when you left the Nickel Plate?" A flash bulb went off.

"About eleven-thirty."

"How do you set the time, Nick?"

"I was watching the clock, because I had to meet Butch and Sunshine at the Cobra Tap at twelve o'clock."

"Did you go immediately to the Cobra Tap?"

"No, sir. I stood in the doorway for a little while watching the rain. It was raining hard and I was hoping it would stop, or a streetcar would come along, when I heard someone yell. It was Grant. He had his car and he drove me down to the Cobra. He went in with me and Butch was already there."

Morton started to put his next question. "Mr. Morton—" Nick said, "there is something else I remember. I gave The Kid a quarter while I was standing in the doorway of the Nickel Plate."

Morton nodded. Then he said, "What happened after you and Mr. Holloway went into the Cobra Tap?"

The jurors, twisted in their swivel chairs until they faced Nick, looked at him intently. They followed every word he said. "Grant had a couple drinks with us and he left. Then, in a little while, maybe fifteen or twenty minutes after Grant left, Sunshine came in. He was excited and he told us that Mr. Riley had been killed—"

I want to live! I want to live!

"Butch and Sunshine were both scared. I told them we hadn't done nothing"— Nick's brown eyes looked at the jurors, looked into them—"and we didn't have nothing to be afraid of. Sunshine and Butch left together at about one o'clock. I stayed there and had three or four more drinks. Then I got to thinking about how cops are and how they had picked me up lots of times for nothing and how they would pick up all the fellows on West Madison—I guess I got scared. . . ."

Kerman was in his chair alongside the counsel table, his legs stretched out across the floor, his face bored. He sat as if he were sleepy.

"What time did you leave the Cobra Tap?" Morton asked Nick.

"I left at about one-thirty. Maybe a little bit earlier or a little later."

"Then from approximately twenty minutes to twelve until about one-thirty you were in the Cobra Tap?" Morton dropped the words into the courtroom slowly and carefully. Nick widened his eyes with innocence. "Yes, sir," he said.

Morton, standing at the end of the jury box, said, "When were you picked up by the police, Nick?"

Nick, looking at the jurors, said, "Two days later."

"Did the police beat you?"

Nick's eyes narrowed angrily, "Yes, sir!"

Morton said, "You have heard the police testify from that stand that they didn't touch you."

"They were lying!" A stir of movement and of anger went across the courtroom. Judge Drake tapped his gavel.

"Mr. Murphy, one of the arresting officers, alleged that he just held you gently by the legs—"

"Yeah—just held me! They cracked me in the face and neck and stomach with their fists—that isn't all!" Again a murmur went over the courtroom.

Morton drew out the whole story of the beatings. He wrung the story dry of its every detail. On the benches jaws and lips began to set angrily. In the jury box eyes grew large with shock and compassion.

"After they had squeezed your genitals what happened?" Morton asked.

"I don't know," Nick said. "I passed out."

The old lady's fingers ran up and down the chain and the cross she wore around her neck. Her face colored with emotion. The

Jewish girl had the end of her handkerchief between her teeth and pulled on it with her fingers. The truck driver was clenching his jaw.

"Nick, did you have any conversation with Mr. Kerman?"

"Yes, sir."

"Tell the jury what was said."

Nick turned to the jury. "When I was arrested he came into the jail to see me once. He offered to buy me out. He said if I'd confess that I killed Riley he'd see that I didn't get anything worse than life. He said if I didn't"—Nick's eyes fastened the jurors— "he was going to see that I got the hot seat."

The jurors' eyes recoiled and looked over the rail at Kerman.

Morton walked to the first row of spectators' benches. He leaned against the rail there with his back to it. "Nick," he said, "you were mercilessly beaten by the police for several days. Why didn't you make a statement or confession if it was only to keep them from beating you?"

"Because," Nick said, "I'm innocent."

The jurors looked at him and believed him.

"Nick, why did you run from the police when they tried to arrest you? Why did you climb a fire escape and run across a rooftop trying to get away from them?"

"Because I was afraid of them," Nick said.

"Why?"

"Because I knew how they treated suspects—and what happened to me proved I was right."

Morton sat down. "Nick—" he asked, "did you have anything to do with this killing of which you are charged?"

"No, sir. I'm innocent."

"Cross-examination," Morton said.

Kerman almost jumped from his chair, almost rushed to the rail of the witness box. "So you're Pretty Boy Romano! You're the good-looking fellow, aren't you?"

"Question excluded," Judge Drake said.

"Well, aren't you?" Kerman shouted, pretending he didn't hear Judge Drake.

"Question excluded!"

"Yeah—I'm good-looking!" Nick said loudly and roughly.

"Know a lot of girls?" Kerman asked in a low, cajoling tone.

"A few." Nick tossed his head.

With a sudden change of manner Kerman yelled, "Why did you kill Riley!"

"I didn't kill him!" Nick yelled as loudly as Kerman had. Nick leaned back in the witness chair and narrowed his eyes at Kerman.

Fuller, Riley, Kerman!

[432]

"Why are you clenching your fists?"

Nick's mind turned on and off like the beer signs on West Madison.

FULLER, Riley, Kerman!

Judge Drake's gavel tapped the rostrum. "Mr. Kerman!"

"Why are you cracking your knuckles?"

Fuller, RILEY, Kerman!

Judge Drake's gavel danced up and down on the rostrum. "Mr. Kerman! —You will not proceed in this manner!"

Fuller, Riley, KERMAN!

Kerman jerked his head and his angry eyes away from Judge Drake and stared at Nick. "You killed Riley—didn't you?"

Nick clenched his teeth.

FULLER

"No!" he said, hard and even.

"Didn't you!" Kerman shouted.

RILEY

Nick held the curse words back.

"No!"

"You stood there in the alley and killed him, didn't you? Isn't that the truth?"

KERMAN

"Didn't you?" Each question had a bullet in it.

"No, I didn't, and I don't know *nothing* about it!" Nick said it loudly, emphasizing each word angrily.

Kerman leaned his face into Nick's. "Are you *sure?*" He hissed the words.

"Sure, I'm sure!" Nick said; then remembering Julian getting nosey about his business and how he always said to Julian, 'Sure, I'm sure!' with his eyes turned up innocently, Nick smiled at Kerman.

It was almost like the blow of a fist to Kerman. He moved back from Nick, his face flushing.

Most of the jurors looked at him with hard, angry eyes. Then their eyes flocked back to Nick protectively. At the counsel table Morton's face was satisfied.

Nick looked at the jurors. His lips were held open a little. Some of his smoothly combed dark hair had begun to lift and curl over his forehead.

Kerman stared through his glasses down into the valise on the counsel table. He snatched the gun from it and walked to the witness stand with it. He held it out in his hand. He went for the jugular vein. "This is the gun you killed Riley with, isn't it? —*isn't it?*"

He pushed the gun out to Nick. "Didn't you stand over him in

[433]

the alley and kill him with this gun? *Didn't you—?*" Nick looked up from the gun in the palm of Kerman's hand to Morton. He saw Morton's face shadowed by his hand and Morton's eyes staring at him, saying, don't touch it! Nick smiled a little. His eyes moved back down to the gun, black and deadly looking in the palm of Kerman's hand. Kerman was shoving it out to him again. Nick slowly reached out—and picked it up.

Morton trembled.

Nick held the gun in his hand, looking down at it with some of his hair spilling over his forehead.

The jurors all looked at the downheld and curly head, at the gun and the eyes looking down at it. The benches leaned forward. The reporters held their breath.

Nick turned the gun over, looking at the other side of it.

I'm glad I did it! I'm glad!

Grant stared at Nick, frightened. Owen pressed his lips together to keep them from trembling. Lottie looked at Nick, fascinated. The tears rolled down Ma Romano's cheeks, down on her worn and aged hands. Morton held his face in the shadow and fastened his eyes to the top of the sunshiny counsel table—and his ears dreaded what they would hear.

The jurors leaned forward staring at Nick.

There was complete silence in the courtroom.

Nick was holding the gun upside down with one finger, balancing it by the trigger guard. He pushed it back at Kerman. He shook his head. "No—I didn't kill Riley." His eyes slanted across the counsel table at Morton mischievously. Morton looked up from the table at him ... they'll *never* break him!

On the benches the carrion crows and the neurotics—and a few of the housewives—sat with disappointed faces.

Kerman had slapped the gun down on the counsel table and walked back to the witness stand. He turned back to Nick, frowning. He was the savage, relentless, heartless prosecutor. He shot question after question at Nick, piling one on top of the other, each with a bullet in it. He tried to scare him. He tried to trip him and convict him in the minds of the jurors. "You're lying, aren't you? Didn't you frame this alibi with Butch and Sunshine? They knew you killed Riley, didn't they? You did the shooting, didn't you?"

I'm Nick Romano and I want to live!

Nick stood up unfalteringly under Kerman's vicious cross-examination. Nick answered Kerman's most penetrating and damaging questions with guiltless eyes and innocent face. Kerman kept him on the stand over two hours.

At last Kerman said angrily, "Excused!"

The jurors looked at Nick gratefully ... he's innocent.

[434]

Kerman heard the squeak of the swivel chair as Nick moved away from it toward the two steps down from the witness box, and whirled around. "Just a minute. Sit down!"

Nick sat down.

Kerman leaned toward him. "Didn't your wife commit suicide?" he shouted.

Morton had jumped up quickly and, buttoning his coat, stood at the foot of Judge Drake's bench. Judge Drake jumped up. Nick was standing in the witness box, his fists clenched. Judge Drake shouted, "He won't answer that!" Nick shouted as loudly as he could, his voice sounding through the courtroom, *"Goddamn you!*—Leave her out of this!"

Morton, standing at the foot of the rostrum, said, "I'm asking your Honor to allow us a short recess."

Judge Drake, staring over the rostrum at Kerman, nodded his head slowly up and down. Nick was taken to the lockup. Judge Drake descended from the bench, looking at Kerman angrily, and went into his chambers.

•••

Nick stood in the lockup behind Judge Drake's beautiful courtroom. His fingers were wrapped around the bars, clutching as hard as he could. His teeth were set. The muscles of his jaw stood in hard, round knots. He heard the door unlock. He heard someone enter and stand inside, and the door lock again. Morton said, looking at Nick's back, "Thanks—you didn't flinch. We're over the worst of it—" He moved across to Nick's side and put his hand on his shoulder. Nick felt himself tremble under his touch. "But for God's sake, Nick, be careful when you go back! He may have more questions to ask you and—hold yourself! *Hold yourself!*"

Nick's mouth crumpled open. "I'm thinking about—about—"

"I know you are—but think of yourself now, and *hold* yourself!"

"Yeah ... yeah," Nick said tonelessly.

"You will, Nick! You will!" Morton said, tapping his shoulder several times. "You will!"

Morton moved out of the lockup, quietly, and left him alone.

Nick stood with his fingers wrapped tightly about the bars, with his eyes staring vacantly and a trembling working through him. He stood clutching—holding himself. His lips trembled. He moved over to the iron bunk and threw himself down on it, face down, with his head in his arms.

Kiss me, Nicky.

Now go to work.

Yes ... the lilacs are blooming.

I'll be waiting for you, Nicky—right where you left me.

Kiss me, Nicky ....

Nick fought the tears. His insides crumbled together like a dried leaf in the fingers of a fist. His insides tightened like a string on a guitar . . . they broke like the string on a guitar snapping.

He lay on the network of iron cot.

Sometimes . . . you don't care . . . whether you live or not.

Sometimes you don't want to live.

···

Nick walked back into the courtroom without a smile on his face for the first time since the trial had opened. He walked woodenly, mechanically. His eyes stared vacantly. He took the witness stand to resume his testimony. Kerman moved to him quickly.

"Were you or were you not at the Cobra Tap the night Riley was killed?"

Kiss me, Nicky . . . now go to work, Nicky. . . .

"Huh?"

"You weren't anywhere near the Cobra Tap the night Riley was killed, were you?"

"I don't re—yes . . . I was there."

"Was Butch there when you arrived?"

"Yes," listlessly.

Kerman stood at the rail of the witness box staring at Nick. Again Nick's mind turned on and off like the beer signs on West Madison Street.

FULLER, Riley, Kerman

"What time was it?"

Fuller, RILEY, Kerman

"About—about . . . eleven-thirty. . . ."

"'Did Sunshine see you when you came from the alley?"

Fuller, Riley, KERMAN

"No . . . I told you—"

Now go to work, Nicky. . . .

"—I wasn't there."

"Weren't you trying to escape the consequences of your crime when you ran from the police and climbed the fire escape to the roof where you were caught?"

"I didn't . . . do it. . . . I told you that."

Kerman's voice rose, speeding the tempo in the courtroom. Kerman lashed questions at him. Kerman beat him with questions. Nick's answers became halting, evasive.

"You hated Riley, didn't you?"

"If a cop beat you up—"

"Answer the question!"

Morton's voice said, calmly, "Mr. Kerman asked him if he hated

[436]

Riley. Mr. Kerman is trying to confuse the witness. He was going to answer why he didn't like Riley. He was going—"

Nick looked at Morton from a long distance. His filmed eyes cleared a little. Nick said, slowly, "I ... I didn't like any of them because ... I was afraid of them ... and they beat me ... before ... this."

And Nick knew vaguely that he owed Morton a responsibility; that he couldn't turn back on him, couldn't break. He tried desperately to think straight ... Mr. Morton, Grant, Butch and Sunshine, Juan ... he couldn't go back on them ... he couldn't ... get them ... in trouble. ...

He strained for clearness.

I'll be waiting for you, Nicky ...

"Didn't you lie when you said I'd see that you got nothing more than life?"

"I didn't lie!" For a moment the fire was back in Nick; in his eyes and his voice. "You did ask me to confess! You did promise me that!"

Kerman questioned him for half an hour, sweating him, grilling him, giving him a verbal third degree.

"You killed Riley! Didn't you—?"

FULLER!

RILEY!

KERMAN!

"Didn't you?"

Nick's mind somersaulted back through the years to a mouse cornered by a cat out along the side of the grocery store when he was eleven ... the boards were green and rotting ... the mouse was cornered ... its little eyes looked up fearfully, black little eyes, scared little eyes. ... The cat's paw reached out, toying, slapping, playing—ripping the mouse's fur. ... Through the legs of the people he saw the cornered mouse and the cat's paw going out sharp, slapping, slapping, slapping! —He was that mouse now. ... Kerman stared into Nick's eyes, fastening him against the back of the chair; and Kerman sensed, from many trials, that he was prepared for the kill, ready for the kill.

The mouse! The mouse!

Kerman brought his finger close to Nick's face, and shouted in a rush of words: "Isn't it true that your wife killed herself because of you?"

Nick jumped up in the witness box. He was standing. He was shouting. His voice trailed loud in the courtroom, filling all the courtroom. "Can the fancy stuff! I know I'm going to burn! Come on! Get it over with! Yes! —I killed that goddamn cop! I'm glad I

[437]

killed him! I'm *glad* I killed him! I'd do it all over again!" Veins stood out bold and hard on his forehead and he shouted it: "Yeah! —I killed him! I'm glad I killed him!"

Gasps—shouts—people standing—staring.

Disbelief—belief—staring—

"He did it! He did it!"

The jurors staring at him with their mouths open and their eyes blinked wide.

Feet shuffling, reporters shouting gleefully over *the story!*

Flash bulbs bursting—

The spectators, Grant's face, Morton's face, Owen's face—

News photographers squatting around him and the flash bulbs going off like firecrackers, like neon signs blinking, like fists striking.

In all the courtroom only Kerman was composed. Kerman sat on the arm of his chair, smiling, tossing his red pencil up in the air and catching it. Tossing it up, catching it, smiling—

And behind him, on the bench, Ma Romano crumpled into herself, sobbing bitterly.

Morton came from his chair, almost overturning it, and stood at the rail of the witness stand trying to quiet Nick while Nick yelled as loudly as he could that he had killed Riley, that he was glad he had done it. Nick pulled away from Morton. "Don't tell me what I'm going to do! It's my life! Yes!— Yes!— I killed him!"

Then, in the awful quiet of the courtroom, Nick suddenly sat down with his face ghastly white and his hands trembling on his knees.

84

MORTON, KERMAN ARGUE TO JURY TODAY

The crowd was larger than it had yet been. The benches were filled, people were lined down the aisles, the corridor was packed outside the courtroom, and the side door had been opened so that the curiosity seekers in the hall could peek over each other's shoulders and by straining their ears could hear the arguments for life and death.

Morton and Kerman stood at the foot of Judge Drake's rostrum. Judge Drake said, "Well, gentlemen, how much time will you need for argument?"

"I'll need three hours." Kerman said immediately.

"Oh—my—my—my!" Judge Drake said.

And Morton, "Oh, there is very little to argue here—forty-five minutes will do me."

"Oh, no, I've got to have time!" Kerman said. "I'll need two hours and thirty minutes for my argument and Mr. Brooks also wants to talk."

Judge Drake rubbed his nose. "Mr. Kerman, I'll accede to your request in large measure and give each side ninety minutes."

"But—your Honor—"

"That's all, Mr. Kerman."

Morton and Kerman went to their chairs at the counsel table. Morton sat squarely at the table, his eyes attentive and reflective. Next to him Nick was slumped in his chair with his head down. He wasn't the smiling killer who had swaggered into the courtroom previously. He was just a scared kid now. His eyes stared at the jury fearfully.

Counsel for the prosecution had finished their whispered conversation. Brooks arranged his coat and prepared to stand up. Brooks, brought in to sit with Kerman and run his errands, Brooks who had spent all the days of his political life working on briefs, formulating opinions for more noisy but less able men, rose to address the jury. He was handsome, with a bearing that indicated the generations of comfortably situated people from whom he was descended. Sartorially correct, in everything the antithesis of Kerman, Brooks approached the bar in front of the jury box.

Brooks brought the scalpel: "Ladies and gentlemen of the jury —in all your life you will never have a harder task imposed upon you than that imposed by your service in this trial. This great State with its millions of people has selected each of you as capable men and women to try this issue in which the honor of the State and the life of the defendant are at stake. That the State made a wise selection is evidenced by the fact that its choice has been approved by that archpriest of criminal procedure, Andrew Morton, and by his Honor, Judge Drake, who has sat as a disinterested umpire and guided this cause with wisdom until now it has come into your hands and your minds for determination. . . .

"I have said hands and minds, ladies and gentlemen, because I am fearful that if you are to be guided by your emotions—sometimes mistakenly called heart—you will forget your duty to the State and be carried away by the suave, polished, mercy-bearing platitudes of the defense counsel who will follow me. And if you were to do this, then justice would be ravaged, statutes desecrated and your oaths forgotten. . . ."

The jurors' eyes became more solemn with his words. Silence had hushed down over the courtroom. Brooks continued: "There is not a great body of evidence to be weighed in this case—but, stripped of all foreign substance, it seems to me—and, I believe, to you—everything *unerringly* points to the guilt of the defendant. The motive is shown by his hatred of all police and in his endeavor to escape arrest for robbery two nights prior to his apprehension. The opportunity presented itself in the darkened alley where, pursued by that gallant Dennis Riley, he fired—death-dealing bullets!—into the body of him who twenty-four years ago escaped the murderous slugs of the Huns only to crash to the ground a lifeless corpse at the hands of this anarchist. . . .

". . . My superior, than whom there is no greater prosecutor, I believe, in the country, will go over the evidence from its inception to now, and with the vigilance that has characterized his every prosecution, he will so weave *a rope* from the threads of evidence that have been introduced that it will lead to no other conclusion than the guilt of Romano." Brooks' voice fell to a low tone. "A sad task . . . my friends . . . a sad task that confronts you surgeons of the State—but—just as the hospital surgeon must face the weeping mother of a dying child whose life he cannot save, you must face your duty and strive to keep aloft the banner of justice!—to keep alive the laws of our nation! *Don't* let Mr. Morton tell you that any of the rights of the defendant have been contravened. *Every one* has been protected by the integrity of the Court . . . and now . . . in conclusion I will say just this—be careful of that man Morton! He talks birds out of trees—but I'm sure he won't affect you intelligent ladies and gentlemen. . . . In conclusion I will say just this—that the defendant is guilty *beyond a shadow of a doubt*— that your duty is clear, and that your verdict *will be,* in accordance with the demands of the prosecution, *death in the electric chair.* . . . Thank you."

And Brooks sat down in the quiet of a courtroom that was disturbed by only the low, almost inaudible sobbing of the defendant's mother.

85

Morton sat for a moment at the counsel table, rubbing his forehead and his eyebrows. For another moment he sat staring at the jury with deep, searching eyes. Then he rose with dignity and calmness and moved to the bar in front of the jury box. He stood there, silent, looking from juror to juror. Every eye in the courtroom was on him. There was a complete silence. The ornate minute hand on the clock over the jury box sprang forward to its next notch.

Morton's deep-set eyes still fixed on the jury. Morton said, "Men and women of the jury, you have just been asked—to take a life." He paused. Finally, in slow-stroked, calm tones he went on. "There sits Nick Romano—" Again the pause; he turned slightly, looking over his shoulder at Nick. The eyes of the courtroom followed his glance; and Morton said, "Nick Romano—accused in the name of Society and of this State—of—murder . . . Nick Romano, twenty-one years old." He took his eyes from Nick and looked at the jury. "He sits before you today for judgment. Today"—he said it looking from face to face until he had starêd into the eyes of all twelve—"you are his life or his death. He sits before you friendless . . . helpless, except for whatever aid I have been able to give him during this trial as his friend and his counsel. You are, today, if you so choose, not only his examiners, but also his judges and his excutioners. The Court has no control over your decision . . . no authority but to fix the day and the hour. In this courtroom . . . today . . . your function is that of twelve gods—givers of life, or takers of life. . . ."

Morton squared his shoulders and moved closer to the jury box. "You have been told to beware of my suave, polished, mercy-bearing platitudes. . . ." He shook his head no. "Platitudes were never farther from my mind. I intend being anything but suave and polished." His voice grew louder. "A young man is on trial for his life!" He cracked the words at them like a whip.

At the counsel table Nick was slumped in his chair, his hands on his lap, his head down, his chin against the front of his shirt.

"...Men and women of the jury—and deliberately I do not address you as"—his voice strode with angry sarcasm—"'ladies and gentlemen, my intelligent peers, my good fellow citizens, defenders of the honor of our great State,' as Mr. Brooks has addressed you, as Mr. Kerman will address you, as all attorneys address all juries, appealing not to their intelligence and their logic and their integrity but actually to their pride and their prejudice and their passions. I appear before you humbly, honestly, simply. Mr. Kerman and I do not count in this case. The young man at the table is all that counts. He is on trial for his life!

"Other Nick Romanos have trooped into our courtrooms." He nodded his head slowly, "Other Nick Romanos will continue to troop into our courtrooms. The innocent—like the boy sitting in the chair there—and the guilty have appeared before us, a long, wretched, endless line. And we have numbered them, or slain them, or—in a few instances—freed them. Numbered, slain, or freed, we have sent them away without illusions. We—Society—have done this." His voice grew loud and questioning in the courtroom, "Who is Society? What is Society?"

Morton stopped a full minute, looking around the courtroom, then at the jury, with angry eyes. When he spoke again his voice was colder, more deliberate. "Society is you and I and all of us. We—Society—are hard and weak and stupid and selfish. We are full of brutality and hate. We reproach environment and call it crime. We reproach crime—or what we choose to label crime—without taking personal responsibility. We reproach the victims of our own making and whether they are innocent or not once we bring them before the court, the law, Society—once we *try* them, we *try* them without intelligence, without sympathy, without understanding!... And—we—cut—down—any—we—choose!"

Morton turned his head, slowly moving his eyes over the jurors and the courtroom crowd. "Platitudes? Suavity...?" And his voice thundered. *"NO! I ACCUSE!"*

When silence was in the courtroom with the sunlight and the tensed listeners, Morton leaned over the jury rail and eye-to-eye with the jury, asked loudly, "Who is Nick Romano?...Unknown half a year ago, he has been picked up by the yellow press and—*made*. Nick Romano has been picked up by the criminal-minded police and the oh! so mighty and just prosecuting attorney's office as another guinea-pig upon whom—*THEY* wish to fasten *THEIR* wrath and revenge! He has been beaten, terrorized, slandered, lied about, perjured against and accused of murder! Why is Nick Romano here in this courtroom?" Morton looked at the jury full-face with his hands spread in front of him on the bar. His voice

[442]

was quiet. "I bring no platitudes. I bring no suavity. I accuse—you and me—this precious thing we call Society—of being the guilty parties who have brought Nick Romano, innocent, here in this courtroom before us!"

The jurors stared at Morton with shocked, curious, unblinking eyes. The silence was so complete that the clock's ticking was like a shout.

At last with a slow gesture of his hand he continued, "You have just sat through the dramatic performance of a murder trial." The edge of sarcasm and bitterness was stiff in his voice. "You have seen a show put on with great theatrical display—a contest not unlike a football game, and played before a packed gallery. The newspapers have seen to that. They have given him a trial by newspaper. They have found him guilty long before this trial opened. They have selected Nick Romano as victim on the altar of their circulation charts. And . . . they have packed the house. . . .

"We are now up to the last act in the play . . . shortly the curtain drops and you retire to the jury room to decide your verdict. . . .

"Men and women of the jury, I stand here with Nick—alone to raise a voice in his defense. The theory of the law is that the jury—and the jury alone—will weigh the evidence and not be confused by the arguments of paid advocates on either side whose interest is not always in doing justice but in securing the applause of the world for their forensic superiority. The gentleman who preceded me did not call to your attention any of the evidence upon which the prosecution relies for a conviction but spent his time—and yours—in eulogizing his associate and insisting that you must pay no attention to my plea for mercy. For many years a talking machine company used as an advertisement an illustration of a small dog sitting at the end of an immense horn and the slogan was 'His Master's Voice.' In this case the urbane gentleman who preceded me listened intently to the sounds from the paid prosecutor and, irrespective of the demands of justice, failed to call your attention to or to explain for your benefit the contradictory testimony of the police and their stooges paraded here. . . .

"Mr. Brooks has told you that this indictment bears on its face the title 'the People of the State against Nick Romano,' but he forgot to tell you that Nick Romano is a citizen too, that he is entitled to the protection of every element of the law and that it is your *duty* to give him the benefit of every reasonable doubt, the safeguard of every guarantee, the *absolute belief* that he is innocent of this offense until the prosecution—*shatters!*—that belief beyond a reasonable doubt. . . . *Mercy*—Brooks told you would be my theme." Morton shook his head decisively. "I—am—not—asking—

mercy. What I am demanding is clear-eyed—clear-eared—unbiased —unprejudiced justice!

"... What is justice? Search your hearts and I believe you must reach the conclusion that the answer is—justice is truth."

Kerman sat stabbing at the counsel table with his red pencil.

"... Believing that, how much truth has been introduced by the State in its endeavor to send to a felon's grave that unfortunate boy sitting before you?" Morton paused a moment, went on, "I propose to take a few minutes of your time to analyze the testimony of the State's witnesses. Nor shall I forget to bring to your attention, as in the trial, every significant episode in the life of the defendant.

"The theory of the State is based upon the assumption that Nick Romano held up and stole five hundred dollars from one Henry Swanson, a barkeeper in a tavern on West Madison, that the killing occurred not later than ten minutes past twelve in the early morning of November 8th. This robbery, the prosecution alleges, was a primary cause for the death of Dennis Riley, who in pursuit of his duties sought the robber of Swanson. *But*—let us go to the truth and ask—in her name—*how, when* and *where*—Swanson!—decided! —that this defendant was the individual who took a sum of money which he alleges was five hundred dollars. A few seconds, according to Swanson's testimony, intervened between the time of the robbery and the time the holdup man backed through the door. He had but a fleeting glance of the thief and on two different occasions at least declared his inability to recognize, or even describe his alleged assailant—and not until the police informed him that they *had the holdup man* in custody, as the murderer of the police officer, did he point him out as the source of the officer's death. You will remember that he said on cross-examination that he had never seen me but eventually admitted that I had talked to him for fifteen minutes and that I accidentally—or purposely—spilled a glass of port wine upon his shirt. At that time he told me that he couldn't identify the holdup man—*but*—after a reward was offered and the melodramatic mind of the police began to wind its web around the defendant—he—put—his—finger—on Nick Romano.

"If the defendant stole five hundred dollars and killed Riley, why was he still on West Madison two nights later? Why, with that sum of money, hadn't he left the city if he killed Riley? Use your common sense, men and women—would you or I have remained in the vicinity of the killing if we had slain Officer Riley?"

From his chair Nick looked at Morton with deep and admiring eyes.

"Some minutes since, I referred to the melodramatic mind of the police. It has *never* been more vividly portrayed or depicted on stage or screen—in books or poems—than in the frantic efforts of the law-enforcing department to fasten the killing of one of its members on the defendant. Not aided alone—*but made*—from the stories of the police, the *moulders* of public opinion, the public prints have from the day of the arrest of Nick Romano screeched with acid voices for his immolation. 'Pretty Boy Romano,' 'Baby-faced Killer,' 'Most Callous Killer,' their headlines have screamed ... these prostitutes of public opinion!

"Killer! That's what they have called this boy here—*before* an indictment!—*before* any evidence whatsoever! Day after day—with every new edition, hate-inciting headlines have been thrust in the eyes of the readers—not to gratify justice!—not to find truth!—but to crucify this youth whom the State, the newspapers and the police have decided must die! For what purpose? To solve the killing? *NO! Not so!* —To add another spray to the laurels of the mouth-pieces of the prosecuting attorney's office, to glorify the police department, and deify the masters of public sentiment—the news-papers!"

The jurors listened, the police scowled, the reporters frowned.

"You read each month the records of the various branches of the police department and of the prosecuting attorneys, showing the number of trials and the convictions secured—but no mention is ever made of the men and women illegally convicted, stripped of all the attributes of humanity, festering mentally, morally and physically in penitentiaries, or lying in graves—forgotten by all save the few who loved these victims of organized persecution and in-justice—and *all in the name of law and Society!*"

Suddenly Kerman leaned across the counsel table and said softly, so that Judge Drake wouldn't hear but the jury would, "How much was your fee? . . . Tell them how much your fee was!"

Morton heard him. Paying no attention, his voice coming back from anger to reasoning, he said, "With all the power of the State, with unlimited money, with thousands of officers, there has not been brought to you *any* uncontradicted evidence that would tend to connect Nick Romano with this crime. Ahhh! I note Mr. Ker-man making a memorandum and he will call to your attention—forgetting Kid Fingers and Squint, his suborned witnesses—the testimony of—*Bailey!* . . . It is fitting that he should," Morton's voice dropped, "because so thoroughly, I believe, have you rejected the testimony of the first two mentioned that he must endeavor to palliate the disgust you felt while listening to their insecurely fixed testimony. Mr. Kerman will tell you, I anticipate, that Mr. Bailey, his surprise witness discovered, mind you, the night before he closed his case, is a"—Morton's voice eased to deriding tones—"respectable business man. I know nothing of Bailey, but I do know from his

[445]

testimony that the 'respectable business' under the euphemistic title of 'hotel for men' is a—West Madison Street flophouse frequently entertaining—*women!* It is of general knowledge that when women frequent these hotels for men the police are not unaware of the fact. What methods were used by the police to make Mr. Bailey realize on which side his bread was buttered, it is easy to conceive. Yet Bailey failed to tie up Nick Romano with the individual whom he saw in a fleeting glance at the mouth of the alley. Use your common sense, men and women of the jury, and again ask yourselves—would you want your husband, your brother, your son or yourself to be convicted on that evidence?"

Morton stuffed his hands down into his coat pockets hard. "Tell them how much your fee was!" Kerman said louder and with biting sarcasm.

Morton turned his head and one shoulder to Kerman. "It was a blank check," he said pleasantly. Turning back to the jury, Morton said, "I like Kid Fingers, self-confessed bum, moocher, panhandler, robber of his own kind, vagrant and jailbird. He had acumen enough to wrench from the prosecution—and its alter-ego, Mr. Kerman"— Morton nodded to Kerman pleasantly—"suitable clothing so that, to use his own words, 'I might look respectable.' I again say—I admire him because he brought to your attention the fact that his testimony was paid for!... Would you want to convict a man on that?" Morton's eyes rested on the truck driver. The truck driver was looking at him squarely, and, Morton felt, was with him.

"Now we come to Squint, whose hatred for the defendant was manifested throughout all his testimony. Squint—actuated only by motives of public policy and a desire to see the perpetrator of the crime pay the penalty for his misdeed—spent two days in prayer and contemplation as to what he should do and made up his mind to volunteer his testimony *after* he had read of the reward to be paid for the killer of the cop. This pure patriot—Squint!—was forced to tell of his weekly honorarium of ten dollars coming from whom or where he knew not. Of course... you men and women... must not imagine that that was a—*bribe!*" His voice grew scornful and mocking. "Far be it for these paragons of purity to do anything so ignoble.... Would—you—want to convict a man—on testimony from that source?"

Morton looked over the spectators' benches, then again to the jury. "And now, we come to his other witness—Juan Rodriguez. I remember very little of this witness's testimony on direct examination except that which fastened itself on my mind, as it must have on yours, in answer to many of the questions of the State—'I don't remember.' And *all* the browbeating of the prosecuting attorney brought out only this. Then—you recall—that on my cross-examination he stated that the police had first offered him money, then beaten and kicked him, and finally forced him to sign a false statement; that Kerman visited him the night before he went on the stand and read his testimony to him. You recall that Juan refused to perjure himself, giving as his reason—that he—*wasn't a rat and wasn't going to lie so that they could burn Nick*."

Morton lifted his head and his shoulders. "Now...men and women...here are the stars that the State has paraded before you and they add up to *absolutely zero!* But...you will be told that the defendant confessed in your presence that he did murder the policeman. That such a statement came from his lips is true. You saw the pleasure of opposing counsel at what he thought was another feather in his cap. You saw his happiness in what he fondly believed was the attainment of his determination to electrocute the defendant. You know that the physician selected by his Honor to examine the defendant told you that Kerman's inhuman cross-examination would be sufficient to produce temporary insanity. The testimony of Mr. Holloway, of Butch and of Sunshine points convincingly to the presence of the defendant from eleven-thirty until almost one o'clock with Holloway or at the Cobra Tap drinking bar. The prosecution will endeavor to tell you that there is a discrepancy between the testimony of Sunshine and Butch as to the kind of beer that was drunk that night. See if you men and women can remember exactly the brand of beer you drank half a year ago."

Morton paused, looking from juror to juror. "One more witness remains to be considered—*Nellie Watkins*. Poor, ragged Nellie Watkins was held at a police station overnight unbooked, and next morning she was conveyed to the office of the prosecution. You remember her testimony! How she was threatened because she refused to testify as counsel would have her. You remember the insinuation in his questions—'He was your lover....' 'Did you ever give him money?'—the implication being that the defendant was almost as low as Squint and Kid Fingers. But there *are* good men and women in the world—and Nellie Watkins proved that she couldn't be seduced by either promises or threats."

Morton's voice was clear, loud, incensed. "I charge that *every* witness called by the prosecution has been thoroughly discredited, from the kindly policeman who with loving hands endeavored to restrain Nick from jumping from the police car while he was being tenderly conveyed to the police station to Captain McGillicuddy who, despite his twenty years in the police department—was denounced as a perjurer and sadist—by the prosecution's own witness—Juan!"

Morton stood looking into the jury box. "In God's name—men

[447]

and women—and it was in His name that you promised to render a fair and impartial verdict—I ask—would you want to be convicted by a conspiracy of policemen?... It is seldom that I indulge in personalities. I have no occasion to, usually, but in this case it is incumbent upon me to bring to your consideration everything that will aid you in reaching a *just* verdict...."

Morton leaned over the rail now, talking in familiar tones to the jury. "As a small boy and a youth I lived in one of the states west of the Missouri River and I became acquainted with the lowest type of animal that roams the prairies. A sneaking—sniveling—slinking quadruped without courage but with the craft of a rattlesnake—not the fairness of the rattler who strikes only in defense of himself and when fearing attack—with not the courage of the wolf who doesn't hesitate to attack superior forces...."

The jury leaned forward on their swivel chairs, hanging to his words, expecting something; the spectators strained their ears and their eyes.

"In that country this animal, this scavenger of the plains, is hated by all people. An open season is declared upon him and a bounty paid for his extermination...." Morton lifted up off the bar. "It—is—called—a coyote!" Morton glanced out over the courtroom, then again looked directly at the jury. "And I have seen its biped counterpart in this courtroom. With a heart that is craven as a coyote's, with a mind that picks unerringly on the weak, with a vindictiveness that is damnable—you too have seen him in the role of prosecuting attorney in this courtroom—the *coyote!*"

Kerman was up, almost knocking his chair over. "*Stop!* —Your Honor! I object! I demand that all that argument be stricken from the record. He slandered me! He's insulted me! He should not be allowed to go on with this cause! Make him apologize to the jury and to me!"

Judge Drake, leaning his face against his hand, said, "Mr. Morton has drawn an unflattering comparison... that's his privilege. He thinks so—or he wouldn't have said it... your objection—did you make an objection, Mr. Kerman, or did you just burst out in anger?"

"I objected, your Honor, and I'm still objecting! That name will stick to me! I must have an apology!"

"Well," Judge Drake said, slow and low, "perhaps the term is strong, but you're overruled—proceed, Mr. Morton—" And Judge Drake spun his swivel away from Kerman and toward the jury; leaning back, he looked down over his rostrum at the jurors and Morton.

Morton walked to the end of the jury box, then back. He stood facing the jurors. "The trial draws near its end. The antagonists

[448]

have been Nick Romano and his persecutors—" Morton put his fists on the jury bar one against the other. "On the one side Grant Holloway, Butch and Sunshine. On the other *Squint* and *Kid Fingers!*—squint and The Kid!—pimps for the prosecution!... On one side Nick and Juan, telling you of the beatings they received from the hands—*and feet!*—of the police. On the other—the police! You have seen them! You know their code! *Ssswoooorn* to uphold the rights of the people, the guarantees of the constitution. You saw their demeanor here in this courtroom. You saw their endeavor to cover up for each other. Policemen are only human. They think in certain channels. They are as prone—more prone—to make mistakes than others. You saw and heard them from that stand: 'I don't remember!'—'I don't know!' These are police officers! These are men who have sworn to uphold the law! —And they're supposed to be impartial!... Third degree?... Ask Nick and Juan—ask Nellie! ... Beatings?... Ask Juan! Ask Nick! Look at the photographs of Nick! They beat Nick for two or three days—but they got no confession—for he had nothing to confess! That didn't stop them from beating him, kicking him, knocking him senseless several times, stripping his clothes off and twisting his testicles!"

Kerman was up shouting, "He's trying to indict me and the whole police department!"

"No—not the *whole* police department—but I *do* indict counsel for prosecution and every witness who has testified for the prosecution—charging either perjury or subornation!"

Judge Drake said nothing.

Morton swung back to the jury. "On the one side," he said, "Nick Romano. On the other the"—he motioned his hand—"the coyote and all his aides. Nowhere are all the corrupt and ugly human elements more vividly on display than in this case—greed, lust for power, dishonesty, ambition of the vilest sort, bigotry, political advancement, the desire to pin the crime on the accused person —*regardless!* A conviction is a personal victory for the prosecuting attorney. Evidence is manufactured as you well know. You heard Nick testify that Kerman offered him life if he would make an untrue confession of guilt or else—*that he would burn!* These are the—" Morton bowed mockingly, "upholders of the people's rights, protectors, guardians!"

Morton stood silent in the courtroom. Defiant. Questioning. Challenging. The minute hand edged a notch. Morton's voice returned to the jury, low, slow. "... Who is Nick Romano?" He motioned toward Nick. "This boy at the table here?" He frowned. "We first meet him on a dirty, rainy, foggy night. All of his life has been a dirty, murky, rainy, foggy night.... I don't know what evil star was in its ascendancy when Nick Romano was born but I know that its

[449]

baleful glare has beaten down upon him for twenty-one years of his young life. There was never any happiness in this boy's life nor was there even any tinge of happiness unless it was when he was serving God at the altar.... Let's get out of the fog and the rain of contradictory evidence... let's get out of the fog and rain of the night of November 7th—let us go over these ten years with Nick and follow the dark shadowings to the bar of this courtroom where he stands charged with murder ... the police, the newspapers and the Attorney's Office have put the finger on Nick ... when and where do we put the finger on him—on the *real* Nick Romano?"

Morton waited a moment; and the courtroom waited. "Is it the boy who sits here in this courtroom?" Morton asked, shaking his head no. "Is he the handsome hoodlum Pretty Boy, leering and scornful, that the newspapers depict?"—shaking his head no. "Is he the boy who walked into this courtroom every day of the trial smiling, showing the people he knows he can take it?"—shaking his head no. "Is he the boy driven insane by the taunts of Kerman?" —shaking his head no. "Let's go back to his home and look for Nick Romano...."

Ang held one hand with a handkerchief in it over her eyes; her face was down in the collar of her coat, her other hand was in Abe's. Ma Romano's lips and arms and legs and shoulders trembled, shaking with dry tears. Julian had his head bent with his fingers up against his forehead. Aunt Rosa wept quietly. Grant leaned slightly toward Nick and stared at Morton's back and head. Owen had his head down, his fingers clutched together in his lap. Juan and Sunshine and Butch and Stash sat tense, hurt, scared. Lottie's make-up ran down her cheeks with her tears, the long knife or razor scar shiny across one cheek. Nellie sat forward on her bench, her eyes staring and wet. The Kid got up and walked out of the courtroom, down the steps, out of the building. A murder case patron flopped down in his vacant place and stared with open mouth, with wild, excited eyes at the drama up in front of the courtroom.

"... to his home and look for Nick Romano.... Come with me to the altar of God with this boy, Nick Romano, aged twelve. The church is dim-lit. Incense moves upward ... let us kneel and pray with this boy, Nick. Let us think with him and feel with him.... This young man you see sitting at the counsel table—waiting—men and women—your pleasure—is the same boy, grown older." Morton paused, smiling slightly and sadly. "In the Catholic Mass there is a line which the altar boy says during his service—'*Et introibo ad altare Dei: ad Deum qui laetificat juventutem meam.*' This same Nick Romano you see before you said this line over and over, morning after morning while he was an altar boy— 'And I go unto the altar of God: to God who giveth joy to my youth....' " Morton shook his head no, slowly. "There was no joy in Nick's youth." Morton paused a moment, then went on; "Let's follow the years.... We might say Nick is guilty—he is guilty of having been reared in desperate poverty in the slums of a big city. He is guilty of having had the wrong environment and the wrong companions. He is guilty of the poolrooms and the taverns whose doors were open to him from the time he was fifteen. He is guilty of learning about sex on street corners from older boys and behind school buildings from older girls. He is guilty of learning police procedure by having been picked up and beaten by the police whenever they chose. He is guilty of the foul treatment of a reform school." Morton frowned. "Come inside the beautiful walls of the reform school with me, where he was incarcerated long months, where he was stripped of his clothes and beaten, where he obeyed a gangster rule—ate, worked, slept, rose, lived by whistles! and curses! and fists! Come with us to the assembly hall where all the boys of the reform school were crowded by their masters to watch the rehabilitation of juvenile delinquency by the end of a leather strap. See, with us, the whip of these—men, they call themselves—as they administer their form of police rule. Hear the curses of the keepers in *your* eardrums. Feel the lash of the whip in *your* flesh. Leave, like Nick, without illusions as to how we reform our youth! That's where we stripped his altar boy garments from him! But—we're not through with him yet! ... Come with us along Maxwell Street where the fences buy anything from a boy—no questions asked. Listen, with him, to the thieves. Look, with him, at the corner prostitutes. Come into the alleys and on the street corners under lampposts where, by older boys, he was taught to shoot craps. Season yourself a year on these streets, then come with us under the neon beer signs past the drunks, past panhandlers, in through the doors of the poolrooms. Sit on a bench and listen to the talk—listen to the jackrollers and thieves. Listen and absorb some of their thinking. Be accepted as an equal by these men and young men. At home, a father who does not understand and who, with a stick or a club, chases you out into the streets. Walk with Nick along West Madison at night when the beat cop comes swaggering down the street. Feel his hand on your shoulder and go with Nick to the police station. Stay two nights in jail for no other reason than that you were walking on the street. Be slapped!—punched!—kicked!—if you so much as answer—*the law!*—back. Be taken to the police line up where people who have been robbed come to point out the alleged robbers. Make the showup, fear the bum fingers anyone can place on you. And ... if you are not fingered—walk out free. As Nick, leave without illusions...."

Morton shoved his hands roughly into his pockets. He frowned at the jury. "Come with him into the adolescent home, the jail. Be garbed in prison clothes. Be numbered! and counted! and hated! And—like Nick—leave without illusions.... Come into this courtroom with us, to stand facing your accusers and your judges. And ...await finally...the decision...the verdict...of your fellow men. If that verdict is death, go with us to the death cell where there is nothing but cold and fear and the moon sifting through the bars at night. Writhe there in fear and pain. Walk to the electric chair with us. Feel the current surge through your blood and your nerves and your heart and your brain with us. Send him out of a dirty, murky life *without illusions*. Send him to a criminal's grave if you dare!"

Then, standing erect—looking straight into the jury box—Morton said, "Nick Romano was murdered seven years ago! I so charge! I accuse—Society!—of the murder of Nick Romano! And I tell you, too, to leave without illusions...." He went on slowly. "Society... you and I ... all of us ... we ... the *good* people!—murdered!—Nick Romano! Why is he here before us? *We ordered him here!* We brutalized and murdered him and we made this rendezvous with him seven years ago..."

And now he said, very emphatically, very slowly, "Nick Romano is any boy anywhere in the world conditioned and influenced as he has been conditioned and influenced. He is your son or brother or mine. We are, all of us, the result of everything that has happened to us and that surrounds us. As Clarence Darrow said, *Before any progress can be made in dealing with crime the world must fully realize that crime is only a part of conduct, that each act, criminal or otherwise, follows a cause; that given the same conditions the same results will follow forever and ever...anyone can reason from cause to effect and know that the crimes of children are really the crimes of the State and Society, which by neglect and active participation have made the individual what he is...."*

Very slowly Morton stood erect. "I say that my client is innocent. Your only duty is to consider whether or not the State has *proved* beyond a reasonable doubt that he—and no one else—caused the death of Dennis Riley. Before God—I submit that it hasn't been proved....

"You know what we—Society—have done to this boy here at the counsel table. Let us pay to Nick what we have never paid him. Let us give him the chance he has never had. It is within our power in this courtroom to do that. To execute an innocent boy would not benefit the State. It will not bring back Dennis Riley. But if your hearts are sympathetic and you want to express that human instinct —carry with you a picture of that toil-worn, sad-eyed woman who sits on the first bench—" Morton nodded toward Ma Romano. "She doesn't believe her boy guilty. But Society takes its revenge on the mothers and families of the men it kills. The man dies. They live on.

"Give him back to the mother who bore him. He's only twenty-one. Give him the opportunity to become the man that woman hoped he would. . . ."

Morton walked slowly backwards from the bar, looking at the jury and talking straight into them. "Give him back to his mother—" His hand touched the counsel table. "To the brother and sister who love him—" He moved around the counsel table and stood behind Nick's chair. "To the aunt who has endeavored to buoy him by her presence throughout the trial." He paused a moment, then went on, "Give him back to those who love him." Morton stood directly behind Nick. He put his hands on the back of Nick's chair and leaned over a little, looking at the jury.

Nick's head was bent. His shoulders were slumped. He stared at his hands. There was no playing to the jury or the crowd now. His face was no longer hard-boiled. The jury saw nothing there but the tumble of black hair over his forehead, his lips pressed in a line, the slightest movement of a quiver at one end of them, sunlight touching the edge of his jaw. And in Nick was a horrible and consuming shame. He was ashamed of himself and his whole life.

Morton looked over the back of the chair and over Nick's bowed head. Morton's deep-set eyes looked into the jury box. "Look at this young man," he said. "Nick Romano, twenty-one years old, is here before you charged with murder . . . look at him and long remember him—whether you find him innocent or guilty. Cut him down if you will—if you dare! Tomorrow ten Nick Romanos will spring up to take his place. A hundred. A thousand." Morton's eyes wouldn't let them go; the spectators' benches quivered and the jurors sat, fascinated. Morton said, slowly, "Nick Romano awaits your decision . . . his life is but a little thing . . . a flame . . . the flare of a matchstick against the wind of—society, newspapers, adolescent homes, reform schools, jails, courtrooms, prosecutors . . . look at him and long remember him. His life is in your hands. If you choose you can now snuff out his life. The law and the bloodletting is in your hands and on your hands. If you so choose you may send this boy to the electric chair. You may send him gasping and struggling into eternity. Should you so decide by your verdict—on the night that he goes to his death the hands of seven women and five men—*your hands*—will be shadowed over the hand that turns the current into this boy's body. Look at him and long remember him. I say he is guilty of no crime against Society. I say he is innocent. The testimony presented to you cries out that he is innocent. I and the testimony ask a verdict of—*not guilty*. I, having pleaded for him with all my heart and soul and strength, now humblv consign my client into your hands."

And Morton sat down.

86

Kerman got up from his chair and before he had quite reached the jury box he said sarcastically, "A very *pretty* and a very *untrue* speech!"

Kerman brought the bludgeon. "With the permission of the Court," he said, bowing to Judge Drake. Turning, he smiled at the jury. "And now, ladies and gentlemen of the jury, we come to the penultimate act of this trial in which you have played so great a part and upon which your verdict will settle. What that judgment will be I am sure is already written in your hearts and minds. I have been convinced from the inception of this matter that but *one* conclusion could be reached—and that would be in the rendition of your opinion that crime doesn't pay—that the wages of sin are death! I would insult your intelligence if I were to intimate for one instant that you could or would render any verdict save that of— *guilty*—as charged—with a punishment as fixed by law—*death in the electric chair!* I cannot believe that you have been beguiled by the sophistries, innuendoes and false assumptions based upon fallacious premises of the counsel for the defendant. It hardly seems necessary to review the evidence introduced after the admission—aye!—not only the admission—but the exultant *boast* of the defendant that— he—did—MURDER!—Dennis Riley. No word of regret—no plea for mercy—no extenuating circumstances were claimed by this hood-lum—"

The jurors began, one and two at a time, looking over the rail at Nick, puzzled, wondering. . . .

"When forced by the vehemence of my cross-examination he— broke away—from his—carefully—fabricated defense! . . .

"Counsel for the defense has ridiculed, insulted, maligned, slandered and traduced every witness for the prosecution in a futile endeavor to put a doubt in your minds. He has directed his venom at the police department, the prosecuting attorney and—the newspapers. Thank God for the newspapers! Our liberties rest upon a free and untrammelled press—and this city is indeed fortunate in having public-spirited citizens who control these great mediums of expression and bring to the knowledge of every member of our community the facts of everyday life. A venal press would be an excrescence upon the body politic—but a *pure—loyal—unafraid* press is the strongest aid that the law enforcement agencies of the country possess in their fight against crime and vice. The public press needs no encomiums from me but I would be neglectful of the aid given us by these honest, straightforward, public-spirited organs of safety if I failed to publicly acknowledge the debt society—owes—them."

Kerman turned his head and scowled at Nick. "Counsel for the sometimes leering and diabolically-grinning—and at other times innocent, acolytish, modest, and smiling Pretty Boy—tells you that the prosecution's witnesses should not be believed. I refer you to Pretty Boy, baby-faced, handsomely combed and clothed Nick Romano himself! You have heard him *shout* from the stand that he killed Riley. Believe *him*—and believe me when I tell you that he told the *truth* from the stand...."

On her front bench Ma Romano suffered. In the jury box the twelve weighed Kerman's words. In his chair Nick sat tense, with his head down, eyes staring at his belt buckle. On his high place Judge Drake looked asleep.

"Use your common sense, ladies and gentlemen, and ask yourselves—would any of you have been found at the location of the murder shortly after midnight? Who but the panhandlers, the jackrollers, the strong-arm men, the vagrants, the denizens of Skid Row —*could* have seen this handsome slayer emerge from the alley after throwing the murder gun in the face of his victim?

"Mr. Ringolsky and Mr. Zinski were—as they admitted—victims of economic conditions and had paid the penalty of their poverty by being incarcerated. But remember this—neither of them evinced any feeling of animosity toward the defendant—the Pretty Boy"—Kerman pointed at Nick with his red pencil, jabbing—"who had been their associate and pal for at least five years prior to the commission of this murder. Every word of testimony extracted from Mr. Ringolsky was reluctantly surrendered. To me there was something of patriotism, of decency, of manhood in Mr. Ringolsky's attitude as with low voice he admitted seeing Baby Face Romano"—again he pointed at Nick with his red pencil—"leave the alley a few seconds after the sound of the final shot brought him to the scene of the crime." Kerman jerked his shoulders angrily and folded his arms.

His muddy eyes, behind the glasses, flashed back and forth over the faces of the jurors.

"Mr. Morton has paid particular attention to the fact that the State supplied Mr. Ringolsky with clothing so that he might make a not unfavorable impression in this courtroom. I erred there—but —it was an error of the mind and not of the heart. There was no attempt on my part to dress the witness so that he might influence, by his sartorial presence, minds which could not be convinced by his sworn testimony. I digress for a moment—you will permit me to mention the fact that silken-hosed, oxford-wearing Pretty Boy—has —appeared before you in at least *three* complete changes of raiment during this trial. *Who supplied them?* They weren't in his possession when he was apprehended running over housetops in an attempt to elude the police! What kindly angel dropped within his cell these garments along with Mr. Morton, ace in the trade of springing crooks, criminals, and murderers! *Who supplied the money?*— Because a look at the garments will convince you that they were *bought*— not on West Madison nor in the subterranean basements of Maxwell Street...."

Kerman leaned against the bar and put the wrist of one arm over his fat-reared coat. "No man who appeared in this action was more bitterly arraigned nor more vituperatively abused than was Mr. Zinski. Much eloquence was displayed—all, I'm sure, was wasted effort, as far as you ladies and gentlemen are concerned—in an attempt to prove that Squint—as he described himself—was paid for his testimony. With the agility that has made counsel for the defendant— *the Ace!*—of all advocates for murderers—Mr. Morton sought to convince you that the witness was activated by greed for a share, if not all, of the reward to be paid for the conviction and execution of this defendant. He would have you believe that the so-called honorarium paid him each week was paid solely for perjured testimony. It—is— not—true. The devil must be fought with fire. And it is common practice of law-enforcing agencies to either keep in seclusion or keep free from want—material witnesses whose testimony is needful in any cause. SO! While admitting that Mr. Ringolsky was supplied with clothing and Mr. Zinski permitted to live free from the attacks which might have been precipitated by the hoodlums of the Romano clique, we openly admit—the truth—of the testimony and make no apology for what we have done, believing, as we believe *you will believe,* that the interests of the State were best served by our conduct. The testimony of these witnesses is—ah—substantiated by that of Bailey—against whom—" and Kerman emphatically shook his head no, "no police records could be introduced. So he stands before you as a reputable business man—and his testimony—*unchallenged!* ... But there is another witness upon whose testimony I

[456]

depended for some corroboration, and that—you recall—was—" Kerman's lips lifted angrily; the mustache porcupined. "The *yellow-skinned,* shifty-eyed, pasty-faced—Mexican, Juan Rodriguez! The *only* thing that this individual seemed ab-so-lute-ly sure of was that he didn't remember! You may ask—why I didn't call the officers to whom he had said that he had seen Romano in the alley. Unfortunately our law, which throws—*every imaginable*—safeguard around a defendant, forbade my calling—any—witness—to impeach him whom I had put on the stand."

Morton was standing. He said calmly, "If it please the Court, I am compelled to express disapproval of counsel's shyster-like methods—I ask your Honor to instruct the jury to disregard all reference to what his witness is alleged by him to have told the police because there is no evidence in support of it."

"Sustained."

Angry, Kerman's voice again shouted in the courtroom, "You ladies and gentlemen know that anything of value must be paid for by influence, by money, by services, by information—and in multitudinous ways. ... *Do not forget* that much money has been spent on behalf of the defendant. You don't get a man of Mr. Morton's cunning ability and springing powers for peanuts! Every man and woman on this jury knows the reputation of the eminent counsel who has so vehemently conducted this defense—and—while I am not able to tell you what remuneration has gone to him, I think it no exaggeration to say that his fee in this case is more than I receive for *one year* of vigilant service in defense of the rights of the people of this state. *In one year* I have sent to the penitentiary twenty-nine felons—and your verdict, when it is returned, will give me a record of thirty cases. *Let no guilty man escape* has been my motto since, at great personal sacrifice, I acceded to the request of the government and took this office. That I have done well is admitted by my associates, my friends, and even my detractors. It isn't egotism that prompts me to unroll this scroll that attests my services to our state —it is simply a desire to convince you that unless I *believed* in the guilt of the defendant I had rather my tongue be silenced, my voice stilled forever in order that no injustice should be perpetrated by me. But *I do* believe in his guilt! I believe in it just as I believe in the honor of my profession, the sacredness of the law, and the vindication of eternal justice. I believe in it as I believe in your hearts *you know!* that there can be—not a scintilla of doubt that—*he—Pretty Boy, Baby Face Romano*—is a—*mur-der-er!*"

Nick sat with his head leaned against the back of his chair, his eyes fixed on the ceiling.

Kerman stood at the rail of the jury box, gesticulating with his pencil like a man swinging an axe. "Counsel for the defendant violated *every* element of courtesy and clean practice when he applied to me the epithet of a"—his voice quivered with anger—"scavenger. Unfair, unjust, untrue—but here, in your presence, and before Almight-y God—I thank my stars that no organized bunch of gangsters, hoodlums and thieves, before starting on a job, has ever drunk to *my* health as they have to the continued good luck of their mouthpiece—*meaning*—that should justice overtake them in their nefarious schemes they may depend upon the ingenuity, the resourcefulness, and the hypnotic powers of the polished—urbane—sophisticated manipulator of passion and prejudice—*Andrew Morton!*"

Morton's name bounced off the wall and Kerman cleared his throat. Kerman now carried his thumbs under his armpits. He leaned forward over the jury rail and went on, "The gentleman has large, luxurious offices, well staffed with alert and cunning investigators and servants and his home on the Gold Coast is one of the show places of Chicago. These things—ladies and gentlemen—cost money! And let nobody tell Andrew Morton that crime doesn't pay! . . . Lest someone may conclude that I accuse counsel of participating in the overt acts of his clients I want to make it plain that I do not mean that he actually participated in the commission of the outrages but—*I do mean*—that he has shared in the profits from these damnable excursions of the underworld . . . !"

Kerman poured his poison into the courtroom:

"Mr. Morton has spent much time—in parading for your benefit that distinguished author, Gold Coast resident, opera lover and socialite—and—*with it all*—radical and denizen of West Madison Street, associate of bums, panhandlers, degenerates and all-around thieves—Grant Holloway. He is *smooth and slick* as the phrases he uses in his pernicious writings. This witness—this Jekyll and Hyde—Holloway—sought to make an alibi with the aid of Sunshine and Butch for their partner and pal—the Pretty Boy! But after all was said and done—to what did Holloway's testimony amount? *Recall*—that he left the Cobra Tap at precisely twelve o'clock—*but!*—there is no intimation that he knew anything of Romano's movements after that. . . . *Why* this devotion on the part of this socialite for this *scum* of the *streets*? What actuated him? How was he paid? Nothing has been said to indicate that Holloway sought to rescue this fallen man—on the contrary, he seems to have found pleasure in his association with Romano and his vicious clique—a kick lacking in his soft life as a parlor pink! The witness put on the stand to aid the defense never helped Pretty Boy but even accelerated his progress down the path of crime!"

Nick lifted his head off the back of his chair and glared at Kerman. Through clenched teeth he whispered, "Why, you sonofabitch!"

Wielding his red pencil Kerman went on in harsh, shouting tones. "Let me digress for a moment so that I may explain to your satisfaction—*why*—I did not bother to contradict the testimony of Juan the Mex and Baby Face as to their treatment by the police. It was too inconsequential, too unimportant, too patently untrue for me to take cognizance of it. For twenty years Captain McGillicuddy has served the City of Chicago and there is not a man or woman—*here* —who would believe the damnable, *slanderous*—perjured!—allegations of these ex-jailbirds! After all, who is on trial here? This ruthless killer or Captain McGillicuddy, a man delegated to defend the security of all of us, even the defense counsel?"

Kerman mopped himself, even his hands and his wrists, and took a swallow of water. "Now, there is one more! And here—I must—make mention—of the testimony of that unfortunate girl whom Morton has lauded as a combination of the Blessed Virgin, Joan of Arc—and—ah—ah—the purified angels! She testified that I had her picked up, kept in the police station overnight, and brought to my office, where I endeavored to procure an admission from her as to the whereabouts of Pretty Boy the night of the killing. *She* was shown to you—as a pooooooor—broken-winged bird—without even a nest where she might withdraw and weep over the sorrow that enveloped her because her lover had—murdered—a man. Courtesy to a female—no matter how low—depraved—she may be, has been a guidepost to me through life—but here—I am constrained to say that *every word* of this unfortunate woman's testimony—so far as it applies to me—was a *lie!*"

Kerman pounded his fist against the bar. His tone became more violent. "More than twelve thousand murders are committed in the United States every year! There are 150,000 murderers at large in this country today! There is a crime committed every twenty-two seconds! There is a murder every forty minutes!" BANG! BANG! BANG! Kerman's fist thundered on the jury rail. "The fate of this one murderer is of small importance. The protection of our city and our decent, upright citizens is paramount in this trial and in every murder trial! Nick Romano is a menace to Society! He must be done away with as you would have a mad dog disposed of!—without sympathy! Only the"—Kerman half-turned toward Morton— "pseudo-sociologist, the sentimentalist, and the—paid benefactors of crime argue otherwise—"

Ma Romano sat on her bench with a handkerchief held to her mouth. Her fingers, moving all the time, moved the handkerchief, slowly, agitatedly, almost as if she were trying to wipe the skin from her face.

"Counsel for the defense has cried to you about his poooooor client. Counsel for the defense would have you believe that he is a poor unfortunate boy, victim of his environment. Counsel for the defense *blames you!—blames Society!*—for the acts of this fiend! AND!—he has the effrontery, the unmitigated gall to dare you!—*dare you!*—to keep your sworn and sacred oath! Counsel for the defense asks you to kiss Pretty Boy and send him off to kill again! If you acquit this murderer because of the foxy tactics of the ace defender of murderers—then—you might as well tear down your churches—burn your schoolhouses—destroy your orphan asylums and hospitals *and*—let each man and woman arm himself or herself in defense of life, property and chastity because—by your verdict you will have sown the seeds of *anarchy!*

"He is a cold-blooded murderer! *He—must—die!* To indulge in sentiment at this time, to let pity for this vicious murderer sway you from your obligation and your oath would be a breach of faith with the people of our state. . . . Our splendid police force must be vindicated! Society must be rid of Romano's kind! Until then none of us is safe! *He must die!*" Kerman stopped and wiped his face again, then went on, "There is little more to be said in conclusion—but I wish that now I had the power such as that possessed by the witch of Endor when she called from the grave the spirit of Samuel to tell his son Saul what the morrow held. I could wish that from out of the little God's acre where Dennis Riley's bones lie mouldering I could call his spirit into this courtroom and he would say to you—as a pure soul—permitted to return to earth to aid God's messenger—Justice—*pointing a finger!*—at the defendant—he would say —'HE!—NICK ROMANO!—MURDERED ME!—May God forgive him.' . . . I wish that you could look into the Riley home night after night and see those fatherless children gathered around their mother in an attempt to console her who bore his offspring. . . . Morton has asked you—to think of Nick Romano's mother and family, but now —I ask you—did the Pretty Boy think of Riley's? . . . Mercy is a wonder-ful attribute of human nature—a godlike gift—to us all. But"—Kerman shook his head no, slowly—"if it ever lodged in this murderer's heart it was suffocated by the vileness that has characterized all his life. . . ."

Nick sat in his chair at the counsel table staring at the ceiling. His mouth was slightly open and he breathed hard to ease the fearful pounding of his heart, scared, scared, staring at the ceiling with his head against the back of the chair.

"He'd do it all over again," Kerman said in an ominous whisper. Then his voice came back to shouting tones, "Free him and we will be back here trying him for murder in less than a year! He *has had* his chance! Society tried *innumerable* times to reform him. He is beyond reform, beyond hope. Four times in institutions, only to come out and murder! These—are the unmistakable facts!

[460]

"And"—Kerman turned, pointing at Nick—"Nick Romano, *this* handsome, *this* innocent-looking young man stood in the alley and pumped *five bullets* into the body of Officer Dennis Riley! A cold-blooded killer!" Kerman's fist pounded the railing. "Send him to the chair! He does not deserve to live! A cold-blooded killer!"

Kerman halted, stood silent a moment, looking from juror to juror, his ugly face dead-serious. Then he spoke slowly, deliberately, his words like bludgeons, "Our city is a great one. Let us keep it so. . . . *Don't* permit yourselves to be swayed by the maunderings of this paid defender! *Don't* tell the inhabitants of the badlands of Chicago they can go unrestricted and unrestrained in their excursions against decency! *Don't* let them destroy our institutions! *Don't* let them annihilate our schools and churches! But—let us go on as for many years we have done—maintaining a respect for law, liberty and life. Let your verdict be such that this proud state may hold high her head in the sisterhood of states and declare that *decent* men and glorious women have said to the world—that the days of gangsterism, the days of Capone, and the days of Romano— *have ended!* I thank you."

87

A dead silence struck the courtroom. The ornamental clock hand quivered, moved a notch. The jury stared over the rail at Nick, Morton, Kerman—then up at Judge Drake. The faces of several of the jurors drained of color; all of them sat nervous, embarrassed and frightened. The case of the State versus Nick Romano was definitely in their hands.

Just beyond their box Kerman sat with his arms folded, his head up stiffly, a slight, tight-lipped smile twisting under the mustache. Across the table Morton sat with his face in the shadow of his hand. Nick took his eyes from the ceiling. He dragged his head up off the back of the chair. His tongue, trying to swallow, was dry against the roof of his mouth. He turned, looking nervously out at the spectators and knew all over again what it was like to be stared at.

White pulpy faces. Eyes pressing in on him, closer, closer; hard, like a wall moving forward to crush. Nick's glance trembled in the glassy, forward-pressing eyes of the murder trial patrons. The fear and the panic choked in his throat.

I'm Nick and I want to live!

He lowered his head quickly. He saw the form of one of the bailiffs assigned to him on the chair next to his. Nick looked up at the bailiff with a smiling mask of a face. "Two to one they get me—bet you a pack of cigarettes I get the chair." He said it fast to cover up the quiver in his voice and the tremble on his lips. A reporter heard.

Judge Drake stood up. He held a sheaf of papers and began reading....

"...The defendant, Nicholas Romano, is charged, as in the indictment, with force of arms, premeditatedly and with malice aforethought.... If you find from the evidence beyond reasonable doubt that the defendant is guilty...."

Sheet three was laid down. Sheet four.

"...You may return but one of four verdicts in this case: guilty as charged, guilty with a recommendation of mercy, guilty of manslaughter, or not guilty...."

Judge Drake's voice droned on, monotonously, reading the instructions to the jury. Nick turned toward Morton and made a slow gesture with his hand. "Thanks, Mr. Morton...," he said. "Thanks...." His voice trembled.

Judge Drake laid down the last sheet. He smiled dryly and said to the jury, "You may now retire to deliberate upon your verdict." The jurors began standing; their swivel chairs made noises under them. They were all standing, now, staring, solemnly over the rail at Nick.

Nick's face began to lose color.

I want to live! I want to live!

But he forced a smile.

The ornate clock hand moved a notch. A man and woman bailiff moved, guardian-like, to the jury box. The third act had come. The trial had reached its closing scene, the dramatic climax, the all-important act played behind the curtain, behind a locked door. The jury had been swayed back and forth. Society was ready, now, to go heroically to work with Nick's twelve peers—the ladies and gentlemen of the jury. The jurors filed out. In their chambers the jurors began arranging themselves in a group around the long, brown-topped table.

ROMANO CASE GOES TO JURY

In the jury room Foreman Joseph Burke stood at the head of the juror's counsel table. Foreman Joseph Burke, who had read all

[462]

about the case in the papers months ago, who had had a fixed opinion half a year ago, said, "Well, let's take a vote right away before any discussions and see where we stand."

Pencils went around the table. Little slips of paper went around the table. The twelve men and women, having been jerked from obscurity into the limelight of a murder trial, pulled the blank slips of paper in front of them. They leaned over the slips of paper, godlike, to fix the fate of a fellow man. The pencils began writing—*Guilty—Guilty—Guilty. . . .*

Foreman Joseph Burke carefully counted the votes. He stood up, cleared his throat, and said slowly, "We have seven for guilty and five for acquittal."

The jurors avoided each other's eyes. Burke sat down. "Let's open the discussions," he said, glancing around at them.

The truck driver leaned back in his chair. "The prosecution hasn't proved his guilt," he said. "You know what the judge said about reasonable doubt—and the State's testimony stunk! I think it's a frame-up."

"What about the confession?" Burke asked, cutting in abruptly.

"Don't you think," said the Jewish girl, "that he could have been driven to it by Kerman's questions about his wife?"

"Temporary insanity," said the social worker, looking around the table with deep eyes in a pale face, "could easily have been—"

"'But his record's bad. What about reform schools and that jail sentence? He's guilty all right." This was Bennett, who owned a shoeshop, was a good Christian and a good citizen.

"Look here—" the truck driver began.

"Well, let's look at it this way—" said one of the housewives, the one with the boy Nick's age. "Ever since he was nothing but a boy he's been a criminal and none of *our* children would have done the things he did. I know my boy wouldn't!"

And another housewife, "I think he's guilty too—but I wouldn't give him the chair. Life in prison would be better and we—"

"I think—" said the blonde.

In the courtroom Nick's family, Nick's few friends waited on the hard benches. In the hallway the spectators waited hungrily. In the press room the gentlemen of the press laughed and cursed, drank, stacked their winnings in front of them, tossed the cards out around the table—waiting for the story.

In the lockup . . . Nick . . . head down . . . alone . . . .

TOUGH GUY ROMANO BETS
PACK OF CIGARETTES
HE'LL GET CHAIR

JURY ROOM. They took another ballot.

7 to 5. The old lady. The blonde. The Jewish girl. The social worker. The truck driver.

PRESS ROOM. "How long they been out? ... Christ! Almost three hours. ... What have they got to argue about? ... Why the hell don't they bring back a verdict? ... Keep your pants on! ... They better bring it back my way, I got my story written up already.... Keep your pants on! —He ain't going to cheat the chair."

JURY ROOM. They were weary and angry and worn out. Mrs. Flint was tired and had a headache and was wondering what the kids were doing and wanted to go home. Paul Majewski, father of a newborn baby, began worrying about his wife. Irene Stewart, touching her blonde curls that were getting a little dark at the roots, began worrying about her beauty shop and the efficiency and honesty of the girl she had left in charge. Margaret Hoffman, the social worker, was quiet and pale. Old Mrs. Green said aloud, "I prayed every night that I might see the truth and not do any injustice to him." Her voice had an emotional quiver. And Rachel Goldberg ... no! ... no! ... no!

"Let's take another ballot," Burke said. White slips again went around the table. Eyes looked at each other, looked away, embarrassed and ashamed. Old Mrs. Green reached slowly for hers. As she reached, her crucifix on the thin gold chain dangled close to the top of the table. Mrs. Green, mother and grandmother, said, "I'm going to change my vote to guilty." Mrs. Green, Christian, follower of the gentle Christ, hesitated—then, writing slowly in her small, precise hand, marked her ballot guilty. Foreman Burke counted the score again.

Nine guilty. Three innocent.

10:22. Judge Drake had gone home to bed.

JURY ROOM. The white slips went around again. The Jewish girl ... no! ... no! ... no! Her pencil wrote—*guilty*.

Down to two. The social worker. The truck driver.

The debate began again. Pressure was on the social worker and the truck driver. All the pressure of these ten upright and honest citizens—all the pressure of Society. The social worker was quietest now, but clung to her verdict. The weary faces, the tired eyes and the impatient voices quarreled and fumed in the night jury room.

In the lockup Nick on the side of the iron bunk, hands hung loosely between his knees, eyes staring through the concrete floor. His long shadow in a long diagonal across the floor. The vertical bars standing stiff and black all around him. Nick in the center of them like an animal caged, his anger, his hate worn out. His fight dried up. His impotence numb. Silhouette in the silhouette of bars.

[464]

Shadow in the shadow of night. Stone on the iron bunk . . . stone in the beautifully heaped stones of the court building. Numb.

JURY ROOM. Her face was very pale. She looked at the foreman of the jury. She opened her lips to speak. She closed them. She dampened her lips. "I am going to"—*the unfit, those who are useless and to themselves and to Society, should be eliminated*— "vote guilty," she said, tonelessly, giving in. And her thoughts crashed around her . . . *into your hands! . . . into your hands!*

COURTROOM. On the second bench the family sat, keeping their miserable watch. The scrubwomen came. They washed down one side of the courtroom and dusted the benches, moving quietly, almost like part of the night and the fear. They finished. They moved to the other side of the courtroom with their pails and their rags. One of them said, not unkindly, to Ma and the family, "Will you please sit on the other side?"

JURY ROOM. They stared at him angrily. "Let's take another vote," the foreman said surlily.

"What for! Why go through with all that?" the truck driver snapped.

"Say! What's the matter with you?" the foreman bellowed.

Erickson looked around at all of them. Their eyes were very angry with him. Everybody wanted to go home. For a moment he hesitated . . . *all of them are better educated than me. They listened to the testimony just as hard as I did . . . they know more than me . . .* his hesitation was a long one. Erickson swung his face and shoulders around at Burke. He apologized first. "Excuse me, ladies—" And to Burke, "Goddamn it, I don't know if he's guilty or not! I don't think he is and if he is I think he had every reason for killing Riley. I ain't going to vote guilty if I have to stay here till hell freezes over!"

ROMANO JURY LOCKED UP
OVERNIGHT; NO VERDICT YET

The sun came. The crowd came. Ma Romano trudged to early morning Mass, then moved fearfully to the courtroom. The crowd was larger than it had yet been. At ten there was no verdict. At eleven the jury hadn't come back. They started a new game in the press room.

JURY ROOM. "Let's agree on twenty years," said the Jewish girl tonelessly.

"Yes," said the social worker.

But Mrs. Jensen, housewife and mother, "I think he deserves the chair—I'm for the chair."

And Bennett, the shoemaker, piously, "No, let's give him life. I know I'd rather get the chair than life!"

The truck driver's voice, loud and angry, "I ain't budging. I'm for acquittal."

···

Grant stood at the tall windows in the hallway outside Judge Drake's courtroom. He stared through the pane. To the west a maze of factory buildings, brute-wide, giant-tall, stretched east. Beyond the pile of factories, below the slowly spiraling smoke—shacks, tenement buildings, crumbling little slum houses. Nick's neighborhood. Ugly, vile, vicious. River, shamed, creeping away from Nick's neighborhood. Look around. A Nick in every block . . . in every third house. Furniture set out on the street . . . gas turned off . . . electric bill overdue . . . politician buying votes . . . police taking bribes . . . beating in heads, making the law . . . greatest percentage of relief, prostitution, unwed mothers, criminality, syphilis, juvenile delinquency, poverty . . . right here, in this pockmark, this hollow, this district . . . man with a gun, boy with a gun.

···

JURY ROOM. Foreman Joseph Burke rapped on the door to signal that a verdict had been reached.

LOCKUP. Nick lay on the iron web of bunk, face down, with his arms stretched up over his head. His fingers were fastened together, twisting, cracking his knuckles.

I can take it . . . whatever they dish out.

Pop!

His knuckles cracked.

I can take it.

They came for him. He heard the key grate in the lock. He sat up, mechanically, with his hands over his face, his lips quivering behind his trembling fingers. A slow, hard, forced smile began to widen his lips.

"Come on, Romano."

Nick stood up as if something beyond himself demanded it. His knees shook under him. He swallowed. Then he grinned. And something outside himself seemed to flood him with a borrowed calmness. "Okay!" he said cockily. He grinned. His feet carried him mechanically toward the waiting bailiffs. Walking—toward it—hearing it—whatever it was—getting it over.

Like a part in a play. This ain't me walking out there to hear—to hear— Just like a part in a play. This is the big scene. I can take it!

"Well, Levant," he asked one of the bailiffs, laughing, "am I going to win my bet?"

And—into the hall—into the anteroom—the leather door facing him—through it—

He moved forward to . . . whatever. . . .

The jurors looked over the rail of the jury box at him, solemn-eyed. He walked, head up, lips twisted in a smile, to the counsel table and sat down in the chair between Grant and Morton.

The cast was complete.

Society was prepared to go heroically to work with its verdict handed down by its prisoner's twelve peers.

Nick looked at the jury from the deep leather of his chair. The smile faded from his lips, leaving them loose. He felt himself fold away from bravado. But he twisted his head and his shoulders and over the back of his chair said to one of his attending bailiffs, casually, "It looks like I win our bet."

Judge Drake leaned over his rostrum. "Have you reached a verdict, ladies and gentlemen?"

"We have," Foreman Burke said, standing.

Grant and Morton leaned forward over the counsel table. They stared at the jury. Nick stared too. His eyes followed the sealed envelope containing the verdict, from the foreman's hand to the hand of the court clerk.

Judge Drake said, "The defendant will rise and face the jury."

Curtain call.

Nick swallowed. He dragged himself to his feet slowly. No smile. Lips loose. Eyes deep. A muscle twitched in his cheek, kept twitching. Each time he breathed his nostrils enlarged and began to quiver. But to the spectators he appeared as nerveless as he had been, save for that one moment, all during the trial.

Nick stood, prisoner at the bar, waiting to hear the verdict.

His eyes saw the court clerk break the seal, unloosen the signed verdict from the envelope.

And the clerk, reading—

"We—the jury—"

Grant gazed intently at the top of the shiny table.

"impaneled and sworn—"

Morton put his hand over his forehead, shielding his eyes.

"in the above entitled cause—"

Owen closed his eyes.

"do upon our oaths—"

Ma had her palms up over her face.

"find the defendant—Nicholas Romano—"

The courtroom waited, absolutely silent, with the voice solemnly reading the verdict.

"guilty as charged—"

The sobs were Ma Romano's.

"and sentence him to . . . death in the electric chair."

The scream was Ma Romano's.

Electric chair!

[467]

The thrill went across the crowd audibly. In a low chorus behind Ma's scream were the voices of the spectators, thrilling together. In the sedate courtroom flash bulbs began to burst, one
after the other, flashing like explosions. In the noisy courtroom
policemen shouted their approval of the decision to one another;
the people of Nick's neighborhood grumbled angrily and cursed
the jury.

The reporters rushed out to their telephones to get the story to
their newspapers.

In the noise Morton's voice spoke and Judge Drake's gavel
rapped. Morton asked, quietly, to have the jury polled.

Calling each member of the jury by name the clerk asked each
in turn, "Was that and is this now your verdict?"

"It was, and is," Foreman Burke said positively.

"It was, and is," said Mrs. Flint, housewife.

"It was, and is," said Rachel Goldberg, with her head down.

"It was, and is," said John Bennett, resolutely.

"It was, and is," said the blonde, uncertainly, her eyes unhappy
on Nick.

"It was, and is," said Paul Majewski, twenty-seven, and six years
Nick's senior.

"It was, and is," said Mrs. Jensen, housewife and mother, firmly.

"It was, and is," said Mrs. Jacoby, staring straight ahead.

"It was, and is," said gray-haired Mrs. Green, mother and grandmother, Christian.

"It was, and is," said Anthony Fontana, proving to the world that
he appreciated his American citizenship and believed in law and
order.

"It was . . . and is," the social worker said with tears in her eyes.

Eleven.

The truck driver left.

His face flushed; then paled. "It was . . ." he said; and he paused.
It was a long, long pause. The delicate minute hand made noise in
the silence, slipping forward a notch. "And is," said the truck
driver.

And Nick, smiling a twisted smile, sat down.

Under the smile a small voice whispered

. . . *I'm all caught up.*

His back slumped against the leather of the chair. Trembling he
turned in his seat and said to the bailiff, in an even and cocky, almost amused tone, "I win. You owe me a pack of cigarettes." The
bailiff handed him a package of cigarettes.

The flash bulbs exploded, picking him off like snipers' bullets.

Judge Drake, standing and facing the jury, said, "This has been
an arduous proceeding for you, ladies and gentlemen of the jury,

[468]

and you are now discharged from further consideration in this matter."

Morton stood at the foot of the rostrum with his head down and his hands behind him, waiting for Judge Drake to finish. He said, as the jury filed from the box, "Now will your Honor consider that the usual motions for a new trial, arrest of judgment, et cetera, are filed and that I may have two days to file the same in writing?"

"Certainly, Mr. Morton," Judge Drake said.

Very close to the rostrum stood Kerman, posing for the photographers and smiling radiantly with his mustache bristling around his lips. "Well, how does it feel to beat Morton, Mr. Kerman?" the reporters asked. "Well, that's number thirty so far this year, Mr. Kerman!"

Judge Drake said, "Court is adjourned until ten o'clock Wednesday morning." The bailiffs snapped handcuffs on Nick's wrist.

Throwing his head up Nick said defiantly, cockily, "Well, the show's over!" Then he brushed past court attendants and walked out of the courtroom, handcuffed to the bailiff.

The spectators walked out.

The courtroom was darkened.

Society, walking majestically, slow-step, firmly, unswervingly, direct as an arrow, had avenged itself. A life for a life.

PRETTY BOY ROMANO
GETS ELECTRIC CHAIR

Nick, in the lockup, leaned his head back against the bars and closed his eyes.

Live fast—

Die young—

And have a good-looking corpse.

Nick blinked his eyes wide. He stared across at the bars at the other end of the cage of bars. He opened his mouth and laughed and laughed. He laughed so loud and so hard that the veins popped out on his forehead and his jugular stood out like a pipe in his neck. He caught his breath and began laughing again. Tears ran down his cheeks. The tears weren't tears that come from hard laughing.

...

They brought Nick in to sentence him. Judge Drake stood on his rostrum looking down sadly. There was no packed courtroom today. There was just Ma Romano, Julian, Ang, Morton, Grant, Owen, a few reporters and court attendants.

The little group stood at the foot of the rostrum in a half circle. Morton and Nick stood just in front of them. Judge Drake began pronouncing the sentence.

"The jury having found you guilty as charged ... it is the judgment of this court that you be taken into custody of the sheriff in the jail of this county until September sixteenth ..."

Morton, looking at Nick, saw his face twitch and his eyes fill.

"when you shall be put to death. . . ."

A reporter's flash bulb exploded.

Nick, head up and defiant, walked swiftly from the courtroom, handcuffed to his guards.

ROMANO TO DIE SEPTEMBER 16TH

The days passed. And Nick in his cell said, Forget it. Don't think about it.

Sun was over the land, over the city, over skyscraper dome and tenement roof. Hot on the long and wide Michigan Boulevard. Hot on the grimy Halsted Street sidewalks.

And the long days passed across the silent cell, as the long thoughts passed across Nick's mind. The days were blue with clouds trailing white over the roof of the jail. And the days were of sun with sun on his stooped shoulders; the sun was warm and bright on his shoulders as he sat, stone on the edge of the iron bunk. The sun was on the toes of his shoes. The sun was a pool of brightness at his feet.

The days turned toward summer. The days turned golden through the summer. And the leaves began to show scarlet, yellow, brown at their edges. And it was September.

PRETTY BOY GETS STAY

And the leaves turned brown to their centers, began to curl in the hot sun, began to drift down from the trees, through the sunlight, through the cooling air. . . . And Morton went to Springfield to argue the case.

SUPREME COURT SAYS
PRETTY BOY MUST DIE

And the days turned golden, the days shortened imperceptibly. The sun thinned. A few leaves rattled, broken and brittle, in the gutters.

ROMANO TO DIE JANUARY 8TH!

And the chill wind blew up out of the north. The chill wind grew colder and the days grew shorter.
The days passed.
The days passed.

Grant sat before the fireplace in the dark. His elbows were on his knees. His folded knuckles were pressed against his forehead.

NO REPRIEVE; ROMANO DIES FRIDAY

Outside the windows was the lake. Outside the windows was the low singsong movement of the lake, cold and alone in the night.
Grant walked to his desk and switched on the light. He pulled writing paper out in front of him. His eyes saw a narrow oblong of paper sticking out from under the edge of a book. He picked up the blank check he had given Morton. Morton had sent it back today, writing across it: *Can't take it. I feel as badly as you do.* Slowly Grant's fingers tore the check in half, tore it again in half. He put his elbows on the desk and his fingers in his hair. He sat a long time. Then he picked up a pen.
Dear Nick, the pen wrote. *"This is to say goodbye. It is also to tell you that I don't blame you for anything. Given the same situations, I'd have done the same thing. . . .*
Words only tongue-tie you. Grant scratched lines across the sheet of paper and took another. He was conscious that he could not write the letter he wanted to write. That he wouldn't really send Nick any letter, but was talking to Nick and trying to place Nick and himself in their relation to the world. *Dear Nick,* he wrote. *It isn't hard to die. It is hard to live and know you are to blame for things being the way they are in the world, because of indifference and lack of doing something about them.* He stopped, rubbed the butt of the pen against his scalp, went on writing. *You have taught me a lot, Nick. And I won't forget you. I'll try to do some-*

[471]

thing about—the pen halted, stumbled on—*these things in the world.
Your friend, Grant.* Under the signature he wrote: *So long, pizon.*

Grant read it over. Then he put his fingers across the sheets of paper. Slowly he tore them. He got up, went to the fireplace, dropped the papers in. With one hand against the mantel he watched them catch, curl into flame.

Grant poured himself a glass of wine. He twirled the thin stem of the glass between his fingers, watching the red wine and the fire reflections swirl round in the glass. Then he drank. He refilled the glass and sat on the edge of the sofa, looking into the fireplace.

89

Seven little miserable, captured days. Only these left.

Time came, in slithers of winter sunlight, through the bars of the jail. Time is nothing. Time stands still and we move through it. Now there was no movement. He stood, frozen in time as his blood would be frozen by the lethal current; and time, the life he had known, the people he had known, moved on into space, into nothing.

Night. Sleep.

Hello, Butch.

Hello, Kid Fingers.

Hello, Squint.

Hello, Juan.

Hello, Sunshine.

Hello, Nellie.

Play "Ti-Pi-Tin."

YOU'RE IN CHICAGO NOW! YIPPEE!

Am I good-looking when I'm dead?

YOU'RE IN CHICAGO! IS EVERYBODY HAPPY?

You got to kill me first.

Don't worry, kid, we will!

FULLER! RILEY! KERMAN!

The gutter gets all of you, every drop of you.

[472]

Pa! Don't kick me, Pa! Ohhhh!—Please, Pa!

I'm Nick and I'm afraid of the darkness. I'm Nick and I want to live.

On the jail cot Nick lay with the bars in black shadows across his face as the dreams passed through him. Along the jail sentry's little aisle of bars leading past each cell with the twisted heads exposed on the bunks for him to see and count, the guard walked slowly, stooping over, clicking his flashlight on, stooping to see better his work, counting.

The light. Behind the lamp, behind the cell, behind the jail was the voice of the mob—KILL! And the guard's shadow, as he moved on, the city safe, fell across Nick's face. And in his sleep Nick's dream changed.

He was wanted for a crime he didn't commit.

■■■

It was a place where they prepared for death. A place where the warden sat in his elegant office and saw the gentlemen of the press. One, a new man, sat in the office today. The young reporter, not yet like the other reporters even in dress, had said that his name was Westbrooke, that this was his first assignment.

"I haven't had much experience," he said diffidently. "Blake told me to hop over here and learn what I could—write a story on the Romano case."

The warden smiled and lit a cigar. "I know Blake well. He's a good friend of mine. Fine reporter, too. Been in here for years. You see, the big daily papers all get two passes to the executions."

The warden was a big man. He looked as if he might have been a professional football player ten years ago. On the wall behind him and stretching all across it were rows of portraits of men, behind glass and in narrow black frames. The men stared out of the frames. The eyes were flooded with fear, or blank, or staring, or dazed. The eyes were focussed on the desk and the warden sitting there; the eyes seemed to listen to the conversation. Hollow eyes. Scared eyes. Fascinated eyes.

"Well—ah—" the new crime reporter said, "tell me something about the setup here when you electrocute a man."

"Well," the warden said, pausing and shaking his head sadly, "we don't enjoy having to electrocute a man. We try to keep the poor fellow who's going from suffering any more than he has to. We do it here in six seconds. In six seconds the current is going through him and it's all over."

The heads on the wall seemed to nod.

"We practice it beforehand, the whole routine, even to the strapping down in the chair. The chair is tested a few days before the execution and once again on the night the man is electrocuted. . . .

[473]

I make it as easy for my boys as I can." The warden leaned back in his chair and nodded toward the black framed photographs.

The eyes looked back at the warden attentively.

"When we move to the control room we take the phone down with us so that there won't be any slip-up. And we always throw the switch two or three minutes late just in case...." His head shook sadly. "It's an awful thing...." He smiled and said, "A lot of them get religion while they're here." Then the warden theorized, "I think what causes so much crime is that they don't get any religion when they're young."

"Is there a death row?" Westbrooke asked, watching sunlight make yellow stripes between the green horizontals of the Venetian blinds.

"Oh, no, we keep them with the heavy cases—high bond cases, men in on three or four robbery charges and with high bonds. It doesn't make it so hard on them that way. And we don't have any regular executioner here. There are four buttons, one being attached to the chair and the others being blank. I pick four guards. Each of them pushes a button—they never know which one turned the current on." And proudly, "We were the first in the country to have this system. Maybe the only one."

"What about visiting?" Westbrooke asked. "Do they get to see their relatives alone in a room?"

"Sometimes open visits are allowed. Then they see their visitors alone downstairs in a large bull pen. Romano gets to see his folks and friends alone the last two days."

...

"Romano!"

Nick heard his name, the sound of stirring and the other prisoners standing alongside their bunks in the dark. "Father O'Neil is here to see you."

Nick stood up woodenly and walked on half-obeying legs to the end of his narrow cell. "Who did you say?" He had to swallow. He was deadly white. And he put his hand against the bars. Then he said, hoarsely, "Tell him I don't want to see him." Nick tossed his head in the dark, black hair whipping wildly off his forehead and back into place. Nick clutched the bars with both hands now. "No! No! I don't want to see him!" he shouted. "I don't want anybody handing me stuff about heaven, see!" He yelled it with his face twisted in the direction of the guard whom he could not see. "I'll die like I lived, see!"

Nick stood against the bars, facing out. His laugh was hard, bitter. Suddenly the laugh choked off. His legs and arms trembled. He turned and walked away into the deeper blackness of his tomb, into the heart of its steel-ribbed darkness. He lay on the cot, face

[474]

down. He bawled like a kid. But quietly. So that nobody would hear.

...the nicest eyes he had ever seen. All saints must have eyes like that....

Lord have mercy! Christ have mercy! Lord have mercy!

God be with you—and with your spirit....

He would be a priest.

He lay, face down, on the prison cot.... In the night ... all night long.

Again he was awake in pain, torture, fear, hopelessness. Awake in body and mind. Awake in his blood. Tensed. Helpless. Pinioned. Alive as are all dead things in their last strugglings for the life that is lost. Every nerve screaming. Every emotion tearing. Every blood vessel pounding.

He carried his torture into unconsciousness. The dream moved to its fortieth reel....

THE MOUSE! THE MOUSE!

Live fast, die young, and have a good-looking corpse.

THE DOG!

90

Daylight, touching, with a gentle finger, the edge of the sky. Smear of gray light over the prison.

It was now the third day from the end. Nick came from his cell, sat in bars with sunlight streaking through, played cards mechanically, grinned, kidded mechanically. His smile was hard-boiled, sneering, when he caught any of the prisoners looking at him.

Morning. Afternoon.

Stash came to see him.

Stash looked through the steel and glass at him, as one looks down into a coffin at someone one knew. "Hello, Nick."

Embarrassed and frightened silence. Then: "The old lady couldn't come—she said—the old lady couldn't come."

Silence. Staring at each other. Nick trying to grin.

"The old man said tell you hello."

Stash with his head down. Nick's eyes traveling up, slowly, expecting to see the white circle of sailor's cap, remembering it there. Stash saying, "I—I—" very huskily, "gotta go, Nick." Stash walking backwards out the steel-barred door and turning, walking away as fast as he could.

···

Late afternoon.

"Nick!" the guard called. The dead man got up to say goodbye to another visitor. Went and peered through the bars. It was Juan, Sunshine and Butch. Their faces were pale, their eyes fearful. "Hello, Nick.... Hello, Nick.... Hello, Nick." There was nothing else to say. They looked at him; he looked at them. Then they avoided each other's eyes. Nothing to say. Yet they were reluctant to go.

Nick pretended nonchalance and swagger.

"You guys working?" (Meaning jackrolling.)

And, "How's the taverns? What's doing at the Pastime?"

And, "How are you and the girls getting along, Juan?"

And, "How do I look, guys? I'm taking a little rest—in bed every night by seven." The laugh was strained.

And, "Next time you see a cop, give him my love." The laugh was bitter and affectionate.

Sunshine's long, sad look cut Nick to the quick. Swift flash of a smile at Sunshine and a wink.

Juan, Sunshine, Butch reluctant to go. Then making themselves strong, feeling Nick inside the glass and steel making himself strong.

Nick, to Juan, "Keep it clean!"

Nick, to Butch, a grin and a playful fist tapping the narrow section of glass near where Butch's chin was.

Nick, to Sunshine, "What you so sad about? Nobody's dead!"

Nick, to all of them, "Live fast—yeah—live fast."

Nick, looking at all of them, one face to the other, eye to eye, slowly, looking longest at Sunshine, a twist of a real and affectionate smile behind the hard mask of a grin.

Nick and all of them making themselves strong, strong to the breaking point. "Well, take it easy, guys!"

Nick turning. His head up. His eyes, hidden from them, filled with tears as, clenching his teeth, he walked away from them.

···

Thursday—then Friday!

These two days, today and tomorrow, were the days of his open visits. The days he saw his friends and family in the large bull pen where he could touch them, where they could touch him.

It was early morning when Aunt Rosa came. She looked as if

she hadn't slept, as if she hadn't slept for a week. "Hello, Nick," she said huskily. Then, after a slight pause, she moved toward him. Older than he remembered, and very unhappy. He lowered his head and continued looking at her with his innocent and contrite eyes. "Hello, Aunt Rosa."

He guessed she had never been happy, really, not getting married and having her own family. Living with Ma instead of having a home of her own. Always jolly and kidding...maybe that was just hiding how she really felt.

"Sit down, Aunt Rosa," softly, and with his face averted.

They sat side by side on the bench against the bars.

He glanced secretly at her. She was staring straight ahead and rapidly blinking her eyes.

He brought his fingers together as if to crack them. Playing the horses and everything just to get a kick out of life...working hard...loving Ma and us kids—especially me. He colored in shame. He felt closer to her, loved her more than Ma. Life was a joke to her, tragedy to Ma. Maybe that was why. She was like a pal to him. Always had been.

Aunt Rosa slowly reached out. Put her hand on his knee. Tightened it. "I don't want you to break down, Nick," she said gruffly. "You're a Romano and—what's more—a Pelitani. They can't hurt you, Nick. Nothing they do to you. And you ain't bad. Whatever you done." She searched for words, dragged them up, "Whatever you done—God—" Again she paused a moment, puzzled. Then she forced a smile and said roughly, "Christ, Nick! I don't want to talk like this." Her hand fastened hard over his knee, shook it. "Come on, grin at your old aunt. Ain't nothing can keep us from grinning, now or ever. We're like that, Nick—you and me—"

She was turned full-face to him, smiling weakly, her eyes watery, unable to keep the quiver from her voice. He took her shoulders between his hands and gently shook her. Then, very gently, one hand moved itself from the cloth of her coat. The fingers gently wiped away the tears that had gathered in her lashes. Then his embarrassed hand came away, lay on his knee. Neither spoke.

For Nick there was relaxation and security in this minute, in the family tie, the remembered existence, the ups and downs of a house and a family living together in that house, a love that would not die with tomorrow's stillness but would exist beyond that tomorrow, beyond many tomorrows. "You been working hard, Aunt Rosa?"

"Not too hard."

He paused, then said, "You been taking care of us a long time, ain't you, Aunt Rosa?" His voice was very low and quivered. "Ma —she did all right. She meant all right. I couldn't tell her, Aunt Rosa, but I can tell you. She taught us right and tried to—to make me do right. But you understand me—all of us—and you—well, you know how to manage better than Ma. You even managed Ma and—kept us together." Color came to his cheekbones and he was silent. Then he said, laughing a little, "How are the horses going, Aunt Rosa?"

"Oh, so-so."

"You win lately?"

"Didn't play since—since—for a long time."

"How's Julian?"

"He's all right."

"How's—Rosemary?"

"She's just fine—and that kid of hers—he's a cute one!" Aunt Rosa took a long time between each answer.

"How's Junior?"

"Getting awfully big, Nick—and bad."

"Aunt Rosa—will you do me a favor?" Then embarrassed and staring at the toes of his shoes. Color deepened on his cheeks and he leaned forward before continuing. "Don't let him get too bad—don't let him end up like— You beat hell out of him, Aunt Rosa! You see that he does right!"

Nodding her head hard and fast without answering.

"Aunt Rosa—"

"Yes, Nick—?"

"I wish you had been my mother."

A pause.

"You keep an eye on Ang too, will you? Ang is all right, Aunt Rosa." He spoke almost frantically, and suddenly he was telling her all about Ang and Abe, blurting it out in compassion and trust. "You help them, Aunt Rosa."

"I will, Nick." She took his hands between hers.

"What's wrong with this lousy world, Aunt Rosa?" And he turned his head away, rubbing his ear against the bars.

"There's nothing wrong with the world, Nick," she said. "There's nothing wrong with people, Nick. There's something good in everybody. I—I don't know how to talk about it—but I know people are all right. People don't do no wrong. Not when they're left alone." She was holding his hand on the palm of one of hers, moving each finger a little to the side and looking at it, gently moving them all together and looking at them as she talked. She smiled a little. "Sometimes I think there's no good or bad in the world. It's just people looking for something—trying to find something—somebody to love—somebody or something to feel good about— Some find it, some don't, but there's nothing wrong with people, Nick."

Somewhere in the jail an iron door clanged. Somewhere outside a wind went searching in a long winter wail. On the floor above feet scraped across concrete. Nick and Aunt Rosa sat in a long silence, side by side, their backs against the bars, their hands touching on the bench between them. And at last they must part. Aunt Rosa stood looking at him, an old woman, beaten here in this farewell. For a long minute she looked at her nephew. Her face worked strangely. Then she smiled slowly. Her old, fat hand patted his cheek. "Kiss your old aunt goodbye," she said. Nick put his arms around her, felt her stoutness fold in around him. The strength of her arms, holding him, passed into him. And she held him with the firm protectiveness of one holding a child from harm.

Neither spoke. She went from the death basement and up into the day.

• • •

In the afternoon Grant came to see him. Grant's face was pale. He stood across the bull pen looking at Nick. Nick lit a cigarette. "Hello, Grant."

"Hello, Nick. How—are you?"

Nick looked up smiling. He blew smoke before answering. "I'm all right."

Grant sat with his back against the bars where Aunt Rosa had sat. Nick stood looking down at him for a moment, then placed himself next to him. They smoked in silence and ground the cigarette butts out against the concrete with their heels. Just outside the bull pen, his back turned to them, stood the guard.

There was a silence. Nick tensed and clenched his teeth, letting the shiver go through him.

"Nick—"

Nick didn't answer and Grant didn't finish what he was going to say. He pulled out his cigarette case instead and pushed it towards Nick.

"Thanks."

Nick took a cigarette lighter from his pocket and snapped it lit. "Remember, you gave me this lighter? It's guaranteed for a lifetime. You know somebody whose lifetime lighter lasted a lifetime." He laughed. "Funny. I never thought it would outlast me. Maybe I'll smash it tomorrow morning." There was contemptuous derision in his tone.

"Nick—!" Grant said roughly. The color bleached out of his face. Looking at Grant, Nick's lips lost their smile. He stopped trying to be funny.

They sat an hour or longer. And neither spoke. They smoked cigarette after cigarette. The floor at their feet was a half-circle of heeled-out butts. Once Grant turned, looked full at Nick, and for a long time. Nick sat with his chin on the front of his shirt in its open V. Part of his hair fell over his forehead. Looking at him,

Grant thought of the first time he had seen him. Nick was aware of Grant's gaze. The last tinge of color left his face.

Grant reached out and with his fingers touched Nick's wrist. "Let's have a cigarette." When they had lit up, Grant said, "Look, pizon. I'm sorry I couldn't do anything for you. You know how I feel...." Grant spoke swiftly his eyes fixed on the bars at the end of the room. "But there's.one thing I can promise you—I'll do everything I can to help other fellows like you always. As long as I live."

Nick said nothing. He lowered his head and rubbed the toe of one shoe against the other.

Time must have moved and life must have gone on elsewhere. They sat immobile, side by side, shoulder to shoulder, on the wooden bench. The only movement was the threads of purple smoke rising above their heads, their hands lifting the cigarettes to their lips.

Grant ran his fingers through his hair. "Well—" He stood up. "Well—" he said again. Nick stood up too, mechanically, and without even hearing Grant, said, "Yeah—" They shook hands blindly. Their eyes came up slowly and looked at each other. Nick felt tears, .cold and wet, run over his lips and down into the corners of his mouth. Their hands were so tightly fastened together that his fingers were numb. Their hands, fastened together, were the only words they could find. And Grant, releasing Nick's hand, turned, walked toward the bull-pen door. Toward life.

The steel door clanged open.

The steel door clanged shut.

•••

Owen had written, *I want to see you, Nicky, terribly—but I can't come there—I can't.* Owen came anyway. Nick stood with one foot up on the bench, his elbow on his knee, his chin in his hand, his eyes staring down through the bars at the floor just outside the bull pen. He heard the door rumble open and close. He twisted his head and chin around on the palm of his hand and saw Owen. Nick immediately put his foot down on the floor, lifted his head and smiled. "Hi, Owen!" he said casually.

"Nicky!"

Owen walked over to him and stood close to him. Nick moved back a little, warily.

"Nicky, I had to see you!"

"You always say that. Remember, that's what you used to tell me up on West Madison." It was a real grin this time, partly amused, partly possessive.

"Nicky—please don't talk like that and please don't say that." Owen stopped. He looked at Nick with pleading eyes. "Let's not

[480]

talk about that, Nicky. Let's—please be decent to me today. It isn't asking much—" Nick, afraid now of the guard outside the bull pen, listened, embarrassed, fascinated, shamed. And Owen went on, "I wish it was me—anybody but you, Nicky!" Owen's voice was very shaky. His lips were quivering. His eyes began to fill.

"Listen—" Nick said softly, but hard-boiled. "Don't you cry! Don't start crying! I'll smash you if you do."

"I won't, Nicky," Owen promised in a voice like a child's.

"Sit down!" Nick said angrily.

Owen slumped down on the bench. Nick sat next to him and put his hand up on Owen's shoulder. He left it there. And he slumped back against the bars with his eyes closed.

Neither knew how long they sat like that. Both seemed content. Owen seemed not to want, ever, to move from under Nick's hand.

Then it was over. Owen stood up in the bull pen. Nick stood facing him. The long bars from the west threw shadows across the floor to them. "Goodbye, Owen," Nick's dark eyes and his lips said. Owen lifted his hands and put them on Nick's shoulders. Owen's eyes looked into Nick's. They were eyes seized with panic and fear. Nick looked back, wonder and pity in his eyes. He didn't try to smile. He didn't try to say anything. He was now the child. And he stood, awed and lonely, before what he saw in the other man.

Nick stood where Owen had left him long after the barred door had banged on another of the threads of his life. He stood blindly. He stood staring at nothing. He thought, in that moment, of all the loves and losses, the twisted and natural longings and frustrations of the world. Then, slowly, everything settled in him. One question asked itself: Why do I like Owen? One answer presented itself: Because he was always decent to me no matter what I did. And liking, love, being pity, sympathy, half-understanding; liking being the recognition of faults along with the good; liking, love, being the circle that ties all things together, Nick went and sat on the bench with his hands at either side of his face. The long shadows of the bars crept out across the concrete like flattened snakes, crept up his trouser legs. Crept up even as his heart sank down reaching for them.

■■■

He must have slept. He awoke with a start.

He wanted—awfully—to see himself. Look at himself. He wanted that more than he had ever wanted anything in his life. He sat on the edge of the cot, looking around the dark cell wild-eyed, for something with which to see himself. Some reflecting surface. Numbly he arose and walked around the five-by-eight cell. Then faster and more frantically. He stooped down, looking at the porcelain of the water fountain. Nothing reflected back. He rolled back the mattress.

and stared at the iron bar of the bunk. No reflection! He looked at the toe of his shoe. No reflection!

I'm Nick Romano, I'm Nick Romano, a little voice inside of him whimpered, went on whimpering like a kicked dog.

Again a coldness, as of ice. He got up off the cot, slowly. Undressed completely. Stood in the circle of his clothes. Stepped out of them. Stood, naked, in the middle of the cell.

He touched his broad square face, his wide cheekbones. He felt his hair, curling across his forehead. He felt his flesh with his hands. His movements were slow and secret. Were lazy and half-asleep as if with a drug, the drug of fear. He drank in the dark prison air. He stepped forward onto new and cold concrete. Felt the cold of the cell floor against the soles of his feet. The shiver of life, running up his spine and into the roots of his hair, felt good to him. Told him something about living and being, feeling and knowing. And the cold concrete at his feet took life from his body, took warmth in a little circle.

He was young. He was healthy.

His palms pressed firmly against his chest, moved slowly down, in their pressing, to his stomach. Felt the smoothness of his flesh, discovered the slight curve of his stomach. The tips of his fingers moved past his navel, slightly tickling. Touched the first hairs. He ran his fingers across the small of his back. Felt the firmness of the flexed muscles of his buttocks. Clamped his fingers into the muscles above his knees. He touched his sex organ. Stooped down and felt the firmness of his calves. Raised up. Again felt his chest, his arms, his face.

Would it burn?

How would he look?

91

"PRETTY BOY" ROMANO DIES TONIGHT!

Over the roof of the court building the initial rays of the weak winter sun began to filter. As a cloud drew back, the sun began yellowing the stone garments of the robed guardians at the top of the building, fell in liquid color across the robe, the sword, the stone jaw—Law.

Today!

The sun fell warm across the side of Nick's face. His hand came up slowly and touched his cheek where the sun lay. He stood up beside the iron cot with bars all around him. He thought of wanting to run away from reform school. Of wanting to get away from there, over the mountains, anywhere....

The jail began slowly to awaken. Twist of a body on a bed. Low murmurings. Sound of footsteps, caged in five-by-eight bars, moving a little closer together. Then suddenly—absolutely no sound whatsoever. As if the whole jail held its breath.

The day a man dies a feeling goes through the jail. This feeling struck now, like a fist. And almost immediately there was a clash of steel doors sliding open. Behind each door a man waited. From each cell, now, stepped a man. Into Nick's bull pen they stepped stiff-legged and cramped. Heads were twisted away from each other in shame, fear, horror. In human compassion. But something more behind all these things. Something that kept their heads bowed and their teeth clenched. And if accidentally their glances met, they saw eyes flared with hatred. Eyes that reflected the shared feeling of the man to go. Then the men moved away from each other and close to the bars, as if to leave plenty of room for Nick; as if they feared, as nothing else, that moment when he would step among them.

Nick put his hands down at his sides and squared his shoulders as best he could.

Today!

To the prisoners he showed a hard-boiled smile. He tried a joke.

[483]

A hard-boiled joke. "Well—I'm getting out of jail today!" he said into their silence.

One paled. Another rolled his eyes away from the sound of Nick's voice. Johnson, who was to go a month after Nick, pulled his shoulders in as if from a cold rain. And the prisoners turned their backs; heads turned away from Nick. They stared at the bars, or at the floor outside. Nick walked over and sat next to Johnson and lit a cigarette. Johnson lifted his hand as if to put it on Nick's knee, seemed to think better of it, and laid it back on his own knee.

And now the sunlight had risen to a higher level on the bars. The frost had loosened its grip. And time threaded out.

•••

An hour before noon the guard, lowering his eyes, yelled, "Nick— you got a visitor." Nick walked stiff-legged between guards to the basement bull pen. Inside the bars Ang waited for him. She looked very small and very frail. Her face was twisted and her eyes looked up through the bars anxiously into his.

They locked him in with her. She swayed a little and put her hands out toward him. She leaned against him. Put her arms around him tightly, tightly. He heard her voice muffled against his chest. "I wanted to come alone, Nick. I didn't want to be with Ma and Julian."

He held her away from him gently, his hands on her shoulders. "Let me look at you, Sis." His voice was soft and tense.

"I'm not going to cry, Nick. I know you wouldn't want me to cry."

She might as well have cried. Her voice cut him like a knife. "Why didn't you bring Abe to see me?" he asked in the same horribly soft voice.

"No," she said, "no, I wanted to see you alone."

He slipped his hands off her shoulders, down her arms to her hands, and took them, held them. "You tell him," Nick said, "that he better be good to you. That I said if he don't I'll knock his block—" and realizing how impossible that would be he grinned.

Ang wrenched her hands free. She folded in against him and, with her face down against his shirt, held on to him as if she would never let go.

High noon was in the sky.

Nick sat again in the bull pen with the other men.

The sun was pale over the prison now and ready to drop down the other side, bringing momentary life to the western bars.

•••

The warden got into his coat. The phone had rung all day long with people on the other end of the line begging to see Nick die. The warden told his secretary that he was going to disappear until it was time to receive the reporters in his office.

[484]

In the bull pen he asked Nick, "What do you want for supper?" The condemned man was to have the traditional privilege of ordering anything he wanted for his last meal.

All the color left Nick's face. But when he spoke he was surprised at the calmness of his voice. "Bring me a big steak—enough for two guys, warden, and peas and mashed potatoes...." He went on ordering more than he could possibly eat, so that when he had gone down to the death chamber, the other prisoners could have what was left. "...And coffee and milk and a couple of pieces of pie and some ice cream. Cake too, if you got it. No—make that fried chicken instead of steak." That was all he wanted and he grinned; but his face was ashy-white, even his neck to where it disappeared into his shirt collar.

···

And now the sun had slipped down beyond the factories, had begun to lower on the residential homes. Long rivers of thin winter sun still lay across wide fields, dimmed by clumps of trees where, west, the city ends in prairie. Over the city factory whistles began to blast in long wails against an ashy-gray sky.

Foreman of the jury Joseph Burke heard the whistles and locked the door of his bakery. He had lived through a day of keen anticipation. On the way home he bought all the evening newspapers. At home he ate supper, pulled off his shoes, sat in an easy chair and spread the newspapers over his knees.

···

In the jail bull pen the guard averted his eyes and said in an unnaturally soft voice, "Nick, your mother is here to see you."

Every man in the bull pen stiffened. Through every man went a shiver. Nick stood up slowly. He had to force himself to walk to the barred door. Every step of the way he had to force himself.

They locked him in the basement bull pen. Then they brought Ma and Julian down. For a long time he couldn't look up into their faces. Then finally he dragged his eyes from the floor. "Hello, Ma." Nick took a halting, half-awkward step toward her.

"Nick! Nick! My boy!"

Nick put his hand on her shoulder and stooped down to kiss her. He saw her aged eyes filled with tears, and the tears falling, hot, fast, on her wrinkled cheeks. "Oh, my boy, my boy!" Her arms were around him, arms skinny from work and worry. He gently patted her shoulder and tried to pull up straight. She clung to him.

This was hell! This was worse than frying!

He pulled away roughly. "Cut it out, Ma!" And he was sorry he said it, hard-boiled and don't-give-a-damn. He lowered his eyes. "Let's sit down. Hello, Julian."

"Nick," Julian said, saying his name instead of hello.

[485]

The three of them sat on the bench, Nick between his mother and his brother. Ma shook all over and tried to pull Nick's head down on her flat breast. Her arm was clutched around his shoulders. Nick held himself stiff and stared down at the floor.

Julian wanted to tell him that Rosemary wasn't able to come but that she was thinking of him. But he couldn't. He couldn't even swallow. Ma grabbed Nick's hands and started kissing the backs of them. He pulled away roughly. And the minutes slipped through the bars and away forever.

Ma whimpered like a child. Nick, listening, knew then that he was guilty and of what he was guilty. He knew that he had broken this woman, his mother, killed her as surely as if he had stood over her in the alley and had pumped the lead into her body. He knew that she would go on living, but that he had killed her. He knew that for months this old woman next to him on the bench had suffered; that for months after tonight she would continue to suffer. He, in that second, remembered the words of Morton as if they stood before him in foot-tall letters: Society takes its revenge on the mothers and families of the men it kills. The man dies. They live on.

Nick lowered his head. He lived again the years of his mother's love of him, her care and protection of him, her suffering because of him, the arguments with Pa because of him. And his mother had always taken his part.

His mother whimpering like a small child. His brother tense, and silent, and sad. Nick was more ashamed, more miserable than he had ever been before.

No words to ask forgiveness. Not even able to say I'm sorry.

Ma clutched him, whispering, whimpering, frantically leaning against him, pulling him close to her, protectively. "Nick, go to confession, please son, confess to the priest. Do this for your Ma." She said it over and over, her voice stabbing at him like red hot needles.

"All right, Ma," he said.

"Oh, *grazie, thank God!*" Ma said, drawing in the jail air deeply.

At last, when it seemed that his mother had no more tears, she told Julian that she wanted to see Nick alone. Julian stood up obediently. His lips began to tremble. And Nick stood up. They looked at each other. Julian put out his hand. Nick grasped it. "Goodbye," he said. For almost the first time in his life, he felt neither envy nor contempt for his brother.

And Nick and his mother sat alone in the wide, barred bull pen. She with her arms around him and sobbing over and over, "My boy! My boy!"

•••

When Nick got back to the upstairs bull pen his supper was waiting for him. The chicken was fried to a golden crisp. The potatoes
were mashed creamy and white. The green peas were richly buttered. There was a whole pie. A cake.

Nick looked down at the tray of food.

My last meal!

He felt he couldn't choke a scrap down. He remembered that
condemned men never had appetites. Looking at the food he
thought the eyes of all the men were on him. Show them you're Nick
Romano! Show them you can take it! He forced the food down.
Mouthful by mouthful. It caught in his throat and he swallowed it
down, took another mouthful. Felt dizzy and sick, but went on,
calmly lifting the fork to his mouth. And he swallowed to force the
food down. Then when he had eaten what he would ordinarily
have eaten he walked to the front of the bull pen and sat down. He
ran his fingers through his hair. "Johnson, take some chicken if
you want." He combed his hair. "You guys will have to cut the pie
mighty thin to all get a piece."

The prisoners sat with their heads down.

"Go ahead, eat!" Nick said, almost in a pleading voice.

They got up automatically and with their heads down walked
slowly to the tray of food.

When they were grouped around it, Nick walked back to the
toilet and was sick.

The minutes limped past. The shadows of night deepened on the
faces of the stoop-shouldered men. Lay deep under Nick's eyes, in
dark triangles under his cheekbones. In the night somewhere near
the jail the leaden tongue of a church steeple began dismally to
count the hour—*oneeee—twoooo—threeee—fourrrr—fiveeee—sixxxx—*
The bell of the church steeple trembled through the bull pen,
hoarse and sad, dimly sounding across the ears of the men. Trembled away into the night, into silence.

The last sound of the steeple gong died and the men sat on without moving. The corpse looked from man to man, at the men who
were holding their silent wake for him. The minutes dragged past.
Nick tensed with the sense of their waiting; and they tensed—waiting—knowing—

And the next sound they heard in that awful silence was the
dreadful sound they awaited, the sound of steel falling on steel, of
bolts releasing their escape-proof clasp. The corpse and the half-
dead men stirred. Through every man there went a shudder. The
guard said in a sigh from the yawning gap in the bars, "All right,
Nick." He didn't look at Nick.

All the men stood up as if each was named Nick. All but Johnson

[487]

—he sat as if he now carried the burden that Nick was to lay down tonight.

Nick got up from the bench. He paused. He looked around, half-smiling. Nick moved from man to man, shaking hands and saying his farewells. Their faces were yellow. Their eyes were downcast.

"Goodbye, Kid—"

"So long—"

"So long, Nick—"

" 'Bye, kid—"

Johnson dragged his eyes up into Nick's. "Well—" Nick said. They shook hands.

"Yeah—" Johnson said.

Nick turned, first his face, then his body away from Johnson and the men. His eyes winced at the gap, like a coffin, that stood in the wall of bars. The men stepped back in embarrassment and made a little clearing for him. A little path through which he must pass from life. Even from this. Nick stepped slowly toward the door where the guard waited with his head down.

92

The death cell is eighteen steps from the chair. The death cell is a squared cage of bars furnished with a toilet, a washstand, a cot and three stools. It is here that the man who is to die spends the last five hours of his life. But not alone. There are two guards in the cell with him. Just outside the cell is another guard with the key, who watches every move the condemned man makes. He is not left alone in these, the last utterly miserable hours of his life, to pray, to cry, to draw into himself or to strengthen himself for what waits when the bars are lifted from around the cage. He sits on a stool in the death cell. The blue-clad guards sit on stools facing him. And beyond the bars the man to die can see a black door with a black handle that leads to the electric chair.

Nick sat now, only eighteen steps from death, staring over the shoulders of the two men who faced him, staring blankly at the wall.

■■■

[488]

While Nick was being moved to the death cell and the other men in the jail were being locked in their separate tombs for the night, Juror Anthony Fontana turned off the light in his little printshop on North Damen Avenue. He went through the dark toward the front door, glancing around the shop in the darkness, seeing the presses loom up, the many cases of type; and Fontana felt a warm beat of pride in himself, in his place in business, his comfortable security, his success as a foreigner who had come to America and made good.

He locked the door and moved under street lamps along the sidewalk toward where his warm room waited. He felt the cold of the night steal in through his heavy overcoat He walked along briskly and proudly, swinging his little fat legs and his fat arms. At the corner, stepping down off the curb he read, as he always did, the evening headline. And tonight it said:

PRETTY BOY ROMANO AWAITS DEATH

He saw it and his eyes, buried by too much good and rich Italian food in a swarthy and greasy face, snapped. All the time they think we Italians are all like—*that dago!*

∎∎∎

And now, after a good supper and a cigar, the warden came down to ask Nick if there was anything he could do for him.

"Smoke, Nick?" the warden asked in a friendly tone, handing him a cigarette.

Nick smiled. He took the warden's cigarette. He let the warden hold the match for him. Tilting his head back he blew smoke.

"I just dropped in on you, Nick," the warden said, "to ask you if there is anything I could do for you—any favor."

Nick dropped the newly lit cigarette and stepped on it. He stepped back a little and looked, panic-stricken, into the warden's eyes. Then his face set itself in its mask once again and cooled to hostility. "Yeah—yeah, I got a favor to ask you. I got nice hair, see, and I don't want it spoiled. I don't want my head shaved."

The warden looked back with cool and unblinking eyes. "All right, Nick," he said "we'll just take a little off the top." He stepped closer to Nick. "You know, Nick, I think you ought to see the priest." He lifted his hand as if to put it on Nick's shoulder. Nick stepped back away from him.

∎∎∎

In another part of the basement the sponges for the electrodes for Nick's scalp and ankle lay in acid where they had been soaking since suppertime and where they must soak for six hours to perform perfectly their function in bringing the electricity into Nick's body.

∎∎∎

[489]

Mrs. Marie Jacoby, juror, had done the dishes and gone to the show by seven-thirty. The picture was very sentimental and she cried softly with her handkerchief up to her face. Cried heartbrokenly over the misfortunes and unhappinesses of celluloid people.

•••

At the same time Nick sat on the edge of the cot in the death cell. He sat waiting—waiting—

His eyes stared out-of-focus at the corner of the floor near his feet. Where they stared they saw the ragged winter web of a spider. Ashy-gray and soot-black. And in the web a wrinkled, leg-agitating spider with fiercely black eyes. And in the web a weak fly. And the spider sewing him in place with black webs like bars. Nick saw it in a blur as his thoughts raced along toward the electric chair and the moment when he would die there.

Yeah, they're burning me in the name of Society.

So what!

And now the spider had wound his web around the fly like a prison. Completely around him. The feeble stirrings of the wings grew less and less with the black strands tight across him.

Today they're going to have their revenge. Fuller and all of them all the way down the line.

I'll walk to that chair like a man.

His eyes stared fascinated at the spider weaving, weaving closer. The feeble attempts of the weak winter fly to release itself. The glisten of light on the taut silk strings. The fly—feebly. And the spider—winding, winding.

I'm hard-boiled.

I'm tough.

No, you ain't.

The hell I ain't!

Nick leaned forward and with his forefinger lifted the fly out of the web.

•••

"Hey, Romano," one of the guards said, unable to sit any longer, watching every twitch of an eyelid, every shudder of a muscle, "you want to play some cards?"

No! No! My God, no!

"Sure!" Nick said, grinning and walking over.

They shuffled the cards.

Tonight I'm going to burn!

Christ! This fellow sure can take it.

They dealt the cards out.

"I can't play for money. I'm broke—unless you'll trust me to pay you tomorrow," Nick wisecracked.

And inside, *I'm going to burn! Me, Nick Romano!*

I thought sure he'd crack. Playing cards cool as you please. You got to take your hat off to a fellow like him.

Me! Me, Nick Romano!

He's got as much nerve as the papers said. Smiling. Imagine that —smiling!

The first witnesses had begun to arrive and, showing their admission tickets, were passed through the police lines toward the building. The crowd on the sidewalk watched enviously.

Old Mrs. Green, juror, prayed for Nick that evening. That night she sat in her comfortable armchair at the window, knitting. The light from the floor lamp was soft on her gray hair, her mother-and-grandmother wrinkled face, her gentle eyes. Once in a while she rocked back and forth. The slim gold chain with the crucifix at its end bounced gently on her bosom. Occasionally her lips moved in prayer for Nick. And once her fingers ran idly along the little gold chain, down to the cross, up, down to the cross again. At nine o'clock she went to bed. She slept.

■■■

At ten o'clock Nick sat on the edge of the cot twisting his fingers. In the corner across the cell Emma was sitting on a chair. Every time he looked up he saw her there. And she would smile. Her hazel no-color eyes would look deeply into his. She would say, *I love you, Nicky! I don't care, Nicky! I'll be waiting for you where you left me. I love you, Nicky, I love you! Now go to work.*

He tried not to look up. But he couldn't help it. She was looking into his eyes and said very slowly, very softly, *Yes, the lilacs are blooming...*

■■■

In the death cell Nick slowly came to accept the inevitable. His body seemed to prepare itself. His blood seemed to course more slowly through his veins, to clot, to run thin and anemic.

Outside the bars the guard smoked a cigarette and took a swig from the bottle of whiskey. Inside the bars the two blue-clad guards turned their eyes away from Nick.

■■■

In Denver someone stepped abruptly from the dark and boarded-up exit of an alley garage. "Are you Tommy?" a voice asked, belonging to a face he couldn't see. The man stepped closer to him. And another man stepped out of the doorway too, and to the side of Tommy. At the same time the first man's fist, wrapped in darkness and coming with the sting of the cold, struck him. Tommy fought back. The attempt was futile against the two bruisers. When he lay unconscious at their feet they kicked him a couple of times. Then they shrugged their shoulders and walked away. All about him on

[491]

the ground were scattered the strikers' leaflets he had been distributing.

...

Nick sat cracking his knuckles.

It ain't long now. It can't be long now.

Don't break! Don't let them break you!

The warden entered the death cell. The barber came with him. The guards stood, ready to give a hand.

They combed his hair straight down over his forehead. The barber moved closer with his shears and razor. Nick sat clenching his teeth, clenching to silence the quivering of his jaws. Sweat ran down his armpits, began to drip in damp beads across his back, and over his face. Began to rise in the curled hairs on his calves.

Looking down at his legs, Nick saw them trembling until his knees were almost knocking together. He put his sweaty hands down between his knees and held his legs still. He grinned sheepishly. Then he lowered his eyes from the warden's and grinned again, knowing that the warden was watching him. Grinned—in shame, fear, impotence.

The barber lifted his clippers. He was wet with sweat and his hands shook. The shears took the long hair. The clippers made the bald spot. The razor scraped it clean. Only a bit of hair was removed from the back of his head. Only a small bald spot for the electrode's paralyzing touch. So little hair was taken away that it couldn't be noticed.

The warden stepped back and looked down straight at Nick. "Do you want to see the priest?"

"Nothing doing, warden," Nick said.

The warden left.

The guards sat down on their stools again.

Outside the death cell the guard took another drink from his bottle of whiskey.

Shivers ran up and down Nick's back, almost visibly shaking him.

...

Only a few steps away, they stood in the small brick theatre. The seventy-four shadows of the seventy-four witnesses fell across the floor blacker than the black concrete. Electric bulbs shed dim yellow light over the audience's part of the execution chamber—but behind the plate glass the little stage blazed with light. The glass was so freshly and brightly polished that it seemed invisible. On the stage the electric chair.

The evening's guests filed in, facing the chair, staring and immobile now, with their eyes fastened to it. Each seemed to suck in his breath. They stood there a moment as if lifeless. And an intoxicated man said in short, sharp tones, "Jesus Christ!"

[492]

Light from the three spotlights overhead poured down upon the chair, showing each cruel attachment and knob. The black leather shone. The chrome threw highlights as if just off a buffer's wheel. The chair gleamed, dominating the whole scene in that dim, low-ceilinged basement where shadows lurked in the far corners. The hard light beat down.

On one side of the small stage and also behind the glass were five other chairs for the jury of doctors who would examine the body and pronounce Nick dead. At the back of the stage on the side was the little black door through which Nick would come.

In front of the stage under the low ceiling were rows of benches. The spectators shuffled in between the rows and sat on the benches. In the last row sat the old priest.

And now the door to the execution chamber was closed and they were locked in.

The spectators sat in silence, looking at the chair.

•••.

At five minutes to twelve the warden walked along the basement corridor toward Nick.

...Steps along the hall, across the black concrete floor. Nick looked up and through the bars. Where he looked he saw only darkness, and in the darkness the sound of steps coming closer. Then the warden stood in the black gap, came slowly toward the death cell. Charlie rose from his stool. His keys struck together, struck so loudly against Nick's ears that he could feel a scream rise in his throat and choke there.

The door was opened. The guards inside stood up, carefully watching Nick.

"This is the last chance," the warden said. "If you have anything to say, now is the time to say it."

Nick sat crouched on the stool looking up at the warden. His lips were stuck together and his tongue swollen to the roof of his mouth. He grinned; weakly, but grinned. And shook his head no.

The warden stepped back. One of the guards stooped down, knelt. With scissors he cut Nick's trousers off above the knees and unlaced his oxfords. He arose with the shorn pieces in his hands. His eyes looked neither at Nick nor the warden. He dropped the pieces on the edge of the cot. "Take off your shirt, Nick," the warden said. Nick paled. He stood up and meekly stripped off his shirt. Stood in his undershirt and the trousers cut off above the knees so that the electrodes could clasp the ankles snugly.

The warden turned away. The barred door opened. The warden left and the door was locked behind him. Nick slumped back on the cot, perspiring profusely. The guards, on their stools, turned their backs to him in pity. The shorn pieces of trousers slipped off

[493]

the cot and lay at Nick's feet where the laces of his opened oxfords trailed across the concrete.

■■■

The whistling notes went up and out. The slim young man, his light brown hair curly under a cap that was twisted around on his head so that the bill was at the back, walked along the down-at-heels street near the tail end of the West Coast town. He grinned a little and looked in through a restaurant window, then in past a grocery store glass. A small pile of newspapers was stacked at one end of the plate glass. The young man glanced down at the headlines, casually, without any real interest. Then in a single column he saw a headline—

PRETTY BOY ROMANO DIES
IN CHICAGO TONIGHT

Rocky stood a full minute in front of the windowpane staring at his feet. Then he moved away down the street, not whistling. Along the railroad tracks his hand mechanically pulled a withered weed-stalk and stripped the dead leaves from it. He sat down near the tracks. In his hand the weed-stalk moved aimlessly back and forth across the hard, bare ground.

■■■

Lost in the maze of neon, Lottie's Place with the door locked, with Lottie sitting in the back room, a bottle of whiskey and a glass near her fat-puffed hand. Lottie's eyes were staring vacantly. She was seeing Nick standing just inside the door dripping with rain, seeing him opening the knife with his teeth and cutting clean blood into the bullet wound, seeing him in court, seeing the hundred dollars he had left in the envelope on top of her dresser.

■■■

Nick sat on the edge of the cot with the half-smoked cigarette held loosely between his fingers. He put it to his lips and sucked in greedily. The harsh smoke cut down into his lungs. He stared, with out-of-focus eyes, at the floor. The purple smoke of the cigarette rose up past his vacant eyes and curled in the tumble of hair on his forehead.

The sound of feet on the concrete—

Nick's eyes blinked rapid-fire.

Feet moving toward him in a muted scraping—

Nick dropped the cigarette on the floor and stepped on it. His eyes went on staring, out-of-focus, at the floor, dimly recording his shoelaces trailing on the concrete.

Feet moving close—halting just outside the barred death cell—

They stood looking in at him, the men who were to take him to

[494]

death. Charlie, the guard, stood up with the key in his hand. And the two guards locked in with him stood up. His mind went cold. His body went numb. He could feel his hair stiffen. A slight moisture came out on his forehead. His armpits began to dampen. Slowly, very slowly, his eyes circled from left to right. Saw the legs in blue trousers. Saw the low verticals of the bars that surrounded him. A prickling of fear itched all over the surface of his skin, up into the roots of his hair and down his fingers to their tips. His skin flushed hot. Then ice cold. He was Nick and he was going to die! It was like being drunk, real drunk. He was almost sure he was going to faint; his head whirled dizzily and he could feel the upper portion of his body swaying. He had to stand up ... go with them. Slowly his head and his eyes came up to meet their eyes.

The sound of steel crashing on steel. The door opening. And the death squad looking in at him.

He stood erect in the cramped death cell. His eyes looked beyond the gap in the bars at Charlie. He smiled with a lazy, deathlike indifference. The corners of his lips were touched with cynicism. "Okay, fellows!" he said. He said it cockily, and heard his voice thrown back at him through a vacuum.

Turning his head slowly to the guard standing next to him in the cell, he said, "Lend me your comb." Without answering the guard handed Nick a comb. Nick pulled it through his curly hair. He felt it scrape, with a little excited thrill of life, against his scalp. He combed his hair slowly and neatly, following up the comb with the palm of his other hand until every hair was perfectly in place and brilliant with highlights above the handsome, tortured face. Then he touched his fingers gently to where the hair covered the bald spot where death would strike him. He handed the comb back to the guard. His fingers shook; he was ashamed of their shaking. He didn't look at the guard. His eyes slanted across the death cell to the floor. Suddenly, where he looked he saw the dog.

The puppy lay in the gutter belching blood.... Trying to whine. Or trying to breathe. Or, perhaps, only trying to die ....

It was yesterday and Nick was a boy on Maxwell Street looking down at the puppy.

Nick looked up from the death-cell floor, feeling the shiver, then the calmness. "Okay, fellows, let's go."

His feet answered. His legs groped forward uncertainly, carrying him from grave to grave. He stepped forward like a sleepwalker, stepped forward into certainty and thus into an uncertainty that knew no time—*past midnight*—and knew all time—*past midnight*.

When he got to the cell door he was soaked with perspiration. Little beads of sweat had gathered on the exposed hairs of his legs and began trickling down his calves.

He was all caught up. Eighteen steps from this spot they would strap him into the electric chair. Death would be swift and cheap in the little brick and plaster execution chamber. The four hands would move upward to the buttons. Touch them. Press them. And one hand with the electricity in it.

...

Peoria near 12th Street ... the Romano house ....

Inside the Romano house ....

Ma Romano lay on a bed. Under her the bed shook with her sobs. Julian and Ang sat in chairs near her.

Rosemary was shut in her bedroom with the baby. The baby was asleep. Rosemary sat in the dark room with her chair drawn up to the window. Her forehead was pressed against the cold pane.

Aunt Rosa was locked up in the bathroom. She sat on the seat cover of the toilet with her elbows on her fat knees, her large hands in half-clasped fists holding the sides of her face. Unchecked tears ran down her cheeks and fell hot on the floor.

Ma Romano lay prostrate on the bed, her eyes clenched tight, her hands at each side of her forehead and her fingers knotted into her long, gray-streaked hair. She was convulsively sobbing, "Oh, Nick, my poor, poor Nick! Oh, God."

Julian and Ang sat chained to their chairs, each broken syllable from their mother shaking them, breaking them.

"Oh, my God. Oh, why did you do this to him?" Ma sobbed.

When Aunt Rosa came out of the toilet she had herself in hand. She heated water to boiling, put two shots of whiskey in a water glass, added a little sugar and, stirring it, carried it to the bedroom.

Ma was still twisting on the bed while she mumbled inarticulately, over and over, "God ... Nick. ..." Sobs burst from her between the strangling phrases. And now she wrung her hands together while her eyes roved wildly across the cracked ceiling.

Aunt Rosa walked squarely to the bed with the glass of whiskey toddy. "Drink this, Lena," she said crisply, almost sternly.

Ma shook her head no.

Aunt Rosa motioned to Ang. Ang sat behind the pillow at the head of the bed, partially supporting Ma. Aunt Rosa put the butt of her hand against Ma's chin and pressed down firmly. She wedged the rim of the glass between Ma's half-clenched teeth and forced her to drink.

Ma lay back again on the bed, sobbing.

In the night a factory whistle blew long and shrill—midnight.

Ma screamed.

The factory whistle roared through the still, waiting rooms. Julian and Ang ran to the bed. Ma pushed them away, screaming, "They've killed him! They've murdered him!"

[496]

Ma Romano's scream rose above the drill of the factory whistle, up, higher and higher.

All along Halsted Street the lights blinked wearily.

...

Nick stiffened. The last mile! It was the longest walk he had ever taken in his life. In the corridor outside, the death squad waited for him. He stood at the cell door, his shoulders almost filling its width. The last mile. Nick's smile quivered, flickered, came more steady. Stayed. In the death cell the guards stood behind him, letting him pass through first. Moving stiffly, Nick stepped out into the corridor. Again a nerve twitched in his eyelid. The corridor . . . bars . . . guards . . . one on each side of him in the corridor, bars down its length, he between the bars and between the guards. The smile went. He lowered his head. His eyes looked down at the pants, cut off at the knees. Yeah, this is the suit I looked good in. . . .

Slowly he lifted his face. He took the first of the eighteen steps forward as in a dream.

Nick took the second and third steps forward. The corridor . . . bars, falling in shadow across his white face.

The nerves went on twitching in his eyelid and his nostril and he put one foot in front of the other, walking toward death. His figure threw a moving shadow against the wall.

. . . Shadows and bars. Walking figures. The shadows of figures walking toward a little black door with a black handle. Nick walked, slowly and steadily, walking with his head down. And inside Nick . . . Tommy didn't bawl on the first lick. It was the second one . . . .

Nick lifted his head then. He walked with his head up. His face set. Teeth clenched. Clenched with resolution. The resolution of taking this.

I'm Nick Romano!

I'm Nick Romano!

Nick took the sixth and seventh steps forward. With each step death came a little closer. But now he had himself under control.

He was Nick Romano! They couldn't break him!

He ground his teeth together and the muscles stood out in his jaws. Maybe they could kill him but they couldn't break him! He threw back his shoulders, widely, and looked straight ahead, a grim tightness of defiance across his lips. With him moved the guards and his shadow. He walked with a little of Rocky's loose, easy grace. With some of Tony's hardness. With something of Vito's *I-don't-give-a-goddamn* in the toss of his head. Butch's razzberry in the twist of his lips.

I'll show every bastard of them!

[497]

The only thing that gave him away was the twitching of an eyelid and one nostril.

The five men in front of him, the guard on either side of him and
. . . against the wall . . . their shadows moving with them. . . .

He wasn't scared now but everything was all jumbled up.

*. . . For a moment he thought he and Tony were carrying the
basket of apples they had stolen. He felt that way. Numb and tingly
all over—or maybe he was in bed with his mother like when he was
a little kid with the covers pulled up over his head. . . . He remembered Ma's nagging and now it was full of a gentle loving. . . . Pa
beating him. . . . Aunt Rosa giving him a little shove. "Clear out of
here while I dress." . . . Julian with the Come-to-Jesus look. But
Julian in the cell with him today. Or was it yesterday? Or last year?
Or did it ever happen? . . . The smell of gas in the kitchen that day.
The day in Ryan's Woods with Emma's lips in his hair, and his ears,
and his neck. . . . Tommy hadn't cried on the first lick . . . it was
the second one . . . .*

●●●

Tommy walked along the Denver street, bruised and sore from
the beating the thugs had given him. He walked in the night toward
his room. It was colder now and the wind blew hard, ruffling the
high-peaked collar of his sweater and slapping blond hair across
his forehead.

Tommy passed the corner newsstand. The headline hit him
squarely between the eyes—

PRETTY BOY ROMANO DIES
IN CHICAGO TONIGHT

—Tommy turned
back in the direction from which he had come. He wandered up
and down the dark night streets, crying like a little kid. The tears
rolled down his cheeks and were icy cold in the cold night. His
nose dripped. Several times he wiped it on the back of his hand.
Aimlessly he wandered up and down streets, carried on by his
aching legs and his aimless feet.

●●●

For one breathless fragment of a minute every heart stood still in
the cramped brick and plaster theatre.

There stood Romano!

For five beats of your heart he did not move but waited for the
door to swing wide enough for him and his guards to get through.
Then, throwing his head up, Nick walked in past the door before it
had come completely open and stepped out onto the stage.

He faced his audience.

[498]

The crowd stared, open-mouthed.

There he was!

Head up!

Smiling!

Pants torn away. In an undershirt. Wavy hair combed back. And his eyes staring straight into you.

There stood the man they were going to kill!

It was his eyes you noticed first. At first glance they alone identified him as the pretty boy killer who through the long trial had sat at the counsel table in the courtroom. They were strangely unblinking eyes. Yet eyes with an awful innocence, an awful accusation.

An eternity of seconds ticked off as the condemned man stood, erect as a soldier, calmly and smilingly looking out at them.

Nick gazed sneeringly at the audience. The smile curled wider, bolder, more defiant. He hated them. He wanted to spit in their faces. Then slowly, and with his proud head up, he turned his eyes —toward it.

One thing stood out in stark dominance in that low-ceilinged basement—the chair. Nick looked at it. The nerves jumped spasmodically in his face. One drip of sweat ran crookedly down his face. The reporters in the first row could see his heart beating wildly under the cotton shirt.

But the smile stayed fixed.

The electric chair was there with its arms outstretched, waiting for him. There was little left of him to kill, little left to die. Just his eyes flaring with hate and defiance; just the twist of a hard smile on his lips. Even white teeth showing. To hell with you! I can take it!

He shook the guards off and walked firmly to the chair. There was a rustle among the newspaper men. He seemed, under their scrutiny, to have courage—if courage means that the brain tells the legs to walk on toward death and the legs obey. The reporters leaned forward, microscopically studying him. Their minds turned out blaring headlines: RUTHLESS KILLER GOES TO CHAIR UNSHAKEN.

He needed no assistance. He took his seat calmly in the electric chair—then lifted from it a trifle in a little shock of surprise at the cold touch of the leather seat. Then again lowered himself onto the black leather.

He was seated now. From the electric chair he took his last look at the world. The world was staring faces and popped eyes striking out at him from the benches like snakes striking.

The spectators sat tense, motionless, only their hearts beating. Curiosity and vengeance and cruelty had been in their faces. And now cowardice replaced the curiosity, the vengeance, the cruelty.

Frightened and shaking, they stared. There was something in this boy who sat calmly before them that defeated them. Fear stood in their eyes and on their faces. And then the emotions of sympathy, pity, compassion. A human being was dying. With him a part of them was dying. And in that hairline of a moment no one of the seventy-four was glad to be there. But it was too late to draw back. They were there now in that tight little room and couldn't get out. They trembled and they were all a part of the man who was going to die.

The death squad was ready now. The death squad stepped forward to its work.

Nick's eyes didn't change. The smile stayed. The nerves in his eyelid and nostril went on twitching. Under the cotton undershirt that clung, wet with perspiration, to his chest, his heart beat like a pneumatic hammer against stone.

The death squad moved in around him efficiently, wavering blue-clad figures with stiff faces.

They were standing all around him now, looking down at him with expressionless eyes in tight faces. He watched them, his breath catching between his lips. There was no fighting back now and he knew it. He sat like stone, waiting to be strapped down for death.

The guards stepped forward. One attendant placed the metal electrode over the shaved spot on his head; and in its placing his black hair fell, curly, over his forehead and partly into his eyes. Another attendant, standing on the right side of the chair, fastened the clamps around one arm. And the third attendant secured the other wrist and arm. And the fourth attendant lashed a strap across his chest and one across his stomach. The chrome brake fastened to the back of the chair was spun by agile hands, snapping Nick unnaturally erect and bruising his shoulders against the back of the chair. The straps grew tighter and tighter. They tightened against his stomach, tightened against his heart. And now the strap was jammed so taut and so close over his heart that it clung to it like a steel band. His heart beat wildly against the strap as if to break it. The lever pulled the straps even closer, choking him, almost suffocating him, pressing now into the flesh and leaving welts, sending the blood pouring up into his dark face and pounding against his temples. The chair embraced him. And the fifth attendant knelt on one knee before Nick. The fifth man moved the bare ankles into place, stepped on the foot lever that snapped the metal hooks and clamped him closer to death. Kneeling before Nick, the attendant fumbled as he lifted the electrode. The electrode touched the flesh and the fingers trembled.

Nick glanced down. "What's the matter, nervous?" And he smiled.

[500]

The attendant, even further shaken at the cold, derisive sound of Nick's voice, continued with bowed head at his work. His fingers were as damp as the damp ankle, putting the electrode around the ankle. One bead of sweat trickled down the attendant's forehead. Slowly he arose. Arose until his face was level with Nick's and Nick's eyes were looking into his. He drew back, shuddering.

And now they had him clamped in. Almost ready now—

The attendants stood around Nick looking at their work in the pause between action.

Enthroned, Nick sat, facing his audience.

No time now—

Life was over—

They poised the hard, black-rubber mask above his head. For an instant his face and his eyes were swept with tragedy. Then he smiled; and his smile was sincerely and cynically fearless. His eyes were level and unclouded. He looked up at the men who were preparing to fasten the death mask over his face. In that glance up, a strap dangling from the mask dropped over one of his eyes, blotting out the brilliance of an electric spotlight overhead and warning him of greater darkness to come. His face was slanted up, his teeth white in the wide smile, the strap over one eye.

This for the spectators to see.

This. Then the rubber closed over him.

The mask closely in cruelly. It tightened against his face and shoved his nose through the one triangular hole in its otherwise completely blank, completely solid, completely black surface. The death mask kissed all of his face. And as it passed down over him the smile dropped from his lips; a shiver passed through him as his body got ready to take the electricity.

The show was over.

You don't have to pretend any more now.

All caught up....

A kid in an electric chair all caught up.

Life had been fast.

Death had come young.

The good-looking corpse would be carried by its arms and legs to a slab in the autopsy room.

The warden carefully examined his watch, and the doctors theirs.

12:03 A.M.

The doctors nodded, giving the warden the okay on the time.

The warden and the four men who would be on the push buttons went into the control room.

...

It was no good. She could not sleep. In the dark the social worker got up, shivering, and dragged a chair to the window. She sat at

[501]

the window in the dark with her head back against the chair and
her eyes closed. Her arms were on the arms of the chair and she
sat unnaturally stiff in the straight-backed chair ... *your hands
shadowing the hand of the executioner ... cut him down—if you
dare! ... Other Nick Romanos. Other Nick Romanos!*

■■■

In the execution chamber all was prepared.

The lights went out.

Went out with the effect of an explosion. With the effect of a
shudder.

Complete blackness.

Complete blackness and complete silence.

The spotlights came on brilliantly over the chair. At angles their
beams struck across each other and encircled the chair like three
lariats thrown. Flooded it in one great spotlight.

He, in the circle of light. The circle of light, white, hard,
brittle. His face hidden. The spotlights picking up the death seat
and thrusting it forward out of the dark and under the eyes of the
spectators.

The spectators strained forward. Waited—for the switch to close.
Waited—to see all his muscles strain to the utmost and every agi-
tated drop of blood rush to strengthen them. Waited—for his body
to thrust itself against the straps and steel clamps. Waited—for the
drone of the dynamo. Waited, with dread, for the jerking of the
figure as it tries to loosen itself from the chair.

And Police Officer Murphy drinks in the scene with narrowed,
vengeful eyes, leaning forward with clamped jaws and angrily
pressed lips, his attention not wavering for an instant.

And the widow Riley reaches an arm around the deputy with
whom she sits, her clenched fist showing on the shoulder of his coat.

And one of the reporters leans forward weakly and covers his
face with his hands. . . .

And now the warden lifts his wrist and carefully examines the
dial of his watch once again. And now the warden lifts his other
hand and gives the okay for the current to be turned on into the
body of Nick. And now the four hands rise, slowly, surely, toward
the four buttons. The hands rise, catch the glint of the bulbs that
light the control room. The hands shadow themselves against the
wall, large, touch in huge shadows on the wall, merge, move as one
huge hand toward death.

■■■

Under the mask Nick blinked his eyes wide open against its
blackness.

And the priest kneels on the concrete floor in the dark. His sad

[502]

voice moans across the basement execution chamber in a mourning
chant of death—

"Out of the depths ... I cry to thee ...

And someone fainted.

"Hear my prayers. ..."

And Riley's widow tightened her fist, harder and harder.

"Let my voice come up to thee. ..."

And under the death mask are Nick's wide, staring eyes, looking
into blackness.

*... He was back in reform school, in the assembly hall with all
the kids in the reform school and Tommy was on the stage.*

"Pull them down," Fuller said.

No boy moved, or made a sound.

Nick closed his eyes and snapped them wide again. His lips
twisted in sobs. His restrained arms and legs tried to move, to
wrestle free.

Tommy's small hands had worked clumsily on his belt.

Nick shut his eyes against the blackness of the death mask.

■■■

The truck driver had had no supper. He walked away from the
factory building where he had just finished a job, and along a small
street lined with taverns, restaurants, bowling alleys and pool halls.
From the blackness of the factory he heard the blast of a steam
whistle. He stood on the sidewalk for a moment with his head
lifted and as if waiting for something. Then slowly he moved a few
steps through the night, thinking, "This is the night Romano
goes."

He walked perhaps a block in gloomy silence, then again spoke
to himself, "Leave without illusions, eh?" He pulled a sack of tobacco from his pocket, and a cigarette paper. Carefully the truck
driver spread the tobacco out on the sheet of cigarette paper. A
little of the tobacco, a few minute flakings, was taken by the wind.
It floated slowly off the edge of the paper, and slowly downward.
A moment in the air. And drifting to the ground.

■■■

And the priest, "... *let perpetual light shine upon him. ..."*

Nick shut his eyes against the blackness of the head hood. Again
he saw the circle of cloth and Tommy grabbing his ankles with
the skin taut across his small behind ... saw the hard light beating
down, Fuller's arm raised with the strap, like a coiled snake, ready
to strike. Ready to cut the flesh, ready to bring blood and screams
and sobbing, whimpering, blubbering.

And the priest, "... *may he rest in peace ..."*

And the hands reaching toward the buttons. ...

And, under the death mask ... Nick, clenching his teeth, opened his eyes to the darkness of the mask and sobbed, seeing the lash fall, bringing blood.

...

Over the jail the wind blows, sharp and cold. Over the jail and over the cartracks the cold wind blows. The streetcar clangs east, turns down Alaska Avenue, and at a diagonal crosses Halsted Street. North and south runs Halsted, twenty miles long. Twelfth Street. Boys under lampposts, shooting craps, learning. Darkness behind the school where you smarten up, you come out with a pride and go look at the good clothes in the shop windows and the swell cars whizzing past to Michigan Boulevard and start figuring out how you can get all these things. Down Maxwell Street where the prostitutes stand in the gloom-clustered doorways. Across Twelfth Street either way on Peoria are the old houses. The sad faces of the houses line the street, like old men and women sitting along the veranda of an old folks' charity home....

Nick? Knock on any door down this street.